In my second werewolf book, *Stolen*, I introduced my witch, Paige Winterbourne, with plans to spin her off into her own story next. At the time my first werewolf book, *Bitten*, hadn't come out yet, so I didn't have any actual readers—unless you include friends and family, but as lovely and supportive as they are, I always figure they're just reading my stuff because they know me. Even when I started *Dime Store Magic*, *Bitten* was barely out, so I had yet to communicate with actual readers. What difference did this make? A huge one, as it turned out.

In *Stolen*, my main character Elena didn't much care for Paige. Their personalities were too different. That was the point—I wanted to explore a very different character. Also, it seemed like an interesting narrative challenge to present a secondary character from one viewpoint, and then see how she changes when the story is told from her point of view.

What happened? Well, when *Dime Store Magic* was finished, I proudly announced that Paige would narrate book three of the Otherworld, and by that time, I had actual readers who replied with a collective . . . well, the response isn't reproducible here. Let's just say it was negative. Resoundingly negative. Elena didn't care for Paige, so neither did they.

The outcry concerned (okay, terrified) me so much that if I had not already sold *Dime Store Magic*, I think I might have given up on Paige. I'm glad I didn't, because *Dime Store Magic* is actually the book that I believe launched my career. New readers bought it, perhaps more comfortable with witches than werewolves. Past readers broke down and picked it up too, and they saw what I was doing, creating a multi-narrator series. They also saw what I was doing with Paige as a character, and they came onboard.

I started with werewolves, and they'll always be my favorites, but I have a special spot for my spell-casters. They were a delightful change of pace, and they performed the greatest magic trick of all—turning me from a "writer with a couple of books" into a career novelist.

Kelley Armstrong

BOOKS BY KELLEY ARMSTRONG

SPELLCASTERS

KELLEY ARMSTRONG

VINTAGE CANADA

VINTAGE CANADA EDITION, 2013

Published in Canada by Vintage Canada, a division of Random House of Canada Limited, Toronto, in 2013. "The Case of the Half-Demon Spy" appeared as an original short story on www.kelleyarmstrong.com in 2013. *Dime Store Magic* was originally published in Canada by Random House Canada, a division of Random House of Canada Limited, in 2004. *Industrial Magic* was originally published in Canada by Seal Books, a division of Random House of Canada Limited, in 2004. *Wedding Bell Hell* originally appeared in *Tales of the Otherworld*, published in hardcover in Canada by Random House Canada in 2010, and simultaneously in the United States of America by Bantam, a division of Random House Inc., New York. Distributed by Random House of Canada Limited.

Vintage Canada with colophon is a registered trademark.

www.randomhouse.ca

LIBRARY AND ARCHIVES CANADA CATALOGUING IN PUBLICATION

Armstrong, Kelley
Spellcasters / Kelley Armstrong.

"Omnibus 2."
Contents: Dime store magic—Industrial magic—Wedding bell hell—The case of the half-demon spy.

Also issued in electronic format.

ISBN 978-0-345-81298-8

I. Title.

PS8551.R7637S65 2013   C813'.6   C2012-908379-8

Text and cover design by Terri Nimmo

Image credit: Nataliya Evmenko / Dreamstime.com

Printed and bound in the United States of America

2 4 6 8 9 7 5 3 1

Contents

The Case of the Half-Demon Spy

A dam watched as Paige put an empty water glass to the meeting room
door and pressed her ear against it. Her brow furrowed in concentration. After a moment, she tried the same thing with a coffee mug.

"What the hell are you—?" he began.

She waved him toward the supply closet. "Go in there."

Adam shook his head, grabbed his new Walkman and changed the
cassette.

"Fine," she said. "*I'll* go in the closet."

"Again . . . what the hell are you—?"

"Stop swearing. It doesn't make you sound cool. Not that anything
could . . ."

He balled up a napkin and pitched it at her. "At least I don't have a
huge zit on my nose. Makes you look like a witch." He snapped his fingers. "Hey, maybe it'll help you cast spells. You can use all the help you
can get."

"Ha-ha. Put the music away and give me a hand. I'm doing this for you."

"Doing what?"

"Saving you from a boring afternoon hanging out in this hallway waiting for the council meeting to end. Now, do you want to go into that
closet or should I?"

"We both could," he said with a sly grin. "That would be one way to
pass the time."

She just gave him a look. Couldn't blame him for trying, though, even if
he knew the answer wouldn't change and, really, he wasn't sure what he'd
do if it ever did. They'd been friends for over a year now, ever since his
father and her mother decided their kids should start attending meetings
of the interracial council, planning for the day when they'd be delegates
themselves. The council was in charge of keeping the peace between supernatural races and protecting them against exposure threats. It sounded
cool and exciting. It never was. Talk, talk, talk, that's all they seemed to do.

So Adam spent a lot of time at those meetings hanging out with Paige. And there were times when, alone like this with a cute girl who at fourteen—his gaze flicked to her chest—was already bigger than a lot of grown women . . . Well, sometimes he *did* entertain thoughts of darkened closets and misplaced hands and—

"Adam?" Paige glowered up at him. "Are you going in there or am I?"

"If you do, can I lock the door?"

A roll of her eyes and she strode past him, opened the closet door and waved him inside.

"What am I supposed to—?"

"Just talk. That should be easy enough."

As he opened his mouth to retort, she shut the door in his face. Christ, like he'd *want* to be in a closet with her. She'd probably spend the whole time giving him orders. Do this, do that . . . kiss me here . . . touch me there . . .

Damn it, stop that. If he ever *did* get Paige in a closet, he'd regret it. She'd make sure of that.

"What am I doing?" he asked.

Her voice was muffled by the door. "Helping me conduct a scientific experiment."

"Science?" He grabbed the handle, but she'd spell-locked the door shut. "You promised you wouldn't spend the weekend doing homework again."

"I'm not." She opened the door and held up the water glass. "Glass works better than china. Or maybe it's because of the shape. I'm not sure."

"Works better for what?"

"Conducting sound." She handed him a glass. "Let's find out why they kicked us out of that meeting."

"We're going to spy on them?"

"Of course not," she said, heading for the boardroom door. "Spying means watching. We're going to eavesdrop."

The interracial council meeting was being held at a remote location in Vermont. When witches, demons, wizards, and vampires got together, you had to be discreet. This particular place was a rustic lodge often rented out to church groups, Boy Scouts, and such. The meeting room was long and narrow with the door at the far end . . . too far from the boardroom table to successfully eavesdrop, they discovered. Even with high-tech spy gear like empty water glasses. After ten minutes outside the door, they'd caught no more than a few words.

"Maybe I should burn a hole in the door," Adam whispered. He was a fire half-demon.

Paige snorted. "If you could scorch it, I'd be surprised."

"Someday I'll be able to put a hole in it."

There was, he knew, no guarantee of that, and Paige could certainly point that out, but she only said, "Not today. Now *shhh.*"

She put her ear to her glass again.

Adam leaned against the wall. "I don't know why we're bothering. They're probably discussing something boring, like interracial politics."

"Do they ever kick us out when they're doing that?"

She had a point. There'd been many times when Adam had wished his dad *would* boot them out of some endless policy discussion.

"If they're going to make us wait out here, it must be something they don't want us to hear." She glanced over at him, brows raised meaningfully. "Something not fit for our young ears."

Adam grabbed his glass and tried again. It was no use. He couldn't hear more than scattered words. Then came a slow thumping, getting louder, almost like . . . footsteps.

The handle turned. Adam backpedaled, hiding the glass behind his back. Paige began studying the list of "rental rules" on the wall. The door opened. His dad stepped into the hall and closed the door.

"I'm afraid this is going to take longer than we thought." Robert took out his wallet, reached for a ten, then paused and plucked out a twenty. "Why don't you two walk into town and see if you can find something to do. I think I saw arcade games at the general store."

Adam reached for the bill, but his dad handed it to Paige, his eyes twinkling. "Just to be sure it's split evenly."

"Or split at all," Paige murmured as his dad retreated into the room.

"Think they knew we were eavesdropping?" Adam whispered.

"Probably. Between my mom and your dad . . ." She shook her head. "We definitely need to work on our stealth skills." She lifted the twenty. "I saw Mortal Kombat in the store."

"Half for games, half to the winner?"

She grinned. "You're on."

Outside, Adam made for the road, but Paige tapped his arm and pointed at the path leading into the woods. "That looks like it heads in the same direction. I bet it's faster."

Inviting him to walk with her into the dark forest? With any other girl, that would mean he was in for something even more fun than video games. But this was Paige. She probably wouldn't even think of that. Not with him anyway.

He watched her walk ahead of him onto the shaded path, her ponytail bobbing as her hips swayed, the darkness of the forest closing in behind her. Maybe she *did* have something else in mind . . .

"Mom said asters grow wild around here," she called back to him. "If I could find some, I might be able to get that second-level wind spell working."

Figures. He sighed and followed along, scuffing his feet as he went.

Something rustled behind him. He turned to scan the path.

"Aster is purple with—" Paige began.

"Shhh. I heard something."

"It's your feet. Try lifting them when you walk. Oh, and while we're here, if you want to practice—"

Another rustle, farther away, like someone moving through a pile of dead leaves.

"Could be a deer," Paige whispered, but her eyes were doubtful as they followed the sound.

"We should check it out," Adam said.

He didn't wait for Paige's nod. He knew she'd be right behind him. As much as she liked to pretend *he* was the adventure-seeking one, it hadn't been his idea to eavesdrop, had it?

Paige was expected to be the responsible one of the pair, only one of many expectations her mother—and others—piled on her. Not a burden he cared to share, but he could lighten it by barreling heedlessly into danger . . . leaving her obligated to follow and "keep an eye on him."

By the time they reached the lodge, Paige had already overtaken him. He tried to brush past her, but she planted a hand against his chest, then leaned to peek around the corner.

She pulled back. "There's someone there."

He peered past her. A man stood to one side of the meeting room window. He was tall and lanky. His hair was short on the sides and long in the back—the way Adam had been trying to grow his, until his mom used the Walkman to bribe him into a haircut. Tattoos covered the man's stringy arms. Adam had seen those tattoos before . . .

As he craned to see the man's face, Paige yanked him back.

"I know—"

She shushed him and gestured for him to follow her back into the woods.

"I know him," Adam said when they were far enough away to speak. "He's a half-demon. He came to Dad's office last week when I was there. He wanted to talk to him."

"About what?"

Adam shrugged. "Dad made me stand outside. But whatever the guy said, it really pissed Dad off, and you know that's tough to do."

"Did your dad say anything afterward?"

"Not to me, but when he was kicking the guy out, I heard something about the council. Dad told the guy that if he ever came to him again with something like that, he'd bring it up to the council himself. The guy was furious. Kept saying Dad would regret—"

Adam turned to run for the lodge. Paige caught his arm. He should have been able to yank free easily enough—she barely came up to his shoulder—but when she dug in her heels, she was tough to budge.

"Robert is in a room with five other delegates, all supernaturals," she said. "If this guy does come for him, he's going to lie in wait. You running in there would only scare the guy off—so he can try another time . . . when you aren't around to help."

As Paige released his arm, she shook her hands, and he could see her palms were red.

"Did I burn—?" he said, reaching for her hand.

"Nothing a little healing salve won't fix." She put her hands behind her back so he couldn't see them. "Wait here. I want to get another look."

When she returned, she was frowning. "It's weird," she said. "He's taking notes. He must be able to hear the meeting, though I'm not sure how."

"Dad called him an Exaudio. That's hearing, isn't it?"

Paige nodded. "A mid-level auditory-enhanced half-demon. Vastly improved general hearing, plus the ability to induce temporary deafness in a single individual."

She'd recited the information as promptly as if he'd asked for her home address. Any other time he'd have ribbed her about spending too much time with the council research books, but today his only thought was "Good thing she knows it," followed by "Maybe I should, too."

He dismissed the second thought as soon as it came. As long as Paige did the research, there was no reason for both of them to waste sunny afternoons poring over dusty books. When they grew up, that could be her job, and he'd do the dangerous stuff better suited to a fire demon.

She cast a reluctant glance at the cabin door. "I suppose we should go in and tell the council."

"He could be gone before we did."

"True . . ."

He could see her thinking it over, trying to figure out an excuse for handling it themselves, an excuse her mother would accept. It wasn't so much that Ruth was overprotective of Paige. She just didn't believe in risk-taking in general—kind of like his dad.

"Hold on." Adam returned to the corner of the building, peeked around and came back. "He looks like he's getting ready to leave. We have to do something."

She agreed, while making no move to check for herself, as if she knew he was lying to give her the excuse she needed.

"I'll take him down," Adam said. "Once I have him, you run in and get my dad—"

She shook her head. "First-degree burns aren't going to stop a guy like that. I'm no help until I learn my binding spell."

"He's not much bigger than me, and I've been working out—"

"Which isn't going to help you if he pulls a knife or a gun."

"Supernaturals hardly ever use that stuff."

"What if this guy is the exception?" She laid her hand on his arm. "As much as I'd like to hog-tie the guy and hand him over, all we really need is that notebook. The council can find out what he was up to and go after him. That's good enough, right?" She looked up at him. "For now."

After a moment, he nodded.

"I'll create a distraction," she said. "You grab the book. You'll need to have your powers ready, in case he turns on you. Have you been practicing?"

He nodded. Almost since the day they'd met, Paige had been trying to help him hone his powers, helping him learn to control them so he could burn on purpose, not just accidentally when he got upset. She'd taught him the techniques she used for spell-casting concentration. Trouble was, they didn't work for him.

To cast a spell, you had to clear your mind and turn off your emotions. To invoke fire, he needed to do the exact opposite—turn his emotional valve on full blast. Telling her how he ignited his powers would only worry her. Sometimes reaching down into that darkest part of himself disturbed even him.

"If something goes wrong, I'll have to go for help. You know that, right? I can't—" She swallowed. "I can't do a damned thing."

"Don't swear."

He smiled when he said it, but she didn't smile back. Paige had noticed that her mother never undertook any council "business" without backup, not even something as simple as delivering a warning. Sure, Ruth was older than most moms, but his dad was almost as old, and he issued warnings by himself. He might not like invoking his darker powers, but at least he had them.

Paige looked at her mother, the most experienced witch she knew, and saw her future. Leader of the Coven, leader of the supernatural council . . . and completely defenseless except for her binding spell.

Adam left Paige in the forest. Then he circled around to the half-demon's other side. He crouched there a moment and watched him, but there wasn't much to see. The guy was still standing beside the window, head tilted, jotting down notes. Exciting stuff.

Across the clearing, a light sparked in the forest. Paige's signal. Adam hunkered down. A moment later, a bright orb bounced from the forest, hovered there a moment, then evaporated. The spy never even saw it. Adam imagined Paige stamping her foot as her light-ball fizzled.

A second later, he heard Paige kick a pile of dried leaves just as she let off another light-ball. The half-demon spun. The ball sputtered out. He shook his head and returned to his spying. But he didn't turn his back on the woods, so when the next light-ball came, he saw it and headed for Paige's hiding spot.

Adam bolted from the bushes. He made a beeline for the notepad hanging from the man's hand. But he'd jumped out too soon. The half-demon caught a movement out of the corner of his eye and whipped his hand back. Adam tried to check himself, but it was too late. He crashed right into him.

The notepad flew to the ground . . . and the man's hands flew to Adam's throat.

Adam managed to duck, but the half-demon caught him by the arm and yanked Adam off his feet. He tried to invoke his power, tried to pull the deepest, darkest emotions from his brain, but all he could think was that he'd made a fool of himself in front of Paige *and* embarrassed his dad. He wasn't sure which was worse. Then, as he hit the ground, he realized he might have something more serious than humiliation to worry about.

The air flew from his lungs, he saw a blur behind the half-demon as Paige charged the man.

Oh, shit. She'd said she would go inside for help, but he should have known she wouldn't run away and leave him alone. Her mouth opened to call for help, to attract the council's attention that way. Before she could get out a syllable, the half-demon turned to meet her charge.

Paige skidded to a stop, eyes going wide, lips moving in some useless incantation. Adam sprang to his feet and grabbed the man's arm. The half-demon yelped and tried to yank away, but Adam tightened his grip, heat flaming through him.

The half-demon fought, panicked. Adam's grip slid. The man pulled free and ran for the forest. Adam tore after him, but the man was faster and Adam reached the road just in time to see him jump into a car.

At a noise behind him, he turned to see Paige. She stopped in front of him, eyes dancing, cheeks glowing, curls flying free from her ponytail.

Whenever his friends asked Adam what his "Boston friend" looked like, he'd say, "Cute, I guess," but as she looked up at him, grinning just for him, she looked way better than cute. Her lips parted, and he knew if he leaned over—

"You did it," she said, waving the notepad between them.

He looked into her eyes then, saw only the glowing happiness of a friend, and he knew that's all he'd seen before, and probably all he ever would. She threw her arms around his neck, and he hugged her back. When she pulled away, she held out the notebook.

"I'll do the talking," she said. "But you give them this. You're the one who got it."

"No, you should—"

She shoved it into his hands. "Don't argue. Take it."

He grinned. "Our first adventure. The first of many."

"Oh, I'm not so sure about that."

His grin widened. "I am."

Robert handed his half-demon friend, Leo, a bottle of salve. "This should work. It's Ruth Winterbourne's recipe and she finds it works particularly well on the burns Adam inflicts . . . though that one seems to be worse than usual. He's making remarkable progress." A soft chuckle. "Though I'm sure you aren't nearly as impressed. I do apologize. This is the first time he's ever caused second-degree burns—"

Leo waved off the apology. "I'm fine. The kid did good, and I owed you."

"Well, thank you anyway for your help. I'll leave the salve with you. I should be getting back to the hotel before anyone realizes I left."

Leo took the jar and they said their good-byes. Then Robert hurried off. He couldn't afford to dawdle—if Ruth found out what he'd done . . . It was the kind of thing that could threaten a very old and very dear friendship.

Yet even if she did learn the truth, he wouldn't regret the ruse. It was training. Necessary training. The council was sliding into old age along with him and Ruth, without ever having become the vibrant, active force he'd once imagined.

With Paige and Adam and the next generation, that could change. The will and the desire for innovation were there. He saw them in Paige and knew they were more than adolescent rebellion. She was questioning her mother's passivity, looking for a more active delegate's path. Adam would follow her on whatever path she proposed, particularly if it offered more excitement than endless talk.

When they'd come running into the meeting, notebook in hand, he'd seen by their expressions that his ploy had succeeded—their glow of victory tempered with the knowledge that they'd picked a fight they may not have been ready for. Someday they'd be ready though. They'd make sure of that now.

Dime Store Magic

PROLOGUE

Todd adjusted his leather power seat and smiled. Now, this was the good life. Driving along the California coast, road stretching empty before him, cruise control set at fifty, climate control at six-eight degrees, Brazilian coffee keeping warm in its heated cup holder. Some might say it'd be even better to be the guy lounging in the backseat instead of his driver, but Todd liked being where he was. Better to be the bodyguard than the guy who needed one.

His predecessor, Russ, had been the more ambitious type, which may explain why Russ had been missing for two months. Odds around the office watercooler were split fifty-fifty between those who assumed Kristof Nast finally tired of his bodyguard's insubordination and those who thought Russ had fallen victim to Todd's own ambitions. Bullshit, of course. Not that Todd wouldn't have killed to get this job, but Russ was a Ferratus. Todd wouldn't even know *how* to kill him.

Todd figured the Nasts were behind Russ's sudden disappearance, but that didn't bother him. When you signed up with a Cabal, you had to know what to expect. Give them your respect and your loyalty, and you had the cushiest gig in the supernatural world. Double-cross them and they'd wreak their revenge right into your afterlife. At least the Nasts weren't as bad as the St. Clouds. If the rumors were right, about what the St. Clouds did to that shaman? Todd shivered. Man, he was glad—

Lights flashed in the side mirror. Todd looked to see a state patrol car behind him. Christ, where had that come from? He checked his speedometer. Dead-on fifty. He made this trip twice a month and knew the speed limit didn't change along this stretch.

He slowed, expecting the police car to whiz past. It stayed on his tail. He shook his head. How many cars had zoomed by in the last hour, going seventy or more? Oh, but they hadn't been custom-designed Mercedes limos. Better to pull over someone who looks as if he might pass you a few twenties to avoid the hassle of a ticket. If so, they'd picked the wrong car. Kristof Nast didn't bribe mere highway patrolmen.

As Todd put on his signal and pulled over, he lowered the shield separating him from his passenger. Nast was on his cell phone. He said something into the phone, then pulled it from his ear.

"We're being pulled over, sir. I had the cruise set at the speed limit."

Nast nodded. "It happens. We have plenty of time. Just take the ticket."

Todd raised the shield and put down his window. Through his side mirror he watched the patrolman approach. No, make that patrol*woman*. A cute one, too. Slender, maybe thirty, with shoulder-length red hair and a California tan. Her uniform could fit better, though. It looked a couple of sizes too large, probably a hand-me-down from a male colleague.

"Morning, Officer," he said, taking off his sunglasses.

"License and registration."

He handed them over with a smile. Her face stayed impassive, eyes and expression hidden behind her shades.

"Please step out of the vehicle."

Todd sighed, and opened his door. "What seems to be the problem, Officer?"

"Broken taillight."

"Aw, shit. Okay, then. Write me up and we'll get it fixed in San Fran."

As he stepped onto the empty road, the woman turned and marched to the rear of the vehicle.

"Can you explain this?" she asked.

"Explain what?"

As he walked toward her, his heart beat a little faster, but he reminded himself that there couldn't be a serious problem. The Nasts never used their family cars for anything illegal. Just in case, though, he flexed his hands, then clenched them. His fingertips burned hot against his palms.

He glanced at the patrol car, parked a mere two feet behind his. It was empty. Good. She didn't have a partner. If things went bad, he'd only have to worry about the woman.

The officer stepped into the narrow gap between the cars, bent and checked something just to the right of the left taillight. She frowned, eased out of the gap and waved at the bumper.

"Explain that," she said.

"Explain what?"

Her jaw tightened and she motioned for him to look for himself. He had to turn sideways to fit between the cars. Couldn't she have backed up? She could see he was a big guy. He bent over as much as he could and peered down at the bumper.

"I don't see anything."

"Underneath," she said curtly.

Bitch. Would it kill her to be polite? It wasn't like he was arguing with her.

He lowered himself to his knees. Christ, was this gap narrower than he'd thought or had he been packing on the pounds? The front bumper of the patrol car pressed against his mid-back.

"Ummm, do you think you could back your car up a little?" he said. "Please?"

"Oh, I'm sorry. Is this better?"

The patrol car pitched forward, pinning him. The air flew from his lungs. He opened his mouth to yell for her to put it into reverse, then realized she was still standing beside the car . . . which wasn't running. He grabbed the limo's bumper and pushed. The smell of burning rubber filled the air.

"Oh, come on," the woman said, leaning over him. "You can do better than that. Put some real firepower into it."

When he swiped at her, she backpedaled out of reach and laughed. He tried to speak, but could only get enough air to grunt. Again he pushed against the bumper. The rubber stripping melted against his fingers, but the car didn't budge.

"Only an Igneus?" she said. "The Cabals must really be hard up for half-demons. Maybe there's an opening for me after all. Sit tight now, and I'll be right back."

Leah opened the driver's door and climbed into the limo's front seat. She looked across the rows of buttons on the dash. Talk about electronic overkill. Now, which one—

The shield between the seats whirred. Well, that saved her the trouble.

"Did everything go—" Nast began.

He saw her and stopped. His hand lifted, just off his lap, fingers moving as his lips parted.

"Now, now," Leah said. "No spell-casting."

Nast's seat belt jerked tight, taking up the slack so fast he gasped.

"Hands out where I can see them," Leah said.

Nast's eyes blazed. His fingers flicked and Leah shot backward, hitting the dash.

"Okay, I deserved that," she said, grinning as she righted herself. She looked at the seat belt. It loosened. "Better?"

"I'd suggest you seriously consider what you're doing," Nast said. He adjusted his suit jacket and eased back into his seat. "I doubt this is a road you wish to take."

"Hey, I'm not stupid or suicidal. I didn't come here to hurt you. Didn't even hurt your bodyguard. Well, nothing a few weeks of bed rest won't cure. I came here to make you a deal, Kristof—oops, sorry. Mr. Nast, I mean. It's about your daughter."

His chin jerked up, eyes meeting hers for the first time.

"And now that I have your attention . . ."

"What about Savannah?"

"Been looking for her, haven't you? Now that Eve's gone, there's no one to stop you from taking what's yours. And I'm just the person to help you do it. I know exactly where she is."

Nast shot his sleeve up and checked his watch, then looked at Leah.

"Is my driver in any shape to resume his duties?" he asked.

She shrugged. "Questionable."

"Then let's hope you can talk and drive at the same time."

CHAPTER 1

BEWITCHED, BOTHERED, AND BEWILDERED

I was in trouble with the Elders. Again.

I'd been a trial to them all my life and now, at twenty-three—no longer a precocious child or a rebellious youth—they were running out of excuses for me.

"Something must be done about Savannah." The speakerphone added a not-inappropriate whine to Victoria Alden's voice.

"Uh-huh." My fingers flew across the keyboard, hammering out the next line of code.

"I hear typing," Victoria said. "Are you typing, Paige?"

"Deadline," I said. "Enhancements to the Springfield Legal Services website. Due in two days. And counting. Look, can we discuss this later? I'll be at the Coven meeting next week, and—"

"Next week? I don't think you're taking this seriously, Paige. Pick up the telephone, stop working, and talk to me. Where did you ever learn such manners? Not from your mother, rest her soul."

I lifted the receiver, gripped it between my shoulder and ear and tried to type quietly.

"It's about Savannah," Victoria said.

Wasn't it always? One of the few perks of having custody of thirteen-year-old Savannah Levine was that my rebellions paled in comparison.

"What's she done now?" I asked. I flipped to my file list of JavaScript functions. I was sure I'd written a function for this last year. Damned if I could find it now.

"Well, I was talking to Grace last night and she expressed concern over something Savannah told Brittany. Now, Grace admits Brittany may have misunderstood the details, which I can certainly see. We don't expose Coven neophytes to this sort of thing, so I'd be shocked if Brittany did understand what Savannah was talking about. It seems—" Victoria paused and inhaled sharply, as if it pained her to go on. "It seems Brittany is having trouble with a few girls at school and Savannah offered to . . .

to help her make a potion that would result in these girls being unable to attend the school dance."

"Uh-huh." Ah, there was that function. A few hours of coding saved. "Then what?"

"What do you mean, 'then what?' Savannah offered to show Brittany how to make these girls sick!"

"She's thirteen. At her age, I would have liked to make a lot of people sick."

"But you didn't, did you?"

"Only because I didn't know the spells. Which was probably a good thing or there'd have been some serious epidemics going on."

"See?" Victoria said. "This is exactly what I've been talking about. This attitude of yours—"

"I thought we were talking about Savannah's attitude."

"That's it exactly. I'm trying to bring a serious matter to your attention and you brush it off with quips. This flippant attitude will never make you Coven Leader."

I stifled the urge to remind her that, as of my mother's death, I *was* Coven Leader. If I did, she'd "remind" me that I was Leader in name only, and this discussion would turn from irritating to ugly in a heartbeat.

"Savannah is my responsibility," I said. "You Elders have made that very clear."

"For good reason."

"Because her mother practiced dark magic. Oooh. Scary. Well, you know what? The only scary thing about Savannah is how fast she's outgrowing her clothes. She's a kid. A normal, rebellious teenager. Not a black witch. She told Brit she could make her a potion. Big deal. Ten to one she can't even do it. She was either showing off or trying to shock us. That's what adolescents do."

"You're defending her."

"Of course I'm defending her. No one else will. The poor kid went through hell last summer. Before my mother died, she asked me to take care of Savannah—"

"Or so that woman told you."

"That woman is a friend of mine. You don't think my mother would have asked me to take Savannah? Of course she would. That's our job. To protect our sisters."

"Not at the risk of endangering ourselves."

"Since when is it more important—"

"I don't have time to argue with you, Paige. Talk to Savannah or I will."

Click.

I slammed down the phone and stalked from my office, muttering everything I wished I'd said to Victoria. I knew when to hold my tongue, though sometimes knowing and doing were very different things. My mother was the political one. She'd spend years working to effect one small change to Coven Law, soothing every rumpled feather and arguing her point with a smile.

Now she was gone. Murdered nine months ago. Nine months, three weeks, and two days. My mind performed the calculation unbidden, springing open the stoppered well of grief. I slammed it shut. She wouldn't have wanted that.

I was brought into this world for one reason. At fifty-two, after a life too busy for children, my mother looked around the Coven and saw no worthy successor, so she found a suitable "genetic donor" and, using magic, conceived me. A daughter born and raised to lead the Coven. Now that she was gone, I had to honor her memory by fulfilling that purpose. And I would, whether the Elders wanted it or not.

I abandoned my computer. Victoria's call had chased all interest in programming from my brain. When I got like this, I needed to do something that reminded me of who I was, and what I wanted to accomplish. That meant practicing my spells—not Coven-sanctioned spells, but the magic they forbade.

In my bedroom, I pulled back the area rug, unlocked the crawl space hatch, and tugged out a knapsack. Then, bending down and reaching farther into the hole, I undid a secret latch, opened a second compartment, and pulled out two books. My secret grimoires. After putting the books into my bag, I headed for the back door.

I was slipping on my sandals when the front doorknob turned. I checked my watch. Three P.M. Savannah didn't get out of school until three forty-five, which is why I figured I had nearly an hour to practice before making her after-school snack. Yes, Savannah was too old for the milk-and-cookies routine, but I did it every day without fail. Let's be honest, at twenty-three I was ill equipped to parent a teenager. Being home for her after school was one thing I could manage.

"What happened?" I asked, hurrying into the hall. "Is everything okay?"

Savannah backpedaled, as if fearing I might do something rash, like hug her. "Teachers' meeting today. Early dismissal. Remember?"

"Did you tell me?"

She rubbed her nose, trying to decide whether she could get away with a lie. "I forgot. But I would have called if I had a cell phone."

"You'll get a cell phone when you can pay for the airtime."

"But I'm too young to get a job!"

"Then you're too young for a cell phone."

Old argument. We knew our lines, and never wavered from them. That was one advantage to being a mere decade older than Savannah—I remembered pulling the same crap with my mom, so I knew how to handle it. Maintain the routine. Give no sign of wearing down. Eventually she'd give up . . . not that I ever did.

Savannah peered over my shoulder to look down at my knapsack, a feat she could easily manage, being two inches taller than my five feet two. Two inches taller and about thirty pounds lighter. I could have explained the weight difference by pointing out that Savannah was very slender, but to be truthful, I was about fifteen pounds over what most women's magazines listed as the ideal weight for my height.

Savannah, by contrast, was very tall for her age: tall, thin, and coltish, all awkward angles and jutting limbs. I told her she'd grow into her body, as she'd grow into her oversized blue eyes. She didn't believe me. Like she didn't believe me when I'd advised her that cutting off her waist-length black hair would be a mistake. Now she had a straight, wispy bob that only made the angles of her face even more prominent. Naturally, she blamed me, because I didn't forbid her to cut her hair, instead of just cautioning against it.

"Heading out for spell practice?" she said, pointing at my knapsack. "What are you working on?"

"Making you a snack. White milk or chocolate?"

Dramatic sigh. "Come on, Paige. I know what kind of stuff you practice. I don't blame you. Those Coven spells are for five-year-olds."

"Five-year-olds don't cast spells."

"Neither does the Coven. Not real spells. Oh, come on. We can work together. Maybe I can get that wind spell working for you."

I turned to look at her.

"You wrote in your journal that you were having trouble with it," she said. "Sounds like a cool spell. My mom never had anything like that. Tell you what—you teach me that one and I'll show you some real magic."

"You read my journal?"

"Just the spell practice journal. Not your personal one."

"How do you know I have a personal one?"

"Do you? Hey, you know what happened at school today? Mr. Ellis told me he's sending two of my paintings to get framed. They're going to hang them at graduation next week."

Savannah headed for the kitchen, still talking. Should I pursue the journal comment? I considered, then rejected it. Instead I hefted my knapsack and headed to my room to return the bag to its hiding spot.

If Savannah did read my personal journal, at least it meant she was taking an interest in me. Which was good. Unless she was snooping in hopes of finding something she could use to blackmail me into buying her a cell phone. Which wouldn't be so good. What exactly did I have in my journal, anyway . . . ?

While I was locking away my bag, the doorbell rang. Savannah shouted "Got it" and thundered into the hallway, making enough noise for someone three times her size. When I walked into the living room a few minutes later, she was standing in the hall doorway, lifting a letter to the light and squinting at it.

"Testing your psychic abilities?" I said. "A letter opener works much faster."

She jumped and jerked the letter down, hesitated, then held it out.

"Ah, for me. In that case, I'd advise steaming it open." I took the letter. "Registered mail? That bumps it up from simple mail fraud to mail fraud plus forgery. I hope you're not using that skill to sign my name to any notes at school."

"As if," she said, heading back toward the kitchen. "What would be the good of skipping school in this town? No mall, no Starbucks, not even a Mickey D's."

"You could hang around outside the hardware store with the rest of the kids."

She snorted and disappeared into the kitchen.

The envelope was standard letter-sized, no unusual markings, just my name and address handwritten in clean, exact strokes and a return address preprinted in the upper left corner. The sender? A California law firm.

I tore it open. My eyes went straight to the first line, which requested— no, demanded—my presence at a meeting tomorrow morning. The first thing I thought was: "Oh, shit." I suppose that's the normal reaction for anyone receiving an unexpected legal summons.

I assumed it had something to do with my business. I created and managed company websites for women tired of male web designers who thought they'd want nothing more technically challenging than floral wallpaper. When it comes to the Internet, the issue of copyright is as murky and convoluted as a celebrity prenup so, seeing a letter filled with legal jargon, I assumed I'd done something like design a Flash sequence that inadvertently bore some passing similarity to one on a website in Zaire.

Then I read the next line.

"The purpose of this meeting is to discuss our client's petition for custody of the juvenile, Savannah Levine . . ."

I closed my eyes and inhaled. Okay, I'd known this could happen. Savannah's only living relative was one of the Coven Elders, but I always assumed Savannah's mother might have had friends who would be wondering what became of Eve and her young daughter. When they discovered that a great-aunt had taken custody of Savannah and handed her over to me, they'd want answers. And they might want Savannah.

Naturally, I'd fight. The problem was that Savannah's aunt Margaret was the weakest of the three Elders, and if Victoria insisted Margaret relinquish custody, she would. The Elders hated trouble; they broke into collective hives at the mere prospect of drawing attention to the Coven. To secure their support, I'd need to persuade them that they'd face graver personal danger by giving up Savannah than by keeping her. With the Elders, it always came down to that: what was best for *them*, safest for *them*.

I scanned the rest of the letter, sifting through the legal jargon to find the petitioner's name. When I found it, my stomach dropped to my shoes. I couldn't believe it. No, strike that. I believed it only too well. Cursed myself for not seeing it coming.

Did I mention how my mother died? Last year, a small group of humans learned about the supernatural world and wanted to harness our powers, so they kidnapped a sampling of powerful supernaturals. One of those was Savannah's mother, Eve. Savannah had the misfortune to be home from school that day and was taken as well.

Eve, however, quickly proved more dangerous than her captors expected, so they killed her. As a replacement, they targeted my mother, the elderly Leader of the Coven. My mother was taken, along with Elena Michaels, a werewolf. There they met another captive, a half-demon who would later kill my mother and blame Savannah—part of an intricate plot to take control of Savannah, and so gain access to a young, malleable, and extremely powerful neophyte witch.

That half-demon's name? Leah O'Donnell. The same name that now stared up at me from the custody petition.

CHAPTER 2

HOME SECURITY

L eah was a telekinetic half-demon of the highest order. A half-demon is the offspring of a male demon and a female human. Half-demons always look human, taking after their mother. What they inherit from their father depends on what kind of demon he is. For Leah, that power was telekinesis. That means she could move things with her mind. Only don't think sideshow spoon-bending. Think of a woman who can mentally hurl a steel desk into a wall—literally *into* a wall, with such force that the desk embeds itself in the plaster and obliterates anything in its path.

Not surprisingly, then, the first thing I did upon reading this letter was rush around securing the house. After fastening the door locks and pulling the blinds, I moved to less conventional security. At each door I cast a lock spell, which would hold them closed even if the dead bolts failed. Next I used perimeter spells at all the doors and windows. Think of perimeter spells as supernatural security systems. No one could enter the house without my knowing it.

All of these were Coven-sanctioned spells, though a few months ago one witch felt it her duty to point out that a lock spell could be used for evil, if we ever took it upon ourselves to lock someone *in* a room, instead of keeping them out. Would you believe the Coven actually convened a special meeting of the Elders to discuss this? Worse yet, the Elders voted two to one to outlaw the second-level spell, leaving us the first-level spell, which could be broken with a strong twist on the doorknob. Fortunately, my vote carried extra weight, so the motion failed.

Savannah walked in as I was casting the perimeter spell across the bottom of our unused fireplace.

"Who are you trying to keep out?" she asked. "Santa Claus?"

"The letter. It's from Leah."

She blinked, surprised but not concerned. I envied her that.

"Okay," she said. "We expected this. We're ready for her, right?"

"Of course." Was it my imagination, or did my voice just tremble? Inhale, exhale . . . now once more, with confidence. "Absolutely." Oh, yeah, that sounded about as confident as a cornered kitten with three broken legs. I turned and busied myself casting perimeter spells at the living room windows.

"So what was in the letter?" Savannah asked. "A threat?"

I hesitated. I can't lie. Well, I can, but I'm lousy at it. My nose might as well grow, my falsehoods are so obvious.

"Leah . . . wants custody of you."

"And?"

"There's no 'and.' She wants to take custody of you, legally."

"Yeah, and I want a cell phone. She's a bitch. Tell her I said so. And tell her to fuck—"

"Savannah."

"Hey, you allowed 'bitch.' Can't blame me for testing the boundaries." She shoved an Oreo in her mouth. "—Go—gi—geen."

"The correct sequence is: chew, swallow, talk."

She rolled her eyes and swallowed. "I said: you know what I mean. 'Witch-slave' wasn't my choice at career day last week. Tell her I'm not interested in what she's selling."

"That's good, but it might take more than that to change her mind."

"But you can handle it, right? You sent her packing before. Do it again."

I should have pointed out that I'd "sent her packing" with lots of help, but my ego resisted. If Savannah thought I'd played a significant role in beating Leah last time, there was no need to enlighten her now. She needed to feel secure. So, in the interest of ensuring that security, I returned to my perimeter spells.

"I'll go do my bedroom windows," she said.

I nodded, knowing I'd redo them when she wasn't looking. Not that Savannah lacked proficiency in second-level spells. Though I hated to admit it, she'd already surpassed me in all levels of Coven magic. I'd redo her spells because I had to, for peace of mind. Otherwise I'd worry that she'd missed a window or rushed through the incantation or something. It wasn't just Savannah. I'd do the same with any other witch. I'd feel better knowing I'd done it myself.

I don't remember what I made for dinner. By seven Savannah was in her room, which might have worried me except that she disappeared after dinner almost every night—before I could ask for help clearing the table—and spent the next few hours in her bedroom, ostensibly doing homework, which somehow involved ninety-minute phone calls to school chums. Group homework. What can I say?

Once Savannah was in her room, I turned my attention back to the letter. It demanded my presence at a ten o'clock meeting the next morning. Until then, I could do little but wait. I hated that. By seven-thirty I resolved to do something, anything.

I had one lead to pursue. The letter was from a lawyer named Gabriel Sandford, who worked at Jacobs, Sandford and Schwab in Los Angeles. Odd. Very odd, now that I thought about it. Having an L.A. lawyer would make sense for someone living in California, but Leah was from Wisconsin.

I knew Leah hadn't moved—I made discreet biweekly inquiries to her station. By "station," I mean police station. No, Leah wasn't in jail—though I knew of few people who belonged behind a stronger set of bars. Leah was a deputy sheriff. Would that help her custody case? No sense dwelling on that until I knew more.

Back to the L.A. lawyer. Could it be a ruse? Maybe this wasn't a real legal case at all. Maybe Leah had invented this lawyer, placing him in a huge city as far from Massachusetts as possible, and assumed I wouldn't investigate.

Though the phone number was on the letterhead, I called 411 to double-check. They provided a matching address and phone number for Jacobs, Sandford and Schwab. I called the office, since it was only four-thirty on the West Coast. When I asked for Gabriel Sandford, his secretary informed me that he was out of town on business.

Next, I checked out Jacobs, Sandford and Schwab on the web. I found several references on sites listing L.A. law firms. All mentions were discreet, none encouraging new business. It didn't seem like the kind of firm a Wisconsin cop would see advertised on late-night TV. Very strange, but I'd have to wait until tomorrow to find out more.

With morning came a fresh dilemma. What to do with Savannah? I wasn't letting her go to school with Leah in town. And I certainly wasn't taking her with me. I settled for leaving her with Abigail Alden. Abby was one of the very few Coven witches to whom I'd entrust Savannah, someone who'd protect her without question and without telling the Elders.

East Falls was only forty miles from Boston. Yet, despite its proximity, people here didn't work in Boston, didn't shop in Boston, didn't even go to concerts or live theater in Boston. People who lived in East Falls liked their small-town ways and fought viciously against any encroachment from the big bad city to the south.

They also fought against incursions of another sort. This region of Massachusetts is overflowing with beautiful villages, replete with gorgeous examples of New England architecture. Among these, East Falls took its place as one of the best. Every building in the downtown area dated back at least two hundred years and was kept in pristine condition, in accordance with town law.

Yet you rarely saw a tourist in East Falls. The town didn't just fail to promote tourism, it actively worked to prevent it. No one was allowed to open a hotel, an inn, or a bed-and-breakfast in town, nor any sort of shop that might attract tourists. East Falls was for East Falls residents. They lived there, worked there, played there, and no one else was welcome.

Four hundred years ago, when the Coven first came to East Falls, it was a Massachusetts village steeped in religious prejudice, small-mindedness, and self-righteous morality. Today, East Falls is a Massachusetts village steeped in religious prejudice, small-mindedness, and self-righteous morality. They killed witches here during the New England witch trials. Five innocent women and three Coven witches, including one of my ancestors. So why is the Coven still here? I wish I knew.

Not all Coven witches lived in East Falls. Most, like my mother, had moved closer to Boston. When I was born, my mother bought a small two-story Victorian on a huge corner lot in an old Boston suburb, a wonderful tight-knit little community.

After she died, the Elders insisted I relocate to East Falls. As a condition of my taking custody of Savannah, they wanted me to move where they could keep an eye on us. At the time, blinkered by grief, I'd seen their condition as an excuse to flee painful memories. For twenty-two years, my mother and I had shared that house. After her death, every time I heard a footstep, a voice, the closing of a door, I'd thought "It's just Mom," then realized it wasn't, and never would be again. So when they told me to sell, I did. Now I regretted my weakness, both in surrendering to their demand and in giving up a home that meant so much to me.

Leah's lawyer was holding the meeting at the Cary Law Office in East Falls. That wasn't unusual. The Carys were the only lawyers in town, and they made their meeting room available to visiting lawyers, for a reasonable fee—the Carys' typical blend of small-town hospitality and big-city business sense.

The Carys of East Falls had been lawyers for as long as anyone could remember. According to rumor, they'd even been around during the East Falls witch trials, though the gossipmongers are divided over which side the Carys served on.

Currently the office had two lawyers, Grantham Cary and Grantham Cary, Jr. My sole legal dealing in East Falls had been the title transfer on my house, which had been handled by Grant junior. The guy invited me out for a drink after our first meeting, which wouldn't have been so bad if his wife hadn't been downstairs manning the receptionist desk. Needless to say, I'd since taken my business legal matters elsewhere.

For as long as the Carys had been lawyers, they'd practiced out of a monstrous three-story house in the middle of Main Street. I arrived at the house at nine-fifty. Once inside, I noted the location of each employee. Grantham junior's wife, Lacey, was at her main floor desk, and a polite inquiry confirmed that both Granthams were upstairs in their respective offices. Good. Leah was unlikely to try anything supernatural with humans so near.

After engaging in the requisite two minutes of small talk with Lacey, I took a seat by the front window. Ten minutes later, the meeting room door opened and a man in a tailored three-piece suit walked out. He was tall, dark-haired, late thirties. Good-looking in a sleek plastic Ken doll kind of way. Definitely a lawyer.

"Ms. Winterbourne?" he said as he approached, hand extended. "I'm Gabriel Sandford."

As I stood, I met Sandford's eyes and knew exactly why he'd taken Leah's case. Gabriel Sandford wasn't just an L.A. lawyer. No, it was worse than that.

Gabriel Sandford was a sorcerer.

CHAPTER 3

A Brilliant Strategy
Four Centuries Too Late

I knew Sandford was a sorcerer the moment I looked into his eyes—a gut-level recognition that registered before I could have told you what color those eyes were. This is a peculiarity specific to our races. We need only look one another in the eye, and witch recognizes sorcerer, sorcerer recognizes witch.

Witches are always female, sorcerers are always male, but sorcerers aren't the male equivalent of witches. We are two separate races with different yet overlapping powers. Sorcerers can cast witch spells, but at a reduced potency, as our ability to use sorcerer spells is handicapped.

No one knows when sorcerers and witches originated, or which came first. Like most supernatural races, they've been around since the beginning of recorded history, starting with a handful of "gifted" people who grew into a full-fledged race—still rare enough to hide from the human world but plentiful enough to form their own microsociety.

The earliest references to true witches show that they were valued for their healing and magical skills, but in Medieval Europe women with such powers were viewed with growing suspicion. At the same time, the value of sorcerers was increasing, as aristocrats vied to have their own private "magicians." The witches didn't need weather-forecasting spells to see which way the wind was blowing, and they devised for themselves a fresh role in this new world order.

Until that time, sorcerers could cast only simple spells using hand motions. Witches taught them to enhance this power by adding other spell-casting elements—incantations, potions, magical objects, and so on. In return for these teachings, the witches asked that the sorcerers join them in a mutually advantageous covenant.

If a nobleman wanted help defeating his enemies, he'd consult a sorcerer, who would take the request to the witches and together they'd cast the appropriate spells. Then the sorcerer would return to the nobleman and collect his reward. In turn, the sorcerer would provide for and protect the witches with his wealth and social standing. The system worked for centuries. Sorcerers gained power, in both the human and supernatural worlds, while the witches gained security, through protection and a guaranteed income. Then came the Inquisition.

Sorcerers were among the first targeted by the Inquisition in Europe. How did they react? They turned on us. The Inquisitors wanted heretics? The sorcerers gave them witches. Freed from the moral restrictions imposed by Covens, the sorcerers turned to stronger and darker magic. While witches burned, sorcerers did what they did best, becoming rich and powerful.

Today sorcerers rule as some of the most important men in the world. Politicians, lawyers, CEOs—search the ranks of any profession known for greed, ambition, and a distinct lack of scruples, and you'll find a whole cadre of sorcerers. And witches? Ordinary women leading ordinary lives, most of them so afraid of persecution they've never dared learn a spell that will kill anything larger than an aphid.

"Figures," I muttered, loud enough for Sandford to hear.

If he knew what I meant he gave no sign of it, only extended his hand and broad smile. I declined both with a level stare, then brushed past him and strode into the meeting room. Inside sat a red-haired woman, average height, lean, thirty-ish, with a blossoming tan and a ready smile. Leah O'Donnell.

Sandford flourished a hand in my direction. "May I present the esteemed Leader of the American Coven."

"Paige," Leah said, rising. "Don't you look"—her eyes took in every one of my excess pounds—"healthy."

"Any more insults?" I said. "Get them off your chest now, 'cause I'd hate for you to be lying in bed tonight, thinking of all the zingers you'd failed to get off."

Leah dropped into her seat.

"Oh, come on," I said. "Go ahead. I won't even retaliate. Cheap one-liners were never my style."

"And what is your style, Paige?" Leah waved at my dress. "Laura Ashley, I presume. How very . . . witchlike."

"Actually," Sandford said, "from what I hear, most Coven witches prefer polyester stretch pants. Blue, to match their hair rinse."

"Want to take a few minutes, think up something more clever? I can wait."

"Oh, let's get on with it," Leah said. "I have things to do, places to be, lives to ruin." She bared her teeth in a grin and rocked back in her chair.

I rolled my eyes, sat, and turned to Sandford. "She's right. Let's get this over with. It's simple. You're not getting Savannah. By arranging this absurd 'custody' meeting all you've done is put me on the alert. If you thought you could wave phony custody papers in my face and scare me into handing her over, you've got the wrong witch."

"Oh, but they aren't phony," Sandford said.

"Uh-huh. On what grounds could you possibly challenge me? My age? Leah's not much older. Because I'm not related to Savannah? Well, neither is she. I have a prosperous business, a house with no mortgage, a solid record of community service and, most importantly, the blessing of Savannah's sole surviving relative."

Sandford's lips twitched in a smile. "Are you sure?"

"Yes, I'm sure. Is that your plan? Persuade Margaret Levine to relinquish custody?"

"No, I mean: are you sure Miss Levine is Savannah's sole surviving relative? Just because her mother is dead doesn't make the child an orphan."

It took me a second to realize what he meant. "Her father? Savannah doesn't even know who her father is. Oh, let me guess. You somehow managed to track him down, and persuaded him to cast his vote behind Leah. How much did that cost?" I shook my head. "Never mind. Take that route. It'll still be my suitability versus Leah's, a battle I'm willing to fight anytime."

"Who said I'm the one who wants custody?" Leah asked from her end of the table. "Did you say that, Gabe?"

"Of course not. Clearly Paige is leaping to conclusions. It says right here—" He raised his copy of the letter he'd sent me and feigned a deep frown—about as believable as smacking himself in the forehead. "I don't believe this. That new secretary of mine. I told her to include your name as a witness. What does she do? She puts you down as the plaintiff. Unbelievable."

Both shook their heads, then left me dangling in silence.

"Who is the plaintiff?" I asked.

"Savannah's father, of course," Sandford said. "Kristof Nast."

When I didn't react, Leah leaned toward Sandford and said in a stage whisper, "I don't think she knows who that is."

Sandford's eyes widened. "Could it be? The leader of the all-powerful American Coven doesn't know Kristof Nast?"

Beneath the table, I dug my fingers into my thighs, willing my tongue to stay still.

"He's heir to the Nast Cabal," Sandford continued. "You do know what a Cabal is, don't you?"

"I've heard of them."

"Heard of them?" Sandford laughed. "Cabals are billion-dollar corporations with international interests. The crowning achievement of sorcerers and she's 'heard of them.'"

"This Nast, he's a sorcerer?"

"Naturally."

"Then he can't be Savannah's father, can he?"

Sandford nodded. "Admittedly it is difficult to comprehend how any sorcerer, particularly one of Mr. Nast's stature, could demean himself by sleeping with a witch. However, we must remember that Eve was a very attractive young woman, and brutally ambitious, so I can understand how she might have seduced Mr. Nast, in spite of the repugnance of such a union."

"Don't forget," Leah said, "Eve wasn't just a witch. She was also a half-demon. A true supernatural."

"Really?" I said. "A supernatural who can't pass on its powers to its children? More an aberration than a race, wouldn't you say?" Before she could answer, I looked over at Sandford. "Yes, I agree that I cannot conceive of any witch screwing around with a sorcerer while there was anyone else with a dick on the planet, but beyond that, there's the biological impossibility. A sorcerer sires only sons. A witch bears only daughters. How could they reproduce? It can't happen."

"Is that a fact?" Sandford said.

"Of course it is," Leah said. "Paige knows everything. She went to Harvard."

Sandford snorted. "The most overrated school in the country, and now they even admit witches. How the mighty have fallen."

"You couldn't get in, huh?" I said. "Sorry to hear it. However, if you do have proof that a witch and sorcerer can procreate, please fax it to my place. Otherwise, I'll assume I *am* right."

"Mr. Nast is Savannah's father," Sandford said. "And now, with her mother gone, he wants to ensure she has the kind of power she deserves, the kind of power Eve would have wanted for her."

"Good argument," I said. "Like to see you take that one before a court."

"We won't need to," Sandford said. "You'll surrender custody long before we reach that point."

"And how do you intend to make me do that?"

Leah grinned. "Witchery."

"What?"

"You give us Savannah or we'll tell the world what you are."

"You mean—" I sputtered a laugh. "You plan to accuse me of practicing witchcraft? Oh, that's a great plan. Or it would have been, four hundred years ago. Witchcraft? Who cares? It's old news."

"Are you sure about that?" Sandford asked.

"The practice of witchcraft is a state-accepted religion. You cannot discriminate against me on the basis of my religious beliefs. You should have done your homework, Counselor."

"Oh, but I did."

He smiled and, with that, they walked out.

Chapter 4

The Furies Descend

We walk a fine line, as supernaturals in a human world. Human rules and laws often have little meaning in our lives. Take Savannah's case. A young girl, a witch, immensely powerful, pursued by dark factions who would kill to woo her to their side while she is still young and malleable. Her mother now dead, who will protect her? Who *should* protect her? The Coven, of course. Sister witches who can help her harness and control her power.

Now look at it from the perspective of human law and social services. A thirteen-year-old child, her mother missing, turned over to a great-aunt whom she's never met, who in turn pawns her off on an unrelated woman barely out of college. Try going before a judge and explaining those circumstances.

To the rest of the world, Eve was only missing, and would remain so, since no one would ever find her body. This had made it easier to take de facto custody of Savannah because, technically, I was only caring for Savannah until her mother returned. So long as I provided a good home for Savannah, no one was about to argue that she should be handed over to child services and enter the foster-care system. To be honest, though, I wasn't sure how well my claim would hold up in court.

The idea of battling a telekinetic half-demon, while daunting, was well within my sphere of understanding. But fighting a legal case? My upbringing prepared me for no such thing. So, faced with this custody suit, I naturally chose to research, not the legal side, but the supernatural aspect, starting with learning more about Cabals.

I had heard of Cabals, but my mother always downplayed their existence. According to her, they were the supernatural world's equivalent of the bogeyman, a seedling of truth that had been twisted and blown out of proportion. They were unimportant, she said. Unimportant to witches, and to the supernatural interracial council.

As Coven Leader, my mother had also led the interracial council, and as her heir I'd been sitting in on meetings since I was twelve. Some wits liken the council to a supernatural United Nations. That's not a bad comparison. Like the UN, we're supposed to keep the peace, to end injustice in our world. Unfortunately, also like its human counterpart, our power lies more in a semi-mythical reputation than in reality.

Last year, I'd overheard my mother and fellow council member Robert Vasic arguing over the importance of Cabals. These days Robert downplayed his role in the council, acting more as a resource and ceding his place to his stepson Adam who, like Robert, was a half-demon. Though Robert claimed he was backing off because of declining health, I often suspected that he was frustrated with the council's limited sphere of influence, its inability to fight the true evil in our world. In the argument I'd overheard he'd been trying to convince my mother that we needed to pay more attention to Cabals. Now, I was ready to agree.

Once I got home I called Robert. No answer. Robert was also a professor of demonology at Stanford, so I tried his office there and left a message on his machine. Then I almost dialed Adam's old number before remembering that he'd moved back home last month, after enrolling at Stanford to take his second shot at a bachelor's degree.

A year older than I, Adam has also been attending council meetings since adolescence, preparing for his role. We've been friends for almost as long—discounting our actual first meeting, where I called him a dumb ox and he roasted me for it, literally, leaving burns that lasted for weeks. Which might give some idea of what kind of half-demon he is.

Next I prepared to make a far tougher call: to Margaret Levine. If Leah and Sandford were serious about this custody suit, they'd have to contact her. I should have thought of this yesterday, but my knee-jerk reaction had been *not* to tell the Elders.

I was still dialing when Savannah emerged from her room, cordless phone in hand.

"You called Adam?" she said.

"No, I called Robert. And how'd you know that?"

"Redial."

"Why are you checking the redial?"

"Did you tell Adam about Leah? I bet he'd like another shot at her. Oh, and how about Elena and Clay? They'd come too, if you asked. Well, Clay wouldn't. Not if *you* asked. But Elena would come, and he'd follow." She thumped down beside me on the sofa. "If we got everyone together again, you guys could kick ass, like back at the compound. Remember?"

I remembered. What I remember most was the smell. The overwhelming stench of death. Corpse upon corpse, littering the floors. Although I'd killed no one, I'd participated. I'd agreed it was necessary, that every human who had been involved in kidnapping supernaturals had to die, to guarantee that our secrets would not leave those walls. That didn't mean I didn't still jolt awake at least once a month, bathed in sweat, smelling death.

"For now, let's see if we can handle this ourselves," I said.

"You haven't told the Elders yet, have you?"

"I will. It's just—"

"Don't. They'll only screw things up. You're right. We can handle this. All we need to do is find Leah. Then we can kill her."

Savannah said this with a nonchalance that took my breath away. Before I could respond, the doorbell rang.

It was the Elders. All three of them, standing on my porch, their expressions ranging from vapid confusion (Margaret) to worried concern (Therese) to barely contained fury (Victoria).

Margaret Levine, Therese Moss, and Victoria Alden had been the Coven Elders for as long as I could remember. They'd been my mother's friends and, as such, part of my life. I remember, even as recently as last summer, seeing the four of them sitting down together for their regular Wednesday Elders meeting, and thinking what a disparate group they made.

Therese fit the image Gabriel Sandford ascribed to witches, right down to the blue rinse and polyester stretch pants. The stereotypical grandmother with a wide lap and a purse that held enough supplies to see her through a three-day siege. Savannah's aunt Margaret was, at sixty-eight, the youngest of the Elders. A beauty in her youth, Margaret was still strikingly attractive, but, unfortunately, fulfilled another stereotype, that of the dim-witted beauty. And Victoria Alden? She was the model twenty-first-century senior, an impeccably groomed, energetic woman, who wore suits to church and khakis on the golf course, and sniffed at less active seniors, as if any physical or mental impairment they suffered was due to self-neglect.

Once I'd undone the perimeter and locking spells and opened the door, Victoria barreled past and strode into the living room, not bothering to remove her shoes. That was a bad sign. Rules of Coven etiquette—which bore a disquieting resemblance to those by Emily Post, circa 1950—dictated that one always removed one's shoes at the door, as a courtesy to the housekeeper. Walking in with your shoes on treaded the border of insult. Fortunately, Therese and Margaret did take off their orthopedic slip-ons, so I knew the situation wasn't critical.

"We need to talk," Victoria said.

"Would you like some tea first?" I said. "I should have fresh muffins, too, if Savannah hasn't finished them."

"We aren't here to eat, Paige," Victoria said from the living room.

"Tea, then?"

"No."

Turning down baked goods was damning enough, but to refuse a hot beverage? Almost unheard of in the annals of Coven history.

"How could you have kept this from us?" Victoria said as I joined them in the living room. "A custody battle is bad enough. A legal custody battle. But—"

"It's not a legal custody battle," Savannah said, slipping around the corner. "Taking custody means kidnapping, like breaking in at midnight and dragging me away kicking and screaming. That kind of custody battle."

Victoria turned to me. "What is she talking about?"

"Savannah? How about you take your aunt downstairs and show her your artwork."

"No."

"Savannah, please. We have to talk."

"So? It's about my life, isn't it?"

"See?" Victoria turned to Therese and Margaret, and waved a hand at Savannah and me. "This is the problem. The girl has no respect for Paige."

"The girl has a name," I said.

"Don't interrupt. You aren't ready for this, Paige. I said so right from the start. We should never have let you take her. You're too young and she's too—"

"We are fine," I said, teeth gritted so hard they hurt.

"Wanna see my art, Aunt Maggie?" Savannah asked. "My teacher says I have real talent. Come see." She bounced off, wearing a "good-girl" grin that looked as painful as my clenched teeth.

"Come on, Aunt Maggie," Savannah called back, her voice a high-pitched singsong. "I'll show you my cartoons."

"No!" I yelled after her as Margaret followed. "The oils, please. The oils."

Somehow I doubted Margaret would see the humor in Savannah's dark cartoons. They'd probably give the Elder a heart attack. Just what I needed.

Once they were gone, Victoria turned on me. "You should have told us about this."

"I just got the notice yesterday after we spoke on the phone. I didn't take it seriously, so I didn't want to upset you. Then, when I met with them this morning, I realized it *was* serious, and I was just about to call Margaret—"

"I'm sure you were."

"Now, Victoria," Therese murmured.

"Do you know what they're threatening to do?" Victoria continued. "Expose you. Expose us. They're alleging you're an unfit guardian because you're a practicing witch."

"So are thousands of mothers in this country," I said. "It's called Wicca and it's a recognized religious choice."

"That's not what we are, Paige. Don't confuse the issue."

"I'm not. Every person who reads that custody challenge will jump to the conclusion that by 'witch' they mean 'Wiccan.'"

"I don't care what they'll conclude. I care about protecting the Coven. I will not allow you to risk exposing us—"

"That's it! Of course. Now I get it. *That's* why Leah's accusing me of witchcraft. Not because she thinks it'll win the lawsuit. She wants to scare us. A witch's worst fear is exposure. She's preying on that weakness. Exploiting it. She threatens us with exposure, and you'll force me to relinquish Savannah."

"A small price to pay—"

"But we can't let her win. If this ruse succeeds, they'll use it again. Every time a supernatural wants something from the Coven, they'll pull the same scam."

Victoria hesitated.

I hurried on. "Give me three days. After that, I promise you won't hear anything more about witches in East Falls."

After a moment, Victoria gave a curt nod. "Three days."

"There's just one other thing. And I'm telling you, not because I believe it, but because I don't want you to hear it from someone else. They say Savannah's father is a sorcerer."

"Wouldn't surprise me. There is definitely something wrong with the girl."

"There is nothing—" I began, then cut myself short. "But it's not possible, is it? For a witch and a sorcerer to have a child?"

"How should I know?" Victoria said.

As Victoria snapped at me, I thought of my mother, how she would have responded. No matter how many questions I asked, or how silly they seemed, she always found the time to answer, or to find an answer. I stifled the sharp pang of grief and pushed on.

"Have you ever *heard* of it happening?" I asked.

"Of course not. Coven witches would never do such a thing. But I'd believe it of Eve Levine. You remember Eve, Therese. She'd do such a thing simply because it *was* unnatural."

"What does Savannah say?" Therese asked.

"She has no idea who her father is. I haven't mentioned the paternity suit. She thinks Leah's the one suing for custody."

"Good," Victoria said. "Let's keep it that way. I don't want anyone in the Coven knowing of this. I won't have them thinking we allowed a witch with sorcerer blood to join our Coven. You'll mention none of this to anyone. I don't want to frighten them into thinking a sorcerer could come to East Falls."

"A sorcerer? In town?" Therese fairly squeaked with terror.

Victoria's eyes narrowed. "He isn't in town already, is he?"

"As far as I know, Kristof Nast is still in Los Angeles," I said, deciding not to complicate the matter by mentioning Sandford. "I'll take care of the witch accusation, and the custody challenge."

Therese nodded. "You need to handle it properly, dear. Get a lawyer. The Carys are good."

Bring a human lawyer into this mess? Not likely—wait, maybe that wasn't so crazy after all. It gave me an idea. I steered the conference to an end.

CHAPTER 5

THE BEAUTY OF SCIENCE

Once the front door had closed behind the Elders, I cast fresh lock and perimeter spells, then grabbed the phone book. Savannah walked in.

"It's a real custody battle, isn't it?" she said, taking a seat on the sofa.

"I thought you knew that."

"When you said Leah wanted custody, I figured you meant she wanted you to just hand me over."

"It doesn't matter. They don't have a case—"

"So Leah has a lawyer and everything? What is he? A sorcerer, I bet."

"Yes, but there's no need to worry."

"Oh, I'm not scared of any sorcerer. Or any lawyer. You know, we should get one."

"I was just about to call Mr. Cary."

"I meant a *sorcerer* lawyer. They're really good at it. All the best sorcerers are lawyers. Well, until they get older and become politicians. That's what my mom always said."

Here was the perfect opening for a query that might help answer the question of Savannah's paternity, something like "Did your mother, uh, know a lot of sorcerers?" Of course I didn't ask. I never asked anything about Eve. If Savannah wanted to tell me, she would.

"Witches don't work with sorcerers," I said.

"Oh, please. That's for Coven witches. A real witch works with anyone who can help her. A sorcerer lawyer could help, as long as we picked carefully. Most of them are real jerks—they won't have anything to do with witches—but Mom knew a few who'd take a case like this, if you paid them enough."

"I'm not hiring a sorcerer. I'm getting a human lawyer."

"Are you serious? Don't be stupid, Paige. You can't—"

"Why can't I? They won't be expecting it. If I get a human lawyer, Leah will need to handle this case by the books. The *human* law books. No secret meetings discussing sorcerers and Cabals—"

"What about the Cabals?"

"I'm just saying, they can't talk about that kind of thing in front of a human lawyer. If they want to play by human laws, let them. I'll play right along."

She frowned, and leaned back into the sofa cushions. "That might not be such a stupid idea after all."

"Glad you approve."

Friday morning started off feeling very familiar. Like the day before, I decided to keep Savannah home from school, picked up her assignments, took her to Abby's, then returned to the Carys' law office for another ten o'clock meeting.

This time my meeting was with Grant Cary, Jr. Yes, I chose Grant junior. Despite my misgivings about the guy's moral compass, he was a good lawyer. He knew me . . . well, not as well as he'd like, but well enough. When I spoke to him on the phone yesterday, he seemed interested in the case and we'd arranged to meet at ten. I'd set up a conference with Leah and Sandford for eleven.

I'd been sitting in Cary's office for twenty minutes, gazing out the oversized window behind his desk while he read through my papers. So far everything had gone well. Other than a lingering look at my boobs when I walked in, he hadn't done anything untoward. I'd probably been too harsh on the guy. I seemed to attract a lot of Cary-types—forty-something married guys who see me, if not as a gorgeous blonde who'd look great on their arm, then as a young woman who might enjoy and appreciate the attention of an older man.

From what I'd seen of Grantham Cary, Jr., he likely hit on every younger woman he met. You know the type. All-American boy of 1975, the town's brightest star, every girl in town wetting her pants if he so much as looked at her. Fast-forward to 2001. His weekly golf game no longer keeps his love handles in check, he's recently resorted to a slight comb-over to cover that growing bald spot, he squints to avoid wearing the bifocals he hides in his desk drawer, and he spends his days in an office filled with decades-old sports trophies. Still a good-looking guy, but these days more likely to be coveted for his bank account than his biceps.

"Well," Cary said, returning the last sheet to the stack. "This certainly is unusual."

"I—I can explain," I said. I could?

"Let me guess," Cary said. "You're not really a witch and this is simply a ploy to gain custody of Savannah by dredging up an uncomfortable element of East Falls's past and playing on the historical paranoia of this particular region of New England."

"Uh, yes," I said. "Something like that."

Cary laughed. "Don't worry, Paige. It's a very transparent scheme obviously dreamed up by folks who don't know much about modern-day Massachusetts. You say this man, Kristof Nast, has no proof that he's Savannah's father? But I assume he's willing to submit to a DNA test?"

"DNA?"

"We can't just take his say-so on the matter."

Of course they couldn't. This was a human court, which played by human rules. A court that wouldn't understand why Kristof Nast couldn't submit DNA. Any supernatural knew that we couldn't risk having humans study our DNA, but to a human judge, it was evidence so easily given that to refuse would be tantamount to an admission of fraud.

"He won't give DNA," I said.

Cary's brows shot up. "Are you sure about that?"

"Absolutely," I said, breaking into a grin. "Is that good?"

Cary leaned back in his chair and laughed. "That's better than good. It's wonderful, Paige. If Sandford's client refuses to submit DNA, he has no case. I'll see to it."

"Thank you."

"Don't thank me yet," he said. "You haven't seen my bill."

He laughed loudly, as if unaware this was a very old joke, but I was in the mood to be generous, so I laughed along. We spent the next thirty minutes discussing the case. Then we wrapped it up and prepared for the meeting with Leah and Sandford. I hadn't told them Cary was representing me. They thought they were coming for a private conference with me.

I do love surprises.

I was sitting in the meeting room, alone, when Lacey ushered in Sandford and Leah on the dot of eleven o'clock. Cary had agreed to wait a few minutes before joining us.

Leah fairly bounced in, like a kid on Christmas morning. Sandford followed, trying—but not very hard—to conceal a self-satisfied smirk.

"Do you have the papers?" I asked, injecting a quaver into my voice.

"Of course." Sandford slid them across the table to me.

For a few minutes, I stared down at the pages that would relinquish my custody rights to Savannah. I inhaled deeply.

"I know this is tough," Leah said, her voice stuffed with gloating sarcasm. "But it's for the best, Paige. It really is."

Another couple minutes of staring at the pages, replete with tortured sighs. Then I said, "I can't do this."

"Yes, you can," Sandford said.

"No, really, I can't." I shoved the papers back to him, with a grin to mirror his. "I'm not giving her up."

"What?" Leah said.

"Oh, it was a clever plan, I'll give you that. Threaten me with exposure and make sure the Elders hear about it. If I don't cave, they'll force me. Well, you underestimated the Coven. With their support, I'm fighting this petition."

The look on their faces was a memory to cherish forever.

"And what does Margaret Levine say about this?" Leah asked.

"You want to know?" I asked. I lifted the phone. "Call her. I'm sure you have the number. Call all the Elders. Ask them if they support me."

"This is bullshit." Leah aimed a glare at Sandford, as if it was his fault.

"No," I said. "It's not bullshit. I assure you, I understand that this is a serious legal matter and, as such, I'm treating it very seriously. To that end, I've hired legal representation."

I walked to the door and waved in Cary, who'd been waiting in the hall.

"I believe you've met Mr. Cary," I said.

Their jaws dropped. Okay, they didn't actually drop, like in the cartoons, but you get the idea.

"But he's a—" Leah began before stopping herself.

"A damn fine lawyer," I said. "And I'm so glad he's agreed to represent me."

"Thank you, Paige." Cary's smile held a bit more personal warmth than I liked, but I was too happy to care. "Now, let's get straight to the heart of the matter. About the DNA test. May I assume your client is willing to submit to one immediately?"

Sandford blanched. "Our—my client is a . . . a very busy man. His business interests make it quite impossible to leave Los Angeles at the moment."

"Otherwise he'd be here now," I said. "Hmmm, doesn't that seem odd? He's so interested in gaining custody of his daughter, but can't find a few days to fly out and meet her."

"He could provide the sample in California," Cary said. "Our firm may be small, but we have contacts in San Francisco. I'm sure they'd be happy to oversee the testing."

"My client does not wish to submit to DNA testing."

"No DNA, no case," Cary said.

Sandford glared at me.

"Checkmate," I said. And grinned.

When Sandford and Leah left, Cary turned to me and smiled.

"That went well, don't you think?"

I grinned. "Better than well. It was perfect. Thank you so much."

"With any luck, it's all over. I can't imagine them pursuing the case without DNA." He checked his watch. "Do you have time for coffee? We can discuss the final details before my next appointment."

"Details? But if it's over . . . ?"

"We hope it is, but we need to cover every contingency, Paige. I'll let Lacey know we're leaving."

CHAPTER 6

SHOT DOWN

Cary and I walked to Melinda's Bakery on State Street. Even by my jaded big-city standards, Melinda's was a first-rate bakery. The coffee alone almost made living in East Falls bearable. And the scones? If I ever persuaded the Elders to let us move, I'd be making weekly runs to East Falls for Melinda's raisin scones.

I would have preferred a window table, but Cary selected one near the back. Admittedly, even the main street of East Falls has little to offer in the way of people-watching and, since we were discussing confidential legal matters, I understood why Cary picked a more private seating arrangement.

When we sat down, he pointed at my scone. "I'm glad to see you're not one of those girls who's always on a diet. I like women who aren't afraid to look like women."

"Uh-huh."

"The girls these days, dieting until they're so thin you can't tell if they're a boy or a girl. You're different. You always look so"—his gaze dropped to my chest—"put together. It's so nice to see a young woman who still wears skirts and dresses."

"So you think they'll drop the case?"

Cary added three creamers to his coffee and stirred it before answering.

"Reasonably certain," he said. "There are a few more things I need to do."

"Like what?"

"Paperwork. Even in the simplest case, there's always paperwork." He sipped his coffee. "Now, I suppose you want to hear how much this is going to cost you."

I smiled. "Well, I can't say I want to hear it, but I should. Do you have an estimate?"

He pulled out his legal pad, ripped off the top sheet, and started tallying figures on a clean page. As the list grew, my eyes widened. When he wrote a total at the bottom, I choked on a mouthful of coffee.

"Is that— Please tell me there's a decimal missing," I said.

"Legal expertise doesn't come cheap, Paige."

"I know that. I have legal work done for my business all the time, but my bills don't look like that." I pulled the legal pad toward me and flipped it around. "What's this? Nine billable hours accrued? We only met today, from ten until"—I checked my watch—"eleven-forty."

"I did need to review your case last night, Paige."

"You reviewed it this morning. In front of me. Remember?"

"Yes, but last night I was researching similar cases."

"For seven hours?"

"'Billable hours' is a complex concept that doesn't necessarily correspond to actual time spent."

"No kidding. And what's this? Three hundred dollars for photocopying? What did you do? Hire Franciscan monks to transcribe my file by hand? I can make copies at the 7-Eleven for ten cents a page."

"We're hardly dealing with the straight cost of copying, Paige. You have to take into consideration the costs of labor."

"Your wife does all your secretarial work. You don't even pay her."

"I understand it may not be easy for you to pay this, Paige. I sympathize. I really do. That's one of the fundamental problems with the practice of law. Those who are most deserving of our help often can't afford it."

"It's not that I can't afford—"

He held up a hand to stop me. "I understand. Really I do. It's a difficult burden to place on someone who's only trying to do what's best for a child. Making you pay this much wouldn't be fair. I only wanted to show you how much something like this could cost."

I eased back into my seat. "Okay. So—"

"Unfortunately, this is how much my father and Lacey will expect me to charge you. What we need to do is discuss this further, see how we can reduce the cost." He checked his watch. "I have a client in twenty minutes, so we can't do this now. How about I finish the case, then we can meet over lunch and discuss the full bill." He took out his DayTimer. "Say Monday?"

"I guess so."

"Good. We'll go someplace nice. Someplace in Boston. Do you still have that dress you wore to the Memorial Day picnic? Wear that."

"Wear—?"

"And find a sitter for Savannah after school. We probably won't be back until evening."

"Evening—?"

He smiled. "I like long negotiation sessions. Very long. Very intense." He leaned forward, leg rubbing against mine. "I know how difficult it must be for you, Paige. Living in East Falls. Caring for a child. Not a lot of eligible young men in town, and I doubt you get many opportunities to get out and meet someone. You're a very attractive young woman. You need someone who can appreciate your . . . special needs. It could be a very profitable alliance for you."

"Oh, I get it. You're saying you'll waive your fees if I have sex with you."

Half the people in the restaurant turned. Cary leaned forward to shush me.

"But the bill's only a couple grand," I said. "For that you'd be lucky to get a hand job."

He motioned me to silence, eyes darting from side to side, trying to see who might have overheard.

"Does Lacey know about this creative financing arrangement?" I continued. "How about I call and ask her? See if she's willing to forgo this much profit so her husband can get laid."

I took my cell phone from my purse. Cary grabbed for it, but I waved it out of his reach. I hit a few buttons. He flew across the table, hands out like a wide receiver lunging for the game-breaking pass. I shoved my chair out of his reach, then leaned over and dropped the phone back into my purse. Cary lay stretched across the table for a few seconds, then slowly raised himself up, adjusted his tie, and glanced around, as if trying to convince himself that not everyone in the bakery was watching.

"I hate to eat and run," I said, standing. "But I have to go pick up Savannah. In case you didn't guess, the answer is no. Don't take it too hard. It's not just because you're married. It's because you've been married longer than I've been alive."

A snicker sounded behind us, followed by an ill-stifled giggle. As I passed the counter, Nellie, the cashier, shot me a discreet thumbs-up.

Savannah went to bed at nine-thirty without protest, after spending the evening helping me with some graphic work for a website contract. Yes, we not only spent quality time together, but she lent me her artistic expertise without even a joking request for compensation. It was one of those perfect one-in-a-million days, a karmic reward for the crap I'd endured.

At ten o'clock, I carried a cup of tea into the living room, preparing to curl up with a book for a much-deserved mental holiday.

As I settled into the sofa, I noticed a wavering light on the front porch.

I set aside my mug, then leaned over, pulled back the curtains, and peered into the night. Someone had placed a burning candle on the far corner of the porch railing. Witches, candles, get it? Next thing you knew, they'd be hanging crystal unicorns from my mailbox. Kids.

I was inclined to ignore the candle until I finished my tea, but if my neighbor across the street, Miss Harris, saw it, she'd probably call the fire department and accuse me of trying to torch the neighborhood.

As I stepped onto the porch, I saw the candle clearly and my breath caught. It was in the shape of a human hand, each fingertip glowing with a tiny flame. The Hand of Glory. This went beyond an innocent child's prank. Whoever did this knew something about the occult and had a very sick turn of mind.

I marched toward the candle. As I snatched it up, my fingers clamped down, not on hard wax, but cold flesh. I yelped and jerked back, throwing the thing to the ground below. A flame flared and a puff of smoke billowed up. I raced down the steps and grabbed the hand, but again, as I touched the icy flesh, my brain balked and I dropped it.

Lights flickered in Miss Harris's house. I dropped to my knees, hiding the hand from view, and whacked at the small fire burning through dead grass clippings that Savannah had shoved under the porch. The flames singed my palm. I stifled a yelp and kept smacking the pile until the fire was out.

Then I closed my eyes, caught my breath, and turned to look at the thing lying in the grass. It was a severed hand, skin grayish brown, a nub of sawed bone sticking from the bottom, the flesh wrinkled and stinking of preservatives. Each finger had been coated in wax and fitted with a wick.

"The Hand of Glory."

I jumped and saw Savannah leaning over the railing.

"Is Miss Harris watching?" I whispered.

Savannah glanced across the road. "She's looking through her blinds, but all she can see is your butt sticking up in the air."

"Go inside and get me something to wrap it in."

A moment later, Savannah tossed me a hand towel. One of my good hand towels. I hesitated, then bundled the hand. This wasn't the time for worrying about linen. Any minute now Miss Harris would venture onto her porch for a better look.

"Must be the sorcerer," Savannah said. "Leah wouldn't know how to make one of those. Is it preserved or dried?"

I didn't answer. I stood, hands trembling around the bundle. Savannah reached over the railing for it. Motioning her back into the house, I hurried up the steps.

Once inside, I shoved the towel-wrapped hand under the kitchen sink, then ran to the bathroom and turned on the hot water full blast. Savannah came in as I was scrubbing.

"I'll bury it later," I said.

"Maybe we should keep it," Savannah said. "They're tough to make, you know."

"No, I wouldn't know," I snapped.

Silence.

Through the mirror, I saw Savannah behind me, her expression unreadable, eyes shuttered.

"I didn't mean—" I began.

"I know what you meant," she said, then turned, went into her room and shut the door. Not slamming it, just closing it softly behind her.

The Hand of Glory is a thief's tool. According to legend, it's supposed to keep the occupants of a house asleep. Criminal, to be sure, but neither harmful nor dangerous. So was Leah planning to break into my place tonight? If so, why leave the hand on my porch railing in midevening? Or did she just put the macabre candle there to attract attention and cause more trouble for me? That also didn't make sense. By placing it outside my front window, chances seemed good that I'd see it first and get rid of it before anyone noticed.

I lay in bed, trying to figure out Leah's motivation, but all I could think about was the hand itself, wrapped under my sink. The stink of it seemed to permeate the house. The feel of the cold flesh clung to my fingers despite my having scrubbed them raw. I couldn't shake the memory of touching it, couldn't forget it was still in my house, couldn't stop worrying about how to dispose of it. I was spooked. And maybe that, after all, was Leah's goal.

I'd set my alarm for two A.M., but I needn't have bothered with the alarm. I didn't sleep, only lay there, counting the minutes. At one-thirty, I decided it was late enough.

Chapter 7

Initiate Phase Two

I covered my silk chemise with the matching kimono before leaving my room. For some reason, this seemed to make more sense than getting dressed. From the hall closet, I selected the old rubber boots my mother had used for gardening. I'd kept them, maybe in the dim hope that someday I'd sprout a green thumb.

I slipped out the back door. I'd left the hand under the sink, so if someone caught me digging, at least they wouldn't see what I was burying. Yeah, like that was going to help matters if anyone saw me in the forest after midnight, digging a hole while dressed in a red silk kimono and black rubber boots.

Once outside, I caught a whiff of smoke. As my stomach clenched, I cursed my fear. In first-year psychology I read a theory that all the major phobias are the result of hereditary memory, that our distant ancestors had good reason to fear snakes and heights, so evolution passed those fears on to future generations. Maybe that explains witches' fear of fire. I fight against it, but seem unable to completely overcome the fear.

Struggling against instinct, I sniffed the air, searching for the source of the smell. Was it smoke from a fireplace extinguished hours ago? Smoldering embers from an evening trash-burning? As I scanned the darkness, I noticed an orange glow to the east, in the forest behind my back fence. A bush party. With the weather warming, local teens must have found something better to do on a Friday night than hang out in the hardware store parking lot. Great, now the hand would have to stay in my house until tomorrow night. I didn't dare bury it with a potential audience looking on.

As I turned to go back in the house, I noticed the silence. Complete silence. Since when did partying teens sit silently around a campfire? I considered other excuses for a late-night fire. East Falls was too small for a homeless population. Could a dropped match or cigarette have ignited the undergrowth? Could someone be secretly burning hazardous material? Either required action.

I tiptoed across the grass, wondering whether I'd have another fire to put out. Two in one evening—coincidence? Oh, God, please don't let this be a second Hand of Glory. I inhaled and pushed past my revulsion. If it was, at least I'd seen it before anyone else had.

As I reached the fence, I was glad I hadn't done anything so foolish as calling the fire department. There, laid out in the grass, was a ring of lit black candles surrounding a red cloth embroidered with a goat's head. A Satanic altar.

With an oath, I raced to put out the candles. Then I saw that they encircled a blood-covered heap. For one terrible, endless moment I thought it was a child's body. Then I saw the face and realized it was a cat. A skinned cat: a lifeless mass of blood and muscle, teeth bared in a lipless snarl.

I twisted away from the sight. Something slapped me in the face, something cold and wet. Frantically shoving it away, I stumbled back, but my hand caught in a loop of spongy elastic. I bit back a shriek. I looked up and saw what I'd hit: another skinned cat, this one hanging from a tree, its belly sliced open, guts spilling out. A loop of intestine was wrapped around my hand.

I yanked free barely in time to bring my hands to my mouth to stifle my scream. I fell to my knees, chest heaving, struggling for breath. My hands were covered in blood. My stomach lurched and I spilled my dinner into the grass. For several minutes, I crouched there, unable to move.

"Paige?" Savannah's whisper floated from the backyard.

"No!" I hissed and sprang to my feet. "Stay there!"

I ran and grabbed her as she rounded the corner. Her eyes widened and I knew she'd seen everything, but I still pushed her away.

"Go—go back in the house," I said. "I—I have to clean it up."

"I'll help."

"No!"

Silence.

"I'm sorry," I said. "I didn't mean—" I realized I was getting vomit and blood all over her bathrobe and pulled back. "I'm sorry. Go inside and clean up. No, wait. Put your robe in a bag. I'll burn it—"

"Paige . . ."

"I— Take a shower," I stammered. "But leave the lights off. Don't turn on any lights. No radio, no lights, nothing. Don't open the blinds—"

"Paige!" Savannah said, grabbing my shoulders. "I can help." She enunciated each word as if I might not understand her. "It's okay. I've seen this kind of stuff before."

"No, you haven't. Get in—"

"Yes, I have. Goddamn it, Paige—"

"Don't swear."

Savannah blinked and, for a second, she looked as if she might cry. "I know what that stuff is, Paige. Like I know what a Hand of Glory is. Why do you keep pretending I don't?"

As she tore off, I started going after her. Then a light flicked on next door and I froze. I looked from Savannah's retreating back to the glow of the candles behind me. I didn't have time to go after her—not now. Leah had composed this horrific tableau for a reason and I doubted she went to all that trouble just to spook me. The police would receive an anonymous phone call: "Go look behind Paige Winterbourne's house." I had to clear this before anyone followed up on that tip.

To the left of the altar was a blackened mound that I hadn't seen earlier. Smoke rose from the mound carrying with it the stench of burned meat. I closed my eyes to compose myself, then approached the smoldering heap and bent to look at it. At first glance, I couldn't tell what it was, or what it had been. I wanted to walk away then, get a shovel, and bury it without ever knowing. But I had to know. If I didn't, I'd lie awake at night, wondering what I'd buried.

I took a stick and prodded at the mound. At the first sharp jab, it fell apart, exposing a sawed-open rib cage. I pressed the back of my hand to my eyes and took a deep breath. The very taste of it filled my mouth and I lurched forward, spilling whatever was left in my stomach.

Oh, God, I couldn't—I just couldn't. No, I had to. This was my problem, my responsibility.

I forced my gaze back to the charred bones, struggling to study them with a scientist's eye. From my few years of biology, I could differentiate between a biped and quadruped ribcage. This was quadruped. To be sure, I poked the stick near the end of the spine, revealing a tail. Yes, definitely an animal. Probably another cat. Okay, I could handle this now. Observe without truly seeing, that was the trick.

I stood and surveyed the site. My brain processed the details, making no judgments, allowing no reactions. There was a chalice filled with blood beside the dead cat on the makeshift altar. Yes, that was to be expected. Black Mass was an inversion and perversion of the Catholic Mass. In a university folklore course I'd done my term project on Satanic cults, debating whether they fit the standard definition of a contemporary legend, so I knew what to look for, what I needed to find and clear away.

There should be an inverted crucifix . . . yes, there it was, hanging from the tree. I strode over and pulled it down. Pentagrams? No, it appeared they'd overlooked . . . wait, there, drawn in the dirt. I started to erase it with my boot, then grabbed a handful of brush instead, so I wouldn't leave footprints. Okay, that seemed to be everything.

Next I needed to bury the corpses. I turned to look at the eviscerated cat in the tree. I willed my gaze past the poor beast to study the hanging device instead, so I'd know what I needed to cut it loose, but I couldn't help seeing the body, swaying in the breeze.

What kind of person could bring themselves not only to kill a cat, but to— My gorge rose and I doubled over, retching. This time, nothing came but a thin string of acid. I spat to clear the taste from my mouth, then, still bent over, wiped my face, took a deep breath of the foul air, and marched to the shed to find a shovel.

Twenty minutes later, I'd buried all three cats and started dismantling the altar.

"Paige?"

Savannah's whisper sent me a foot into the air. I spun to see her jogging across the lawn.

"There's a car circling the block," she said. "I've been watching out the front window."

Her eyes were red. Had she been crying? Why did I make such a mess of everything? Before I could apologize, she grabbed my arm and dragged me across the yard.

As we stepped through the back door, I glimpsed myself in the hall mirror. Blood, vomit, and dirt streaked my face, hands, and kimono. Just then lights flashed through the living room sheers. A car engine died.

"Oh, God," I said, staring into the mirror. "I can't—"

"I'm clean," Savannah said. "I'll answer it. You go wash up."

"But—"

The doorbell rang. Savannah shoved me into the living room. I ducked below window level and ran for the other side of the house.

Leah hadn't settled for placing an anonymous call to the station's overnight answering service. No, she'd called the local sheriff, Ted Fowler, at home, babbling hysterically about strange lights and screams coming from the woods behind my house.

Fowler had thrown on clothing that looked like it came from his bedroom floor and driven straight over. In reward for his haste, he found the smoldering remains of a Satanic altar a scant ten feet beyond my backyard.

By dawn my house and yard were crawling with cops. By disposing of the cat corpses, I'd only made things worse. When Fowler saw traces of blood and no bodies, his imagination leaped to the worst possible conclusion. Murder.

Since East Falls wasn't equipped to deal with homicide, the state police were called in. On the way, the detectives woke up a judge and got him to sign a search warrant. They arrived shortly before five, and Savannah and I spent the next several hours huddled in my bedroom, alternately answering questions and listening to the sound of strangers tearing apart our home.

When I heard the oven door open, I remembered the Hand of Glory under the sink. I bolted for the hall, then checked my pace and walked into the kitchen. One officer rifled through my cupboards as another waved some kind of light wand over the contents of my fridge. They glanced at me, but when I didn't speak, they returned to their work.

Heart thudding, I waited as the cupboard searcher moved to the cabinets under the counter. When he reached for the sink cupboard, I whispered a spell under my breath. It was a form of cover spell that would distort the appearance of an object. While it wouldn't have worked on the entire Satanic altar site outside, it would do fine for the wrapped bundle under the sink.

As he threw open the cupboard, I said the last words and directed the spell at the object to be hidden. Only there was no object there. The hand and the towel were gone. The officer did a cursory search, then closed the cupboard. I hurried back to the bedroom.

"What did you do with it?" I whispered.

Savannah looked up from her magazine. "With what?"

I lowered my voice another notch. "The Hand of Glory."

"I moved it."

"Good. Thank you. I completely forgot. Where'd you put it?"

She rolled onto her stomach and returned to her magazine. "Someplace safe."

"Ms. Winterbourne?"

I spun to see the lead detective from the state police in my bedroom doorway.

"We found cats," he said.

"Cats?" I repeated.

"Three dead cats buried a short distance from the scene."

I motioned toward Savannah and lifted a finger to my lips, gesturing that I didn't want this discussed in front of her. The detective moved to the living room, where several officers were lounging on my sofa and chairs, muddy shoes propped on my antique coffee table. I swallowed my outrage and turned to the detective.

"So it was cat's blood?" I said.

"Apparently, though we'll run tests to be sure."

"Good."

"Killing cats might not be on the same scale as murder, but it's still a serious offense. Very serious."

"It should be. Anyone who'd do that . . ." I didn't have to fake my shudder, needing only to remember the sight of those maimed bodies. "I can't believe someone would do that, stage a Satanic altar behind my yard."

"Stage?" the detective said. "What makes you think it was staged?"

"It looked real to me," one of the officers said, waving a cookie that looked suspiciously like the same cookies that were in my cupboard.

His wave scattered crumbs across my ivory carpet. I looked at those crumbs, looked at the muddy boot prints surrounding it, looked at the bookcase behind it, my books and photos and mementos shoved into haphazard piles, and I felt a snap. Just a small one.

"And you say that based on witnessing exactly how many Satanic altars?" I asked.

Silence.

"We've seen photos," he muttered at last.

"Oh, right. The photos. There's probably one genuine photo circulating endlessly around the entire country. Attention all units: Beware of Satanic cults. Do you know what Satanic cults are? The biggest hoax ever perpetrated by the American media. Do you know who builds all those so-called Satanic altars you hear about? Kids. Bored, angry teenagers trying to shock the establishment. That and the occasional homicidal moron who's already planning his defense: the devil made me do it. Satanic altar, my ass. What you saw out back there is a prank. A very, very sick prank."

Silence.

"You sure seem to know a lot about this stuff," one officer said.

"It's called a college education." I wheeled on the detective. "Are you charging me with anything?"

"Not yet."

"Then get the hell out of my house so I can clean up your mess."

After a tersely worded admonition against leaving town and a suggestion that I "may want to retain legal counsel," the police left.

CHAPTER 8

BLACK MASS PIZZA

The police were barely out the door when Savannah appeared from her room and dropped down beside me on the sofa.

"Black Mass," she said. "I can't believe they still believe in that stuff. Humans are so stupid."

"You shouldn't say that," I said, without much conviction.

"It's true. About the Satanism stuff at least. They get all weird about it. You try to tell them the truth, that Satan's just one of tons of demons and that he doesn't give a crap about us, and they still figure you can conjure him up and he'll give you anything you want. As if." She sunk back into the sofa cushions. "My mom had this friend, a necromancer, who used to make really good money selling Black Masses."

"Selling Black Masses?"

"You know, setting them up for people. He ran this business, 'Satanic Rites by Jorge.' His real name's Bill, but he figured he could charge more with 'Jorge.' He'd supply all this fake stuff, set it up, give them scripts, the whole thing. If he did a full Black Mass, which cost a lot, he'd buy us pizza. Black Mass pizza, we called it. We tried eating it upside-down, but the toppings fell off, so we settled for eating it backward." She sat up. "There's still pizza left from last night, isn't there? That's what I'll have for breakfast. Black Mass pizza. You want some?"

I shook my head.

Savannah trotted off to the kitchen, still chattering. I collapsed back into the sofa.

Two hours later, I was still on the couch, having ignored eight phone calls and three answering machine messages, all from reporters dreaming of a "Satanism in a Small Town" scoop. Like the police, these people knew nothing about true Satanism—not to say that I agree with that belief system, either, but at least it has nothing to do with mutilated cats and bloody pentagrams.

The Satanic cult scares that crop up periodically are just a new form of witch-hunts. People are always looking to explain evil, to find a rationale that places the blame outside the realm of human nature. The scapegoats change with remarkable ease. Heretics, witches, demonic possession, the Illuminati, they've all been targeted as hidden sources of evil in the world.

Since the sixties, Satanic cults have been the favored group. The damn tabloids publish so much crap on the subject that it's a self-perpetuating cycle—they print one story, some psycho reads it and copies the methods described, so they print his story and so on. In 1996, the government spent $750,000 to reassure the American public that Satanic cults weren't operating in the nation's day care facilities. I sleep so much better knowing they cleared up that one.

With this new development, I'd have been reluctant to send Savannah to school. Fortunately, it was Saturday, so that wasn't an issue. After lunch, she went down to the basement to work on her art. Yes, I know, most artists like big airy studios filled with natural light and soothing silence. Not Savannah. She liked the semidark basement and blaring music.

When the doorbell rang, I suspected it was one of the reporters, deciding to try something more proactive than making phone calls. So I ignored it and continued emptying the dishwasher. It rang again. I realized then that it might be the police come to renew their search. The last thing I needed was cops busting down my door. They'd done enough damage already.

I hurried to the front hall, undid the spells, and flung open the door to see a young man. He was about six feet tall, thin, with a face so average I doubted anyone remembered him five minutes after meeting him. Short dark hair, clean-shaven, Hispanic. Presumably dark eyes behind his wire-frame glasses, but he wouldn't meet my gaze. He stood there, eyes downcast, clutching an armful of papers with a beat-up satchel slung over one shoulder. Oh, did I mention he was wearing a suit? On a Saturday? Wonderful. Just what I needed. A Jehovah's Witness.

"Lucas Cortez," he said, shifting the papers to his left hand and extending his right. "Your new legal counsel."

"Look, I'm not interested—" I stopped. "Did you say 'legal counsel'?"

"I'll be taking your case from here, Ms. Winterbourne." Despite his lowered gaze, his voice was confident. "We should step inside."

He brushed past me without waiting for an invitation. As I stood, momentarily dumbfounded, Cortez took off his shoes, walked into the living room, and surveyed his surroundings, as if assessing my ability to pay for his services.

"I assume the disarray is from the search," he said. "This is unacceptable. I'll speak to them about it. I presume they had a warrant? Ah, here it is."

He picked up the warrant from the coffee table, added it to his papers, and walked into the kitchen.

"Wait a second," I said, hurrying after him. "You can't just take that."

"Do you have a copier?"

I swung into the kitchen. He'd already established himself at the table, moved my things aside, and started spreading his papers.

"I take my coffee black."

"You can take your coffee down at the doughnut shop unless you tell me who sent you here."

"You are in need of legal services, are you not?"

I hesitated. "Oh, I get it. No one sent you. What do they call you guys? Ambulance chasers? I'm not interested. And if you try to bill me for this visit—"

"I'll do nothing of the sort. This visit is entirely free. A sampling of my services. I've taken the liberty of acquainting myself with your case, and I've devised a strategy for defending you." He moved two papers across the table, and turned them to face me. "As you'll see, this is a simple contract stating that, by agreeing to speak to me today, you are in no way committing yourself to retaining my services and will not be charged for this meeting."

I scanned the contract. For a legal document, it was surprisingly straightforward, a simple statement that relieved me of any obligation for this initial consultation. I glanced at Cortez, who was busy reading the warrant. He couldn't be more than late twenties, probably just out of law school. I'd once dated a newly graduated lawyer, and I knew how tough it could be to find work. As a young entrepreneur myself, could I really blame this guy for hard-selling his services? If, as the police suggested, I did need a lawyer, it certainly wouldn't be someone this young, but there was no harm in hearing him out.

I signed the contract, then passed it to him. He said nothing, just added his signature and handed me a copy.

"Let's start by discussing credentials," I said.

Without looking up from his papers, he said, "Let me assure you, Ms. Winterbourne, there is no one more qualified to handle your case."

"Humor me, then. Where'd you go to school? Where do you practice? How many custody cases have you handled? What percentage have you won? Any experience handling defamation of character? Because that may be a possibility here."

More paper gazing. Some paper shuffling. I was two seconds from showing him to the door, when he turned, eyes still downcast.

"Let's get this over with then, shall we?" he said.

He looked up at me. I dropped the contract. Lucas Cortez was a sorcerer.

CHAPTER 9

SPELL-BOY

"Get out of my house," I said.

"As you can see, I'm quite qualified to handle your case, Paige."

"So now it's 'Paige'? Did Savannah hire you?"

"No." He said this without surprise, as if the thought of a child witch hiring a sorcerer lawyer wasn't at all peculiar.

"Then who sent you?"

"As you've already determined, no one sent me. You called me an ambulance chaser and I didn't argue the point. Though, admittedly, I find the phrase reprehensible, the motivation it implies can be accurately applied to me. There are two ways for a lawyer to rise in the supernatural world. Join a Cabal or gain a reputation for successfully fighting them. I have chosen the latter route." He paused. "May I have that coffee?"

"Sure. Just go out my front door, make a left at the end of the road, and look for the big neon doughnut. You can't miss it."

"As I was saying, being a young lawyer seeking to make a name for myself outside the Cabals I must, unfortunately, chase down my cases. I heard of Mr. Nast's intent to seek custody of Savannah and, seeing an opportunity, I followed it. I understand Mr. Nast has not yet abandoned his challenge?"

"He refuses to submit to DNA testing, meaning he can't prove he's Savannah's father, meaning I don't see a case and don't need a lawyer. Now, if you'd like those directions again—"

"While his refusal to surrender a DNA sample may seem advantageous, let me assure you, it doesn't eliminate the problem. Gabriel Sandford is an excellent lawyer. He'll find a way around this, likely by bribing a medical laboratory to provide phony test results."

"And willingness to bribe officials makes one an excellent lawyer?"

"Yes."

I opened my mouth, but nothing came out. How could I answer that? Cortez continued, "If he does attempt such a maneuver, I will insist that the court supervise the testing." He returned to his papers. "Now, I've prepared a list of steps we should take to—"

Savannah walked into the kitchen and stopped short, assessing Cortez and his accoutrements.

"What's with the salesman?" she asked. Then she looked Cortez in the face. She didn't even blink, only tightened her mouth. "What do you want, sorcerer?"

"I prefer Lucas," he said, extending a hand. "Lucas Cortez. I'm representing Paige."

"Repres—" Savannah looked at me. "Where'd you find him?"

"The yellow pages," I said. "Under 'U.' For unsolicited, uninvited, and unwanted. He's not my lawyer."

Savannah sized Cortez up. "Good, 'cause if you want a sorcerer lawyer, you can do much better than this."

"I'm sure you can," Cortez said. "However, since I am the only one who's here, perhaps I can be of some assistance."

"You can't," I said. "Now, if you've forgotten the way to the door—"

"Hold on," Savannah said. "He's pretty young, so he's probably cheap. Maybe he'll do until we can get someone better."

"My services are extremely reasonable and will be agreed upon in advance," Cortez said. "While it may seem at this point as if Nast doesn't have a case—"

"Who's Nast?" Savannah asked.

"He means Leah," I said, shooting Cortez a "don't argue" glare. "It's O'Donnell, not Nast."

"My mistake," Cortez said without missing a beat. "As I was saying, Leah has not withdrawn her petition for custody and shows no signs of doing so. Therefore we must assume that she plans to pursue that endeavor. Thwarting her efforts must be our primary purpose. To that end, I have drawn up a list of steps."

"The twelve-step program for un-demonizing my life?"

"No, there are only seven steps, but if you see the need for more, we can discuss making the additions."

"Uh-huh."

"Who cares about lists?" Savannah said. "All we have to do is kill Leah."

"I'm glad to see you're taking such a keen interest in this, Savannah," he said. "However, we must proceed in a logical, methodical manner, which, unfortunately, precludes running out and murdering anyone. Perhaps we should begin by going over the list I prepared for you. Step one: Arrange to have your homework brought to the house by a teacher or student known to both you and Paige. Step two—"

"He's kidding, right?" Savannah said.

"It doesn't matter," I said. "I'm not hiring you, Cortez."

"I really do prefer Lucas."

"And I'd prefer you found your way to my front door. *Now*. I don't know you and I don't trust you. You might very well be what you say you are. But how do I prove that? How do I know Sandford didn't send you here? Hey, Paige's lawyer quit, let's send her one of ours, see if she notices."

"I don't work for Gabriel Sandford or anyone else."

I shook my head. "Sorry, no sale. You're a sorcerer. No matter how hard up you were for a job, I can't believe you'd offer to work for a witch."

"I have no quarrel with witches. The limitations of your powers are hereditary. I'm sure you endeavor to use them to their full potential."

I stiffened. "Get out of my house or I will show you the limitations of my powers."

"You need help. My help. Both as legal counsel and added protection for both you and Savannah. My spell-casting is not outstanding, but it is proficient enough."

"As is mine. I don't need your protection, sorcerer. If I need help, I can get it from my Coven."

"Ah, yes. The Coven."

Something in his voice, a nuance, an inflection snapped the last restraint on my temper.

"Get the hell out of my house, sorcerer."

He gathered his papers. "I understand you've had a difficult day. While we must go over this list soon, it's not necessary to do so immediately. My advice would be to rest. If you'll allow me to listen to your telephone messages, I can return calls from the media, after which we can review this list—"

I grabbed the paper from his hands and ripped it in two.

"If that makes you feel better, by all means, go ahead," he said. "I have copies. I'll leave you a new one. Please add any concerns that may have escaped my—"

"I am not going through any list. You are not my lawyer. Want to know when I'd hire a sorcerer to represent me? Ten minutes after being hit by a transport and declared a vegetable. Until then, scram."

"Scram?" His eyebrows rose an eighth of an inch.

"Leave. Go. Get lost. Beat it. Take your pick. Just take it with you."

He nodded and returned to his writing.

"Listen," I said. "Maybe I'm not making myself clear—"

"You are." He finished his note, then put the papers into his satchel and laid a card on the table. "In the event that you reconsider—or experience an unfortunate collision with a large trucking conveyance—I can be reached at my cell number."

I waited until he was gone, then cast fresh lock spells at all the doors and vowed never again to answer the bell. At least not for a few days.

After Cortez left, Savannah decided to watch TV, so I slipped downstairs for some spell-casting. After what happened last night I could hardly let my neighbors catch me sneaking into the woods to cast spells. The forest is my preferred location for spell practice. Not only does nature provide peace and solitude, but something about the very primordiality of it seems to provide an energy of its own. From the earliest times, shamans and spell-casters have trekked into the forest or the desert or the tundra to reconnect with their powers. We need to. I can't explain it any better than that.

My mother taught me to spell-cast out-of-doors. Yet, as strongly as she believed in it, she was never able to impose that belief on the Coven. For several generations now the Coven has taught its children to practice indoors, preferably in a locked room with no windows. By forcing neophytes into locked rooms, it seems to me that they reinforce the idea that we are doing something wrong, something shameful.

That idea is also reinforced in neophytes by the way the Coven handles their first menses ceremony. First menses marks the passage into true witchhood, when a witch comes into her full powers. A witch's abilities increase automatically, but she must also undergo a ceremony on the eighth day, which fully releases her powers. Skip the ceremony and you forever forfeit that extra power. The Coven's stance on this was that if a mother wished her daughter to go through the ceremony, she had to find the ingredients, study the rituals, and perform them herself. Understandably, few did. My mother had performed it for me, though, and when the time came, I would do the same for Savannah.

I headed down to the basement. It's a large, unfinished single room that stretches the length of the bungalow. The far corner, under Savannah's bedroom, was the spot she'd staked out for her art studio. So far, I'd only thrown down an area rug for it, but eventually I planned to finish it into a separate room for her.

I won't say I understand Savannah's art. Her dark-themed paintings and cartoons tend toward the macabre. When her choice of theme began to worry me last fall, I talked to Jeremy Danvers, the werewolf Pack Alpha, who's the only artist I know. He looked at her work and told me not to worry about it. In that, I trust his judgment, and I appreciate the encouragement and help he's been giving Savannah.

This past year has probably been a nightmare for Savannah, and she's been so strong about it that sometimes that very strength worries me. Perhaps here, on canvases covered with angry splotches of crimson and black, she finds an outlet for her pain and, if so, then I must not interfere, however strong the temptation.

When I spell-cast in the basement, I do it in the laundry area, right near the bottom of the steps. So, I settled myself on the floor, then laid the grimoire before me and leafed through the yellowed pages. I had two such spellbooks, ancient and ripe with the stink of age, a smell that was somehow simultaneously repulsive and inviting. These did not contain Coven-sanctioned spells. Yet they were Coven property.

That might seem like the Coven was asking for trouble, having these books around where any rebellious young witch could get hold of them. But the Coven wasn't worried about that. Why? Because, according to them, the spells didn't work. And, I fear, after three years of tinkering with them, that they were mostly right.

Of the sixty-six spells contained in these tomes, I'd managed to successfully cast only four, including a fireball spell. Admittedly, with my fire phobia, I'd been nervous about the fireball spell, but that very fear made it all the more alluring, and made me all the more proud of myself when I'd mastered it. That bolstered my determination to learn the rest, convinced me that all I needed to do was find the right technique.

Yet, in the ensuing two years, only one other spell had showed any sign that it might work. Sometimes I wondered if the Coven was right, that these were false grimoires, passed down only as historical oddities. Still, I could not put the books aside. There was so much magic in here, magic of true power—elemental spells, conjuring spells, spells whose meaning I couldn't even decipher. This was what witch magic should be, what I wanted it to be.

I worked on the wind spell Savannah had seen mentioned in my practice journal. That was the spell that had shown signs it might eventually work. It was actually a spell to "wind" a person. That is, to deprive someone of oxygen. A lethal spell, yes, but my experience in the compound last year had taught me that I needed at least one lethal spell in my repertoire, a spell of last resort. Now, with Leah in town, I needed this spell more than ever, but the added determination didn't help. I still couldn't cast it.

After thirty minutes, I gave up. Knowing Savannah was alone upstairs, even if she was protected by security spells, played havoc with my concentration.

Savannah was watching television in the living room. I paused in the doorway, wondering what she could have found to watch on a Saturday afternoon. At first, I thought it was a soap opera. The woman filling the screen certainly looked like a soap opera actress—a sultry redhead in her late thirties who'd been outfitted in glasses and an upswept hairdo in a laughable attempt to make her look scholarly.

When the camera pulled back, I saw that she was walking through an audience with a mike clipped to her blouse, and revised my assessment. An infomercial. No one smiled that much unless they were selling something. From the way she was working the crowd, it almost looked like a religious revival. I caught a few sentences and realized she was selling a different kind of spiritual reassurance.

"I'm getting an older male," the woman said. "Like a father figure, but not your father. An uncle, maybe a family friend."

"Oh, please," I said. "How can you watch this crap?"

"It's not crap," Savannah said. "This is Jaime Vegas. She's the best."

"It's a con, Savannah. A trick."

"No, it's not. She can really talk to the dead. There's this other guy who does it, but Jaime's way better."

A commercial came on. Savannah picked up the remote and fast-forwarded.

"You have it on tape?" I said.

"Sure. Jaime doesn't have her own TV show. She says she prefers traveling around, meeting people, but *The Keni Bales Show* has her on every month and I tape it."

"How long have you been doing this?"

She shrugged.

"Oh, hon," I said, walking into the room. "It's a con job, don't you see that? Listen to her. She's making guesses so fast that no one notices when she's wrong. The questions are so open—did you hear that last one? She said she has a message from someone who had a brother die in the past few years. What's the chance that nobody in the audience has recently lost a brother?"

"You don't get it."

"Only a necromancer can contact the afterworld, Savannah."

"I bet *we* could do it if we tried." She turned to look at me. "Haven't you ever thought of it? Contacting your mother?"

"Necromancy doesn't work like that. You can't just dial up the dead."

I walked into the kitchen and picked up the phone. Lucas Cortez's visit had one positive outcome, in that it reminded me about my Cabal questions, which reminded me that Robert hadn't returned my call.

It wasn't like Robert not to call back, so when I made the rounds again—phoning his house, phoning his office, checking my e-mail—and got no response, I began to worry. It was now nearly four, so I phoned Adam's work again, though I doubted the campus bar would be open in the afternoon. Silly me. Of course it was.

When I spoke to one of the servers, I learned that Adam was away for the week. At some conference, she said. Which sparked a memory flash and a big, mental "duh!" I returned to my computer and checked my recent e-mail, finding one from two weeks ago in which Adam mentioned going with his parents to a conference on the role of glossolalia in the Charismatic movement. Not that Adam gave a damn about Charismatics or glossolalia (A.K.A. "speaking in tongues"), but the conference was being held in Maui, which had more than its share of attractions for a twenty-four-year-old guy. The dates of the conference: June 12 to 18. Today was June 16.

I thought about tracking them down in Maui. Neither Robert nor Adam carried a cell phone—Robert didn't believe in them and Adam's service had been disconnected after he'd failed to pay yet another whopping bill. To contact them, I'd need to phone the conference in Hawaii and leave a message. The more I thought about this, the more foolish I felt. Robert would be home in two days. I'd hate to sound like I was panicking. This wasn't critical information, only background. It could wait.

Lucas Cortez's visit had, in fact, prompted me to remember two things I needed to do. Besides contacting Robert, I needed to line up a lawyer. Though I hadn't heard back from the police, and doubted I would, I really should have a lawyer's name at hand, in case the need arose.

I called the Boston lawyer who handled my business legal matters. Though she did only commercial work, she should be able to provide me with the names of other lawyers who could handle either a custody or criminal case. Since it was Saturday, there was no one in the office, so I left a detailed message, asking if she could call me Monday with a recommendation.

Then I headed to the kitchen, picked up a cookbook, and looked for something interesting to make for dinner. As I pored over the possibilities, Savannah walked into the kitchen, grabbed a glass from the cupboard, and poured some milk. The cupboard creaked open. A bag rustled.

"No cookies this late," I said. "Dinner's in thirty minutes."

"Thirty minutes? I can't wait—" She stopped. "Uh, Paige?"

"Hmmm?" I glanced up from my book to see her peering out the kitchen door, through to the living room window.

"Are there supposed to be people camped out on our front lawn?"

I leaned over to look through the window, then slammed the cookbook closed and strode to the front door.

CHAPTER 10

HELL HATH NO FURY LIKE A MIDDLE-AGED MAN SCORNED

I threw open the door and marched onto the porch. A camcorder lens swung to greet me.

"What's going on?" I asked.

The man with the camcorder stepped back to frame me in his view-finder. No, not a man. A boy, maybe seventeen, eighteen. Beside him stood another young man of the same age, swilling Gatorade. Both were dressed in unrelieved black, everything oversized, from the baggy T-shirts to the backward ball caps to the combat boots to the pants that threatened to slide to their shoes at any moment.

On the opposite side of the lawn, as far as they could get from the young cinematic auteurs, stood two middle-aged women in schoolmarm dresses, ugly prints made into unflattering frocks that covered everything from mid-calf to mid-neck. Despite the warm June day, both wore cardigans that had been through the wash a few too many times. When I turned to look at the women, two middle-aged men appeared from a nearby minivan, both wearing dark gray suits, as ill-fitting and worn as the women's dresses. They approached the women and flanked them, as if to provide backup.

"I asked: what's going on?" I said. "Get that camera— What are you doing?"

"There she is," one of the women whispered loudly to her companions. "The poor girl."

"Look," I said. "It's no big deal. I appreciate your support, but—"

I stopped, realizing they weren't looking at me. I turned to see Savannah in the doorway.

"It's okay, sweetie," one man called. "We won't hurt you. We're here to help."

"Help?" she said, between cookie bites. "Help with what?"

"Saving your immortal soul."

"Huh?"

"You needn't be afraid," the second woman said. "It's not too late. God knows you're innocent, that you've been led into sin against your will."

Savannah rolled her eyes. "Oh, please. Get a life."

I shoved Savannah back into the house, slammed the door, and held it shut.

"Look," I said. "Not to deny you folks your right to free speech, but you can't—"

"We heard about the Black Mass," the boy without the camera said. "Can we see it?"

"There's nothing to see. It's gone. It was a very sick prank, that's all."

"Did you really kill a couple of cats? Skinned them and cut them all up?"

"*Someone* killed three cats," I said. "And I hope they find the person responsible."

"What about the baby?" his camera-wielding friend asked.

"B—baby?"

"Yeah, I heard they found some parts they couldn't identify and they think it's this baby missing from Boston—"

"No!" I said, my voice sharp against the silence of the street. "They found cats. Nothing else. If you want more information, I'd suggest you contact the East Falls or state police, because I have nothing further to add. Better yet, how about I call them myself? Charge you with trespassing? That's what this is, you know."

"We must do as conscience dictates," the second man said in a deep orator's voice. "We represent the Church of Christ's Blessed Salvation and we have committed ourselves to fighting evil in every form."

"Really?" I said. "Then you must have the wrong address. There's no evil here. Try down the street. I'm sure you can find something worth denouncing."

"We've found it," one of the women said. "The Black Mass. A perversion of the most sacred rite of Christianity. We know what this means. Others will know. They will come. They will join us."

"Oh? Gee, and I'm fresh out of coffee and doughnuts. I hate to be a bad hostess. If they don't mind tea, I'll put on the kettle. I make a really wicked brew."

The boy dropped the camcorder. For a second, I thought it was the tea comment. Then, as he stumbled forward, I glanced up to see Savannah peering through the front curtains. She grinned at me, then lifted her hand and the boy jerked backward, falling to the grass.

"That's not funny," I said, glaring at the teen as he struggled to get up. "I won't stand here and be mocked with pratfalls. If you have something to say to me, contact my lawyer."

I stormed into the house and slammed the door.

Savannah lay collapsed on the sofa, giggling. "That was great, Paige."

I strode across the room and yanked the curtains shut. "What the hell did you think you were doing?"

"Oh, they wouldn't know it was me. Geez. Lighten up." She peeked under the curtain. "He's checking his shoelaces. Like maybe he tripped or something. Duh. Humans are so stupid."

"Stop saying that. And get away from that window. Let's just ignore them and make dinner, okay?"

"Can we eat out?"

"No!"

We ended up eating out.

Savannah didn't railroad me into it. As I was defrosting chicken for dinner, I kept thinking of the people on my lawn, and the more I thought about them, the angrier I got. The angrier I got, the more determined I was to not let them upset me . . . or, at least, not to let them know they'd upset me. If I wanted to go out to dinner, damned if they'd stop me. Actually, I didn't really want to go out to dinner, but after I made up my mind, I decided to proceed, if only to prove my point.

No one stopped us from driving away. The teenagers filmed our exit, as if hoping my car would transform into a broomstick and take flight. The Salvationists had retreated to their minivan before we made it to the corner, probably grateful for the excuse to sit down.

Savannah decided she wanted takeout from Golden Dragon. The local Chinese restaurant was run by Mabel Higgins, who'd never set foot outside Massachusetts in her life, and, judging by her cooking, had never cracked open an Asian cookbook. To Mabel, bean sprouts were exotic. Her idea of Chinese cooking was American chop suey—A.K.A. macaroni and ground beef.

Unfortunately, other than the bakery, the Golden Dragon was the only restaurant in East Falls. The bakery closed at five, so I had to buy my dinner from the Golden Dragon as well. I decided on plain white rice. Even Mabel couldn't screw that up.

I parked on the street. Most parking in East Falls is curbside, particularly in the village core, where all the buildings predate the automotive age. I've never mastered parallel parking—I'd rather walk an extra block than attempt it—so I pulled over in the empty stretch in front of the grocer, which had also closed at five.

"Geez, can't you park a little closer?" Savannah said. "We're, like, a mile away."

"More like a hundred feet. Come on. Get out."

She launched into a moaning fit, as if I was asking her to trudge twenty miles through waist-high snow.

"Wait here then," I said. "What do you want?"

She gave me her order. Then I warned her that I was locking her in and did so, with both the car remote and spells.

As I headed back to the car, I noticed an SUV parked behind my Accord and quickened my pace. Yes, I was being paranoid. Yet, considering there were no other cars within a half-dozen spaces of mine, it did seem odd, even alarming. As I jogged toward my car, I saw the face of the SUV driver. Not Leah. Not Sandford. Grantham Cary, Jr.

"Great," I muttered.

I slowed to a quick march and yanked my keys from my purse. Under my breath, I undid the locking spells, then hit the remote unlock, so I could hop in my car without stopping long enough for him to approach me. As I drew near, I heard the soft rumble of his engine idling. I kept my gaze fixed on my car, listening for the sound of his door opening. Instead I heard the clunk of his transmission shifting into gear.

"Good," I said. "Just keep going."

Out of the corner of my eye, I saw him reverse to pull out. Then he drove forward. Straight forward, hitting my car with a crash. Savannah flew against the dashboard.

"You son of a bitch!" I shouted, dropping the take-out bag and running for the car.

Cary veered out and tore off.

I raced to the passenger door and yanked it open. Inside, Savannah cupped a bloody nose.

"I'm okay," she said. "I just hit my nose."

I grabbed a handful of tissues from the box behind her seat and passed them to her, then examined the bridge of her nose. It didn't feel broken.

"I'm okay, Paige. Really." She glanced down at her blood-streaked T-shirt. "Shit! My new shirt! Did you get a license number? That guy's paying for my shirt."

"He's paying for more than your shirt. And I don't need a license number. I know who it was."

While Savannah went to retrieve the take-out bag from the sidewalk, I pulled out my cell phone, called the operator, and asked for the police.

"I'm not doubting it was Cary," Willard said. "I'm asking if you can prove it."

Of the three East Falls deputies, Travis Willard was the one I'd hoped they'd send. The town's youngest deputy—a couple of years my senior—he was the nicest of the bunch. His wife, Janey, and I had served at several charity functions together, and she was one of the few townspeople who'd made me feel welcome. Now, though, I was questioning the wisdom of phoning the police at all.

Although Willard was considerate enough to sit in my car, instead of making us stand on the sidewalk, everyone who passed did a double take. Only twelve hours ago the police had found a Satanic altar at my house, news of which I was sure had flown through the town before noon. Now, seeing me pulled over talking to a deputy, tongues would wag with fresh speculation. If that wasn't bad enough, I was quickly realizing that accusing a respected town member of intentional hit-and-run was no easy sell.

"Someone must have seen it," Savannah said. "There were people around."

"None of whom stuck around to do their civic duty," I said. "But there's bound to be evidence. He didn't do a lot of damage, but the paint's scratched. Can't you check his truck?"

"I could," Willard said. "And if I find silver paint on his bumper I can ask Sheriff Fowler to requisition a lab test and he'll laugh in my face. I'm not trying to give you a hard time, Paige. I'm suggesting maybe this isn't the way you want to pursue this. I heard you had a run-in with Cary at the bakery yesterday."

"You did?" Savannah said. "What happened?"

Willard turned to the backseat and asked Savannah to step outside the car for a moment. When she was gone, he looked back at me.

"I know he hit on you. The guy's a—" Willard cut himself short and shook his head. "He hits on every cute girl in town. Even made a pass at Janey once—after we were married. I could have—" Another headshake. "But I didn't. I didn't do anything. Some things are more trouble than they're worth."

"I understand that, but—"

"Don't worry about the car. I'll write it up for your insurance company as a hit-and-run. And maybe I'll pay Cary a visit, drop a hint that he should pay the deductible."

"I don't care about the damage. It's a car. I'm upset because Savannah was inside. She could have gone through the windshield."

"Do you think Cary knew she was there?"

I hesitated, then shook my head.

"That's what I figure, too," Willard said. "He wouldn't have seen her over the headrest. He was driving by, saw your car, and pulled in behind, thinking it was empty. When he saw you walking up, he slammed into the rear end. An asshole, like I said. But not a big enough asshole to intentionally hurt a kid."

"So you won't do anything."

"If you insist, then I have to make the report, but I'm warning you—"

"Fine. I get the idea."

"I'm sorry, Paige."

I fastened my seat belt and waved Savannah into the car.

Next stop: 52 Spruce Lane. Home of Mr. and Mrs. Grantham Cary, Jr.

The Carys lived in one of East Falls's finest homes. It was one of five stops on the annual East Falls garden walk. Not that the gardens were spectacular. Quite mundane, in fact, tending to overpruned shrubbery and roses with fancy names and no scent. Yet each year the house made the tour and each year the people of East Falls paid their fee to troop through the house and gardens. Why? Because each year Lacey hired a top-notch decorator to redo one room in the house, which then set that season's standard for interior design in East Falls.

"Do you think this is a good idea?" Savannah said as I stalked up the front walkway.

"No one else is going to do it for us."

"Hey, I'm all for putting the boots to the guy, but there are other ways, you know. Better ways. I could cast a spell that'll—"

"No spells. I don't want revenge. I want justice."

"A good case of body lice would be justice."

"I want him to know what he did."

"So we'll send him a card. Cooties courtesy of Paige and Savannah."

I tramped up the steps and whammed the cherub knocker against the wooden door. From inside came the scuffling of shoes. A curtain fluttered. Voices murmured. Then Lacey opened the door.

"I'd like to speak to Grantham, please," I said, with as much courtesy as I could muster.

"He isn't here."

"Oh? That's odd. I see his car in the lane. Looks like he scraped up the front bumper."

Lacey's surgically tightened face didn't so much as ripple. "I wouldn't know about that."

"Look, could I please talk to him? This doesn't concern you, Lacey. I know he's in there. This is his problem. Let him handle it."

"I'm going to have to ask you to leave."

"He hit my car. On purpose. Savannah was inside."

Not a flicker of reaction. "I'm going to have to ask you to leave now."

"Did you hear me? Grantham hit my car. He—"

"You're mistaken. If you're trying to get us to pay for damages—"

"I don't care about the car!" I said, pulling Savannah over and waving at her bloodied nose and shirt. "This is the damage I care about! She's thirteen years old."

"Children get bloody noses all the time. If you're hoping to sue—"

"I don't want to sue! I want him to come out here and see what he's done. That's it. Just bring him out here so I can speak to him."

"I'm going to have to ask you to leave."

"Stop covering for him, Lacey. He doesn't deserve it. The guy chases—"

I stopped there. My quarrel was with Grantham, not Lacey and, as good as it would have felt to tell Lacey what else her husband was doing, it wasn't fair. Besides, she probably already knew. I'd only be lowering myself to cheap shots.

"Tell him this isn't finished," I said, then turned and stomped down the steps.

As I approached my car, I realized Savannah wasn't behind me. I turned to see her in front of the house. Inside the lights flickered on and off. A television soundtrack blared, then faded, then blared again.

"Savannah!" I hissed.

A main floor curtain drew back. Lacey peered out. Savannah looked up and waved her fingers. Then she jogged toward me.

"What do you think you're doing?" I said.

"Just a warning," she said, grinning. "A friendly warning."

When we got home, the teens were filming my neighbor's black cat. I ignored them and pulled into the garage.

While Savannah reheated her dinner, I listened to my messages and returned calls to several Bostonian friends who'd seen my plight on the news. My Satanic altar made the Boston news? They each assured me it had been only a cursory mention on one channel, but that didn't make me feel better.

The teenagers left at nine forty-five, probably to make curfew. The older quartet stayed, taking turns sitting in the minivan and standing vigil on my lawn. I didn't phone the police. That would only call more attention to myself. If I didn't react, the Salvationists would tire soon enough and go home, wherever home was.

I went to bed at eleven. Yes, sad but true, I was young, single, and going to bed at eleven on a Saturday night, as I had almost every night for the past nine months. Since Savannah's arrival, I've had to struggle to maintain even friendships. Dating is out of the question. Savannah is very jealous of my time and attention. Or, perhaps more accurately, she dislikes not having me at her convenience. Like I've said, stability was one of the few things I could offer her, so I didn't push it.

Before retiring for the night, I peeked out the front curtain. Two men still stood on my front lawn, with two women in a nearby car, but the faces and the vehicle had changed. Replacement workers? Great.

I spent way too much time that night brooding about Cary. As if dealing with a Satanic altar wasn't enough, now I had a maturity-challenged lawyer stalking me. How did I get myself into these messes? Maybe publicly humiliating Cary wasn't my brightest idea ever, but how was I to know the guy would retaliate like a sixteen-year-old turned down for a prom date?

Then there was Travis Willard. I liked Willard, which made his cop-out only that much worse. If he wouldn't support me against Cary, who would? I could say East Falls was a typical small town, insular and protective, but I grew up in a small community and it hadn't been like this at all. If the Elders would only let me move . . . but that led into a whole new area of brooding. I already had enough to last me the entire night.

All was quiet the next morning. Not surprising, given that it was Sunday and this was East Falls. At nine A.M. the phone rang. I checked caller ID. Private caller. Whenever someone doesn't want you to know who they are, it's a good bet they aren't someone you care to speak to.

I let the machine pick up and set the kettle on the stove. The caller hung up.

Ten minutes later, the phone rang again. Another mystery caller. I sipped my tea and waited for the hang up. Instead, the caller left a cell-phone-static-choked message.

"Paige, it's Grant. I want to speak to you about last night. I'll be at the office at ten."

I grabbed the receiver, but he'd already hung up, and *69 didn't work. I considered my options, then dumped my tea down the sink and walked down the hall to Savannah's bedroom.

"Savannah?" I called, rapping at the door. "Time to get up. We've got an errand to run."

CHAPTER 11

FLYING THROUGH THE AIR
WITH THE GREATEST OF EASE

When we arrived at Cary's office, the reception desk was deserted. No surprise there. I doubted Cary wanted Lacey to overhear this conversation.

Our footsteps echoed through the emptiness as we crossed the hardwood floor.

"Hello!" Cary's voice drifted from his second-story office. "I'll be right with you!"

I headed up the stairs, Savannah behind me. A rustling of paper erupted from Cary's office, followed by the squeak of his chair.

"Sorry about that," he said, still hidden from view. "No reception on a Sunday, I'm afraid. The wife doesn't—" He stepped from his office and blinked. "Paige? Savannah?"

"Who were you expecting?"

He disappeared back into his office. I followed and waved for Savannah to do the same.

"New client," Cary said. "Not until ten-thirty, though, so I guess I can spare a few minutes. Lacey tells me you stopped by the house last night. Apparently I bumped your car on State Street. I did go downtown to pick up some dry cleaning. I can't say I recall hitting anything, but I did notice a scratch on the front bumper. Of course, I'm extremely sorry—"

"Cut the crap. You know what you did. If you called me here to make excuses, I don't want to hear them."

"Called you here?" He frowned as he settled into his chair. I studied his face for any sign of dissembling but saw none.

"You didn't call me, did you?" I said.

"No, I . . . well, of course, I was *going* to call—"

"Where's Lacey?"

A deeper frown. "At church. It's her week to help Reverend Meacham set up."

"It's a trap," I murmured. I whirled to Savannah. "We have to get out of here. Now."

"What's going on?" Cary said, rising from his desk.

I pushed Savannah toward the door, then thought better of it and yanked her behind me before starting forward. She grabbed my arm.

"Careful," she mouthed.

Right. Barreling out the door probably wasn't the best idea. I had too little experience with running and fighting for my life. Savannah already had too much.

After motioning Savannah back, I inched around the doorway, pressed myself against the wall, and peered into the hall. Empty.

"Is something wrong?" Cary asked.

I reached for Savannah. Tugging her at arm's length behind me, I ventured into the hall. We sidestepped along the wall, moving toward the stairs. Halfway there I stopped and listened. Silence.

"Are you in some kind of trouble?" Cary's voice fluttered from his office and echoed down the hall.

I slipped back to the office and closed the door, then cast a lock spell to seal him inside. I needn't have bothered. Cary obviously had no intention of risking his neck, and chose instead to sit behind his big desk and play dumb.

The hallway was fully enclosed, flanked by rows of shut doors, with the stairs along the left wall. I motioned for Savannah to follow, then quickstepped across the hall and wheeled around so my back was against the other wall. Again, I slid sideways, this time stopping two feet from the stairs.

"Wait," Savannah whispered.

I waved her to silence and leaned toward the stair opening. Savannah grabbed my sleeve and jerked me back, then gestured for me to crouch or bend before looking out. Okay, that made sense, instead of sticking my head out exactly where someone would expect to see it. I crouched and glanced down the stairwell. Empty. I scanned the waiting room below. Also empty. Five feet from the base of the stairs lay my goal. The front door.

As I pulled back, I caught a glimpse of reflected sunlight, froze, then checked again. The front door was open an inch or two. Had Savannah left it ajar when we came in?

I turned to Savannah.

"Cover," I mouthed.

Her lips tightened. Defiance flashed in her eyes. Before she could open her mouth, I locked glares with her.

"Cover now," I hissed.

Another flare of anger, then she lowered her eyelids. Her lips moved and, when they finished, she was gone. Invisible. So long as she didn't move, no one would see her. I paused a second, making sure she was staying covered, then crept into the stairwell.

It took an eternity to descend. Step down, pause, listen, duck and look, step down again. Coming down a staircase is more dangerous than you'd imagine. If the stairs are enclosed, as these were, then someone standing on the lower level will see you long before you can see them. Hence the stopping, ducking and looking, which made me feel safer, though I doubted it would have saved me from anyone standing below with a gun.

Actually, I wasn't too worried about guns; supernaturals don't usually use them. If Leah *was* down there, she'd more likely use telekinesis to yank my feet from under me and drag me down the stairs, breaking my spine so I'd still be alive, lying at the bottom, paralyzed, when she crushed me with a flying file cabinet. Much better than being shot. Really.

When I finally reached the bottom, I lunged for the door handle. I grabbed it, yanked—and nearly flew face first into the wall when the door didn't move. Once I'd recovered my balance, I looked around and tugged the handle again. Nothing. The door stood an inch open, yet would neither open nor close. A barrier spell? It didn't seem like one, but I cast a barrier-breaking incantation anyway. Nothing happened. I grabbed the door edge. My fingers passed through the crack without resistance, but I couldn't pull it open. I cast an unlock spell. Nothing.

As I stood there I was keenly aware of time passing, of standing here in plain sight, yanking on the door, an easy target, and of Savannah hiding in the upper hall, undoubtedly losing patience. After one last round of breaking spells, I flung my back against the wall and caught my breath.

We were trapped. Really trapped. Any moment now, Leah and Sandford and God knows what other kind of supernaturals would arrive and we'd—

For God's sake, Paige, get a grip! The front door's barred. Big deal. How about another door? How about windows?

I glimpsed sunlight glinting through the doorway behind Lacey's reception desk. Staying close to the wall, I eased a few feet left, so I could glance through the doorway. It led into a large meeting room and at the back of that room was a huge set of patio doors.

I hunkered and bolted across the room. Then I inched along the opposite wall toward the doorway. As I slipped into the other room, a shadow flashed across the sunlit floor. I ducked behind an armchair, barely daring to breathe, knowing the chair did little to hide me. I cast a cover spell.

The shadow danced across the floor again. Had I already been spotted? I glanced left, being careful to move only my eyes. The shadow returned, skipping over the floor. Realizing it was too small to be a person, I looked up and saw tree branches fluttering in the wind just outside the patio doors.

As I was easing from behind the armchair, footsteps pattered across the front hall. I zipped back and cast another cover spell. The steps turned left, receded, then returned, went too far right, nearly vanishing into silence, then came back again. Searching the rooms. Were they coming my way now? Yes . . . no . . . they paused. A squeak of shoes turning sharply. More steps. Growing louder, louder.

I closed my eyes and prepared a fireball spell. When a shape moved through the doorway, I launched the ball. A fiery sphere flew from the ceiling. I tensed, ready to run. As the ball fell, the intruder yelped, raising her arms to ward it off. Catching sight of her face, I flew from my hiding spot and knocked her out of the fireball's path. We hit the floor together.

"You promised to teach me that one," Savannah said, disentangling herself from my grip.

I clapped a hand over her mouth, but she pulled it away.

"There's no one here," she said. "I cast a sensing spell."

"Where'd you learn that?"

"Your mom taught me. It's fourth level. You can't do it." She paused, then offered an ego-consoling, "Yet."

I took a deep breath. "Okay, well, the front door's barred somehow, so I was going to try that one." I waved at the patio doors. "They're probably jammed, but maybe we can break the glass."

Again, we moved against the wall, in case someone outside was looking in. When I reached the doors, I peeked out. The patio opened into a tiny yard, grass-free, low-maintenance, covered with interlocking brick and raised beds of perennials. As I reached for the door handle, a shadow flickered across the yew hedge at the rear of the yard. Assuming it was another waving tree branch, I stepped forward. Leah was standing against the bushes. She lifted a hand and waved.

As I whirled toward Savannah, time slowed and I saw everything, not in a blur of movement, but in distinct, slow-motion frames. Leah raised both hands and gestured toward herself, as if beckoning us closer, but her gaze was focused on something over our heads. Then came the crash of glass. And the scream.

I lunged at Savannah, slamming us both to the floor. As we rolled, a dark shape plummeted toward the ground outside. I saw the chair first—Cary's chair—dropping like a rock. No, faster than a rock; it flew so fast it I heard it hit the brickwork before my brain had processed the image. In my mind, I still saw the chair in midair, tilted backward. Cary sitting in it, arms and legs thrust forward by the force, mouth open, screaming. I could still hear that scream hanging in the air as the chair slammed onto the brick, and bright drops of blood sprayed outward.

As I lifted my head, Leah caught my gaze, smiled, waved, and walked away.

I scrambled to my feet and raced out the patio doors, which opened without resistance. Even as I ran to Cary, I knew it was too late. The force of the impact, that horrible shower of blood. Two feet away, I stopped, then doubled over, retching.

I squeezed my eyes shut against the sight, but it was too late. I could see it against the backdrop of my eyelids. Grantham Cary, Jr., toppled from the chair, spread-eagled on the ground, his head crushed like an overripe fruit, bursting into a puddle of blood and brains. The force so great that a huge shard of glass had impaled his stomach clear through; so great that his arm, striking the corner of a perennial bed, had been severed, his detached hand still gripping the armrest. I saw that, and I remembered Leah, smiling, waving, and I wasn't sure which was worse.

"Paige?" Savannah whispered. Looking up, I saw her face, stark-white, staring at Cary as if unable to look away. "We—we should go."

"No," said a voice behind us. "I don't think you should."

Sheriff Fowler stepped through the open patio doors.

CHAPTER 12

LAWYER ROULETTE

Leah had framed me for the murder of Grantham Cary.

Take a woman accused of witchcraft and Satanism, a woman known to have engaged in a public feud with the murdered man, who then accused him of intentionally hitting her car and injuring her ward. This woman conspires under false pretenses to meet her former lawyer in his office, on a Sunday when his wife will be at church early. The police receive a call—a neighbor worried about the angry shouts emanating from the lawyer's office. The police arrive. The lawyer is dead. The house is empty except for the woman and her ward. Whodunit? You don't need Sherlock Holmes to figure that out.

Again, the East Falls police department wasn't equipped to handle such a case, so they called in the state cops, who took me to their station. The police interrogated me for three hours. The same questions over and over, badgering, bullying, until I could still hear their voices echoing in my head when they left for a cigarette or a coffee.

They'd taken everything I'd done in the last two days and twisted it to fit their theory. My tirade about Satanism? Proof that I had a wicked temper and was easily provoked. My bakery blowout? Proof that I was paranoid, misconstruing a simple coffee invitation as a sexual proposition. My accusation about the car accident? Proof that I had a vendetta against Cary.

All my arguments about Black Mass were now seen as protesting too much, denying the very existence of Satanic cults so I could cover up my own participation in such practices. Maybe Cary had learned the truth and refused to represent me further. Or maybe I'd hit on him and thrown a shit-fit when he rebuffed me. Maybe he *had* made a pass at me, but did I really expect them to believe he'd been upset enough over my rejection to slam his new Mercedes SUV into my six-year-old Honda? Grown men didn't do things like that. Not men like Grantham Cary. I was paranoid. Or delusional. Or just plain crazy. Hadn't I stormed off to his house like a madwoman, shrieking wild accusations and vowing revenge? What about Lacey's reports of electrical malfunctioning after my visit? Not that the police were accusing me of witchcraft. Rational people didn't believe in such nonsense. But I had done *something*. At the very least I was guilty of murdering Grantham Cary.

After the third hour, the two detectives left for a break. Moments later, the door opened and in walked a thirty-something woman who introduced herself as Detective Flynn.

I was pacing the room, my stomach knotted from three hours of worrying about Savannah. Was she here at the station? Or had the police called Margaret? What if this was Leah's plan, to get me locked up while she grabbed Savannah?

"Can I get you something?" Flynn asked as she stepped inside. "Coffee? A cold drink? A sandwich?"

"I'm not answering any more questions until someone tells me where Savannah is. I keep asking and asking and all I get is 'She's safe.' That's not good enough. I need to know—"

"She's here."

"Exactly where? Savannah is the subject of a custody battle. You people don't seem to understand—"

"We understand, Paige. Right now Savannah is in the next room playing cards with two officers. Armed state troopers. Nothing will happen to her. They gave her a burger for lunch and she's fine. You can see her as soon as we're done."

Finally, someone who didn't treat me like a tried-and-convicted murderer. I nodded and took my seat at the table.

"Let's get it over with, then," I said.

"Good. Now, are you sure I can't get you something?"

I shook my head. She settled into the seat across from me and leaned across the table, hands almost touching mine.

"I know you didn't do this alone," she said. "I heard what happened to Grantham Cary. I doubt Mr. Universe could do that to a person, let alone a young woman your size."

So this was the good cop. The one who was supposed to make me spill my guts, an older woman, maternal, understanding. I wanted to leap to my feet and tell her to take her act and go.

As I sat there, I realized why such an overused police routine worked. Because, after hours of being yelled at and made to feel like a lowlife degenerate, I was desperate for validation, for someone to say, "You're not a cold-blooded killer and you don't deserve to be treated this way."

I knew this woman didn't give a damn about me. I knew she only wanted a confession so she could high-five her colleagues watching through the one-way glass. Yet I couldn't help wanting to confide in her, to gain a smile, a look of sympathy. But I knew better, so I fixed her with a cold stare and said, "I want a lawyer."

A smirk tainted Flynn's warmth. "Well, that could be difficult, Paige, considering he's just been taken to the morgue. Maybe you don't understand the seriousness—"

The door opened, cutting her short. "She understands the seriousness perfectly well." Lucas Cortez walked in. "That is why she's asking for her lawyer. I will assume, Detective, that you were just about to honor that request."

Flynn pushed back her chair. "Who are you?"

"Her lawyer, of course."

I tried to open my mouth, but couldn't. It was sealed shut, not by desperation or fear, but by a spell. A binding spell.

"And when did Paige hire you?" Flynn asked.

"It's 'Ms. Winterbourne,' and she retained my services at two o'clock P.M. yesterday, shortly after firing Mr. Cary for sexual harassment."

Cortez dropped a file folder onto the table. Flynn read the first sheet, frown lines deepening with each word. I managed to strain my eyes far enough left to see Cortez. He pretended to study the poster behind my head, but his eyes were on me, as they had to be during a binding spell.

So spell-boy knew some witch magic. Surprising, but not shocking. I knew better spells, several of which I deeply yearned to cast his way at that moment, but being unable to speak curtailed that impulse. A bit disconcerting, too, that he could cast a binding spell, something even I hadn't fully perfected. Wait. Brain flash. If I couldn't cast a perfect binding spell, could Cortez? Hmmm.

"Okay, so you're her lawyer," Flynn said, pushing Cortez's papers aside. "You can sit down and take notes."

"Before I have a few minutes in private to consult with my client? Really, Detective. I didn't pass the bar exam yesterday. Now, if you'll please find us a private room—"

"This one's fine."

Cortez gave a humorless half-smile. "I'm sure it is, complete with one-way glass and video camera. Once more, Detective, I'm requesting a private room and a few minutes alone . . ."

Cortez was still talking, but I didn't hear him. All my mental power went into one final push. Pop! My leg jerked. Cortez kept talking, unaware that I'd broken his spell.

I stayed still, saying nothing, waiting. A minute later, Flynn stalked from the room to find us a private chamber.

"Forging my signature on legal documents, sorcerer?" I murmured under my breath.

To my disappointment, he didn't jump. Didn't even flinch. I thought I saw a flicker of consternation in his eyes when he realized I'd broken his spell, but it may have been the lighting. Before Cortez could answer, Flynn came back and escorted us to another room. I waited until she closed the door behind her, then took a seat.

"Very convenient," I said. "How you just happen to be around every time I need a lawyer."

"If you are implying that I am somehow aligned with Gabriel Sandford or the Nast Cabal, let me assure you that I would not debase my reputation with such an association."

I laughed.

"You're too young to be so cynical," he said, returning to his papers.

"Speaking of young, if you are working for Sandford, tell him I'm pretty insulted that he couldn't even bother sending a full-fledged sorcerer. What are you? Twenty-seven? Twenty-eight?"

He sifted through his papers. "Twenty-five."

"What? You really did only pass the bar exam yesterday. Now I *am* insulted."

He didn't look up from his file or even change expression. Hell, he didn't have an expression to change. "If I was working for the Nasts, then, logically, they would send someone older and presumably more competent, would they not?"

"Maybe, but there are advantages to sending a guy closer to my age, right?"

"Such as?"

I opened my mouth to answer, then took another look at Cortez—the cheap suit, the wire-frame glasses, the perpetually funereal expression— and I knew no one was playing the seduction card in this game.

"Well, you know," I said. "I might be able to relate better, be more sympathetic . . ."

"The disadvantages of my youth would far outweigh the advantages of our age similarity. As for how I conveniently show up whenever you need a lawyer, let me assure you, that doesn't require insider information or psychic powers. Murders and Satanic altars are hardly everyday occurrences in

East Falls. An enterprising lawyer simply has to cultivate an equally enterprising local contact, and persuade him to make contact with any new rumors regarding your situation."

"You bribed someone in town to inform on me?"

"Sadly, it's easier—and cheaper—than you might think." Cortez pushed aside his papers and met my gaze. "This could be a career-making case for me, Paige. Normally, the competition for such a case would be stiff, but, given that you are a witch, I doubt any other sorcerers will be vying for it."

"But you're willing to make an exception. How . . . big of you."

Cortez adjusted his glasses, taking more than a few seconds, as if using the pause to decide how best to proceed. "It's ambition. Not altruism. I won't pretend otherwise. I need your case, and you need a lawyer."

"Then I'll find one myself."

"If you choose to replace me later, that's fine. But, for now, I'm the only person here. Your Coven is obviously uninterested in helping or they'd have found a lawyer for you. At the very least, they'd be here to offer moral support. But they aren't, are they?"

He'd almost done it, almost gained my confidence, but then, with those last comments, he undid all his efforts. I stood, strode to the door, and tried the handle. Locked from the outside, of course. An unlock spell was out of the question. I was in enough trouble already. As I lifted my fist to pound on the door, Cortez caught my hand from behind. Didn't grab it. Just caught and held it.

"Let me work on your release," he said. "Accept my services, free of charge, in this one matter and, afterward, if you aren't satisfied with my performance, you may discharge me."

"Wow. A free trial run. How can I refuse? Easy. No deal, Counselor. I don't want your help."

I wrenched my hand from his and lifted my fist to bang for the detective. Cortez put his hand against the door, fingers spread, blocking my fist's path.

"I'm offering to get you out of here, Paige." The formality fell from his voice and I thought, just for a second, that I detected a note of anxiety. "Why would I do that if I was working for the Nast Cabal? They want you in here, where you can't protect Savannah."

"I'll get out. They'll set bail and I can make it."

"I'm not talking about setting bail. I'm talking about getting you out. Permanently. No charges."

"I'm not—"

"What if they don't set bail? How long are you willing to stay in jail? To leave Savannah in the care of others?" He met my eyes. "Without you to protect her."

The arrow hit its mark. My Achilles' heel. For one brief moment, my resolve wavered. I glanced at Cortez then. He stood there, waiting for me to agree. And, though there was no smugness in his face, I knew he assumed I would agree.

I whammed my fist against the door, catching Cortez off guard. On the second bang, Flynn yanked it open.

"This man is not my lawyer," I said.

I turned my back on Cortez and walked into the hall.

After Cortez left, they put me back in the private meeting room. Another hour passed. Flynn didn't return to question me. No one did. They just left me there. Left me to sit and stew, then to pace, then to bang on the door trying to get someone's attention.

Savannah was out there, unprotected, with strangers who had no idea of the danger she faced. Yet again I was constrained by human laws. By law, they could hold me here for any "reasonable length of time" before charging me. What was reasonable? Depended on the person supplying the definition. Right then, for all I cared, they could go ahead and charge me with murder, so long as I could post bail and take Savannah home.

Nearly two hours passed before the door opened.

"Your new lawyer," said an officer I hadn't met.

For one fleeting moment, one desperate moment of naive hope, I thought the Elders had found someone to represent me. Instead, in walked . . . Lucas Cortez. Again.

Chapter 13

A Twelve-Step Plan

"Goddamn it!" I said. "I told you people this man is not my—"
Before I could finish, I found myself, once again, caught in a binding spell. The officer, having paid no attention, closed the door and left me alone with Cortez. When the door shut, he undid the spell. I grabbed for the door handle, but Cortez caught my hand. I spun to face him.

"You scheming son of a bitch! I don't believe this. I told them—I told that detective—no one's listening to me! Well, they're going to listen now. I didn't sign anything and if you have papers with my signature, I'll prove it's a forgery. Whatever the penalty is for misrepresenting a client—"

"They aren't going to charge you."

I stopped. "What?"

"They don't have enough evidence to charge you now and I doubt they will ever find the evidence they need. The injuries to Mr. Cary make it impossible to argue that you pushed him out the window. Furthermore, I have proven that there is no evidence to indicate you came in physical contact with Mr. Cary at the time of his death. His office was cleaned Saturday night. The only fingerprints found within belong to Mr. Cary and his cleaner, as do the only footprints on the vacuumed carpet near his desk. The scene shows no sign of a struggle. Nor does his body. It would appear that Mr. Cary's chair was lifted from the floor without human intervention and propelled with great force out the window."

"How are they explaining that?"

"They aren't. While they may believe you did it, they cannot prove it."

"How do—" I stopped. "They think I used witchcraft?"

"That is the general consensus, though wisely left unmentioned on all official papers. Since such an accusation would never pass a Grand Jury, you are free."

Cortez checked his watch. "We should leave. I believe Savannah is growing quite restless. We have to complete some paperwork before you can be released. I must insist that you refrain from speaking to any law enforcement officers we encounter during our departure. As your lawyer, I will handle all external communications herein."

"As my lawyer . . . ?"

"I believe I have proven my intentions are—"

"Above reproach?" I turned and met his gaze, keeping my voice soft, reasonable, letting no trace of anger escape. "But they aren't, are they?"

"I am not working for—"

"No, you probably aren't. I accept your story, that you're here to offer your services to further your career . . . at my expense."

"I'm not—"

"Do I blame you for it? No. I run a business. I know what someone our age needs to do to get ahead. I need to undercut the competition. You need to take cases the competition won't touch. If you want to bill me for today, go ahead. I'll pay. You earned it. But I can't—won't—work with you."

I opened the door and walked out.

Finishing the paperwork proved an ordeal; the grim-faced desk clerk filled out forms so slowly you'd think his wrist was broken. Worse yet, Flynn and the other detectives stood off to the side, watching me with glares that said I wasn't fooling them, I was simply another criminal who'd gotten away with murder.

Cortez, as one might expect, didn't accept defeat so easily. He stuck around to help me with the paperwork, and I let him. Why? Because six hours in captivity was enough for me. If the police knew that my freedom had been arranged by a man misrepresenting himself as my lawyer, could they toss me back inside? Accuse me of fraud? Probably not, but I didn't know the legalities involved and, now that I was free, I wasn't about to start posing any hypothetical questions that might land me in a jail cell. I didn't say that Cortez was my lawyer and I didn't say he wasn't. I ignored him and let the police draw their own conclusions.

When I went to collect Savannah, Cortez took his leave. He said nothing more than a murmured good-bye. To be honest, I felt a bit sorry for him. Sorcerer or not, he had helped me, and it hadn't done him a damn bit of good. I hoped he took me up on my offer of payment. At least then his efforts would have some reward.

I found Savannah in the waiting room. The public waiting room, amidst a half-dozen strangers, none of them the "armed state troopers" Detective Flynn had mentioned. Anyone could have walked into that room, including Leah. On the heels of my flare of anger came another silent thanks to Lucas Cortez for getting me out. If he didn't bill me, I promised myself I'd track him down and pay him anyway.

The waiting room looked like waiting rooms everywhere, with cheap furniture, yellowing posters, and stacks of year-old magazines. Savannah had laid claim to a row of three chairs and was lying across them, sound asleep.

I knelt beside her and gently shook her shoulder. She mumbled something and knocked my hand away.

"Savannah, hon? Time to go home."

Her eyes opened. She blinked and struggled to focus.

"Home?" She pushed up onto her elbow and smiled. "They let you out?"

I nodded. "I'm free to go. They aren't going to charge me."

At my words, an elderly woman turned to stare at me, then mumbled something to the man beside her. I was struck by the overwhelming urge to explain, to turn to these strangers and tell them I hadn't done anything wrong, that my being here was a mistake. I bit it back and tugged Savannah to her feet.

"Have you been out here the whole time?" I asked.

She nodded sleepily.

"I'm so sorry, hon."

"Not your fault," she said, stifling a yawn. "It was okay. There were cops around. Leah wouldn't try something here. So, what happened in there? Did they fingerprint you and everything? Are you going to have a record?"

"God, I hope not. Come on. Let's get out of here and I'll explain what I can."

There was a small crowd at the front door. Well, "small" in comparison to, say, the crowd at Fenway Park on opening day. I saw some media types, some placard-waving types, some rubbernecker-ghoul types, and decided I'd seen enough. They were probably there covering a "real" event, something completely unrelated to me, but I opted for the back door anyway, so I wouldn't disturb their vigil.

The police had towed my car to the station, which removed the problem of finding transportation, but also meant they'd searched it. Though I keep a very tidy car, they'd managed to move everything that wasn't nailed down, and there were traces of powder everywhere. Fingerprint powder, I suspected, though I had no idea why they'd be dusting my car for prints. Given the low homicide rate in this area, they probably used each one as an opportunity to practice every technique they'd learned in police college.

I had a seven-thirty Coven meeting in Belham, so Savannah and I grabbed a quick dinner, then headed straight there without returning home.

It was seven twenty-seven when we arrived at the Belham community center. Yes, I said *community center*. We had a standing reservation for the third Sunday of each month, when our "book club" would meet in the center's main hall. We even had the local bakery cater the event. When women from town asked to join our club, we told them, with deep regret, that our ranks were full, but took their names for our waiting list.

Our Coven had fourteen initiated witches and five neophytes. Neophytes were girls from ten to fifteen years of age. Witches attain their full powers when they first menstruate, so the neophytes were the girls newly coming into their powers. On their sixteenth birthday, assuming they've reached first menses, witches are initiated, meaning they receive voting rights and begin learning second-level spells. At twenty-one they graduate to the third level and, at twenty-five, to the fourth and final tier. Exceptions could be made. My mother had moved me to third level at nineteen and fourth at twenty-one. And I'd be really proud of that, if Savannah hadn't already surpassed me—and she hadn't even come into her full powers yet.

As Savannah and I crossed the parking lot, a minivan pulled in. I stopped and waited as Abby's older sister, Grace, and her two daughters climbed out. Fourteen-year-old Brittany saw us, waved, and jogged over.

"Hey, Savannah, Paige," she said. "Mom said you guys weren't—"

"I thought you weren't coming," Grace said, frowning as she approached.

"I nearly didn't make it, that's for sure," I said. "You wouldn't believe the day I've had."

"I heard."

"Oh? Word gets around, I guess."

Grace turned to yell at seventeen-year-old Kylie, who was still inside the van, chatting on her cell phone.

So the Coven already knew about Cary's death? I'd hoped they hadn't. If the news hadn't reached them yet, then that would explain why no one had come to my aid.

Cortez's words about the Coven still stung. I understood why they hadn't rallied around me at the police station. They couldn't take the risk of associating themselves with me. But they could have discreetly found me a lawyer, couldn't they? Or, at the very least, brought Margaret to check up on Savannah.

Grace and I walked in silence to the doors, then she suddenly remembered something she'd left in the van. I offered to walk back with her, but she waved me off. When Brittany tried to follow Savannah inside, her mother called her back. I could still hear them whispering as I pushed open the community center doors.

As I walked in, all chatter stopped dead and everyone turned. Victoria was at the front of the room talking to Margaret. Therese saw me and motioned to Victoria. Victoria looked up and, for a moment, seemed stunned. Then she snapped something to Margaret and strode toward me.

"What are you doing here?" she hissed when she'd drawn close enough for no one else to overhear. "Did anyone follow you? Did anyone see you come in? I can't believe you—"

"Paige!" called a voice from across the room.

I looked up to see Abby bearing down on me, her arms spread as wide as her grin. She caught me up in a hug.

"You made it," she said. "Thank God. What a horrible day you must have had. How are you feeling, hon?"

I could have sunk into her embrace, I was so grateful.

"They dropped the charges," Savannah said.

"There weren't any charges," I corrected quickly. "The police didn't charge me."

"That's wonderful," Abby said. "We're just so glad to see you're okay." She turned to the others. "Aren't we, everyone?"

A few murmured noises of assent answered. Not exactly a deafening show of support but, right now, it was good enough.

Abby hugged me again, and used the embrace to whisper in my ear. "Just go sit down, Paige. You belong here. Don't let them say otherwise."

Victoria glared at me, then swept to her place at the front of the room. I followed and took my seat in my mother's chair. And the meeting began.

After discussing Tina Moss's new pregnancy and eight-year-old Emma Alden's nasty case of chicken pox, Victoria finally deigned to acknowledge my problem. And she made it clear that this was indeed *my* problem. They'd argued against letting me take custody of Savannah from the start and this only confirmed their fears. Their biggest concern now was not that I'd lose Savannah, but that I'd expose the Coven. It all came back to fear. I was to handle this on my own. In handling it, I was not to involve any other Coven witch. I was forbidden to even ask Abby for help babysitting Savannah, because it created a public link between us.

When Victoria finished, I stormed out of the building, undoing the door lock spell, then crashing through the security perimeter and hoping the mental alarm gave the Elders a collective migraine. How dare they! The Coven existed for two purposes, to regulate and to help witches. They'd all but abdicated the first role to the interracial council. Now they were denying responsibility for the second. What the hell were we becoming? A social club for witches? Maybe we should become a real book club. At least then we might have some hope of intelligent conversation.

I strode across the empty baseball field, fuming but knowing I couldn't leave. Savannah was still inside. The Elders wouldn't allow her or anyone else to come after me. Like a child throwing a tantrum, I was expected to walk it off and return.

"May I assume it's not going well?"

I wheeled to see Cortez behind me. Before I could blast him, he continued, "Yesterday I noted a seven-thirty book club appointment on your calendar, which I feared you might be obstinate enough to attend, despite the danger inherent in pursuing regular activities—"

"Speak English," I snapped.

He continued, unperturbed, "However, I now realize that you were not acting rashly in attending a mere book club but, instead, wisely conferring with your Coven and enlisting their help implementing our plan. As you may recall, step three of the initial list requires enlisting the members of your Coven to discreetly support you—"

"Forget it, Counselor. They aren't going to be supporting me, discreetly or otherwise. I am hereby forbidden to impose my problem—*my* problem—on any member of the Coven."

I regretted the words as they left my mouth. Before I could backtrack, though, Cortez murmured, "I'll handle this," and strode off, leaving me trapped in a split second of blind panic, as I realized what he was about to do. By the time I tore after him, he was at the community center doors. He gestured sharply, undoing any spells, and marched through.

CHAPTER 14

FOX IN THE HENHOUSE

I got to the meeting room door as Cortez started to speak. "Ladies," he said. "I apologize for interrupting your meeting."

A collective gasp drowned him out as eighteen witches realized they had a sorcerer in their midst. And what did they do? Hex him? Cast repelling spells? To my embarrassment—to my shame—they drew back, gasping and chattering, like a bunch of chickens seeing a fox in the henhouse. Witches in their prime, witches with fifty years of spell-casting experience, cowering before a twenty-five-year-old sorcerer. Only Savannah stayed where she was, perched on the pastry table.

"You again?" she said. "You don't take a hint, do you?"

"He's—" Therese stammered. "He's a—"

"A sorcerer," Savannah said. "Get over it."

"Lucas Cortez," he said, striding to the front of the room. "As you know, Paige is undergoing a custody challenge and, as a result, has now been implicated in a murder investigation. In order to prevent further legal proceedings and protect Paige's reputation, there are several actions I will require from each of you."

At this point, I could have jumped in and explained that he wasn't my lawyer. But I didn't. I was still smarting from the Coven's rejection. Maybe if they thought I was forced to accept outside help—from a sorcerer, no less—they'd change their minds. And maybe, yes, maybe a small part of me liked watching the Elders squirm.

Cortez hefted his satchel onto the front table. "I don't suppose you have access to an overhead projector."

No one answered. No one even moved. Savannah jumped off the table, crossed the room, handed him a marker, and pointed to the flip chart. Then she sauntered back to the pastry table, grinning, and winked at me before resuming her perch.

I'd have to speak to Savannah about taking pleasure in the discomfort of others. Still, it was kind of funny, Cortez standing up there, writing down his list, explaining each point, so serious and intent, as the Coven sat and gawked, each one of them hearing nothing but the endless loop of an internal voice, repeating, "A sorcerer? Is that really a sorcerer?"

"Are there any questions?" Cortez said after his presentation.

Silence.

Eleven-year-old Megan, the youngest neophyte, raised her hand. "Are you a bad sorcerer?"

"I lack some proficiency in the higher-order spells but, at the risk of sounding overconfident, I must say there are worse sorcerers."

I sputtered a laugh, covering it with a cough.

"Mr. Cortez is right," Abby said. "We all need to come together and help Paige in any way we can."

Silence.

"And on that note," I muttered under my breath.

"Cortez," murmured Sophie Moss who, at ninety-three, was the oldest witch in the Coven and fast succumbing to Alzheimer's. "I knew a Cortez once. Benicio Cortez. Back in '72, no, '79. The Miami affair. Horrible—" She stopped, blinked, frowned, then looked at Cortez. "Who are you, boy? This is a private meeting."

On that fitting note of mental acuity, the meeting ended.

After the meeting adjourned, Savannah walked over to Cortez as every other witch practically tripped over her own feet getting as far from him as possible. I was heading to the front of the room to join Savannah and Cortez when the Elders waylaid me.

"Now I have seen everything," Victoria said. "Your mother must be rolling in her grave. Hiring a sorcerer—"

"I haven't hired him," I said. "But I have to admit, I'm considering it. At least someone is offering to help me."

"A sorcerer, Paige?" Margaret said. "Really, I can't help but wonder if you're doing this to spite us. Even speaking to a sorcerer is against Coven policy, and you've obviously been doing that." She glanced toward the front of the room, where Savannah was chatting with Cortez. "And allowing my niece to do the same."

"Only because your niece is getting zero help from her aunt," I said.

Therese motioned for me to lower my voice. I didn't.

"Yes, I've talked to him. Why? Because he is the only person who's offered to help me. He got me out of jail today. You three couldn't even bother sending Margaret to the police station to make sure Savannah was safe. You guys don't seem to get it. You know I'm not the type who likes to ask for help, but I'm asking now."

"You don't need a sorcerer."

"No, I need my Coven."

"Get rid of the sorcerer," Victoria said.

"And then you'll help me?"

"I'm not making a deal," she said. "I'm giving an order. Get rid of him. Now."

With that, she turned and left, the other two trailing in her wake.

Cortez materialized at my shoulder.

"Perhaps you'd care to reconsider my offer?" he murmured.

I saw the Elders watching us. Victoria's glare ordered me to get rid of Cortez. The urge to flip her the finger was almost overwhelming. Instead, I did the figurative equivalent.

"You're right," I said to Cortez, voice raised. "We should talk. Savannah, come on. We're going."

I motioned for Cortez to lead the way.

We drove to Starbucks in Belham—taking separate cars, of course. After I'd parked, Cortez took the spot in front of me and still managed to be standing beside my door before I pulled my keys from the ignition. He didn't try to open the door for me but, once I pushed it open, he held it steady while I got out of the car.

Once inside, I ordered Savannah a child-sized hot chocolate. She changed it to a venti café mocha. I downsized that to a small decaf café mocha. She negotiated a chocolate chip brownie and we settled. Here this stuff was finally getting easier for me, and Kristof Nast wanted to spoil it all. Very unfair.

Although the place wasn't exactly booming at nine-thirty on a Sunday night, Cortez opted for a side room where the staff had already put the chairs upside down on the tables. As we headed in, the cashier leaned over the counter, a half-pound of necklaces and amulets clanging against the laminate.

"That section's closed," she said.

"We'll tidy up when we're done," Cortez replied, and nudged us back to the farthest table. Once we were seated, he turned to Savannah. "I'm afraid this is going to be another of those very boring conversations. There's a magazine stand over there." He reached for his wallet. "May I buy you something to read?"

"Nice try," she said and slurped a mouthful of whipped cream.

"All right, then. Let's review that list I gave you."

"Didn't bring it."

"That's quite all right." He hoisted his satchel to the table. "I have extra copies."

"Fine," she said, taking the five-dollar bill from his hand. "I don't know why you're bothering. We aren't going to hire you. If we wanted a sorcerer lawyer, I could get someone a whole lot older and more experienced than you."

"I'll remember that."

While I watched Savannah buy her magazine, Cortez shuffled papers. Only when she'd settled at a table across the room did I turn my attention to him.

"Okay," I said. "You want to persuade me that you're on my side? Skip the lists. Tell me everything you know about Cabals. And I mean *everything*."

"Everything?" He checked his watch. "I believe they close in a couple of hours."

"You have thirty minutes," I said. "Fill it."

He did—the full thirty minutes. I figured he'd toss me a few tidbits and hope that would be enough to shut me up. Instead he laid it all on the table, literally, drawing me diagrams, maps, listing key figures and so on.

Here's the condensed version. Pretty much everything I'd heard about Cabals was true. Cabals were very old, established groups formed around a central sorcerer family. Like a family-run business, only think Mafia, not the neighborhood deli. That's my comparison, not Cortez's. He never mentioned the Mafia, though the parallels were obvious. Both were ultra-secretive, family-oriented organizations. Both insisted on complete employee loyalty, enforced through threats of violence. Both mixed criminal activity with legitimate enterprise. Cortez didn't try to gloss over the uglier parts, simply stated them as fact and moved on.

In structure, though, the Cabal was more Donald Trump than Al Capone. At the top was the CEO, the head of the sorcerer family. Next came the board of directors, composed of the CEO's family, radiating out in power from sons to brothers to nephews to cousins. Within the lower ranks you had unrelated sorcerers, half-demons, necromancers, shamans, whomever the Cabal could hire. No werewolves or vampires, though. According to Cortez, the Cabals had strict policies against employing any supernatural being that might mistake them for lunch.

Everyone in the Cabal, high and low, pursued the same goals: gaining money and power for the Cabal. The more business they brought in, the quicker they rose in the ranks. The more profitable the company was, the more the employees received in year-end bonuses and stock options. Yes, Cabals were listed on the NYSE. Might have been a nice investment, too, if you didn't mind a little blood on your dividends.

On the surface, Cabals seemed more benign than the Mafia. No car bombs or shoot-outs. Sorcerers were not common hoodlums. Oh, no. These guys were serious businessmen. Double-cross a Cabal and they wouldn't blow up your house and family. Instead, they'd have an incendiary half-demon torch the place, making it look like an electrical accident. Then a necromancer would torture your family's souls until you gave the Cabal what they wanted.

If all this was true, why didn't the interracial council do something about it? The council was dedicated to pursuing misuse of supernatural power. Here was the biggest, most widespread misuse. Now I understood Robert Vasic's concern.

"What part is Leah playing in all this?" I asked.

"Only a member of the Nast Cabal could answer that with any certainty. Whatever information I could impart would be based purely on rumor, and I prefer to deal in fact."

"I'll settle for hearsay. What have you heard?"

"I'm not comfortable—"

"Let me start, then. Last year, Leah and a sorcerer named Isaac Katzen infiltrated a human project to kidnap supernaturals, Katzen as an informant and Leah as a captive. Their plan was for Katzen to point out powerful supernaturals, let the humans take the risks of capturing and containing them, then have Leah win their confidence while imprisoned. A cheap and easy way to recruit supernaturals for the Nast Cabal—"

"They weren't working for any Cabal. That much I know as fact. It is assumed that they were attempting to build their own organization, a scaled-down version of a Cabal."

"Go on."

He hesitated, then said, "They say Leah approached the Nast Cabal after you killed Katzen."

I bit back a denial. I hadn't killed Katzen, had only brought about the circumstances leading to his death, but if this sorcerer thought I was capable of killing his kind, maybe that wasn't such a bad thing.

Cortez continued, "There have been rumors about Savannah's paternity for years, though Kristof was either unable to locate the girl or unwilling to incur Eve's wrath by interfering in their lives. With Eve gone, Leah offered to help him get Savannah."

"So you think Nast really is her father?"

"I don't know, and I think it has little or no bearing on the case. The Nasts want Savannah. That's all that matters."

I sipped my chai. "How bad is he? This Kristof? Well, I mean, you may not consider him 'bad,' I guess, but how . . . criminal is he?"

"I understand the concept of good and evil, Paige. Most sorcerers do. They simply choose the wrong side. Among sorcerers, Kristof Nast's reputation is average, meaning you should consider him a dangerous man. As heir to the Nast Cabal, he is backed by immense resources."

I leaned back and shook my head. "At least now I know where the Illuminati myth comes from."

"If it arises from the Cabals, the connections are tenuous at best. The Illuminati were believed to be a secret group of powerful men using supernatural means to overthrow the government. A Cabal's interest in politics is minimal, and far more mundane. Yes, there are Cabal members in government, but only to support fiscal policies that benefit the Cabal. It's all about money. Remember that, Paige. The Cabal does nothing that acts against its own financial interests. It's not the Illuminati or the supernatural Mafia or a Satanic cult. It doesn't ritually murder people. It doesn't abduct, abuse, or kill children—"

"Oh, right. Savannah's thirteen, so technically, she's not a child."

He continued in the same calm voice, "What I meant is that they don't follow the classic description of a Satanic cult in that they do not abduct children for ritualistic purposes. To the Cabal, Savannah means profit. Always look at the bottom line and you'll be better prepared to deal with the Cabals."

I checked my watch.

"Yes, I know," Cortez said. "My time is up."

I sipped my nearly cold chai and stared down at the diagrams Cortez had made. Now what? Send Cortez packing again? I didn't see the point. He'd only come back. To be honest, though, it was more than that. The guy had helped me. Really helped me.

It was a sad world when a witch had to rely on a work-starved sorcerer for help, but I couldn't waste my time whining about how things should be. Cortez was offering to help when no one else would, and I'd be a fool to refuse. I had seen absolutely no proof that he was anything other than what he claimed to be, a young lawyer willing to take on the shittiest cases to launch his career.

"What would you charge?" I asked.

He took a sheet from his satchel and spent the next few minutes explaining the fee schedule. His terms were reasonable and fair, with a written guarantee that every charge would be explained in advance and he would do no work that I hadn't preapproved.

"The moment you feel my services are no longer fulfilling expectations, you may dismiss me," he said. "All that will be clearly outlined in a contract, which I would strongly suggest you have examined by another legal professional before signing."

When I hesitated, he folded the fee schedule in half and passed it to me, then placed his business card on top.

"Take tonight to think about it. If, in the meantime, you have any questions, call me, no matter what the hour."

I reached for the paper, but he laid his fingertips lightly on it, holding it to the table, and met my gaze.

"Remember, Paige, I can offer you more than normal legal help. No human lawyer you could engage will understand this situation as I do. More than that, should you require additional protection, I will be there. As I've said, I'm not the most proficient sorcerer, but I can help, and I'm quite willing to do so. It may come to that."

"I know."

He nodded. "I'll speak to you in the morning, then."

He gathered his papers, and left.

CHAPTER 15

ALOHA!

On the way home Savannah asked what Cortez had said. In the midst of brushing her off, I stopped myself and, instead, told her Cortez's Cabal story.

"I don't get it," she said when I finished. "Okay, maybe Leah wants me for her Cabal. That makes sense. These Cabals, they're always recruiting. Mom told me, if someone ever tries to sign me up, I should—" Savannah paused. "Anyway, she said they're bad news. Like joining a street gang. You join, you join for life."

"Your mom say . . . anything else about the Cabals?"

"Not really. She said they'd come after me, so this makes sense, what Leah's Cabal is doing. But if she wants me, why doesn't she take me? She's a Volo. She could run our car off the road and grab me before we knew what hit us. So why doesn't she?"

Savannah peered at me through the darkness of the car's interior. I glanced into my side mirror, averting my eyes from hers. Okay, this had gone too far. I had to say something.

"Cortez says Leah works for the Nast Cabal."

"Huh."

"You've heard of them?"

She shook her head. "My mom never mentioned names."

"But she said they might come for you. Did she mention any Cabal in particular? Or why they'd want you?"

"Oh, I know why they'd want me."

I held my breath and waited for her to go on.

"Cabals only hire one witch, see? They'd probably rather not hire any at all, but we've got special skills, so they overlook the whole witch-sorcerer feud just enough to hire one of us. Anyway, they figure, if they have to hire a witch, they want a good one. My mom was real good, but she told them where to stick it. She said they'd come for me, and I wasn't to listen to any of their lies."

"Lies? Was there any lie in particular?"

Savannah shook her head.

I hesitated, then forced myself to press on. "It might be tempting, to be offered a place in a Cabal. Money, power . . . they probably have a lot to offer."

"Not to a witch. A Cabal witch is strictly an employee. You get a pay-check, but no perks."

"But what if you *did* get the perks? What if they offered you more than the standard package?"

"I'm not dumb, Paige. Whatever they offered me, I'd know they were lying. No matter how good a witch I might be, to them, I'm still only a witch."

Such a chillingly accurate answer, so easily given. What was it like, to be so young, and yet so keenly aware of your place in the world?

"It's funny, you know," she continued. "All those times my mom warned me and I barely listened. I thought, 'Why is she telling me this? If they come after me, she'll be here. She'll always be here.' You just figure that. You don't think . . . maybe she won't. Did you ever think—with your mom—that something like that could happen? That one day, she'd be there, and then she wouldn't?"

I shook my head.

Savannah continued, "Sometimes . . . sometimes I have these dreams. Mom's shaking me and I wake up and I tell her what happened, and she laughs and tells me I was just having a nightmare, and everything's okay, but then I really wake up, and she's not there."

"I've had those."

"Hurts, doesn't it?"

"More than I ever imagined."

We drove a few miles in silence. Then Savannah shifted in her seat and cleared her throat.

"So, are you hiring Lucas?"

I managed a forced laugh. "It's 'Lucas' now?"

"It suits him. So are you hiring him or what?"

My natural inclination, as always, was to give her a simple pat answer, but I'd felt as if in these past few days we'd cracked open the door between us, and I didn't want to slam it shut now. So I told her Cortez's alleged motivation for taking the case, then went a step further and asked her opinion of it.

"Makes sense," she said. "He's right. With the Cabals, either you're for them or against them. Especially if you're a sorcerer. Those lawyers my mom knew, the ones I said might help you, they do the same thing Lucas is doing. They take cases against the Cabals."

"Isn't that dangerous?"

"Not really. It's weird that way. If a supernatural goes up against the Cabals, they'll squash him like a bug. But if he's a lawyer whose client went against the Cabals, or a doctor who fixed up a supernatural attacked by the Cabals, they leave him alone. Mom says the Cabals are pretty fair that way. You don't bother them, they don't bother you."

"Well, I didn't bother them, and they sure are bothering me."

"But you're only a witch. Lucas is a sorcerer. Makes a difference, you know. So, are you hiring him?"

"Maybe. Probably." I glanced over at her. "What do you think?"

"I think you should. He seems all right. For a sorcerer."

There were people outside my house. More than a few. When I neared the house, no one turned, probably not recognizing my car—yet. From twenty feet away, I hit the garage door opener and zoomed inside before anyone could stop me. We went in through the little-used door linking the garage to the front hall, avoiding any potential confrontations.

After sending Savannah to bed, I faced down the dreaded answering machine. The display flashed 34. Thirty-four messages? My God, how many did the thing hold?

Fortunately most calls only required an intro. This is Chris Walters from KZET—delete. Marcia Lu from *World Weekly News*—delete. Jessie Lake from Channel 7—delete. Of the first twelve calls, seven were media, including three from the same radio station, probably trying to land an impromptu interview on their show.

Of the nonmedia calls, one was an ex-boyfriend and one was a friend I hadn't seen since she moved to Maine in the seventh grade. Both were calling to see how I was doing. That was nice. Really nice. Better than the other two. The first began (extreme profanity omitted): "You're a lying, murdering *bleep.* Just wait, you *bleep*ing *bleep.* You'll get yours. Maybe the *bleep*ing cops don't—"

My finger trembled as I hit the delete button. I cranked down the volume before going on to the next call. Savannah didn't need to hear that crap. *I* didn't need to hear it, either, but I told myself I'd have to get used to it, grow a thicker skin.

The next call was more of the same, so I deleted it after the first exple-tive. Then came a message that I listened to all the way through, one that began "Ms. Winterbourne, you don't know me, but I'm so sorry to hear what's happening to you out there," and went on to dispense more sympathy and a promise to pray for me. I needed that. I really did.

A scan through the next nine messages revealed seven media persons, one irate woman damning my soul to eternal fire, and one really sweet Wiccan from Salem offering moral support. See? Not so bad. Only 60 percent of strangers were calling for my corpse on a pyre.

I fast-forwarded through four more media calls, then heard one that jolted my spirits.

"Paige? Paige? Come on, pick up!" a familiar voice bellowed over loud rock music and high-decibel chatter. "I know you're there! It's eight o'clock at night. Where else would you be? On a date?"

A whoop of laughter, then an ear-piercing whistle to catch my attention from whatever corner of the house I might be lurking in.

"It's Adam! Pick up!" Pause. "Okay, fine, maybe you aren't there. I'm still in Maui. I called home and got your message. Dad's in a conference right now. I was just out having a drink, but you sounded pretty upset, so I'll head back to the hotel and give him the message. Aloha!"

What hotel? A name? Maybe a phone number? Typical. I fast-forwarded through the final messages, praying I hadn't missed Robert's call but, sure enough, there it was.

"Paige? It's Robert. I called home and retrieved your messages—one can never rely on Adam for coherent message-taking. As impatient as ever, it seems he only listened to your first one. I won't tell him about the one concerning Leah, or he'll be on the next plane to help out, which I'm sure is the last thing you want. I assume you're looking for the information you asked me to gather on Volo half-demons. As luck would have it, that's right here with me. You know how I pack: one carry-on of clothes and two suitcases filled with books and notes I don't need. I'm faxing the Volo notes to you right now. We leave for our flight in an hour, but if you get home before then, call me at (808) 555–3573. Otherwise, I will speak to you tomorrow."

I'd asked Robert for Volo information several months ago, in a spurt of foresight that I'd then forgotten to follow up on. I'd have to wait until tomorrow to find out Robert's thoughts on Cabals. Until then, it wouldn't hurt to know all I could about Leah.

CHAPTER 16

DEMONOLOGY 101

The fax was lying on the floor where my machine had spit it. Thank God the police hadn't stopped by for another search. Imagine what they'd have thought if they found this. "No, Detective, I'm really not a Satanist. So why am I receiving faxes on demonology? Well, uh, it's this new web-design idea I'm working on . . ." From now on, I'd be a lot more careful about what I left lying around.

To make sense of what Robert told me about Volos requires some background on demons. Demonology 101, so to speak.

Demons exist, both in the physical and spiritual worlds. They are arranged into hierarchies according to their degree of power. There is probably a ruling demon, someone you *really* don't want to conjure up, but I'd suspect the position changes hands, much like leadership roles in our world.

Among all the various levels, from courtier to archduke, you have your good demons and your bad demons, or to use the correct terminology, eudemons and cacodemons. When I say "good" demons, or eudemons, I don't mean they run around helping people in our world. Most demons couldn't give a damn about us. By eudemons, I'm referring to those who don't actively seek to screw up the human world.

A more accurate description would be chaotic and nonchaotic demons. "Chaotic" demons or cacodemons are almost exclusively the kind who come into contact with the rest of us. A sorcerer or witch could summon a eudemon, but most of us know so little about demonology that we wouldn't know a eudemon from a cacodemon anyway. Even if one said he was a eudemon, he'd probably be lying. A wise spell-caster abjures conjuring altogether.

Move from demons to half-demons. One way cacodemons like to cause trouble in our world is by fathering babies. They're pretty darned keen on the sex part, too. To do so, they take human form, having found that any woman with less than a forty-ounce bottle of whiskey coursing through her bloodstream does not respond favorably to seduction by large, scaled, cloven-hoofed beasts.

To be honest, we don't know what a demon's true form is, and it probably bears no resemblance to the cloven-hoofed monster of myth. When they come into the physical world, they take the shape of whatever will accomplish their goal. Want to seduce a young woman? Pull out the old "drop-dead-gorgeous twenty-year-old male" disguise. My advice to young women who like to pick up guys in singles bars? Condoms prevent more than venereal disease.

Half-demons inherit the main power of their fathers. Adam's power is fire. Robert is a Tempestras, meaning he was fathered by a storm demon, and has some control over weather elements like wind and rain. The degree of power depends on the demon's ranking within the hierarchy. Take the so-called fire demons. An Igneus can induce only first-degree burns. An Aduro can induce burns plus ignite flammable objects. An Exustio, like Adam, can not only burn and ignite, but incinerate. The number of demons decreases per level. There are probably a dozen Igneus demons out there making babies. There is one Exustio, meaning Adam probably has only two or three "siblings" in the world.

On to Leah, then. She is a Volo, which is the top telekinetic demon category. Like Adam, she is a rarity, fathered by a singular high-ranking demon. The difference is that Adam, at twenty-four, only recently learned to use his full powers. As with spell-casters, the progression takes time. Although Adam started being able to inflict burns by twelve, it took another dozen years before he could incinerate. Leah, at thirty-one, has likely been in full use of her power for at least five years now, giving her plenty of practice time.

Cary's death was a good indication of what Leah can do. Yet it was the only clear example of her powers I had. Yes, we'd encountered her last year and, yes, lots of objects had gone flying through the air, but there was a problem. Not only hadn't I witnessed anything firsthand, but there'd been a sorcerer involved, meaning it was difficult to tell where his contributions to the chaos left off and Leah's began.

Robert's research indicated that a Volo could propel an object as large as a car, though precision, distance, and speed drop as weight increases. A parked car they could probably shift a few feet. They could hurl an object as small as a book across a room with enough force to decapitate a person. Nor do they need to see what they are moving. If they can picture a nearby room from memory, they can displace objects within it. Sound scary? Try being in a room with the woman, knowing she could kill you without moving a muscle.

Why hadn't Leah killed me already? I don't know. Maybe the Cabal was holding her back. Cortez said they preferred using legal methods to resolve disputes, thereby minimizing the risk of exposure. So they probably hoped to win Savannah in a court battle, though that didn't mean they wouldn't let Leah off her leash if that failed.

As disturbing as Robert's report was, it was little more than I'd already expected, based on my dealings with Leah to date. Yet he did uncover two tidbits that bolstered my optimism. Two possible methods of thwarting Leah. No, not crosses and holy water. Such things belong in fairy tales.

First, Robert's research indicated that, unlike Exustio half-demons such as Adam, Volos' powers plummeted as their tempers flared. Piss them off enough and they'd become too flustered to concentrate. Simple psychology, really.

Second, all Volos had a tell, a physical mannerism that preceded an attack. It could be as discreet as an eye blink or as obvious as a bloody nose, but they all did something before lashing out. Of course, that meant you had to provoke them a bunch of times before you'd discover their tell.

Upon waking, I forced myself to peek through the drawn front curtains. The street was empty. Whew. I showered and dressed, then roused Savannah for breakfast. After we ate, I called her school and left a message saying she wouldn't be in again today, but we'd stop by later for her assignments.

Then I made another call. On the third ring, he answered.

"Lucas Cortez."

"It's me, Paige. I think . . ." I swallowed and tried again. "I'd like to give this a shot. I want to hire you."

"I'm glad to hear that." His cell phone buzzed, as if he was moving. "May I suggest we meet this morning? I'd like to formulate a concrete plan of action as soon as possible."

"Sure. Do you want to come here?"

"If you're comfortable with that, it would doubtless afford the most privacy."

"That's fine."

"Shall we say . . . ten-thirty?"

I agreed and rang off. As I hung up, relief washed over me. It was going to be okay. I'd done the right thing. I was sure of it.

By nine-thirty Savannah and I were both at work, me in my office and Savannah at the kitchen table. At nine forty-five I gave up any hope of getting something done and turned my attention to my e-mail.

My inbox had filled up over the weekend, and 95 percent of it was from addresses I didn't recognize. That's what I got for running a business and having my e-mail address, home phone, and fax number listed in the yellow pages.

I created a folder entitled: "Hell: Week One," then scanned the list of senders and, if I didn't recognize the name, dumped the e-mail into the folder unread. I'd have preferred to delete them, but common sense told me I shouldn't. If some maniac broke into my house and knifed this "Satan-worshipping bitch" in her sleep, maybe the police would find my killer's name buried in this heap of electronic trash.

I did the same with my faxes. A quick scan of the first page and if it contained the words "interview" or "burn in hell," I dumped it into a file folder, then stuck the whole thing under "H." By the time I finished sorting, I was quite proud of myself for handling things so calmly and efficiently. Over two dozen faxes and e-mails condemning me to eternal damnation and my hands barely shook at all.

Next I made the incredibly stupid mistake of searching the Internet for references to my story. I told myself that I needed to know what was out there, what was being said. After reading the first headline, "Satanic Witch Cult Surfaces Near Salem," I really should have quit. But I had to keep going. Of the three articles I scanned, two mentioned the "missing Boston baby" rumor, one said I'd been seen skulking around at the local humane society, two accused me of being a member of some Boston "Hellfire Club," and all three said I'd been found at the site of Cary's murder "covered in blood." After that, I decided ignorance really was bliss, and turned off my computer.

It was now ten-fifteen. Time to put on a pot of coffee for Cortez. As I was measuring coffee into the filter, the phone rang. I checked the display. Unknown caller. To answer or not to answer? I chose the latter, but poised my hand over the "talk" button in case a friendly voice came on.

"Ms. Winterbourne, this is Julie calling from Bay Insurance . . ."

Insurance? Did I have insurance with a place called—oh, wait, no, Bay

Insurance was a new client. As the voice continued, I hit the talk button, but the machine kept running.

"... cancel our order. Given the, uh, publicity, we've decided that's for the best. Please bill us for any work you've done to date."

"Hello?" I said. "Hello?"

Too late. She'd hung up. I'd lost a contract. I closed my eyes, inhaled, felt the sting. Why hadn't I imagined this, that my business could be hurt by the publicity? But I couldn't worry about it. If they didn't want my services, screw 'em. It wasn't like I had trouble finding customers. Once or twice a week I had to turn someone down because my schedule was full. Besides, sure, I might lose a few contracts, but I might also gain some.

While I waited for the coffee to brew, I decided to slog through the rest of my phone messages. As if to prove me right, three calls later, I hit this message:

"Hi, it's Brock Summers from Boston. I'm with the New England Perception Group and we'd love to have you do something for our website . . ."

Maybe the old saying is right. There's no such thing as bad publicity.

"... already have a website," Mr. Summers continued. "But we're very interested in having you do some enhancements. I've seen your work and I know several people in our field who'd also be interested . . ."

This was good. Really good.

"... please check out our current website at www dot exorcisms r us dot com. That's e-x-o-r-c-i-s-m-s-r-u-s, all one word. We do séances, poltergeist exterminations, exorcisms of course—"

I hit delete and sank into a kitchen chair.

"Uh, Paige?"

I turned to see Savannah in the kitchen doorway, binoculars in her hand, a troubled look in her eyes. She glanced over her shoulder, toward the front window.

"Let me guess, we have new lawn ornaments."

She didn't smile. "No, that's not—well, yes we do, but they've been there for a while. I was peeking out now and then, seeing how many there were. Then, a few minutes ago, I thought I saw a woman with red hair standing down the street, so I grabbed these to check."

I jolted up from the chair. "Leah."

Savannah nodded and fidgeted with the binoculars. "I was watching her—"

"You don't need to worry, hon. Robert faxed me some notes last night about Volos, and if she's more than twenty yards away, she's too far to hurt us. One good thing about having a crowd out front is that she won't dare get too close."

"It's—it's not that." She glanced at the window again and squinted, as if trying to see Leah in the distance. "I was watching, right? And this car drove up. She walked onto the road, and the driver pulled over, and . . ." Savannah inhaled and passed me the glasses. "I think you need to see this. You can see better from my room."

I went into Savannah's room and walked to the window. There were at least a half-dozen cars lining our street, but my gaze immediately went to one parked five doors down, across the road. As I saw the small, white four-door, my breath caught. I told myself I was wrong. It was a common type of car. But even as I lifted the binoculars to my eyes, I knew what I would see.

There were two people in the front seat of the car. Leah sat in the passenger's seat. And on the driver's side? Lucas Cortez.

"Maybe there's an explanation," Savannah said.

"If there is, I'm getting it now."

I strode into the kitchen, picked up the cordless phone, and hit redial. The line connected to Cortez's cell phone. Again, he answered on the third ring.

"Lucas Cortez."

"Hey, it's me, Paige," I said, forcing lightness into my voice. "Any chance you could pick up some cream on the way into town? There's a corner store right off the highway. Are you there yet?"

"No, not yet. I'm running a few minutes behind."

The lie came smoothly, without a millisecond of hesitation. You bastard. You lying bastard. I clutched the phone tighter.

"Do you prefer table cream or half-and-half?" he asked.

"Half-and-half," I managed to say.

I lifted the binoculars. He was still there. Beside him, Leah leaned back against the passenger door.

I continued, "Oh, and be careful when you drive in. I've got people hanging around my place. Don't pick up any hitchhikers."

A pause now. Brief, but a definite hesitation. "Yes, of course."

"Especially redheaded half-demons," I said. "They're the worst kind."

A long pause, as if he was weighing the possibility that this was a coincidental joke.

"I can explain," he said finally.

"Oh, I'm sure you can."

I hung up.

CHAPTER 17

GRIEF ON THE RUN

After hanging up on Cortez, I stormed into the kitchen and slammed the phone into the cradle so hard that it bounced out again. I scrambled to grab it before it hit the floor. My hands were shaking so badly I could barely get it back into the cradle.

I stared down at my hands. I felt . . . I felt betrayed, and the depth of that feeling surprised me. What had I expected? It's like the parable about the scorpion and the frog. I knew what Cortez was when I let him into my life. I should have expected betrayal. But I hadn't.

At some deep level, I'd trusted him and, in some ways, that betrayal stung even more than the Coven's. With the Coven, I'd hoped for support, but deep down I knew better than to expect it. They'd told me from the start that they wouldn't help. That was rejection, not betrayal. Cortez had taken advantage of that rejection to insinuate himself in my life.

"Paige?"

I turned to Savannah.

"I thought he was okay, too," she said. "He tricked us both."

The phone rang. I knew who it was without checking caller ID. He'd had just enough time now to get Leah out of his car. I let the machine answer.

"Paige? It's Lucas. Please pick up. I'd like to speak to you."

"Yeah," Savannah muttered. "I'm sure you would."

"I can explain," he continued. "I was driving to your house and Leah hailed me. Naturally I was curious, so I pulled over and she asked to speak to me. I agreed—"

I grabbed the receiver.

"I don't care why the hell you spoke to her," I said. "You lied about it."

"And that was a mistake. I fully admit that, Paige. You caught me off guard when you called and—"

"And you had to stumble and stammer for an excuse, right? Bullshit. You lied without a moment's hesitation. You lied so smoothly I bet a lie detector wouldn't have caught it. I don't care about why you spoke to

Leah, I care about how easily you lied, and do you know why? Because now I know you've got a talent for it."

A slight pause. "Yes, that's true, but—"

"Well, at least you're honest about that. You're a skilled liar, Cortez, and that tells me that I can't believe anything you've said to me so far."

"I can see where—"

"What I saw out there today only convinces me that my first instinct was right. You're working for the Nasts. I told myself that doesn't make sense, but now I get it. They made sure it wouldn't make sense."

"How—?"

"I'm a programmer, right? I think logically. Send me a smooth, sophisticated, well-dressed sorcerer, and I'd see through that scam in a minute. But send you and I'll say, this guy can't work for a Cabal. It doesn't make sense. It's not logical. And that was the whole idea."

A pause, so long I wondered if he'd hung up.

"I believe I can clear this up," he said at last.

"Oh, you do, do you?"

"I haven't been entirely forthright with you, Paige."

"*Wow.* Really?"

"I don't mean about being associated with the Nasts. I'm not. Nor was my motivation, as stated, entirely inaccurate, though I am guilty more of omission than deceit."

"Stop right there," I said. "Whatever you tell me next will just be more lies. I don't want to hear them."

"Paige, please. Just listen. I told you the version of my story that I believed you would find most palatable and would therefore—"

"Hanging up now," I said.

"*Wait!* You are, I believe, well acquainted with Robert Vasic. You're friends with his stepson, Adam? Would I be correct in assuming you trust him?"

"Adam?"

"Robert."

"What does Robert have—?"

"Ask Robert who I am."

"What?"

"Ask Robert who Lucas Cortez is. He doesn't know me personally, but we have mutual acquaintances, and if Robert is not inclined to vouch for my integrity, then he will be able to recommend someone who can. Will you do that?"

"What's he going to tell me?"

Cortez paused again. "I think, perhaps, at this stage it would be better if you heard it from Robert first. If I tell you, and you choose not to believe me, you may decide not to follow up with a call to Robert. Please call him, Paige. Then phone me back. I'll be at my motel."

I hung up.

"What'd he say?" Savannah asked.

I shook my head. "Honestly, I have no idea."

"Yeah, sometimes I can't figure it out either. Too many big words."

I hesitated, then dialed Robert's number, but got the machine again and didn't bother leaving a message. My finger was still on the disconnect button when the phone rang. "Williams & Shaw Legal" and a Boston phone number scrolled across the call display. Had my commercial lawyer found someone willing to represent me? God, I hoped so.

"May I speak to Paige Winterbourne?" a nasally female voice asked.

"Speaking."

"This is Roberta Shaw. I'm an attorney with Williams and Shaw. Our firm works with the Cary Law Office in East Falls. Mr. Cary has asked me to assist with the disposal of his son's current caseload. I've come across your folder among the deceased's files."

"Ummm, right. Actually, I am looking for someone to take over the case. If anyone at your firm would be interested—"

"We would not," Shaw said, the chill in her voice bordering on arctic. "I am simply calling to request that you take possession of your file immediately. It is not in perfect order, but I am not about to ask Mr. Cary or his daughter-in-law to transcribe any of the notes. Under the circumstances, they shouldn't need to look at this file again. Out of consideration to the family, I will ask that you refer all questions to me. The billing will also come from my office."

"Look," I said. "I don't know what you heard, but I had nothing to do with Mr. Cary's—"

"It is not my place to dispute that matter. I have many files to go through today, Ms. Winterbourne. I would like you to collect yours this afternoon."

"Fine. I'll pick it up at the office—"

"That would hardly be appropriate, would it?"

I gritted my teeth. "Where do you suggest—"

"I will be at the Barton Funeral Home all afternoon. They've established an office for me in the funeral parlor, so I may consult with Mr. Cary easily while disturbing him as little as possible. You may meet me there at one o'clock."

"At Grant Cary's visitation? Now that's what I'd call inappropriate."

"You will come to the service door," she said, biting off each word as if it cost her untold effort to speak to me. "There is a parking lot at the side of the building. You turn off"—papers shuffled—"off Chestnut. I assume you know where the funeral home is?"

"On Elm," I said. "Beside the county hospital."

"Good. Meet me there at one, in the side parking lot by the service door. Good day, Ms. Winterbourne."

So, with Cortez out of the picture, I was now officially on my own. If this had all happened a year ago I'd have said "no problem," and been glad for the chance to prove myself. Last fall, when the rest of the council had been reluctant to rescue Savannah, I'd been ready to go in on my own. Had I done so, I'd be dead. No question about it. I'd be dead and I might have got Savannah killed doing it. I'd learned my lesson then.

Now, faced with another big threat, I knew I needed help and was prepared to ask for it. But who? If I asked someone in the council, I'd put their life at risk for something that was a witch problem, and should therefore be handled by witches. But our Coven had abandoned us. Where did that leave us?

I tried instead to concentrate on doing exactly what Cortez had been coming over to do. Formulate a plan of action. But here I was stuck. If I went out and tracked down Sandford and Leah, I'd have to take Savannah along, and would probably end up delivering her straight into their hands. For now, the wisest course of action seemed to be to lie low, defend us against their attacks, and hope they simply decided Savannah was more trouble than she was worth. While it irked me to take a defensive position, at this point I refused to take chances with Savannah's life.

At twelve-thirty, I checked the crowd outside. Maybe I was being optimistic, but it seemed to be shrinking. When I went to tell Savannah to get ready, I found her lying on her back in bed. She opened her eyes when I walked in.

"Napping?" I asked.

She shook her head. "Not feeling so good."

"You're sick?" I hurried to the bedside. "You should have told me, hon. Is it your head or your stomach?"

"Both . . . I mean, neither. I don't know." She scrunched her nose. "I just feel . . . weird."

I didn't see any obvious signs of illness. Her temperature was normal, her skin wasn't flushed, and her eyes looked tired but clear. Probably stress. I hadn't been feeling so hot myself lately.

"You could be coming down with something," I said. "I was supposed to go out, but it can wait."

"No," Savannah said, pushing herself up from the covers. "I want to go. I'll probably feel better once I get outside."

"Are you sure?"

She nodded. "Maybe we can rent some videos."

"All right, then. Get ready."

"I bet it's a closed casket," Savannah said as I turned onto Chestnut.

An image of Cary's mangled corpse shot through my brain. I forced it back.

"Well, we aren't finding out," I said. "I'm not setting foot anywhere near that room."

"Too bad it wasn't one of those drive-through viewings. Then we could see him without anyone knowing."

"Drive-through viewings?"

"Haven't you heard about those? They had one in Phoenix when my mom and I lived there. We drove by once to see it. It's like a drive-through bank teller, only you look in the window and there's the dead guy."

"Grief on the run."

"People are real busy these days. You gotta make it easy." She grinned and shifted in her seat. "Isn't that weird? I mean, think about it. You drive up and then what? Talk into some drive-through speaker? Tell the guy how much you'll miss him?"

"Just as long as he doesn't sit up and ask if you'd like fries with that."

Savannah laughed. "Humans are so weird."

She shifted in her seat again.

"Do you have to go to the bathroom?" I asked.

"No. I'm just getting sore from sitting still."

"We've only gone five blocks."

She shrugged. "I dunno. Maybe I've got the flu."

"How's your stomach?"

"Okay, I guess."

I flashed back through everything she'd eaten in the last day. Then my gut knotted. "Did Cortez get near your café mocha last night?"

"Huh?" She looked over at me. "You think he poisoned me? Nah. He didn't touch my drink. Besides, potions aren't like that. If someone gives you one, you get sick all at once. This comes and goes. Oh, wait . . . there, it's gone. See?" She twisted to look over her shoulder. "Isn't the funeral home on Elm?"

"Yes—damn!"

I swung the car into the nearest laneway and turned around. As I'd said, the funeral home was next to the local hospital. Actually, the two buildings were attached, maybe for ease of transporting those who didn't respond favorably to treatment. The hospital also affords an excellent view of the adjacent local cemetery, which the patients must find most heartening.

The lot beside the funeral home was full, so I had to park behind the hospital. With Savannah trailing along behind me, I fairly scampered around to the mortuary, so worried about being seen that I wiggled through a tall hedge rather than walk along the road. Once in the funeral home parking lot, I checked to make sure no one was coming or going, then dashed across to the side door and knocked.

"I think a branch scratched my back," Savannah said. "Who cares if someone sees us? You didn't kill the guy."

"I know, but it would be disrespectful. I don't want to cause any more trouble."

Before she could answer, the door swung open. A woman in her mid-forties peered out, her doughy face fixed in a scowl that seemed more habit than intent.

"Yes?" Before I could answer, she nodded. "Ms. Winterbourne. Good. Come in."

I would rather have stayed outdoors, but she released the door and vanished into the room before I could protest. I ushered Savannah inside, then stepped through into a storeroom. Amidst the piles of boxes was a folding chair and a table covered with files.

Shaw wore a linen dress, smartly fashionable and tailor-made—my mother ran her own dressmaking business, so I can tell a good piece from a Wal-Mart bargain. Though the dress was top-of-the-line, the expense was wasted. Like too many large women, Shaw made the mistake of choosing oversized clothing, turning an expensive dress into a shapeless piece of sackcloth that fell in folds around her.

As my eyes adjusted to the dimly lit storeroom, Shaw settled into her chair and busied herself with her papers. I waited a few minutes, then cleared my throat.

"I'd—uh—like to get going," I said. "I'm not comfortable being here."

"Wait."

I did. For another two minutes. Then, before I could comment again, Savannah sighed. Loudly.

"We don't have all day, you know," Savannah said.

Shaw glared, not at Savannah, but at me, as if Savannah's rudeness could be no one's fault but my own.

"I'm sorry," I said. "She's not feeling well. If you're not ready, we could grab lunch, then come back."

"Here," she said, thrusting a file folder at me. "The bill is on top. We require a certified check, which you can courier to the address shown. Under no circumstances are you to contact the Carys regarding payment or anything else related to your case. If you have questions—"

"Call you. I get the idea."

I walked to the door, yanked on the handle, and stumbled backward when it failed to open. How's that for a gracious exit? Regaining my balance and my dignity, I grasped the handle again, turned, and pushed. Still nothing.

"Is there a lock?" I said, peering down at the handle.

"Just turn and pull, as with any exterior door."

Bitch. I almost said it aloud. Unlike Savannah, though, my upbringing did not permit me to do any such thing. I tried the door again. Nothing happened.

"It's jammed," I said.

Shaw sighed and heaved herself from the chair. Crossing the room, she waved me out of the way, took hold of the handle, and yanked. The door remained closed. From the other side, I heard voices.

"Someone's out there," I said. "Maybe they can open the door from the outside—"

"No. I will not have you bothering the mourners. I'll call the custodian."

"There's a front door, isn't there?" Savannah said.

Again, Shaw glared at me. This time, I didn't apologize for Savannah.

"For obvious reasons, you are not exiting through the front," Shaw said, picking up her cell phone.

I sighed and leaned against the door. As I did, I caught a muffled exchange from outdoors. I recognized the voices.

"—really too easy," Leah said.

Sandford laughed. "What do you expect? She's a witch."

The voices faded, presumably walking around the front. I yanked on the door again, this time murmuring an unlock spell. Nothing happened.

"Leah," I mouthed at Savannah, then turned to Shaw. "Forget the custodian. We're leaving. Now."

"You can't—" Shaw began.

Too late. I already had the interior door open and was propelling Savannah through. Shaw grabbed the back of my blouse, but I pulled free and pushed Savannah into the hallway.

CHAPTER 18

A Memorial to Remember

Once in the hall, I prodded Savannah forward.

"Take the first door you see," I whispered. "Hurry. I'm right behind you."

To the left, an empty corridor snaked off into unknown territory. Sunlight radiated through a door less than twenty feet away to the right—twenty feet of hallway clogged with somber-suited mourners. I turned left. Following my advice, though, Savannah turned right, toward the front door, through the crowd.

"Sav—!" I whispered loudly, but she was out of reach and moving fast.

Taking a deep breath, I lowered my eyes, prayed no one recognized me, and followed her. I'd gone less than five feet when Shaw's voice boomed from behind me.

"Paige Winterbourne, don't you dare—"

I didn't hear the rest. A dozen heads turned toward me and a dozen pairs of eyes met mine. My name hurtled down the hallway on a blast of whispers.

"Winterbourne?"

"*Paige* Winterbourne?"

"Isn't she—"

"Oh, my God—"

"Is that her?"

My first impulse was to hold my head high and march to the door. As Savannah said, I hadn't done anything wrong. But consideration won out over pride and, in deference to the mourners, I ducked my head, murmured my apologies, and hurried after Savannah. The whispers snaked after me, petering out before turning to slander.

"Did she . . . ?"

"I heard . . ."

"They say . . ."

I forced more apologies to my lips and pushed through the crowd.

Ahead, a huddled quartet swallowed Savannah's thin form and I lifted my head, picking up speed, bobbing on my toes, trying to see her.

The crowd around me rustled, whispers swelling into chatter. A brief commotion erupted ahead to my left, inside two large double doors. I paid no attention as I moved forward, gaze scanning hostile faces, struggling to find Savannah while not making eye contact with the mourners. Someone grabbed my arm. I only half-turned, catching a glimpse of blond hair under a black hat.

"I'm sorry," I murmured, eyes still roving the crowd ahead, searching for Savannah.

Without looking, I brushed the hands from my arm, tugging away. Someone gasped. There! The back of a dark head appeared near the exit. Savannah. I lunged forward, but the hands caught me again, nails digging into my arm.

"I'm sorry," I said again, distractedly. "I really have to—"

I turned to brush my assailant off, then saw her face and stopped cold. Lacey Cary stared down at me with eyes rimmed in red grief and black mascara. Around us, the crowd went silent.

"How dare you?" she hissed. "Is this some kind of sick joke?"

"I'm so, so sorry," I said. "I didn't mean—it was a mistake—I needed my file."

"Your file?" Lacey's face twisted. "You—you interrupted my husband's visitation to come and ask me about your file?"

"No, I was told to pick it—" I stopped, realizing this wasn't the time to correct her. I glanced down the hall for Savannah, but didn't see her. "I'm so sorry. I'll just leave—"

Someone pushed through the crowd behind me. The ripples of movement caught my attention and I saw Shaw move into an open gap a dozen feet down the hall.

As I turned away, Shaw took something from the folds of her dress. A doll. The sight was so unexpected that I paused, just long enough to see her lips move . . . and to see that the doll wasn't a doll at all.

"A poppet," I whispered. "Oh, God—"

I whirled to run, but not before I saw Leah step up behind Shaw. She lifted a hand and finger-waved at me.

"Savannah!" I shouted, wrenching free from Lacey and throwing myself against the crowd that blocked my path.

Something popped overhead. A small explosion. Then another and another. Glass flew everywhere, tiny razor-sharp shards of glass. Lightbulb glass. Even the sconces on the walls exploded, sinking the hallway into twilight, lit only by the curtained exit at the end. I scrambled for the front door, clawing at everything in my path. An interior door slammed, blocking the way into the front vestibule and plunging the hallway into darkness. Other doors slammed. People screamed.

Someone hit me. No, not just someone, the whole crowd. Everyone around me seemed to fly off their feet, and we shot in a screaming, seething, kicking mass through a doorway. The huge double doors slammed shut behind us, deadening the shouts and cries of those trapped in the hallway.

As I struggled up from the carpet, I looked around. We were in a large room festooned with hanging curtains. Scattered pockets of mourners stared at us. Someone ran to help Lacey to her feet.

"What's going—"

"Has someone called—"

"Goddamn it—"

With the confused shouts, my own senses returned and I leaped to my feet. I heard a small pop. A now-familiar sound. I glanced up to see a chandelier over my head and dove to the ground, covering my head just as the tiny bulbs began to explode.

Only when the shards stopped falling did I peek out, expecting pitch dark. Instead, I found that I could see, a little. Light flickered from one single unbroken chandelier bulb, giving just enough illumination to allow me to make out my surroundings.

Again I sprang to my feet, searching for an exit. People were shouting, screaming, sobbing. They banged at the sealed door and yelled into cell phones. I noticed little of it. My brain was filled with a single refrain. *Savannah.* I had to find Savannah.

I stood, oddly clearheaded amidst the confusion, and took inventory of my situation. Main door blocked or sealed shut. No windows. No auxiliary doors. The room was roughly twenty feet square, ringed with chairs. Against the far wall was . . . a coffin.

In that moment, I realized where I was. In the viewing room. Thankfully, as Savannah had guessed, there was no actual viewing. The coffin was closed. Still, my gut twisted at being so close to Cary's body.

I forced myself to be calm. Around me, everyone else seemed to be calming as well, shouts turning to quiet sobbing and whispered reassurances that help was on the way.

I returned to surveying my surroundings. No windows . . . Through the muffling cushion of whispers and sobs came a low moaning. A moaning and a scratching. I hardly dared pinpoint the source. I didn't need to. I knew without turning, without looking, that the noise came from the far wall. From the coffin.

In my mind, I saw Shaw again, holding the poppet and reciting her incantation. I saw her and I knew what she was: a necromancer.

The scratching changed to a thumping. As the noise grew, the room went silent. Every eye turned to the coffin. A man stepped forward, grasping the edge of it.

"No!" I shouted. I dove forward, throwing myself at him. "Don't—"

He undid the latch just as my body struck his, knocking him sideways. I tried to scramble up, but our legs entwined and I tripped, falling against the casket. As I fought free, the lid creaked open.

I froze, heart hammering, then closed my eyes, squeezed them as tight as I could, as tight as I had when I was four years old and mistook the creaking of the pipes for a monster in my closet. The room went quiet, so quiet I could hear the breathing of those closest to me. I opened one eye and saw . . . nothing. From my vantage point on the floor, I saw only an open coffin lid.

"Close it," someone whispered. "For God's sake, close it!"

I exhaled in relief. Shaw wasn't a necromancer. Leah had probably simulated the noise in the coffin by moving something within it, hoping to trick a mourner into opening it and displaying Cary's broken remains. Another grotesque prank, designed to slow me down, to stop me from getting to Savannah.

A moan cut short my thoughts. I was still bent over, pushing myself to my feet. Rising, I turned and saw the man who'd hurried over to close the coffin. He stood beside it, hand on the open lid, eyes round. Another moan shuddered through the room and for one moment, one wildly optimistic moment, I persuaded myself that the sound came from the man. Then a battered hand rose above the satin lining of the casket.

No one moved. I am certain that for the next ten seconds, not a heart beat in the entire room. Every gaze was glued to the casket. The hand grasped the side of the coffin, squeezed, then relaxed and inched down, as if stroking the smooth wood. Another moan. A gurgling, wet moan that raised every hair on my body. The tendons in the hand flexed as it grabbed tighter. Then Cary sat up.

In the dimness of that room, there passed a brief second in which Grantham Cary, Jr., looked alive. Alive and whole and well. Maybe it was a trick of the darkness or the deception of a hopeful mind. He sat up and he looked alive. Lacey let out a gasp, not of horror, but of exultation. Behind me, Grantham senior sobbed, a heartbreaking cry of joy, his face fixed in such a look of longing, of hope, that I had to turn away.

Cary lifted himself out of the coffin. How? I don't know. Having seen him after his death, I knew that there shouldn't be an unbroken bone in his body. Yet I understood little of this part of necromancy. I can say only that, as we watched, he struggled from the coffin and stood. Then, as his form caught the light, that blessed illusion of wholeness evaporated.

The morticians had done their work, cleaning away the blood and gore . . . and it did nothing but unmask the monstrous reality of his injuries. The opposite side of his head was shaved and torn and sewn and crushed, yes, crushed, the eye gone, the cheek sunken and mangled, the nose—no, that's enough.

For a moment, the silence continued as Cary stood there, head swaying on his broken neck, his remaining eye struggling to focus, the wet moan surging from his lips as rhythmic as breathing. As he turned, he saw Lacey. He said her name, a terrible parody of her name, half-spoken, half-groaned.

Cary started toward his wife. He seemed not to walk, but to drag himself, teetering and jolting, pulling himself forward. His one hand reached out toward her. The other jerked, as if he was trying to lift it, but couldn't. It flopped and writhed, the fabric of the sleeve rasping against his side.

"—ac—ee—" he said.

Lacey whimpered. She stepped back. Cary stopped. His head swayed and bobbed, lips contorting into a twisted frown.

"—ac—ee?"

He reached for her. She fainted then, dropping to the ground before anyone could catch her. With her fall, the whole room snapped to life. People ran for the door, pounding and shrieking.

"—ad—" Cary groaned, wobbling as he turned.

His father stopped short. As he stared at his son, his lips moved, but no sound came out. Then his hand went to his chest. Someone pulled him back, shouting for an ambulance. Across the room, a woman began to laugh, a high-pitched laugh that quickly turned to hiccuping sobs. Cary lurched around and stared at the sobbing woman.

"—wha—wha—wha—"

"Peter!" a woman's voice shouted. "Peter, where the fuck are you!"

Everyone who wasn't shocked into immobility turned to see a woman in a green dress emerge from the curtains behind Cary's casket.

"Peter, you fuck! I'm going to kill you!"

The woman strode into the middle of the room, then stopped and surveyed the crowd.

"Who the hell are you people? Where's Peter? I swear to God, I'm going to kill the fucker this time!"

The woman was young, maybe only a few years older than me. A thick layer of makeup barely concealed a blackened eye. She was thin, rail-thin, the kind of thinness that speaks of drugs and neglect. As she cast a scowl across the room, she swept a fringe of dark-rooted blond bangs from her face . . . and away from a bullet-sized crater in her temple.

"She's—she's—" someone sputtered.

The woman wheeled on the speaker and lunged at him. The man shrieked and stumbled back as she landed on him, nails ripping at his face.

An elderly woman backpedaled into Cary. Seeing what she'd hit, she screamed and turned sharply, tripping over her feet. Falling, she reached out instinctively, grabbing his useless arm. Cary stumbled. As he collapsed, his arm yanked free, the woman still holding his hand, ripping the stitches the morticians had used to reattach the severed limb.

I turned away then, as Cary saw his arm fly from his body, as his garbled screams joined the cacophony. Only half aware of what I was doing, I ran for the curtained wall from which the dead woman had emerged.

I raced through the curtain-hidden door and found myself in a tiny darkened room. An empty casket sat on something that looked like a hospital gurney. Behind the coffin I could make out the shape of a doorway. I thrust the gurney aside, grabbed the door handle, turned it, and pushed, nearly falling through when it actually opened. I stumbled through.

CHAPTER 19

DIME STORE MAGIC

I raced down the empty hall. From behind me came the screams of those trapped with the corpses. Other screams hurtled down the hall, seemingly from both directions, different in pitch, but no less panicked. I looked both ways, but saw only doors and adjoining halls.

A dim glow emanated far off to my right. I ran toward it. Behind me, I heard a distant thumping, like someone climbing stairs. I kept running.

As I passed an adjoining hallway, I glanced down it and saw a mob of people, all pressed against a closed door, banging and shouting. This struck me as odd, made me wonder why my own hallway was empty, but I didn't slow. As I rounded the corner, my salvation came into view: an exit door, sunlight peeping around the edges of the dark curtain.

I dashed for the door and got about ten feet when a flash of crimson reared up in my path. For a moment, the indistinct cloud of red and black writhed and pulsated. Then it exploded into a gaping mouth of fangs and shot for my throat.

I screamed, wheeled around, and collided with a body. As I screamed again, hands grabbed my shoulders. I pummeled and kicked, but my attacker only tightened his grip.

"It's okay, Paige. Shhh. It's nothing."

Recognition penetrated my panic. I looked up to see Cortez. For one second, relief flooded through me. Then I remembered his betrayal. As I pushed away from him, I saw that his glasses were gone. In fact, the downtrodden-lawyer getup had been replaced by khakis, a leather jacket, and a Ralph Lauren Polo shirt. An outfit far more befitting a young Cabal lawyer. How had I been so easily deceived?

"Oh, God, Savannah—" I said.

I dove for the door. The demon dog sprang to life, lunging at me. I spun on my heel and shoved Cortez hard, trying to get past him and run the other way. He grabbed me around the waist and yanked me off my feet.

"Savannah is this way, Paige. You have to go through it."

He started pushing me into the jaws of the beast. I clawed at him, scratched, kicked, flailed. My nails connected with something and he gasped, loosening his grip just enough for me to squirm free. I lunged forward, but he grabbed me again, wrapping his arms around my chest.

"Goddamn it, Paige! Listen to me! Savannah is that way! There's nothing there! It's a hallucination!"

"I'm not halluc—"

He wrenched me around to face the demon beast. It was gone.

"Damn it, watch!" he grunted as I elbowed him in the stomach.

Holding me in one arm, he waved his hand into the air before us. The cloud of red smoke returned, contorting into a massive pair of snarling jaws. I fought with renewed strength, but Cortez managed to keep hold of me and force me to watch.

The smoke writhed and pulsed, changing into something that resembled a dragon, with fangs, a forked tongue, and blazing eyes. Then, the dragon vanished, becoming the demon dog again, slavering and straining as if on a short lead.

"A vision," he said. "A conjuring. Dime store magic. It acts like a trip wire. Gabriel Sandford set them up by all the exits. Now, Savannah is safe and waiting for us—"

I wrenched free and dashed in the opposite direction. Ahead of me, a shape emerged from a doorway. I didn't slow, just put out my hands, ready to push the person aside. Then he turned toward me. It was a man, naked, skin glowing pale in the dim light. The top of his head was missing. His chest was cut open in a Y from shoulder to chest and down to his pelvis. I could see ribs, sawed open. As he stepped forward, something fell from his chest, hit the floor with a splat. He looked at me, lips parting. I screamed.

Cortez's hands closed around my waist. He yanked me into the air and half-carried, half-dragged me down the hall. When we hit the spot where we'd struggled earlier, the dragon reappeared. I closed my eyes and fought harder.

Seconds later, I felt a rush of air and opened my eyes to see Cortez pushing through the exit door. Behind us, the demonic dog slavered and snarled at nothing. Cortez heaved me off my feet and carried me out the door. Only when we were in the parking lot did he let me down.

"If you'll look over there," he said, panting, "you'll see Savannah in your car."

When my feet touched earth, I shoved him away and looked out over the hospital parking lot. I saw my car—and I saw no one in it.

"Goddamn it!" he said, looking about as he wiped blood from the furrows I'd left in his cheek. "Where the hell is she?"

"I swear, if you've hurt her—"

"There," he said, striding away. "Savannah! I told you to stay in the car."

"And you thought I'd listen?" Savannah replied from behind me. "You cast a lousy lock spell, sorcerer. Hey, Paige, come over here. You've got to see this."

Even as I was turning, she ran off, leaving me with only a glimpse of her T-shirt. I raced after her, Cortez jogging behind. We rounded the corner to see her at another door. Before I could stop her, she vanished inside. I dashed forward, catching the door before it closed. Savannah stood inside, her back to us.

"Watch," she said.

She waved her hand in front of her. For a second, nothing happened. Then particles of gray floated in from all directions until they formed a loose ball above Savannah's head. I braced myself for the snarling beast. Instead the gray dust assembled itself into a woman's face, then pieces of it fell away, revealing a grinning skull. The mouth opened in silent laughter and the skull spun three times, then vanished.

"Cool, huh?" Savannah said. "It's sorcerer stuff. Can you do this, Lucas?"

"Dime store magic," he said, wheezing to catch his breath.

She grinned at him. "You can't, can you? Bet I could." She waved her hand again, triggering the spell. "That is so cool. You get near the door and it goes off. They're at all the doors." She looked at me for the first time. "You don't look so good, Paige. Are you okay?"

"Leah . . . Sandford," I managed, still winded from panic. "We have to go. Before they—"

"They're long gone," Savannah said. "When I got outside, I saw Leah, and I was just about to run when Lucas grabbed me. I slugged him one, and—" She stopped and pointed to the scratches on his face. "Hey, did I do that?"

"No, I believe that would be Paige. The bruise from your blow hasn't had time to rise yet. Now, as Savannah is trying to say, Leah and Sandford have left—"

"Oh, right," she continued. "So, Lucas grabs me and I fight, then Leah does her stuff and sends us flying. Before she can get to me, though, this other guy—Sandford, I guess—cuts her off, and he says something to her and they leave."

"They just walk away?" I said, turning to Cortez. "How . . . convenient."

"No, wait," Savannah said. "That's the good part. See, they can't touch Lucas because he's—"

"Not now, Savannah," Cortez said.

"But you have to tell her. Or she won't understand."

"Yes," I said. "You have to tell me. Or I'm walking away and the next time I see you—"

"You didn't call Robert, I presume?"

"He's out of town. And I want to hear it from you. Right now."

Cortez shook his head. "I'm afraid you'll require the extended explanation, for which there isn't time at the moment. However, I will explain as soon as we are safely away from this place."

"Hey, Paige," Savannah said. "Did you see Lucas's bike?"

She raced around the corner before I could stop her. When I caught up, I found her crouching beside, not a bicycle, but a motorcycle.

"It's a Scout," she said. "An Indian Scout. It's, like, an antique. What year did you say again?"

"It's from 1926, but we need to leave, Savannah."

"It's a collector's item," Savannah said. "Really rare."

"Expensive, huh?" I said, shooting a look at Cortez. "Like the designer shirt. Pretty sharp for a struggling lawyer."

"I restored the bike. As for the clothing, a suit is hardly appropriate for motorcycle riding. My wardrobe contains a limited supply of casual wear, the majority of it gifts from my family whose budget and taste exceed my own. Now, we really should—"

"I'm not going anywhere," I said.

Cortez made a noise that sounded remarkably like a growl of frustration. "Paige, this is not the time—"

"I'm not being difficult. I don't think it's a good idea to run. People in there saw me. They'll tell the police, who'll come after me and wonder why I took off."

He hesitated, then nodded. "Quite right. I'd suggest we find an officer to take your statement."

"First, I'm getting those people out, before someone has a heart attack."

Savannah rolled her eyes. "Oh, please. Who cares about them? They wouldn't help you. Tell her, Lucas."

"She's right. Paige, I mean. We should get them out."

"Not you, too," Savannah said. "Oh, God. I'm surrounded."

I waved her to silence and we headed for the back door.

I won't give a play-by-play of what happened next. Between the two of us, Cortez and I managed to undo all of Sandford's spells, unlocking the jammed doors and disengaging the trip-wire illusions.

As for Cary and the other walking dead, they simply stopped walking. By the time everyone escaped and the authorities got inside, the necromancer's incantation had worn off. Or so Cortez explained. As I've said, I know nothing about raising the dead. Any necromancer can do it, but I've never met one who dared. The necromancers I know use their power only for communicating with spirits. Returning a soul to a dead body is against every moral code in the supernatural world.

In the chaos outside the funeral home, it took me twenty minutes to find a police officer, who insisted I follow him to the station and give my statement.

Of course, the police thought I'd played a role in what happened. Yet they didn't know *what* had happened. Sure, they heard the stories, witness after witness babbling about dead people walking and talking. But when the police had finally entered the building, they found only corpses strewn across the floor. Horrifying, yes, but hardly proof of the unthinkable.

When I told my story, I repeated only those portions I deemed believable. I'd been lured to the memorial service and tricked into entering the crowded hallway of mourners. Then the lights had gone out. Someone had shoved me into the visitation room and bolted the door. I'd heard people screaming, but could see very little in the near-dark. Soon I found my way into a back passage and escaped.

I did admit that, while escaping, I encountered a frightening image blocking the hall, but I'd passed through it without incident and figured it must have been some kind of hologram. Finally, themselves dazed with disbelief and information-overload, the police had to let me go. My story made sense and it checked out against that of the witnesses—barring the fact that I hadn't seen the dead rise. With no small reluctance, they released me.

CHAPTER 20

REBEL WITH A CAUSE

We'd taken my car to the police station, Cortez leaving his motorcycle at the funeral parlor. By the time we exited the station, it was nearly five o'clock and Savannah reminded me that she hadn't yet had lunch. Since Cortez still owed me an explanation, we decided to pick up something to eat at a drive-through on the highway and find a quiet place to talk.

We stopped at the first fast-food restaurant we hit. The plan was to go through the drive-through, but then Savannah announced she needed to use the bathroom, and I had to agree I could use one as well, so we went inside. As we walked in, a few people turned to look. I tried to tell myself it was simply the idle curiosity of bored diners, but then one woman leaned over and whispered something to her companions and they all turned to stare. No, not stare. Glare.

"If you'll give me your order, I'll get it while you use the ladies' room," Cortez murmured.

"Thanks."

We told him what we wanted and I gave him some money, then we slipped off to the bathroom.

When we came out, Cortez was waiting by the condiment stand, take-out bags in hand.

"I should do the same before we leave," Cortez said, glancing toward the bathrooms. "Shall I walk you to the car first?"

"We're fine."

I took the bags and shepherded Savannah out. A few glares flew our way, but no one said anything. A few minutes later, Cortez joined us in the car.

"Took out your contacts?" Savannah said as he climbed in. "How come?"

"They're well suited for wearing under a helmet but, for all other situations, I prefer glasses."

"Weird."

"Thank you."

I sneaked a fry from the bag while they were still warm. "Speaking of helmets, what's with the motorcycle? You had a rental car this morning."

"And I still do, back at my motel. After our . . . altercation this morning, I thought it best to undertake discreet surveillance, should my assistance be required. In my experience, a motorcycle is much more conducive to surveillance work. It operates very well in alleyways and other places where one couldn't hope to fit a car. As well, the full helmet provides an excuse for shielding one's face. Usually, it's less conspicuous, though I realize now that may not be the case in East Falls."

"Motorcycle population: zero. Until today."

"Quite right. After this, I shall park the bike and rely on the rental car."

I pulled into a deserted picnic area just off the highway. As I locked the car, Cortez said a few words to Savannah. She nodded, took her take-out bag, and headed to a picnic table on the far side of the lot. Cortez led me to one closer to the car.

"What'd you say to her?" I asked.

"Simply that it might be easier for you and me to speak privately."

"And how many bribery bucks had to go along with that suggestion?"

"None."

I looked over at Savannah unpacking her bag. She saw me watching, smiled, and finger-waved, then sat down to eat.

I turned to Cortez. "Who are you and what have you done with the real Savannah?"

He shook his head and settled on the bench. "Savannah is a very perceptive young woman. She understands the importance of enlisting aid in this situation. She's willing to give me a second chance, but she realizes it may not be as easy for me to persuade you to do the same."

He unfolded his burger and tore open a ketchup package.

"So that brings us to the first part of my last question," I said. "Who are you?"

"I told you that I am in no way associated with the Nast Cabal, nor do I work for any Cabal. That is entirely accurate. However, I may have intentionally fostered the misconception that I am not associated with any Cabal."

I nibbled the end of a fry while I untangled that last sentence.

"So you *are* 'associated' with a Cabal," I said. "Like what, a contract employee?"

"No, I work for myself, as I said." Cortez folded the half-empty ketchup package and laid it aside. "At the Coven meeting, an older woman mentioned a Benicio Cortez."

"Ah, a relative, I presume?"

"My father."

"Let me guess . . . your father works for a Cabal."

"It would be more accurate to say a Cabal works for him. My father is CEO of the Cortez Cabal."

I coughed, nearly sputtering up a half-eaten fry. "Your family runs a Cabal?"

Cortez nodded.

"Is it . . . big?"

"The Cortez Cabal is the most powerful in the world."

"I thought you said the Nast Cabal was the biggest."

"It is. My father's is the most powerful. I say that as a matter of record, not out of any pride in the fact. I play no role in my father's organization."

"You just told me yesterday that Cabals are family-based, led by a sorcerer and his sons."

"In practice, that's true. The son of a Cabal head is introduced to the organization at birth and, in virtually every instance, that is where he remains. However, while a son may grow up in the Cabal, he is still required to undergo formal initiation on his eighteenth birthday. Since Cabal membership is, theoretically, voluntary, it is possible for a son to refuse initiation, as I did."

"So you just said, 'Sorry, Dad, don't want to be part of the family business'?"

"Well . . ." He adjusted his glasses. "Technically, of course, since I failed to accept the initiation, I'm not a member of the Cabal. Nor do I consider myself one. Yet, because, as I said, such a thing is extremely rare, I find myself in a position where most people still consider me part of my father's organization. It is generally accepted that this rebellion is a temporary situation, a perception which my father, unfortunately, shares and promotes, meaning I am accorded the privileges and protections such a position would provide."

"Uh-huh."

"This position provides me with some stature in the Cabal world and, though I'm loath to take advantage of that association, in some cases it is beneficial, allowing me to initiate activities the Cabals would not permit, were I not who I am."

"Uh-huh." A headache was forming behind my eyes.

"I've decided that the best use of my position, a position I neither want nor encourage, is to use it to counteract some of my race's worst abuses of power. Clearly, taking a young witch away from the Coven and placing her into the hands of a Cabal is such an abuse. Upon learning of Kristof Nast's initiative, I followed Leah and Gabriel and waited for an opportune time to introduce my services."

"Uh-huh. Let me get this straight. Having abandoned the family fortunes, you now use your power to help supernaturals. Like the Caped Crusader . . . in permanent Clark Kent disguise."

I would have sworn he smiled. His lips twitched, at least. "The Caped Crusader is Batman, whose alter ego would be Bruce Wayne. Clark Kent is Superman. Neither analogy, I'm afraid, is quite accurate. I lack the tormented brooding sexiness of the Dark Knight and, sadly, I've not yet learned to fly, though I did manage to sail a few yards when Leah threw me this afternoon."

I couldn't resist a small laugh. "Okay, but seriously. You know how this whole 'Rebel with a Cause' routine sounds?"

"Unlikely, I know."

"Try crazy. Insane. Preposterous."

"I haven't heard those particular adjectives before, doubtless only because no one dares say them to my face." He pushed aside his untouched burger. "Before you dismiss my story completely, please speak to Robert Vasic. I am confident that he will have sources who can vouch for my sincerity."

"I hope so."

"I can help you, Paige. I know the Cabals, know them more intimately than anyone you could hope—or would want—to meet. I can operate within that world with little fear of reprisals. As Savannah saw today, the Nasts don't dare touch me. That can be very useful."

"But why? Why go through all this to save a stranger?"

He glanced over at Savannah. "Preposterous, as you said. I can't imagine anyone doing such a thing."

I tore a crispy fry tip off, stared at it, then tossed it onto the grass. A crow tottered over for a closer look, then fixed me with a cold, black eye, as if to ask whether it was safe to eat.

"You still lied," I said. "About Leah."

"Yes, and, as you've said, I'm very good at it. For a Cortez, it's a skill we learn as other boys are learning to swing a baseball bat. For me, lying is a survival reflex. Placed in a situation where truth-telling may be risky, I often lie before I even make a conscious decision to do so. All I can say in my defense now is that I will make every effort not to do so again."

"You do, and that's it. I've got serious trust issues with this arrangement already, aligning myself with a sorcerer."

"Perfectly understandable."

"And I am going to speak to Robert first. I need to do that, for my own peace of mind."

"Again, understandable. You expect him back soon, I hope."

"He's probably already called the house, trying to find me."

"Good. Then I will accompany you home, you can go in and return his call, then we'll come up with a plan of action."

"What about your bike?"

"I'll retrieve it later. Right now, getting this situation straightened out is my first priority."

Chapter 21

Feeding Frenzy

As I rounded the second-last corner to my street, Cortez turned sideways in his seat, so he could see both me and Savannah.

"Now, as I said, it is possible that some members of the media may have established themselves in the vicinity. You must be prepared. Perhaps we should go over the plan again. The most important thing to remember is—"

"No comment, no comment, no comment," I said, with Savannah chiming in.

"You're quick studies."

"Keep the script simple and even us witches can learn it."

"I'm very impressed. Now, when we get out of the car, stick close to me—"

Savannah leaned over the seat. "And you'll protect us with lightning bolts and hail and hellfire."

"I cannot protect you at all if Paige hits the brake and you go flying through the windshield. Put on your seat belt, Savannah."

"It is on."

"Then tighten it."

She slipped back into her seat. "God, you're as bad as Paige."

"As I was saying," Cortez said. "Our primary objective is to— Oh."

With that one word, my breath caught. A simple word, not even a word really, a mere sound, an exclamation of surprise. But for Cortez to *be* surprised, worse yet, for him to stop in the middle of explaining one of his grand plans to make such an exclamation—well, it boded no good.

I'd just rounded the corner onto my street. A quarter-mile ahead was my house. Or so I assumed. I couldn't be sure because both sides of the street were lined with cars, trucks, and vans, crammed into every available space, some even double-parked. As for my house, I couldn't see it, not because of the cars, but because of the crowd of people spilling over the lawn, onto the sidewalk and across the road.

"Pull in the next driveway," Cortez said.

"I can't park here," I said, taking my foot off the accelerator. "I'm sure my neighbors are pissed off enough already."

"You're not parking. You're turning around."

"You want me to run?"

"For now, yes."

I gripped the steering wheel. "I can't do that."

I kept my face forward, but I could sense his gaze on me.

"Getting into your house won't be easy, Paige," he said, his voice softer. "This type of situation . . . it doesn't bring out the best in people. No one would blame you for turning around."

I looked through the rearview mirror at Savannah.

"Paige is right," she said. "If we back down now, Leah will know we're spooked."

"All right, then," Cortez said. "Pull in wherever you see an opening."

As I scouted for a parking space, nobody spoke. My eyes traveled from group to group. To the national news crews sipping coffee from the Belham Starbucks. To the scattered clusters of people with camcorders and curious eyes. To the state police arguing with five bald people in white robes. To the men, women, and children pacing the sidewalk, carrying signs condemning my soul to damnation.

Strangers. All strangers. I scanned the crowd and saw not a local newsperson, not a village cop, not a single familiar face. Up and down the street every door was closed, every curtain drawn. Everyone willing to shut out the June sun and cool breezes if it meant they could also shut out whatever was happening at 32 Walnut Lane. Shut it out and wait for it to go away. Wait for us to go away.

"When Paige stops the car, get out immediately," Cortez said. "Undo your seat belt now and be ready. Once you're out, keep moving, don't even pause to look around. Paige, take Savannah's hand and head to the front of the car. I'll meet you there and clear a path."

When we'd turned the corner, a few people had looked over, not as many as you might expect, considering they were waiting for a stranger to arrive, but maybe they'd been there so long, seen so many strangers drive by, that they'd stopped jumping every time a new car appeared.

When the car slowed, more glanced our way. I saw their faces then. Bored, impatient, almost angry, as if ready to snap at the next rubbernecker who falsely aroused their expectations. Then they saw me. A shout. Another. A ripple of movement, escalating to a stream, then a wave.

I turned the wheel to wedge in sideways behind a news van. For a second, I saw nothing but the call letters of a TV station in Providence.

Then a rush of people swallowed the van. Strangers jostled against the car, rocking it.

A man, knocked flying by the mob, sprawled across the hood. The car bounced. The man scrambled up. I met his eyes, saw the hunger there, the excitement, and for one second, I froze.

As the flood of people engulfed the car, I saw the very real possibility that I'd be trapped. I grabbed the handle and flung the door open, putting all my strength behind it and not caring who I hit. I leaped from the car, wheeled, and grabbed Savannah as she got out.

"Ms. Winterbourne, do you—"

"—have you—"

"—allegations—"

"Paige, what do you—"

The cacophony of questions hit me like a fifty-mile-an-hour wind, almost knocking me back into the car. I heard voices, words, shouts, all blending into one screaming voice.

I remembered Cortez saying to meet him at the front of the car. Where was the front of the car? The moment I stepped away from the vehicle, people surrounded me, the noise engulfed me. Fingers grabbed my arm. I jerked away, then saw Cortez at my side, his hand around my elbow.

"No comment," he said and pulled me from the fray.

The crowd released me for a moment, then swallowed me again.

"—do you—"

"—living dead—"

"—Grantham Cary—"

"—dragons and—"

I opened my mouth to say "no comment," but couldn't get the words out. Instead, I shook my head and let Cortez say them for me.

When he managed to free us again, I pulled Savannah closer, my arm going tightly around her waist. She didn't resist. I tried to look over at her, but everything around us moved so fast, I caught only a glimpse of her cheek.

The crowd tried closing in on us again, but Cortez barreled through, pulling us in his wake. We'd gone about ten feet when the mob swelled. Others joined the newspeople, and the tone of that single, shouting voice went from predatory excitement to vicious rage.

"—killer—"

"—Satanist—"

"—witch—"

A man shoved a newswoman out of our path and stepped in front of Cortez. His eyes were wild and bloodshot. Spittle flew from his lips.

"—Devil's whore! Murdering bitch—"

Cortez lifted his hand chest-high. For a moment, I thought he was going to deck the guy. Instead, he simply flicked his fingers. The man stumbled back, tripping over an elderly woman behind him, then wheeling to scream deprecations at her for pushing him.

Cortez steered us through the gap. If anyone didn't move fast enough, he shouldered them aside. If they tried to block us, he flicked his fingers at waist level, propelling them back with just enough force to make them think someone had pushed them. After five long minutes, we finally reached the porch.

"Get inside," Cortez said.

He turned fast, shoving Savannah and me toward the door as he blocked the porch steps. I fumbled to unlock the door, my mind racing in search of a spell, something that might distract or repel the mob until Cortez could get inside.

Mentally thumbing through my repertoire, I realized I had nothing. Yes, I knew some aggressive spells, but my selection was so limited that I had nothing to suit the situation. What was I going to do? Make one person faint? Rain down fireballs? They probably wouldn't even notice the former, and the latter would attract too *much* notice. The rebel Coven Leader, so proud of her forbidden spells, was useless. Completely useless.

While we got inside the house, Cortez staved off the crowd, physically blocking the narrow steps, one hand planted on each side of the railing. It lasted just long enough for us to get through the door. Then someone pushed hard, and a heavyset man pitched against Cortez's shoulder.

Cortez backpedaled just in time to avoid being knocked over. His lips moved and, for a moment, the crowd held at the steps, stopped by a barrier spell. Cortez shot for the door and undid the spell before it became obvious. The front row of the crowd tumbled forward.

I threw open the screen door. Cortez caught it. As he dashed through, a shadow passed overhead. A young man leaped off the side railing. The spell flew from my lips before I had time to think. The man stopped short, head and limbs jerking back. The binding spell broke then, but he'd lost his momentum and fell onto the porch several feet from the door. Cortez slammed the screen shut, then the inner door.

"Good choice," he said.

"Thanks," I said, choosing not to mention that it was my only choice and that I was lucky it worked for even those few seconds. I bolted the door, cast lock and perimeter spells, then collapsed against the wall. "Please tell me we don't have to go out again . . . ever."

"Does that mean we can order pizza for dinner?" Savannah called from the living room.

"You got the fifty bucks for a tip?" I yelled back. "Ain't no pizza boy coming through that mob for less than a Ulysses S. Grant."

Savannah let out a cry, half-shriek, half-shout. As I raced into the living room, she said something I couldn't make out. A man's body flew across the rear hall. He struck the wall headfirst. There was a sharp crack, then a thud as he collapsed in a heap on the carpet. Savannah stepped from her bedroom doorway as Cortez and I arrived. He dropped to the man's side.

"Out cold," Cortez said. "Do you know him?"

I looked at the man, middle-aged, receding hairline, pinched face, and shook my head. My gaze traveled up the wall to a four-inch hole with cracks radiating from every side, like a giant spider.

"Leah," I said. "She's here—"

"I don't believe Leah did this," Cortez said.

There was a moment of silence, then I turned to look at Savannah.

"He surprised me," she said.

"*You* knocked him out?" I said.

"She has excellent reflexes," Cortez said, fingers moving to the back of the man's head. "A possible concussion. A definite goose egg. Nothing serious. Shall we see who we have?"

Cortez reached around and pulled the man's wallet from his slacks. When I looked toward Savannah, she retreated into her room. I was about to follow when Cortez lifted a card for my inspection.

As I took the card, the phone rang. I jumped, every frayed nerve springing to life. With an oath, I closed my eyes and waited for the ringing to stop. The machine picked up.

"Ms. Winterbourne? This is Peggy Dare from the Massachusetts Department of Social Services . . ."

My eyes flew open.

"We'd like to speak to you regarding Savannah Levine. We have some concerns . . ."

I ran for the phone. Cortez tried to grab me as I passed and I dimly heard him say something about preparing and phoning back, but I couldn't listen. I raced into the kitchen, grabbed the receiver, and whacked the stop button on the answering machine.

"This is Paige Winterbourne," I said. "Sorry about that. I've been screening my calls."

"I can well imagine." The voice on the other end was pleasant, sympathetic, like that of a kindly neighbor. "There seems to be a bit of excitement at your place these days."

"You could say that."

A mild chuckle, then she sobered. "I do apologize for adding to what must be a very difficult time for you, Ms. Winterbourne, but we have some concerns about Savannah's well-being. I understand you're undergoing a custody challenge."

"Yes, but—"

"Normally, we don't interfere in such matters unless there is a serious threat of harm to the child. While no one is alleging Savannah has been mistreated, we are concerned about the current climate in which she is living. It must be very confusing for Savannah, having her mother disappear, then once she's settled in with you, this happens."

"I'm trying to keep her out of it as much as possible."

"Is there anyplace Savannah could go? Temporarily? Perhaps a more . . . stable environment? I believe there is an aunt in town."

"Her great-aunt. Margaret Levine. I thought of letting Savannah stay there until this is over." Yeah, right.

"Please do. As well, I've been asked to pay you a visit. The board is anxious to assess the situation. A home visit is usually best. Is two o'clock tomorrow afternoon convenient?"

"Absolutely." That gave me less than twenty-four hours to clear the circus outside.

I signed off, then turned to Cortez. "The Department of Social Services is paying a home visit tomorrow afternoon."

"Social Services? That is the last thing—" He stopped, pushed up his glasses, and pinched the bridge of his nose. "All right. We should expect they'll take an interest. A minor concern. Tomorrow afternoon, you said? What time?"

"Two."

He pulled out his DayTimer and made the note, then handed me the card I'd dropped while running for the phone. I looked at it blankly for a second, then saw the unconscious man lying in the hallway and groaned.

"Back to crisis number twenty-one," I said.

"I believe this is twenty-two. The angry mob was twenty-one. Or, given that they show no signs of leaving, I should say they *are* twenty-one."

I moaned and collapsed onto a kitchen chair, then lifted the card. The unlucky B&E artist's name was Ted Morton. If anyone had told me a week ago that I'd be sitting at my table, collaborating with a sorcerer about how best to dispose of a stranger that Savannah had knocked out cold, I'd have . . . well, I don't know what I would have done. It was too ludicrous. Yet, considering all that had happened in the past week, this really wasn't so bad. It certainly ranked a few rungs below watching a man hurtle to his death or seeing his shattered corpse come to life before his family and friends.

Mr. Morton was a so-called paranormal investigator. I have no patience with these guys. I've never met one who wasn't in serious need of a real life. Maybe I'm being intolerant, but these guys are a bigger nuisance than cockroaches in a Florida flophouse. They poke around, inventing stories, attracting con artists and, once in a while, stumbling onto a bit of truth.

All through high school I worked at a computer store where my boss was head of the Massachusetts Society for Explaining the Unexplained. Did she ever explain how I vanished every time she came looking for someone to make a fast-food run? She'd walk into the back office, I'd cast a cover spell, she'd murmur, "Gee, I could have sworn I saw Paige come back here," and go in search of another victim.

"Figures," I said, tossing the card back to Cortez. "How do the Cabals handle these people?"

"Chainsaws and large cement blocks."

"Sounds like a plan." I glanced over my shoulder at Morton and sighed. "Guess we should do something before he wakes up. Any suggestions?"

"Chainsaws tend to be quite noisy. I don't suppose you have a ready supply of quicklime?"

"Tell me you're joking."

"Unfortunately, yes. We require a somewhat more discreet solution. Our best answer would be one that sees Mr. Morton outside the house, but does not require taking him far, which would risk calling attention to the endeavor. It would also be preferable if he could be made to forget having been inside the house which, again, would risk attention when he retells the story. You wouldn't know hypnosis, would you?"

I shook my head.

"Then we'll have to settle—"

Savannah appeared in the doorway. "I have an idea. How about we dump him in the basement, right beneath the hatch. We can break the lock on the hatch, maybe leave it ajar. Then, when he wakes up, he might think he came in through there, fell, and hit his head."

Cortez nodded. "That might work. Paige?"

"If it means we don't have to go outside again, it works for me."

Cortez got to his feet and headed for the back hall.

"Sorry," Savannah said. "I didn't mean to cause more trouble. He surprised me, that's all."

I squeezed her shoulder. "I know. We'd better give Cortez a—"

Someone rapped at the back door. This, unlike the ringing phone and doorbell, was a first. When I'd looked through the kitchen window earlier, my backyard had been empty, possibly because no one dared be first to climb the fence. Now even that sanctuary had been invaded.

As I listened to the impatient rapping, anger surged through me and I stomped off to confront my newest "visitor." I glanced out the back door window to see Victoria and Therese. Worse yet, they saw me.

CHAPTER 22

THE THREAT

I backed into the living room.

"The Elders," I hissed at Cortez, who was in the bedroom returning Morton's wallet to his pocket. "It's the Coven Elders."

"Don't answer the door."

"They saw me."

He swore under his breath.

"I'm sorry," I said.

"It's not you. Hold them off. Count to five, let them in, then stall for a few minutes. Keep them in the hall."

I ran back to the rear door, pulled open the sidelight curtain, and motioned that it would take a minute to open the door. Then I undid the lock spell and perimeter spell and spent so much time turning the dead bolt, you'd think I had fifty of them. Then I ushered the Elders inside while blocking their path down the hall.

"You made it through the crowd?" I said. "Geez, it took us—"

"We had to come through the woods," Victoria said. "A most unpleasant experience. Therese has ripped her blouse."

"We had to come," Therese said. "Is it true? What they say? About poor Grantham?"

"We came because you lied to us, Paige. You said there wasn't a sorcerer in town."

"I never said—"

"You implied as much, leaving us all vulnerable to attack. Look what's happened now. This sorcerer brought Mr. Cary back to life."

"No, that was the necromancer. Sorcerers can't raise the dead."

"Which makes us feel so much better," Victoria said, her face contorting into a most unladylike snarl. "We have been invaded, Paige. Not only by a half-demon, but by a sorcerer and a necrophiliac—"

"Necromancer," I said. "A necrophiliac is someone who has sex with dead people. Necromancers don't—or, at least, I hope they don't . . . On second thought, let's not go there."

"Paige Winterbourne! I have had enough of your—"

Thud! Something crashed in the stairwell. Then Savannah's whisper floated up, "Shit! I'm sorry, Lucas. I slipped."

He shushed her, but too late. Victoria thrust me aside and strode toward the cellar door. I ran after her and caught up when she was one step from the basement stairs. I lunged to slam the door shut, but I was too late.

"What in God's name—"

"Oh, my lord," Therese said, looking over Victoria's shoulder. "They've killed a man."

"We haven't killed anyone," I snapped. "The guy broke into our house and . . . and I—"

"There was a struggle," Cortez said, from the bottom of the steps. "I accidentally knocked him unconscious. We're moving him to the basement where he can leave through the hatch. Having been struck on the head, he'll be disoriented and will likely believe he fell in that way. As you can see, we have everything under control."

"Under control?" Victoria wheeled on me. "Is this what you call having things under control, Paige? Dead people wandering around mortuaries? Mobs of strangers on your lawn? A sorcerer in your house, dragging a half-dead man into your basement? You took a simple situation and with each passing day, no, with each passing *hour* you have made it worse."

"Victoria," Therese said, reaching for her friend's arm.

Victoria shook her off. "No, it has to be said. We asked her to leave things alone—"

"I haven't done anything!" I said.

"You disobeyed us. Blatantly disobeyed us as you have been disobeying us for years. For your mother's sake, Paige, we put up with it. In accordance with her dying wish, we let you take the child, though God knows I wouldn't trust a parakeet to your care."

"That's enough," Cortez said, starting up the stairs.

I waved him back and turned to Victoria. "Tell me what I've done wrong. Please. I consulted a lawyer, as you advised. I cooperated with the police when Leah killed that lawyer. I sat in the police station and I answered their questions and I waited for help. For *your* help."

"The Coven doesn't exist to help those who bring trouble on themselves. You took the girl, knowing this demon woman was after her, knowing she was Eve's daughter and therefore didn't belong anywhere near the Coven."

"The Coven exists to help all witches. No one doesn't belong."

"That's where you are mistaken." Victoria looked down the steps at Savannah, then back at me. "You have twenty-four hours to make alternate arrangements for her care. Permanent arrangements. If you do not, you are no longer welcome in the Coven."

I froze. "What did you say?"

"You heard me, Paige. Fix this now or you will be banished."

"You can't banish me. I'm the Coven Leader."

Victoria laughed. "You are not—"

"Victoria," Therese said again. "Please."

"Please what? Please continue this charade? We're too old for these games, Therese. We should have put a stop to them last year. You are not Coven Leader, Paige. Do you really think we'd allow ourselves to be led by a girl so incompetent she manages to turn a simple custody challenge into an all-out witch-hunt?"

Cortez appeared at my shoulder. "Please leave. Now."

"Or you'll do what? Knock me out and put me in the basement with that poor man?"

"He's not the one you should be afraid of," said a soft voice. Savannah climbed the steps and smiled at Victoria. "Would you like to see what my mother really taught me?"

I shushed her with a quick shake of my head. Victoria strode from the kitchen, Therese at her heels. Before reaching the back door, she turned and met my eyes.

"This is not an idle threat, Paige. Find a home for the girl and clean this up—or you aren't welcome in the Coven."

What did I do next? Retreat to my bedroom, have a good cry, and wonder where my life had gone so horribly wrong? While the temptation was there, I couldn't afford the luxury of self-pity. I had a feeding frenzy on my front lawn, an unconscious paranormal investigator on my stairs, and, somewhere out there, an entire Cabal special projects team devoted to ruining my life. At this point, getting kicked out of the Coven seemed the least of my worries. Deep down, I knew that it was a threat that could destroy my very purpose in life, my mother's dream that I would lead the Coven into a new age, but I couldn't worry about that now. I just couldn't.

I headed for the kitchen and began listening to messages. I made it through two before Cortez slipped behind me, reached over, and hit the stop button.

"You don't need to listen to that," he said.

"I do. Robert . . . or someone . . ." My voice quavered as badly as my hands. I clenched my hands into fists and tried to steady my voice. "I should listen. It could be important."

"You can check the call display records, Paige."

I shook my head. "I need—I need to do something."

He hesitated, then nodded. "I'll make you a coffee."

"She likes tea," Savannah said from behind us. "Here, I'll show you."

He followed Savannah to the pantry and I resumed telephone detail.

Caller number six was a familiar and welcome voice.

"Paige? It's Elena. Jeremy read something about you in the paper. Sounds like you're in a bit of trouble. Give me a shout when you get a chance."

"Can I call?" Savannah asked, bouncing down from her perch on the counter, where she'd been supervising Cortez's tea-brewing.

"I'd better," I said. "You can talk to her when I'm done."

I went into my room, phoned Elena, and explained everything that had happened. It felt good to get it off my chest, to talk to someone who'd understand. She offered to come and help, and I can't describe how good it felt to hear that. Unfortunately, I had to refuse.

Leah and Elena knew each other from the compound, having both been captives. Leah had befriended, then betrayed Elena. Later, when we returned for Savannah, Elena's lover, Clayton, had killed Leah's lover, Isaac Katzen. Undoubtedly, Leah still felt she had a score to settle with the werewolves. If Elena showed up here, Leah might very well decide to take her revenge, and the last thing any of us needed right now was a werewolf/half-demon grudge match unfolding in downtown East Falls.

Elena understood, but promised to stick close to home for a few days. Should I change my mind, I only needed to call. I don't think she knew how much I appreciated that.

Before I signed off, I put Savannah on and returned to the kitchen.

"Do you take anything in your tea?" Cortez asked.

"No, black's fine." I took the mug from him. "Thank you."

"Perhaps you should call Robert. I'll feel better—"

A moan from the basement cut him off. Morton was awake. Or, I should say, I hoped it was Morton but, considering the events of the last few days, I wouldn't have been surprised to pop open the basement door and find a decomposing zombie tramping up the stairs. Neither of us moved as footsteps sounded. When there was a bang at the door, even Cortez hesitated before responding.

Any hopes that Morton would awake and beat a hasty retreat vanished as he continued to pound and shout. He was in the house and, damn it, he wasn't leaving without a fight. Cortez gave it to him. Not a literal fight, of course. No offense, but I couldn't picture Cortez rolling up his sleeves and coldcocking anyone. His strength was in words and, after going a few rounds with him, Morton beat that hasty retreat trailing apologies, convinced he really had fallen through the hatch.

CHAPTER 23

THE ORIGINAL CABAL

After Morton was gone, I heard Savannah say good-bye to Elena. She wasn't even out of the bedroom when the phone rang again. It rang once, then Savannah's animated voice floated down the hallway. Hearing only the lilt in her tone, and none of the conversation, I knew who was calling.

"No way," she said as she walked into the kitchen, phone to her ear. "Yeah, right. Like we'd need you." She snorted. "Oh, sure. You can, like, incinerate them. Dream on."

She paused, listening, then stifled a giggle. There was only one person Savannah giggled for, though she'd sooner die than admit it—and would probably kill anyone who had the nerve to mention it.

"It's for you," she said, holding out the phone. "Adam. He thinks he's going to help us. As if."

"Hello," I said.

"It's about time. Do you know how many times I've called there since this afternoon? Dad gave up hours ago. Either it's busy or we get your machine. Where have you been?"

"You don't want to know."

"I bet I can guess. My mom was watching the satellite news earlier, some show from out there, and guess whose picture she saw?"

"Mine. Lemme guess. It said I was a Satanist, right?"

"Hell, no. It said you were a witch. You're a Satanist now, too? Cool. If you see the big guy, can you ask him to pass along a message for my father? Tell him he's way behind in his child support payments."

"Ha-ha."

"So what's going—" Adam stopped and sighed. "You'll have to tell me later. Dad's here, tapping his foot and making faces. You'd better talk to him. Then get back to me, okay?"

The phone crackled as Adam passed it to Robert.

"Paige." Robert's warm voice rushed down the line. "You should have tracked me down at the conference. This sounds absolutely horrible."

"You don't know the half of it," I said, heading back into my room.

"Tell me then."

I did.

"How can I help?" he asked when I finished.

I could have cried. I feel foolish admitting it, but those four words meant so much.

"The stuff on Leah is great," I said. "But I also need some information on Cabals." I hesitated, almost afraid to go on. "Have you heard of the Cortez Cabal?"

"Certainly." He paused. "Is that who's after Savannah?"

"No."

"I'm glad to hear that. The Cortezes are the most dangerous of a dangerous lot. The original Cabal."

"The first one, you mean?"

"Yes. Hold on. I'm in my study. Let me pull up the file." A stream of keystroke clicks followed, then, "Here it is. The Cortez Cabal was founded during the Spanish Inquisition. They precipitated the Break."

My breath caught. "The break between witches and sorcerers. They were the ones who handed us over."

"Exactly. After doing so, the Cortez family formed a group originally based on the witch concept of a coven, though it quickly took on an entirely different focus. The name 'cabal' came later, after they relocated to the New World. It's a play on words, a mingling of truth and irony. You know what the word means, I assume."

"A secret society formed to conspire against something, usually the government."

"That's the joke, of course. A joke at the expense of the Illuminati myth. The only thing a sorcerer Cabal conspires to do is make money. The name also derives from 'cabala,' linking it to sorcery and mysticism. Finally, there's the allusion to 'caballero,' meaning a Spanish gentleman, which, of course, they were."

"About the Cortez Cabal . . ."

"Oh, yes. I'm sorry." He chuckled. "I suppose etymology doesn't help you much, does it? Was there anything in particular you wanted to know about them? If they aren't behind the attack on Savannah—"

"It's related. I need to know about the family. The main family."

"The Cortez Cabal is headed by Benicio Cortez and his sons. I believe there's a brother or two, plus assorted nephews and cousins."

"The sons . . . Do you know their names?"

"Let me see. There's Hector, then . . . I'm not certain of the middle two brothers, but the youngest, of course, is Lucas."

"*Of course?*"

"Outside the Cabals, Lucas Cortez is the best-known of the four brothers. He has quite a reputation—" Robert stopped, then laughed. "I think I see where this is leading. Dare I presume you've met young Cortez?"

"You could say that."

"Let me guess. He wants to help you protect Savannah from this other Cabal."

"I'm guessing he does this kind of thing a lot, huh? What's your take on this . . . crusade of his?"

"Well, let's see. The most unflattering view of the situation is that it is nothing more than youthful hell-raising. A spoiled delinquent protected by a blindly doting father. The middle ground, and the view most widely subscribed to, is that this is simply a developmental stage. The prodigal son rebelling against his family, a moral revolt that will last only until he realizes poverty isn't much fun, whereupon he'll return to the fold. The most optimistic view, of course, is that he truly is committed to what he's doing."

"Saving the world from the evil Cabals."

"He's around your age, isn't he? The age of idealism. The time to join protests and causes. To enlist in the Peace Corps. To fight evil Cabals. To put your life on hold to raise a thirteen-year-old stranger."

"Hmmm."

"If Lucas Cortez is offering to help, don't turn him away. No matter what people in the Cabal world say about him, no one denies the honesty of his intentions. For your situation with Savannah, I'd say the boy is perfectly suited to help. No one knows more about the Cabal world, and he can operate in it with impunity."

"About the Cabals," I said. "They seem much more . . . important than I thought. Than my mother thought."

Silence hummed down the line. "Your mother and I had different views on some subjects concerning the council and its mandate."

"She chose to ignore the Cabals."

"She . . ." He paused, as if choosing his words with care. "She thought our efforts were better directed. I wanted to investigate Cabals more, if only to further our understanding of them. Your mother disagreed."

"So you left the council."

"I—" He inhaled. "I felt I was no longer the right person for the job. My interests lay elsewhere." He paused. "Your mother and I were getting older, getting tired and discouraged. I thought we should pass on the torch to the younger generation, to you and Adam. She wasn't ready for that."

Maybe because she thought I wasn't ready.

"I . . . I should go," I said. "Can I call you back? If I have more questions?"

"Even if you don't, I'd appreciate an update when you get time, and I'm sure Adam would like to speak to you. I'll stave off his questions for now, but call him when you have a chance."

I promised I would, then signed off.

I found Cortez alone at the table, reading a week-old copy of the Boston Globe.

"Where's Savannah?" I asked.

He folded the paper and laid it aside. "In her room, if the music is any indication. You were speaking to Robert?"

I nodded. "He confirmed everything you said. I'm sorry I gave you a hard time."

"Perfectly understandable. If I'd expected you to trust me, I'd have told you the truth from the start. You have every reason to be wary, both of sorcerers and of anyone connected to Cabals. A wariness I would suggest you maintain. In nearly all cases, your mistrust will be well-founded."

I stood in the middle of the kitchen and looked around, not sure what I was looking for.

"Is there something else?" he asked.

I shook my head. "I'm just feeling . . ." I shrugged. "Out of sorts, as my mother would say."

As I mentioned my mother, I thought about what Robert had said, about my mother's reluctance to give me a bigger role in the council. She'd always made me feel like there was nothing I couldn't do, no challenge I wasn't strong enough to meet. Had that just been motherly support?

Victoria's words replayed in my head: "God knows I wouldn't trust a parakeet to your care . . . a girl so incompetent she manages to turn a simple custody challenge into an all-out witch-hunt."

"Paige?"

I realized Cortez was watching me.

"It's going to get rougher, isn't it?" I said. "This is only the beginning."

"You're doing fine."

I turned, suddenly uncomfortable, and put my teacup in the microwave. I reheated it, keeping my face to the microwave until it was done. When I turned around, I forced a smile.

"I'm the world's lousiest hostess, aren't I? Letting my guest make me tea. What can I get you? Coffee? Soda? Beer? Something stronger?"

"Tempting, but I'd better forgo anything harder than coffee tonight. I don't want to sleep too soundly with that crowd out there. You, on the other hand, have more than earned a few shots of anything you can dredge up."

"If you're keeping sober for guard duty, so am I." I sipped my tea, made a face, and dumped it. "I'll make that coffee for two."

Savannah burst into the kitchen, startling us both.

"Good, you're off the phone finally," she said. "Lucas and I wanted to talk to you."

"No, we didn't," Cortez said, shooting a look at Savannah. "Tomorrow, I said. Tonight we all need our rest."

"Tomorrow? I can't wait until tomorrow! They're driving me crazy now!"

"Who's driving you crazy?" I said.

"Them!" She waved her arm toward the living room. When I didn't respond, she whirled on Cortez. "See? I told you she's in denial."

"She means the crowd outside," Cortez said. "We are not in denial, Savannah. We are ignoring them, which, as I explained, is the best course of action under the circumstances. Now, perhaps tomorrow—"

"They're bugging me *now*!"

"Have they done something?" I asked, looking from Savannah to Cortez.

"They're there! Isn't that bad enough? We need to do something."

"Like what?"

Cortez shot Savannah a warning look, but she ignored him.

"You know," she said. "Magic. I was thinking hail."

"Hail? Are you serious, Savannah? Do you have any idea how much trouble I'm in already?"

"We've already discussed this," Cortez said. "I've explained to Savannah that, as useful as magic might be, in some cases, such as this, it would be far more detrimental than beneficial."

"What's wrong with hail?" she asked. "It's normal weather stuff."

"Not when the temperature hasn't dropped below sixty in a week," I said. I turned to Cortez. "Don't worry about it. She doesn't know how to make hail."

"No, but you do," Savannah said.

Cortez turned to me. "Really? I've heard of such spells, but I've never encountered one."

"That's 'cause it's witch magic," Savannah said. "Special witch magic. Paige has these really cool grimoires she's working on, and—"

"And we're not conjuring up a hailstorm," I cut in. "Or using any other kind of magic to get rid of those people. They'll leave on their own."

"Denial," Savannah whispered loudly to Cortez.

"Bedtime," I said. "It's nearly eleven."

"So? It's not like I'm going to school ever again."

"You're going as soon as this mess calms down. Until then, you should keep to your normal routine. It's already past your bedtime. Now go."

She stomped off.

CHAPTER 24

PARTY GAMES

I pulled the coffee bean bag from the cupboard.

"I don't suppose you'd let me see that hailstorm spell," Cortez said.

"Hail*storm* is an exaggeration. I can conjure up a handful of nearly frozen ice pellets. More like a slush shower. How bad is it out there, anyway?"

"Let's just say, if the temperature plummets tonight, I'd recommend testing out that hail spell."

I walked into the living room and parted the curtains to see a solid mass of people, even more than had been there when we'd got here. Though it was eleven at night, all the flashlights and camping lanterns lit up the yard bright enough for a ball game.

Camera vans lined the road, their windows rolled down, crews waiting inside, sipping coffee and talking, like cops on a stakeout. While the media stuck to the road, strangers covered nearly every square inch of my yard. Strangers on lawn chairs drinking soda. Strangers with camcorders filming everything in sight. Strangers huddled in circles clutching Bibles. Strangers carrying placards reading "Satan Lives Here" and "Thou Shalt Not Suffer a Witch to Live."

Cortez walked up behind me.

Still holding the curtain, I half-turned and looked up at him. "This afternoon, when we got here, you thought we should go to a motel. Do you think . . . That is . . ." I shook my head and smiled wryly. "I'm not good at this. Asking for advice."

"You want to know if I still think we should leave?"

"Yes. Thank you."

"I don't. My initial concern pertained to the dangers and difficulties of getting past the crowd. Having done that, I believe, as I told Savannah, that we are best to stay here and ignore them."

He gently plucked the curtain from my hand, then let it fall closed.

"The mob mentality is, naturally, a concern. However, the presence of media should counteract any urge to violence, and the size of the crowd itself makes it unlikely that any rogue element could take control."

"But I know what Savannah means." I glanced at the closed curtain and shivered. "I feel . . . under siege."

"True, but think of it instead as an insulating buffer. No Cabal would act with such a crowd of witnesses. You are much safer here than you would be in an isolated motel."

"But if they won't act in front of witnesses . . . what was that at the funeral parlor? Not exactly a private demonstration."

"No, and I can promise you whoever came up with that scheme is in line for a serious reprimand. Someone acted without proper authorization, and will be duly punished. I've already reported the incident. It will be handled by an intra-Cabal judiciary review."

"Uh-huh. And that, I'd guess, is a bad thing."

His lips curved in the barest smile. "I won't bore you with an explanation but, yes, it's a bad thing. From herein you can expect Gabriel Sandford's team to act in accordance with standard Cabal rules of engagement."

"They have rules for . . . ?" I shook my head. "Let me get that coffee going before I do need something stronger."

I walked into the kitchen, then turned around. "How about a snack? I don't think either of us ate our burgers this afternoon."

"If you're having something, then I'll join you, but don't—"

"How about cookies? Do you like chocolate chip?"

He nodded. After turning on the oven, I took a sheet from underneath the stove, and grabbed a Tupperware container from the freezer. I pulled off the lid, then tipped the box to show Cortez the tiny balls of cookie dough within.

"Instant fresh cookies," I said.

"Good idea."

"My mom's, not mine. Mothers know all the tricks, don't they?"

"Cooking was never my mother's forte. We tried cookies once. The dog wouldn't touch them."

I paused in transferring the cookie dough to the sheets. Had he lived with his mother, then? Obviously. Mother *and* father? Did sorcerers leave their sons with their mothers? Or did they marry? I wanted to ask, to compare stories. I was always curious to see how other races did things. It was like learning baking tricks from my mother—other races were bound to have learned tactics for living in the human world, tactics that I might be able to apply to the Coven and make our lives easier, less furtive. I thought of asking, but it seemed too much like prying.

Once the cookies were in the oven, I loaded up the coffeemaker, then excused myself to use the bathroom. When I returned, Cortez was pouring brewed coffee into mugs.

"Black?" he said.

"Black for tea, cream for coffee," I said, opening the fridge. "Strange, I know, but black coffee's just too strong. That's how you take yours, right?"

He nodded. "A taste acquired in college. Spend enough late nights poring over law texts and you learn to take caffeine hits strong and black."

"So you really are a lawyer. I'll admit, when you said you misrepresented yourself in the beginning, I was hoping you didn't mean that part wasn't true."

"No need to worry. I passed the bar last year."

"Pretty young, isn't it?" I said. "You must have fast-tracked your way through school." I turned on the oven light and crouched to check the cookies.

"I condensed my studies," he said. "As I believe you did."

I smiled up at him as I stood. "Did your homework, huh, Counselor?"

"A degree in computer science, completed nearly three years ago. From Harvard no less."

"Not nearly as impressive as it sounds. There are far better schools for computer science, but I wanted to stick close to home. My mother was getting older. I was worried." I laughed. "Wow, I've gotten so used to saying that I can almost convince myself. Truth is, my mom was fine. I wasn't ready to leave the nest. Mom ran a successful business, and we always lived simply, so she'd put aside enough for me to have my pick of schools. I got a partial scholarship, and we decided Harvard made sense. And, of course, it looks great on a résumé." I took two small plates from the cupboard. "So where'd you go to school? No, wait. I bet I can guess."

He lifted his brows quizzically.

"It's a theory," I said. "Well, more of a party game actually, but I like to give it the veneer of scientific respectability. My friends and I have this hypothesis that you can always tell where someone went to school by the way they say the name of their alma mater."

Another brow arch.

"I'm serious. Take Harvard, for example. Doesn't matter where you came from originally, after three years at Harvard, it's *Hah-vahd*."

"So before you went to Harvard, you pronounced the 'r'?"

"No, I'm a Bostonian. It's always been *Hah-vahd*. Wait, the cookies are almost done."

I turned off the timer with five seconds to go, then pulled out the tray and moved the steaming cookies onto the rack.

"So let me understand this theory," he said. "If someone was from the Boston area and went to college elsewhere, he would cease to pronounce Harvard as *Hah-vahd*."

"Of course not. I didn't say it was a perfect theory."

He leaned back against the counter, lips curving slightly. "All right, then. Test this hypothesis. Where did I go to school?"

"Have a cookie first, before they harden."

We each peeled a cookie from the rack. After a few bites, I cleared my throat with a swig of coffee.

"Okay," I said. "I'm going to list some colleges. You repeat each one in a sentence, like 'I went to blank.' First, Yale."

"I went to Yale."

"Nope. Try Stanford."

I listed all the major law schools. One by one, he repeated them.

"Damn," I said. "It's not working. Say Columbia again."

He did.

"Yes . . . no. Oh, I give up. That sounded close. Is it Columbia?"

He shook his head and reached for another cookie.

"May I suggest that your logic is flawed?" he said.

"Never. Oh, okay. Like I said, it's not a perfect theory."

"I'm referring not to the theory, but to the assumption that I attended a top-tier law school."

"Of course you did. You're obviously bright enough to get in and your father could afford to send you anywhere, ergo you'd pick from the best."

Savannah appeared in the doorway, dressed in a lily-print flannel nightgown. The plastic tag still hung from the sleeve. Someone from the Coven had given her the gown for Christmas, but she'd never worn it. She must have dug it up from the depths of her closet, a concession to having a man in the house.

"I can't sleep," she said. She glanced at the rack on the counter. "I knew I smelled cookies. Why didn't you come get me?"

"Because you're supposed to be sleeping. Take one, then get back to bed."

She took two cookies from the rack. "I told you I can't sleep. They're making too much noise."

"Who?"

"The people! Remember? Mobs of people outside our house?"

"I don't hear anything."

"Because you're in denial!"

Cortez laid his empty mug on the counter. "All I hear is a murmur of voices, Savannah. Less than you'd hear if we had the television on."

"Go sleep in my room," I said. "You shouldn't hear the noise from there."

"There are people out back, now, too, you know."

"To bed, Savannah," Cortez said. "We'll reevaluate the situation in the morning and discuss taking action then."

"You guys don't understand anything."

She grabbed the last cookie and stomped off. I waited until her door slammed, then sighed.

"This is tough on her, I know," I said. "Do you think they're really keeping her awake?"

"What's keeping her awake is the knowledge that they're there."

"It would take a lot more than an angry mob to scare Savannah."

"She isn't frightened. She simply finds the idea of being trapped by humans quite intolerable. She believes, as a supernatural, she shouldn't stand for such an intrusion. It's an affront. An insult. Hearing them is a constant reminder of their presence."

"Sure, I suppose surrounding our house could be seen as an indirect threat, but no one's throwing rocks through the windows or trying to break in."

"That doesn't matter to Savannah. You have to see it from her point of view, in the context of her background and her upbringing. She's been raised—"

"Wait. Sorry, I don't mean— Do you hear that?"

"What?"

"Savannah's voice. She was talking to someone. Oh, God, I hope she's not trying to provoke—"

Leaving the sentence unfinished, I hurried to Savannah's room. When I got there, all was silent. I knocked, then opened the door without waiting for an invitation. Savannah was glaring out the window.

"Did you say something to them?" I said.

"As if."

She retreated to her bed and thumped onto the mattress. I glanced at the phone. It was across the room, untouched.

"I thought I heard you talking," I said.

Cortez appeared at my shoulder. "What spell did you cast, Savannah?"

"Spell?" I said. "Oh, shit! Savannah!"

She collapsed onto her back. "Well, you guys weren't going to do anything about it."

"What spell?" I said.

"Relax. It was only a confusion spell."

"A sorcerer confusion spell?" Cortez asked.

"Of course. What else?"

Cortez spun and disappeared down the hall, sprinting for the front door. I raced after him.

Chapter 25

The Riot

Savannah had cast a confusion spell once before. Though I hadn't witnessed the results, Elena told me what had happened. During their escape attempt at the compound, Elena had been heading down a darkened hall to disarm a pair of guards. An elevator filled with guards responding to the alarm touched down behind her. The doors opened. Savannah cast a confusion spell. The guards started firing—at each other, at Elena, at everything in sight. She hadn't told Savannah that she'd nearly been killed, and I hadn't seen the sense in bringing it up later. Now I saw the sense.

Cortez started for the front door, then stopped and turned toward the rear.

"Wait here," he said, pulling open the back door. "I'm going to countercast."

"Can't you do that from inside?"

"I need to be at the locus of her cast, the presumed target area."

"I'll go to her window and direct you."

"No—" He stopped, then nodded. "Just be careful. If anything happens, get away from the glass."

He checked to make sure no one was looking, then ducked out. People had only begun congregating in the backyard an hour or so ago, so the crowd there was less than a third of that out front, no more than a dozen people. With the patio lights off and the additional shadow cast by the roof overhang, the back door was in darkness, so Cortez was able to slip through without being seen.

I hurried to Savannah's bedroom. She was still lying on her bed, arms crossed. I moved to the window.

Cortez appeared a moment later. There must have been people out there who'd seen him escort me into the house earlier, but no one gave any sign of recognizing him now.

As Cortez slipped through the crowd, I looked over the sea of faces, searching for a sign of panic or confusion. Nothing. Cortez moved behind a couple selling cans of soda and glanced toward the window. I shifted left, positioning myself where Savannah had been. Standing on tiptoes brought me to her height.

"You're both as bad as the Elders," Savannah said. "Making a big fuss out of nothing."

I waved Cortez to the right a few steps, then motioned for him to stop. His lips moved as he countercast. When he finished, he glanced around, as if trying to determine whether the spell was broken. Yet there was still no sign that Savannah's spell had worked at all.

I motioned for him to come inside. He shook his head, waved me away from the window, and headed into the crowd.

I released the curtain, but didn't step away, only shifting out of his direct view. He traversed the crowd, pausing here and there before moving on.

"I don't think it worked," I said.

"Of course it did. *My* spells always work."

I bit my tongue and kept my attention on Cortez. When someone shouted, I jumped. A man laughed and I followed the sound to see a couple of young men jostling one another and laughing between gulps from a paperbag-covered bottle. Guess my lawn had replaced the Belham Raceway as the leading source of community entertainment.

As I shifted my gaze away to search for Cortez, one of the men's shouts turned angry. The other whirled and slammed his fist into his companion's jaw. The bottle flew from the first man's hand and struck the shoulder of a woman in a lawn chair. As the woman cried out, her husband leaped to his feet, fists raised.

Cortez came running from the other side of the crowd. I waved my arms, gesturing for him to stop, trying to communicate that the fight had nothing to do with Savannah's spell. Then someone saw me. A cry went up.

I stumbled back from the window. A clod of dirt struck the glass. Someone screamed. The shouts lost their edge of excitement and turned angry, then seemed to drift away from the window.

"Go into my room," I said.

Savannah only set her jaw and stared at the ceiling.

"I said get to my room!"

She didn't move. The shouting became frenzied. Someone howled. I grabbed Savannah by the arm and hauled her into my bedroom, away from the front of the house. Then I raced to the living room.

I cracked open the curtains, hoping to see Cortez and make sure he was okay. The moment I moved the drapes, something hit the glass. I fell back, curtain still in my hand. When I looked up, a man was plastered against the window. Two matronly women held him by the hair while a third pummeled his stomach. I let the curtain fall and ran to the front door.

I once dated a soccer buff. One afternoon, as we watched a European game on television, a riot broke out and I'd stared at the screen in horror, unable to believe such an outpouring of violence could occur over something as trivial as a sporting event. The scene outside reminded me of that soccer riot. I had to help, to do something. If this was anything like the riot I'd seen, people would be hurt, and one of them might be the innocent guy who'd gone outside trying to stop it.

I hurried onto the front porch. No one noticed me. The loosely gathered crowd had become a seething mass of bodies, hitting, kicking, biting, scratching. Stranger attacked stranger while others huddled on the ground, protecting themselves from the onslaught. A half-dozen people had escaped the crush and stood at a distance, gaping as if unable to tear themselves away further.

From a car window, a video camera lens panned across the scene. When I saw that, I had to stifle the urge to march over, grab the camera, and smash it against the pavement. I don't know why, but even with all that was happening, that bothered me the most. After a glare at the cameraman, I diverted my attention to the crowd, searching for Cortez.

Finding one person in that mob would be like spotting a friend at a Columbus Day sale. I climbed onto the porch swing for a better look. Then, bracing myself against the house, I stepped onto the railing. As I did, it occurred to me that I was making myself much more visible than was safe. It also occurred to me that this might be the best thing I could do, to somehow divert the crowd's attention by revealing the long-hidden object of their vigil.

"Hey!" I shouted. "Anybody want an interview?"

Nobody even turned. No, strike that, someone did turn. From the very bowels of the brawl, someone looked my way. Cortez. He was restraining a huge man intent on attacking an elderly woman. Cortez had the guy in a headlock, but the man must have outweighed him by a hundred pounds and, every time the man swung his arm, Cortez flew off his feet. I jumped from the railing and dashed into the fray.

I moved through the crowd with surprising ease. Sure, a few fists flew my way, but when I kept moving, my would-be attackers found less-active targets. With a confusion spell, no one cares who they attack, so long as they attack someone.

When I reached Cortez, I grabbed the elderly woman to lead her to safety.

"You fucking bitch!" she screeched. "Get your filthy hands off me!"

She clawed my face, and punched me in the stomach, then knocked me down as I doubled over. A man tripped over my prone form, righted himself, and kept running. As I struggled to my feet, Cortez lost his grip on the other man, who scrambled up and barreled into the crowd after the elderly woman. I lunged for him, but Cortez caught my arm.

"We can't," he panted, wiping blood from his mouth. "It doesn't help. We need to break the spell. Do you know the countercast?"

"No." I turned to see a woman crawling through the crowd, ducking blows. "It doesn't seem to be affecting everyone."

"It is. They're all confused. Some don't react violently to it."

"I'll get those people to safety, then. You keep working on the spell."

I hurried to the crawling woman, helped her to her feet, and ushered her through the throng. At the road, we crossed and I left her sitting on the far curb before heading back. It took several minutes to find someone else trying to escape, and several more to get him out of the mob.

As I went back for a third time, I realized my mission was like saving single seal cubs from the slaughter. While I rescued one person, at least two more were beaten unconscious. Either Cortez's countercast wasn't working or the violence had picked up enough momentum to continue on its own.

"Thought you could get away, did you?" a voice said at my ear.

I turned to see one of the Salvationists. He slammed a Bible into my face.

"Get thee hence, Satan!"

I whirled away. A hand caught my arm. I looked into the rolling eyes of a young woman.

"Bitch!" she shouted. "Look what you did to my shirt!"

She grabbed it, pulling the front forward with a seam-ripping wrench. It was covered in dirt and blood. More blood smeared her hand. In the opposite fist she held a Swiss Army knife, bloodied blade exposed.

Without thinking, I grabbed for the knife. The blade sliced across my palm. I yelped and fell back. Cortez appeared, grabbing the woman from behind. She spun and struck. The short blade plunged into Cortez's side. She yanked it out and pulled back for a second stab.

I cast a binding spell. The woman stopped in mid-strike. I threw myself on her, knocking her down and grabbing the knife. The spell broke then and she fought, kicking and screaming. Cortez dropped to his knees and tried to help me restrain her, but adrenaline seemed to triple her strength and it was like restraining a wild animal. We both cast binding spells, but neither worked. If only we could calm people— Yes, of course. A calming spell. I cast one, then another, reciting the spell in an endless loop until I felt her limbs go slack beneath me.

"Hey," she said. "What— Get off me. Help! Fire!"

Around us, people had stopped fighting and were milling about, wiping bloodied noses and muttering in bewilderment.

"Perfect," Cortez said. "Keep casting."

I did. We got to our feet and, with Cortez shielding me, we moved through the crowd as I repeated the calming spell. It didn't work on everyone. As I'd feared, the aggression had taken on a life of its own and some people didn't want to stop, yet enough people did that they were able to restrain those who kept going.

"Now, to the house," Cortez said. "Quickly."

"But there's more—"

"It's good enough. Any longer and people will start recognizing you."

We ran for the front door.

Once inside, Cortez called the police. Then I led him to the bathroom, where we could assess injuries. Savannah stayed in my room, door closed. I didn't tell her it was over. Right then, I was afraid of what else I might be tempted to say.

The slice across my hand was the worst of my injuries. Hardly fatal. I slapped on a bandage, then turned my attention to Cortez, starting with a cold compress for his bloodied lip. Next, the knife wound. The blade had passed through his right side. I pulled up his shirt, cleaned the wound, and took a better look.

"It looks okay," I said. "But it could use a couple of stitches. Maybe when the police get here, we can take you to the hospital."

"No need. I've had worse."

I could see that. Though I'd only pulled his shirt up a few inches, I could see a thick scar crossing his abdomen. He was reed thin, but more muscled than one might expect from his build. I guess there's more to fighting Cabals than courtrooms and paperwork.

"I'll make a poultice," I said. "It usually pulls the wound together better than stitches anyway. Less chance of scarring, too."

"Handy. I'll have to ask for a copy of the recipe."

I opened the bathroom cupboard and took out the poultice ingredients. "This is my fault. She's cast that spell once before, with even worse results. I should have warned her about it. I should have told her to wipe it from her repertoire."

"I wouldn't go that far. The confusion spell can be very useful, under the right circumstances, or as a spell of last resort. The caster has to understand it, though, which Savannah obviously doesn't."

"Does it always work like that?"

"No. Her casting is surprisingly strong. I've never seen a confusion spell affect so many people in such a clearly negative fashion. The spell always exacerbates any underlying tendency toward violence. Perhaps under these circumstances, I should have expected such a reaction, assuming the sort of people who congregate around such a story are not the most mentally balanced of individuals."

"That's an understatement."

The doorbell rang then.

"The police," I said. "Or so I hope."

It was the police. They didn't stay long. Outside, people had either left or resumed their vigil as if nothing had happened. The police took some statements, helped people to the paramedics, and secured the area. Afterward they left behind a cruiser and two officers to keep watch.

Savannah finally appeared as I was putting the poultice on Cortez.

"Don't expect me to say I'm sorry," she said.

I turned to face her.

She stood in the bathroom doorway. "I'm not sorry."

"You—do you know what you've done?" I stalked across the bathroom and pushed open the window. "Do you see that? The ambulances? The paramedics? The blood? People got hurt, Savannah. Innocent people."

"They shouldn't have been there. Stupid humans. Who cares about them?"

"*I* care about them!" I ripped the bandage off my hand. "I suppose you don't care about this, either. Well, there is something you should care about—"

I grabbed her shoulders and turned her to face Cortez, then pointed out his swollen lip and wounded side.

"Do you care about that? This man is here to help you, Savannah. To help *you*. He could have been killed out there trying to undo the spell you cast."

"I didn't ask him to undo it. If you got hurt, it's your own fault for going out there."

"You—" I flung her arm down. "Get to your room, Savannah. Now."

Her eyes glistened with tears, but she only stomped her foot and glared at us. "I'm not sorry! I'm not!"

She turned and ran for her room.

CHAPTER 26

ALL ABOUT EVE

"I am so sorry," I said as we walked into the living room. "I know I should be able to handle her. I really should. I keep telling myself I'm making progress, teaching her control, but then something like this happens and it's—it's pretty obvious I haven't taught her anything at all."

I dropped onto the sofa. Cortez took the armchair and moved it around to face me before sitting.

"She doesn't like humans," I continued. "She hates the Coven. She probably hates me. Sometimes I wonder why she sticks around."

"Because her mother told her to. Before Eve died, she told Savannah that if anything happened to her, she was to find the Coven and take refuge there."

I looked up at him. "Who told you that?"

"Savannah. We talked earlier this evening. She has some concerns and hoped I might be able to mediate on her behalf."

"What'd she say? No, let me guess. I'm a wonderful guardian. I understand her and I always know exactly the right thing to do and say."

A slight smile. "She admitted you two don't always get along. Naturally, she says you don't understand her, you don't give her enough responsibility, you're overprotective, all the things every teenager says to every adult. Do you know what else she says? That you have potential."

"I have . . ." I couldn't stifle a small laugh. "*I* have potential."

"Don't take it too hard. She says I have potential, too. Neither of us is measuring up to her standards quite yet, but at least there appears to be hope for us."

I turned to stare at the front curtains. "Still, potential or not, I don't think I'm what Eve had in mind when she told Savannah to take refuge with the Coven. The problem is—" I stopped. "God, I'm blathering. What time is it anyway?"

"Not that late. You were saying?"

I hesitated. I wanted to keep talking. Maybe exhaustion had worn down my defenses. Or maybe Cortez just seemed like someone I could talk to.

"Sometimes I . . . I wonder if the Elders aren't right. If I'm not endangering the Coven by keeping Savannah here."

"Do you mean you want to find someone else to take her?"

"God, no. What I mean is that maybe we're both endangering the Coven by staying. That I should leave and take her with me. Only I can't. This . . . this is my life. The Coven. Being Coven Leader. I want . . . I want to . . ." I heard the passion in my voice, the near-desperation. My cheeks heated. "I want to do a lot. I can't leave."

I looked away, embarrassed by my outburst. I wanted to stop but, having started, couldn't until I'd said everything I wanted to say.

"About Savannah," I said. "I want to show her how to take that power and use it for good. Only sometimes, like tonight, that seems completely delusional. I can't—I can't seem to make her understand the difference between right and wrong. I can't make her *care*."

He glanced toward Savannah's room. "Should we use a privacy spell?"

I nodded. A privacy spell was witch magic. It allowed two people to converse without being overheard. Both speakers had to cast it, which we did. Cortez fumbled the first time, but recast and got it to work.

"How much do you know about Eve?" Cortez asked.

"She was kicked out of the Coven for using dark magic. But after that . . . I don't know. She couldn't have been too bad or the council would have gotten involved." I shook my head. "Okay, that's a cop-out. We knew she was into bad stuff. Not bad enough to warrant attention, but she was definitely practicing dark magic. It's just that, well, we can't chase after everyone. We have to choose—"

"Which cases warrant your attention. You don't need to explain that to me, Paige. As difficult as it is, sometimes we have to forgo chasing down the worst offenses and pick the battles we can win. Yes, Eve practiced dark magic. Not just dark. The darkest of the dark. Her focus, however, was not on using it but on teaching it to other spell-casters—witches, sorcerers, whoever could pay her fees."

"Teaching? Why?"

He shrugged. "It was a very lucrative business. Such information is very difficult to obtain through standard sources."

"So she didn't use dark magic for her own gain. She just taught it to dozens of others. That's no better, maybe even worse."

"Exactly as I see it, yet in most supernatural circles, Eve's choice gave her the veneer of respectability. She was highly regarded as a teacher."

A car door slammed outside. I jumped and reached for the curtain, then heard an engine start.

"Another departing guest," I said. "Do you think Savannah's spell scared them off? Or is it just past their bedtime?"

He opened his mouth, then snapped it shut.

I managed a small smile. "You were going to lie, weren't you? Tell me what I want to hear, that they're running for their lives, never to darken my doorstep again."

"I caught myself."

"Thanks," I said, my smile turning genuine. "I appreciate the sentiment, but I appreciate the honesty more."

We looked at each other for a moment, then I reached down and picked up a pillow that had been knocked off earlier. I plumped it and returned it to its spot.

"So," I said. "Back to Eve. She was a teacher. Any Cabal connection? Did they ever hire her?"

"No. All of the Cabals had censured her, meaning that their members were forbidden to seek her teachings."

"Because she was a witch?"

"No, because she imparted dangerous spells without teaching the requisite methods of control for using them. I'm not defending the Cabals. If they set limits on the type of magic they allow, they are limits of practicality, not morality. As the degree of darkness increases, so does the risk of danger. Eve's magic was the worst sort. I can say that based, not on rumor, but on experience."

"You met Eve?"

"'Met' would be an exaggeration. I encountered her. Several years ago, I investigated a sorcerer who'd been casting spells far too advanced for his abilities and was responsible for several rather gruesome deaths. After handling the situation, I traced the source of his spells, and it led me to Eve Levine. I managed to confiscate several of her grimoires, but not before getting a taste of her power."

"She bested you?"

Cortez rubbed a hand across his mouth. "Ah, one could . . . say that." When he lowered his hand, a tiny smile played at his lips. "In the interests of being honest, I must admit it was a bit . . . more humiliating than that, and certainly not a story I'd wish to hear repeated."

"My lips are sealed."

"Eve used sorcerer magic against me and I consider myself lucky to have escaped. Her proficiency far outstripped that of most sorcerers. That's why Isaac Katzen targeted her for recruitment."

"You mean by having her kidnapped last year."

"Exactly. An unwise move. Again, we move into the realm of gossip, but given my firsthand knowledge of Eve's power, I'm inclined to believe the story. They say that Eve survived only one day in captivity before her captors killed her. Katzen had assumed that his powers would be greater than those of even the strongest witch and therefore led the humans to believe Eve would be easily handled. They were unprepared for her level of expertise and, given the very real possibility of losing both her and Savannah, chose to kill her and keep the more manageable child. Their biggest mistake, though, was taking Savannah in the first place. You don't corner a lioness with her cub."

"Do you think—" I stopped, tried again. "I mean, when you met Eve, did you get any sense of her as a mother? Was she good to Savannah?"

"I never saw Savannah. From what I've heard, that was typical. No one outside Eve's immediate circle of friends was permitted contact with the child. Certainly, I'm not qualified to make such a judgment, but from what I've seen of Savannah, I would assume Eve was a decent mother, perhaps better than decent. In some ways, it might have been better if Eve had been negligent. Savannah has a very strong bond with her mother. You have to remember that. When you speak against dark magic, you speak against Eve."

"I need to understand Eve better. I know that." I paused. "But I can't—it's not—this wasn't how I was raised. I know . . ."

I looked over at Cortez. His eyes were on mine, waiting with a mixture of quiet interest and understanding that made me want to go on.

"I should have talked to Savannah about the confusion spell," I said. "I should have told her what happened the last time. We should have discussed when and when not to use it. I *know* all this. I see it, but I can't do it. Dark magic . . ."

I looked down and picked at the bandage on my hand. Cortez was still watching me, that same look of patient waiting on his face.

"It's not—my mother taught me—I was raised to see dark magic as bad. Always. No exceptions. And now I see exceptions, but—" I stopped and pressed my hands to my eyes. "God, I am so tired. I can't believe I'm babbling like this."

"You're not—"

I interrupted him by undoing the privacy spell, then scrambled to my feet. "You're staying the night, I assume?"

"Yes, I thought that would be best. But—"

"Here, I'll show you where I keep the guest supplies." I headed for the back hall. "I've got extra toothbrushes . . . there should be some unisex deodorant."

"That's not necessary, Paige. I brought the saddlebags from my bike and they're fully equipped with overnight provisions."

"Are they out in the car?"

"Yes, I can retrieve them later. I know this is difficult for you, Paige. If you'd like to talk—"

"Talked your ear off already, haven't I?" I forced a laugh as I turned and walked instead into the front hall. I took my keys from the rack. "Here are my car keys. You go grab those saddlebags and I'll put bedding on the sofa bed. You'll find fresh towels in the bathroom closet, along with shampoo, soap, and whatever else you might need."

I headed into the living room. By the time he'd returned from getting his saddlebags, I was in my room.

CHAPTER 27

THE ARRIVAL

"**Y**ou're up!"
I bolted awake as Savannah sailed across the room and thudded onto my bed.

"Thank God, 'cause Lucas is cooking breakfast and I'm getting kinda worried. When's the last time you tested the fire extinguisher?"

I pulled myself upright. Looked around. Looked at Savannah. Was I dreaming? The last time we'd spoken, she'd stormed off to her room. Now she was rifling through my closet, chattering away as if nothing had happened.

"He says he's making an omelet. But I'm not so sure. Doesn't look like any omelet I've ever seen. Are you getting up today? It's nearly eight-thirty." She whirled around, held my green cashmere sweater up to her chest, and grinned. "Whaddaya think? This winter, maybe?"

"Who else are you going to fit in there with you?"

"You know, you're not supposed to talk like that in front of me. Young women are very susceptible to negative body image perceptions. I read that last month in *Seventeen*. You're not fat. Not by a long shot. At least you've got boobs." She turned to the mirror, pulled her T-shirt tight against her nearly flat chest, and frowned. "You think maybe I'm a late bloomer? Or is this it?"

Was this the same girl who'd caused a riot on my front lawn? Who'd then vowed that she didn't care who'd been hurt? I'd told Cortez that I needed to understand her. How? One minute she was making strangers attack one another, the next she was a normal thirteen-year-old girl, worried about clothes and breast size.

"—time we go shopping, I want new bras and panties. Stuff like yours. Lace and satin and colors. Real lingerie, not that white cotton stuff. I'm starting high school next year, don't forget. I'll have to change for gym with other girls. Even if I don't have boobs, I can't be looking like a little kid."

"Savannah," Cortez said from the hall. "I asked you not—"

He stopped, seeing me sitting up in bed in my chemise. He quickly stepped back, out of view.

"My apologies. Savannah, I asked you not to bother Paige. She needs her sleep. You were supposed to be doing homework, remember?"

"Oh, please. I'm in danger of being handed over to a psycho half-demon and brainwashed into slavery for supernatural mobsters. You think anyone cares whether I know how to conjugate verbs?"

"Go conjugate, Savannah," I said. "Please."

"And close Paige's door so she can rest."

Savannah sighed and flounced out of my room, swinging the door half-closed behind her. I collapsed back onto my bed and considered staying awhile but I knew, if I did, I might never get up again. Time to face the day . . . whatever it might bring.

When I walked into the kitchen, Cortez was at the stove, his back to me.

"Savannah has vetoed my omelet, but I assure you it's quite edible. If you prefer, I can probably manage toast."

"The omelet will be fine. Better than fine. Tomorrow, I'll set my alarm. Guests shouldn't need to fend for themselves in the morning."

"You don't need to play hostess for me, Paige. You have quite enough to worry about."

I grabbed two glasses and filled them with orange juice. "Look, about last night. I didn't mean to unload on you."

"You didn't unload. You have justifiable concerns and I think we should discuss them. If you'd like to talk—"

"I'd like to talk about coming up with a plan. Yesterday was crazy and I know I was running around like a chicken with its head cut off, but I'm not usually that disorganized. After breakfast, I'd like to sit down and discuss a plan of action."

"Excellent idea."

Contrary to what Savannah had implied, the omelet looked good, and tasted just fine. Once we were both sitting down eating, I noticed the ringer light on the phone flashing. Cortez followed my gaze.

"I turned the ringer off to let you sleep," he said. "Shall I—"

"No, leave it off. You were right yesterday. I should just start reviewing call display records. I don't need to hear a constantly ringing phone and I really don't need to hear those messages. Is the machine off?"

He shook his head. "I just turned the volume down. That seemed safest."

"Good idea." At a loud bass thump from Savannah's room, I glanced toward the back hall. "Did she even apologize to you?"

"I believe her mood is intended as an apology."

"Making nice."

"Exactly."

I lowered my voice. "Do you think she regrets it? At all?"

"That's difficult to say."

"Hey," Savannah said, swinging through the kitchen doorway. "Anyone notice how quiet it is this morning? I just looked out my window and guess what? They're gone. Poof." She grinned. "Like magic."

"Yes, I'd noticed that," Cortez said, taking another bite of his omelet.

"Are you going to say anything?"

"Such as?"

She sighed. "Oh, come on, Lucas. You aren't still mad at me, are you? Don't be like that. Admit it. It wasn't such a bad idea after all."

"What wasn't?" I said. "The confusion spell? I hope you're kidding, Savannah."

Her eyes clouded. "No, I'm not. Look outside. Look. They're gone. I made them leave."

"First, they are not all gone," Cortez said. "There is still a small contingent remaining. Most, however, have left, due perhaps in part to your actions, but quite probably owing more to this." He stood, walked to the counter, and picked up several sheets of paper. "It appears East Falls has grown weary of its recent influx of tourists."

He laid the sheets on the table for Savannah and me. They were printouts from a website covering local news.

"I hope you don't mind, Paige, but I took the liberty of using your computer this morning. After last night's problem, I feared the number of onlookers might increase. When I saw that the reverse had occurred, I was curious."

I scanned the articles. The one I wanted was right at the top of the page, with the biggest headline. "Old-Fashioned Shunning Shuts Down Media Onslaught." In colonial New England one of the most severe punishments a Puritan community could inflict on its members was shunning. Instead of exiling you, they banished you socially. They pretended you didn't exist. Parents have always known how infuriating such a punishment is. The worst thing you can do to a child is to ignore her. That's what East Falls had done to the crowds of strangers drawn to my story.

After a half-day of being beset by the plague of locusts, the people of East Falls had withdrawn into their homes, locked the doors, and taken the phones off the hook. That left the media searching in vain for quotes and sound bites. Then, when dinnertime came, no one could find an open restaurant within twenty miles of East Falls. Even the grocery and variety stores had closed early. Then, when they tried to find lodgings, every motel, hotel, and bed-and-breakfast in the county was suddenly full.

Sure, people could drive to Boston for food and shelter—if they had enough gas. All the local stations had closed at nine. This didn't stop the most intrepid reporters and ghouls from hanging around, but more than enough had decided it simply wasn't worth their while. No one was giving interviews. I wasn't coming out of my house. The dead weren't rising in the local cemetery. There was really nothing much worth seeing in East Falls. For now, at least.

"This is bullshit," Savannah said, swiping the papers to the floor. "People didn't leave because of this. They left because of me. Because of my spell."

"Your spell may have frightened off a few," Cortez said. "But, under normal circumstances, it would have only increased the level of public interest. Yes, some would have left . . . those who were merely victimized by the spell and who played no active role in the violence. A confusion spell exacerbates violent tendencies. Those who enjoyed the emotional release would stay. And more would come—the sort of people hoping for a replay. Without this shunning, the situation would have only worsened." He paused. "I know that you didn't understand the full ramifications of the spell you cast, Savannah."

Her eyes hardened. "I knew exactly what I was doing, sorcerer."

"Don't you talk to him like that," I said.

Cortez lifted his hand. "You didn't understand it, Savannah. I know that. No one holds you responsible—"

"I am responsible! I got rid of them. Me! You—you two—you have no idea—"

She grabbed the tablecloth, wrenching it and spilling dishes to the floor. Then she turned and stalked away. When I stood to go after her, the doorbell rang.

"Goddamn it!" I said. "Does it never end?"

"Let me get the door. Ignore Savannah for now."

He headed for the door. I followed.

Cortez persuaded me to wait around the corner while he opened the door. Though I hated any perception of hiding, he had a point. There were still nine or ten people on my lawn waiting for me to make an appearance.

After last night's riot, I couldn't risk another scene.

"Good morning, Officer," Cortez said.

I slumped against the wall. Now what? I'd seen more cops in the last few days than on a weekend *Law & Order* marathon.

"Department of Social Services," the officer said. "Come to see Miss Winterbourne. I thought I'd better escort them to the door."

What could be worse than a police visit right now? A child welfare visit.

"I believe your appointment was for this afternoon," Cortez said. "While we appreciate your interest in Savannah's well-being, I really must ask you to return then. We had an incident here last night. A very upsetting incident and, as you might imagine, my client had a difficult night and is not yet prepared for visitors."

"That 'incident' is the reason we're early," a woman's voice replied. "We're very concerned for the child."

The child? Oh, right . . . my loving ward, currently barricaded in her room. Oh, God. Would they want to see Savannah? Of course they would. That's what they were here for. To evaluate my parenting skills. I would have laughed . . . if I hadn't been so close to crying.

Cortez argued for several minutes, but it soon became apparent that he was wavering. I didn't blame him. If we refused to admit Social Services, they would think we had something to hide. Well, we did have something to hide. Plenty, in fact. But, God knew, if we didn't let them in now, things might be even worse when they returned.

"It's okay," I said, walking into the hall. "Come in, please."

A fiftyish woman with an auburn bob introduced herself as Peggy Dare. I didn't catch the name of the timid blond with her. It didn't matter. The woman whispered hello and never said another word. I escorted them to the living room, then offered coffee or tea, which they refused.

"May we see Savannah?" Dare asked.

"She's resting," Cortez said. "As I said, last night was very hard on all of us. Naturally, Savannah, given her youth, was particularly affected by the violence."

"She's very upset," I managed.

"I understand," Dare said. "But that, of course, is why we're here. If you would let us speak to her, perhaps we can verify the extent of the damage."

"Damage?" Cortez said. "That seems rather judgmental."

"It wasn't intended that way. We've come with an open mind, Mr. Cortez. We only want what's best for the child. May we see her, please?"

"Yes, but unless I'm mistaken, part of your mandate is to assess the physical environment. Perhaps we can begin with that."

"I'd like to begin by speaking to Savannah."

"As I've said, she's sleeping, but—"

"I am not, Lucas!" Savannah shouted from her room. "You are such a liar!"

"She's very upset," I repeated.

Cortez turned toward the hall. "Savannah? Could you please come out for a moment? There are some people here from Social Services who would like to speak to you."

"Tell them to go piss up a rope!"

Silence.

"Haven't heard that one in a while," I said, struggling to smile. "Sorry. I've been working on her language. She's very upset."

"More than upset," Cortez said. "The events of last night were extremely traumatic. Paige has been trying to soothe her all morning. Professional help may be necessary."

"I'm not the one who needs professional help!" Savannah shouted. "You don't see me running around trying to save the world. Wonder what a therapist would say about that?"

"What is she talking about?" Dare asked.

"She's confused," I said.

"I'm not the one who's confused! And I didn't just mean Lucas. I meant you, too, Paige. You're both crazy. Fucking looped."

"Excuse me," I said, hurrying for the back hall.

When I got to Savannah's room, the door opened. She glared at me, then marched into the bathroom and locked the door. I grabbed the handle and rattled it.

"Open this door, Savannah."

"Can I take a pee first? Or are you controlling that now, too?"

I hesitated, then walked into the living room. Dare and her partner sat on the sofa like dumbfounded bookends.

"You—you seem to be having some discipline issues," Dare said.

Savannah screamed. I raced for the door, casting an unlock spell under my breath as I ran. Before I could grab the handle, the door flew open. Savannah burst into the hall.

"It's here!" she said. "Finally! I was starting to think it was never going to come."

"What's here?" I said, hurrying to her. "What's wrong?"

"Nothing's wrong." She grinned. "I'm bleeding."

"Bleeding? Where? What happened?"

"You know. My period. My first period. It's here."

She lunged into my arms, hugged me, and kissed my cheek. The first spontaneous display of affection she'd ever shown, and I could only stand there like an idiot, thinking "Well, that explains a lot."

"Your . . . you got your period?"

"Yes! Isn't that great?" She whirled around and punched the air. "Watch out, Leah. I'm—" She stopped, seeing Dare and her partner standing in the hallway. "Who the hell are you?"

CHAPTER 28

At Last, a Plan

Getting rid of the social workers proved remarkably easy. After that display, they couldn't wait to run back to their office and file their report. I tried to get them to stay and conduct the complete interview—now that Savannah was soaring high and eager to please—but they were having none of it.

Within minutes, they were gone. Cortez had done nothing to help me persuade them to stay. The moment they'd left, he ushered us into the living room, waved us onto the sofa, and began to pace. Cortez pacing. Not a good sign.

"You're quite certain?" he asked Savannah.

"About Paige being a good guardian? Sure. That's why I said so, but I don't think they were listening. I told the blond girl that I wanted to keep living here, but she jumped back like I had mono or something."

"I'm not referring to your statement," Cortez said. "Your menses. You're certain it's arrived?"

"Duh, yes. Girls don't start bleeding down there for no reason."

"It makes sense," I said. "She hasn't been feeling well, probably cramps. Plus the mood swings."

"What mood swings?" Savannah said.

"Never mind, hon. You're fine. I'm very happy for you. We both are."

Cortez didn't look happy. He looked agitated. Not a powerful description when applied to most people, but in Cortez, it was the equivalent of a breakdown.

"Do you know about the ceremony?" he asked.

"I was going to talk to Paige about it," she said. "And how do you know about the ceremony, sorcerer?"

She said it with a smile, but he waved the question away and turned to me.

"Yes," I said. "I know about the first menses ceremony."

"Do you know about the variations?" he asked.

"Variations?"

"I take that as a no."

He paced to the window and back. Then he stopped, ran his hand through his hair, adjusted his glasses, and collected himself. Before continuing, he settled into the armchair across from us.

"I mentioned before that the Nast Cabal's interest in Savannah is largely contingent upon capturing her at such a young age. That is not without reason. Good reason. If a witch is taken before she begins to menstruate, she's much easier to turn."

"Brainwash," I said.

"Recruit, persuade, brainwash, call it what you will. A witch who has not reached puberty is the ideal candidate. That in itself is not surprising, as anyone with any knowledge of youth psychology can tell you it's a very vulnerable age."

Savannah snorted.

Cortez continued, "However, in the case of a witch, it's more than that. By varying the menses ceremony, it's possible to secure the loyalty of a witch."

"You mean enslave her."

"No, no. Altering the ceremony can impose certain limitations on a witch's powers, which can then be used to persuade her to remain with the Cabal. It's difficult to explain. There are nuances and implications I don't fully comprehend. The crux of it is this: Alter the ceremony and you have the ideal recruit. Allow the ceremony to proceed unchanged and you might as well forget the whole thing."

"So if we can get through the ceremony, they won't want Savannah? Nothin' wrong with that, Counselor."

"Except for two small considerations. First, if they discover Savannah has reached her menses, they'll do everything in their power to get her before the eighth night."

"How would they know that?" she asked.

"Shamans," I said. "They have shamans, don't they?"

Cortez nodded. "The Cabals have everything."

"A shaman can diagnose illness. A shaman would know whether she'd matured to the point of first menses yet. All a shaman has to do is touch you, Savannah. Jostling you in a crowd would be enough. They must have had one check you out before they started all this."

"Are you saying I need to stay indoors for a week? You're kidding, right? I have graduation next week, you know. If the school still lets me graduate after all this."

"They will," Cortez said. "I'll make certain of it. Our most pressing concern, however, is preventing the Nast Cabal from learning of your good news. Paige, is the house protected against astral projection?"

"Always," I said.

"Then there's the second consideration. Once Savannah has completed the unaltered ceremony, they won't want her. However, given the reputation of her mother and the problems she caused the Cabals, the Nasts won't simply walk away. If they can't have Savannah, they'll make sure no one else can."

"You mean they'll kill me," she said.

"She doesn't need to hear this," I said.

"I think she does, Paige."

"Well, I disagree. Savannah, go to your room, please."

"He's right, Paige," she said quietly. "I need to hear this."

"She needs to know exactly what danger she faces," Cortez said. "So we need to protect her until after the ceremony, then tell them their opportunity has passed."

"What?" I said. "But if they know that, they'll kill her. You said so yourself."

"No, I said they might kill her if they believe she's completed the unaltered ceremony. However, if the eighth night were to pass without a ceremony, Savannah's powers would be irrevocably weakened. Hence, she'd pose no threat."

"I'm not skipping the ceremony," she said.

"You won't," I said. "We just need to convince them that you did."

"Exactly."

We worked on the plan for three hours, sharing information, floating ideas, drawing up lists—Cortez's lists, of course. Savannah stuck around for the first hour before deciding verb conjugation sounded like more fun.

We had a week to wait. A long time to spend locked in the house. We debated the wisdom of staying here versus finding a safe place to hole up for the week. After considering the options, we agreed that we'd stick around until we'd figured out the Nast Cabal's next move. They'd gone through a lot of trouble to make my life hell, and Cortez suspected they might now simply sit back and wait for me to cave. If we ran, they'd surely follow. For now, it seemed best to play "wait-and-see" for a day or two.

Although Savannah's ceremony wouldn't take place for eight days, there were a few things that had to be done the first night, such as gathering the juniper. That meant we had to go out. As well, the ceremony book was kept at Margaret's house, and Cortez agreed that I needed to look through it as soon as possible, so we added that to our list of chores for the evening. Until then, we'd just sit tight.

After lunch, while Cortez made some legal-type calls related to the DSS visit, I decided to clear my mind with some spell practice. I took the grimoires from my knapsack and put them into another bag, which I hid in the second compartment. I got as far as the hall when someone banged at the front door.

I winced and returned my knapsack to its hiding place. By the time I got to the front hall, Cortez was undoing his lock spells. When he reached for the dead bolt, I waved him back.

"I've got it."

He hesitated, then stepped behind me as I opened the door. There stood two state cops. I'd probably seen them before—the county detachment wasn't large—but I'd moved past the point of bothering to attach names to faces.

"Yes?" I said through the open screen.

The older officer stepped forward, but made no attempt to open the door or demand admittance. Maybe he enjoyed having a wider audience. Unfortunately for him, most of the crowd and all the TV crews were gone, though the kids with the camcorder had returned.

"We were asked by town council to escort these good people to your door."

He stepped back. A man and a woman, both of whom I knew only vaguely, stepped forward.

"Councilor Bennett and Councilor Phillips," the man said without indicating who was who. "We'd like to bring to your attention—" He cleared his throat, then raised his voice for the small smattering of people below. "We'd like to bring to your attention a request by the East Falls town council."

He paused, as if for effect.

"The council has agreed, most magnanimously, to divest you of this property for a fair market value."

"Div—did you say divest—?"

"Fair market value," he said, voice rising another notch. He glanced around, making sure he had his audience's full attention. "Plus moving expenses. Furthermore, we will assess the value of your home as it stood before any damage occurred."

"Why not just tar and feather me?"

"We have a petition. A petition signed by over fifty percent of the voting population of East Falls. They are asking you, in light of recent events, to consider relocating and, with their signatures, they are endorsing the town's generous offer."

The woman held out a roll of paper, letting the end fall to the ground like some kind of medieval proclamation. On it I saw dozens of names. Names of people I knew, neighbors, shopkeepers, people I'd worked with on the Christmas charity dinner, parents of children at Savannah's school, even teachers who'd taught her. All asking me to move out. To leave.

I grabbed the list, tore it up the middle and thrust half into each of the councilors' hands.

"Take this back to the council and tell them where they can stuff their generous offer. Better yet, tell everyone on this damned list that they'd better get used to me, because I'm not leaving."

I slammed the door.

I stood in the doorway between the living room and front hall, held there as if by a binding spell. I kept seeing that list, mentally repeating the names. People I knew. People I thought knew me. Granted, they didn't know me well, but I wasn't a stranger. I'd helped with every school and charity event. I'd bought cookies from every Girl Scout, apples from every Boy Scout. I'd donated time, money, effort, whatever was needed wherever it was needed, all because I knew how crucial it was to Savannah's future that I fit in. And now they overlooked all that and turned their backs on me. Not just turned away, but thrust me away.

Yes, what had happened in East Falls was terrible: the appalling discovery of the Satanic altar and its mutilated cats, the unspeakable horror of Cary's death and funeral. I didn't blame the town for not rushing to my aid with casseroles and condolences. They were confused, afraid. But to judge so blatantly, to say, "We don't want you here." Such a rejection burned worse than any epithet hurled by a stranger.

When I finally broke from my trance, I crossed the room and dropped onto the sofa. Savannah sat beside me and put her hand on my knee.

"We don't need them, Paige," she said. "If they don't want us here, screw 'em. We can take their money and get a better place. You like Boston, right? You always said that was where you wanted to live, not this backwater dump. We'll move there. The Elders can't complain. It's the town's fault, not ours."

"I won't go," I said.

"But, Paige—"

"She's right, Savannah," Cortez said. "At this point, it would appear an admittance of guilt. When this is over, Paige may well decide to reconsider the offer. Until then, we can't dwell on it." His voice softened. "They're wrong, Paige. You know they're wrong and you know you don't deserve this. Don't give them the satisfaction of upsetting you."

I closed my eyes and pressed my fingers to the lids, cutting off impending tears. "You're right. We have work to do."

"There's nothing we need to do right now," Cortez said. "I'd suggest you rest."

"I'll go practice my spells."

Cortez nodded. "I understand. Perhaps I could—" He stopped short. "Yes, that's a good idea. Spell practice should help take your mind off things."

"What were you going to say?"

He took his DayTimer from the end table. "There were a couple of spells . . . I thought . . . Well, perhaps, later, after I've made some more calls, and you've had some time to yourself . . . if you wouldn't mind, there are a few witch spells I'd like to ask you about."

He flipped through his DayTimer, eyes on the page, as if he wasn't awaiting an answer. I couldn't help smiling. The guy could handle homicide cops, bloodthirsty reporters, and the walking dead with implacable confidence, but turn the conversation to something as remotely personal as asking to discuss spells with me and suddenly he seemed as flustered as a schoolboy.

"I'll show you mine if you show me yours," I said. "Spell for spell, even trade. Deal?"

He looked up from his book with a crooked smile. "Deal."

"Make your calls then, and give me an hour to clear my head, then we'll talk."

He agreed and I headed downstairs.

An hour passed. An hour of practice. An hour of failure. Was there not some benevolent force in the world that rewarded perseverance and good intentions? If such a being existed, couldn't it look down on me, take pity, and say, "Let's toss the poor kid a bone"?

One good killing spell to protect Savannah. That's all I asked for. Well, okay, if there was such a benevolent force out there, it probably wasn't about to give anyone the power to kill. But I needed to know how to do it. Couldn't whatever supreme being who governed witchcraft realize that? Yeah, right. If such an entity existed, it was probably looking down and laughing, shouting, "Those spells don't work, you little fool!"

"Those spells don't work," said a voice at my ear.

I jumped about a foot, nearly toppling from my kneeling position. Savannah peered down at my grimoire.

"Well, they don't, do they?" she said. "Other than those few you got working, the rest just fail, right?"

"You've tried them?"

She dropped down beside me. "Nah. I can never find where you hide the grimoires. But I know what you're practicing from your journal, remember? I wondered if I should tell you they don't work, but I didn't figure you'd listen. Lucas thinks I should tell you, so you stop wasting your time."

That stung, the thought that she'd been talking to a near-stranger about things she didn't feel comfortable discussing with me. Yet I had to admit she was right. I wouldn't have listened. I didn't want to hear anything that might relate to her background, to her mother. That had to change.

"Why don't you think they'll work?"

"Know, not think."

"Okay, then, why do you *know* they won't work?"

"Because they're witch magic."

"And what's wrong with witch magic? There's nothing—"

"See, I told Lucas you'd do this."

I settled back onto the floor. "I'm sorry, Savannah. Please continue."

She grinned. "Wow. I like that."

"Don't get too used to it. Now talk."

"None of the strong witch spells work because the middle spells are missing. That's why my mom and other witches—non-Coven witches—use sorcerer magic for all their strong spells."

"They use sorcerer magic?"

"You didn't know that?"

"Ummm, well, I—" I forced the words out. "No, I didn't know that."

"Oh sure, all the really powerful spells are sorcerer magic. We can all do the simple witch stuff, like the Coven spells, plus a bunch of others, but for the strong spells, we need to use sorcerer magic. That's the problem, see? My mom used to get all worked up about it. She blamed the Coven for losing the middle spells. At least, they said they lost them, but she always figured they threw them away. It was wrong, she said, because it denied witches—"

Savannah stopped as Cortez appeared in the doorway.

"Sorry to interrupt," he said. His lips twitched, as if suppressing a smile. "We appear to have a situation out back. I don't mean to intrude on your practice, but I thought perhaps you could use a break."

"Just a sec," I said. "Savannah was telling me something important."

"It can wait," she said, jumping to her feet. "What's outside?"

"I don't believe I could do it justice with a verbal description," he said. And smiled.

With that, Savannah was off and up the stairs.

CHAPTER 29

THEY AREN'T NAKED, THEY'RE SKYCLAD

When I got upstairs, I shooed a near-hysterical Savannah away from the kitchen window, lifted the blind, and looked out to see five women kneeling in a circle on my lawn. Five naked women. I mean butt-naked, not just topless or scantily dressed, but absolutely without clothing.

I jumped back so fast I collided with Cortez.

"What the hell is that?" I said.

"I believe the commonly accepted term is 'Wiccan.'"

"Wiccans?"

"Or, I should say, that is how they introduced themselves when I ventured out to request that they dress themselves and vacate the premises. They indicated that they are members of a small sect of Wicca from a coven somewhere in Vermont. No relation to your Coven, I presume?"

"Ha-ha."

"They seem quite harmless. They're performing a cleansing ceremony for your benefit."

"How . . . nice."

"I thought so." He grinned then, an action I'd never have thought his face capable of performing. "One other thing it behooves me to mention. On their behalf. A request. One that I really would advise you to honor."

"What is it?"

"They've asked you to join them."

I whirled around and, had I not been a firm believer in nonviolence, I swear I would have slugged him. Instead, I collapsed against the counter, laughing. Laughing far harder than the situation warranted. After one week of hell, I must admit, naked Wiccans on my back lawn was a welcome diversion.

"I take it that's a no?" Cortez said, still grinning.

"'Fraid so."

"I'll convey my regrets, then. And I'll ask them to leave."

"No," I said. "I'll do it."

"Are you sure?"

"Hey, these are the first supporters I've seen. The least I can do is tell them to get lost myself."

"Can I come?" Savannah asked.

"No," Cortez and I said in unison.

I peered out the back door before exiting.

Except for the Wiccans, my yard was empty. When I stepped outside, the Wiccans stopped, turning as one body and bestowing beatific smiles on me. I approached slowly. Cortez followed at my heels.

"Sister Winterbourne," the first one said.

She threw open her arms, embraced me, planted a kiss on my lips, then another on my left breast. I yelped. Cortez made a choking noise that sounded suspiciously like a stifled whoop of laughter.

"My poor, poor child," she said, clasping both my hands to her chest. "They've frightened you so. Not to worry. We're here to offer the support of the Goddess."

"Praise be to the Goddess," the others intoned.

The first one grasped my hands. "We've begun the cleansing ceremony. Please, unburden yourself of your earthly vestments and join us."

Cortez choked again, then leaned down to my ear and murmured, "I should check on Savannah. If you decide to comply with their request, let me know. Please."

He retreated to the house, racked by a sudden fit of coughing. I grabbed the nearest discarded robe.

"Could you please put this—could you all put these—could you get dressed, please?"

The woman only bestowed a serene smile on me. "We are as the Goddess requires."

"The Goddess requires you to be naked on my lawn?"

"We aren't naked, child. We're skyclad. Clothing impedes mental vibrations."

"Uh, right. Look, I know this is all very natural, the human form and all that, but you just can't do this. Not here. It's illegal."

Another beatific smile. "We care not for the laws of men. If they come for us, we will not go without a fight."

"Oh, God."

"God*ess*, dear. And take not her name in vain."

"Blessed be the Goddess," the other intoned.

"That's—uh—very—I mean—" I stammered. Be polite, I reminded myself. Witches should respect Wiccans, even if we didn't quite get the whole Goddess-worship thing. I knew some Wiccans and they were very nice people, though I must admit they'd never arrived in my backyard naked and kissed my tits before.

"You're—uh—from Vermont, I hear," I managed. That was polite, wasn't it?

"We're from everywhere," the first one said, still refusing to relinquish my hands. "We're roving missionaries, free spirits not enslaved by any traditional system of belief. The Goddess speaks to us directly and sends us where she will."

"Praise be to the Goddess," her companions chanted.

"Oh, well, that's very nice," I said. "While I do appreciate your support"—oh, God, please get out of my yard before someone sees you!—"this really isn't a good time to talk."

"We could come back," the leader said.

"Gosh, could you? That'd be so great. How about next Monday? Say, eight o'clock?"

I grabbed the robes and passed them out, nearly tripping in my haste. Soon the Wiccans were dressed and heading for the side gate.

"Um, actually, you know, you should go out the back," I said. "Through the woods. It's a great walk. There's lots of, uh . . . nature."

The leader nodded and smiled. "Sounds lovely. We'll do that. Oh, wait." She reached into the folds of her robe and passed me a card. "My cell phone number and e-mail address, should you care to contact me before Monday."

"Uh, right. Thanks."

I unlatched the gate leading into the woods and held it as they filed through. As the last one was leaving, a figure brushed past them and caught the gate before it closed. Leah stepped through, twisting to watch the Wiccans go.

"Nice friends," she said. "Witches, I presume?"

"Piss off."

"Oww, getting testy, I see. Rough week?"

"What do you want?"

"I came to"—she snatched a twig from the ground and brandished it—"challenge you to a duel. No, wait. That's not it. I came to talk, though a duel would be kind of fun, don't you think?"

"Get off my property."

"Or you'll—" She glanced over my shoulder and stopped. "Oh, look who's still here. The baby Cortez."

Cortez stepped up beside me. "This is inappropriate, Leah."

She laughed. "Oh, I like that. Inappropriate. Not surprising, rude, foolhardy. No, it's inappropriate. He has such a way with words, don't you think?"

"You understand me perfectly well," Cortez said.

"Yes, I do, but perhaps we should explain, for the benefit of our non-Cabal friend. What Lucas means is that my presence here, unaccompanied by Gabriel Sandford, the sorcerer and, therefore, the project leader, is a direct violation of Cabal rules of engagement." She grinned. "There, I almost sound like him, don't I? Between you and me, Paige, these guys have way too many rules. So, Lucas, does your daddy know you're here?"

"If he doesn't, I'm quite certain he'll learn of it. Though, as you're well aware, that will hardly impact the situation."

Leah turned to me. "In English, that means Daddy Cortez doesn't give a damn . . . so long as his darling baby boy doesn't get hurt. If you think I'm nuts, you should meet his family." She twirled a finger beside her head. "Certifiable. This one runs around acting like he's the last of the Knights Templar. And what does Daddy do about it? Brags about him. The kid ruins profitable business ventures, even for his own family, and Daddy couldn't be prouder. Then there's his stepmother . . . Can you call someone your stepmother when she was married to your father both before and after you were conceived?" Leah leaned toward me and said in a stage whisper, "Born on the wrong side of the sheets, this one."

"I believe the technical term is bastard," Cortez said. "Now, if you're quite done—"

"What's the bounty up to now, Lucas?"

"I'm asking you to leave."

"Humor me. What is it? One million? Two? I could really use that kind of cash."

"I'm sure you could. Now—"

"Does Paige know about the bounty? I bet she doesn't. I bet you neglected to mention that tidbit, like you probably neglected to mention the reason for it. Here's a tip, Paige. If you ever want to make a fortune, have a talk with Delores Cortez. Or one of Lucas's brothers. They're all willing to pay very well to get rid of him. Can you guess why?"

"Because my father has named me as his heir," Cortez said. "A political ploy, as you well know, Leah, so please stop trying to make trouble. I'm sure Paige could care less about my personal situation."

"You don't think she'd have a problem being indebted to a future Cabal leader?"

"I'm sure she's aware that such a coronation will never take place. Even if my father insists on pursuing his course, I have no interest in the position."

"Oh, come on. We've all seen *The Godfather*. We all know how this turns out."

"Take your gossip and go," I said. "I'm not interested."

"No? What if I make you an offer you can't refuse?" She grinned and winked at me. "Gotta talk to these Cabal guys in language they understand."

There was something so disarming, so childlike about Leah that it was hard to stand before her and remember how dangerous she was. As she mugged and teased, I had to keep repeating to myself, "This is the woman who killed your mother."

"I'm going inside now," I said.

"We both are," Cortez said, putting his hand against my back.

She rolled her eyes. "Geez, you guys are no fun at all. Fine. I'll get serious then. I want to talk."

I walked away. Cortez followed. When we were inside, I made the mistake of looking out the kitchen window. Leah stood there, waving a cell phone. I turned and saw the ringer light flickering on my phone. I picked up the receiver.

"Is this better?" she asked. "A Volo's range is about fifty feet, which I'm sure you already know, being the genius you are. How about I just start walking backward and you tell me when you feel safe?"

I slammed down the phone and stood there, struggling for composure.

"I can't do this," I whispered. "She—she killed my mother."

"I know." Cortez laid his hand against my back. "Let me handle it."

A shout rang out from the front lawn. Steeling myself, I walked into the living room and peeked out the curtain. A video camera wheeled across the lawn like a tumbleweed, the teenage owner stumbling after it. The dozen or so onlookers watched and laughed. Then a woman's hat flew off.

"That bi—" I bit off the epithet, wheeled around, and strode into the kitchen. "She wants to talk? Fine. We'll talk. I'll go out there and show her that she doesn't frighten me."

"No," said Savannah's quiet voice behind us. "Let her come in. Show her that she really doesn't frighten us."

We let Leah in. As Cortez said, she could do no worse damage in here than she could out there. Sad but true. If Leah wanted to kill us, she had a fifty-foot radius from which to act. No walls could stop her. All we could do was be on alert.

"She has a tell," I said to Cortez. "Whenever she's about to move something, she'll give herself away. Watch for tics, jerks, sudden movements, anything."

He nodded, then went out back to escort Leah inside.

A minute later, the rear door opened. Leah walked in, looked around, and smiled. Then her eyes lit on Savannah.

"Savannah," she said. "My God, you've gotten big, kiddo. You're almost as tall as me."

Savannah looked at her for ten long seconds, then turned on her heel and marched off to her room. Leah stared after her, frowning as if perplexed by her welcome.

"What have you done to her?" she asked.

"Me? You're the one who—"

Cortez lifted his hands. "As Leah pointed out, we sorcerers are very fond of rules. The cardinal rule of mediation, as I'm sure Leah is well aware, is that neither party is permitted to mention past wrongs or disparage the other. Is that understood?"

"Why are you looking at me?" Leah said. "She started it."

"No, I believe you did. Paige is, without question, the injured party in this matter. Upset her and the mediation is over."

"What makes you think I'm here to negotiate?"

"If you aren't, you may leave now."

She rolled her eyes. "God, he's so much fun, isn't he?" She walked into the living room and plunked herself down on my sofa. "Nice little place you have here, Paige. Must have been a tidy inheritance."

"Out," Cortez said. "Get out now, Leah."

"What did I do? I was only complimenting Paige on her house and commenting that—whoops—" She grinned. "Guess I can see how that last remark might be, uh, 'inappropriate.'"

"Let her talk," I said, clenching my fists so tight I felt blood well up where my nails dug into my palms. "What did you come here for?"

"I don't like the way this is going," she said, lounging back against the cushions. "These Cabals, they're as bad as Isaac said. All their rules and codes of conduct. And the paperwork. Honest to God. You would not believe it, Paige. Kill some dumb-ass human and they make you fill out a zillion forms in triplicate. Once I accidentally shot a perp and even Internal Affairs didn't make me fill out so many forms. Would you believe Kristof reprimanded us for that great gag in the funeral home? We 'exceeded authority' and 'exercised questionable judgment,' and now he's fuming because there's going to be some kind of joint-Cabal disciplinary hearing over it. God, I'm telling you, those Cabal watchdogs have about as much of a sense of humor as baby Cortez here."

"What do you want, Leah?" I said.

"First, immunity. If I back out of this deal, the Nast Cabal will be all over my ass. I want Lucas here to promise me his daddy's protection."

"I play no role in the Cortez Cabal—" Lucas began.

"Oh, stuff it. You're a Cortez. If you say I'm protected, I am. For my second demand, I want joint custody of Savannah."

"Is that all?" I said. "Whew. I thought you wanted something big. How about weekends?"

Leah wagged a finger at Cortez. "I don't think she's taking this seriously."

"Imagine that," Cortez murmured.

"Dare I ask why you want joint custody of Savannah?" I asked.

"Because I like the kid. Because I think you'll ruin her. And because she could prove useful."

"So in return for granting these two demands, you'll do what? Take on the whole Nast Cabal for us?"

She laughed. "I'm not suicidal, Paige. If you give me what I want, I'll back out of the fight."

"That's it?"

"It should be enough. I'm the best damned weapon they have. You'd do well to get on my good side now, Paige. Something even you should consider, Lucas."

"Truly an offer we can't refuse," he said. "I believe I speak for Paige in saying get the hell out, Leah. You're wasting our time."

She sat upright and leaned forward. All humor drained from her eyes. "I'm making you a serious offer, sorcerer. You don't want me in this fight."

"No? If your position is so strong, surely you wouldn't be here right now. The Cabals always reward talent. Shall I hazard a guess as to why you've had this sudden change of heart?"

"Wait," I said. "Let me give it a shot. I'm a newbie at this Cabal stuff, so I want to be sure I'm getting it right. You say you're here because you don't like the choice you made, teaming up with the Cabal. I think you're telling the truth. But not because they have too many rules. Because, suddenly, you're not in charge anymore. Sure, you have one incredible power, but that's it. A one-trick pony. Put you in a room full of magical races and you're a nobody, a grunt worker. Am I getting close?"

Her eyes blazed.

I continued, "This all started because you went to the Nast Cabal and offered them a deal. Maybe you found out about Savannah's father or maybe you just picked them out of a hat and they invented the paternity story. They took you up on the offer, and then took over. All you'll probably get is a nice year-end bonus and an office with a window. Worst of all, you lose Savannah. You sold out for an office with a view."

A brass urn flew from the bookshelf, sailed across the room, and smashed into the wall. Leah flung herself from the sofa, skewering me with a glare before turning that glare on the urn.

"Whoops," I said. "Did you miss? Maybe you aren't as good as you think you are."

This time, the whole bookshelf jerked free from its moorings. It shuddered, rocked once, and came to rest, still upright. I cast a binding spell before she could try again.

"When I let go, you leave," I said. "Don't think I've forgotten what you did to my mother. And don't think for one second that I can't kill you where you stand, or that I'm not considering it at this very moment."

When I released the binding spell, Leah glared at me once, then stormed from the house, slamming the door in her wake.

"So her power decreases as her emotions escalate," Cortez said. "Very interesting."

"And handy. Did you figure out her tell?"

Cortez shook his head.

"Damn. Well, I can't worry about that now. I need to discuss something with Savannah." I started to leave, then turned to him. "Should I be worried? About retaliation?"

"From Leah?" He shook his head. "The Cabals have clipped her claws. She knows the penalty for acting without their assent, particularly if those actions jeopardize a current project. It's considered treason. Punishable by death. A very unpleasant death."

"Good."

Cortez adjusted his glasses. "I have, uh, finished my work. Once you've spoken with Savannah, perhaps we could . . . that is, if you feel up to it—"

"The spell swap," I said with a smile. "Don't worry. I haven't forgotten. It's next on my list. Just let me finish with Savannah."

CHAPTER 30

THE KEY

"Tell me about the sorcerer spells again."

We were sitting cross-legged on Savannah's bed.

"Almost any strong spell a witch casts is sorcerer magic," Savannah said. "Like the knock-back spell I used on that paranormal guy? Same thing Lucas used on those people out front. You know some sorcerer spells, right?"

"A few."

"I can teach you more. Or Lucas can. They're pretty good, but witch magic would be better. You know, that whole thing about us each being better at our own spells. Except witches don't have a choice. I mean, we have all the primary spells and some of those are good, like the binding spell. Sorcerers can't beat us at the protection and healing stuff. That's why the Cabals recruit witches. If we had our own spells, though, we'd be way stronger."

"But the grimoires I have *are* witch magic. Strong witch magic."

"Right. That's what my mom said, too. Those were her books, you know."

"My grimoires?"

"Yep." Savannah picked up her stuffed bear and smoothed its fur, keeping her gaze on the toy as she continued, "She used to talk about them. The lost books. Only they weren't lost, I guess. The Coven just hid them. She kinda figured that. Anyway, she talked about them all the time, how much she wanted them back, even though they didn't work."

I struggled to keep up with her, to piece the fragments together. A million questions ran through my mind, but I decided to start at the end.

"She couldn't get any of the spells to work?"

"None. But you could, which is weird. You're an okay spell-caster and all, but my mom was amazing. But, then, she was probably only your age when she tried them, so maybe—" Savannah stopped. "That's weird, huh? I hadn't thought of that. You guys both trying them, both being around the same age. That means . . ." Her lips moved as if calculating. "You were around when my mom left, weren't you?"

I nodded. "I must have been four or five, but I don't remember her. You know, I never thought of this, but I bet we've got photos of your mom around here somewhere, in one of my mother's old albums. She was always snapping pictures at Coven picnics and parties. There must be photos."

"You think so?" Savannah laid down her stuffed bear. "That'd be cool. I don't have any pictures."

"You don't—oh, God. Of course you don't. I never thought . . ."

"That's okay," she said. "When we moved . . . I noticed you didn't put the pictures of your mom back up. I kinda wondered why not, but then I kinda understood, too. It's tough enough sometimes, without being reminded."

Our eyes met. I felt mine well up and rubbed my hand over them.

"I'll look for the photos as soon as I can," I said.

Savannah nodded. "Okay. Lucas is waiting for you, so let's talk about the grimoires."

"Right. Now why did your mother say they didn't work?"

"'Cause they're tri—uh, tre—tertiary spells, that's it. That means you need to know the middle spells first. Only we don't have them. The witches, I mean. We've only got the primary ones. The Coven got rid of the middle ones."

"Got rid of them?"

"That's what my mom figured. The Coven decided the spells were too strong, so they burned them or something."

"Who told her that? My mother?"

"No, no. My mom never had any problems with your mom. It wasn't her fault, what happened. It was the Elders."

"So the Elders claimed they destroyed the books."

"No. I meant it was the Elders' fault my mom left the Coven. They didn't know anything about the secondary books. Another witch told my mom about those."

I rubbed my temples. This wasn't making any sense. I longed to tell her to stop, to go back and proceed logically from the beginning, but I was almost afraid that if I did, I'd lose everything, like a wisp of smoke I had to catch before it vanished.

"So a non-Coven witch told your mom that these intermediate spells were missing."

"Right. Mom found this witch who had a copy of one of those grimoires."

"The grimoires I have now?"

"Right. Mom stole the grimoires from Aunt Margaret's library. She was the keeper of the books or whatever they called it. Aunt Margaret, I mean."

"She still is. So your mother took the books and found out they didn't work."

"Right. So she went back to Aunt Margaret and asked why. Aunt Margaret figured out that my mom stole them, so she told the Elders. Your mom said it didn't matter, since the spells didn't work, but Victoria flipped out and caused a big stink about it and my mom got fed up and left the Coven."

"Uh-huh." My head was starting to hurt.

"So how'd you get them?"

"Hmmm?"

"Where'd you find the grimoires?"

I had to pause and clear my mind even to remember. "I found them in the Coven library. In Margaret's collection."

"Wow. So she didn't throw them out after all? Weird."

"Very weird. When we go there later, to get the ceremony book, I'll have some questions for her."

Savannah nodded. We finished talking, then I went to find Cortez.

When I heard Cortez rustling around in the kitchen, I smiled and quickened my pace, suddenly eager to— To what? I stopped in the hallway, and it took a moment to realize that I'd been hurrying to tell him the news about the grimoires.

Naturally, I was excited. If I could unlock the secret of these spells, it would mean not only that I'd have stronger spells to protect Savannah, but that I'd have stronger spells to offer all witches. This could truly be the key to everything I'd dreamed of. With these spells, I could help witches regain their rightful place in the supernatural world.

The implications were mind-boggling, and of course I wanted to share them with someone, but there was more to it than that. I didn't want to tell just anyone. I wanted to tell Cortez. Logically, as a sorcerer, he probably couldn't care less about newly discovered witch spells or, if he did, he'd want to suppress them, to ensure his race's supremacy. Yet I couldn't imagine Cortez doing that. Somehow, as foolish as it might sound, I felt he'd be happy for me or, perhaps even more importantly, that he'd understand. I could take this news to every witch in the Coven, and some might congratulate me, might even be pleased for me, but they wouldn't really understand. With Cortez, I felt it would be . . . different.

I paused in the hall and considered telling him. Seriously considered it. But I decided to speak to Margaret first and then, if I really had what I thought I had here, I'd talk to Cortez about it.

I walked through the kitchen door to see Cortez eyeing two canisters of tea.

"You don't want the one on the left," I said. "It's a sleeping brew."

"That's what I was trying to figure out. Savannah told me the sleeping brew was on the right, but I believe she returned the canisters to the wrong places."

"I don't doubt it. Sometimes I think she puts things back in the wrong places on purpose, so I won't ask her to tidy up. I remember trying that with my mom. Only she decided it just meant I needed more practice tidying up." I took the canisters. "Both of these, however, are caffeine free, so for today I think I'll stick with coffee."

"I just brewed a pot."

"Damn, you're good. Let's grab some, then, and start the spell swap."

CHAPTER 31

SPELL-CASTING MONOPOLY

Before we started, I popped a frozen lasagna into the oven for dinner. Then I brought out my Coven grimoire and spell-casting journals, and ushered Cortez into the living room. With his help, I moved the coffee table aside. Then I settled onto the carpet, cross-legged.

"This okay?" I said.

He nodded and sat across from me.

"This is all I've got," I said, laying out my grimoire and journals. "Well, all that works, anyway. These are the Coven-approved spells, and in my journals I've written down a few others that I picked up. I may not have what you're looking for."

"No, you probably do. I believe they'd all be Coven-sanctioned, probably level three or four. I'm still struggling through third level, but there are several fourth level spells I'd like to discuss, in the expectation—or hope—that I progress that far."

"You know your levels, then," I said. "Good. But how come—no offense, but you are a Cabal CEO's son, so you must have access to the best spells available, even witch spells."

"Obtaining witch spells is not as simple a matter as you might expect, largely due to the ongoing animosity between the races. Most sorcerers won't avail themselves of witch magic, no matter how practical it might be. For those, such as myself, who wish the knowledge, it can be very difficult to obtain. Witches, quite understandably, are loath to give us access to their power. The lower-level spells are commonplace, but the higher ones are well guarded by the few witches who can cast them."

"Any decent witch can cast them. Even fourth level isn't tough, if you have the experience." I hesitated, remembering what Savannah had said. "Unless, of course, you're a witch who prefers sorcerer magic, in which case, I suppose, you might never gain that level of experience."

"Precisely. Even Cabal witches, who can cast the more difficult witch spells, don't like to part with the information. Given my Cabal standing, they don't dare refuse my requests, but I suspect they leave out a critical word or two of the incantation, so it will appear that I simply lack the skill to cast it properly."

"Passive-aggressive witches. Got a few of them around here, too." I reached out and took a cookie from the plate Cortez had laid between us. "Okay, so what do you want to know?"

"First, the cover spell."

I pretended to choke on my cookie. "Let's just start at the top, shall we? Next to the binding spell, that's probably the best defensive weapon we've got. No wonder the Cabal witches are giving you phony spells."

"Is that a no?"

"It's a yes, but it's gonna cost ya, and I don't mean dollars, either, though that might be a good way to knock down my bill."

Cortez picked up a cookie. "Speaking of my bill, I should point out that such payment was only part of my initial money-hungry-lawyer guise. My services are offered 'pro bono,' so to speak. If you are inclined to pay me, though, given the choice between monetary and magical remuneration, I would far prefer the latter."

"You'd rather have new spells than cash?" I grinned. "My kinda guy. I'll warn you, though, being of the same bent myself, I'd rather pay your bill with a check and trade on the spells."

A crooked smile. "Quite acceptable. For the cover spell, then . . ."

"Well, here you have the advantage, because I don't know of many sorcerer spells. There's the one you did the other day—I think Savannah called it the knock-back spell—but she knows that, so I'll get it from her. There's that anticonfusion spell which, granted, didn't seem to work, but with Savannah around, I may need to know it."

"And you had the calming spell, which did work. I'd certainly like that."

I sipped my coffee as I racked my brain for more sorcerer spells. "Barrier spell. I definitely want that."

"Barrier spell?" His brows arched. "That one is, as you say, gonna cost ya. I'm still working on that one myself."

"Cover spell for barrier spell?"

He nodded and took another cookie.

"And calming for anticonfusion." I laughed. "I feel like I'm trading baseball cards here. Or playing Monopoly. I'll give you Broadway for Atlantic and one railroad."

"Is that how you play Monopoly? I always suspected my father was doing it wrong."

"How did your father play it? Or dare I ask?"

He bit into his cookie and chewed before answering. "He took the title rather seriously. Global domination was the goal, at any cost. To win, one had to control all the property and drive one's competitors to bankruptcy. Bribery, usurious interest rates, housing development kickbacks—it was a very complicated, cutthroat game."

"Sounds like . . . fun."

"It was not without challenge, but it left one with the feeling of having accomplished relatively little of consequence at an overwhelming moral price. And, as you might imagine, ultimately, not much fun. I eventually started arguing the case for a more equitable division of assets, with needs-driven interest rates and financial aid for those experiencing a temporary downturn in fortunes. My father, of course, disagreed, but was ultimately unable to sway my beliefs and I soon stopped playing with him. An early sign of things to come, I fear."

I laughed and shook my head. "So, you don't play Monopoly any more, I'm guessing."

"It wasn't my game."

"What is your game? What do you like to do when you're not saving the world?"

He finished off his cookie. "Games have never been my forte. Sports even less so. I am, however, reasonably proficient at poker. I bluff quite well, a skill that has made me a few dollars when the need arose."

I grinned. "I can imagine that."

"How about you?"

"Not big on the sports, either. I do like games, though. Anything that's fun. Pool's a favorite."

His brows went up. "*Pool?*"

"What? I don't strike you as the pool shark type? Pool's great. Helps me build up concentration and precision for spell-casting. If you can sink a shot in a noisy pool hall, with friends trying to spoil your shot and with a few bottles of beer swimming through your system, then you can cast a spell under the worst circumstances."

"That makes sense. I'll admit, I could use more practice spell-casting under adverse conditions. Do you find—"

A shrill whistle cut him short. He frowned, then looked in the direction of the sound, through the kitchen doorway and toward the answering machine on the counter.

"It appears your overloaded machine has finally surrendered," he said.

I pushed myself to my feet as the machine whistled again. "That's not it."

I walked into the kitchen and turned up the volume.

"Paige! Pick up!" Adam's shout reverberated through the kitchen. "You don't answer, I'm going to assume the worst and catch the next plane—"

I lifted the receiver.

"Good excuse," I said. "I'm sure you can very well guess why I'm not answering the phone."

"Because you're overwhelmed and understaffed . . . or under-friended."

"Under-friended?"

"Lacking the support of friends. There should be a word for that. Point is, you could obviously use my help."

"To do what, answer the phone? Hold on."

I covered the mouthpiece and turned to Cortez, who was still in the living room.

"I'm sorry," I said. "I really should take this. I'll be back in a few minutes."

I took the phone to my room and told Adam what was going on. I didn't tell him about the grimoires. If I had, I can imagine his response. I'd tell him that I might have finally unlocked the secrets of true witch magic and he'd have said something like: "Whoa, that's great, way to go, Paige . . . oh, and that reminds me, I finally got my Jeep to stop making that knocking noise." Adam is a great guy, and a wonderful friend, but there are things in my life he just doesn't get.

We chatted until I heard the distant ding of the oven timer.

"Whoops," I said. "Lost track of time. Dinner's ready. I have to go."

"You sure you don't need me?"

"Positive. And don't bother trying to call here. I'll phone you with an update as soon as I can."

I ended the conversation and headed into the hall.

Savannah's voice floated from the kitchen. "—just friends. Good friends, but that's it."

The oven door clanged shut. I walked in to see Cortez taking the lasagna from the oven as Savannah watched from her perch on the counter.

"Supervising?" I said.

"Someone has to," she said.

"While you're up there, grab the plates." I leaned over to turn off the oven. "I'll take it from here. Thanks."

Cortez nodded. "I'll wash up."

Savannah watched him leave, then jumped from the counter and scurried to my side.

"He was asking about Adam," she said in a stage whisper.

I took the foil off the lasagna. "Hmmm?"

"Lucas. He was asking about Adam. You and Adam. I came in, you were gone, he said you were on the phone, so I checked call display on my phone and told him it was Adam. Then I said you'd be a while because you guys, like, talk forever, and he said, 'Oh, so they're pretty good friends,' or something like that."

"Uh-huh." I sliced into the middle of the lasagna, making sure it was cooked through. "I think the lettuce is wilted, but could you check it for me?"

"Paige, I'm talking to you."

"And I heard you. Lucas asked if Adam was a friend."

"No, he didn't ask if he was a friend. Well, yes, he did, but he meant, you know, is Adam a *friend*. He wasn't just asking, he was *asking*. Get it?"

I frowned over my shoulder at her. Cortez walked into the kitchen. Savannah looked at me, threw up her hands, and stomped off to the bathroom.

"Mood swings?" Cortez asked.

"Communication breakdown. I swear, thirteen-year-old girls speak a language no linguist has ever deciphered. I remember some of it, but rarely enough to decode entire conversations." I turned around. "Is wine with dinner okay? Or should we avoid alcohol tonight, too?"

"Wine would be wonderful."

"If you can get the glasses from above the stove, I'll run downstairs and grab a bottle."

After dinner, while Cortez and Savannah cleared the table, I changed my clothing. Retrieving the juniper might require some backwoods searching, so I exchanged my skirt for my sole pair of jeans. With a mother who was a dressmaker, I'd grown up loving fabrics, the luxurious swish of silk, the snug warmth of wool, the crisp snap of linen, and I'd never understood the allure of stiff jeans and limp cotton T-shirts—unless, of course, you plan to go tramping through the forest for spell ingredients. I considered changing into a sweatshirt, but opted instead to leave on my short-sleeved silk blouse and throw a jacket over it. Some sacrifices are just too great.

Once dressed, I went into the living room and pulled back the curtain, to see whether the crowd was still small enough for us to make an easy escape. But I couldn't see anything. The window was blacked out, covered with paper.

"Well, I don't want to see you people either," I muttered.

I was about to let the curtain fall back into place when I noticed writing on the papers. No, not writing. Print. They were newspapers. Someone had cut out newspaper articles about me and plastered them over my front window.

There were dozens of articles, taken not just from tabloids, but from webzines and regular newspapers. The tabloids screamed the loudest: "Lawyer Murdered in Gruesome Satanic Rite." "Mangled Corpses Return to Life." The webzines were quieter, but nastier, less constrained by the threat of slander. "Kidnapped Baby Brutally Murdered in Black Mass." "Zombie Cult Raises Hell in Funeral Homes Across Massachusetts."

The most disturbing voice, though, was the quietest. The somber, almost clinical headlines from the regular press: "Murder Linked to Allegations of Witchcraft." "Mourners Claim Corpses Reanimated." I scanned the headers atop the articles. *The Boston Globe, The New York Times,* even *The Washington Post.* Not front-page news, but still there, tucked farther back. My story. My name. Splashed across the most prominent papers in the nation.

"They're still out there." Cortez tugged the curtain from my hand and let it fall, hiding the papers from view. "Not many, but I wouldn't advise we take the car. The Nasts have undoubtedly assigned someone to watch the house, and we don't want them following us."

"Definitely not."

"Since we have to stop at Margaret Levine's, I would suggest we walk there, going through the woods, and borrow her car."

"If she'll let us. What about your rental—oh, geez, your bike. We left it at the funeral home. I should call a tow truck—"

"I've done that."

"Good. Did they tow it someplace safe?"

He hesitated, then said, "It wasn't there when they arrived. Could you get Savannah? I knocked at her door, but she has her music too loud to hear and I didn't dare intrude."

"What do you mean, your bike wasn't there? Someone stole it?"

"So it would appear. No matter. The police have been informed and, failing that, I had an excellent insurance policy."

"Oh, God, I'm sorry. I should have thought— I completely forgot about it yesterday."

"Given everything that happened, the bike was the last of my concerns. You suggested we return for it before we came here, and I decided against that, so it's entirely my own fault. Now, if you'll get Savannah—"

"I'm so sorry. You should have mentioned it. God, I feel awful."

"Which is precisely why I didn't mention it. Compared to what you've lost these last few days and what you stand to lose, a motorcycle is quite inconsequential. As I said, I have insurance and I can replace it." He glanced at his watch. "We really have to go. Collect Savannah and meet me at the back door."

He gently moved me out of the way and went into the kitchen to gather his papers. I was about to follow when the clock struck six-thirty, reminding me that we did indeed need to hurry. The Salem shop that carried some of the material for Savannah's ceremony closed at nine.

I banged on Savannah's door.

"Just a sec," she called.

The music clicked off, followed by the slam of the closet and various drawers. Finally she opened the door and handed me a plastic grocery bag.

"Hold this," she said, then grabbed her hairbrush and ran it through her hair. "I figured out how we can get around without being seen. I should have thought about that earlier, but I forgot about it."

"Forgot about what?"

She pointed at the bag. "That."

I opened it and screamed.

CHAPTER 32

Tools of the Trade

Okay, I didn't scream. More of a yelp, really. Maybe a shriek.

What was in the bag? The long-lost Hand of Glory. Just what I wanted to see.

At my cry, Cortez came flying down the hall. Once we assured him that no one was mortally wounded, I explained how Savannah came to be in possession of the Hand.

". . . and then I forgot about it," I finished.

"So did I," she said. "Until now when I was putting away my home-work and saw my bag."

"You put that thing in your schoolbag?" I said.

"Wrapped up, of course. The cops would never look in there. Now we can use it to sneak out of the house. We just light the fingers on fire and carry it outside. It'll make us invisible. Well, maybe not invisible, but it'll stop people from seeing us."

Cortez shook his head. "I'm afraid that's a myth, Savannah. The Hand of Glory only prevents sleeping people from waking and it does that very poorly."

"You've tried it?" she asked.

"Several times, until I learned a spell that worked better." He lifted the hand from the bag. "And smelled better. This Hand is very crudely done. Quite fresh, too. That weakens its power. Whoever made this didn't even follow the proper methods of anointing and preserving. I'd be surprised if it worked at all. I'd say its purpose is more fright than sleight."

"Dime store magic?" Savannah said.

"Definitely. See here? Where the bone comes through? Now, if this was done correctly—"

I shivered. "Am I the only one totally grossed out by that thing?"

They both looked at me blankly.

"Apparently so," I muttered. "Can I skip this lesson? I'll start walking to Margaret's and you two can catch up."

"Paige is right," Cortez said, returning the Hand to the bag. "We haven't time for this. I would suggest, though, that we take the Hand along, so we can dispose of it away from the house."

I nodded and we headed for the back door. Cortez grabbed his leather jacket, then wrapped the bag as small as it would go and shoved it into the pocket. I couldn't suppress a shudder. Yes, I know I'd resolved to better accept the darker side of Savannah's nature, but I couldn't imagine ever toting around body parts as if they were tools like chalices and grimoires.

When we stepped outside, the evening was already growing cool and Savannah, dressed in a midriff-baring T-shirt, decided to run back in for a sweater.

Once she was gone, I pointed at the bag. "You really use stuff like that?"

"I use whatever works."

"Sorry. I didn't mean to sound . . ."

"A lot of magical objects aren't things I would otherwise choose to handle. It's like magic. You can refuse to learn the stronger, more distasteful spells, or you can acknowledge that they may, under some circumstances, be necessary."

"I know that. With the spells, I mean. But I'm . . ." I hesitated, then pushed on. "I'm having trouble with it. Getting my head around the idea that I might have to . . ."

"Do bad to do good?"

I managed a small smile. "Good way of putting it. I've been thinking about that a lot. Killing someone to protect Savannah. I know it might come to that, but I've never . . . And what if I had to do more than disable an enemy? What if protecting her meant hurting an innocent bystander? I'm really . . ." I took a deep breath. "I really have trouble with it."

"So do I."

I looked up at him, but before I could say anything, Savannah burst through the door.

"All set?" I asked.

She nodded and off we went.

I spent the ten-minute walk to Margaret's thinking about the grimoires. What bothered me most of all was the realization that if only Savannah had felt comfortable talking to me about her mother, we could have cleared this up months ago. Now that I'd finally been ready to listen, it might be too late.

I was still working through Savannah's story. She said that the Coven-sanctioned spells were primary spells, which you had to master before you could progress to secondary spells. Only once you knew the secondary spells could you hope to successfully cast a tertiary spell, like the ones in my secret grimoires. I'd never heard of such a thing before.

Although Coven spells are divided into four levels, hypothetically, a witch could start at fourth level. It would be excruciatingly difficult, but not impossible. It's like programming languages. They start you out with something easy, like C. You learn that, then move on to the higher languages like C++. That's not to say you can't jump straight into a higher-level language. People do it all the time. But, if you've mastered something like C, the learning curve on other languages decreases significantly. You understand concepts like data structures and functions, which can be ported into any language.

What Savannah said implied something altogether different. If I understood her correctly, every Coven witch spell was a primary spell, the bottom building block for witch magic. Yet that didn't explain why I'd mastered four spells from the "tertiary" grimoires. Savannah said Eve hadn't been able to make any work. Now, I'd love to believe that I'd mastered them due to my superior spell-casting abilities, but even I'm not that smug.

Eve had stolen the grimoires from Margaret. I'd . . . well, I'd pretty much done the same thing. The Coven maintains a library. The books are kept in a fortified closet in Margaret Levine's house. With advance notice, witches may visit the collection. Some books may not leave the house. Others may be borrowed. To borrow one, you have to fill out a card and return the book within a week. I think the only reason the Elders haven't instituted late fines is because I'm the only one who ever borrows anything.

Coven witches aren't even permitted to step into the closet and peruse the collection. Margaret keeps a list posted inside the door, from which they must choose their books.

Three years ago, as I was pestering Margaret for a better reference book on herbs, someone knocked at the front door and she took off to answer it, leaving the library. It was like leaving a kid with an open closet full of candy. The moment she was gone, I was in that closet. I knew exactly what I wanted. The prohibited spellbooks.

So why was I returning to Margaret's house now? Because I wanted answers. More than that, I had a hope, a slim hope, that Savannah was both right and wrong. That she was right about the existence of a grimoire that would unlock the spells I now possessed, and that she was wrong in thinking the Coven had destroyed it.

We arrived at Margaret's place, a two-story house on Beech. I opted for the rear door, both as a courtesy and so she couldn't freak out about me showing up on her front doorstep for all of East Falls to see. Being the village pariah does make social calls most trying.

I persuaded Savannah to wait outside with Cortez. Savannah understood her great-aunt well enough to know that Margaret would speak more freely to me alone.

I rang the doorbell. A minute later, Margaret peeped through the curtain. It took another minute for her to decide to answer it. Even then, she only opened the inside door, keeping one hand on the knob of the screen door.

"You shouldn't be here," she whispered.

"I know."

I wrenched the screen door open and stepped inside. Rude, I know, but I didn't have time for courtesy.

"Where's Savannah?" she asked.

"She's safe. I need to talk to you about some grimoires."

She peered over my shoulder, scanning the yard, as if I'd brought an entourage of reporters with me. When she didn't see anyone, she closed the door and ushered me farther into the living room, which was filled with boxes of books.

"Please ignore the mess," she said. "I've been organizing the donations for the library book sale. A nerve-wracking task. Absolutely horrible."

I thought of offering to switch places, let her handle the Black Masses and walking dead for a while, but clamped my mouth shut and settled for a quasi-sympathetic nod.

Margaret was the volunteer head librarian at the East Falls library (open two evenings per week plus Saturday afternoons). She'd taken the position after retiring as librarian at the East Falls high school. If this gives the impression that Margaret Levine was a timid little old lady with a steel-gray bun and wire-rimmed glasses, let me correct that. Margaret was five feet ten and had, in her youth, been pursued by every modeling firm in Boston. At sixty-eight she was still beautiful, with the kind of long-limbed, graceful beauty that her gangly great-niece showed every sign of inheriting. Margaret's one physical flaw was a blind insistence on dying her hair jet black, a color that must have been gorgeous on her at thirty, but looked almost clownish now.

The one librarian stereotype Margaret did fulfill was that she was timid. Not the studious timidity of the intellectual, but the vacuous timidity of the, well, the . . . intellectually challenged. I've always thought Margaret decided to become a librarian not because she loved books, but because it gave her a chance to look intelligent while hiding from the real world.

"Victoria is very angry with you, Paige," Margaret said as she cleared books from a chair. "You shouldn't upset her so. Her health isn't good."

"Look, I need to talk to you about a couple of grimoires I borrowed from the library." I tugged the knapsack from my shoulder, opened it, and removed the books. "These."

She frowned at them. Then her eyes went wide. "Where did you get those?"

"From the library upstairs."

"You aren't supposed to have those, Paige."

"Why? I heard they don't work."

"They don't. And we shouldn't have them, but your mother insisted we keep them around. I forgot all about them. Here, give them to me and I'll see what Victoria wants done with them."

I shoved the books back into my knapsack.

"You can't take those," she said. "They're library property."

"Then fine me. I'm in enough trouble with Victoria already. Keeping these books isn't going to matter."

"If she finds out—"

"We won't tell her. Now, what do you know about these grimoires?"

"They don't work."

"Where did they come from?"

She frowned. "From the library, of course."

Okay. This wasn't getting me anywhere. One look at Margaret's face and I knew she wasn't holding anything back. She wouldn't know how. So I explained what Eve had told Savannah about the books.

"Oh, that's nonsense," Margaret said, fluttering her long fingers. "Absolute nonsense. That girl wasn't right, you know. Eve, I mean. Not right at all. Always looking for trouble, trying to learn new spells, accusing us of holding her back. Just like . . ."

She stopped.

"Like me," I said.

"I didn't mean it like that, dear. I've always liked you. A bit impetuous, but certainly nothing like that niece of mine—"

"It's okay," I said. And, to my surprise, it was. I knew I wasn't "just like Eve," and didn't want to be, but the comparison didn't rankle as it once would have. I continued, "You said these spells don't work, right? So how come I can cast four of them?"

"That's not possible, Paige. Don't be telling stories—"

"Shall I demonstrate?" I grabbed the first grimoire from my bag, opened it to a marked page, and thrust it at her. "Here. Follow along. It's a fireball spell."

Margaret clamped the book shut. "Don't you dare—"

"Why? You said the spells don't work. I say they do. And I think you know why."

"Be sensible, Paige. If they worked, why would we keep them?"

And that, I believe, was the smartest thing Margaret Levine ever said. No one was covering up anything. The Coven really didn't think these spells worked; otherwise, they wouldn't have kept them. What a horrible thing to admit, that the very group designed to support and aid witches would have destroyed their strongest source of magic.

"I want to see the grimoires," I said. "All of them."

"We aren't trying to hide anything from you, Paige. You have to stop accusing us—"

"I'm not accusing you of anything. I just want to see the library."

"I don't think—"

"Listen to me. Please just listen. Why do you think I'm here? Some sudden whim to learn new spells? I'm here because I need to know that I've done everything I can to protect Savannah. To protect your niece. That's all I want. Let me see the library and, I swear, when this is over, you can tell Victoria what I've done. Tell her I stole the grimoires. I don't care. Just let me see what's up there."

Margaret threw up her hands and headed for the stairs. "Fine. If you don't believe me, come up and see. But you're wasting your time."

Chapter 33

Stopping By for a Spell

The first thing I did was inspect the library closet for hidden compartments. You know, sliding panels, loose floorboards, massive books with incredibly boring titles that really contained forbidden grimoires—that sort of thing.

While I looked, Margaret paced behind me making noises of exasperation. I ignored her. Finally, though, I had to concede that there was no secret niche of hidden books, so I scanned the rows of titles, looking for the ceremony tome. When Margaret paced out of sight, I slid the thin volume into my knapsack. She probably would have let me take it anyway, but I wasn't taking the chance.

With the ceremony book in my bag, I turned my attention to looking for potential secondary-spell grimoires. That didn't take long. Of the forty-three books in the library, there were only four that I hadn't read before. A flip through each assured me they were just as dull and useless as their titles implied.

"The grimoires are all right here," Margaret said, waving at a half-shelf near chest level. "All of them."

"All of them" comprised exactly six books. One contained the current collection of Coven-sanctioned spells. Another held spells that had been removed in the past few decades, which my mother had let me copy from her grimoire into my journals. The other four were books of spells long forbidden to Coven witches. There were two reasons why these hadn't been destroyed. First, my mother would never have permitted it. Second, the damn things were practically useless.

For years, I'd known that these "forbidden" spellbooks existed. For years, I'd pestered my mother to let me see them. She finally capitulated by sneaking them out for me as an eighteenth birthday gift. Inside I found useless spells, like ones to evaporate a puddle of water or extinguish a candle. I hadn't bothered to master more than two dozen of the hundred-odd spells in these books. Most of them were so bad, I almost didn't blame the Elders for removing them from the Coven grimoire, if only to conserve space.

As a last resort, I flipped through one of these grimoires. I paused at one spell I'd learned, an incantation for producing a small, flickering light, like a candle. The Coven-sanctioned light-ball spell was far more useful. I'd learned this one only because it involved fire, and I was always trying to overcome my fear of flames.

When I glanced at the spell, something in it snagged in my brain, made me pause. Under the title "Minor Illumination Spell" the writer had added "elemental, fire, class 3." I'd seen that notation before . . . just a few minutes ago, in fact. I yanked one of the two secret grimoires from my bag and flipped to the dog-eared page for the fireball spell. There it was, under the title: elemental, fire, class 3.

Oh, God, could that be it? My hands trembled as I flipped to another spell I'd mastered in that grimoire, a wind-summoning spell. Beneath the title: elemental, wind, class 1. I racked my brain for the names of the two dozen spells I'd learned in the forbidden manuals. What was that one . . . Yes, that was it! A spell for extinguishing fire. A silly little spell that summoned a mere puff of wind, barely enough to blow out a candle. I'd tried it a few times, got it to work, then moved on. Grabbing another grimoire from the shelf, I flipped through until I found it. "Minor Wind-Summoning Spell: elemental, wind, class 1."

These were the secondary grimoires. I knew now why I'd mastered four tertiary spells, because I'd learned the secondary spells from these books. Eve had been unable to cast any tertiary spells because she'd probably taken one look in the secondary spellbooks and decided they were too useless to risk stealing.

The doorbell rang. Margaret jumped like a spooked cat.

"It's Savannah," I said.

I scooped all four grimoires from the shelf, shoved them into my bag with the other two, and headed for the stairs.

"You can't take those," Margaret called after me.

I bounded down the stairs and opened the back door.

"Lucas says we have to go," Savannah said. "It's getting late."

"I'm done. Just let me grab my shoes." I remembered our other purpose and turned to Margaret. "Could I borrow your car? Just for tonight. Please?"

"I don't think—"

"I'll be careful. I'll fill it up, wash it, whatever. Please, Margaret."

"Savannah?" She noticed her niece for the first time and turned to me. "Did you leave her outside alone? What are you thinking, Paige?"

"I didn't leave her alone. Now, I really need to borrow your car."

"Who—" She stopped, peering outside, her eyes picking out Cortez's form in the yard. She slammed the door. "That's—you—you left my niece with a sorcerer?"

"Oddly enough, I'm having trouble finding babysitters."

"Lucas is fine, Aunt Margaret," Savannah said. "Can we borrow your car? I need the stuff for my first menses—"

"Savannah just got her period," I cut in. "I'm out of supplies for menstrual tea, and she's having very bad cramps."

Savannah pulled a face of sheer agony. Margaret looked at her and blinked.

"Oh, yes. I see." Her voice softened. "This is your first time, isn't it, dear?"

Savannah nodded, lifting wounded-puppy eyes to her great-aunt. "It really hurts."

"Yes, well . . . I suppose, if you need to use my car . . ."

"Please," I said.

Margaret retrieved the keys and handed them to me. "Be careful in parking lots. I had someone dent the door just last week."

I thanked Margaret and prodded Savannah toward the door before Margaret could change her mind.

Next stop: Salem, Massachusetts, world-renowned epicenter of the American witch-hunt craze.

One can argue about the causes of the witch craze that visited Salem in 1692. Theories abound. I even read something recently that attributed the madness to some kind of blight on the rye crops, a mold or something that drives people crazy. What we do know, without question, is that life wasn't a whole lotta fun for teenage girls in Puritan America. In the harsh New England winters, it was even worse. At least the boys could go out hunting and trapping. Girls were confined to their homes and household tasks, forbidden by Puritan law to dance, sing, play cards, or engage in basically any form of entertainment.

As we drove into Salem, I imagined Savannah plunked into that world. Regimented, repressed, and restricted. Bored as hell. Is it any wonder they'd be eager for diversion? Maybe a little mischief? In the winter of 1692 the girls of Salem found exactly that, in the form of an old woman, a slave named Tituba.

Tituba belonged to Reverend Samuel Parris and was nursemaid to his daughter, Betty, whom, by all accounts, she doted on. To amuse herself during those long winter months, Tituba showed Betty and her friends some magic tricks, probably mere sleight-of-hand learned in Barbados. As the winter passed, word of this new entertainment swept through the community of teenage girls and, one by one, they found reasons to visit the parsonage.

In January, Betty, the youngest of the group, fell ill, her Puritan conscience perhaps made uneasy by all this talk of magic and sorcery. Soon other girls caught the "fever." Reverend Parris and others insisted that the girls name their tormentors. Betty named Tituba, and at the end of February the old slave was arrested on a charge of witchcraft.

And so it started. The girls soon grew addicted to the attention. No longer relegated to house and hearth, they became celebrities. The only way to prolong their fifteen minutes of fame was to up the ante, to act wilder, more possessed. To name more witches. So they did. Soon any woman that the girls might have had reason to dislike fell victim.

Four Coven witches died. Why? The witch-hunts often targeted social or gender deviants, particularly women who didn't comply with accepted female roles. This described many Coven witches. Outspoken and independent, they often lived without a husband—though the fact that they weren't necessarily celibate was a lifestyle choice that wouldn't have been too popular in Puritan New England. That lifestyle, in my opinion, is what put those witches on the gallows.

I tried telling that to the Coven once. How did they react? They agreed with me completely and declared that if those women had had the sense to keep their heads down and conform, they wouldn't have died. I could have beaten my head against the wall.

Today the Salem witch-hunts are a tourist attraction. Makes my skin crawl, but the upside is that there are plenty of practicing Wiccans in the area, and several New Age shops in Salem that sold ingredients I'd have had a hard time finding elsewhere.

Most of "tourist" Salem had shut down around dinner hour, but the shop we wanted was open until nine. The streets were quiet and we found parking easily, then headed to the tourism core, several tree-lined streets restricted to pedestrian traffic. It took less than twenty minutes to gather what I needed, then we were back in Margaret's car and heading for the highway.

"We have two hours to kill," I said as I turned back onto 1A. "Any ideas? We can't collect the juniper until after midnight."

"What do we need juniper for?" Savannah asked.

"It'll protect us against interference by evil spirits."

"Oh, right. So when are we getting the grave dirt? That needs to be gathered right at midnight."

"Perhaps we can find a juniper tree at the cemetery," Cortez said.

"What cemetery?" I said. "There's nothing about grave dirt in the ceremony, Savannah. We have everything we need except the juniper."

"Uh-uh. We need grave dirt."

"Savannah, I know the ceremony. I went through it myself and I double-checked my mother's notes last night."

"Yeah? Well, *my* mother told me everything about the ceremony and I know I need grave dirt."

"You need earth. Regular dirt collected anytime, anywhere."

"No, I need—"

"May I make a suggestion?" Cortez cut in. "In the interest of avoiding later trouble, I would advise that you clarify your respective understandings of the ceremony."

"Huh?" Savannah said.

"Compare notes," he said. "There's a sign for a park ahead. Pull off, Paige. As you've said, we have time."

"That's not part of the ceremony," I said, pacing between two trees as I listened to Savannah. "Absolutely not. It couldn't be."

"Why? Because the Coven says so? This is what my mother told me to do, Paige."

"But it's not the right ceremony."

Cortez cleared his throat. "Another suggestion? Perhaps we should consider the possibility that this is a variation on the Coven ceremony."

"It's not," I said. "It can't be. Listen to the words. They say—no, never mind."

"My Latin is perfectly serviceable, Paige. I understand the additional passage."

"You might understand the words, but you don't understand the meaning."

"Yes, I do. I have some knowledge of witch mythology. The additional passage is an invocation to Hecate, the Greek goddess of witchcraft, a deity the Coven and most modern witches no longer recognize. The invocation asks Hecate to grant the witch the power to wreak vengeance on her enemies and to free her from all restrictions on her powers. Now, as to the ability of Hecate to grant such a wish, I admit I place little credence in the existence of such deities."

"Same here. So, you're saying that the passage doesn't do anything, so there's no harm in including it?"

He paused, giving the question full consideration. "No. While I doubt the existence of Hecate per se, we must both admit that there is some force that gives us our power. Hecate is simply an archaic reference to that force." He glanced at Savannah, who was sitting on a picnic table. "Could you excuse us, Savannah? I'd like to speak to Paige."

Savannah nodded and, without protest, headed off to the empty swing across the park. I really had to learn how he did that.

"I told you about the Cabal's variation on your ceremony," Cortez said when she was gone. "Isn't it possible that other permutations exist?"

"I guess so. But this . . . this is . . ." I shook my head. "Maybe the extra passage doesn't mean anything, maybe it doesn't make any difference, but I can't take that chance. I'd be asking that Savannah be granted something I don't think any witch should have."

"You'd be asking to grant Savannah her full powers, without restriction. An ability you don't think any witch should have."

"Don't twist my words around. I went through my mother's ceremony and I'm fine."

"Yes, you are. I'm not saying—"

"And I'm not asking for reassurances. Savannah's already a stronger spell-caster than I am. Can you imagine how dangerous she could be with more power?"

"I can't argue this for you. You're the witch. You're the only one who can perform the ceremony for her." He stepped closer, putting his fingertips on my arm. "Go talk to her, Paige. We have to settle this before midnight."

CHAPTER 34

A Grave Dilemma

"I won't!" Savannah shouted, her voice echoing across the vacant park. "I won't do your stupid Coven ceremony! I'd rather have no ceremony at all than be a useless Coven witch."

"Like me."

"I didn't mean that, Paige. You aren't like them. I don't know why you waste your time with them. You can do so much better."

"I don't want to do better. I want to *make* things better. For all of us."

She shook her head. "I won't do your ceremony, Paige. I won't. It's mine or nothing. Don't you understand? This is what my mother told me to do. It's what she wanted for me."

When I didn't respond fast enough, Savannah's face contorted with rage.

"That's it, isn't it? You won't do it because it comes from my mother. Because you don't trust her."

"It's not that I don't trust—"

"No, you're right, it isn't. It's because you hate her. You think she was some kind of monster."

I stepped toward Savannah, but she flung me off with such force that I tripped and fell against the picnic table.

"My mother looked after me. She wouldn't have let Leah come near me again."

I flinched. "Savannah, I—"

"No, shut up. I'm sick of listening to you. You think my mother was evil because she practiced dark magic? That didn't make her evil. It made her smart. At least she had the guts to get out of the Coven, not hang around, learning stupid little baby spells and thinking she's queen of the witches."

I stepped back, bumping the table again and falling hard onto the bench. Cortez hurried from the woods, where he'd been burying the Hand of Glory. I shook my head to warn him off, but Savannah stepped into my line of vision and towered over me.

"You know what?" she said. "I know why you won't do that ceremony for me. Because you're jealous. Because your mother made you go through that useless Coven ceremony and now it's too late. You're stuck. You can't go back and do it over again. You can't get more powerful. So you're going to hold me back because your mother didn't—"

"Enough," Cortez said, pushing Savannah away from me. "That is enough, Savannah."

"Back off, sorcerer," she said, turning on him.

"You back off, Savannah," he said. "Now."

Savannah's face fell, as if all that anger suddenly gave way.

"Go back to the swings and cool down, Savannah," he said.

She obeyed, giving only a tiny nod.

"Let her go," Cortez whispered when I made a motion to stand. "She'll be fine. You have a decision to make."

With that, he sat beside me and didn't say another word while I made that decision.

Would I force Savannah to settle for less than her full potential? Once the choice was made, there was no reversing it. A witch had exactly one night to turn the tide of her destiny. Melodramatic, but true.

Was I jealous of Savannah for still having the opportunity to become a more powerful witch? No. The thought hadn't occurred to me until she mentioned it. Now that she had, though, it did give me something to think about. The chance had passed for me. If, as Eve claimed, this other ceremony would make a witch stronger, then yes, it stung to think I'd missed out. Given the choice, I'd have picked the stronger ceremony without question. Even without knowing whether it worked, even without knowing how much more power it could give me, I would have taken the chance.

Did I trust Savannah with this power? Give me the ability to kill and you'd never need to worry about me suffocating some jerk who cut me off on the freeway. Knowing I possessed the power would be enough. But Savannah was different. She already used her power at the slightest provocation. Yesterday, when we found that investigator in our house, Savannah had thrown him into the wall. Would she have settled for that if she could have killed him? Yet I couldn't wait around to see whether she'd outgrow her recklessness. Either I performed that ceremony tomorrow or I never did it at all. With that came another responsibility. If I gave Savannah those powers, I would need to teach her to control them. Could I do that?

Savannah's mother may have passed along some attitudes with which

I strongly disagreed, but Eve had loved her daughter and had wanted the best for her. She'd believed that the "best" was this ceremony. Did I dare dispute that?

How could I make a decision like this so quickly? I needed days, maybe weeks. I had only minutes.

I walked up behind Savannah as she swung, her sneakers scuffing the dirt into clouds.

"I'll do the ceremony," I said. "Your ceremony."

"Really?" She twisted to look up. Then, seeing my expression, her grin collapsed. "I didn't mean it, Paige. What I said."

"What's said is said."

I turned and walked back to the car.

I drove in silence, answering only questions directed at me.

"Can I see the grimoires, Paige?" Savannah asked, bobbing from the backseat.

I nodded.

"Maybe I can help you learn these. Or we can learn them together."

I had to say something. I'm no good at holding grudges. It feels too much like sulking.

"Sure," I said. "That . . . sounds good."

Cortez glanced back at the grimoire in Savannah's hands, then looked at me. He didn't say anything, but his look oozed curiosity.

"Later," I mouthed.

He nodded, and silence prevailed until we reached the outskirts of East Falls.

"Okay," I said as we drove into town. "We've got a decision to make. We need this grave dirt, but I'm not going near the East Falls cemetery. The last thing I need is for someone to look down from the hospital and see me darting among tombstones. So, we have two choices. One, we can go to the county cemetery. Two, we can go to the one here in town and you can get the dirt, Cortez."

He sighed.

"Okay, I guess that answers my question. We head to the county cemetery."

"It wasn't the proposition to which I was registering my objection," he said.

"So what's wrong?"

"Nothing."

Savannah leaned over the seat. "He's pissed because you're still calling—"

Cortez cut her off. "I'm not 'pissed' about anything. The town cemetery is closer. I'll get the dirt."

"You don't mind?"

"Not at all. I should be able to retrieve dirt through the fence without having to enter the cemetery proper and therefore without risk of being seen."

"Is that where they buried Cary?" Savannah asked. "By the fence?"

"I think he was cremated."

Cortez nodded. "A course of action which, had it not been determined prior to the visitation, I'm quite certain would have been considered afterward."

"No kidding," I said with a shudder. "After that, I'm a cremation convert."

"Wait a sec," Savannah said. "If they cremated Cary, how are we going to take dirt from his grave?"

"We aren't."

"Lucas can't take it from just anyone," Savannah said. "It has to be from the grave of someone who was murdered."

"What?"

"Uh, didn't I mention that?"

"No."

"Ummm, sorry, guys."

"We have"—I checked the clock—"forty-five minutes to find the grave of someone who was murdered. Great. Just great."

"Pull over again," Cortez said. "We're going to need to give this some thought."

We'd been sitting at the side of the road for nearly ten minutes. Finally I sighed and shook my head.

"I can't even think of the last person who was murdered in East Falls. The Willard girl was killed by a drunk driver before Christmas, but I'm not sure that counts."

"We ought not to take the chance."

I thudded back against the headrest. "Okay, let me think." I bolted upright. "I've got it! The woman in the morgue. The one behind the curtain. Someone shot her. I don't know the story, probably because I've been avoiding the papers, but that's murder, isn't it? Or could it be manslaughter?"

"Premeditated or not, it appears a clear case of homicide, and that will be sufficient. Is she buried in town?"

"Oh, God. I don't know. I didn't recognize her. She probably wasn't from East Falls, but I can't be sure. Shit! Oh, wait. It would say in the local paper, right? If we could get last week's paper—"

"How are we going to do that?" Savannah asked.

"Hold on. Let me think." I paused, then smiled. "Got it. Elena. She's a journalist. She should have resources, right?"

"She'll have access to online newswire services." Cortez passed me his cell phone. "Tell her to search for anything on Katrina Mott."

"Where'd you get the name?" Savannah asked.

"From the notice board outside the funeral home on Monday. There were only two services listed."

"Good memory," I said.

He nodded and turned on the phone for me.

As I'd hoped, Elena hadn't gone to bed yet, though it was past eleven on a weeknight. Not that her social calendar was any busier than mine—she stuck pretty close to home, which was several hours from any late-night city clubs—but she had the advantage of having housemates over the age of thirteen, neither of whom had to get up early for work or school. Plus there was the whole werewolf thing, which often necessitated late nights. When I called, she was outside playing touch football with visiting Pack mates. Rough life, huh?

She took the information and called back within five minutes.

"Katrina Mott," she said. "Died Friday, June fifteenth. Shot to death by her common-law husband during an argument because he—and I quote—'wanted to shut her (obscenity deleted) mouth for good.' Sounds like murder to me. Hope the bastard gets life."

"Life in prison and a lifetime of haunting, if there's any justice in the world. Does it say where she was being buried?"

"Uh . . . oh, here. Memorial at East Falls Funeral Parlor followed by interment Tuesday morning at Pleasant View Cemetery."

"The county cemetery. Perfect. Thanks."

"No problem. You sure you don't need help? Nick's here for the weekend. The three of us could come. Clay, Nick, and I. Or is that exactly what you *don't* need?"

"Something like that. No offense, but—"

"None taken. If you need more subtle muscle, I can sneak down without Clay. For a while, at least. Until he finds me. Sounds like you have everything under control, though."

I made a noncommittal noise.

"Call me if you need me, okay?" she continued. "Even if you just want a bodyguard for Savannah. She's still coming up here next month, right?"

"Absolutely."

She laughed. "Do I hear relief in your voice? We're looking forward to having her."

"Uh-huh. Let me guess, 'we' as in you and Jeremy."

Another laugh. "Clay's fine with it. Not counting down the days, but not complaining either. With Clay, that's a sign of near-approval."

"Approval of Savannah, not me."

"Give it time. You're still staying for the weekend, right? And we're driving down to New York? The two of us?"

"Absolutely."

Savannah was waving for the phone.

"I have to go," I said. "Savannah wants to talk."

"Pass her over and I'll talk to you soon."

As I passed Savannah the phone and started the car, I couldn't help smiling. For two minutes there, I'd forgotten everything else. Two minutes in which I could again see the future progressing exactly as I'd planned it before all this started. I'd get through this. Then I'd go on to enjoy my summer. I'd have a Savannah-free week to squeeze in some social time with my Boston-area friends, plus a New York weekend to develop my friendship with Elena.

For the first time since Leah arrived in East Falls, I could envision a time when all this would be a memory, something to talk about with Elena over drinks at an overpriced New York nightclub. With that came a renewed burst of optimism. I would get past this.

Now, I just had to gather dirt from a murdered woman's grave before the stroke of twelve. I could handle that.

Chapter 35

A Good Walk Spoiled

Pleasant View Cemetery did, surprisingly, have a pleasant view, though I doubted any of the residents appreciated it. Pleasant View was less than a hundred years old, but already quadruple the size of its East Falls counterpart, owing to a century-old municipal bylaw prohibiting any "newcomers" from buying a plot within town.

The argument was that the East Falls cemetery couldn't expand, so to ensure that people could be buried beside their ancestors, you had to already have a family plot there. This is East Falls's version of a country club. Seriously. At my first town picnic, three people found a way to work into conversation his or her eventual inclusion in this elite society. "Have you seen our local cemetery? Quite beautiful, isn't it? My family has a plot there, you know." "See that oak tree by the swing set? There's one just like it on our family plot in the cemetery." "I'm Emma Walcott. My family owns the mausoleum in the town cemetery. Pass the dip, please."

Though it already holds more graves than East Falls, the Pleasant View site is so large that the burials are spaced out, some tucked in valleys, some nestled in wooded groves, some amidst meadows of wildflowers. Legend has it that an unnamed philanthropist donated the land and decreed that nature be left as unspoiled as possible. Members of the East Falls elite say the old guy gave away the property to save on taxes and the county was too cheap to clear it. They're just jealous because they're gonna spend eternity surrounded by a hospital, a funeral home, and a 7-Eleven.

The parking lot for Pleasant View was empty, as one might expect at eleven-thirty on a Tuesday night. Eschewing the lot, I pulled over along the side road.

"How are we going to find her?" Savannah said, squinting into the darkness beyond the car.

"At the front gates, there's a map showing where everyone's buried."

"That's handy."

"Handy and necessary," I said. "Some of these graves are almost hidden in the trees. The only problem is that they may not have added Ms. Mott yet, in which case we'll have to do some searching."

As we neared the map, a horrible thought struck me. What if Mott hadn't been buried today? The newspaper article listed the funeral for this morning, but that was before her corpse got up and started slugging people. To my relief, Katrina Mott's grave had been penciled in on the map.

"Would you like me to collect the dirt?" Cortez asked.

I shook my head. "There's no risk of being seen here, so I'll do it. You two can wait back at the car."

"Uh-uh," Savannah said. "It's my dirt. I'm helping you get it."

"I'll stand watch within the cemetery," Cortez said.

"You don't have to," I said. "It's dark, secluded. No one can see us."

"Humor me."

Katrina Mott's grave was near the middle, nestled in a U-shaped cluster of cedars. Sounded easy enough to find, and it probably was . . . during the day. At night, though, all trees look alike, and my ability to judge distances was severely compromised by the fact I could see only five feet in either direction. If there was a moon overhead, it went into hiding the moment we entered the cemetery.

After stumbling over two graves, I cast a minor illumination spell. A tiny glowing ball appeared in my palm. I tossed it and it hovered before me, lighting my way.

"Now that is definitely handy," Cortez said.

"You don't know this one?" I said.

He shook his head. "You'll have to teach me."

"She's teaching it to me first," Savannah said. "After all, *I'm* the witch."

Cortez was about to answer, then stopped and looked around. "There," he said. "Ms. Mott is buried over that hill."

"How do you know that?" Savannah asked.

His lips twitched in a tiny smile. "Magic."

"He memorized the map," I said. "It went gully, hill, three oaks, then another hill. There's the oaks. Now let's get moving. We've only got ten minutes."

"It doesn't need to be precisely on the stroke of twelve," Cortez said. "That, I fear, is a romantic, yet illogical embellishment. Illogical because—"

"Because the 'stroke of twelve,' according to someone's watch, probably won't be dead-on." I glanced at the graves near my feet. "Sorry, folks. No pun intended."

"So what does it mean, then?" Savannah asked.

"Simply that you must gather the dirt in the dead of night—" He looked around. "That is to say, roughly at midnight, give or take an hour or so."

"Well, I'm not hanging around," I said. "If I can grab it now, I'm doing that and getting out of here."

"Go ahead," Cortez said. "I see some juniper over there. I'll gather that, then stand watch partway up the hill."

"Don't you think it's spooky out here?" Savannah asked as we tramped up the hill, having left Cortez behind.

"Peaceful, actually. Very peaceful."

"Do you think that's what it's like when you die? Peaceful?"

"Maybe."

"Kinda boring, don't you think?"

I smiled over at her. "Yes, I suppose so. Maybe just a little peace, then. A break."

"Before what?"

I shrugged.

"Come on, Paige. What do you think happens? After all this."

"I'll tell you what I'd like to happen. I'd like to come back."

"Reincarnation?"

"Sure. Come back and do it all over again. All the good and all the bad. That's what I'd want for my eternity."

"Do you believe what they say? That you keep coming back with the same people? All the people you cared about?"

"It would be nice, don't you think?"

She nodded. "Yeah, that would be nice."

We climbed in silence to the top of the hill. When we got there, Savannah paused.

"Do you hear that?"

I stopped. "What?"

"Voices. Like whispers."

"I hear the wind."

I started forward again, but she grabbed my arm.

"No, really, Paige. Listen. I hear whispering."

The wind rustled through the trees. I shivered.

"Okay," I said. "Now you're scaring me. So much for a peaceful walk."

She grinned. "Sorry. I guess it is just the wind. Hey, what if Leah's necromancer buddy followed us here? This place would be even worse than the funeral parlor, wouldn't it?"

"Thanks for bringing that up."

"Oh, I'm kidding. There's no one here. Look." She turned and gestured at the vista beyond the hill. "You can see all the way to the entrance. Nobody's there. Anyway, Lucas is guarding the path. He's an okay sorcerer. Not great, but at least he could shout and warn us."

"Sure, but Leah would probably knock him unconscious before he finished whatever he was trying to shout."

Cortez's voice floated up on the still night air. "I can hear you perfectly well. This is a cemetery. There isn't much in the way of noise interference."

"Sorry," I called down.

"Did you hear me, too?" Savannah asked.

"The part about me being an 'okay sorcerer'? 'Not great'? No, I believe I missed that."

"Sorry."

A sound floated up, something suspiciously like a chuckle. "Quiet down and get moving before we learn whether it really is possible to make enough noise to wake the dead."

"What are we putting the dirt in?" Savannah asked as we approached the trees surrounding Mott's grave.

I took a sandwich bag from my pocket.

"A Baggie?" she said.

"A Ziploc Baggie."

"You're putting grave dirt in a Ziploc? Shouldn't we have a fancy bottle or something?"

"I thought of bringing a jam jar, but it could break."

"A jam jar? What kind of witch are you?"

"A very practical one."

"What if the Baggie breaks?"

I reached into my pocket and pulled out another one. "Backup Baggie."

Savannah shook her head.

I pushed through the cedars. Three graves lay in the cup formed by the U. I didn't need to check the headstones to find Mott's. The fresh dirt had not yet been covered with sod. Perfect.

I took a small trowel from my coat pocket, bent over, and was blinded by a sudden glare of light. As I stumbled backward into Savannah, I dowsed my light-ball. Yet the light was still there. Someone was shining a flashlight into our faces.

Savannah started an incantation, but I clapped my hand over her mouth before she could finish.

"See?" a woman's voice said. "It is her. I told you so."

The flashlight dropped and I found myself standing before four people, ranging in age from college-bound to mid-retirement.

"Wow," whispered the youngest, a woman with rings through her lower lip. "It's the witch from the newspapers."

"I'm not—" I cut off the denial. "What are you doing here?"

"Seems we should ask you the same thing," a twenty-something man in a ball cap said.

An older woman, the one who'd spoken first, shushed him. "She's here for the same reason we are."

"To find the treasure?" the man said.

She glared at him. "To communicate with the spirit world."

"Is it true you saw her rise from the dead?" the younger woman asked, pointing at Mott's grave "That is so cool. What was it like? Did she say anything?"

"Yeah," Savannah said. "She said, 'Bother me again and I'll rip your—'"

I prodded her to silence. "Do you people know what you're doing? It's called disturbing a grave site. A—uh—" I slipped my trowel behind my back. "A very serious offense."

"Nice try," the young man said. "My brother's a cop. We can't get in trouble unless we dig her up. We aren't stupid."

"No," Savannah said. "You're just hanging around a cemetery looking for buried treasure. Hey, wait, I think I found something. Nope, just another rotting corpse."

"Mind your tongue, child," the older woman said. "While I disagree with the concept of using the spirits for material gain, necromancers in the ancient world often did exactly that. They believed that the dead could see all—the past, the present, and the future—thus allowing them to locate hidden treasures."

The elderly man beside her made a noise.

"Quite right," she said. "Bob wishes me to clarify that the dead are believed to be able to find *any* treasure, not just that which they themselves may have buried."

"He said all that with a grunt?" Savannah asked.

"Mental telepathy, dear. Bob has moved beyond the realm of verbal communication."

"Maybe so, but he hasn't moved beyond the realm of human justice," I said, bending to pick up a saucer of dried mushrooms, which I doubted were shiitake. "Bet these help with the mental telepathy. Maybe you can explain this to the police."

"There's no need to threaten us, dear. We're no danger to you or anyone else. We simply want to communicate with poor Miss Mott. A spirit who has been raised once remains very close to the surface, as I'm sure you're aware. If we can contact her, perhaps she can relay a message from the other side."

"Or tell us where to find treasure," the young man said.

The younger woman rolled her eyes. "You and Joe, always on about your treasure." She looked at me. "Joe's another member of our group. Joe and Sylvia. Only Joe had bowling tonight and Sylvia doesn't like to drive after dark."

"Uh-huh."

"We don't need to worry about these guys raising the dead, Paige," Savannah said. "They're so dumb they couldn't raise—"

I elbowed her to silence. "I'm going to ask you, once more, to leave."

The young man stepped forward, towering over me. "Or what?"

"Better be careful, or she'll show you," Savannah said.

"Is that a threat?"

"That's enough," I said. "Now, we're all leaving—"

"Who's leaving?" the young man said. "I'm not leaving."

The older woman's mouth set. "We aren't leaving until we've communicated with the spirit world."

"Fine," Savannah said. "Here, let me help you."

Her voice rose, words echoing through the silence as she recited an incantation in Hebrew. I whirled to stop her. Before I could, she finished. All went silent.

"Damn," she muttered, leaning in so only I could hear her. "It's supposed to—"

Her body went rigid, head jerking back, arms flying out. A deafening crack ripped through the silence, like the thunder of a hundred guns fired at once. A flare of light lit up the sky. Savannah stood on tiptoe, barely touching the ground, body shaking. I dove for her. As my fingers grazed her arm, something hit me in the gut, throwing me against a tombstone.

CHAPTER 36

KINDA COOL . . .
IN A BAD WAY

When I recovered from my fall, I saw that Savannah had collapsed. The four would-be necromancers stood ringed around her prone body. I pushed myself up and ran to Savannah. She was unconscious, her face white.

"Call an ambulance," I said.

Nobody moved. I checked Savannah's pulse. Weak but steady.

"Wow," the young woman said. "That was, like, so cool."

"Call a goddamned ambulance!" I snarled.

Still no one moved. Around us, the air had gone still, but I could still feel the crackle of energy. At a sound near the trees, I looked up and saw a shape moving toward us. Someone was coming.

Cortez. Perfect. He had a cell phone.

I raised my head to tell him to hurry, then saw the figure emerge from the trees. It wasn't a figure at all, but a writhing mass of reddish light that twisted on itself, turning blue, then green, then yellow. To my left, wisps of light wafted from the ground, congealing into a mass that hovered over the earth, then shot into the air. We all stared, transfixed, as one after another of these airy phantasms of colored light rose from the soil around us.

"Oooh," the young woman said. "They're so pretty."

Light shot up around us, gaining in speed, hurling into the air. One soared up right beside me, then swerved and dove at my head. The breath flew from me, literally was sucked from my lungs. I gasped. The light darted off into the trees.

Suddenly, the ground began to shake. Light streamed from the earth. Something knocked me hard, pushing me away from Savannah. A deafening howl rent the air. I dove toward Savannah, but a geyser of light erupted between us, pushing me back. The ground quaked, knocking me to my knees. Howl after howl tore through the night.

"Savannah!" I shouted.

The moment my mouth opened, the air was ripped from my throat. A globe of light surrounded my head, sucking the air from me. Pain cleaved through my chest. I couldn't breathe. As I fought, the light seemed to take form. I clawed at my attacker, but my fingers passed through it.

"Stop fighting!" a voice said at my ear.

I struggled harder, legs and arms flailing against the thing.

"Goddamn it, Paige. Don't fight! You're making it worse!"

Cortez? As my brain registered his voice, my body went still for a brief second. The light evaporated and I fell back, hitting the ground and gulping air. Cortez bent over me.

"They're koyut," he said. "They feed off energy. If you fight, you only produce more."

I pushed him away and sat up, wildly looking about for Savannah.

"She's right here," Cortez said, pointing at a prone form behind him. "She's fine. I'll carry her. We need to move past the trees."

He grabbed her up and we ran. When we reached the meadow beyond the trees, Cortez stopped me.

"We need to wake her," he said. "What did she cast?"

"I—I don't know."

I turned back toward the grove. Light trumpeted up from treetops. The howls were muted, as if soundproofed within the grove. A man screamed.

"I need to help the others," I said, turning to run.

Cortez lunged and grabbed me. "Koyut don't kill. As soon as people lose consciousness, the koyut leave them alone. We need to concentrate on Savannah. What did she say?"

"It was Hebrew. I'm not good at Hebrew. I think—" I closed my eyes and willed my thumping heart to slow so I could concentrate. "She said something about summoning forces. Forces or energies, I'm not sure which."

"Summoning the energies of the earth. It's a sorcerer spell."

"You know it?"

"I know *of* it. I haven't learned it because it's not something I can ever imagine needing to use. It calls on the spirits of the earth, not to perform any particular task, but simply to respond and do as they wish. It's considered a chaos spell."

"No kidding," I said. "What was Savannah thinking?"

"It—it's never worked before," Savannah's thin voice said beside us. "All it ever does is make some noise and flashing lights. Like a prank. Dime store magic. Only this time—"

"Only this time, it behaved precisely as intended," Cortez said. "Owing, no doubt, to your increasing strength. Plus the fact that you chose to cast it in a cemetery, a place rich in energy."

I knelt beside Savannah. "Are you okay?"

She pushed herself up onto her elbows. "Yeah. Sorry about that, guys."
She gave a tiny smile. "Only it was kinda cool, wasn't it?"

We both glared at her.

"I mean, kinda cool in a bad way."

"I would suggest that is one spell you can safely remove from your
repertoire," Cortez said. "I would also suggest that we return to the car
before the lights attract—"

"I still need the dirt," I said.

"I'm fast," Savannah said. "I can get it."

"No!" we said in unison.

Cortez insisted on following me to the edge of the trees, so he could
jump in if anything went wrong. It didn't. By now the lights had dimmed
to a soft glow, illuminating the glade and the four figures lying blissfully
unconscious within. I scooped dirt into both bags, shoved them into my
pocket, and headed back to Cortez and Savannah.

"So that's what spirits look like?" Savannah asked, watching the swirling, multicolored glow.

"Not human spirits," I said. "Nature spirits and their energy. Let's go."

Savannah stepped away from the trees, then stopped and stared,
transfixed.

"Yes, very pretty," I said, reaching for her arm. "Now move!"

Her body went rigid. A wave of physical energy shot from her, knocking both Cortez and me off our feet. The ground shivered. A low, nearly
inaudible moan seemed to emanate from the earth itself. Geysers of dirt
erupted, borne up on rocketing streams of light. Then the wind began to
scream—not wail, but scream a high-pitched endless shriek that made me
double over, hands clamped to my ears.

Cortez grabbed my shoulder and shook me, mouthing "To the car"
once he had my attention. He hoisted Savannah's limp form over his
shoulder and began to run. I followed.

As we crested the hill, I saw lights in the distance. Not the glow of
spirits, but the very human illumination of flashlights and headlights. I
looked at Cortez, but he had his head down, struggling to get Savannah
to the top of the steep hill. I shouted for him, but the wail of the wind
sucked the words from my mouth.

Lunging forward, I snagged the back of his shirt. He twisted, nearly
tumbling onto me. I steadied him and gestured toward the road.

The flashing lights of police cars now cut through the night, joining a
mob of flashlight beams spilling through the cemetery gates. Cortez's lips

moved in a soundless curse and he wheeled around. I pointed at the woods to our left and he nodded.

As we raced for the woods, the shrieks and lights pursued us. No, that's a poor choice of words, implying the spirits were trying to attack us. They weren't. They simply followed, arising from the ground in our tracks. Elsewhere, the commotion seemed to be dying down. Or maybe it just seemed that way, in comparison to the chaos erupting around us. I wasn't about to stop for a scientific survey of the situation.

Once we reached the woods, Cortez lowered Savannah's body to the ground. Then he turned, raised his hands, and said a few words. As he swept his right hand across the air, the spirits vanished.

"I thought you couldn't do that kind of magic," I said, wheezing as I struggled for breath.

"I said I saw no need to learn how to conjure such spirits. I did, however, see a distinct need to learn how to un-conjure them. Unfortunately, it's a geographically limited spell."

"Meaning if we leave the woods, they'll return. Fine by me. I haven't run that fast since grade school. No, strike that, I've *never* run that fast."

I lowered myself to the ground beside Savannah and checked her vital signs. She was unconscious, but breathing fine.

"How come they keep following her?" I asked.

"To be honest, I have no idea. Perhaps they're feeding off her energy. I would assume, from my knowledge of witch folklore, that the sudden surge in a witch's powers during first menses renders those powers unpredictable."

"That's an understatement."

I leaned against a tree and exhaled. At my feet, a wisp of light floated from the earth. I jumped up so fast I banged my head against an overhanging limb.

"I thought you—"

Cortez waved me to silence. As I watched, the light drifted upward. Unlike the earlier spirits, this light was pure white. It floated up as lazily as smoke from a dying fire. When it reached a height of about five feet, it stopped and shimmered, growing denser.

At a motion to my left, I looked and saw four other towers of light, each a different height. I looked at Cortez, but he lifted a hand, as if telling me to watch and wait. The cones of light took on form. Particles of light flowed from all sides, adding to the shapes and giving them definition.

Before me stood five people dressed in Colonial-era clothing. A man and a boy in doublets and breeches, a woman and a teenage girl in fitted jackets, skirts, and white caps, and a toddler, its gender indeterminate in its long white gown. Though the light remained white, the forms were so solid I could see the wrinkles around the man's eyes. Those eyes stared directly into mine. The man turned to the woman and spoke, lips moving soundlessly. She nodded and replied.

"Ghosts," I said.

The girl tilted her head and frowned at me, saying something to her mother. Then the boy reached out toward Cortez. His father leaped forward and caught his arm, lips moving in a silent scolding. Even the toddler stared up at us, wide-eyed. When I stepped toward the child, the mother swept up the little one in her arms, glaring at me. The father stepped toward his wife, motioning the other two children closer. The boy's hands moved in the sign of the evil eye.

"Only they don't know who the ghosts are," I said.

Cortez gave a tiny smile. "Do you?"

The family, now clustered together, turned and began walking away. The toddler grinned and waved at us over his mother's shoulder. I waved back. Cortez extended his left hand. I thought he was going to wave, but he said a few words in Latin. As he balled his hand into a fist, the family began to fade. Just before they vanished, the daughter glanced over her shoulder and shot us an accusing glare.

"Rest in peace," I whispered. I turned to Cortez. "I thought you said Savannah cast a spell for summoning nature spirits, not ghosts."

"It is. But Savannah's spell seems to be doing a lot it was never intended to do."

"How do we stop it?"

"By getting her out of this graveyard."

"That'll end it?"

"I hope so. Now, when we leave these woods, the spirits will return but, as you saw, they intend no harm. You simply have to move through them, as you moved through that sorcerer illusion in the funeral home."

"Got it. If we head south, we'll hit the road. There's no fence, so we can—"

A howling cut me off. Not the howls of the spirits, but the distinct howl of a dog on a scent.

"The hounds of hell, I presume," Cortez said.

"I wouldn't bet against it. But I think those are tracking dogs, probably with the police."

"Ah, I forgot about the police. Problem number sixty-three, I believe."

"Sixty-four. The unconscious bodies scattered around Katrina Mott's grave are sixty-three. Or they will be, when they wake up." I took a deep breath. "Okay. Let's think. There's a stream to the west. Dogs can't follow a trail through water. Plus, it's in the opposite direction, so we'll get a head start."

"West it is, then." He hauled Savannah's limp form over his shoulder. "Lead the way."

So we ran . . . away from the gun-toting state troopers, through a swirling mass of spirits, pursued by baying hounds, surrounded by the screams of the damned. You know, I think the mind has a saturation point, beyond which it just doesn't give a damn. Spirits? Hounds? Cops? Who cares? Just keep running and it'll all go away.

This whole running-away business is getting tedious, so here's the condensed version: Run to water. Tramp through water. Fail to evade hounds. Throw fireballs at hounds. Make mental note to send sizable donation to the SPCA. Reach road. Jog to car. Collapse, wheezing, beside car. Get dragged into car by Cortez. Mutter excuse about childhood asthma. Make mental note to join a gym.

"Do you have the dirt?" Cortez asked.

"Dirt?"

I cannot describe the look on his face. The shock. The disbelief. The horror.

"Oh, *that* dirt." I pulled both bags from my pocket. "Got it."

I relinquished the driving to Cortez so I could stay in the backseat with Savannah, who was still unconscious. Good thing, too, because, while I consider myself an excellent driver, I have little experience at it, having always preferred to walk or ride my bike. The upshot being that, had I been behind the wheel, I would have been ill-prepared to handle what happened next.

Cortez pulled onto the road, not turning us back toward the highway, but heading farther down the dirt road, away from the cemetery front gates. Before we reached the first crossroad, sirens sounded behind us. I twisted to look out the rearview mirror and saw a state police car bearing down on us, lights flashing.

"Shit!" I said. "Don't pull over!"

"I wasn't about to. Are you both buckled in?"

"Yes."

"Hold on, then."

With that, he turned off the headlights and hit the gas.

Chapter 37

The Conscientious Car Thief

Margaret's car was an Oldsmobile. An old Olds, probably from the mid-eighties. This meant that it went like a bat out of hell, but didn't corner so well, as Cortez discovered the first time he sailed around a bend and nearly went into the ditch. On the plus side, the Olds, being a wide-bodied car, was also good at off-roading.

Yes, I said "off-roading," as in leaving the road and cutting through a farmer's field. Imagine it, please. It's past midnight, with no discernible moon or stars, the headlights are off, and you're rocketing across a rutted field at forty miles an hour. Let me assure you, for sheer terror, it ranks right up there with getting your breath sucked out by a koyut.

How we managed to get to the other side without flipping over is beyond me. The car never even slid. Before we'd gone fifty feet into the field, the police cruiser backed off.

We shot out the other side onto empty country roads.

"Are you okay?" Cortez asked as he slowed the car.

"Jostled, but fine. That was some driving."

"Where are we?" Savannah asked, sitting up.

"Heading home," I said.

Cortez glanced in the rearview mirror. "Unfortunately, we have something of a predicament. I would presume those officers made a note of our license plate."

"You're right. I didn't think of that."

"Not to worry. It simply means we have to abandon the car outside town and walk in through the woods. When we get to your house, you'll need to call Miss Levine and apprise her of the situation. If the police arrive before morning, she can claim the car was stolen while she slept. If they don't contact her by nine, I would advise that she call and report the car missing herself."

"Police?" Savannah said, blinking sleepily. "What police?"

"Don't ask," I said. "And don't ever cast that spell again. Please."

"I conjured cops?"

"In a manner of speaking," Cortez said. "I'm going to pull over up here. I believe that leaves us with about a twenty-minute walk."

He parked the car with the nose pulled into a stretch of forest, leaving the tail end out, so it could be found, but not easily.

"Should we leave the keys in the ignition?" I said as I hoisted my knapsack onto my shoulder.

"No. That would raise too many questions as to how the thieves obtained the keys. Better to make this look like a typical car theft."

He opened his jacket and pulled out a tiny tool case.

"You're going to hot-wire the car?" Savannah said, leaning over the seat. "Cool. Did you boost cars when you were a kid?"

"Certainly not."

"Let me guess," I said. "Another of those questionable, but necessary skills. Like knowing how to un-conjure ghosts and drive a getaway car."

"Precisely."

"How many cars have you boosted?" Savannah asked as we got out of the car and headed down the road on foot.

"Two. Both times, I assure you, it was an absolute last resort. I found myself without transportation and in urgent need of it. Fortunately, neither vehicle was damaged and I was able to leave it in a safe place, after washing it and filling the tank."

I grinned. "Bet that had the cops scratching their heads. A conscientious car thief."

Savannah rolled her eyes. "Don't you guys ever do anything bad?"

"I lifted a tube of lipstick when I was twelve."

"Yeah. You told me about that one." She looked at Cortez. "Know what she did? Stole it, then felt so bad she mailed the money to the store. Tax included. You guys are really setting a bad example, you know."

"A *bad* example?"

"Sure. How do you expect me to live up to it? I'm going to need serious therapy someday."

"Don't worry," I said. "I've budgeted for that."

"She probably has," Savannah muttered. "What about—"

"Car coming," I said. "Off the road."

We tramped into a field.

"Do you do this a lot, Lucas?" Savannah asked. "Car chases and evading the cops and stuff?"

"On occasion, though I would hesitate to say it qualified as 'often.'"

"The real question is: How often do you have to do it this often?" I said.

He smiled. "Not often."

"So, we're special?" Savannah said.

"Very special."

"I don't think that's good," I said.

I transferred the knapsack to my other shoulder. Cortez reached to take it from me, but I waved him back.

Savannah tripped in a groundhog hole, then jogged up beside Cortez. "So what kind of case is this? Compared to your other ones?"

"Frenetic."

She glanced at me for clarification.

"He means we're keeping him busy," I said. "Mainly because we're causing half the trouble ourselves."

Cortez smiled. "I must admit, you two do have a unique predilection for creating new challenges."

"Unique," Savannah said. "He means we're special."

"Uh-huh."

We reentered the house the same way we'd left, coming through the woods, then darting across the yard and in the back door. A quick peek out the front confirmed that such caution was still warranted. There were still three or four people camped out on my lawn. One of them had even erected a pup tent. Maybe I should have started charging site rental fees.

After sending Savannah off to bed, I called Margaret. The conversation went something like this:

Me: Ummm, we had a problem with your car . . .

Her: An accident! Oh, dear, no. My insurance rates—

Me: Not an accident. We're all fine, including the car. We just had to ditch it.

Her: You drove it into the ditch?

Me: Sorry, I meant "abandon." The police saw the license number and—

Her: Police?

Me: Everything's fine, but when the police find it, say it was stolen.

Her: Stolen?

Me: Right. Say it was in the driveway when you went to bed and you never saw it again. Don't mention the keys. And if the police say anything about the cemetery—

Her: Cemetery?

Me: Tell them you don't know anything about it.

Her: But I don't!

Me: Good. Whatever they say, you know nothing. You haven't seen me in days. If they find my prints in your car, it's because I borrowed it last month, okay?

Her: Prints? Do you mean fingerprints? What on earth have you—

Me: Gotta go. Thanks for letting us borrow the car. I'll make it up to you. Bye.

When I walked into the living room, Cortez was standing in front of the television, flipping through channels.

"TV," I said as I collapsed onto the sofa. "Great invention. The perfect mindless antidote for a hellish day. So what's on?"

"*Night of the Living Dead.*"

"Ha-ha."

"I'm quite serious."

He turned back a few channels and stopped on a black-and-white image of the moaning undead lurching around a farmhouse.

"Kinda looks familiar," I said. "Haven't I seen this before?"

"Yesterday," he said. "In the funeral home."

"No, that's not it. Those undead were much scarier. And they didn't lurch. Well, Cary did, but only 'cause he was kind of squashed. Hmmm, where have I seen this? Ghouls surrounding a house, trapping the inhabitants within, refusing to leave. Wait! That's my front lawn. Look, there's a naked woman! Bet she's a Wiccan."

Cortez chuckled. "I'm glad you can laugh about it."

I hesitated, then glanced over at him. "You know, if this gets to be too much . . . I mean, this isn't quite the nice, easy court case you probably imagined. I'd understand if you wanted to back out."

"And miss all the fun?" He shot a crooked grin my way. "Never."

We looked at each other a moment, then he quickly turned to the TV and started channel-surfing.

"No, wait," I said. "Go back to the movie. I could use some light entertainment. Flesh-eating zombies might be just the ticket."

He returned to the old movie, then glanced from the recliner to the couch, as if trying to decide where to sit. I gestured at the other end of the sofa. He nodded and sat beside me.

"What're we watching?" Savannah said, bouncing into the room wearing her nightgown.

"Paige and I are watching *Night of the Living Dead*. You are going to bed."

"I just conjured a cemetery full of spirits. I think I'm old enough to watch a horror movie." She plopped into the recliner. "Do we have chips or anything?"

"You think I've been shopping lately?" I said. "Pretty soon we'll be down to pickles and preserves."

"Are those the zombies?" she said. "Talk about lame."

"It's an old film," I said. "The special effects aren't very advanced."

"What special effects? That's a guy with mascara smeared under his eyes. I've seen scarier people at the mall."

"Did Paige tell you to go to bed, Savannah?" Cortez said.

"Oh, fine," she said. "It's a dumb movie anyway."

She flounced from the room. A few minutes later, I sighed.

"It is a pretty dumb movie," I said. "But I'm too wired to sleep."

"I, uh, believe you mentioned something about new grimoires?"

I sat up. "Geez, that's right. I almost forgot. I wanted to try them out tonight."

"You were, I believe, going to tell me . . ." He let the sentence fade out.

I grinned. "I was going to tell you about them, wasn't I?"

So I did.

CHAPTER 38

PRESSURE VALVE

"It's possible," he said when I finished telling him about the grimoires. "Possible? Are you saying my logic is flawed?"

"I wouldn't dare. I'm simply saying that it makes sense and, therefore, it's possible. Non-Coven witches have been using sorcerer magic for generations. It would be good to see them get their own back."

I smiled. "Would it? You know what it would mean, don't you? These spells could level the playing field."

"As it should be."

I leaned back into the sofa cushions. "Is this the same guy who made a crack about the 'hereditary limitations' of witch powers?"

"I effected the persona with which I thought you'd be most comfortable. I've dealt with enough witches not to underestimate their abilities. Not every sorcerer hates or even dislikes witches. Many do, though, even those who'd be considered decent, moral men."

"Decent moral sorcerers?"

"No, that's not an oxymoron. Not every sorcerer is evil. To say that would be akin to saying that every witch is weak and fearful, which I'm sure you wouldn't appreciate. A stereotype becomes a stereotype when a significant percentage of a population appears to conform to it. Unlike some stereotypes, that of the morally corrupt sorcerer is, unfortunately, valid."

"Absolute power corrupts absolutely."

"Exactly. Those who chase the dream of absolute power, as many sorcerers do, find themselves obsessed by it."

"So you don't crave stronger powers?"

He met my gaze. "What I crave, as I believe you do, is stronger knowledge. The best possible repertoire of spells and the power to do my best with them. When I say I'm pleased that you found these grimoires, I must admit, I can't help but see it as an opportunity to acquire new spells."

"Can't blame you for that." I shifted and turned toward him. "Don't you think maybe we're being naive? Believing that we'll never be corrupted by our own quest for power?"

"Perhaps."

"There's a definitive answer."

"Wouldn't it be naive of me to think I couldn't possibly be naive?"

"Enough," I said. "You're making my head spin. Time to try out a new spell."

He shifted forward. "Would you . . . object to an audience?"

I grinned. "Not at all."

I gathered my books and we went down to the basement.

When I said I hoped to learn a new spell, I meant exactly that: one new spell. As much as I longed to test-drive the whole book, even hoping to learn one spell might be pushing it. To cast a spell from the tertiary-level grimoires, I first had to master a new one from the secondary spellbook, which would take time.

I further dampened my own enthusiasm by insisting on proceeding in a logical fashion. Tonight I wanted not only to learn something new, but also to test my theory. Was it necessary to learn the corresponding secondary spell before one could cast the tertiary?

To test this, I selected the suffocation spell. Since I'd practiced it already for hours without success, it was the perfect choice. If I could cast it after learning the secondary spell, it would support my hypothesis. The suffocation spell was classified as an elemental, air, class five.

The corresponding air spell was one that caused hiccups. Maybe in grade school that would have been fun, but for anyone over the age of ten, it was a pretty silly spell. Logically, though, it made sense. Both hiccups and suffocation are interruptions to breathing.

When I'd run through these grimoires the first time, I'd tried this spell, just for fun, but stopped before mastering it. If my theory was right, that might explain why the suffocation spell had shown some signs that it might eventually work—because I'd partially learned the secondary spell.

Struck by a thought, I dug out my Coven-sanctioned grimoire and flipped to a page near the end. A spell to cure hiccups, which I'd learned years ago. That one was an elemental, air spell, class five. The primary spell. First you learn to cure hiccups, then you learn to cause them, then you learn to cut off breathing altogether.

"Mind if I give you hiccups?" I asked Cortez.

"What?"

"Hiccups. I need to give you a case of hiccups. Is that okay?"

"I can't say I've ever had a girl offer to give me that."

"It's a spell," I said. "Don't worry. I know one to cure them, too."

"You'll have to teach me that one. The curing, not the giving. I've never had much luck with holding my breath."

"No? Then just wait until you see the spell I'm going to try next."

Before I could hope for a successful cast on the hiccup spell, I needed to practice it. Having Cortez there wasn't a distraction, probably because he was considerate enough to sit behind me, so I wouldn't feel like I was performing.

After twenty minutes of tinkering with the spell, the rhythm felt right, so I asked Cortez to move in front of me. When he did, he faced the wall, rather than looking straight at me. That made it easier. So easy, in fact, that the spell worked on the second try. Then, of course, I had to do another half-dozen trial runs, to be sure I had it right. When I debated another try, Cortez proclaimed me fully proficient in the spell, and begged leave to regain his breath.

Next I moved on to the suffocation spell. I'd start by casting it on myself. Lucas had been through enough that night and I wasn't in danger of suffocating myself. As with a binding spell, the moment I stopped concentrating, the spell would break.

It took twenty minutes before I could recite the suffocation spell. It wasn't a difficult incantation. It being Latin, it was in the spell-casting language with which I was most familiar. The delay resulted from one simple factor. Nerves. So many of my hopes rode on this spell that I stumbled over the words. I tried to tell myself that it didn't matter that much, that if I failed, I'd find another way, but to no avail. I knew how important this was and couldn't persuade myself otherwise. I scarcely dared utter the words for fear I'd fail. As if, in fumbling just this once, the magic would somehow vanish, never to be recovered.

After tripping over the incantation a few times, I changed tack and began with the second line. By leaving off the opening, I was guaranteed that the spell would fail, so I could concentrate on the recitation. Having tried this spell many times before, I quickly picked up the rhythm.

The words flowed, the inflections and tones rolling off my tongue. A well-cast spell is true music. Not a chant or a song, but the music of pure language, the music of Shakespeare or Byron. Put emotion and conviction behind those words and it has the power of opera—without even understanding the words, you can feel their meaning.

I closed my eyes and poured my heart into it, poured in every ounce of longing and frustration and ambition. My voice rose until I couldn't feel the words coming from my throat, could only hear them echoing around me. Again and again I repeated the incantation. I heard the first line flow from my lips, unbidden. The words rose to a crescendo and, with the final line, the breath flew from my lips. I gasped, almost choked.

The moment my breath returned, the words started again, as if of their own accord. The window above my head rattled as I recited the incantation. Rosebush branches lashed and scratched against the pane. When the words finished, I sputtered, breathless.

Again I started anew. The hatch doors buckled and groaned. As the spell neared the end, the doors suddenly blew open. A gust of wind whooshed in, knocking over the baskets of clean laundry. With the last word, my breath was sucked out with such force that I fell forward and blacked out.

The next thing I knew, Cortez was grabbing my shoulders.

"Are you all right?" he asked as my eyes opened.

I turned, lips curving in a slow grin. "I think it worked."

"I should say so," he said, surveying the windswept piles of laundry surrounding us. "Now, having proven that the spell works and you can cast it successfully, I don't suppose you'd mind if I had a try."

I yanked the grimoire away. "No. Mine."

With a laugh, I waved the spellbook, just out of reach. He grinned and grabbed for the book, but I whisked it away, nearly falling backward. He lunged for it. As his face came to mine, he paused and blinked. I knew what he was thinking. And I knew he wouldn't do it. So I did. I lifted my mouth to his and kissed him.

Cortez's eyes widened. I laughed, nearly breaking the lip-lock, but before I could fall back, he pulled me to him. His lips went to mine, surprising me with the force of his kiss. Whatever Cortez lacked in technique, he more than made up for in zeal, and in that kiss I tasted something that made my head spin and set my insides afire and brought to life every other romantic cliché I'd ever laughed at. The intoxication of the spell-casting still lingered, now infused with a fresh passion and the sheer elation of feeling that passion returned. I felt giddy, electrified, invincible. For the first time in days I felt I was everything I'd once believed myself to be.

We tumbled into the pile of clean laundry, still kissing. Cortez rolled over, pulling me on top of him. His hands moved to the back of my head and fumbled with my hair clip. I reached back and released it. As my hair fell free, Cortez entwined his fingers in it and kissed me harder. Then he slipped one hand from my hair and snapped his fingers over our heads. The light went out. He murmured a few words against my mouth and the unlit candles from my spell-casting practice ignited.

My chuckle vibrated between our lips. "Show-off."

He pulled back and arched his brows. "It's called being romantic." His lips curved in a grin. "And maybe showing off. A little."

"Well, don't. This is my seduction."

"Is it?"

"I started it, didn't I?"

"Quite right. I'll leave you to it, then."

I cast the witch spell to extinguish the candles, then the one to relight them. Cortez chuckled and pulled me onto him again. We kissed for a few minutes. When he tugged my blouse from my jeans, I shook my head and backed up, breaking the kiss.

"My lead, remember?" I said.

I wrapped my fingers in his shirtfront and pulled him until he was sitting. Then I straddled his hips, kneeling, and wriggled until I felt his erection exactly where I wanted it. His breath caught. I smiled and tugged off his glasses.

"Do you need these?" I asked.

He shook his head.

I laid them aside, then began unbuttoning his shirt. After three buttons, I pressed my lips to his throat, tickling my tongue along it, feeling him swallow. I moved my fingers down to the next button and undid it, then slid my tongue down, tracing circles down his chest. Between each unfastening, I ran my fingers across the bared skin.

When I got to the final button, I shimmied back, so I was sitting by his knees. Then I bent forward and teased his bellybutton with my lips, my tongue dipping lower until I undid the button on his pants, then, slowly, tugged down the zipper. I could hear his breathing above me, raspy and uneven, and my own hunger ignited.

I ran my tongue along the top of his underwear, letting it slide just underneath. Then I slid my body forward, lips moving back up his chest until I was straddling him again. When I was back at eye level, he wrapped his hands in my hair and pulled my mouth to his. His hands slid under my shirt, but I backed off again and grinned.

"Not yet," I said.

He opened his mouth, but I put my finger to his lips and scuttled backward, pushing myself up. Then I stepped back, grinned down at him, and pulled off my shirt. My socks followed, then my jeans, falling in a puddle at my feet. I stepped out and kicked them aside. I unbuttoned my shirt and let it slide away. Then I took my time with the rest, the bra and panties.

When I let the panties fall, for a few seconds, Cortez only stared. Then he grinned, scrambled to his feet, and covered the ground between us in one stride.

I arched onto my tiptoes to kiss him and we nearly tumbled down. As my balance faltered, he caught me and redirected our fall onto the pile of clean clothes. I tugged his shirt off his shoulders, running my fingers across and down his back. His pants were still undone. I wriggled my hands under the waistband and pushed them down, leaving his briefs in place.

He kicked off his pants and moved his hands under my rear, pulling me against him. Then his right hand shifted and, from the corner of my eye, I saw him reach out. He murmured something against my lips and Savannah's stereo turned on.

"Ah-hem," I said, pulling back. "My seduction."

"Consider me seduced."

As he lowered his mouth to mine, the crooning of a boy band filled the room. Cortez's eyes widened and his hand flicked again, moving the tuner. I laughed. He flipped past a jazz station, then returned and, with another flick, adjusted the volume to a whisper.

"Not bad," I said.

I cast the wind incantation, softening the emphasis in the right places, so a cool breeze tickled across our skin. Cortez kissed me, then moved his lips over my chin and down my neck. As he kissed my throat, he murmured something and flicked his fingers. The candle flame refracted into a hundred shards of light. I chuckled and arched my back as his lips went to my breast. I let myself enjoy that for a minute, then tugged away and pulled myself up until I was sitting, straddling his chest.

I whispered a spell and a small fireball appeared in my hand. Cortez looked from it to me, and tilted his head, eyes questioning. I grinned and cast a dampening spell, putting out the ball and leaving only my fingers glowing.

"Interesting," he said. "But I don't see—"

I pressed my hot fingers against his chest. He gasped. I traced the heat down his chest, then slid my hand under his briefs and stroked him. He moaned, closing his eyes and leaning back.

"See now?" I asked.

"Teach me that," he said hoarsely.

I grinned. "Maybe."

I peeled off his briefs and slid one hot hand under his balls, caressing them as I stroked his shaft with the other. He arched back, moaning. I continued, measuring his breathing until I heard just the right tempo, then stopped, still holding him tight.

"Do I win?" I asked.

"Yes. God, yes." He paused, then pulled free of my grasp, eyes flying open. "No."

"Changed your mind?" I said with a grin. "That's okay. You're right. Maybe it isn't such a good idea." I started backing off him. "We should keep this professional. After all—"

He lunged for me, knocking me onto my back and stretching over me.

"I meant 'no' as in I don't concede defeat. Not yet."

He kicked off his briefs, then grabbed me by the hips. We rolled, entangling ourselves in the linen. The soft sheets and clean scent of lemon engulfed us. As we kissed, I felt Cortez's lips move and opened my eyes to see his hand arc above us. A low thrumming drowned out the radio, then a fog of purple and blue light rose from the floor.

"Tell me that isn't the koyut," I murmured against his mouth.

He chuckled and slid his fingers between my thighs, teasing. I arched back and closed my eyes. When I opened them, the fog was wafting toward us. It touched my arm first, sending a tingle of energy through it. I gasped. Cortez chuckled again and pushed his fingers into me. The fog wrapped around us. Every hair on my body rose and I pressed my head into the sheets, luxuriating in the sensation.

"That is—" I gasped after a few minutes. "You have to teach me that."

He smiled, pulled out his fingers, and slid on top of me. "I'll teach you anything you want."

Chapter 39

Good Morning

Afterward, I disentangled myself from the sheets and his arms, and got to my feet. He lifted his head and frowned.

"Wait," I said.

I went to the cold cellar and grabbed a bottle of wine. When I returned, Cortez was still wrapped in the clean sheets, watching me.

"Good?" I said, holding out the bottle.

"Hmmm?" He blinked, then looked at the bottle. "Oh, yes. Wine. Good. Great."

I laughed. "I suppose I'd be insulted if it *was* the wine you were staring at."

He grinned then, a slow lazy grin that did something to my insides.

"Guess I'm still in shock," he said.

"Don't tell me I'm the first damsel in distress who's ever seduced you."

"I can say, with absolute certainty, that you are the first woman who has ever even *tried* to seduce me, on or off a case." He reached for the bottle. "Do you need a corkscrew for that?"

"Of course not. I'm a witch."

I said a few words and the cork flew out.

"I don't suppose you know how to conjure glasses," I said.

"Sorry."

"The kitchen's so far away. Do we need glasses?"

"Absolutely not."

He hooked his arm around my waist and pulled me down onto his lap. We each took a drink from the bottle.

"I'm sorry about your bike," I said.

"My . . . ? Oh, right. As I said, it's nothing. I had insurance."

"Still, I am sorry. I know replacing it won't be the same thing, if you restored it and all."

"*If* I restored it?"

"I didn't mean—"

He chuckled. "You don't need to explain. I'm well aware that I hardly seem the type to be tinkering with transmissions and carbure-tors. To be honest, short of that particular hobby, my mechanical skills approach nil."

"You can hot-wire cars."

Another chuckle. "Yes, I suppose there's that. As for the motorcycles, one of my mother's boyfriends got me started restoring them when I was Savannah's age. At first, I must admit, I took it up in hopes it would add a certain cachet to my social life."

"You hoped it would help you pick up chicks. Did it?"

"Hardly. I quickly outgrew that notion. Or so I thought, though I must admit that part of my motivation in choosing to take the motorcycle to the funeral home was a semiconscious desire to present myself in a more attractive light."

"I was very impressed."

He fell back onto the sheets and laughed, startling me. "Oh, I could tell. You were *very* impressed. About as impressed as you were when you discovered I was the son of an infamous Cabal CEO."

"The heir to an infamous Cabal CEO."

I said it teasingly, but the humor drained from his eyes. He nodded and reached for the wine bottle.

"I'm sorry," I said. "New topic. So, where do you live?"

"Back to the heir question first. It's true and it's not a subject I want to avoid. I want to be honest with you, Paige. I want—" He hesitated. "My father has very good reasons for naming me heir, reasons that have noth-ing to do with me and everything to do with the politics of succession and keeping my older brothers in line."

"A purely strategic decision? I can't believe that."

"My father harbors some delusions regarding the nature of my rebel-lion. He's wrong. I will never be the employee—or leader—of any Cabal. Nor am I naive enough to take the reins of leadership in hopes of reform-ing it into a legitimate business."

"Is it true—" I shook my head. "Sorry, I don't mean to pry—"

"It's not prying, Paige. I'd be far more concerned if you didn't care. Ask away. Please."

"About the bounty. Is it true? I mean, if you're in danger—"

"I'm not. Or, if I am, it's a permanent situation and nothing that impacts the present circumstances. No one in Nast's organization would dare collect such a reward. Let me say, first, that Leah has a tendency to get her facts confused. My father's wife and my three half-brothers do not all have contracts out on me. Last I heard, only Delores and my eldest brother were offering bounties. Carlos, the youngest, did at one time, but recent debts have forced him to withdraw the offer. As for William, he's never tried to hire anyone to kill me, probably because he hasn't the wits to think of it."

"Are you serious?"

"About William? Unfortunately. He's intelligent enough, but lacks initiative."

I bumped his shoulder. "Ha-ha. You know what I mean. The bounty. You're serious?"

"Quite, though I wouldn't suggest you mention it to my father. He's convinced he cleared this matter up years ago. Killing the bastard heir is absolutely forbidden. Any family member caught attempting it will be severely punished. He tried threatening them with death, but that didn't work, so he revised it to the worst possible fate: disinheritance."

"You guys raise the dysfunctional family to a whole new level, don't you?"

"The Cortezes have always been overachievers."

We passed the bottle again.

"You asked where I lived," he said.

"Right."

"I believe the standard expression for my situation is 'no fixed address.' Since graduating, I haven't been in one place long enough to even sublet an apartment. My work—legal and otherwise—keeps me on the move. With my extracurricular activities, I'm obviously ill suited for a steady job at a law firm. Instead, I do piecemeal legal work for supernaturals."

"Lawyer to the paranormal."

"Almost as bad as 'superhero,' isn't it? It provides me enough to live on, no more and no less. More importantly, it gives me the opportunity to do what I really want."

"Save the world?"

"Something which I'm sure you know nothing about."

"Hey, I don't want to save the *whole* world. Just my corner of it."

He laughed and tightened his arms around me. We kissed for a few minutes, then I reluctantly pulled back.

"I want to know more," I said. "About you, about what you do. But I suppose we should get some sleep."

"Probably. If these last two days have been any indication, we'll need our rest." He reached over and retrieved his glasses, then looked at me.

"Any chance we can avoid separate sleeping quarters tonight? I know Savannah's presence is a concern—"

"One easily handled by a locking spell or two."

The next morning I awoke to find myself alone. At first I thought Cortez slipped out in the night and returned to the sofa. Which would be a bad sign. But, as I stretched, I noticed his side of the bed was still warm.

I glanced at the clock. Eleven A.M.? I hadn't slept this late since college. No wonder Cortez was up.

I tumbled from bed, still groggy, pulled on my kimono, and headed for the bathroom. The door was ajar, so I gave it a shove and whacked it against Cortez, who was bent over the sink, shaving.

"Sorry," he said.

"For what? Standing near a door?"

A small smile. "For leaving the door open, thereby causing you to believe the room was vacant." He waved to the mirror, which was fogged from his shower. "I opened it for some air. I couldn't find the—"

I flicked a switch outside the door and a whoosh filled the room.

"Ah, the fan," he said.

"Lousy setup," I said. "I'll be in my room. Just knock when you're done."

Before I could leave, he grabbed my arm, tugged me inside, and closed the door. Then he pulled me against him and lowered his mouth to mine. Well, that certainly alleviated any "morning after" awkwardness.

I kissed him back, wrapping my hands around his neck. Tendrils of damp hair tickled my fingers. The clean tang of soap filled my nose. When my tongue slipped into his mouth, I tasted mint. Toothpaste.

I jerked back and slapped my hand over my mouth. "I have to brush my teeth." As I spun to face the mirror, I caught sight of my hair, which frizzed out in a way that could only be called "witchy." "Shit! My hair!"

Cortez wrapped a handful around his fist and bent to kiss my neck. "I love your hair."

"Which is more than you can say for my breath."

As I reached for the toothpaste, he turned me around.

"Your breath is fine."

Then, as if to prove it, he kissed me again, deeper this time, lifting me up onto the counter and pressing against me. I slid my fingers under his open shirt, to push it off his shoulders, but he caught my hands.

"This, I believe, is my seduction," he said. "Not, of course, that I wish to discourage you from taking the initiative in future. Nor to discourage you from disrobing me or from disrobing yourself, particularly in the . . . enchanting fashion you employed last night. But—"

"Are you seducing me or talking about it?"

He grinned. "I could talk about it, if you like. In terms perhaps more amenable to the situation."

"Tempting," I said. "Very tempting. If I wasn't worried about Savannah waking up—"

"Quite right," he said. "There will be plenty of time for talk later."

His mouth came down to mine as he undid my sash. He slipped his hands inside my kimono, and traced his fingers up my sides, slowly, then moved to cup my breasts. As his thumbs found my nipples, I arched my back and moaned.

Something hit the door, hard enough that we both jumped, me falling into his arms.

"Is someone in there?" Savannah said between pounds.

Cortez looked at me. I motioned for him to answer.

"I am," he said.

"Are you almost done?"

"Umm, no, I'm afraid not, Savannah. I'm just starting."

"Oh, geez," she groaned.

The door creaked, followed by a rasp and a thump as she dropped to the floor. Cortez exhaled and shook his head. We waited another minute. Not only didn't Savannah leave, but her noises of impatience escalated in frequency and volume.

Cortez leaned down to my ear. "Are you sure you *want* to keep her?"

I smiled, shook my head, and waved him toward the door.

"What about you?" he mouthed.

I slid off the counter, then backed into the corner by the toilet and cast a cover spell. Cortez nodded, then opened the door.

"Finally!" Savannah said. "There's only one bathroom here, you know."

He brushed past her without a word, footsteps echoing down the hall.

"Grouchy this morning, aren't we," she called after him.

Savannah closed the door and proceeded to her urgent business. That business, contrary to what one might expect, had nothing to do with the toilet. First she brushed her hair—with my brush. Then she sampled some new lipstick—my lipstick. Then she rooted around under the cupboard and pulled out my hidden stash of high-priced shampoo and conditioner. Hair products which, may I point out, were intended for curly hair. Finally, she grabbed my French perfume and sprayed it around as if it was air freshener. I had to bite my lip to keep from yelping.

Next, a shower. As Savannah began to undress, I averted my eyes, shifting my gaze all the way to the right. After several minutes in that position, my eyes began to water. When I finally had to glance back, she was standing in front of the mirror, just standing there, looking at herself and frowning. I looked away again.

"Well, I'm a woman now," she muttered to her reflection. "Hurry up and do something." She snorted. "What a rip-off."

With that she stamped to the shower and got in. When the water began, I eased from my hiding spot and darted to the door, then stopped, stepped back, did a quick swish with mouthwash, and left.

After dressing, I walked into the kitchen to find Cortez surveying the fridge. He looked up when I entered, glanced behind me for Savannah, then pulled me in for a kiss.

"Last one for today, I presume," he said, then sniffed. "You smell nice."

"Not intentionally," I muttered. "My mom always said never to use the cover spell to spy on someone or you might see something you don't want to. Well, I just learned why my shampoo and perfume disappear so fast. And now I know why my friends always complained about their siblings using their stuff." I grabbed the fridge door. "Did you get that growing up?"

"No," he said, as I peered into the nearly empty fridge. "I was an only child, like you."

I paused, confused. I knew he had three older brothers—oh, wait. I recalled what Leah said about his parentage, that he was . . . Words failed me. Oh, I knew a few. Illegitimate, conceived out of wedlock, plus the "B" word, which I wouldn't mention, even if Cortez had used it himself. Everything sounded so negative, so archaic. Maybe the terms were archaic because there was no need for such a designation at all. If a child is conceived during an extramarital affair, the burden for any questionable judgment rests with the parents, not the child. In the twenty-first century, we should be enlightened enough to realize that. Yet, by the way Leah had brought it up, such a casually tossed barb, I knew it wasn't something the rest of the Cabal world let Cortez forget.

"Not much in there," he said, looking over my shoulder. "If the eggs are still good, I could make an omelet. Yes, I know I made that yesterday, but my repertoire is exceedingly limited. It's that or, possibly, a hard-boiled egg, though I have been known to boil them into golf balls."

"You've done enough. I've got breakfast. Eggs, pancakes, or French toast?" I glanced at the bread, the edges blooming a lovely shade of periwinkle. "Forget the French toast."

"Whatever is easiest."

"Pancakes," Savannah said as she swung into the kitchen.

"You set the table, then, and I'll cook."

CHAPTER 40

THE VOTE

By the time breakfast—or should I say brunch—ended, it was past noon. Cortez insisted on cleaning up and also insisted on Savannah's help. I took my mug of coffee and was heading into the living room when the phone rang. Cortez checked the call display.

"Victoria Alden," he said. "Shall we let the machine pick up?"

"No, I'll get it. After the last few days, Victoria is one problem I can handle."

"Hello, Victoria," I said as I picked up the phone.

Silence.

"Call display, remember?" I said. "Great invention."

"You sound very cheerful this morning, Paige."

"I am. The crowd's gone. The media has stopped calling. Things are definitely looking up."

"So stealing Margaret's car and leading the police through a cemetery last night are things you would consider to be an improvement in your current situation?"

"Oh, that was nothing. We were very careful, Victoria. The police won't know it was me. They haven't even called."

"I'm phoning concerning the future of one of our Coven members."

I paused, then winced, my euphoria fading. "Oh, geez. It's Kylie, isn't it? She's decided not to stay with the Coven. Look, I've been talking to her and I'll speak to her again when all this is over."

"This isn't about Kylie. It's about you."

"Me?"

"After hearing of your latest escapade, we called an emergency Coven meeting this morning. You've been banished from the Coven, Paige."

"What—you—" Words dried up in my throat.

"The vote was eight to three with two abstaining. The Coven has decided."

"N—no," I said. "Eight to three? That can't be. You rigged it. You must have—"

"Call Abigail, if you wish. I'm sure she is one of the three who voted to allow you to stay. She'll tell you it was a fair and open count. You know the rules of banishment, Paige. You have thirty days to leave East Falls and you are prohibited from taking any of your mother's—"

"No!" I shouted. "No!"

I slammed down the phone. Without turning, I sensed Cortez behind me.

"They banished me," I whispered. "They voted to kick me out of the Coven."

If he replied, I didn't hear it. Blood crashed in my ears. Somehow I managed to cross the three steps to the recliner and drop into it. Cortez sat on the armrest, but I turned away from him. No one could understand what this meant to me and I didn't want anyone to try. As he bent over me, his lips moved, and I braced myself against the inevitable "I'm sorry."

Instead he said, "They're wrong."

I looked up at him. He leaned down and brushed the hair from my face, using the movement to stroke my cheek with his thumb.

"They're wrong, Paige."

I buried my face against his side and began to sob.

I knew the Elders were beyond help. All the older witches were. They were set in their ways and their beliefs, and I could do little to change that. I wouldn't waste my time trying. Instead, I wanted to focus on the younger generation, the ones like Kylie, who was heading off to college this fall and seriously contemplating breaking with the Coven.

Save the younger generation and let the older one wither away. From there, I could reform the Coven, make it a place witches came to, not escaped from. Once the Coven had regained its strength and vitality, we could reach out to other witches, offer training and fellowship and a powerful alternative to those, like Eve, who saw power only in dark magic. I'd make the Coven more flexible, more adaptable, more attractive, better suited to fulfilling the needs of all witches. A grand plan, to be sure. Maybe not one I could even realize in my lifetime. But I could start it. I could try.

This was more than a vision; it was the embodiment of every hope I'd had since I'd been old enough to form hopes. I couldn't imagine leaving the Coven. Literally could not envision it. Never at anytime in my life had I wondered what life would be like outside the Coven. I'd never dreamed of living outside Massachusetts. I'd never dreamed of falling in love and marrying. I'd never even dreamed of children. The Coven was my dream and I'd never considered anything that would interfere with that mission.

So what was I to do now? Roll over and cry? Let the Elders drive me away? Never. When the initial pain of being banished subsided, I stepped back for a logical assessment of the situation. So the Coven had kicked me out. They were scared. Reacting to an age-old fear instilled in them by Victoria and her cronies. Terrified of exposure, they took the easiest route—rid themselves of the cause of that threat. The people of East Falls had done the same thing with their petition. Once the danger passed, both would welcome me back. Well, maybe "welcome" is optimistic, but they'd allow me to stay, in the town and in the Coven. With the right amount of will and determination, anything can be fixed.

"Wh—where's Savannah?" I said, drying my eyes.

"In the kitchen. Making tea, I believe."

I pulled myself upright. "Seems everyone's been doing a lot of that lately. Taking care of Paige."

"Hardly. You—"

"I appreciate it, but I'm okay," I said, squeezing his hand as I got to my feet. "We've got things to do today. For starters, I should go through Savannah's ceremony with her. I know it's still a week away, but I want to make sure she remembers everything Eve told her and that we have all the ingredients."

He nodded. "Good idea. While you do that, if you don't mind, I'll toss my other set of clothing in the laundry."

"Oh, that's right. You've only got the two sets. Here, give me your dirty clothes—"

"I've got it, Paige. You go on with Savannah."

"Later, we should get your bags from the motel and bring them back here." I paused. "That is, if we're staying here. We should discuss that, too."

He nodded and I walked to the kitchen doorway. Savannah looked up from measuring tea.

"Leave that, hon," I said. "Thanks for thinking of me, but I'm fine. How about we run through that ceremony of your mom's, make sure I get it right?"

"Sure."

"Let me get my stuff, then, and we'll head downstairs."

Savannah followed me into my room. As I pulled my knapsack from its hiding place, the window smashed behind me. Savannah screamed and I wheeled around just as a football-sized rock crashed into the far wall. It hit the throw rug, rolling once and leaving a trail of red. Thinking it was blood, I spun to face Savannah, but she was running to the window, unharmed.

"Get away from there!" I yelled.

"I want to see who threw—"

"No!"

I grabbed her arm and wrenched her back. As I turned, I saw a word smeared in red paint on the large rock: BURN.

I dragged Savannah from the room as Cortez came sprinting from the kitchen.

"I was in the basement," he said. "What happened?"

I grabbed the phone and dialed 911 as Savannah explained about the rock. Cortez's face went grim and he marched to the kitchen window to look out back. As I was telling the 911 dispatcher what had happened, he took the phone from me.

"Get the fire department here now," he said to the 911 operator. "Police and fire. Immediately."

While he gave details, I ran to the window. My shed was engulfed in flames, fueled by the gasoline for the lawn mower and God knew what other flammable liquids.

Suddenly the shed exploded. The boom resounded through the house. When the next crash came, I thought it was still the shed—until shards of glass hit my face and something struck my shoulder.

Cortez yelled and dove at me, grabbing the back of my shirt and yanking me backward so hard I flew off my feet. As he pulled me from the kitchen, I saw what had hit me. A bottle stuffed with a flaming rag. I was barely out of the room when whatever filled the bottle ignited. A ball of fire flared, filling my kitchen with flame and smoke.

"Savannah, get down!" Cortez shouted. "Crawl to the door!"

From the back of the house, I heard another window break. My office! Oh, God, all my work was in there. As I wrenched free of Cortez's grasp, I remembered what other room was at the back of the house and what even more precious contents it held.

"My room! The ceremony material and the grimoires."

Cortez tried to grab me, but I lunged out of his reach. Sirens and shouts sounded, nearly drowned out by the crackle of fire. Two steps from my room, a cloud of smoke hit me. I reeled back, gagging. Instinctively I breathed deeper, gasping for air and filling my lungs with smoke. After a split second of animal panic, sense returned and I dropped onto all fours and crawled into my room.

My bed looked like a demonic fire-beast, a four-legged mass of flame, devouring everything within reach. A gust of wind billowed through the broken window, blowing smoke into my face and blinding me. I continued forward, moving from memory, fingers outstretched. I found the knapsack first and wrapped the straps around one hand as the other continued to search. When I touched the edge of the trapdoor, I stopped and began feeling around it. My fingers connected with the white-hot metal of the clasp and I jerked away, backing into the flaming throw rug.

For one moment, it was too much. The ancient fear of fire gnawed away reason, filling my brain with the smell, sound, taste, and feel of the flames. I froze, unable to move, certain I would die here, condemned to a witch's death. The horror of that thought—the very idea of curling up and surrendering to fear—restored my senses.

Ignoring the pain, I flipped the clasp and opened the trapdoor. A moment later, I had the second knapsack. I seized the straps, yanked it from the cubbyhole, and started to creep backward, crab-like, toward the door. I'd barely gone two feet when Cortez grabbed my ankle and dragged me out.

"That way," he said, pushing me forward. "To the door. Don't stand up. Oh, shit!"

He tackled me, knocking me to the floor just as I felt flames lick my calves. As he beat at flames on my back, I twisted to see that the hem of my skirt had also ignited. I kicked against the wall, but the sharp movement only made the flames burn brighter. Cortez slapped out the fire with his hands. Then he grabbed the knapsacks from my hand.

"I have them," he said. "Don't look back. Just keep moving."

I started forward. The rear of the house was ablaze. Tongues of fire licked across the house toward the front and, when I passed the living room, I turned to see the drapes ignite. Breathing through my mouth, I pushed forward, willing myself to crawl over small pockets of fire in my path. At the front hall, I paused to glance over my shoulder for Cortez. He waved me forward. I crawled to the open back door and toppled outside.

A man in a uniform caught me and shoved a cloth over my nose and mouth. I inhaled a deep breath of something cold and metallic. I grabbed the man's arm, gesturing that I could breathe without medical help. Above me, his face wobbled out of focus. I wrenched around, looking behind me for Cortez. I saw the open doorway and empty hall. Then my limbs gave way and everything went black.

CHAPTER 41

PACKAGE DEAL

I awoke with a headache that felt like a chisel striking behind my eyes. When I lifted my head, bile rushed to my mouth and I hunched over, gagging and spitting. Every time I tried to rise, nausea forced me down. Finally I gave up and collapsed.

Where was I? When I opened my eyes, I saw only darkness. The last thing I remembered was drifting off to sleep with Cortez beside me. Flashes of nightmare illuminated the darkness. The taste of smoke made me retch again. As I did, my fingers clenched the sheets and I hesitated, running my thumb over the cloth. These weren't my sheets.

"Cortez?" I shifted onto my side. "Lucas?"

As I squinted into the darkness, my eyes adjusted enough to make out shapes. Another twin bed to my left. A nightstand beside me. I reached for the light and flicked the switch, but nothing happened. My fingers crept to the bulb and found an empty socket. I jumped up, stomach lurching with the sudden movement.

Across the room Savannah muttered in her sleep.

"Savannah?"

She made a noise, half-stirring.

The door swung open. A woman stood in the entrance, illuminated by the hall light. I blinked twice but my eyes wouldn't focus.

"Finally. We thought you girls were going to sleep all day."

With that voice, my heart stopped. *Leah.* I flung myself from the bed and tried to locate Savannah but my legs buckled under me and I fell to the carpet.

"Stay in bed," a man's voice said. "You won't be ready to walk yet."

I tried to push myself up from the floor, but couldn't. Leah and her partner stood outside the door, neither making any move to help me. A staccato series of beeps filled the silence, then the man murmured something.

"A cell phone?" Leah said when he finished the call. "Jesus, Friesen. He's in the next room."

"Standard communication procedure. Mr. Nast wants to see them immediately."

The man—Friesen—moved into the light and I recognized him as the "paramedic" who'd helped me out of the burning house. Early thirties, dirty blond brush cut, with the oversized build of a quarterback and the misshapen face of a boxer.

But who was Nast? I should have known, but my brain wouldn't focus any better than my eyes. I repeated the name in my head, my stomach clenching with each iteration. Nast was . . . wrong. Someone I didn't want to meet. My gut told me that. But . . .

"My throat hurts," Savannah said.

"We'll get you a cold drink in a sec, kiddo," Leah said. "You just lie there and relax."

Savannah. Nast. The connection fired. Savannah's father. Kristof Nast. Oh, God.

"Sa—Savannah?" I managed, struggling to my feet. "I have to ta—talk to you, hon."

"No talking," Friesen said. "Mr. Nast will want her to save her energy."

I made it to Savannah's bed and sat down on the edge. I had to swallow several times before my throat would open. "Nast is—" I stopped, realizing I couldn't just blurt it out. She needed to know more. "Kristof Nast. He's a sorcerer. He's the head . . . no, the son of the head of the Nast Cabal."

She blinked. "Like Lucas?"

"No, not like Lucas." At the mention of Cortez's name, I remembered the last time I'd seen him, crawling behind me in the burning house. I hadn't seen him get out. Had they—? Oh, God. I swallowed hard and tried not to think of that. "The Nast Cabal—"

"Enough," Leah said. "If you haven't told her by now, we should leave it for a surprise. Do you like surprises, Savannah?"

Savannah glared at her. "Don't talk to me."

"Savannah, there's something else—" I began.

"Nope," Leah said, grabbing my shoulders and propelling me off the bed. "It's gonna be a surprise. Trust me, kiddo, you're gonna love this one. You've hit the genetic jackpot."

Before I could argue, Friesen lifted Savannah up, ignoring her protests, and took her from the room. Leah followed. I stood there, staring at the partly open door, waiting for it to close. A moment later, Leah popped her head back in.

"Those drugs make you stupid, girl?" she said. "Come on."

I only looked at her.

"I told them they OD'd on the stuff," she said. "What are you waiting for? Shackles and chains? You aren't a prisoner here. Nast wanted to talk to Savannah and this was the only way he figured he could do it."

"So . . . so I can leave here? I'm free to go?"

"Oh, sure." She grinned. "If you don't mind leaving Savannah behind." She disappeared. I followed.

Nast may have been "in the next room" as Leah said, but he must have decided to hold the meeting elsewhere because we headed downstairs, taking a circuitous route to the living room.

During the walk, my mind cleared. My head and throat still felt like they were stuffed with cotton, but at least I could think and take in my surroundings. We were in a house. A farmhouse, judging by the vista outside the windows. The windows were unbarred, some even propped open. We passed a front and side door and neither Leah nor her partner so much as glanced back to see if I'd make a break for it. They didn't need to. As long as they had Savannah, I wasn't going anywhere.

Any hope that I could still tell Savannah about Nast vanished when we walked into the living room. Sandford stood by the fireplace. Seated next to him was a tall man with thinning blond hair and broad shoulders. As we entered, he turned and smiled, and I found myself looking into an exact replica of Savannah's big blue eyes. My heart dropped and I knew then that Kristof Nast was indeed Savannah's father.

"Savannah," he said. "You have no idea how long I've waited for this."

"Tell this guy to let me go!" She wriggled, trying to get free. "Put me down. *Now!*"

Nast waved for Friesen to release Savannah. "My apologies, princess." He chuckled and glanced at Sandford. "Still any doubt she's mine?"

"I'm not yours," Savannah said, pulling her shirt into place. "Not yours. Not hers." She jabbed a finger at Leah. "Not anyone's. Now take me home or there's going to be trouble."

"Savannah, hon," I said. "I need to tell you something. Remember I was telling you about Kristof Nast—"

"This is him?" Her gaze raked over Nast, dismissing him with a snort. "He's the CEO's son? He's what, fifty? By the time he takes over, he'll be ready to retire."

"I'm forty-seven, actually," Nast said with an indulgent smile. "But I take your point. All the better for you, then, isn't it?"

"Isn't what?"

"If I'm so old. All the quicker to get your inheritance."

"Why? What are you, sorcerer? My mom's lawyer?"

Nast looked at me. "You haven't told her?"

"Savannah," I said. "This is—"

"I'm your father," Nast said.

He smiled and reached for Savannah. She jumped back, arms flying up to ward him off. She looked from me to Nast, then back to me.

"That's not funny," she said.

"Savannah, I—" I began.

"No one's joking, Savannah," Nast said. "I know this must come as a shock, but you are my daughter. Your mother—"

"No," she said, voice quiet. She turned to me. "You would have told me, right?"

"I—" I shook my head. "I'm so sorry, hon. We don't know for sure. Mr. Nast claims he's your father. I couldn't believe that. I wanted proof before I told you."

Nast laid a hand on Savannah's arm. When she flung him off, he bent to her height.

"I know you're angry, princess. This wasn't how I planned this. I thought you knew."

"I . . . I don't believe it."

"You don't have to. Now that we've moved beyond human courts, we can clear this up with a simple blood test. I've arranged for our doctors to conduct the test as soon as we get back to California."

"California?" Savannah said. "I can't—I'm not—I won't go. I won't."

"My apologies, I'm getting ahead of myself. I'm not taking you anywhere against your will, Savannah. This isn't a kidnapping. I'm sorry I had to resort to such drastic measures to get you here, but I feared it was the only way Paige would allow me to present my case."

"Case?" she said.

"For custody."

She looked from me to him. "We're going to court?"

He laughed. "No, thank God. I've decided to circumvent the horrors of the legal system. No human judge can decide where you belong, Savannah. No person can decide that. It's your life and it should be your decision."

"Good. Then I'm staying with Paige."

"Don't I get to argue my side? Paige has had nearly a year to make her case. Surely you can grant me thirty minutes to make mine. That's all I ask, princess. Thirty minutes to explain why you should stay with me."

"And if I don't want to?"

"Then you're free to go back to East Falls with Paige."

"Bullshit," I said.

Nast looked up, startled, as if the walls had spoken. When he turned to me, his gaze focused somewhere above my head, as if I was literally beneath his notice.

"You doubt my word, Paige?" All indulgent humor drained from his voice. "I'm a Nast. My word is inviolable."

I felt the weight of Savannah's gaze on me. In that moment, I realized what I had to do. I had to shut my mouth. Nast was right. This was her choice. Coven or Cabal. White magic or dark. If I swayed her decision, I'd always feel the pull of the other side working against me. Let her hear what Nast was offering and she'd see that Eve had made the right decision in sending her to the Coven. Though I doubted Nast would let her leave that easily, I'd jump that hurdle when it came. If I dragged her out kicking and screaming, I'd lose her forever.

Before stating his case, Nast insisted on feeding us. He'd ordered pizza. He even had a delivery guy bring it, further underscoring the point that we weren't being held captive at some top-secret location.

Though Leah and Friesen shared in our meal, Nast looked at the pizza as if expecting the mushrooms to start crawling. He assured us, as if we cared, that he'd be eating lunch later, at a business meeting in Boston.

So we were still in Massachusetts? As I thought this, I realized he'd said lunch, not dinner or supper. With that came the shock that we'd slept through Wednesday and had been gone now nearly twenty-four hours. Again, I thought of Cortez, but I knew there was no sense asking. They'd only tell us what we wanted to hear.

"Can we get started?" Savannah said. "The pizza's great and all that, but I want to get this over with."

Nast nodded. "First, let me say that your mother was a remarkable woman and I loved her very much. It just . . . it didn't work out for us. After you were born, she asked me to stay away, so I did, but I always planned to be part of your life someday. With your mother's death, that's happened earlier than I expected."

"How come she never mentioned you to me?"

"I have no idea, Savannah."

"Get on with your case, then, so I can go home."

Nast reclined without putting a single rumple in his suit. "Well, I hardly know where to start. Do you understand how a Cabal is organized?"

"Sort of."

Nast gave her a quick rundown, concentrating on the importance of the head sorcerer family. "As my daughter, you would be an important part of that family, with all the rights and privileges that entails."

"May I ask a question?" I said.

"I don't think—"

"It's a reasonable question," I said. "I'm not challenging or disagreeing with anything. I just want to clarify a point. As I understand it, sorcerers typically have only sons, meaning Savannah would be the only girl—or woman—in the family. How would that impact her position?"

"It wouldn't." Nast paused, then said, "Let me expand on that. I want to be completely forthcoming with you, Savannah. Within our Cabal, the Nast family's power is absolute. If we say you are to be accepted, you will be. Now, as regards matters of succession, there would likely be some dispute over whether you could inherit leadership. However, that point is moot. I have two very capable sons, and the oldest has already been named as my heir."

"So what do I get?" she asked.

"Everything else." He shifted forward, leaning toward her. "I'm a very wealthy, very powerful man, Savannah. One who can give you everything you've ever wanted. I'm sure Paige has done her best, but she can't offer you the advantages I can. More than money, Savannah. I'm talking about opportunity. Access to the best tutors, the best spellbooks, the best materials."

"Sure. In return for my immortal soul. I'm not a dumb little kid, sorcerer. I know why you grabbed me. Because of the ceremony."

My heart shot into my throat and I motioned her to silence.

"It's quite all right, Paige. We've been aware of Savannah's menses since yesterday morning."

"Before you grabbed us?" I said. "Who told you?"

"We can discuss that later. The point is—"

"The point is," Savannah said. "That you grabbed me so you can change the ceremony and make me a Cabal slave."

"Cabal slave?" Nast laughed. "Is that what Paige told you?"

"It wasn't Paige."

"Ah, Lucas, I presume. Well, as much as I respect the Cortezes, I must say that Lucas Cortez is a very confused young man. He's had some . . . unfortunate experiences with Cabal life and has formed some rather wild opinions. As for the ceremony—"

"Wait," Savannah said. "I want to know about Lucas first. Is he okay?"

"He's fine, Savannah. Now—"

"What happened to him?"

"We delayed his escape, but not unduly. Last time we saw Lucas, he was in the hands of the paramedics. Unconscious from smoke inhalation, but otherwise uninjured."

As he spoke, Savannah kept darting concerned glances at me, taking in my reaction. Gabriel Sandford followed those glances with interest.

"So you didn't hurt him?" she said.

"Harming Lucas Cortez would cause a diplomatic incident of epic proportions. Killing him would start a blood feud the likes of which the Cabals haven't seen in over a century. A Cabal son has absolute immunity. That's what I'm offering you, Savannah. You'll never need to hide again."

He paused, checking to see if he had her full attention now. He did.

"About the ceremony," he continued. "Yes, there is a version that enhances a witch's employability in a Cabal, though it's a far cry from enslavement. You won't undergo that, though. There are several other ceremonies you can choose from—"

"I want the one Paige was going to do. The one my mother wanted."

"Done."

She blinked, then recovered and sat straighter. "And I want Paige to do it. No one else."

"Done." Nast stood and crossed the room to sit beside her. "I'm your father, Savannah. I want what's best for you and, in matters of witchcraft, I trust your mother's judgment. If you wish to have a more experienced witch perform the ceremony, I'll provide that. But if you want Paige, that's fine. She can stay with you until next Wednesday and she'll perform the ceremony your mother chose for you."

"Then what will happen to Paige? After the ceremony?"

"She'll be free to go."

Savannah slanted me a look. "What if I don't want her to go?"

Nast hesitated. "I'm sure Paige has her own responsibilities with the Coven—"

"They kicked her out. They're all stupid and useless. She's too good for them anyway. If I stay, Paige stays. She can be my tutor."

"No offense to Paige, but we have far superior teachers of witchcraft."

"Then she'll be my companion or my nanny or something. That's what rich kids have, isn't it? Servants? I want Paige. She stays with me and she gets to learn everything I learn."

"I don't think—"

"Package deal," Savannah said. "Take it or leave it."

He took it.

CHAPTER 42

MR. NAST'S WITCH

"I didn't mean it," Savannah said after we'd returned to our bedroom, which had now been equipped with a working light. "About the servant part. I was just saying that."

I barely heard her. I couldn't remember the walk back to the room, couldn't remember who'd brought us or what they'd said. All I could hear was Savannah's voice, accepting Nast's proposition.

"You're mad at me, aren't you?"

"No, I'm not mad. Just . . . confused. It's a lot to take in. I'm sorry I didn't tell you earlier, about him claiming to be your father."

"Things got pretty crazy. You wanted proof first. I guess I understand that."

The truth was, I'd held back out of fear that something like this would happen, that Nast would breeze in and offer Savannah the world. In failing to tell her, I'd lost my chance to warn her. Anything I said now would seem churlish, disgruntled lies woven to sway her to my side. Even as she bounced around the room, chattering, I could feel her slipping away. As Nast said, I'd had nearly a year to make my case. Why hadn't I done a better job? She'd called the Coven stupid and useless. That's the alternative I'd shown her—a world where witches were stupid and useless.

I knew I should stay silent, let her see things for herself, but it took every bit of restraint to keep from shaking her and shouting "What are you doing?" Instead, I settled onto the bed before saying, "I'm glad you want me around, Savannah, but you know I can't do this. I'm Coven Leader. I can't just leave—"

"They kicked you out!"

"Yes, they're angry, but—"

"You said you'd stay with me. You promised."

"I know and I will, but—"

"Well, this is my decision. I want to be here and if you want to help me, you have to stay."

She plopped onto the opposite bed, turned her back to me, and crossed her arms. We sat like that for a few minutes. A few times she half-turned, as if waiting for me to argue. When I didn't, she twisted to face me.

"Don't be mad, Paige," she said. "Did you hear what he said? The best tutors, the best books, the best materials. I'll get all that and I'll share it with you. Isn't that what you wanted?"

I didn't answer.

"You're worried because it's a Cabal, right?" she continued. "I know what Lucas said, but, well, maybe he—my—Nast is right. Not that Lucas is lying. I don't mean that. But he could be confused. Maybe he saw some really bad stuff. Stuff that doesn't normally happen."

Again, I said nothing.

"Fine. Be that way. Go back to stupid little East Falls, to your burned-down house. I won't go. They don't want us there. Every time you walk down the street, people are going to be pointing and saying stuff. Well, they won't say stuff about me. I'll be in California. I bet Adam will come visit me. He won't be like this."

"I'll stay with you, Savannah. You know I will."

She hesitated, then smiled and leaned across the beds to hug me. "It's going to be okay, Paige. You just watch. This will be the best thing that's ever happened to us."

Still drowsy from the drugs, we dozed for an hour or so. Then a knock at the door woke us both. A woman peeked through.

"May we come in?" she asked.

Without waiting for a response, she pushed open the door and walked in. She was in her early forties, more handsome than pretty, with an angular jaw and a salt-and-pepper brush cut. Behind her was another woman, about twenty years older, with the same jawline and silver hair cut in a stylish bob.

"I'm Greta Enwright," the younger woman said. "This is my mother, Olivia."

"Livy, please," the older woman said. "We're so pleased to meet you. Both of you." She bustled in behind her daughter and laid a silver tray on the nightstand. "I know your mother liked her tea, Paige. I took a chance on guessing you'd developed the same tastes."

I blinked. "You knew my mother?"

"From years back. More years than I care to count." A tinkling, girlish laugh. "I grew up in the Coven. My mother left when I was a teenager."

"You're—you're a witch?"

"Oh, I'm so sorry. An incomplete introduction, Greta. I've always thought that strange, that we should be able to recognize sorcerers but not our own sisters. Greta is Mr. Nast's witch." Another laugh. "That sounds perfectly horrible, doesn't it? And much too familiar. Cabals, as you may know, have only one witch. A very prestigious and exclusive position, which I was fortunate enough to be able to pass on to Greta when I retired. And now—" She turned a broad smile on Savannah. "We meet our official successor. I can't tell you how pleased we are."

Savannah hesitated, and looked from mother to daughter. "You're not mad? I mean, I'll be replacing you, won't I?"

Greta laughed, a throaty chuckle that was the very opposite of her mother's. "It'll be some years before you're ready for that, Savannah. By then, I'll be ready to retire myself. An early retirement, most likely, but Mr. Nast has promised me a full pension. If anything, I should be thanking you."

Olivia nodded. "And Mr. Nast has brought me out of retirement to help you get adjusted, for which he is more than adequately compensating me, so I should be thanking you as well."

"You guys'll be teaching us?"

"Us?" Greta repeated.

"Her," I said. "So you'll be her tutors?"

"In witch magic only," Olivia said. "For the rest, you'll have proper tutors. Sorcerers, I mean. They have the true magic."

"Maybe not for long," Savannah said, jumping from the bed. "Paige has these grimoires—"

I tried to stop her, but only halfheartedly. As much as I wanted to keep the grimoires secret, I was curious to hear the opinion of these women. I'd never met a Cabal witch. I'd expected—let's be honest, I expected them to be a lot different, more intimidating, more dangerous, more, well, evil.

Savannah told them about the grimoires and our theory.

"Of course, Paige still has to test it," she said. "We could be wrong."

I refrained from telling the other witches that I *had* tested them, successfully. For now, better to keep that to myself.

"It sounds promising," Greta said. "But I wouldn't get my hopes up, ladies. Sorcerer magic is the magic of power. With all respect to women and equal rights, witch magic just doesn't measure up."

"I wouldn't waste my time on it," Olivia said. "Your tutors will teach you everything you need to know. As for those grimoires, I doubt they survived the fire."

"No, Paige went back for them." Savannah stopped and turned to me. "Where are they?"

"Cor—Lucas had them. I gave them to him."

"Lucas Cortez?" Olivia said. "Oh, my, that's right. I heard young Lucas was involved. He has quite the reputation, but we've never had the chance to meet him, have we, Greta? That must have been quite an experience. You'll have to tell us all about him. Let me pour the tea first."

Once the tea was poured, we sat on the edge of the bed. Olivia asked about Cortez. I let Savannah reply, discreetly cutting her short after a few sentences.

"Oh, he is an odd one," Olivia said, clucking. "I feel so sorry for his father. Mr. Cortez is handling the situation remarkably well, though I must say, he lets the boy get away with far too much. All parents do, don't they? A Cabal leader is no different from any father. You'll see that, Savannah. Mr. Nast dotes on his boys and I'm sure he'll treat you just the same."

"As for Lucas Cortez," Greta said, "young men are always looking for dragons to slay. And pretty damsels to rescue." She slid a smile my way. "It's only a stage. Soon he'll come to see that Cabals aren't the monsters he thinks they are."

"What are they?" Savannah asked. "I mean, what are they really like?"

"Excellent employers," Greta said. "Everything an employee could ask for. They offer comprehensive benefits, stock options, a solid pension plan, and excellent remuneration."

Olivia laughed. "None of which interests you in the least, does it, Savannah? And with good reason. You won't ever need to worry about those things. Your biggest concerns now will be whether you want to spend your summer vacation in France or Italy."

"And what kind of sports car you want for your sixteenth birthday," Greta added.

"I want a Porsche," Savannah said, turning to me with a grin. "A Porsche convertible, like Clay's. Only red. I want it in red."

"You'll get it," Greta said. "This will be a whole new life for you, Savannah. A life any girl, and any witch, would envy."

CHAPTER 43

GOOD AND EVIL

Before dinner, Greta and Olivia decided to squeeze in Savannah's first lesson. They took us outdoors to a grove of forest beyond an unused barn. Leah and Friesen came along, presumably to guard Savannah from any external threat, but more likely to guard against any joint escape plan I might hatch. They needn't have bothered. As long as Savannah wanted to stay, I was staying right beside her.

Greta started with witch magic, but it was clear her heart wasn't in it and, as soon as she'd ascertained that Savannah already knew the basics, she moved on.

"Now, we're going to show you some sorcery," Greta said. "Of course, you'll have a better tutor for this later, but I thought you might like to see a sampling of what you'll learn. When we get back to Los Angeles, we can work more on your witch skills."

Olivia grinned. "For now we'll have some fun."

Over the next hour, Greta and Olivia demonstrated a half-dozen spells. One was a variation on Cortez's fog spell. Another shot a bolt of electrical energy from the caster's hand. A third conjured colored lights. Obviously they were showing off, selecting spells that were little more than the magical equivalent of Fourth of July fireworks. Dime store magic, as Cortez would say. I wanted to turn up my nose at it, but the truth was, I was impressed.

As they cast, I couldn't help thinking of all the possible uses for their spells. The fog spell would be handy for escapes, particularly in conjunction with the cover spell. The electrical bolt seemed an excellent variation on the fireball spell, something else to add to my repertoire of nonlethal defense. I wanted to find fault, to find evil, but I couldn't. There was nothing wrong with this magic. Although it wasn't any better than the magic in the tertiary witch grimoires, it wasn't any worse, either—at least, not in the sense of being any less moral.

"Could you cast that fog spell again?" I asked.

Greta smiled. "You like that one?"

"It's interesting. It contains components of wind and fire elemental witch spells, but the construction is much different. The invocation to Boreas is particularly unique. I suppose that's a leftover vestige of its origin."

Greta and Olivia stared at me as if I was speaking Greek, which, in a way, I was, since the spell itself was in Greek. After a moment of silence, Olivia laughed.

"To tell the truth, Paige, we have no idea what it says. We've never translated it."

"You don't know Greek?" Savannah said. "I thought all witches had to know Greek. And Latin and Hebrew. Enough to understand the spells, at least."

"We don't bother with that," Olivia said. "I know some Latin from my school days, but it's not important. The grimoires tell you what the spells do, and your tutors will explain the pronunciation."

"Would you like to try a casting?" Greta asked Savannah.

"Sure."

"Which one?"

Savannah grinned at me. "All of them. Teach us all of them."

That evening Nast hosted a formal dinner party for Savannah. Savannah received her first little black dress, which was about two sizes too small in length and two sizes too big in width, but she was too excited to notice. She also received her first pair of heels and her first makeover, as Greta and Olivia fussed and primped her into a "little princess." Only Nast and Sandford joined us for dinner, both in tuxes. I didn't recognize half of what I ate.

Afterward, Nast presented Savannah with a family crest ring. Then he gave me an amulet, a gesture that clearly pleased Savannah, which was, I'm sure, the intent. It was a pretty piece, but nonmagical, probably something he'd grabbed at an antique jewelry store that afternoon in Boston.

Next everyone else in the house, from Sandford to the witches to the half-demon guards to the shaman cook, filed through with gifts. Once, in a museum, I saw a mural depicting an ancient pharaoh sitting in his throne as a parade of foreign dignitaries presented him with exotic offerings. That's what this looked like. And, like any normal thirteen-year-old girl, Savannah lapped it up.

After dinner, we retired to our room. It was only eight-thirty, but we couldn't keep our eyes open.

"Did you see what Greta gave me?" She pulled an amethyst-encrusted silver ritual dagger from the pile by her bed. "A new athame. Isn't it great? I bet it was expensive."

"Very."

"Can I see the amulet Kristof gave you?"

Nast had asked Savannah to call him by his given name, until she felt ready for something more indicative of their relationship. A wise move, I had to admit.

I passed Savannah the necklace.

"Cool. Bet it's an antique."

"I'm sure it is."

"It was nice of him, don't you think? To get you something?"

I nodded.

Savannah yawned and stretched back on the bed. "I'm so tired." She lifted her head to look at me. "Do you think they put something in our cocoa?"

I wanted to shout, "Yes! Don't you see? Don't you see everything? The gifts, the party, it's all a sham." Yet the truth was that I wasn't so sure of that myself. Yes, it was over the top. And patently unfair, since I could never compete. But was it a sham? I didn't know, so I settled for answering Savannah's question as honestly as I could.

"I think they probably gave us something to help us sleep," I said. "It doesn't feel any stronger than a sleeping potion. Probably valerian root, judging by the aftertaste."

"Well, I don't know about you, but I'm going to bed. Greta said she has a surprise for me tomorrow. A really good surprise."

"I'm sure she does," I said.

Someone knocked at the door. When I called a welcome, Olivia popped her head in.

"Paige? Mr. Nast would like to speak to you."

Savannah moaned. "Can't it wait until morning? I'm so tired."

"He only wants to speak to Paige, dear. I'll stay and keep you company while she's gone."

Savannah sat up. "I want to go with Paige."

Olivia shook her head. "Your father was very clear. Paige only."

"But—"

"I'll be fine," I said.

"Of course she will," Olivia said. "Nothing's going to happen to her,

Savannah. Your father understands how much you've come to rely on her." She turned to me. "Mr. Nast is in the living room."

I nodded and left.

No one escorted me downstairs. I passed Friesen and another half-demon guard, whom I'd only heard called Anton. Both cast subtle glances my way, but gave no sign that they were watching me. I knew they were, though.

Despite my intent to stay with Savannah, I'll admit to an inkling of temptation as I passed the front door. Earlier I hadn't thought of running. Now, though, as I neared the living room, I had to ask myself what Nast wanted.

I knew Nast had no intention of taking me back to Los Angeles. So long as I was alive, I'd be a threat. A minor one, but a threat nonetheless. Once I'd served my purpose, he'd have me killed. The only question was: When?

As I passed the door, I wondered whether I'd already outlived my usefulness. I hesitated, but only for a second. Nast's hold on Savannah wasn't strong enough to risk incurring her wrath. I had a few more days at least. Enough time to come up with a plan.

When I pushed open the living room door, Nast was inside, laughing as Sandford relayed an anecdote about a shaman.

"Paige, come in," Nast said. "Have a seat."

I did.

"Would you like a drink? Port? Claret? Brandy?"

"Claret would be fine. Thank you."

Sandford's brows arched, as if surprised I'd accept a drink. I had to trust in my conviction that they wouldn't kill me yet, and behave as if I trusted them.

Once Sandford passed around glasses of claret, Nast settled back in his chair.

"You asked earlier how we knew about Savannah's menses. I thought you should know the truth, though dinner hardly seemed an appropriate time to discuss it." He sipped his drink, taking his time before continuing. "I'll be blunt, Paige. Victoria Alden told us."

The glass almost fell from my hand.

"I realize you won't believe me," he continued. "Let me offer proof that I've been speaking to Miss Alden. As for the ceremony, the Coven disapproved of it, but your mother did it for you. Miss Alden believes you borrowed Margaret Levine's car Tuesday night, not to get the tea ingredients, as you told Margaret, but to get the required ceremonial materials."

I leaped to my feet. "What did you do to Victoria?"

"I beg your pardon?"

"You said Victoria told you. You forced her to talk, didn't you? What—" Sandford's laugh cut me short.

Nast smiled. "Touching, isn't it? How she jumps to the defense of her Coven sister, even after that very person has exiled her from the Coven? We didn't hurt Victoria, Paige. We never even contacted her. She called us."

"No. She wouldn't do that."

"Oh, but she did. She got Gabe's number from Mr. Cary's office, then called and offered us a deal. Information for protection. She'd tell us crucial details about Savannah if we'd promise to take my daughter and leave town."

"No! She'd never—!"

"You don't believe me?" Nast lifted a cell phone from the table by his arm. "Call her yourself."

I made no move to take the phone.

"No? Allow me, then."

He dialed the number, lifted the phone to his ear and said a few words, then passed it to me. I snatched the phone from his hand.

"Tell me he's lying," I said.

"He isn't," Victoria said. "I have the Coven's interests to consider, Paige. I will not—"

"You— Do you have any idea what you've done?"

"I've given Savannah to her father."

"No, you've given her to a—"

"A Cabal. Yes, I realize that. I know all about them, despite what I said the other day. Savannah is the daughter of a sorcerer and a black witch. She deserves to be where she's going. Evil begets evil."

"No!" I shouted, flinging the phone into the fireplace.

"Hear that crash, Gabe?" Nast said. "It's the sound of illusions shattering." He looked at me. "I thought you should know, so you're fully aware of the situation. You may leave now."

Without even waiting for me to go, he turned back to Sandford and resumed their conversation. I stormed from the room.

CHAPTER 44

COMPREHENSIVE
INSURANCE POLICY

Savannah was asleep when I returned to our bedroom. Olivia left with only a murmured good-bye, perhaps realizing I was too stunned to hear her, much less respond.

How could the Elders have betrayed us? Banishing me from the Coven I could understand—barely—but this, this was beyond fathoming. They'd sold Savannah for their own peace of mind. How could their own security be worth so great a price?

No matter how much I railed against the Elders, I believed them to be good women. They'd spent their lives fighting the temptation of evil and rooting it out of their Coven. Yes, they went too far, placed too many restrictions on us, robbed us of our potential. Yet I never doubted that their intentions were good.

Here, though, I was faced with something I could not deny—that they had acted in a way that made them no better than the Cabals, perhaps even worse. In chasing so relentlessly after morality, the Elders had become the very thing they'd fought so hard against: evil. I blanched at the word, instinctively feeling the need to justify, to moderate. Yet there it was. What else could you call their betrayal but an act of unforgivable evil?

Perhaps now more than ever I wanted to save the Coven. If I did, though, I'd never forget this lesson.

We had a late breakfast with Nast, who was heading back into Boston for business that day, but promised to return before dinner. After breakfast, we spent an hour in our room—Nast having not yet given us free run of the house. At eleven, Greta and her mother came to give Savannah her surprise.

"What is it?" Savannah asked as we trooped downstairs.

"If I told you, it wouldn't be a surprise, would it?" Greta said.

"We'll tell you this much," Olivia said. "It's for your ceremony. Only five more days."

"But I thought—" Savannah glanced at me. "Kristof said Paige could do the ceremony."

"Oh, yes, Paige will be conducting it. We'll have to use our own material, though. All Paige's things were lost in the fire. A shame, really. I warned—mentioned to Mr. Nast that he might want to rescue the magical items first, but he didn't see the need."

"You'll get all new tools anyway, Savannah," Greta said. "Better, too. Also better materials for your ceremony. Do you know whose grave we got the dirt from? Abby Borden, Lizzie Borden's stepmother. She was killed near here, you know."

"Really?"

"Really. Now *there's* someone who was definitely murdered."

"When did you gather it?" I asked. "It has to be on the first night of her menses."

"Oh, that's an old wives'—or old witches'—tale," Olivia said. "That's one thing you'll learn, Savannah. A lot of what you've heard is nonsense. Gathering items on certain days, performing rituals at specific times—"

"You mean I don't need to wait until the eighth day?"

"No, that one's true. Or so we believe, though no witch I know has ever been willing to test the theory and risk hampering her daughter's powers."

When we arrived at the back door Roberta Shaw and Anton were waiting to escort us outside. I hadn't seen the necromancer since Monday, at the funeral home. Shaw hadn't been among the staff who'd presented Savannah with gifts, so I'd assumed she'd been sent packing for her role in that horror show. Seeing her still here made me wonder whether Nast's condemnation of the funeral home debacle had been more show than substance.

"What's she doing here?" Savannah said, shooting a glare at Shaw.

"I asked Mr. Nast if Roberta could accompany us instead of Leah," Greta explained. She lowered her voice. "I don't know about you, but I don't trust that Volo."

"Well, I don't trust that necro, either," Savannah said.

Olivia hushed her. "She was only doing her job, Savannah. Now come along."

We passed the barn and entered the forest.

"So are we practicing the ceremony?" Savannah asked.

"No, we're performing a rite. A special protection rite."

"Cool."

"Very cool," Greta said. "Not many young witches get this. It requires very unique ingredients. When we mentioned it to Mr. Nast, though, he gave us carte blanche. Anything to help his little girl on her special day."

I resisted the urge to make retching noises. "What kind of protection does it give?"

"The best. Think of it as a comprehensive insurance policy. It'll prevent everything from demonic interference to having Savannah wake up with the flu next Wednesday."

"Huh," I said. "Sounds good."

"It's sorcerer magic."

"Of course."

They led us into the woods. We passed the spot where we'd practiced the afternoon before and kept going. As we walked, Savannah glanced back at Shaw and Anton.

"Who's carrying the material?" she asked.

"What material is that, dear?" Olivia said.

"For the ritual."

"Everything we need is at the site."

"I should have brought my new athame."

Both Greta and Olivia frowned, then Olivia laughed.

"Oh, that's right. Coven witches still use their tools. You'll find we've moved beyond that. We all still have an athame as a keepsake—a reminder of our past. As I'm sure you know, the tools aren't actually required for casting."

"My mom used them," Savannah said.

"That's because she was raised Coven. It takes a while to shake the old ways. I clung to my tools for years, like a security blanket. You'll find we only use tools that are imperative for casting."

"The same goes for materials," Greta said. "We've done away with all the nonessentials. Gemstones with symbolic meanings. Incense for mood. Candles for atmospheric lighting. All they do is complicate and prolong a ceremony."

"Maybe," Savannah said. "But don't you think they make it kinda . . . fun?"

Greta laughed. "Cabals don't have a budget for fun."

"Modern witches have made witchcraft modern," Olivia said. "You'll come to appreciate that, Savannah. It makes things much easier if we discard the baggage, both literal and figurative."

"And here we are," Greta said.

She stepped off the path, then pulled back a bush and waved us through.

Savannah stepped into the clearing first. Through the bushes, I saw her walk forward, eyes on the towering trees. Then she stopped short and yelped. I dove through the bushes to find her standing over a prone figure. It was a boy, maybe fifteen or sixteen. I hurried forward, then saw the steady rise and fall of his chest.

"He's sleeping," Savannah said. "Weird. He must live around here, huh? Guess we should find someplace else—"

"He's supposed to be here," Greta said.

Savannah stared at the young man. He wore a faded denim jacket and jeans. He had light brown hair tied at the nape of his neck and the kind of soft, pretty face that markets so well to teenage girls.

"Who is he?" Savannah asked.

"Prince Charming," Greta said. "You've heard of Sleeping Beauty? Well, this is the girl-power version."

Savannah gave a half-laugh, turning away as her cheeks went scarlet. "No, really, who is he? A sorcerer?"

"He's nobody. Just a human boy." Greta grabbed a small bag from the side of the clearing. "Now, as I've said, we skip all the ritual preliminaries, so you can just go right ahead and kneel beside him."

"What? Why?"

My gut went cold. "What's going on here?"

"The protection ritual, as we said. Savannah, kneel beside the young man and put your hand on his chest."

Savannah hesitated, then started to kneel.

"No," I said. "Get up, Savannah." I turned to Greta and Olivia. "We aren't doing anything until you tell us exactly what this ritual entails."

Greta turned her back on me.

"Hey—!" I said.

I was cut off after the first word, frozen in a binding spell. Savannah started scrambling to her feet, but Anton put his hands on her shoulders and pressed her down.

"Hey! Don't—! Paige!" Savannah swung her gaze up to Olivia, who stood behind me and was undoubtedly casting the binding spell. "Let her go! Now!"

"Paige is a Coven witch," Greta said. "She doesn't understand."

She pulled a thin-bladed knife from her bag and knelt on the other side of the boy.

"Wh—what are you doing?" Savannah asked.

"A top-level protection spell requires an exchange. A life protected for a life lost. You should know this, Savannah. Your mother did."

"No! My mother never—she wouldn't—" Savannah looked at the boy, then wrenched her gaze away and struggled against Anton's grip. "You can't do this! I forbid it."

"You *forbid* it?" Greta's lips twisted. "Did you hear that, Mother? She's giving orders already. Well, 'princess,' it's your father who gives orders around here, and he told us to do whatever was necessary to keep his little girl safe. Anton, put her highness's hand on the boy's chest. Over the heart, please."

Anton forced Savannah's hand to the boy's left breast. Greta moved the blade to the boy's throat.

"No!" Savannah said. "You can't do this! You can't! He didn't—he didn't do anything."

"He's a nobody, Savannah," Olivia said from behind me. "A runaway. The only meaning his life has is in protecting yours."

"Don't bother, Mother," Greta said. "It's obvious Eve coddled the girl. What do you think dark magic is, Savannah?"

"It's not this. I know it isn't. My mother never did this."

"Of course she did. She just never let you see it."

Greta pressed the blade against the boy's throat.

"No!" Savannah struggled harder, forcing Anton to put all of his weight into holding her down.

"He's a pretty boy, isn't he?" Greta said. She put her left hand behind the boy's head and lifted it. "Would you like to give him a kiss, Savannah? A last kiss? No? All right then."

She slashed the knife over the boy's neck so fast that it seemed not to have left a mark. Then his throat split open. Anton shoved Savannah's head forward. Blood jetted into her face and she started to scream.

CHAPTER 45

BROTHERLY LOVE

I won't detail the next few minutes. I can't. It broke my heart the first time, and even thinking about it is enough to bring me to tears. Savannah's terror and rage were indescribable. All I could do was stand there and watch, trapped in a binding spell.

Twenty minutes later I was in the bedroom, tucking Savannah into bed. Ringed around us were Nast, Sandford, and Leah.

On hearing the screams, Leah had come running. In the chaos that ensued, no one had escaped Savannah's blind fury. Leah had a bloodied nose and even I had a scratch across my upper arm. Eventually Shaw managed to sedate Savannah, and she'd collapsed where she stood. Then Sandford had carried her back to the house.

Once I'd finished getting Savannah into bed, Nast waved for everyone to leave the room. When I tried to stay, he motioned for Leah to remove me. I brushed her off and followed Nast and Sandford into the hall.

"I can't believe they did that," Nast said.

"They say you gave them carte blanche," Sandford said.

"Not for this."

"It's a common spell, Kris. Not too common, given the risk that comes with kidnapping and killing humans, but it's common enough."

"But to take her, unprepared, without a word of warning, of explanation . . ."

"I did warn you, Kris," Sandford said, lowering his voice so Leah couldn't hear. "They expected Greta's daughter to succeed her."

"You think they did this intentionally?"

"Duh, no, really?" I said, stepping forward. "Of course it was intentional! I can't believe you placed Savannah in the hands of women who had every reason to want her gone. I'm surprised they didn't kill her instead of the boy." I looked from Sandford to Nast. "Oh, I see. You figured they'd toe the party line because they're witches. Too stupid, or too cowed, to plot against you."

"Are we done with her yet?" Sandford asked, jerking his chin at me.

Nast looked at me, but his gaze was unfocused, distracted. "Just get her out of here. I'll decide what to do with her later. I haven't time for this right now."

The moment Sandford asked his question, I'd started whispering the fog spell. I flicked my hand and a cloud of smoke burst from my fingertips, swirling up like a smoke screen. I raced into the bedroom, slammed the door, and cast a lock spell. Then I ran to the window and tugged on the frame. It was painted shut. I grabbed a chair and threw it through.

"Savannah!" I said, shaking her shoulder.

She gave only a low groan. I grasped her around the waist and pulled her off the bed. Then I looked out the window. We were on the second story. Maybe I could jump, but I could hardly throw Savannah out.

Leah pounded at the door. Sandford shouted orders, calling the others. I thought fast. Did I know any spells for getting Savannah down? No. Either I could find a way to lower her to the ground or I'd have to carry her. The first would take too long. I tried lifting her, but could barely get her off the floor.

The door flew open. Friesen burst through and grabbed Savannah from me. Leah followed at his heels.

"See, guys?" she said. "No rush, like I said. She wasn't going anywhere."

"Take her to the secured room," Nast said.

Leah leaned over me and said in a mock-whisper, "Just a tip. Next time, run for the front door."

Friesen and Sandford laughed.

They put me in a secured basement room, but bound and gagged me, leaving me incapable of spell-casting. Then Shaw shot a dose of sedative into my arm. I was unconscious before they left the room.

I don't know how much time passed, but when I awoke, I found myself staring into Cortez's eyes. I struggled to sit upright, smiling behind my gag. The eyes blinked and I saw within them something so cold I shuddered and skittered backward. Somewhere in the room Gabriel Sandford laughed.

"Scared of her own shadow," Sandford said. "Just like a witch."

The man bending over me blinked and the illusion shattered. They were Cortez's eyes, but older. Older and soulless. He moved back and I saw that the resemblance ended at the eyes. This man was in his early forties, shorter than Cortez, with a severe, patrician look that might have been handsome if he smiled, but with frown lines that suggested he never did.

"You're certain?" he said. "About the relationship?"

"Certain?" Sandford said. "What do you want? A videotape of your brother banging her?"

The man turned a cold stare on Sandford, who straightened and cleared his throat.

"I can't be absolutely certain, as she's not likely to admit to it," Sandford said, his tone formal. "Yet all evidence points to that conclusion. Your brother is searching frantically."

"Frantically?"

"Very."

The other man's brows lifted. "I don't think I've ever seen Lucas frantic about anything. That seals the matter, then. Kill her."

"And put her head in his bed?"

The man's lip curled ever so slightly. He only shook his head, as if Sandford's quip wasn't worthy of an answer. Sandford stiffened, then dropped his gaze.

"Would you prefer I sent a videotape, then?" Sandford said. "Of her death?"

"That should do."

"Degree of suffering?" Sandford asked.

"Average. Enough to hurt him, not enough to convince him it was overtly personal."

"I'll send my best."

"No, you'll send your most expendable. An independent contractor. That will be more cost-effective and will make it more difficult for Lucas to trace it back to you. You'll involve no one else from the Nast organization in this matter, and you'll eliminate the contractor once he's finished the job. As soon as I leave, you'll move her to a second location. From there you'll arrange for the contractor to kidnap and kill her. You'll then include this note with the videotape."

The man handed an envelope to Sandford. When Sandford looked down at it, the man went on, "The note simply makes it clear that her death is his fault, that had she not become involved with him, and his 'crusade,' she'd still be alive."

Sandford smiled. "A little guilt's always good for the conscience."

"Now make sure this cannot be linked to you or the Nast Cabal. As for me, I was never here."

"That goes without saying. We have a deal, then?"

The man nodded.

"Just to, uh, be clear . . ." Sandford continued. "If I do this, I'm guaranteed a position in the Cortez Cabal, at a twenty-percent salary increase."

"That's what I said, isn't it?"

"I just wanted to be sure. I'm taking a big risk here. It would have been easier if I could have persuaded Kristof to get rid of her, but he's still stalling, worried about that witch-brat of his. When he finds out this one disappeared on my watch, I'll probably be out of a job, friend or not. So, of course, I want to be sure—"

The man's gaze hardened. "Did I give you my word?"

"Y—yes, sir. Forgive me."

"I appreciate your having brought this . . . unique opportunity to my attention, Gabriel. You will be very well compensated for it." The man turned toward me, lips curving in a humorless smile. "I must say, it's almost a shame she has to die. My father's been worrying that Lucas will never provide him with grandsons. It's hard to perpetuate a dynasty when the current heir shows no inclination to father future heirs. He'd be so pleased to hear that Lucas has finally found someone. Then he'd meet her . . . and probably drop dead of shock." The man shook his head. "A witch? Unbelievable, even for Lucas."

"Not *just* a witch," Sandford said. "The head of the American Coven."

"Oh, there's a dynastic alliance guaranteed to make the Cortez Cabal the laughingstock of the supernatural world. I'm doing my father such a favor, it's a shame I can't tell him about it."

The man turned to leave. As he walked out, a fireball flew from the ceiling and struck the side of his head. He whirled to Sandford.

"Don't look at me," Sandford said, stepping back. "That wasn't one of our spells."

The man turned to me. I glared at him, pouring every bit of hate and fury into that glare. The man opened his mouth, as if to say something, then shut it and settled for returning my glare before stalking out the door.

"I want her dead by sundown tomorrow. FedEx the tape to Lucas's motel room. Overnight express."

CHAPTER 46

SEND-OFF

D espite Cortez's brother's warning about involving others, Sandford had at least one ally: the half-demon Friesen. Less than thirty minutes after Sandford left me alone again, Friesen walked in. Without a word, he tossed me over his shoulder. He carried me from the room and across the basement to a hatch, much like the one in my house. Then he opened the hatch and pushed me through it.

I tumbled out the hatch door into a weed-choked garden. After being in the near-dark so long, the blast of sunlight made my eyes water. I struggled to wiggle free of my bonds, but they were tied tight. Friesen hefted himself out of the hatch, then picked me up, oblivious to my struggles, and slipped across the backyard to the barn. Inside the barn, a panel van was waiting. So was Gabriel Sandford. As Friesen carried me toward the van, Sandford snapped shut his cell phone.

"Done," Sandford said. "He'll be at the cabin in two hours."

Friesen nodded. With me still over his shoulder, he flipped open the van's rear gate. He laid me inside, faceup, then stepped back. His gaze traveled slowly over me, pausing at my chest and bared legs.

"Shut the door and get moving," Sandford said. "Before someone notices she's gone."

Friesen gave me another slow once-over, then slid his gaze toward Sandford. "I was just thinking . . . you're sending Lucas Cortez a video, right? Of her death? Why not . . . you know . . . bump it up a little." His gaze shot back to me, a gleam of hunger alighting in his eyes. "I'll do it for you."

"You'll do what?" Sandford caught the look Friesen was giving me and his lip curled. "Rape wasn't part of the deal, and it's not going to be. Just take her to the cabin, and let the professional do his work."

"Seems like a waste, don't you think?"

"No, I'd prefer not to think about it at all, thank you very much." Sandford started to turn away, then frowned at Friesen, who was still staring as if I was a free buffet dinner. He shook his head and threw up his hands. "Oh, hell, do what you like, but do it away from the house and before you get to the cabin, okay? You've got two hours. Now move."

Friesen smiled and slammed the door.

As we pulled away from the house, I started to count. I had to get out of here before Friesen got far enough to pull over, and by the looks he'd been giving me, he wasn't going to wait longer than necessary.

When I reached a hundred, I decided we were out of sight of the house, so I closed my eyes and concentrated on mentally casting the suffocation spell, aiming it at Friesen. Nothing happened, not surprising, since I couldn't speak. Yet, back at the house, someone had lobbed a fireball. The spell came from my secret grimoires, so it had to have been me, though I wasn't sure how I'd done it. Had my fury somehow manifested itself in an unintentional spell? I hoped so, as I hoped I could do it again, this time choosing my spell.

The van slowed, then pulled to the side of the road. Already? We couldn't be more than a half-mile from the house. Friesen put the van in park. Then he swiveled, undid his seat belt, and squeezed through the front seats. I fought the urge to struggle and instead put everything I had into a mental cast. Nothing happened.

Friesen loomed over me. I started to fight against my bonds, inching backward across the floor.

"Not yet, honey," he said, crouching over me. "Nothing to worry about yet. I'm just going to take a better look."

As he unbuttoned my blouse, I rocked and twisted, but couldn't move enough to even hamper him. He spread my shirt apart, then grinned.

"Red," he said, gaze glued to my bra. "Black's okay, and white's kinda nice, but there's nothing like a girl who wears red." He stroked a finger across the bra cup. "Silk, I bet. A girl who really knows how to dress."

While he fiddled with the front clasp, I squeezed my eyes shut and concentrated on casting something, anything. My bra popped open. Friesen inhaled sharply.

I opened my eyes and tried to wriggle away. He reached down for my breast, then stopped before his fingers touched me. He held his hand there a moment, then squeezed it into a fist and pulled back.

"Not yet," he murmured. "Prolong the fun."

He grabbed my hips. I kicked at him, but he only tugged me sideways, so I was facing the front of the van. Then he reached down and hiked my skirt up around my waist. I writhed and bucked, trying to get away, but he only grinned broader.

"Red silk," he said, chuckling as he touched my panties. "A matching set, of course. Very nice. Poor Lucas. That boy probably didn't know what hit him. You sure knew what you were doing, honey. I gotta give you credit for that. A first-class ticket to the good life . . . even if it did mean screwing that geek sorcerer." He smiled and ran a finger up the inside of my thigh. "If you gotta go, I figure the least I can do is give you a better send-off."

He took another look at me, then straightened and went back to the driver's seat. As the van pulled onto the road, he readjusted the rearview mirror so he could see me.

"There now, that's better," he said. "Couldn't ask for a better view."

My fear crystallized to rage, blind rage. The van swerved onto the shoulder. Friesen swore. My head bounced up, then slammed down on the metal floor. Something jabbed into my scalp as Friesen yanked the van back onto the road.

"Damn," he said glancing in the mirror and chuckling. "More of a distraction than I thought."

The cut in my scalp throbbed. I twisted to see the corner of a metal strip of edging protruding from the van's side. I wriggled upward until I'd aligned the jutting metal with my gag. Then I lifted my head, trying to snag the top edge of the cloth. The van hit a washboard of ruts and the metal sliced my cheek.

Friesen's gaze went back to the mirror. I stopped and waited until he'd looked his fill and returned his attention to driving. I brushed my cheek against the metal strip. This time the gag caught.

I wriggled the cloth down over my top lip. Then the van hit a bump and the snag came loose. I worked my jaw until enough of my mouth was free that I could mumble. Then I cast the suffocation spell. Friesen coughed and I froze.

He glanced in the mirror again and smiled. "Seem to be getting a bit short of breath. Must be those red panties. Let's see if I can't find a place to pull over."

When he looked away, I cast again. Nothing. Quickly I recast. He coughed, then wheezed. The van swerved. Friesen fought to keep it on the road, gasping for what seemed like an eternity. Then the van went off the road, thudding over grass.

The right side dipped. For a moment, the van continued thumping along, slowing, sliding into the ditch. Then the world spun. I flew from the floor, hit the side, then struck the roof, knocking around in the van until I didn't know which end was up. Then everything stopped.

When I lifted my head, the seats were over my head. The van had come to rest on its roof. I shifted, trying to flip onto my back. The van groaned and trembled, then settled and went still.

I looked around, searching for something that had broken off sharp. The window nearest to me had broken, but it was safety glass. Useless. I looked overhead. One of the seats had broken, exposing a metal rod that looked suitably sharp. It took about twenty minutes and plenty of cursing, but I finally cut through the bindings on my hands. I undid my legs, then crawled out through the broken window.

Friesen was still in his seat belt, hanging upside down. He had a gash on his head. His eyes were closed. I crept forward and saw that he was unconscious but alive. Though I was tempted to do something more painful to the bastard, I let him be. Unconscious was good enough.

I spent the next few minutes searching Friesen and the van for a cell phone. Of course I couldn't find one. That would be too easy. Finally I gave up and sealed the doors with the strongest lock spells I had. As I fastened my bra and buttoned my blouse, I looked around. The van had landed in a field. When I got to the road, I paused to get my bearings. I had a decision to make. To return to the house or to go for help? It seems an obvious choice, doesn't it? I'm not stupid. Surely I should have realized that the wisest course of action would be to get to safety, bring in some muscle, then go back for Savannah. But I couldn't do that. Right now, I knew where to find her. If I went for help, she might not be there when I returned. Yes, it was insane, but I had to go back.

I headed deeper into the fields, out of sight of the road, then began the long walk back to the house. What would I do when I got there? I didn't know. If I could rescue Savannah, I would. It seemed unlikely I could do it alone. I admit that. If it wasn't possible, maybe I could get a message to her, telling her I'd return. At the very least, I could assess the situation, go for help, then hurry back to keep watch over her from a distance.

We must have driven at least three miles. Fortunately, Friesen had turned only once and the roads were spaced far enough apart that I could easily guess where to turn. After about a mile of tramping through the fields, I heard a distant motor and froze.

Though I was too far from the road to be spotted, I crouched and waited for the vehicle to pass. A farm pickup finally drove by, moving well below the speed limit. Once it was out of sight, I straightened and resumed walking.

I'd gone about another mile when the faintest notes of a scream blasted through the silence. I dropped to the ground like a shot. The fields were silent. I waited another minute, but when all remained quiet, I rose and began moving forward, slower now.

I'd gone about another hundred yards when I saw a stretch of trees surrounding what looked like a two-story white house. Yes, there had been huge evergreens along each side, as a windbreak. Before I could break into a run, I picked up the sound of voices. I dove for the ground again and lay flat on my stomach in the long grass.

"I'm not going back in there!" Sandford, his voice shrill.

"If I tell you to, you will." Nast, cool and calm.

"No, I will not. As of now, I'm no longer a member of your fucking organization. I quit, you got that? Quit!"

"You have a contract."

"You want me to tell you where you can shove that contract? I am not going in that house. She's your daughter. *You* get her out."

A yelp and a thud in quick succession. Then silence. I inched forward until I could see the two men through the trees. They stood in the side yard. Sandford crouched on the ground, nose and mouth streaming blood. Nast stood a few feet away, arms crossed, waiting.

"Please, Kris, be reasonable," Sandford said, pulling himself to a sitting position, but making no effort to stand. "You're asking me to risk my life for a witch."

"I'm asking you to help my *daughter*."

"How long have we known each other? You asked me to take this assignment as a special favor and I did. Now it's all gone to hell, but I'm still with you, aren't I?"

"You'll be well rewarded for that loyalty, Gabriel. Bring Savannah out of that house and you can expect a six-figure bonus."

Sandford wiped a bloodied hand across his shirt. Then he looked up at Nast. "A bonus plus a vice presidency. With a twelfth-floor office."

"A tenth-floor office . . . and I'll forget who was supposed to be looking after the witch when she vanished."

Sandford hauled himself to his feet and nodded. "Done."

"I want her unharmed. Not a scratch. Understood?"

Sandford nodded again, then headed toward the front door. I waited until he was out of sight, then I scurried to the woods and circled around to the other side of the house.

CHAPTER 47

A Lesson in Respect

Moving behind the trees, I circled the house. The side door stood open. I scampered across the yard and in the open door.

When I stepped into the house, the first thing I saw was the necromancer Shaw's body. She lay crumpled at the foot of a narrow set of stairs. I checked each way before stepping through the door. Overhead I heard one, maybe two, pairs of footsteps. I crept to Shaw's body. From the angle of her head, I guessed she'd fallen down the stairs and broken her neck.

What had happened here? It hadn't been more than an hour or so since Friesen had loaded me into the van. Now Shaw was dead, Nast was standing around outside, and Sandford was searching, with great reluctance, for Savannah. From what Sandford said, I gathered Savannah was at the root of all this. But how? Whatever the reason, I needed to find her before anyone else did.

As I moved past Shaw, the look on her face made me stop in my tracks. Her eyes were open so wide the whites showed all around the irises. Her lips were curled back over her teeth. And the expression . . . stark terror. Perhaps at the moment of her dying, an image flashed through her mind, that of some other necromancer sucking her soul from eternity and plunking it back into her broken corpse. Fitting, really.

I stepped over her and began ascending the stairs. They were enclosed on both sides and the passage was so narrow it was a wonder Shaw had fallen down them at all, and not become wedged in halfway. These must have been back steps, a secondary set probably leading from behind the kitchen.

The stairs exited through an open door on the second floor. When I had climbed high enough to see past the door, I paused for a better look. The door was at the end of the upstairs hallway. At the opposite end were the main stairs, the ones I'd been using when I was here. Of the six bedroom doors, one was wide open, two were partially open, and the other three were closed.

"Savannah?" someone called.

I jumped, then recognized the voice. Sandford.

"Savannah . . . come on, sweetie. No one's going to hurt you. You can come on out now. Your dad's not mad."

Oh, yeah, like *that* was a big concern. How old did he think Savannah was? Five? Hiding in a corner, cowering in fear of a spanking?

I listened for any return noise, but none came. Except for Sandford's voice and the creak of his shoes, the house was silent.

As I eased into the hall, something rustled overhead. Sandford's shoes squeaked as he stopped, as if pausing to listen. Footsteps sounded above me. I closed my eyes to follow them, then shook my head. They were too heavy to be Savannah. I guessed Anton or one of the witches was searching the attic for Savannah.

Sandford's shadow advanced out an open doorway near the end of the hall. I ducked into the other open room and slid behind the door while he passed. Another door opened, then shut. Footsteps receded.

I glanced around, finding myself in the bedroom I'd seen Greta and Olivia using. The dresser top was bare, the closet open and empty except for a sweater that had fallen on the floor and been forgotten. It looked as if the two witches had left in a hurry. Had they fled when they realized Nast suspected their motives in killing the boy? Or had something else scared them off?

I looked around again, then returned to the hall and pulled the bedroom door half-shut behind me, as it had been when I found it.

Hands grabbed me, one going over my mouth. Then an exclamation of disgust and the hand shoved me aside.

"You don't give up, do you?" Sandford said. "I'm almost impressed."

"What happened?" I asked. "What's Savannah done?"

Sandford only snorted. He turned away and headed for the next closed door.

"Hey," I said, jogging after him. "Tell me what's going on. I can help."

"I don't need a witch's help. Just stay out of my way."

He flicked his fingers, sending me flying into the far wall. As his hand closed on the door handle, I cast a lock spell.

"Either I help you or I hinder you," I said, getting to my feet. "Now which—"

The door flew open. For a second, I thought he'd broken the lock spell. Then a man walked through, stepping off the bottom riser of the attic stairs.

"Anton," Sandford said. "You're okay. Good."

Anton turned, fixing Sandford with bright green eyes, a brighter green than I remembered.

"Did you call me?" he asked. His voice was nothing short of beautiful, a melodious tenor that reverberated through the hall.

Sandford frowned, as if confused by the voice, and shook his head sharply. "I'm guessing you haven't found the girl, have you? Come on, then. We'll head downstairs."

"I asked you a question, sorcerer," Anton said, stepping eye-to-eye with Sandford. "Did you call me?"

"No, but I can use you now. We'll—"

Anton turned to face me. In the dim light, his skin seemed to give off a glow of its own.

"Ignore her," Sandford said. "We need—"

"Did you call me, witch?"

As Anton stepped toward me, I instinctively backed up, hitting the wall. His hand reached out, as if for my throat, but instead cupped my chin and tilted my face up to his. At the touch of his hand, I jumped. The skin was hot.

"Did you summon me?"

Even if I knew how to answer, his hand held my jaw too tightly to speak. His grip was iron hard, strong but not painful. His eyes searched mine, as if looking for his answer there.

"The girl?" he murmured. "A mistake. Yes, clearly a mistake. A forgivable one, I suppose. This time."

I knew then, instinctively, what had taken control of Anton's body. A demon, a high-ranking one, the kind that should never—and usually *could* never—be summoned.

I dropped my gaze. The demon loosened his grip on my chin and stroked my cheek with his forefinger.

"Smart witch," he murmured. "Don't worry. It was a mistake."

Behind us, Sandford's lips moved in an incantation. Though no sound reached my ears, the demon swung around, letting me go and turning on Sandford.

"What are you doing?" the demon said.

Sandford's lips kept moving, but he shrunk back as the demon bore down on him.

"What do you think I am?" the demon thundered, bringing his face to Sandford's. "You dare try to send me back? With a spell to dispel some mewling spirit?"

Sandford's voice rose, words spilling from his mouth.

"Show some respect, sorcerer!"

The demon grabbed Sandford by the shoulders. Sandford squeezed his eyes tight and kept casting.

"Fool! Disrespectful fool!"

With a roar, the demon pulled back his hand and slammed it into Sandford's chest. Slammed it *into* his chest, fingers disappearing inside Sandford's torso. The muscles on the demon's arm tightened, as if squeezing. Sandford's mouth opened in a silent scream. The demon withdrew his hand, bloodless, and let Sandford's body fall to the floor. Then he turned to me.

A protective spell flew to my lips, but I swallowed it back and forced myself to stand up straight, meeting his gaze, firm but not defiant.

He strode back to me and his hand cupped my chin again, lifting my face to his. His eyes searched mine. I fought the urge to look away. For a long minute, he just stared at me . . . into me. Then his lips curved in a smile and he released my chin.

He stood there, watching me for a moment, then turned and headed down the hall. After a few steps, he lifted his hands and Anton's body dropped to the floor. A sharp wind, as hot as a furnace blast, encircled me, then was gone.

I wrapped my arms around me, shaking despite the heat. Looking down at Sandford, I saw his shirt was neither torn nor bloodied, as if I'd only imagined what I'd seen. Shivering, I stepped over his lifeless body.

Anton's corpse lay several feet away, also blocking the hall. He was on his stomach, face turned toward the wall, eyes closed. As I lifted my foot to step over him, his body convulsed. I jerked back, stumbling into Sandford. Anton's body shook and twisted, bucking off the floor. Then it went still.

I fought to control my racing heart, then lifted my foot slowly. Dime store magic, I told myself. Yet that mantra no longer worked, no longer held true. There were things here that could hurt me, things my brain could barely fathom.

As my foot passed over Anton's head, his eyes opened and I fell back with a shriek. Anton's head rose and jerked from side to side. Then it turned nearly full around, bones snapping. His eyes met mine. The bright green irises were gone, replaced by dull yellowish disks with huge pupils. Those reptilian eyes fixed on mine, wide and unblinking. The mouth opened and a stream of high-pitched gibberish flew out. Then the thing that had been Anton rose up onto its fingertips and toes, lifting itself just inches from the floor and skittered into the next open room. From within the room came more gibbering, then the scratching of nails moving fast against the wooden floor.

I dove past the open door and ran for the front stairs, taking them two at a time. Halfway down, the step beneath me split in two. I stumbled and grabbed the railing. The next step cracked, then the next and the next, pieces dropping into the empty hole below. I raced back up the stairs, hearing the steps crackle and splinter in my wake.

I dashed for the back stairs, gaze trained on the doorway ahead. Something hissed in my path and I stopped short. Anton—or what had been Anton—was now back in the hall, crouched over Sandford's corpse. The creature hissed and snuffled at my approach, but kept its face against Sandford's torso, as if sniffing it.

I looked back at the front steps, now a twelve-foot sheer drop. Then I glanced at the creature. It still hadn't lifted its head, didn't even seem to know I was there. If I could just step over—oh, God, you must be kidding! I bit back my horror and steeled myself. A short run, a jump, and I'd be at the back stairs. I just couldn't think about what I was jumping over.

As I prepared to sprint, I changed my mind. I'd flunked track-and-field in elementary school, being unable to clear even the lowest hurdle. If I ran and jumped, I risked kicking the creature and pissing it off. Instead I tiptoed across the hall, then pressed myself against the wall and began slowly sidestepping toward Sandford's body. His arm was stretched over his head. Carefully I stepped over it, then continued inching sideways, past his head and along his upper chest. The creature was still crouched over Sandford's stomach, with its feet braced against the wall.

I lifted my foot to step over. Its head shot up and twisted full around, yellow eyes meeting mine. Strings of Sandford's flesh hung from its mouth and teeth. It hissed, spraying me with gore. I screamed then, screamed as loud as I could and wheeled, instinctively heading back to the front steps. I only got as far as Sandford's outstretched arm, tripped over it, and sailed to the floor. Something moved across my legs and I reared up, kicking and screaming. I couldn't stop screaming. Even knowing I was wasting energy—and possibly attracting more horrors—I couldn't stop.

The thing that had been Anton squirmed over me, pinning me to the floor. As hard as I punched, I couldn't even make it flinch. It moved up my chest until its face was over mine, dribbling bits of bloodied flesh onto my mouth and cheeks.

I shut my mouth then. Shut it fast. In my head, though, I was still screaming, unable to focus or think, seeing only those yellow eyes boring into mine. The thing opened its mouth and gibbered, a high-pitched stream of noise that stabbed through my skull.

It lowered its face to mine. I squeezed my hands between its shoulders and mine, and pushed with everything I had. It bared its teeth and hissed louder, spraying me with saliva and blood, but I kept pushing and finally managed to wriggle from under it.

I scrambled to my feet and kicked it in the head. It shrieked and gibbered. I turned to run, but a woman blocked my path. I recognized her as the shaman cook.

"Look out!" I shouted. "Run!"

She only bent and waved her hands at the creature, as if shooing a cat. It hissed and snarled. As I glanced back at the thing, it lifted itself onto its fingers and toes and skittered through another open door.

"Oh, God, thank you," I said. "Now let's get—"

The woman grabbed my arm as I turned to run for the back steps.

"He was here," she said.

"Yes, a lot of things are here. Now let's—"

The woman stepped in front of me, blocking my path again. I looked her full in the face for the first time. Her eyes were white—pure white, devoid of irises and pupils. I wheeled to run the other way, but she grabbed my arm with a viselike grip and pulled me to her.

"He was here," she said, her voice a breathless whisper. "I can smell him. Can you smell him?"

I struggled to get free. She didn't even seem to notice my efforts. She licked her lips.

"Yes, yes, I smell him. One of the masters. Here. Here!"

She moved her face down to mine, nostrils flaring.

"I smell him on you." Her voice and body quivered with excitement. "He spoke to you. He touched you. Oh, you have been blessed! Blessed!"

Her tongue shot out and licked my cheek. I yelped and dove past her. She grabbed for me, but I kept running.

I tore down the hall and back steps, vaulting over Sandford, then Shaw without so much as a stumble. At the bottom of the stairs, I didn't pause to look around. I dove through the first open door and slammed it behind me, then leaned against it, gulping air. I was shaking so badly the door itself quavered under me. Then I realized it wasn't me making the door shake. The whole house was quaking.

Beneath my feet, the floor rattled and groaned. I looked around wildly. The floorboards buckled, then gave way, splinters spraying upward as a wave of spirits flew through, formless rays of light, like the ones in the cemetery. The force of them hurled me into the air. As I rocketed across the room, a huge gaping maw appeared before me. Before I had time to scream, I sailed through the apparition and hit the floor.

All around me, spirits jetted into the air, moving so fast that I could feel their passing. The very fabric of the house moaned and shifted, threatening to blow apart. I fought to move, but the force of the passing spirits was like a gale-force wind, holding me still and snatching the breath from my lungs.

It stopped as suddenly as it had begun. The spirits had broken through the ceiling and were gone.

I took a minute to breathe, just breathe, then looked around. Between me and the door, the floor was gone, leaving a gaping hole into the basement. I glanced at the window, but it was barely eighteen inches square. My hips definitely weren't less than eighteen inches, round or square.

After a few more deep breaths, I approached the hole in the floor. Then, from below, I caught a sound that made my heart leap. Savannah's voice. She was in the basement, chanting an incantation.

I dropped to my knees, grabbed the edge of the hole, and leaned into it.

"Savannah?" I called. "It's me, hon. It's Paige."

She continued chanting, her voice a distant whisper. I cleared my throat.

"Savannah?" I said, louder. "Can you—"

The house rocked suddenly, like a boat cut from its moorings. I flew, face-first, through the hole and somersaulted, landing hard on the dirt floor beneath. For a moment, I couldn't move. The commands wouldn't travel from my brain to my muscles. Panic washed through me. Then as if in a delayed reaction, all my limbs convulsed, throwing me awkwardly into a sprawl. I scrambled to my feet, ignoring the pain that slammed through me.

From somewhere beyond came Savannah's faint voice. I looked around, seeing I was in an empty cold cellar. I moved to the only door and opened it. Savannah's voice became clear. I caught a few words of Greek, enough to tell me, if I hadn't already guessed, that she was conjuring. Conjuring what, though, I couldn't tell. I hurried toward her before I found out.

CHAPTER 48

SHOW & TELL

As I followed Savannah's voice, I heard another. Nast's.

"You have to stop, sweetheart," he said. "You can't do this. It isn't possible."

Savannah kept chanting.

"I know you're angry. I don't know what happened—"

Savannah stopped in mid-incantation and howled, "You killed her!"

"I didn't kill anyone, princess. If you mean that boy—"

"I mean Paige! You killed her. You told them to kill her."

"I never—"

"I saw her body! Leah showed me! I saw them carry her to the van. You promised she'd be safe and you killed her!"

I stepped into the furnace room and walked around the mammoth wood-burning furnace to see her on the other side, kneeling, facing the far wall.

"I'm right here, Savannah," I said. "Nobody killed me."

"Oh, thank God," Nast said. "See, sweetheart? Paige is fine."

"You killed her! You killed her!"

"No, hon, I—"

"You killed her!" Savannah screamed. "You killed her! You promised! You promised and you lied!"

Tears streamed down Savannah's face. Nast stepped forward, arms wide to embrace her. I lunged forward to grab him, but missed.

"Don't—!" I shouted.

Savannah's hands flew up and Nast shot backward. His head slammed against the concrete wall. His eyes widened, then closed as his body slumped to the ground, head falling forward.

I ran to him and felt for a pulse, but there was none. Blood trickled from the crushed back of his head, wending down his neck and over my fingers.

"Oh, God. Oh, God." I gulped air, forcing calm into my voice. "It's okay, Savannah. It'll be okay. You didn't mean it. I know that."

She'd started chanting again. I turned. Her hands were clenched and raised, her head down, eyes squeezed shut. I tried to decipher the spell, but the words flowed so fast, they were almost unintelligible. I could tell she was summoning, but what?

Then I caught a word. A single word that told me everything. Mother. Savannah was trying to raise her mother's spirit.

"Savannah," I said, keeping my voice soft, but raised loud enough for her to hear. "Savannah, hon? It's me. It's Paige."

She kept casting, repeating the words over and over in an endless loop. My gaze moved to her hands, caught by a flash of something. Something red. Blood streamed down her wrists as her fingers bit into her palms.

"Oh, Savannah," I whispered.

I moved toward her, hands outstretched. When I was only inches from touching her, her eyes flew open. Her eyes were blank, as if seeing only a shape or a stranger. She shouted something and banged her hands against her sides. My feet flew from under me and I sailed into the far wall.

I stayed on the floor until she returned to her incantation. Then I pushed myself to my knees.

From my new angle, the light from the basement hall caught Savannah's face, glistening off the tears that streamed down, soaking the front of her shirt. The words flew from her lips, more expelled than spoken, moving seamlessly from spell to spell, language to language, in a desperate bid to find the right words to call forth her mother's spirit.

"Oh, baby," I whispered, feeling my own eyes fill with tears. "You poor baby."

She'd tried so hard, moving from one life to another, trying to fit into a new world populated by strangers who couldn't, wouldn't understand her. Now even that world had fallen apart. Everyone had deserted her, failed her, and now she was desperately trying to summon the one person who'd never failed her. And it was the one thing she could never do.

Savannah could call forth every demon in the universe and never reach her own mother. She might have accidentally raised the spirits of that family in the cemetery, but she could not call on her mother, buried in an unknown grave, hundreds of miles away. If such a thing were possible, I would have contacted my own mother, despite every moral qualm against such a thing. How many times in this past year would I have called her, to ask for advice, for guidance, for anything, just to speak to her?

My own grief washed through me then, my own tears, breaking past the dam I'd so carefully erected. How different everything would have been if my mother had been here. She could have told me how to deal with the Coven, could have interceded on my behalf. She could have rescued me from jail, comforted me after that hellish afternoon in the funeral parlor. With her there, it would never have been this way. I would never have *fucked up so badly*!

I hadn't been ready. Not for Savannah, not for Coven Leadership, not for anything that had befallen me since her death. Now I was here, in this strange basement, listening to the howling chant of Savannah's grief and knowing, if I did not stop her, she would summon something we couldn't control, something that would destroy us both.

I knew this, yet I could do nothing. I didn't know what to do. Hearing Savannah shout her mother's name, voice rising to a crazed crescendo, I did the only thing I could think of. I asked my mother for help. I closed my eyes and called to her, summoning her from the depths of my memory and pleading for help. When Savannah paused to gulp breath, I heard someone calling my name. For one second, my heart leaped, thinking I had somehow succeeded. Then my mind cleared and the voice came clear.

"Paige? Savannah? Paige!"

It was Cortez, upstairs. I whispered a word of thanks to my mother, or providence, or whatever had sent him, then raced past the furnace and up the stairs. When I reached the top, I saw Cortez run past the end of the hall.

"Here!" I called. "I'm here!"

The house shook. I braced myself in the doorway, tensed for the next quake, but nothing came. As the house shuddered and went still, I flew down the hall, meeting Cortez halfway. He grabbed me in a fierce hug.

"Thank God," he said. "Where's Savannah? We have to get out. Something's happening."

"It's Savannah. She's—"

"Well, look at that," Leah's voice said behind us. "The white knight arrives just in time. You're such a lucky girl, Paige. All my knights die and leave me to finish their battles."

We pulled apart and turned to face her.

"You have your deal, Leah," Cortez said. "We don't have time for you. I'll speak to my father. You'll be immune from any repercussions."

"Repercussions?" She laughed. "What repercussions? I'm about to save Thomas Nast's son and granddaughter, risking my life for theirs. I'll make VP for this."

"No, you won't," I said. "There is no son to save. Kristof Nast is dead."

Cortez blinked, but recovered in a heartbeat. "You understand what that means, Leah. If you walk out of here alive, you'll be the sole survivor of a Cabal disaster. A disaster that killed the Nast heir. Thomas Nast won't reward you. You'll be lucky if he doesn't kill you."

"He will when he finds out that you initiated this tragedy," I said. "You told Savannah that I was dead, that her father killed me. You set her off. Whatever plan you had, it backfired. Take the offer and go before we change our minds."

A clay pot flew from beside the front staircase. Cortez shoved me and twisted, but it hit him in the gut so hard he flew back against the wall. He slid to the floor and doubled over, gasping. I ran to him, but Leah shoved me back.

"If there's one thing I know," she said, stepping over Cortez as he retched and coughed. "It's how to turn a sow's ear into a silk purse. A Cabal project gone horribly wrong. One Cabal heir dead. Why not make it two? And collect a very nice bounty in the process. With a houseful of bodies, no one's going to question two more."

I cast the suffocation spell, but it failed. As she bent over, I launched a fireball, my one foolproof offensive spell. The ball hit her in the back of the head. As she whirled, a knickknack table flew up and smashed against my side, knocking the next spell from my lips.

Leah advanced on me. Behind her, Cortez struggled to sit, coughing up gobs of crimson phlegm. His eyes widened and his right hand shot up, fingers flicking. The spell knocked me sideways. As I stumbled, a splintered table leg slammed into the wall, right where I'd been standing.

Leah turned on Cortez. She strode over, grabbed his face, and shoved him backward to the floor. Cortez struggled, but his eyes blazed with pain.

Again I tried the suffocation spell. This time it took hold. Leah gasped. She released Cortez and turned on me. Something hit me in the side of the head and I went down, breaking the spell. When Cortez moved, she wheeled and sent the clay pot crashing into his stomach again. He fell back, eyes wide, face contorting.

I recast the suffocation spell. Again it caught. Again Leah broke it, this time by hitting me in the back of the head with a ceramic knickknack and knocking me to my knees. She stepped forward, towering over me.

"Seems you've learned a new trick since you got Isaac killed," she said. "It doesn't really work any better than the fireballs, does it? Another useless witch spell. Or is it just another useless witch?"

I dropped and rolled out of her reach. When I came up, Leah bore down on me. Behind her, Cortez lifted his left hand and squeezed it into a fist, then opened it and repeated the motion in rapid succession, lips moving soundlessly. A spell?

As I turned, I saw Leah copy the motion, balling her left hand into a fist. Cortez slammed his hand to the floor, motioning me down. I dove as another knickknack flew past, shattering against the wall. The tell! That was it. Leah's tell.

I leaped to my feet and cast the suffocation spell. On the first gasp, her left hand clenched. I hit the floor and rolled without breaking my concentration. The clay pot flew past, and crashed against the wall. Her hand balled again and I scampered to the side, narrowly avoiding an ottoman that sailed in from the living room.

"Running out of things to throw?" I said. "Maybe we should move to the kitchen. Plenty of pots and pans there. Maybe even a knife or two."

Her face contorted with rage as she gasped for air. Her hand clenched, but this time nothing happened.

"Oooh, impotence," I said. "Never good."

Another fist. Again, nothing happened. Leah's face was purpling now, eyes bulging. She leaped at me and hit me in the chest, sending us both down. Her fist hit my cheek and the spell broke. I recast it, nearly tripping over the words in my haste, but it worked and she only got a sniff of air before I cut off her oxygen again.

Leah began to choke. I grabbed her by the shoulders and threw her off me, pinning her to the floor. Her eyes widened and bulged. She was suffocating now, dying. Indecision flitted through me. Could I do this? I had to. Around us, the house groaned. Pieces of plaster fell from the walls. It was starting again, and I had to get Cortez and Savannah out. We'd given Leah the chance to leave and she'd refused. She'd never let us walk out alive. I had to kill her. Yet I couldn't look into her eyes and watch her die. I couldn't. So I shut my eyes, concentrated as hard as I could and waited for her body to go still. Once it did, I waited another thirty seconds, then scrambled off her, not looking back, and stumbled to Cortez's side.

He'd pushed himself onto all fours. I opened my mouth, but the house shook again and a rumbling howl drowned me out. Cortez jabbed a finger toward the front door. I shook my head, but he pushed himself to his feet, grabbed my arm, and started to drag me. When we made it to the porch, the house rumbled. A beam supporting the porch snapped and we dove onto the grass just as the porch collapsed on itself. Then the house went still and the howling fell to a drone.

CHAPTER 49

SUMMONING EVE

"It's Savannah," I said, words tumbling out. "She's trying to raise her mother's spirit."

"She can't."

"I know, but she won't stop. She doesn't even seem to know I'm there. I can't get near her."

The house groaned and shuddered. I spun toward it, but Cortez grabbed my arm, then started coughing uncontrollably, splattering blood-soaked sputum.

"I need to stop her," I said. "Before she summons something else or brings the house down."

"I know a spell"—coughing obliterated his next words—"look like Eve."

"What?"

"A spell that'll make you look like Eve. It's not perfect. The success depends on whether the viewer is inclined to believe the deception. Savannah obviously is."

"Impersonate her mother?" I shook my head hard. "That's . . . that's . . . I can't do it. I won't betray her that way. It isn't right."

"You have to, Paige. Any minute now that house is coming down. Would Eve rather you let her daughter die in there? Yes, it's wrong, but it's justified. We'll never tell Savannah the truth. You're giving her one last moment with her mother, Paige. I know you understand how much that means to her."

"Oh, God." I rubbed my hands over my face. "O—okay. Do it. Hurry, please."

Cortez cast the spell. It seemed to take forever. Twice he fell into a coughing fit, and my heart seized. How badly was he hurt? What if he— No, I couldn't think of that. I couldn't.

Finally, he finished. When I opened my eyes and looked down, I saw my own short fingers, my own silver rings.

"Did it—" I glanced up at him. "Did it work?"

"If you need to ask, then you won't see it. The illusion depends on the viewer's inclination to believe."

I closed my eyes and forced myself past my own doubt. I needed this to work. I needed to become Eve.

When I looked again, my fingers shimmered, then lengthened, nails growing long and manicured, rings disappearing. I nodded and got to my feet, expecting disorientation but finding none. My body moved as it always had. As Cortez said, the illusion was in the eye of the beholder.

Since the front door was now inaccessible, I jogged around to the side entrance. As I swung through, I saw Cortez limping along, using the side of the house for support.

"Go on," he said. "I'll meet you downstairs."

"No," I said. "You need to stay here."

"I won't let Savannah see me, Paige. The illusion will be complete. I'm only coming along as backup, in case of an emergency."

I hurried to him and put my hand against his chest, halting his progress. "Please. Stay out here. You're hurt."

"I can still cast—"

"No, please." I met his eyes. "If something goes wrong, you'll never get away in time. I need to know you're okay. I'll be fine."

The house creaked. Shingles slid off, one striking me on the shoulder. Cortez nudged me toward the house. I didn't need a second hint. With one backward glance, I was gone.

I raced down to the basement. From inside the furnace room, Savannah continued her pleas, voice rising and falling. I pressed my hands to my face and inhaled deeply, fighting to control my hammering heart. I had to believe. *She* had to believe.

When I rounded the corner into the room, Savannah stopped. She went still, completely still, as if sensing me there but fearing to turn and face disappointment.

"Savannah?" I said.

To my ears, my voice still sounded like my own and, as she turned, I nearly broke and ran. Instead, I held my breath and waited. Her eyes met mine. She blinked, then rubbed her palms over her eyes.

"Mom?"

"I heard you calling," I said.

"Mom!" She leaped from her knees and ran to me, arms flinging around my chest. Burying her head against my shoulder, she started to sob. "Oh, Mom, it's such a mess. I . . . I did everything wrong."

Instinctively I reached to stroke her hair, forgetting who I was supposed to be and speaking as myself. "You didn't do anything wrong. Nothing at all."

"Yes, I did. I made Paige stay here with me, and now she's gone." Her voice broke in a sob. "I—I think she's dead, Mom. It's my fault. I made her stay and they killed her."

"No," I said sharply, putting my hand under her chin. "Paige is fine. You need to get out of this house, Savannah, before it collapses."

As if to emphasize the point, the house began to shake. Splinters of wood popped from the beams overhead.

"I—I didn't mean to do this. I just kept casting and casting and things kept coming, but they weren't you. I only wanted you."

"I'm here now." I kissed her forehead, realizing as I did that, for once, I had to bend to do it. "But you have to go, Savannah. I love you very much, but I can't stay. You know that."

"Oh, Mom. I miss you so much."

My voice caught. "I know. I miss you, too. So much."

A beam broke over the furnace, then another. Chunks of the ceiling fell through.

"You have to go, Savannah," I said. "Please."

I hugged her tight, so tight her ribs crackled in protest. She gave a hiccuping laugh, then reached up to kiss my cheek.

"Can I see you again?" she asked.

I shook my head. "I'm sorry, sweetheart, but it only works once. I'll be with you, though. Even if you can't see me. You know that." I hugged her again and whispered in her ear, the words flowing unbidden, as if someone else was speaking. "You were my whole world, Savannah. The best thing I ever did."

She gave me a crushing hug, then stepped back. The ceiling above groaned.

"Go," I said. "I'll be right here watching. Go on."

She walked backward, eyes never leaving mine. Overhead, the beams began to pop like matchsticks.

"Hurry!" I called. "Up the stairs now. Run!"

"I love you, Mom."

"I love you too, baby."

She threw me a kiss, then turned and ran. I waited, listening to her footsteps, needing to make sure she was gone before I bolted. I heard Cortez shout. Heard Savannah answer. Then the ceiling caved in.

THE EIGHTH DAY

I'm still not quite sure how I made it out. Sheer luck, I suppose. Guess I was entitled to one miracle. I managed to duck inside a crawl space while the house collapsed around me. After that, well, after that is a bit of a blur, but I made it out with only cuts and bruises.

Savannah never realized I'd impersonated her mother. She assumed I'd been trapped in the house while searching for her. As Cortez said, we'll never tell her. She deserves that fantasy, one I envied her, a few last minutes with the person who meant more to her than anyone in the world.

We still had to do Savannah's ceremony in a few days but, with Leah and Nast dead, no one would impede that now. So it was all over. All over. I should feel relief at those words. Yet I couldn't, because it truly was over. My life as I'd always known it was over.

I didn't get my happy ending. Maybe I've seen too many Hollywood movies, but I honestly believed everything would turn out okay. If I survived, if I saved Savannah, then I would get my karmic reward. My tattered life would miraculously mend. The media would forget about me overnight. The town would forgive me, welcome me back. The Coven would overthrow Victoria and reinstate me as Coven Leader. I'd return to find my house hadn't been burned to the ground, but barely scorched, all my belongings still intact.

But my house was a hollow shell. Anything that hadn't burned had been scavenged by human vultures. When we returned to survey the damage, we were beset by reporters. The tabloids screamed, "Mob Justice: Vigilantes Try to Burn Massachusetts Witch." Some claimed I'd caused the fire accidentally while conducting a Satanic ritual, using body parts dug up from the cemetery the night before. Hordes of screaming strangers banged against the taxi windows, chasing us up the street. The front page of every Boston paper carried the story of the burning, augmented with news of "renewed efforts" by townspeople to cleanse East Falls of my presence. Within a day, the more enterprising reporters began drawing links between me and the "unholy" destruction of a farmhouse thirty miles away.

I called every Coven member, assuring them that Nast was out of our lives for good. I told them what Victoria had done. It didn't matter. I'd tainted the Coven. Only a handful would even consider having me back.

We stayed in Massachusetts only long enough to file an insurance claim and get the paperwork done. Between the money from the claim, and money I still had from my mother's estate, I had enough to move anywhere I wanted and start over. For most women my age, this would be a dream come true. It wasn't my dream, but I'd make it mine. I swore I would.

When we pulled out of Boston three days later, I watched the city lights fade behind me, perhaps for the last time, and a wave of sadness washed over me, but no tears came. Surprisingly few tears had come in the last few days. Even as I'd surveyed the ruins of my life, I'd realized that I still had exactly what I'd fought for.

I had Savannah. I'd known that I might lose everything I had in my quest to protect her, and I'd told myself that didn't matter. I guess that's what happens when you make a deal with the Fates. They take you at your word. Still, they did leave me with two consolation prizes, which I valued more than I could have imagined.

First, I still had the grimoires. When the firefighters rescued Cortez from my burning house, he'd still been carrying the two bags, the one with the grimoires and the one with my tools and the material for Savannah's ceremony.

My second bonus reward? Cortez was fine, and still with us. Through his network of contacts, he'd found a doctor in Boston willing to examine him, no questions asked. He had three cracked ribs, internal bruising, and a possible concussion. The doctor had advised a hospital stay, but Cortez settled for a chest binding and some painkillers, then we'd set out on the road.

I hadn't told him of his brother's plan to have me killed. What would be the use? He already knew his brothers hated him. If I told him, he might decide he was putting my life in danger and leave, and I wasn't risking that.

We'd been driving for two days now. I still didn't know where we were going. For now, it was a cross-country summer tour. Savannah thought that was pretty cool. She'd tire of it soon. Hopefully I'd find a place to settle before she did.

We'd stopped this morning. Some town in Virginia. At least, I think we were still in Virginia, though we may have crossed into Kentucky. Today was the big day. The eighth day.

Since dawn we'd been preparing for the ceremony. Now that it was dark, we'd driven to a state park, slipped past the locked gates, and headed into the forest. I'd found a site almost immediately, a good-sized clearing ringed with trees, as the ceremony prescribed. We were still early, though, so Savannah had grabbed a flashlight and taken off to see if she couldn't find something better. My choice was fine, but I suspected she was simply too excited to sit still.

I'd found a fallen log and sat down to pore over my notes. I was reading them through for the third time when a hand pressed between my shoulder blades, fingers rubbing the knot of tension there.

"How are you doing?" Cortez said, taking a seat beside me.

I managed a shaky smile. "It feels like I'm about to do my SATs, driver's test, and thesis presentation all rolled into one."

He squeezed my hand. "You'll do fine."

I leaned against him and he put his arm around my shoulder.

"What would you think about heading out to the Coast?" he asked. "Washington or Oregon. You might like it there. Lots of open space, and the ocean. It's not the East Coast, but . . ."

"I visited Portland once. I liked it."

"We'll go there, then."

"So you're going to—?" I hesitated. "I mean, we haven't discussed . . ." I took a deep breath and plowed on. "Are you coming with us? For now, I mean?"

"For now . . . and for as long as I'm welcome." He slid a quarter-smile my way. "The problem, as you undoubtedly have already discerned, will not be keeping me around, but getting rid of me."

"I can live with that."

I leaned over and kissed him. When we pulled apart, he adjusted his glasses, then looked at me.

"When I, uh, mentioned the Pacific Northwest, it wasn't a random suggestion. Oregon is one of the few states without a Cabal satellite office. With Kristof dead, on a case in which I was involved, I may need to lie low for a while."

"What will happen?"

"I don't know. I can say, with certainty, that my presence won't place you or Savannah in danger. I'd never do that. The matter of Kristof's death will be handled through proper Cabal channels. If I'm in danger, I'll hear of it long before anyone comes for me. My father should be able to handle it." He shook his head. "It seems no matter how far and how fast I run, I always end up relying on my father to—" He stopped. "I'm sorry."

"Tell me."

He entwined his fingers with mine and smiled. "Later. I only wanted you to know that I'm not placing you in danger, but that it would be wise for me to keep out of sight for a while. My father may—will summon me home to Miami. I'd prefer to be as far away as possible when that happens."

Savannah burst from the forest. "Is it time?"

I nodded. "Wait here. I'll cast a perimeter spell around the site."

"We'll have everything set up when you return," Cortez said, dropping the knapsack from his shoulder.

"No, I'll do—" I bit my lip. "Sure. Thanks."

I walked until I could no longer hear the murmur of their voices, then continued another ten feet before casting the perimeter spell. Fighting my way through the thick woods, I circled the site, casting as I went. Then I looped around again, just to be sure. When I returned to the clearing, Cortez and Savannah were kneeling on the ground, laying out the final objects.

Cortez shifted to a crouch. "Is this correct?"

I took the notes from him and walked around the tableau, scrutinizing it from every angle. Along both the north and south sides of the cloth they'd laid a quartet of tools—a small pot, an athame, a candle, and a chalice. The north candle was purple, for power. The south one blue, for wisdom and truth. Off the cloth they'd left the Baggies of dirt, the juniper, and a bottle of water.

Savannah handed me a necklace, a lodestone on a strip of rawhide, like the one now around her own neck. I put it on, surveyed the tableau once again, and bent to move the blue candle an inch to the left and rotate the northern athame about twenty degrees east. They'd probably been fine to begin with, but I felt better making the adjustments. Control isn't a habit you can break overnight.

"Okay. We're almost ready. Savannah, have you buried the cloth?"

She nodded.

"Good, then you need to kneel on the north side, in front of the purple candle."

"Shall I move elsewhere?" Cortez said.

"Only if you want to."

"I'll sit back on the log and watch. If that bothers you, tell me and I'll get out of sight."

"Thanks."

When he went to take his seat, I cast a protective circle around us. Then I turned to Savannah.

"Before we start, I want you to know that I really want this to work. It's possible, though, that I might not have the power or the experience to do it properly. If it seems to fail, I'll keep trying, but—"

"It's okay," she said. "I'll know you tried. Thanks, Paige. For doing this, I mean. I know it's not what you had in mind for me."

"It's what your mother wanted. That's good enough for me."

I laid my notes before me.

"Okay, first the elements. If anything sounds wrong, stop me. Even if you aren't sure, don't be afraid to speak up. Better to restart partway through than repeat the whole thing later."

She nodded.

"Here we go then. Air."

I slashed the athame through the air.

"Earth."

I poured the grave dirt from the Baggie into each shallow clay pot.

"Water."

I uncapped the Evian bottle and filled both chalices.

"Fire."

I struck a match and lit the candles.

I paused then, closing my eyes and clearing my mind. When I opened my eyes, I focused straight ahead, seeing nothing. With a brief Latin invocation, I called on the power of the elements to heed my will. Then I blinked, allowing myself to see again, and motioned for Savannah to watch carefully, since she'd need to repeat the next steps.

"Air to the north," I said, taking my athame and placing it before me.

"Earth to the east." I put my clay pot to my right.

"Water to the west." I moved my chalice to my left.

"Fire to the south." Taking the blue candle, I twisted, being careful not to fall, and laid it behind me.

I touched each in turn, the athame, the dirt, the water, and the flame. When it came to the last, panic darted through me and I hesitated, then gritted my teeth and forced my finger into the flame.

"Air, earth, water, fire. At their center, I sit in balance. All nature in harmony."

I turned to Savannah and motioned for her to copy me. She did, intoning each phrase without faltering. When she'd finished, we repeated the last part together. Then Savannah shifted onto her knees, lighting the candles as I resumed my place. Fingers trembling, I held the juniper branch over my candle's flame.

"With this offering, I beg protection," I said in Latin. "Hecate, Selene, Artemis, goddesses three, hear my plea. We ask this in your name. Grant this, your child, all the powers you can bestow."

I looked Savannah in the eyes, lifting my hands and voice.

"Grant her power without bounds. Give her the strength to wreak vengeance on her enemies."

The ground beneath me rumbled, but I held Savannah's gaze and kept going.

"Give her the power to overcome and the wisdom to do right by this gift. Give her all that you have to give."

The earth quaked, toppling the candles and igniting the cloth beneath. I raised my hands to the sky and stood, closing my eyes and pouring everything into the last few words.

"Hecate, Selene, Artemis! Hear my plea!"

For a split second, all went still. Preternaturally still and silent. I could hear nothing, feel nothing. No, I did feel something. I felt peace. Complete peace.

"It worked!" Savannah said, launching herself across the space between and falling into my arms. "Can you feel that, Paige? It worked! You did it!"

"Yes," I said, smiling. "We did it."

Industrial Magic

PROLOGUE

"Got another *CSI* question for you," Gloria said as Simon walked into the communication hub with an armload of papers. "If you're not busy."

"Perfect timing," Simon said. "I'm just about to start my coffee break." He started pulling a chair to Gloria's workstation, then hesitated. "Can I get you something?"

Gloria smiled and shook her head. Simon moved the chair beside hers, being careful not to block her view of the digital-display city map on the side wall. That's what Gloria loved about shamans, they were so damned considerate. You want a nice guy, you get a shaman. You want a self-centered jerk, you get a half-demon.

Her shift partner, Erin, hated it when Gloria said that. Racial discrimination, she called it. Of course Gloria didn't really believe every half-demon was a jerk—she was a half-demon herself—but that didn't keep her from saying so to Erin. Night shift in the communication hub could get deathly dull, and there was nothing like a good political correctness debate to liven things up.

Gloria pushed her chair back, one eye still on her monitor. "Okay, so I'm watching *CSI* last week, and they trick this guy into giving them DNA. Then, like five minutes later, they tell him it's a match. Can you really analyze DNA that fast?"

"Can *they*? Or can *we*?" Simon said. "For a municipal crime lab, it's damn near impossible. With our lab, though, there's no political wrangling about overtime and budgets and case precedence. We can't analyze a DNA specimen in five minutes, but—"

Gloria's headset beeped twice: an incoming call on the emergency line. She lifted a finger to Simon, then swung around. Even before the call connected, data began flashing on her computer screen as the call tracer went to work. She glanced over her shoulder to see the map of Miami replaced by another city: Atlanta.

Gloria reached for the button to page Erin back from lunch, but Simon beat her to it, simultaneously grabbing Erin's headset to put it on.

The line clicked.

"Cortez emergency services," Gloria said.

A female voice came on, shrill and garbled with panic. "—help— park—man—"

Gloria soothed the caller with reassurances that help was on its way. She could barely make out a word the caller said, but it didn't matter. The computers had already pinpointed the location, a pay phone in an Atlanta park. The Cabal had an office in Atlanta, which meant they had an emergency crew there, and the computer automatically dispatched them the moment it located the call's origin. Gloria's only job was to keep the caller calm until the team arrived.

"Can you tell me your name, honey?"

"D—na M—ur."

Sobs punctuated the words, rendering them unintelligible. Gloria glanced at her monitor. The computer was analyzing the voice, trying to match what it heard against the roster of Cabal employees and employee families. A list of several dozen names appeared. Then the computer factored in gender, an age estimate, and the call location. It came back with a list of five names. Gloria focused on the top one, the computer's best guess.

"Dana?" she said. "Are you Dana MacArthur, honey?"

A muffled "Yes."

"Okay, now, I want you to find someplace—"

The line went dead.

"Damn!" Gloria said.

"The Atlanta team just phoned in," Simon said. "Ten-minute ETA. Who is it?"

Gloria waved a hand at her screen. Simon leaned over to look at the photo. A teenage girl grinned back.

"Ah, shit," he said. "Not another one."

The driver swung the SUV into the park and dowsed the lights. Dennis Malone stared out the window into the overcast night. He turned to tell Simon they'd need good lighting, and saw that the crime-scene tech was already fiddling with his flashlight, replacing the batteries. Dennis nodded, stifled a yawn, and rolled down the window for some air. On the jet, he'd loaded up on caffeine, but it wasn't kicking in. He was getting too old for this. Even as the thought flitted past, he dismissed it with a smile. The day he retired without a fight would be the day they found him cold and stiff in his bed.

He had the best damned job a cop could want. Head of the finest investigative unit in the country, with the kind of resources and funding his old buddies in the FBI could only dream about. And he didn't just get to solve crimes, he got to plan them. When the Cortezes needed to get rid of someone, they came to Dennis and, together with his team, he'd devise the perfect crime, one that would stump the authorities. That was the best part of his job. What he was doing tonight was the worst. Two in one week. Dennis told himself it was a coincidence, random attacks unconnected to the Cabal itself. The alternative . . . well, no one wanted to consider the alternative.

The SUV stopped.

"Over there," the driver said, pointing. "To the left, behind those trees."

Dennis swung open his door and stepped out. He rolled the kinks from his shoulders as he surveyed the site. There was nothing to see. No crime-scene tape, no television crews, not even an ambulance. The Cabal EMTs had been and gone, arriving silently in an unmarked minivan, then speeding back into the night, headed for the airport, where they'd load their passenger on the same jet that had brought Dennis and Simon to Atlanta.

Over by a stand of trees, a flashlight signaled with an on-off flicker.

"Malone," Dennis called. "Miami SD."

The light went on and a heavyset blond man stepped out. New guy, recently come over from the St. Cloud Cabal. Jim? John?

Greetings were a brief exchange of hellos. They only had a few hours until daybreak, and a lot of work to do before then. Both Jim and the driver who'd brought them from the airport were trained to assist Dennis and Simon, but it would still take every minute of those remaining hours to process the scene.

Simon moved up behind Dennis, camera in one hand, light source in the other. He handed the light source to the driver—Kyle, wasn't it?—and pointed out where he wanted Kyle to aim it. Then he started snapping pictures. It took a moment for Dennis to see what Simon was photographing. That was one advantage to having shaman crime techs—lead them to a scene and they instinctively picked up the vibes of violence and knew where to start working.

Following the angle of Simon's camera lens, Dennis looked up to see a rope dangling from an overhead limb, the end hacked off. Another length lay on the ground, where the EMTs had removed it from the girl's throat.

"It took me a while to find her," Jim said. "If I'd been just a few minutes faster . . ."

"She's alive," Dennis said. "If you hadn't been that fast, she wouldn't be."

His cell phone vibrated. He took it from his pocket. A text message.

"Have you updated Mr. Cortez?" he asked Jim. "He hasn't received a site report yet."

From Jim's expression, Dennis knew he hadn't sent one. With the St. Cloud Cabal you probably didn't phone anyone in the family at three A.M. unless the Tokyo stock market had just crashed. Not so when you worked for the Cortezes.

"You've filled out a preliminary report sheet, right?" Dennis said.

Jim nodded and fumbled to pull his modified PalmPilot from his jacket.

"Well, send it to Mr. Cortez immediately. He's waiting to notify Dana's father and he can't do that until he knows the details."

"Mr . . . ? Which Mr. Cortez?"

"Benicio," Simon murmured as he continued snapping pictures. "You need to send it to Benicio."

"Oh? Uh, right."

As Jim transmitted the report, Simon moved back to photograph the rope on the ground. Blood streaked the underside of the coil and Dennis flinched, imagining his granddaughter lying there. This wasn't supposed to happen. Not to Cabal children. You worked for a Cabal, your kids were protected.

"Randy's girl, wasn't it?" Simon said softly behind him. "The older one?"

Dennis could barely picture Randy MacArthur, let alone know how many kids he had. Simon was almost certainly right, though. Lead the man once around a corporate picnic, and the next day he'd be sure to ask Joe Blow in Accounting whether his son's cold was improving.

"What is her father?" Jim asked.

"Half-demon," Simon said. "An Exaudio, I believe."

Both Jim and Dennis nodded. They were half-demon, as were most of the Cabal's policing force, and they knew what this meant. Dana would have inherited none of her father's powers.

"Poor kid never had a chance," Dennis said.

"Actually, I believe she *is* a supernatural," Simon said. "If I'm not mistaken, her mother is a witch, so she would be one as well."

Dennis shook his head. "Like I said, poor kid never had a chance."

CHAPTER I

THAT CORTEZ BOY

I sat in a hotel room, across from two thirty-something witches in business suits, listening as they said all the right things. All the polite things. How they'd heard such wonderful accounts of my mother. How horrified they'd been to learn of her murder. How delighted they were to see that I was doing well despite my break with the Coven.

All this they said, smiling with just the right mixture of sadness, commiseration, and support. Wendy Aiken did most of the talking. While she did, her younger sister Julie's eyes darted to where Savannah, my thirteen-year-old ward, perched on the bed. I caught the looks Julie shot her, distaste mingled with fear. A black witch's daughter, in their hotel room.

As Wendy's lips moved in rehearsed platitudes, her gaze slipped past me to the clock. I knew then that I would fail . . . again. But I gave my spiel anyway. I told them my vision of a new Coven for the technological age, linked by sisterhood instead of proximity, each witch living where she chooses, but with a full Coven support system only a phone call or e-mail away.

When I finished, the sisters looked at each another.

I continued, "As I mentioned, there's also the grimoires. Tertiary-level spells, lost for generations. I have them and I want to share them, to return witches to their former glory."

To me, these books were my trump card. Even if you didn't give a damn about sisterhood or support, surely you'd want this power. What witch wouldn't? Yet, as I looked at Wendy and Julie, I saw my words wash right over them, as if I was offering a free set of steak knives with the purchase of a complete living-room suite.

"You're a very compelling saleswoman," Wendy said with a smile.

"But . . ." Savannah muttered from the bed.

"But we must admit, we have a problem with the . . . present company you keep."

Julie's gaze slid toward Savannah. I tensed, ready to leap to her defense.

"That Cortez boy," Wendy said. "Well, young man, I should say. Yes, I know he's not involved with his family's Cabal, but we all know how things like that turn out. Youthful rebellion is all very well, but it doesn't pay the bills. And I hear he's not very successful in that regard."

"Lucas—"

"He's still young, I know, and he does a lot of pro bono work. That's very noble, Paige. I can see how a young woman would find it romantic—"

"But," Julie cut in, "like Wendy says, it doesn't pay the bills. And he *is* a Cortez."

Wendy nodded. "Yes, he is a Cortez."

"Hey," Savannah said, standing. "I have a question." She stepped toward the sisters. Julie shrank back. "When's the last time you saved a witch from being murdered by Cabal goons? Lucas did that just last month."

"Savannah . . ." I said.

She stepped closer to the two women. "What about defending a shaman set up by a Cabal? That's what Lucas is doing now. Oh, and Paige does charity work, too. In fact, she's doing it right now, offering two-faced bitches like you a spot in her Coven."

"Savannah!"

"I'll be in the hall," she said. "Something in here stinks."

She wheeled and marched out of the hotel room.

"My God," Wendy said. "She is her mother's daughter."

"And thank God for that," I said, and left.

As I drove out of the city core, Savannah broke the silence.

"I heard what you said. It was a good comeback."

The words "even if you didn't mean it" hung between us. I nodded and busied myself scanning traffic. I was still working on understanding Savannah's mother, Eve. It wasn't easy. My whole being rebelled at the thought of empathizing with a dark witch. But, even if I could never think of Eve as someone I could admire, I'd come to accept that she'd been a good mother. The proof of that was beside me. A thoroughly evil woman couldn't have produced a daughter like Savannah.

"You know I was right," she said. "About them. They're just like the Coven. You deserve—"

"Don't," I said quietly. "Please."

She looked at me. I could feel her gaze, but didn't turn. After a moment, she shifted to stare out the window.

I was in a funk, as my mother would have said. Feeling sorry for myself and knowing there was no good reason for it. I should be happy—ecstatic even. Sure my life had taken a nasty turn four months ago—if one can call "the end of life as I knew it" a nasty turn—but I'd survived. I was young. I was healthy. I was in love. Damn it, I should be happy. And when I wasn't, that only added guilt to my blues, and left me berating myself for acting like a spoiled, selfish brat.

I was bored. The website design work that had once fired a passion in me now piled up on the desk—drudgery I had to complete if anyone in our house intended to eat. Did I say house? I meant apartment. Four months ago, my house near Boston had burned to cinders, along with everything I owned. I was now the proud renter of a lousy two-bedroom apartment in a lousier neighborhood in Portland, Oregon. Yes, I could afford better, but I hated digging into the insurance money, terrified I'd wake up one day with nothing in the bank and be forced to spend eternity living beneath a deaf old woman who watched blaring talk shows eighteen hours a day.

For the first two months, I'd been fine. Lucas, Savannah, and I had spent the summer traveling. But then September came and Savannah had to go to school. So we set up house—apartment—in Portland, and carried on. Or, I should say, Savannah and Lucas carried on. They'd both lived nomadic lives before, so this was nothing new. Not so for me. I'd been born near Boston, grown up there, and never left—not even for school. Yet in my fight to protect Savannah last spring, my house hadn't been the only thing to burn. My entire life had gone up in smoke—my business, my private life, my reputation—all had been dragged through the tabloid cesspool, and I'd been forced to relocate clear across the country, someplace where no one had heard of Paige Winterbourne. The scandal had fizzled out quickly enough, but I couldn't go back. The Coven had exiled me, which meant I was forbidden to live within the state boundaries. Still, I hadn't given up. I'd sucked in my grief, dried my tears, and marched back into the fight. My Coven didn't want me? Fine, I'd start my own. In the last eight weeks I'd met with nine witches. Each one said all the right things, then turned me down flat. With each rejection, the abyss widened.

⚜

We went out for dinner, followed by an early movie. My way of apologizing to Savannah for inflicting another witch-recruitment session on her.

Back at the apartment, I hustled Savannah off to bed, then zoomed into my room just as the clock radio flipped to 10:59. I grabbed the cordless phone, jumped onto the bed, and watched the clock. Two seconds after it hit 11:00, the phone rang.

"Two seconds late," I said.

"Never. Your clock must be running fast."

I smiled and settled back onto the bed. Lucas was in Chicago, defending a shaman who'd been set up by the St. Cloud Cabal to take the fall for a corporate espionage scheme gone awry.

I asked Lucas how the case was going, and he filled me in. Then he asked how my afternoon had gone, specifically my meeting with the witches. For a second, I almost wished I had one of those boyfriends who didn't know or care about my life outside his sphere of influence. Lucas probably noted all my appointments in his DayTimer, so he'd never do something as inconsiderate as fail to ask about them afterward.

"Shot down," I said.

A moment of silence. "I'm sorry."

"No big—"

"Yes, it is. I know it is. However, I'm equally certain that, given the right circumstances and timing, you'll eventually find yourself in a position where the number of witches clamoring to join your Coven will far exceed your requirements."

"In other words, give it time and I'll need to beat 'em off with a stick?"

A soft chuckle floated down the line. "I get even less coherent after a day in court, don't I?"

"If you didn't talk like that once in a while, I'd miss it. Kind of like I'm missing you. Got an ETA for me yet?"

"Three days at most. It's hardly a murder trial." He cleared his throat. "Speaking of which, another case was brought to my attention today. A half-demon killed in Nevada, apparently mistaken for another who was under Cabal warrant for execution."

"Whoops."

"Exactly. The Boyd Cabal isn't admitting its mistake, let alone conducting a proper investigation and procedural review. I thought perhaps you might be able to assist me. That is, if you aren't busy—"

"When can we leave?"

"Sunday. Savannah could spend the night at Michelle's, and we'd return Monday evening."

"Sounds—" I stopped. "Savannah has an orthodontic appointment Monday afternoon. I'd reschedule, but . . ."

"It took six weeks to get it, I know. Yes, I have it marked right here. Three o'clock with Doctor Schwab. I should have checked before I asked." He paused. "Perhaps you could still come along and leave early Monday morning?"

"Sure. That sounds good."

The words came out empty, the elation that surged only a moment ago drained by this sudden glimpse of my future, calendar pages crammed with orthodontic appointments, Saturday morning art classes, and PTA meetings stretching into eternity.

On the heels of that thought came another. How dare I complain? I'd taken on this responsibility. I'd wanted it. I'd fought for it. Only a few months ago, I'd seen the same snapshot of my future and I'd been happy. Now, as much as I loved Savannah, I couldn't deny the occasional twinges of resentment.

"We'll work something out," Lucas said. "In the meantime, I should mention that I took advantage of a brief recess today to visit some of Chicago's lesser-known shopping venues, and found something that might cheer you up. A necklace."

I grinned. "An amulet?"

"No, I believe it's what they call a Celtic knot. Silver. A simple design, but quite elegant."

"Sure. Good . . . great."

"Liar."

"No really, I—" I paused. "It's not a necklace, is it?"

"I've been told, on good authority, that jewelry is the proper token of affection. I must admit I had my doubts. One could argue that you'd prefer a rare spell, but the jewelry store clerk assured me that all women prefer necklaces to musty scrolls."

I rolled onto my stomach and grinned. "You bought me a spell? What kind? Witch? Sorcerer?"

"It's a surprise."

"What?" I shot upright. "No way! Don't you dare—"

"It'll give you something to look forward to when I get home."

"Well, that's good, Cortez, 'cause God knows, I wasn't looking forward to anything else."

A soft laugh. "Liar."

I thumped back onto the bed. "How about a deal? You tell me what the spell does and I'll give *you* something to look forward to."

"Tempting."

"I'll make it more than tempting."

"That I don't doubt."

"Good. Now here's the deal. I give you a list of options. If you like one, then you can have it when you get home if you tell me about the spell tonight."

"Before you begin, I really should warn you, I'm quite resolved to secrecy. Breaking that resolve requires more than a laundry list of options, however creative. Detail will be the key."

I grinned. "You alone?"

"That goes without saying. If you're asking whether I'm in my hotel room, the answer is yes."

My grin broadened. "Good, then you'll get all the detail you can handle."

I never did find out what the spell was, probably because, five minutes into the conversation, we both forgot what had started it and, by the time we signed off, I crawled under the covers, forgetting even the most basic nighttime toiletry routines, and promptly fell asleep, my curiosity the only thing left unsatisfied.

CHAPTER 2

DEATH BEFORE DISHONOR

Come morning, I bounded out of bed, ready to take on the world. This would have been a positive sign had I not done the same thing every morning for the past two weeks. I awoke, refreshed, determined this would be the day I'd haul my ass out of the pit. I'd cook breakfast for Savannah. I'd leave a cheerful message of support on Lucas's cell phone. I'd jog two miles. I'd dive into my website projects with renewed vigor and imagination. I'd take time out in the afternoon to hunt down season-end tomatoes at the market. I'd cook up a vat of spaghetti sauce that would fill our tiny freezer. The list went on. I usually derailed somewhere between leaving the message for Lucas and starting my work-day . . . roughly around nine A.M.

That morning, I sailed into my jog still pumped. I knew I wouldn't hit two miles, considering I'd never exceeded one mile in my entire running career, which was now in its fifth week. Over the last eighteen months it had come to my attention, on multiple occasions, that my level of physical fitness was inadequate. Before now, a good game of pool was as active as I got. Ask me to flee for my life, and we could be talking imminent heart failure.

As long as I was reinventing myself, I might as well toss in a fitness routine. Since Lucas ran, that seemed the logical choice. I hadn't told him about it yet. Not until I reached the two-mile mark. Then I'd say, "Oh, by the way, I took up running a few days ago." God forbid I should admit to not being instantly successful at anything.

That morning, I finally passed the one-mile mark. Okay, it was only by about twenty yards, but it was still a personal best, so I treated myself to an iced chai for the walk home.

As I rounded the last corner, I noticed two suspicious figures standing in front of my building. Both wore suits, which in my neighborhood was extremely suspicious. I looked for Bibles or encyclopedias, but they were empty-handed. One stared up at the building, perhaps expecting it to morph into corporate headquarters.

I fished my keys from my pocket. As I glanced up, two girls walked past the men. I wondered why they weren't in school—dumb question in this neighborhood, but I was still adjusting—then realized the "girls" were at least forty. My mistake arose from the size differential. The two men towered a foot above the women.

Both men had short dark hair and clean-shaven, chiseled faces. Both wore Ray-Bans. Both were roughly the size of redwoods. If there hadn't been a one-inch height difference between them, I'd have sworn they were identical twins. Other than that, my only way of distinguishing them was by tie color. One had a dark red tie, the other jade green.

As I drew closer, both men turned my way.

"Paige Winterbourne?" Red Tie said.

I slowed and mentally readied a spell.

"We're looking for Lucas Cortez," Green Tie said. "His father sent us."

My heart thumped double-time, and I blinked to cover my surprise.

"Fath—?" I said. "Benicio?"

"That'd be the one," Red Tie said.

I pasted on a smile. "I'm sorry, but Lucas is in court today."

"Then Mr. Cortez would like to speak to you."

He half-turned, directing my gaze to a king-size black SUV idling just around the corner, in the no-stopping zone. So these two weren't just messengers; they were Benicio's personal half-demon bodyguards.

"Benicio wants to talk to me?" I said. "I'm honored. Tell him to come on up. I'll put on the kettle."

Red Tie's mouth twisted. "He's not going up. You're going over there."

"Really? Wow, you must be one of those psychic half-demons. Never met one of those."

"Mr. Cortez wants you—"

I put up a hand to cut him off. My hand barely reached the height of his navel. Kind of scary if you thought about it. Luckily, I didn't.

"Here's how it works," I said. "Benicio wants to speak to me? Fine, but since I didn't request this audience, he's coming to me."

Green Tie's eyebrows lifted above his shades.

"That's not—" Red Tie began.

"You're messengers. I've given the message. Now deliver."

When neither moved, I cast under my breath and waved my fingers at them.

"You heard me. Shoo."

As my fingers flicked, they stumbled back. Green Tie's eyebrows arched higher. Red Tie recovered his balance and glowered, as if he'd like to launch a fireball at me, or whatever his demonic specialty might be. Before he could act, Green Tie caught his gaze and jerked his chin toward the car. Red Tie settled for a glare, then stomped off.

I reached for the door handle. As the door swung open, a hand appeared over my head and grabbed it. I looked up to see the green-tie-wearing body-guard. I expected him to hold the door shut, so I couldn't escape, but instead he pulled it open and held it for me. I walked through. He followed.

At this point, any sane woman would have run for her life. At the very least, she would have turned around and walked back out onto the street, a public place. But I was bored and such boredom has a detrimental effect on my sanity.

I unlocked the inner door. This time, I held it open for him. We walked to the elevator in silence.

"Going up?" I asked.

He pushed the button. As the elevator gears squealed, my resolve faltered. I was about to get into a small, enclosed place with a half-demon literally twice my size. I'd seen too many movies not to know how this could turn out.

Yet what were my options? If I ran, I'd be exactly what they expected: a timid witch-mouse. Nothing I did in the future would ever erase that. On the other hand, I could step on the elevator and never step off. Death or dishonor? For some people, there's really no choice.

When the elevator doors opened, I walked on.

The half-demon followed. As the doors closed, he took off his sunglasses. His eyes were a blue so cold they made the hairs on my arms rise. He pressed the Stop button. The elevator groaned to a halt.

"You ever seen this scene in a movie?" he asked.

I looked around. "Now that you mention it, I think I have."

"Know what happens next?"

I nodded. "The hulking bad guy attacks the defenseless young heroine, who suddenly reveals heretofore unimagined powers, which she uses to not only fend off his attack but beat him to a bloody pulp. Then she escapes"—I craned my head back—"out that handy escape hatch and shimmies up the cables. The bad guy recovers consciousness and attacks, whereupon she's forced, against her own moral code, to sever the cable with a fireball and send him plummeting to his death."

"Is that what happens?"

"Sure. Didn't you see that one?"

His lips curved in a grin, defrosting his icy gaze. "Yeah, maybe I did." He leaned back against the wall. "So, how's Robert Vasic?"

I blinked, startled. "Uh, fine . . . good."

"Still teaching at Stanford?"

"Uh, yes. Part-time."

"A half-demon professor of demonology. I always liked that." He grinned. "Though I did like it better when he was a half-demon priest. Not nearly enough of those around. Next time you see Robert, tell him Troy Morgan said hi."

"I—I'll do that."

"Last time *I* saw Robert, Adam was still a kid. Playing baseball in the backyard. When I heard who Lucas is dating, I thought, that's the Winterbourne girl. Adam's friend. Then I thought, whoa, how old is she, like, seventeen, eighteen . . . ?"

"Twenty-three."

"Man, I'm getting old." Troy shook his head. Then he met my gaze. "Mr. Cortez isn't leaving until you talk to him, Paige."

"What does he want?"

Troy arched his brows. "You think he'd tell me? If Benicio Cortez wants to relay a message in person, then it's personal. Otherwise, he'd save himself the trip and send some sorcerer flunky. Either way, half-demon bodyguards are not in the know. The only thing I do know is that he really wants to talk to you, enough that if you insist on inviting him upstairs, he'll come. The question is: Are you okay with that? It's safe. Hell, I'll come up and stand guard if you want. But if you'd feel more comfortable in a public place, I can talk to him—"

"No, that's fine," I said. "I'll see him if he comes up to the apartment."

Troy nodded. "He will."

CHAPTER 3

An Offer I Can Refuse

The moment I stepped into my apartment, I had to grip my fists tight to keep from slamming the door and throwing shut the dead bolt. I was about to meet Benicio Cortez. And to my shame, I was afraid.

Benicio Cortez headed the Cortez Cabal. The comparison between Cabals and the Mafia was as old as organized crime itself. But it was a bad analogy. Comparing the mob to a Cabal was like comparing a gang of teenage neo-Nazis to the Gestapo. Yet I feared meeting Benicio, not because he was the CEO of the world's most powerful Cabal, but because he was Lucas's father. Everything that Lucas was, and everything he feared becoming, was embodied in this man.

When I'd first learned who Lucas was, I'd assumed that, having dedicated his life to fighting the Cabals, Lucas wouldn't have any contact with his father. I soon realized it wasn't that simple. Benicio phoned. He sent birthday gifts. He invited Lucas to all family functions. He acted as if there was no estrangement. And even his son didn't seem to understand why. When the phone rang and Benicio's number appeared on the caller ID, Lucas would stand there and stare at it, and in his eyes I saw a war I couldn't imagine. Sometimes he answered. Sometimes he didn't. Either way, he seemed to regret the choice.

So now I was about to meet the man. What did I truly fear? That I wouldn't measure up. That Benicio would take one look at me and decide I was't good enough for his son. And the worst of it? Right now, I wasn't sure he'd be wrong.

A single rap at the door.

I took a deep breath, walked to the door, and opened it. I saw the man standing there, and my heart jammed into my throat. For one second, I was certain I'd been tricked, that this was not Benicio but one of his sons—the son who'd ordered my death four months ago. I'd been drugged and, coming to, the first thing I'd seen were Lucas's eyes—a nightmare version of them, their deep brown somehow colder than the icy blue of

Troy Morgan's stare. I hadn't known which of Lucas's half-brothers it had been. I still didn't know, having never told Lucas what happened. But now, as I stared into those eyes, the steel in my spine turned to mercury and I had to grip the door handle to steady myself.

"Ms. Winterbourne."

As he spoke, I heard my mistake. The voice I'd heard that day was riveted in my skull, words bitten off sharp, staccato, and bitter. This one was velvet-soft, the voice of a man who never has to shout to get anyone's attention. As I invited him inside, a harder look confirmed my error. The son I'd met had been in his early forties, and this man was another twenty years older. It was an understandable mistake, though. Smooth some of the deeply etched lines on his face and Benicio would be a carbon copy of his son. Both men were wide-shouldered, stocky, and no more than five seven, in contrast to Lucas's tall, rail-thin physique.

"I knew your mother," Benicio said as he crossed the room. No "She was a good woman" or "I'm sorry for your loss" tacked on. A statement as emotionless as his stare. His gaze swept the room, taking in the secondhand furniture and bare walls. Part of me wanted to explain, and another part of me was horrified by the impulse. I didn't owe this man an explanation.

Benicio stepped in front of the couch—part of a perfectly serviceable if threadbare set. He looked down at it as if debating whether it might soil his suit. At that, a small inkling of the old Paige bubbled to the surface.

"Don't bother sitting," I said. "This isn't a tea-and-crumpets kind of visit. Oh, and I'm fine, thank you for asking."

Benicio turned his empty stare on me and waited. For at least twenty seconds, we just looked at one another. I tried to hold out, but I broke first.

"As I told your men, Lucas is in court, out of town. If you didn't believe me—"

"I know where my son is."

A chill tickled the nape of my neck as I heard the unspoken qualifier: "I *always* know where my son is." I'd never thought of that, but hearing him now, there was no doubt in my mind that Benicio always knew exactly where Lucas was, and what he was doing.

"Well, that's funny," I said. "Because your men said you had a message for him. But if you know he's not here, then . . . Oh, I get it. That was only an excuse, right? You know Lucas is gone and you came here pretending to want to deliver a message, hoping for a chance to meet the new girl-friend. You wouldn't want to do that with Lucas around, because you might not be able to control your disappointment when you confirm that your son is indeed dating—whoops, living with—a witch."

"I do have a message," he said. "For both of you."

"I'm guessing it's not 'congratulations.'"

"I have a case that might interest Lucas," he said. "One that might be of particular interest to you as well." While we'd been talking, his eyes had never left mine, but now, for the first time, he truly seemed to be looking at me. "You're developing quite the reputation, both for fending off the Nast Cabal's attempt to take Savannah and for your role in ending that business with Tyrone Winsloe last year. This particular case would require someone with such expertise."

As he spoke, a thrill of gratification rippled through me. On its heels came a wave of shame. God, was I that transparent? Throw a few empty words of praise my way and I wriggled like a happy puppy? Our first meeting and Benicio already knew what buttons to press.

"When's the last time Lucas worked for you?" I asked.

"This isn't working for me. I'm simply passing along a case that I believe would interest my son—"

"And when's the last time you tried that one? August, wasn't it? Something about a Vodoun priest in Colorado? Lucas turned you down flat, as he always does."

Benicio's cheek twitched.

"What," I said, "you didn't think Lucas told me about that? Like he didn't tell me how you bring him a case every few months, either to piss off the other Cabals or to trick him into doing something at your request? He's not sure which it is. I'm guessing both."

He paused. Then he met my gaze. "This case is different."

"Oh, I'm sure it is."

"It involves the child of one of our employees," he said. "A fifteen-year-old girl named Dana MacArthur."

I opened my mouth to cut him off, but couldn't. The moment he said "fifteen-year-old girl," I needed to hear the rest.

Benicio continued, "Three nights ago, someone attacked her while she was walking through a park. She was strangled, hung from a tree, and left to die."

My gut clenched. "Is she . . . ?" I tried to force out the last word, but couldn't.

"She's alive. Comatose, but alive." His voice softened and his eyes filled with the appropriate mix of sorrow and indignation. "Dana wasn't the first."

As he waited for me to ask the obvious question, I swallowed it and forced my brain to switch tracks.

"That's . . . too bad," I said, struggling to keep my voice steady. "I hope she recovers. And I hope you find the culprit. I can't help you, though, and I'm sure Lucas can't, either, but I'll pass along the message."

I walked toward the front hall.

Benicio didn't budge. "There's one more thing you should know."

I bit my lip. *Don't ask. Don't fall for it. Don't—*

"The girl," he said. "Dana MacArthur. She's a witch."

We locked gazes for a moment. Then I tore mine away, strode to the door, and flung it open.

"Get out," I said.

And, to my surprise, he did.

I spent the next half-hour trying to code a customer feedback form for a client's website. Simple stuff, but I couldn't get it to work, probably because 90 percent of my brain was endlessly cycling through what Benicio had told me. A teenage witch. Strangled and strung up from a tree. Now comatose. Did this have something to do with her being a witch? Benicio said she wasn't the first. Was someone targeting witches? Killing witches?

I rubbed my hands over my eyes and wished I'd never let Benicio into our apartment. Even as I thought that, I realized the futility of it. One way or another, he'd have made sure I knew about Dana MacArthur. After all these years of bringing cases to Lucas, he'd found the perfect one, and he wouldn't quit until we knew about it.

A faint rustling from the kitchen interrupted my brooding. My first thought was "We have mice," followed by "Well, doesn't that just make my day complete." Then the loose floorboard by the table creaked, and I knew whatever was in the kitchen was a lot bigger than a rodent.

Had I fastened the dead bolt? Cast the lock spell? I couldn't remember, but somehow I suspected I'd been too overwhelmed by Benicio's visit to take care of such mundanities. I mentally readied two spells, one to deal with a human intruder and another, stronger spell, for the supernatural variety. Then I pushed up from my chair and crept toward the kitchen.

A dish clattered, followed by an oath. No, not an oath, I realized as I recognized the voice. Simply a wordless exhalation of pique. Where anyone else would mutter "shit" or "damn," this was one person who never uttered even a profanity without first considering its appropriateness to the situation.

I smiled and peeked around the corner. Lucas was still dressed for court, wearing a dark gray suit and equally somber tie. A month ago,

Savannah had bought him a green silk tie, a splash of color she declared long overdue. Since then, he'd made three trips out of town, each time packing the tie and, I was certain, never wearing it.

When it came to his appearance, Lucas preferred the disguise of invisibility. With wire-rimmed glasses, dark hair cut short, and an unexceptional face, Lucas Cortez didn't need a cover spell to pass through a room unnoticed.

Now he was trying very hard to be silent as well as invisible as he poured coffee from cardboard cups into mugs.

"Playing hooky, Counselor?" I said, rounding the corner.

Anyone else would have jumped. Lucas only blinked, then looked up, lips curving in the crinkle I'd learned to interpret as a smile.

"So much for surprising you with a midmorning snack."

"You didn't need that to surprise me. What happened with your case?"

"After the debacle with the necromancer, the prosecution began pursuing a twenty-four-hour recess, to find a last-minute witness. Initially I was reluctant, wanting to end the matter as quickly as possible, but, after speaking to you last night, I decided you might not be opposed to an unexpected visit. So I decided to be magnanimous and agree to the prosecution's request."

"Won't it hurt your case if they find their witness?"

"They won't. He's dead. Improper handling of a fire-swarm."

"Firearm?"

"No, fire-swarm."

I shook my head and sat down at the table. Lucas placed two scones on a plate and brought it over. I waited until he took his first mouthful.

"Okay, I'll bite. What's a fire-swarm and what did it do to your witness?"

"Not *my* witness—"

I tossed my napkin at him. His quarter-smile broadened to a grin and he launched into the story. That's one thing about being a lawyer to the supernatural. The pay is crap and the clientele can be lethal, but any time you take supernatural events and try to present them in a human courtroom, you're bound to get some great stories. This time, though, no story, no matter how amusing, could distract me from what Benicio had said. After the first few sentences, Lucas stopped.

"Tell me what happened last night," he said.

"Last—?" My mind slowly shifted gears. "Oh, the Coven thing. Well, I gave them my spiel, but it was pretty obvious they were more interested in not missing their dinner reservation."

His gaze searched mine. "But that's not what's bothering you, is it?"

I hesitated. "Your father came by earlier this morning."

Lucas stopped, fingers tightening around his napkin. Again he searched my eyes, this time looking for some sign that I was making a very poor joke.

"He sent his guards in first," I said. "Supposedly looking for you, but when I said you weren't here, he wanted to talk to me. I . . . I decided it was best to let him. I wasn't sure—we'd never discussed what I should do if—"

"Because it shouldn't have happened. When he found I wasn't here, he shouldn't have insisted on speaking to you. I'm surprised he didn't already know—" He stopped, eyes meeting mine. "He knew I wasn't here, didn't he?"

"Er, uh . . . I'm not sure really."

Lucas's mouth tightened. He shoved back his chair, strode into the front hall, and pulled his cell phone from his jacket. Before he could dial out, I leaned into the hall and lifted a hand to stop him.

"If you're going to call him, I'd better tell you what he wanted or he's going to think I refused to pass along the message."

"Yes, of course." Lucas tucked the cell phone into his pocket, then pinched the bridge of his nose, lifting his glasses with the motion. "I'm sorry, Paige. This wasn't supposed to happen. Had I thought he might come here, I would have forewarned you, but no one from my father's organization was supposed to contact you or Savannah. He gave me his word—"

"It was fine," I said, managing a smile. "Short and sweet. He just wanted me to tell you he's got another of those cases that might interest us—well, you."

Lucas frowned and I knew he'd caught my slip.

"He said it would interest both of us," I said. "But he meant you. He was just throwing in the 'us' part to pique my curiosity. You know, get the new girlfriend intrigued and maybe she'll pester you to give in."

"What did he say?"

I told him Benicio's story. When I finished, Lucas closed his eyes and shook his head.

"I can't believe he'd—no, I *can* believe he'd do that. I should have warned you."

Lucas paused, then steered me back into the kitchen.

"I'm sorry," he said. "These last few months haven't been easy for you, and I don't want you affected by this part of my life any more than necessary. I know I'm the reason you can't find any witches to join your Coven."

"That's got nothing to do with it. I'm young and I haven't proven myself—well, not beyond proving that I can get kicked out of the Coven. But whatever their hang-ups, it's got nothing to do with you."

A small, wan smile. "Your lying hasn't improved."

"Well, it doesn't matter. If they don't want—" I shook my head. "Why are we talking about me anyway? You have a call to make. Your father is already convinced I'm not going to relay his message, so I'm going to hound you until you do."

Lucas took out his phone, but only stared at the keypad. After a moment, he looked over at me.

"Do you have any critical projects to complete this week?" he asked.

"Anything due this week would have been done last week. With Savannah around, I can't let deadlines creep up on me, or an emergency could put me out of business."

"Yes, of course. Well . . ." He cleared his throat. "I'm not due in court until tomorrow. If Savannah was able to stay at a friend's tonight, would you be able—or should I say *willing*—to join me on an overnight trip to Miami?"

Before I could open my mouth, he hurried on, "I've postponed this long enough. For your own protection, it's time to formally introduce you to the Cabal. I should have done this months ago, but . . . well, I hoped it wouldn't be necessary, that I could take my father at his word. Apparently not."

I looked at him. It was a good excuse, but I knew the truth. He wanted to take me to Miami so I could hear the rest of Dana MacArthur's story. If I didn't, worry and curiosity would gnaw at me until I found some way to get the answers I needed. This was the reaction Benicio wanted, and I desperately didn't want to give it to him. And yet, was there really any harm in hearing what had happened, maybe seeing this witch and making sure she was all right? Benicio said she was a Cabal employee's daughter. The Cabals looked after their own. That much I knew. All we had to do was say "No, thanks," and the Cabal would launch an investigation, and Dana MacArthur would get her justice. That was good enough for me. It had to be.

So I agreed, and we made plans to leave immediately.

CHAPTER 4

MASTERMIND OF
MANIPULATION

We booked seats on a flight for Miami. Then we arranged for Savannah to stay at a friend's house overnight, called her at school, and gave her the news. An hour later, we were at the airport.

We hadn't had a problem booking last-minute tickets, and we hadn't expected to. Just over a month ago, terrorists had driven planes into the World Trade Center, and many travelers opted not to fly the not-so-friendly skies if they could avoid it. We'd arrived early, knowing that passing through security wouldn't be the speedy process it had once been.

The guard opened Lucas's bag and rifled through it, then pulled out a cardboard tube. He passed his metal detector over it, then gingerly removed the end cap and peered inside.

"Paper," he said to his partner.

"It's a scroll," Lucas said.

Both men glowered at him as if this might be a new street name for an automatic rifle.

"A sheet of paper bearing ancient text," Lucas said.

One guard pulled it out and unrolled the scroll. The paper was brand-new, gleaming white, and covered in precise, graceful strokes of calligraphy. The guard screwed up his face.

"What does it say?" he asked.

"I have no idea. It's Hebrew. I'm transporting it for a client."

They handed it back, unfurled and creased. As they checked out my laptop and overnight bag, Lucas straightened the scroll and rolled it. When they finished, Lucas hoisted both bags and we headed toward the boarding area.

"What *is* that?" I whispered. "My spell?"

"I thought you might need a distraction after today."

I smiled up at him. "Thanks. What does it do?"

"I'm choosing option two."

I remembered the option game and laughed. "Too late, Cortez. The deal was that you had to tell me last night. You're home now, so the scroll is mine, option-free."

"I would have selected an option, had you not distracted me from my purpose."

"What, my listing the options prevented you from choosing one?"

"Most effectively. Option two."

"Hand it over, Cortez."

He thumped the scroll into my outstretched hand. "I've been robbed."

"Well, there is a solution. You could get me another spell."

"Greedy," he said, steering me to a quiet spot along the wall. "An unquenchable thirst for spell-casting power and variety. This does not bode well for our relationship."

"Why? Because you're just as bad as I am?"

With a fluid two-step, Lucas moved from my side to my front, and turned to face me. He arched one brow.

"Me?" he said. "Hardly. I'm a disciplined and cautious spell-caster, well aware of my limitations and with no desire to overcome them."

"And you can say that with a straight face?"

"I can say everything with a straight face, which makes me a naturally gifted liar."

"So how many times did you try my spell?"

"Try your spell? That would be wrong. Grievously impolitic, not to mention impolite, rather like reading a novel before you wrap it as a Christmas gift."

"Twice?"

"Three times. I would have stopped at two, but I had a modicum of luck with the second effort, so I tried again. But, sadly, a successful cast eluded me."

"We'll work on it. So what does it do?"

"Option two."

I socked him in the arm and started unrolling the spell.

"It's a rare gamma-grade sorcerer ice spell," he said. "When cast upon an object, it acts much like a beta-level ice spell, freezing it. However, if cast upon a person, it induces temporary hypothermia, rendering the target unconscious. There were four options, weren't there?"

"Three . . . no, the movie theater makes four."

"Four options. Ergo, if I provide you with four spells . . ."

"Now who's greedy?"

"I'm only asking whether the implied promise of one spell for one option could be reasonably translated to mean four spells would get me—"

"Oh, for God's sake, pick an option already. It's not like you wouldn't get any of them anytime you wanted."

"True," he said. "But I like the added challenge of attaining it. Four spells for four options."

"That wasn't—"

"There's our flight."

He picked up our carry-ons and headed for the boarding area before I could get in another word.

The official "meet-the-parents" visit. Has there ever been a greater torture in the history of dating? I speak from hearsay, not experience. Sure, I'd technically met plenty of old boyfriends' parents, but never through the formal introduction process. More like bumping into them on the way out the door. The "Mom, Dad, this is Paige. See ya" kind of introduction.

I'd met Lucas's mother, but there hadn't been a lead-up. She'd appeared at our door one day, housewarming gifts in hand. Had I known she was coming, I'd have been terrified. Would she disapprove because I wasn't Latina? Wasn't Catholic? Was living with her only child after exactly zero weeks of dating? It didn't matter. If Lucas was happy, Maria was too.

The Cortezes were another matter. Benicio had four sons, of whom Lucas was the youngest. The older three worked for the Cabal, as was traditional for all members of the central family. So Lucas was already the odd man out. His position wasn't helped by the fact that Benicio and Maria had never married, likely because Benicio had still been married to his wife at the time of Lucas's conception, which would make Lucas . . . not the most popular guy at family reunions.

In a Cabal central family, like any "royal" family, matters of succession are all-important. It is assumed that a son of the CEO, usually the oldest, will inherit the business. Not so with Benicio. While his three eldest sons spent their adult lives toiling to improve the family fortunes, who had Benicio named as his heir? The illegitimate youngest son who had devoted *his* adult life to destroying the family business, or at least buggering it up real good. Does this make any sense to anyone besides Benicio? Of course not. Either the man is a mastermind of family manipulation or just plain fucked in the head. I don't use that word much, but in some cases, nothing else fits.

We took a cab from the airport into the city. Lucas had the driver let us out in front of a café, where Lucas suggested we stop for a cold drink because it was at least ninety degrees and, with the full sun beating down, felt more like a hundred, especially after the chill of an Oregon autumn. I argued that I was fine, but he insisted. He was stalling. I scarcely believed it, but after twenty minutes of sitting on the café patio, pretending to drink our iced coffees, I knew it was true.

Lucas talked about the city, the good, the bad, and the ugly of Miami, but his words were rushed, almost frantic in their desperation to fill time. When he took a sip of his drink, more reflex than intention, his cheeks paled and, for a moment, he looked as if he might be sick.

"We don't have to do this," I said.

"We do. I need to make the introduction. There are procedures to be followed, forms to be completed. It must be official. You aren't safe if it isn't." He lifted his gaze from the table. "There's another reason I've brought you here. Something else that's worrying me."

He paused.

"I like honesty," I said.

"I know. I'm just afraid that if I pile on one more disadvantage to being with me, you're going to run screaming back to Portland and change the locks."

"Can't," I said. "You put my return ticket in your bag."

A soft laugh. "A subconsciously significant act, I'm sure. By the time today is over, you may very well want it back." He sipped his coffee. "My father is, as we expected, less than overjoyed by our relationship. I haven't mentioned this because I felt there was no reason to confirm your suspicions."

"It was a given, not a suspicion. I'd be suspicious if he *was* overjoyed at the thought of his son dating a witch. How loudly is he complaining?"

"My father never voices his objections in anything above a whisper, but it is an insidious, constant whisper. At this point, he is merely raising 'concerns.' *My* concern, though, is that with his trip to Portland he appears to already be assessing your influence over me. If he decides that your influence will negatively affect his relationship with me, or my likelihood of becoming heir . . ."

"You're afraid I'll be in danger if your father thinks I'm coming between you two?"

Lucas paused.

"Honesty, remember?" I said.

He looked me square in the eye. "Yes, I'm concerned. The trick, then, is not to allow him to think that will happen. It would be even better if I could convince him that my happiness with you will be beneficial to him.

That the strength of our relationship might bolster, rather than tear down, the other relationships in my life."

I nodded, as if I understood, but I didn't. Nothing in my own life had prepared me to understand a parental relationship where a simple visit home had to be planned with the strategic cunning of a military engagement.

"I hope this doesn't mean you're planning to accept this case," I said.

"No. My intention is simply not to refuse as vehemently as I normally do, or he'll blame you, however illogical the reasoning. I will hear him out, and I will endeavor to be more receptive to his paternal attentions than is my wont."

"Uh-huh."

Lucas smiled. "In other words, I'll make nice." He pushed his half-filled glass to the middle of the table. "We have a few blocks to walk. I know it's hot. We could call a cab—"

"Walking is good," I said. "Though I can just imagine what the humidity has done to my hair. I'm going to meet your family looking like a poodle with a live wire shoved up its butt."

"You look beautiful."

He said it with such sincerity, I'm sure I blushed. I grabbed his hand and tugged him to his feet.

"Let's get this over with. We meet the family. We fill out the forms. We find a hotel, buy a bottle of champagne, and see if I can't get that spell working for you."

"*You'll* get it working?"

"No offense, Cortez, but your Hebrew sucks. You're probably mispronouncing half the words."

"Either that or my spell-casting simply lacks your expert proficiency."

"Never said it. Well, not today. Today, I'm being nice to you."

He laughed, brushed his lips across my forehead, and followed me out of the café.

I'd never been to Miami before, and coming into the city by cab I hadn't been impressed. Let's just say, if the taxi had got a flat tire, I wouldn't have left the vehicle, not even armed with a passel of fireball spells. Now, though, we walked through the southeast section of the downtown core, along a dramatic row of steel and mirrored-glass skyscrapers overlooking the impossibly blue waters of Biscayne Bay. The tree-lined streets looked like they'd been scrubbed clean, and the only people hanging out on the sidewalk were sipping five-dollar coffees on café patios. Even the hotdog vendors wore designer shades.

I expected Lucas to lead me to some seedy part of town, where we'd find the offices of the Cortez Corporation cleverly disguised in a run-down warehouse. Instead, we stopped in front of a skyscraper that looked like a monolith of raw iron ore thrust up from the earth, towers of mirrored windows angled to catch the sun and reflect it back in a halo of brilliance. At the base of the building the recessed doors opened to a street-front oasis with wooden benches, bonsai, overhanging ferns, and a circular waterfall ringed with moss-covered stones. Atop the waterfall was a carved granite pair of Cs. Over the double-width glass doors a brass plate proclaimed, with near-humble simplicity, "Cortez Corporation."

"Holy shit," I said.

Lucas smiled. "Reconsidering that vow never to be the CEO's wife?"

"Never. Co-CEO, though, I might consider."

We stepped inside. The moment the doors closed, the noise of the street disappeared. Soft music wafted past on an air-conditioned breeze. When I turned around, the outside world truly had vanished, blocked out by dark mirrored glass.

I looked around, trying very hard not to gawk. Not that I would have been out of place. Just ahead of us, a gaggle of tourists craned their necks in all directions, taking in the twelve-foot-high tropical aquariums that lined two of the walls. A man in a business suit approached the group and I tensed, certain they were going to be kicked out. Instead, he greeted the tour guide and waved them over to a table where a matron poured ice water.

"Tour groups?" I whispered.

"There's an observatory on the nineteenth floor. It's open to the public."

"I'm trying not to be impressed," I said.

"Just remind yourself where it all comes from. That helps."

It did, dowsing my grudging admiration as quickly as if someone had dumped that pitcher of ice water over my head.

As we veered near the front desk, a thirtyish man with a news-anchor smile nearly knocked his fellow clerk flying in his hurry to get out from behind the desk. He raced toward us as if we'd just breached security, which we probably had.

"Mr. Cortez," he said, blocking our path. "Welcome, sir. It's a pleasure to see you."

Lucas murmured a greeting, and nudged me to the left. The man scampered after us.

"May I buzz anyone for you, sir?"

"No, thank you," Lucas said, still walking.

"I'll get the elevator. It's running slow today. May I get you both a glass of ice water while you wait?"

"No, thank you."

The man darted ahead of us to an elevator marked "Private." When Lucas reached for the numeric pad, the clerk beat him to it and punched in a code.

The elevator arrived, and we stepped on.

CHAPTER 5

THE WAGES OF SIN
PAY VERY NICELY INDEED

Inside, the elevator looked as if it had been carved from ebony. Not a single fingerprint marred the gleaming black walls and silver trim. The floor was black marble veined with white. How much money does a company need to make before it starts installing marble floors in the elevators?

A soft whir sounded and on what had appeared to be a seamless wall, a door slid open to reveal a computer panel and small screen. Lucas's fingers flew over the keypad. Then he pressed his thumb against the screen. The computer chimed, the panel slid shut, and the elevator began to rise.

We exited on the top floor. The executive level. At the risk of sounding overimpressed, I'll stop describing the surroundings. Suffice to say it was exquisite. Simple and understated, yet every surface, every material, was the best money could buy.

In the middle of the foyer, a marble-paneled desk rose, as if erupting from the marble floor. A beefy man in a suit sat behind a panel of television screens. When the elevator chime announced our arrival, he looked up sharply. Lucas steered me off the elevator and toward the left side of the foyer. A solid wood door swung open. Lucas glanced at the guard, nodded, and led me through.

We headed into a long corridor. As the door behind us closed, I slowed, sensing something out of place. It took a moment to realize what it was. The silence. No piped-in Muzak, no voices, not even the clatter of keyboards. Not only that, but the hall itself was unlike any office corridor I'd ever seen. There were no doors along either side. Just a long hallway, branching off in the middle, and ending in a huge set of glass doors.

As we passed the midway intersection, I snuck a glance down each side. There were actually two diagonal corridors off each side, each ending in a glass door. Through each of the four glass doors I could see a reception desk and secretarial staff.

"Hector's office to the left," Lucas murmured. "My eldest half-brother. To the right, William and Carlos's offices."

"Who has the other office?" I asked. "Beside Hector's?"

As soon as I said the words, I knew the answer, and wished I hadn't asked.

"It's mine," Lucas said. "Though I've never worked an hour in it. An absurd waste of prime real estate, but my father keeps it staffed and stocked, because any day now I'm bound to come to my senses."

He tried to keep his tone light, but I could hear the tightness creeping in.

"And if that ever happens, which office do I get?" I asked. "'Cause you know, I'm not going to be one of those silent-partner wives. I want a seat on the board and an office with a view."

He smiled. "Then I'll give you this one."

We'd come to the end of the hall. Through the glass door I saw a reception area three times as large as the ones I'd glimpsed down the side hallways. Though it was now past six o'clock, the office was manned by a squadron of secretaries and clerks.

Like the other door, this one was automatic, and, like the last time, someone had it open before we came within ten feet. As the doors opened, the sea of staff parted to give us a path to the reception desk. The younger secretaries heralded our arrival with unconcealed gapes and stammered hellos. The older ones welcomed us with subdued smiles before quickly returning to their work.

"Mr. Cortez," the receptionist said as we approached the desk. "A pleasure to see you, sir."

"Thank you. Is my father in?"

"Yes, sir. Let me—"

"He's in a meeting." A heavyset man walked from an interior hall and headed for a bank of filing cabinets. "You should have called."

"I'll buzz him, sir," the receptionist said. "He's asked to always be notified of your arrival."

The man across the room shuffled papers loudly enough to draw our attention. "He's busy, Lucas. You can't show up unannounced and drag him out of meetings. We're running a business here."

"Hello, William. You're looking well."

William Cortez. Middle brother. I could be forgiven for not reaching that conclusion earlier. The man bore little resemblance to either Lucas or Benicio. Average height and about seventy pounds overweight, with soft features that might have been girlishly handsome once, but had faded into doughy blandness. William turned to us for the first time, zapping

Lucas with an irritated glare. His gaze crossed over me with only a small headshake.

"Don't page my father, Dorinda," William said. "Lucas can wait like the rest of us."

She glanced at her fellow secretaries for help, but they worked harder, pretending not to notice her sinking into the quicksand of conflicting authority.

"Perhaps we should ascertain the exact nature of the request," Lucas said. "Did my father say he *could* be notified or that he *should* be notified?"

"Should, sir. He was very clear on that." She snuck a sidelong glance at William. "Very clear."

"Then I'm sure neither William nor myself wishes to get you into any trouble. Please notify him that I've arrived, but tell him I'm not here on a matter of any urgency, so I can wait for his meeting to end."

The receptionist fairly sighed with relief, nodded, and picked up the phone. While she called, Lucas steered me over to William, who was still at the filing cabinet.

"William," Lucas said, dropping his voice. "I'd like to introduce you to—"

William slammed the drawer, cutting him short. He hefted a pile of folders under his arm.

"I'm busy, Lucas. Some of us work here."

He turned on his heel and stalked out the main doors.

"Mr. Cortez?" the receptionist called from the desk. "Your father will be right out. He'd like you to wait in his office."

Lucas thanked her and led me down the hall to the glazed-glass double doors at the end. Before we reached them, a door to our left opened and a trio of men in standard-issue middle-management suits strode out, then stopped to stare at Lucas. After a quick recovery, they offered welcomes and handshakes to the crown prince, their greetings falling just a hair short of obeisance. I snuck a peek at Lucas. As someone who normally passed through life unnoticed, what was it like to be recognized here at every turn, to have VPs twice his age falling over themselves to pay their respects?

Once they were gone, we headed through the double doors, into a small reception room, and through yet another set of double doors before we reached Benicio's inner sanctum. Had I seen a picture of his office earlier, I'd have been shocked. Now, having seen the rest of the building, it was exactly what I'd expect. Simple, understated, and no larger than the office of the average corporate VP. The only remarkable thing about it was the view, made all the more spectacular by the window itself, which was a single pane of glass stretching floor-to-ceiling across the entire wall. The glass was spotless and the lighting in the room had been arranged so it cast no reflection, meaning you saw not a window, but a room that seemed to open right into the bright blue Miami sky.

Lucas walked to his father's computer and typed in a password. The screen blinked to life.

"I'll print off a copy of the security forms while we wait," he said.

While he did that, I perused the photos on Benicio's desk. The first one to catch my eye was of a small boy, no more than five, at the beach, staring at the camera with the most serious expression any five-year-old at the beach has ever had. One look at that expression and I knew it was Lucas. Beside him, a woman pulled a face, trying to get him to smile, but only making herself laugh instead. The broad grin infused her plain face with something approaching beauty. Maria. Her grin was as unmistakable as Lucas's sober stare.

What did Benicio's other sons think when they saw their father's former mistress's picture so prominently displayed, yet none of their own mother, his legal wife? Not only that, but of the three photographs on Benicio's desk, Lucas occupied two while the three of them shared one group portrait. What went through Benicio's head when he did something like that? Did he just not care what anyone thought? Or was there a deeper motive at work, purposely fanning the flames between his legitimate sons and the "bastard heir"?

"Lucas."

Benicio wheeled through the door, a broad smile lighting his face. Lucas stepped forward and extended his hand. Benicio crossed the room in three strides and embraced him.

The two bodyguards who'd accompanied Benicio to Portland slipped inside, surprisingly unobtrusive for men of their size, and took up position against the wall. I smiled at Troy, who returned it with a wink.

"Good to see you, my boy," Benicio said. "This is a surprise. When did you get in?"

Lucas extricated himself from his father's embrace as he answered. Benicio had yet to acknowledge me. At first, I assumed this was an intentional slight, but as I watched him talk to Lucas, I realized Benicio hadn't even noticed me there. From the look on his face, I doubted he'd notice a raging gorilla if it was in the same room as Lucas. I searched his face, his manner, for some sign that he was dissembling, putting on an act of fatherly affection, but saw none. Which made everything else all that much more inexplicable.

Lucas stepped back beside me. "I believe you've met Paige."

"Yes, of course. How are you, Paige?" Benicio extended a hand and a smile almost as bright as the one he offered his son. Apparently Lucas wasn't the only Cortez who could make nice.

"Paige told me you wanted to speak to me," Lucas said. "While that could, of course, be easily accomplished by telephone, I thought perhaps this would be a good time to bring her to Miami and ensure the proper security clearance forms are completed, so there is no misunderstanding regarding our relationship."

"There's no need for that," Benicio said. "I've already sent her vital stats to all our field offices. Her protection was assured the moment you told me about your . . . relationship."

"Then I'm simply clarifying it with a paper trail, to please the insurance department. Now, I know you're busy, Father. When would be the best time to discuss the details of this case?" He paused, then pushed on. "Perhaps, if you don't have plans, the three of us could have dinner together."

Benicio blinked. A small reaction, but in that blink and the moment of silence that followed, I read shock, and I suspected it had been a while since Lucas had voluntarily shared a meal with his father, much less extended an invitation to do so.

Benicio clapped Lucas on the back. "Perfect. I'll make the arrangements. As for discussing these attacks, though, we'll leave dinner as social time. I'm sure you're both anxious to hear more—"

A rustle at the door cut him short. William stepped in, gaze riveted on his father, probably so he didn't have to acknowledge us.

"I beg your pardon, sir," William said. "But as I was dropping off the Wang report, I overheard Lucas's offer and wanted to remind you that you have a dinner engagement with the governor."

"Hector can take my place."

"Hector's in New York. He has been since Monday."

"Reschedule, then. Tell the governor's office that something important came up."

William's mouth tightened.

"Wait," Lucas said. "Please don't rearrange your schedule on my account. Paige and I will be staying the night. We can have breakfast together."

Benicio paused, then nodded. "Breakfast tomorrow then, and drinks tonight if I can get away from the governor early enough. As for this other matter—"

"Sir?" William said. "About breakfast? You have an early morning meeting."

"Reschedule it," Benicio snapped. When William turned to leave, he stopped him. "William, before you go, I'd like you to meet Paige—"

"The witch. We've met."

He didn't so much as glance my way. A line creased between Benicio's eyebrows and he rattled off something in Spanish. Now, my Spanish was pretty good, and Lucas had been helping me improve—if only so we could talk without Savannah listening in—but Benicio spoke too fast for my translation skills. I didn't need an interpreter, though, to guess that he was upbraiding William for his rudeness.

"And where is Carlos?" Benicio said, reverting to English. "He should be here to see his brother and meet Paige."

"Is it past four?" William said.

"Of course it is."

"Then Carlos isn't here. If you'll excuse me—"

Benicio turned away, as if William had already left. "Where was I? Yes. This other matter. I've convened a meeting in twenty minutes to provide you with all the details. Let's get Paige a cold drink and we'll head to the boardroom."

Chapter 6

Familial Violence Insurance

Twenty minutes later, Lucas opened the conference room door for me. His eyes slanted a silent question my way. Did I want him to go first? I shook my head. Though I wasn't looking forward to confronting what I knew lay within that meeting room, I had to do it without hiding behind Lucas.

As I stepped inside, my gaze swept across the dozen or so faces within. Sorcerer, sorcerer, sorcerer . . . another sorcerer. Over three-quarters of the men in the room were sorcerers. Each pair of eyes met mine. Chairs shuffled and voices murmured wordless noises of disapproval. The word "witch" snaked through the room on a chorused whisper of contempt. Every sorcerer in the room knew what I was without being told. One look in the eyes, and witch recognized sorcerer, sorcerer recognized witch, and the introduction rarely pleased either.

Benicio waved Lucas and me to two empty chairs next to the vacant head of the table.

"Good afternoon, gentlemen," he said. "Thank you for staying late to join us. You all know my son Lucas."

The men within handshaking distance extended their hands. The rest offered spoken salutations. No one looked my way.

"This is Paige Winterbourne," Benicio continued. "As I'm sure most of you know, Paige's mother, Ruth, was Leader of the American Coven. Paige herself has been a member of the interracial council for several years, and I'm pleased to say, in that capacity, she has expressed an interest in the MacArthur case."

I held my breath waiting for some comment about my exile from the Coven or my embarrassingly short term as Leader. But Benicio said nothing. As much as he might dislike me, he wouldn't upset Lucas by insulting his girlfriend.

Benicio gestured toward a stocky man near the foot of the table. "Dennis Malone is our head of security. He's most familiar with the case, so I'll ask him to begin with an overview."

As Dennis explained, Dana MacArthur was indeed the daughter of a Cabal employee but not, as I'd assumed, of the Cabal witch. Like Savannah, Dana claimed supernatural blood from both parents, her father being a half-demon in Cortez Corporation sales. Randy MacArthur was currently overseas establishing a commercial foothold in the newly capitalist areas of Eastern Europe. Dana's mother was a witch named Lyndsay MacArthur. I'd hoped to recognize the name, but I didn't. Coven witches had little contact with non-Coven witches. Even my mother had only taken notice of outside witches when they'd caused trouble. One of the many things I'd wanted to change about the Coven, and now never would.

According to the background information Dennis provided, Dana's parents were divorced and she lived with her mother. Dennis mentioned that her mother lived in Macon, Georgia, and the attack had taken place in Atlanta, so I assumed Dana had been traveling or visiting friends. She'd apparently been out walking by herself around midnight—which seemed very strange for a fifteen-year-old girl, but I'd get an explanation later. The important thing was that during that walk, she'd cut through a park and been attacked.

"Where is Dana now?" I asked when Dennis finished.

"At the Marsh Clinic," Benicio said.

"That's a private hospital for Cabal employees," Lucas explained. "It's here in Miami."

"And her mother is with her?" I said.

Benicio shook his head. "Unfortunately, Ms. MacArthur has been . . . unable to come to Miami. We have every hope, though, that she'll change her mind."

"Change her mind? What's the problem? If she can't afford airfare, I'd certainly hope someone would—"

"We've offered her both commercial airfare and a flight on our private jet. Ms. MacArthur has some . . . concerns over air travel at this time."

At a noise from across the table, my gaze slid down the row of faces until it came to the youngest attendee, a sorcerer in his thirties. He met my gaze with a half-smirk. At a glare from Benicio, the smirk changed into a cough.

"Concerns over air travel," I said slowly, trying to wrap my head around the idea that a witch would let anything stop her from racing to her daughter's sickbed. "That's not unusual these days, I guess. A bus ticket might be—"

The smirking sorcerer cut in. "She doesn't want to come."

"There's been some estrangement between Dana and her mother," Benicio said. "Dana had been living on her own in Atlanta."

"On her own? She's fifteen—"

I stopped, suddenly aware that a dozen pair of eyes were on me. I could imagine nothing more humiliating for a witch than this, to sit in a room filled with sorcerers telling you that one of your race, who pride themselves on their family bonds, had let her teenage daughter live on the streets. Not only that, but she didn't even care enough to come to her daughter's side when she lay comatose and alone in a Cabal hospital. It was inconceivable.

"Maybe if I could speak to her," I said. "There might be a misunderstanding . . ."

"Or we could be lying," the sorcerer said. "Here's my cell phone. Anyone got Lyndsay MacArthur's number? Let the witch—"

"Enough," Benicio said, his voice sharp enough to cut diamonds. I'd heard that tone before . . . from his son. "You are excused, Jared."

"I was only—"

"You are excused."

The sorcerer left. I struggled to think of some way to defend my race. Lucas's hand squeezed my knee. I looked at him, but he'd turned to the table, mouth opening to speak for me. I quickly interrupted. As much as I longed for the support, the only thing that could make this worse would be for him to jump to my rescue.

"Is Dana's father aware of the situation?" I said.

Benicio shook his head. "Randy has been in Europe since spring. If he'd known about Dana's estrangement from her mother, he would have requested leave to come home."

"I meant the attack. Does he know about that?"

Another headshake. "He's currently in a very unstable location. We've tried contacting him by telephone, e-mail, and telepathy, but haven't been able to deliver the news. We expect him to be back in a major city within the week."

"Good. Okay. Back to the case, then. I'm guessing we're here because you want Dana's attacker found."

"Found and punished."

Somehow, I doubted that punishment would involve the local authorities, but after hearing what had been done to Dana, I couldn't bring myself to care.

"But the Cabal can investigate by itself, right?"

A reedy voice from down the table answered. "Mr. MacArthur is a class C employee."

352 • KELLEY ARMSTRONG

I looked at the speaker, a specter-thin, specter-pale man dressed in a mortician-black suit. Necromancer. It's a stereotype, I know, but most necros have a whiff of the grave about them.

"Paige, this is Reuben Aldrich, head of our actuarial department. Reuben, Ms. Winterbourne isn't familiar with our designations. Would you explain for her please?"

"Of course, sir." Watery blue eyes looked my way. "Employees range from class F through A. Only class A and B employees are entitled to familial violence insurance."

"Familial . . . ?"

Lucas turned to me. "It's insurance that covers corporate investigations into criminal matters such as kidnapping, assault, murder, psychic wounding, or any other dangers one's family might face as a result of their employment with the Cabal."

I looked at Reuben Aldrich. "So Mr. MacArthur, being class C, isn't entitled to a paid investigation into his daughter's attack. So why bring it to us—to Lucas?"

"The Cabal is offering to hire him," said the man beside me. "The reallocation of resources and man-hours would make the cost of an internal investigation prohibitive. Instead, we're offering to retain Mr. Cortez in a contract position."

Lucas folded his hands on the table. "Paying for an outside investigation into an assault not covered by the benefit package is a generous and considerate offer, but"—he met his father's gaze with a level stare—"unlikely to meet corporate profitability standards. You mentioned to Paige that the attack on Miss MacArthur wasn't the first."

"There's a second, possibly related, case," Benicio said. "Dennis?"

Dennis explained. Eight days ago another Cabal employee's runaway teen had been attacked. Holden Wyngaard was the fourteen-year-old son of a shaman. Someone had followed him for several blocks at night, then jumped him in an alley. Before anything could happen, a young couple had wandered into the alley and Holden's attacker had slipped away. The Cabal was not investigating.

"Let me guess," I said. "Mr. Wyngaard is a level C employee."

"Level E," Reuben said. "Substance-abuse problems have caused his status to drop. He is currently on suspension, and therefore entitled only to the most basic health-care benefits."

"But you think the cases are connected?"

"We don't know," Benicio said. "If we had clear proof of a pattern, we'd conduct our own investigation. As it stands, it's a troubling coincidence.

While the expense of a full-scale investigation isn't warranted, we'd like to be proactive and hire Lucas to look into the matter."

"Not me," Lucas said, his voice soft, but firm enough to carry through the room. "Paige."

"Of course, if Paige was interested in helping you—"

"I'm currently in the midst of defending a client, and couldn't possibly pursue this in the timely manner you'd require."

Benicio hesitated, then nodded. "Understandable. You have other obligations. I can't argue with that. If you'd like to set Paige on the case then, and supervise—"

"Paige doesn't require my supervision. You approached her with this case, hoping it might interest her because it concerns a witch. Whether she decides to take it is her choice."

Every pair of eyes turned to me. I felt the eager words of agreement leap to my throat. No one in this room gave a damn about Dana MacArthur. She needed someone on her side, and I longed to be that someone. Yet I locked my mouth shut and gave my brain time to override my heart.

One tragedy, and one near-tragedy, both involving the runaway kids of Cortez Cabal employees. Did I think they were related? No. The streets were a harsh and violent place for teens. That's a cold fact. I had to make an equally cold decision. I had to let someone else find justice for Dana. If I took this case, it would involve Lucas, if only by forcing him to act as middleman between the Cabal and me. I wouldn't do that to him. So I thanked everyone for coming out . . . and turned them down.

CHAPTER 7

TIME TO EMPTY THE MINIBAR

After the meeting, Benicio walked with us back to his office to get our overnight bags.

"I'd like you to take Troy tonight," Benicio said. "I'm concerned. If someone's targeting Cabal children—"

"I believe I'm a decade or so above fulfilling that requirement," Lucas said.

"But you're still *my* child. You know Troy; he'll be as unobtrusive as possible. I just . . . I want you to be safe."

Lucas lifted his glasses and rubbed the bridge of his nose, then glanced over at me.

I nodded.

"Let me take a guard from the security pool, then," Lucas said. "You should keep yours—"

"I'll still have Griffin," Benicio said, nodding at Troy's partner. "That will be enough tonight."

When Lucas finally agreed, Benicio slid in a few more "requests." He wanted to pick up the tab for our hotel, to compensate for bringing us here. Lucas refused. Benicio backed off, but followed with another demand. With the combination of this new threat and 9/11, he didn't want Lucas flying on a commercial airline. He'd make sure the corporate jet was fueled up to take us home. Again Lucas refused. Now Benicio dug in his heels, and kept them dug in until Lucas finally agreed to accept the hotel room, just to get us out of there.

By the time we escaped to the street, Lucas's forehead had gained ten years of stress-furrows. He stood beside the garden, closed his eyes, and inhaled.

"The sweet smell of freedom," I said.

He tried to smile, but his lips faltered and fell into a tired line. He squinted up and down the street, then headed east. Troy fell into position two paces behind. After a few yards, Lucas glanced over his shoulder.

"Troy? Please, walk beside us."

"Sorry," Troy said, striding up. "Habit."

"Yes, well, when a two-hundred-and-fifty-pound half-demon follows me, it's never a good thing. Fleeing for my life is usually involved."

Troy grinned. "You need a bodyguard."

"I need a saner life. Or faster feet. Right now, though, we need . . ."

"Wheels," I said. "Followed by stiff drinks."

"Uh, sir?"

Lucas winced.

"*Lucas*, I meant," Troy said. "The parking garage is beside the office. We needed to take the walkway across to get the car."

Lucas sighed. "Now you tell me."

"Hey, it's not my place to think. That's for you sorcerer guys. Me? I'm paid to keep my mouth shut, glare at strangers, and, on a good day, break a couple kneecaps."

"Cushy job," I said.

"It has its moments. The kneecap-breaking gets a little stale, though. I've tried tossing in the occasional jaw-busting and skull-smacking, but Mr. Cortez, he's a kneecap man."

Lucas shook his head and headed back toward the building.

At the hotel, Troy cased our room before allowing us inside. Seemed like overkill to me, but that was his job.

"All clear," he said, coming out. "There's a door between our rooms. Knock if you need me. If you go out to dinner . . ."

"We'll tell you," Lucas said.

"I'll keep out of the way, sit at a corner table, whatever."

"We'll probably have a quiet night, order room service."

"Hey, it's all paid for, so go for it." Troy caught Lucas's look. "Yeah, I know, you don't like using the old man's money, but you're his kid, right? If it was my dad . . ." He grinned. "Well, if it was *my* dad, I suppose he'd be offering me a lifetime supply of fire and brimstone, and personally, I'd prefer the cash, but that's just me. Seriously, though, take advantage of it. Clean out the minibar, rack up the room-service bill, steal the bathrobes. Worst thing that can happen, you'll piss off the old man and he won't talk to you for a year."

"Not the worst punishment I can imagine," Lucas murmured.

"Exactly. So live it up. And call me if you need help with the minibar."

I closed the door, cast a locking spell, and collapsed on the couch.

"I'm sorry," Lucas said. "I know that was difficult for you, turning them down."

"Let's just—let's not think about it. Not now. Maybe in the morning . . . Will we have time to stop by the hospital in the morning? See how she's doing?"

"We'll make time."

"Good. I can make sure she's okay, see if there's anything I can do from that angle and try to forget the rest. Now, let's help ourselves to that drink."

I started pushing to my feet, but Lucas waved me down.

"Stay there. I'll get it."

He glanced at the minibar, then at the door.

"The minibar's closer," I said. "And if you go out for booze, you'll have to take Troy. Your father brought us running down here, the least he can do is pay for our hotel and a drink."

"You're right. First, the drink. Then dinner. We'll order in—" He stopped and shook his head. "No, we're going out. Someplace nice. Followed by a show or a walk on the beach or whatever you want. My treat."

"You don't have to—"

"I want to. And, though I neglected to mention it earlier, I have money. Well, some money. I received payment on a legal matter, and I am, for the first time in months, reasonably flush."

"Is this for the case you're working now? With the shaman?"

"No, this is from a few years ago, a client whose financial situation has improved and who wanted to repay me. As for the current case, there is the possibility of a payment. A barter, so to speak. He has—" Lucas paused, then shook his head. "A matter we can discuss later, if and when it comes to fruition. For now, I have enough money to treat you to a proper evening out, and pay the rent for the next few months. Let me mix that drink, then I'll tell Troy we'll be leaving for dinner within the hour."

I didn't miss the "pay the rent" part, however skillfully he slipped it in. I paid the lion's share of the household expenses. Paid them by choice, I should add. I knew this bothered Lucas—not in an "I am man; I am breadwinner" kind of way, but as a subtler matter of pride.

Lucas barely earned a living wage. Most of his court and investigative work was pro bono, helping supernaturals who couldn't afford a lawyer or PI. What little money he made usually came from doing legal paperwork for wealthier supernatural clients, many of whom could easily and more conveniently have hired a local lawyer, but who retained Lucas as a way of supporting his pro bono efforts. Even that made Lucas uncomfortable, smacking too much of charity, but his only alternative would be to stop taking nonpaying cases, which he'd never do.

It hurt like hell to see him sleeping in fleabag motels, barely able to afford public transit, saving every penny so he could pay part of our expenses. I had enough for both of us. But how could I turn down his contributions without belittling his efforts? Yet another kink in the relationship we had to work out.

We stumbled back into the hotel room just before midnight, having followed dinner with a few rounds of pool and more than a few rounds of beer. Definite advantage to the whole chauffeur/bodyguard deal: built-in designated driver. The downside, though, was that Troy beat me in two out of three pool games, a serious blow to my ego. I blamed it on the booze. Deadened my reflexes . . . though it did wonders for helping me forget the rest of the day. As for Lucas, he was feeling better, too.

"I did not cheat!" I said, struggling to wriggle free of the upside-down over-the-back-of-the-sofa position in which I found myself pinned.

He pulled my blouse from my skirt and tickled my ribs. "You *so* cheated. Second game. Seven ball, left corner pocket. Minor telekinesis spell."

I squealed and swatted his hands. "I—the ball rolled."

"With help."

"Once. Only once. I—stop—" Another embarrassingly girlish shriek. "You—third game—the eight ball. You moved it out of the way of your shot."

He toppled us over onto the couch and slid a hand under my skirt.

"Diversionary tactics, Counselor," I said.

"Guilty." He hooked his fingers over my panties and peeled them off.

"Not so fast, Cortez. You promised me spell-casting."

"I think you did enough of that at the pool hall."

He stifled my sputtering with a kiss.

"Wait. No—" I wiggled sideways and dropped to the floor, then scooted out of reach. "How about a game? Strip spell-casting."

"Strip—?" He rubbed at his smile. "Okay, I'll bite. How do you play?"

"Just like strip poker, only with spell-casting. We take turns trying the new spell. Each time we fail, we remove a piece of clothing."

"Given the difficulty of that spell, we'll likely both run out of clothing first."

"Then we'll have to get more creative."

Lucas laughed and started to say something, but a knock cut him off. He looked at the main door. I pointed at the one linking our suite to Troy's. Lucas sighed, heaved himself to his feet, and peered around. I picked up his glasses from the floor.

"Thank you," he said, taking them. "I'll be right back."

"Better be. Or I'm starting without you."

Lucas buttoned his shirt on the way to the door. I crawled onto the sofa, straightened my skirt, and stuffed my panties between the cushions.

Lucas pulled open the adjoining-room door.

"There's been another attack," Troy said.

"Where?" I said, popping up from the sofa.

"Here. In Miami." Troy ran a hand through his hair. His face was pale. "I just got the page. They—I'm on call this week. No one took me off the list tonight. Can you phone in and let them know I can't make it?"

"Come in," Lucas said.

"I need—I've got some calls to make. It's—it's Griffin. His oldest boy. Jacob. I should—"

"You should come in. Please." Lucas closed the door behind Troy. "Are you saying Griffin's son has been attacked?"

"I—we don't know. He called the emergency line and now he's missing. They've sent out a search team."

"Why don't you go with them?" I said. "We'll be fine."

"He can't," Lucas said. "He'd be severely reprimanded for leaving me behind. A problem easily solved if I go along. Care to join us?"

"You need to ask?" I said, getting to my feet.

"No way," Troy said. "Dragging the boss's son and girlfriend along on a search-and-rescue wouldn't get me reprimanded, it'd get me fired. Or worse."

"You aren't dragging me anywhere," Lucas said. "I'm going to help, therefore you're obligated to follow. I'll phone in for details on the way."

CHAPTER 8

WELCOME TO MIAMI

I sat in the front seat of the SUV, giving Lucas privacy in the back as he called the security department for an update.

A drizzling rain pattered on the roof, just enough to make the road slick and shimmery in the darkness. Our windshield, though, was dry, improving Troy's visibility tenfold. Seeing that, I understood how Troy knew Robert Vasic. Like Robert, Troy was a Tempestras, a storm demon. The name, like many half-demon cognomens, tipped into melodrama and bordered on false advertising. A Tempestras couldn't summon storms. He could, however, control the weather within his immediate vicinity, calling up wind, rain or, if he was really good, lightning. He could also, like Troy, do something as small but practical as keeping rain off his windshield. I thought of commenting, but one glance at Troy's taut face told me he was in no mood for a discourse on his powers. He was so intent on his driving, he probably didn't even realize he was shunting the rain from the windshield.

"Can I ask something?" I said quietly. "About Griffin's son?"

"Hmm? Oh, yeah, sure."

"Is he a runaway?"

"Jacob? Shit, no. They're tight. Griffin and his kids, I mean. He's got three. His wife passed away a couple years ago. Breast cancer."

"Oh."

"Yeah, Griff's great with his kids. Real close." Troy eased back in his seat, as if grateful for the chance to fill the silence with something other than the patter of rain. "Griffin comes off like an asshole, but he's a good guy. Just takes the job too serious. He used to work for the St. Clouds, and they run things different. Like the fucking military . . . pardon my French."

"The St. Clouds are the smallest Cabal, right?"

"Second smallest. About half the size of the Cortezes. When Griffin's wife was sick, the St. Clouds made him use vacation time for every minute he took off driving her to chemo and stuff. After she died, he gave two weeks' notice and took an offer from Mr. Cortez."

At a click from the backseat, Troy glanced in the rearview mirror.

"Any news?" he asked.

"They have two search teams out. Dennis—" Lucas looked my way. "Dennis Malone. You met him at the meeting today. He's been called in to coordinate the operation from headquarters. He advises that we begin several blocks from where Jacob phoned. The teams are currently searching the blocks on either side of that point."

I twisted to face Lucas. "Do we have any idea what happened to Jacob?"

"Dennis replayed his phone call for me—"

"Nine-one-one?"

Lucas shook his head. "Our personal emergency line. All Cabal employee children are given the number and told to call it instead. The Cabals prefer to avoid police involvement in any matter that may be supernatural in nature. An employee's family is told that phoning this number ensures faster response times than calling nine-one-one, which it does. The larger Cabals have security and paramedic teams ready to respond twenty-four hours a day."

"So that's who Jacob called."

"At eleven twenty-seven P.M. The call itself is indistinct, owing to both the rain and poor cellular reception. He appears to say he's being followed, after leaving a movie and becoming separated from his friends. The next part is unclear. He says something about telling his father he's sorry. The operator tells him to stay calm. Then the call ends."

"Shit," Troy said.

"Not necessarily," Lucas said. "The cellular signal may have been disrupted. Or he may simply have decided he was making too big a deal out of the matter, become embarrassed, and hung up."

"Would Griffin let him go to a late movie with his friends?" I asked Troy.

"On a school night? Never. Griff's real strict about stuff like that."

"Well, then, that's probably it. Jacob realized he'd be in trouble for sneaking out and hung up. He'll probably crash at a friend's place, and call his dad once he works up the nerve."

Troy nodded, but didn't look any more convinced than I felt.

"Jesus," Troy said as he pulled into the area where Dennis had advised us to park.

He'd squeezed the SUV between two buildings and come out in a tiny parking lot only a few feet wider than the alley itself. Every building in sight was rife with boarded-up windows, the boards themselves rife with bullet holes. Any security lights had long since been shot out. The rain swallowed the glow of the new moon overhead. As Troy swung into a parking spot, the headlights illuminated a brick wall covered in graffiti. My gaze swept across the symbols and names.

"Uh, are those . . . ?"

"Gang markings," Troy said. "Welcome to Miami."

"Is this the right place?" I said, squinting into the darkness. "Jacob said he was at a show, but this doesn't look . . ."

"There's a theater a few blocks over," Troy said. "A gazillion-screen multiplex plopped down in the middle of hell. Just the place you want to drop off the kiddies for a Saturday matinee." He shut off the engine, then dowsed the lights. "Shit. We're going to need flashlights."

"How's this?" I cast a spell and a baseball-size blob of light appeared in my hand.

I opened the car door and lobbed the light out. It stopped a few yards away and hung there, illuminating the lot.

"Cool. I've never seen that."

"Witch magic," Lucas said. He cast the spell himself, conjuring a weaker ball of light, and leaving it in his palm. "It has a more practical orientation than ours. I'm not as accomplished at this spell as Paige yet, so I'll keep my light at hand, so to speak. If I throw it out . . . well, it rarely cooperates."

"Splats on the sidewalk like an egg," I said, tossing him a quick grin. "Okay, then, we have the flashlights covered. Troy, I'm assuming you can handle umbrella duty. So we're all set."

We walked to the edge of the parking lot. The skeletal remains of a building rose from a vacant slab of land at least the size of a city block. Scrubby trees, half-demolished walls, piles of broken concrete, ripped-open trash bags, discarded tires, and broken furniture cluttered the landscape. I bent to lift a sodden sheet of cardboard draped over a large lump. Troy kicked a syringe out of the way and grabbed my hand.

"Not a good idea," he said. "Better use a stick."

I peered across the field, in one glance picking out a score of places where Jacob could lie low and wait for help.

"Should we try calling him?" I asked.

Troy shook his head. "Might attract the wrong kind of attention. Jacob knows me, but he's a smart kid. If he's hiding out here, he's not going to answer us until he sees my face."

Though none of us said it, there was another reason for not just calling his name and moving on. He could be injured, unable to answer. Or worse.

"The rain is easing and Paige's ball casts sufficient light for us all to search," Lucas said. "I suggest we split up, each taking a ten-foot swatch, and make a thorough sweep." He stopped. "Unless . . . Paige? Your sensing spell would be perfect for this."

"A spell?" Troy said. "Great."

"Uh, right. The only problem . . ." I glanced at Troy. "It's a fourth-level spell. Technically, I'm still third level, so I'm not . . ." God, this stung. "I'm not very good—"

"She's still refining her accuracy," Lucas said. That sounded so much better than what I was going to say. "Could you give it a try?"

I nodded. Lucas motioned for Troy to follow him and start searching, giving me privacy. I closed my eyes, concentrated, and cast.

The moment the words left my mouth, I knew the spell had failed. Most witches wait for results, but my mother had taught me to use my gut instinct, to feel the subtle click of a successful cast. It wasn't easy. To me, intuition always seems like some flaky New Age thing. My brain seeks the logic in patterns; it looks for clear, decisive results. As I move into harder spells, though, I've been forcing myself to develop that inner sense. Otherwise, with the sensing spell, if I didn't detect a presence, I wouldn't know whether it was because no one was there or because the spell had failed.

I recast. The click followed, almost as a subconscious sigh of relief. Now came the tough part. With a spell like this, I couldn't just cast it and leave it on, like the light-ball. I needed to sustain it, and that took concentration. I held myself still and focused on the spell, measuring its strength. It wavered, almost disappeared, then took hold. I resisted the urge to open my eyes. The spell would still work, but I'd rely too much on what I was seeing instead of feeling. I turned slowly, and sensed two presences. Troy and Lucas. I pinpointed their location, then peeked to double-check. There they were, exactly where I'd sensed them.

"Got it," I said, my voice echoing through the silence.

"Good," Lucas called back as they headed my way.

"So how does this work?" Troy asked.

"If I walk slowly, I should be able to detect anyone within a twenty-foot radius."

"Great."

I inhaled. "Okay, here goes."

I had two choices. Be led around with my eyes closed, like some wack-job spiritualist, or open my eyes and keep my gaze on the ground. Naturally, I went for option two. Anything to avoid looking like an idiot.

Lucas and Troy followed. After a few yards, I felt the spell waver. I told my nerves there was no need to panic, no pressure here. They called me a liar, but agreed to fake it for a while. I relaxed and the spell surged to full strength.

Weak presences tickled at the edges of awareness. When I focused on them, they stayed amorphous. Small mammals, probably rats. An image flashed through my mind: a novel a friend and I had "borrowed" from her older brother when we'd been kids. Something about rats going crazy and eating people. There was this one scene with . . . I forced the image back, my gaze skittering across the ground looking for rat turds.

The spell fluttered, but I kept walking. We finished one twenty-foot strip and started up the next. I weaved through a minefield of beer cans and around the black scar of a campfire pit. Then I picked up a presence twice as strong as the others.

"Got something," I said.

I hurried toward the source, climbed over a three-foot wall remnant, and startled a huge gray tabby. The cat hissed and tore off across the field, taking the presence I'd sensed with it. The spell snapped.

"Was that it?" Troy said.

"I can't—" I shot a glare at Lucas. I knew he didn't deserve it, but couldn't help myself. I stamped off to the end of the swath, grabbed a stick, and poked at a pile of rags.

"Paige?" Lucas said, coming up behind me.

"Don't. I know I'm overreacting, but I hate—"

"You didn't fail. The spell was working. You found the cat."

"If I can't tell the difference between a cat and a sixteen-year-old boy, then, no, it's not working. Forget it, okay? I should be looking for Jacob, not field-testing spells."

Lucas moved up behind me, so close I could feel the heat from his body. He dropped his voice to a murmur. "So you uncover a cat or two along the way. Who cares? Troy doesn't know how the spell's supposed to work. We have a lot of ground to cover."

Too much ground. We'd been here at least thirty minutes and barely searched a thousand square feet. I thought of Jacob being out there, waiting for rescue. What if it was Savannah? Would I be plodding through the field, bitching at Lucas then?

"Can you guys keep up the manual search?" I whispered so Troy couldn't overhear. "I don't want . . . I don't want you relying on my spell."

"That's fine. We'll cover ground faster that way. We have my light spell, as poor as it is. You take yours, go to the opposite side of the field, and start there."

I nodded, touched his arm in apology, and headed off with my light-ball trailing after me.

This time the sensing spell worked the first time. Or, I thought it worked, but something was wrong. The moment I cast, I felt a presence, a dozen times stronger than the cat's. I broke the cast, and tried again. Failure, then success. But the presence was still there, down a narrow alley between two buildings. Should I alert Lucas and Troy? And what, drag them over to help me uncover a whole litter of cats? This I could check myself. No sixteen-year-old boy would be scared off by the sight of me.

I ended the sensing spell and directed my light-ball to stay around the building corner. There it would cast a dim glow, enough to see by, but not enough to spook a kid who likely knew little about the supernatural.

I slipped into the alley. The presence had come from a few yards down, along the east side. Less than ten feet away I saw a recessed doorway. That'd be it. I picked my way through the refuse, making as little noise as possible. Beside the doorway, I pressed myself against the wall. A smell wafted past. Cigarette smoke? Before I could process the thought, my body followed through on its original course of action, swinging around the doorway. There, in the shadows, was a teenage boy.

I smiled. Then I saw another boy beside the first, and another behind him. Something rustled behind me. I turned to see my exit blocked by another bandana-wearing teen. He said something in rapid-fire Spanish to his friends. They laughed.

Something told me this wasn't Jacob.

CHAPTER 9

THE LOCAL WILDLIFE

Attitude is everything. Therefore, when faced with four—oh, wait, there's another—five inner-city gang members, the worst thing you can do is turn tail and run. And why should you? Well, the presence of lethal weaponry might answer that question, but that's not how I see it. These are kids, right? People, just like everyone else. As such, they could be reasoned with, so long as one took the right stance. Firm, but polite. Assertive, but respectful. I had every right to be here, and furthermore, I had good cause. A cause that they might be able to assist.

"Hello," I said, standing tall and looking up to meet the eyes of the one I assumed was the leader. "I'm sorry to disturb you. I'm looking for a teenage boy who went missing around here. Have you seen him?"

For a moment, they just stared at me.

"Yeah?" one in the back said finally. "Well, we're looking for some money. Have you seen any? Maybe in your purse?"

A round of snickers. I turned to the speaker.

"As you've probably noticed, I'm not carrying a purse. I—"

"No purse?" He turned to his friends. "I think she is hiding it, under her shirt. Two big purses." He made the universal male gesture for large breasts.

I waited through the inevitable guffaws and resisted the urge to tell them that, as boob jokes went, this was one of the lamer ones I'd heard.

"He's sixteen," I said. "Tall. Dark hair. White. Someone was chasing him. He may be hurt."

"If we saw him, he would be hurt. No one comes here and just walks out again." He met my gaze. "No one."

"Ah," a voice said behind us. "Well, perhaps this evening you gentlemen could make an exception." Lucas took my arm. "We apologize for the misunderstanding. Please excuse us."

The thug behind me stepped up to Lucas and flicked open a switchblade, keeping the knife down at his side, a covert threat.

"Nice suit, *pocho*," he said, then dropped his gaze over my skirt and blouse. "Where did you two come from? The fucking mission?"

"Out of town, actually," Lucas said. "Now, if you'll excuse us—"

"When we're done," the knife-thug said. "And we aren't done."

He smirked at me and reached out his free hand toward my breast. I started murmuring a binding spell, but before I could cast it, Lucas lifted his hand and blocked the youth's.

"Please don't do that," Lucas said.

"Yeah, and who's gonna stop me?"

"I am," a voice rumbled.

Everyone looked up—way up—to see Troy. He plucked the knife from the thug's hand.

"The mission bodyguard," I said. "Sorry, guys, but we have work to do. Thanks for your cooperation, and don't stay out too late. It's a school night."

A chorus of muttered Spanish, none of it complimentary, I'm sure, followed us from the alley, but the kids stayed in their doorway.

When we were out of earshot, Lucas glanced over at Troy.

"You realize, of course, that you robbed me of a rare opportunity to display my martial prowess, and win untold weeks of feminine appreciation."

"Sorry 'bout that."

I grinned and squeezed Lucas's arm. "Don't worry. I know you were mere milliseconds from blasting them with an energy-bolt spell."

"Absolutely." He glanced over his shoulder at Troy. "You'll have to forgive Paige's overenthusiastic attempt to befriend the local wildlife. Not many of their type where she comes from."

"Hey, we have gangs in Boston."

"Ah, yes. I believe they're particularly bad down by the wharf, where they're liable to descend upon the unwary, surround him with their yachts, and shout well-chosen and elegantly elocuted epithets."

Troy laughed.

Lucas continued, "When dealing with gang members, Paige, it's best to treat them as you would a rabid dog. Whenever possible, avoid their territory. If you inadvertently run into one, avoid eye contact, back away slowly . . . then blast them with a good energy bolt."

"Got it."

"Shall we continue—"

Lucas's cell phone beeped. He answered it. Fifteen seconds later, he hung up.

"They found him?" Troy said.

Lucas shook his head. "Just checking in to see if we had."

"Like we wouldn't call if we did." Troy gazed around the field. "Aw, fuck this. He's not here. You know what? I think you're right. I think he's lying low at a buddy's house. Griffin knows all about the other attacks. That's why he gave Jacob the cell phone, and told him to report anything unusual. Jacob probably spotted one of the neighborhood bad boys, panicked, and phoned it in. Then he felt stupid and took off."

We looked at one another.

"So," I said. "Do you guys want to take the north end again and I'll cover the south?"

They nodded. We were just about to split up when Lucas's phone buzzed. Another brief conversation.

"Griffin showed up in the second sector," Lucas said.

Troy winced. "Oh, shit."

"Precisely. He's making things difficult for the searchers. Unintentionally, of course, but he's quite distraught. They're understandably concerned, considering his abilities."

"What kind of half-demon is he?" I asked.

"A Ferratus," Lucas said.

Not one of the more common half-demons. So rare, in fact, that I had to translate the name from Latin before I remembered it. Ferratus. Iron-plated. A one-trick half-demon, but that one trick was a doozy. When a Ferratus half-demon invoked his power, his skin became as hard as iron. No wonder Benicio had snapped up Griffin from the St. Clouds. He was the perfect bodyguard . . . and the last guy you'd want going on a rampage.

"Dennis has asked me to intercede," Lucas said. "They're only a block over. I suggest we walk, and cover the intervening area along the way."

"I could stay here and—" I began.

"No," both men chorused.

I followed them into the alley.

As we walked, I drifted behind Lucas and Troy. So long as we were moving, I might as well cast my sensing spell and see whether I picked up anything. No reason to let them know what I was doing—that would only increase the pressure to provide results. Since they were both examining every nook and cranny on the way, they assumed I was doing the same and didn't notice as I fell farther behind.

I found two more alley cats. My alternate career with Animal Control was looking bright. On the positive side, as soon as I sensed kitty number three, I knew it was feline, which meant I was learning to distinguish between presence strengths.

I'd just finished finding my fourth stray cat when a distant voice hailed us. I peered down the alley to see several men approaching Troy and Lucas. The second search party. I quickened my pace. I'd gone about ten feet when I sensed another presence. Stronger than a cat, but . . . I stopped walking and concentrated. No, too weak to be human. I took another step. My feet felt lead-weighted, as a niggling uncertainty plucked at my brain. Too strong to be a cat, too weak to be human. So what was it?

Ahead, the men stood in a huddle, voices carrying to me only as waves of sound. Lucas saw me, but didn't wave me over. Tacit permission to continue searching. So no harm in checking out that presence. I traced it to an adjoining alleyway. I turned to show Lucas where I was going, but he'd left the group. Gone to find and calm Griffin, no doubt. I'd zip down the alley and be back before he noticed I was gone.

I tracked the presence along the connecting alley to a doorway. The door had been propped open by a wadded-up piece of cardboard. Wet cardboard, bracing a door that opened inward. I checked the door itself for signs of dampness, but it was dry. A windless night and a drizzling rain wouldn't explain the sodden cardboard, meaning it had been brought in from the alley within the last hour or so.

I hesitated outside the door, readied a fireball, then shifted my light to the entrance, where it would illuminate the room within. I eased around the doorway. The room was empty, save for a pile of rags in the corner. The presence I was sensing came from that corner, somewhere under those rags. As I pulled the light-ball closer, I saw that the heap wasn't rags, but a moth-eaten filthy blanket. Protruding from under it was a high-top sneaker emblazoned with the ubiquitous Nike swoosh.

I ran across the room, dropped to my knees, and yanked away the blanket. Underneath was a man, curled in fetal position. I touched his bare arm. Cool. Dead. The presence had weakened even more since I'd first detected it. Dissipating as the last traces of body heat faded. A pang of sadness ran through me, chased by a guilty surge of relief that this wasn't the boy I was seeking.

I moved back. As I did, my shadow fell from the man's face, and I realized it wasn't a man at all. The size had fooled me, but now, seeing the soft features and frightened eyes, I knew I was looking at Griffin's son.

My hands flew to his neck, feeling for signs of life, but I knew I'd find none. I rolled him onto his back to check for a heartbeat. As his arms fell from his chest, I inhaled, seeing the bloody patchwork of his T-shirt, criss-crossed with stab wounds.

"Paige!" Lucas called from somewhere outside.

"In—" My voice came out as a squeak. I swallowed and tried again. "In here."

I got to my feet, then caught sight of Jacob's bloodied shirt and bent to pull up the blanket. His wide eyes stared at me. People used to believe you could see the last moment of a man's life imprinted in his eyes. I looked into Jacob's eyes and I did indeed see that last moment. I saw bottomless, impotent terror. I bit my lip and forced myself to tug the blanket up.

A noise at the door. A large shadow filled the door frame.

"Troy," I said. "Good. Keep everyone else back until I've had a chance to tell Lucas—"

The man crossed the room in a few long strides. Even before I saw his face, I knew it wasn't Troy.

"Griffin," I said, jumping back to block Jacob's body. "I—"

He grabbed me by the shoulder and threw me out of the way. I hit the floor. For a moment, I lay there, dazed. That moment was just long enough for Griffin to kneel beside his son and pull back the blanket.

A howl split the air. A curse, a scream, another howl. The slam of fist against brick. Another. Then another. I looked up to see a fog of brick and mortar dust and, through it, Griffin beating the wall, each blow punctuated with an unearthly howl.

"Griffin!" I shouted.

He was past hearing me. I cast a binding spell, too quickly, and it failed. From outside came the sound of voices and running feet, then Griffin's enraged grief drowned them out. A hail of broken brick pelted down, mingled with slivers of wood and stone. A falling shingle glanced off my shoulder as the building quaked under the force of Griffin's blows.

In a few minutes, something would give—the roof, a wall, something. Through the dust, I could see the open doorway, beckoning me to safety. Instead, I closed my eyes, concentrated, and cast the binding spell again. Halfway through the incantation, a chunk of brick hit my arm, and I stumbled backward. More brick rained down, larger pieces now, big enough to hurt. I gritted my teeth, closed my eyes, and cast again.

The pounding stopped. I held the spell for a few seconds before I dared to open my eyes. When I did, I saw Griffin, his fist stopped in midair. He grunted, then snarled, trying to break free, but I put everything I had into holding him still. Our gazes met. His eyes darkened with rage and hate.

"I'm sorry," I said.

Lucas and the others swung through the doorway.

CHAPTER 10

EVIDENCE OF A PATTERN

Two draining hours later, we returned to the SUV. The EMTs had taken Jacob's body to the Cabal morgue for examination and autopsy. A forensics team was processing the scene. Investigators were combing the area for witnesses and clues. Standard procedure for a murder investigation. Yet every one of these professionals, from the coroner to the photographer, was a supernatural, and a Cortez Cabal employee.

None of this would ever make the six o'clock news. The Cabals were a law unto themselves in the purest sense of the phrase. They had their own legal code. They enforced that code. They punished the transgressors. And nobody in the human world knew any different.

"Do you want to stay with Griffin?" I asked Troy as he escorted us to the car. "I'm sure we could grab another bodyguard from the security team."

Troy shook his head. "They're taking Griffin to see his kids. He doesn't need me there."

As we neared the SUV, Troy lifted the remote. Heavy running footfalls sounded behind us. It was Griffin.

"I want to talk to you," he said, bearing down on Lucas.

Troy put up a hand to stop him, but Lucas shook his head. I readied a binding spell. Griffin stopped inches from Lucas, well within anyone's personal comfort zone. Both Troy and I visibly tensed. Lucas only looked up at Griffin.

"I want to hire you," Griffin said. "I want you to find whoever did this."

"The Cabal will investigate. My father will see to it."

"Fuck the Cabal."

"Griff," Troy warned.

"I mean it," Griffin said. "Fuck the Cabal. They won't do shit until some sorcerer's kid gets hurt. I want you to find this son of a bitch and bring him to me. Just bring him to me."

"I—"

"I can pay you. Whatever the going rate is for a PI, I'll double it. Triple it." He raised his fist for emphasis, then looked at his hand, shoved it into his pocket, and lowered his voice. "Just tell me what you want, and I'll get it."

"You don't need to do that, Griffin. My father will order an investigation, and he has resources I can't match."

"I'm class C. I'm not *entitled* to an investigation."

"But you'll get one."

"And if I don't?"

"Then I'll do it," I said quietly.

Griffin glanced over, as if he hadn't noticed me there. For a long minute, he just looked at me. Then he nodded.

"Good," he said. "Thank you."

He turned and walked back into the night.

"Oh, God, what did I just say?" I murmured, thumping my head back against the leather rear seat. I looked at Lucas, buckling his seat belt beside me. "I am so sorry."

"Don't be. If you didn't say it, I would have. You set his mind at ease. That's what he needed. As for following through, that won't be necessary. My father will call for an investigation, if for no other reason than to reassure his employees that the Cabal is taking action."

This time when Troy searched our room, he found someone there. Benicio. Lucas took one look into the room and slumped, as if the strain of the night had just hit him full force.

"Minibar?" I whispered.

"Please."

Benicio and I traded nods, and I skirted past him to the bar fridge. I took out two glasses, then stopped and turned to Benicio.

"Can I get you something?"

"Water would be fine," he said. "Thank you, Paige."

I fixed drinks as the two men talked behind me.

"I wanted to thank you for joining the search," Benicio said. "It meant a lot to everyone, having someone from the family helping."

"Yes, well, you're welcome. It's been a long night. Perhaps—"

"I couldn't get your brothers there on a direct order, let alone voluntarily. They think leadership is showing up at the office every day, issuing orders, and signing papers. They have no concept of what the employees expect, what they need."

I peeked at Lucas. He stood there with the pained expression of a child forced to sit through the thousandth rendition of his father's favorite lecture.

"I'm sure Hector would have gone."

Benicio snorted. "Of course Hector would go. He'd go because he knows I'd want him to. He'd have killed the boy himself, if he thought it'd win my favor."

Lucas winced. I handed him a straight Scotch. He mouthed a thank-you. I gave Benicio his water and he nodded his thanks before continuing.

"We've had more evidence of a pattern. A St. Cloud VP got wind of our problem, prompting a call from Lionel. One of their necromancer's daughters, who was living with relatives after some family trouble, was attacked last Saturday, the night before Dana."

"Is she okay?" I asked.

Benicio shook his head. "Like Jacob, she managed to place a call to their emergency line saying she was being followed but was dead when they found her. I've placed calls to Thomas Nast and Guy Boyd asking whether they know of any attacks on employees' children. Thomas tentatively confirmed that they've had two incidents, but he wouldn't provide details over the phone. The Cabals are meeting in Miami tomorrow to share information."

"They're launching a joint investigation, I presume," Lucas said.

"Yes, which is why I'm asking you to reconsider."

"Reconsider?" I said. "If the Cabals are investigating, you don't need us."

"No. If the Cabals are *jointly* investigating, I need your help more than ever. As Lucas can tell you, an intra-Cabal operation—"

Lucas lifted a hand. "We're tired, Papá," he said softly. "It's been a very long night. I understand this new concern, and I agree that it *is* a concern. May I ask, though, that you let me explain the situation to Paige tonight, try to get some sleep, then discuss it with you over breakfast?"

"Yes, of course," Benicio said. "What time do you need to be in court tomorrow?"

"Noon."

"Then let's reschedule our breakfast from seven to eight, to give you time to sleep. I'll have the jet fly you to Chicago afterward."

Lucas hesitated, then nodded. "Thank you."

He turned toward the door.

"One last thing," Benicio said.

Lucas paused, still facing the door, one hand on the knob, lips parting in a silent sigh. "Yes, Papá?"

"In light of this latest tragedy, I think we must assume that the killer's intent is to hurt the Cabals where they expect it least and will feel it most. Given that, we have to also assume that the ultimate prize for him would be a member of a CEO's family."

"Yes, of course, but we can discuss this—"

"I'm not talking generalities, Lucas. I'm bringing this to your attention because it obviously affects you and Paige, and you need to consider that immediately."

"He's targeting teenagers. I'm not a teen—"

"I'm not referring to you. This killer is obviously smart enough to attack the edges, pluck from the herd the most vulnerable, those children farthest removed from Cabal protection. If he wanted a teenager from a Cabal CEO's immediate family, there is only one who doesn't live with a Cabal and who isn't under twenty-four-hour guard."

"Oh, God," I said. "Savannah."

CHAPTER 11

THE MOST ENDANGERED KID ON THE PLANET

Earlier this year, when Kristof Nast sued for custody of Savannah, he'd done so by claiming to be her father. At first, I hadn't believed him. Savannah, as the daughter of a notoriously powerful woman who was both a witch and a half-demon, showed every sign of matching or surpassing her mother's powers, and as such she'd be a prize acquisition for any Cabal.

As for Kristof being her father, it was preposterous. No witch would ever get involved with a sorcerer, much less a high-ranking Cabal sorcerer. Then I'd met Kristof, seen Savannah's eyes staring back at me, and knew there was no question of paternity.

Even if I'd still doubted it, his actions proved he wasn't trying to recruit a potential employee. Kristof hadn't just made a halfhearted attempt to kidnap Savannah. He'd put his all into getting custody, and he'd died trying to stop Savannah from hurting herself. A sorcerer like Kristof Nast would never do that for a witch who wasn't his daughter.

This story had been churning in the Cabal gossip mill for months now. Anyone looking for Cabal children would know about Savannah. They'd also know that, unlike every other child and grandchild of a Cabal CEO, she wasn't ferried to and from a private school in an armored car filled with half-demon bodyguards. She had only Lucas and me, and right now, she didn't even have us.

I will say, with some modicum of pride, that I did not panic. Okay, I did have a few moments of heart palpitations and rapid breathing, but I managed to pull myself together before hitting the clinical anxiety stage.

It took only a few minutes for Lucas and his father to come up with a plan that kept me from barreling out the door and grabbing the next plane home. Benicio had already dispatched the corporate jet to Portland. By the time he mentioned the possible danger to Savannah, Cabal guards were en route to pick her up. I will admit to a brief moment of "What if this is all a setup and he's going to snatch Savannah" anxiety, but I managed to stifle it before I blurted out any wild accusations. Lucas trusted his father to bring Savannah here, so I trusted him.

Lucas made the call to Michelle's parents, apologized for waking them, and tossed together a plausible story to explain why several huge men would be arriving at their door to collect Savannah. Or I assume he came up with a plausible story. I heard none of it. I knew enough about Lucas, though, to know he was capable of manufacturing the most convincing lies at a moment's notice—yet another birthright from his father.

At my request, Lucas also talked to Savannah. What did he tell her? The truth. I'm sure of that. If it was me on that phone, I'd have sugar-coated it for her. I couldn't help it. The urge to make her life easier was too great. So I'd have given her a watered-down version, and she'd have listened, then asked to speak to Lucas to get the truth.

Once Benicio was gone, Lucas walked to the sofa, sat down beside me, and took my hand.

"You okay?" he murmured.

I squeezed his hand and managed a wan smile. "I'll be better when she's here, but I'm okay."

"About this case," he said. "Am I correct in assuming you want it?"

"I want it, but—"

"After what happened tonight, we've moved beyond the luxury of worrying about conflict of interest. Someone needs to investigate this."

"You don't think the Cabals can handle it?"

"Individually, I'd say the Cabals are quite capable of handling the situation. But together? Together they work at a fraction of their capacity."

"Infighting?"

He nodded. "Precisely. It's like two warring countries teaming up against a common enemy. Each will want to lead the attack. Each won't share their information for fear of divulging contacts and techniques. Each will want the other to put *their* men at risk. A plan of action won't be decided so much as negotiated."

"And in the meantime, more kids will be hurt."

"Collateral damage. I won't say the Cabals don't care; they aren't monsters. But they are structured around profit-making and self-preservation. Those priorities will always come first, intentionally or not."

"But obviously your father foresees this or he wouldn't still be asking you to take the case. Why doesn't he tell the other Cabals, 'Thanks for the offer, but we'll go it alone'?"

Lucas leaned back into the sofa. "Politics. At this level, even my father's hands are tied. If he refuses to cooperate, it'll not only affect his standing with the other Cabals but also cause internal dissent. Understandably, his employees will question why he'd refuse extra help."

"So it's down to us. In that case, then, I definitely want to—" I stopped. "Wait. What about Savannah? I certainly can't let her tag along and—"

"I have a thought on that. Someone who could look after her."

I shook my head. "You know how I am. Either I look after her myself, or I'll go crazy worrying. I don't trust anyone—"

He told me who he had in mind.

"Oh," I said. "That might work."

Benicio called to say that Savannah was on the jet and would arrive in Miami just after six. Lucas told him our decision, that I would take the case, starting immediately. As for Lucas's role, we'd decided on honesty over subterfuge. Of course he'd help me. Yes, this meant working alongside the Cabals, but the cause was right, and he wouldn't cheapen that by hiding his involvement. If Benicio felt he'd won a victory, we had to let him have that satisfaction. Our only defense was that we wouldn't accept a Cabal paycheck for the job. We were doing this on our own, for our own reasons.

With securing Savannah's safety now our top priority, Lucas asked his father for a rain check on breakfast. Instead, Benicio would bring a copy of the case files for me later in the morning, after Lucas was gone and I'd had time to settle Savannah in at the hotel. Benicio promised Lucas that he would help with protection arrangements for Savannah, and Lucas wisely refrained from telling him we'd already done so. While we appreciated Benicio's help, neither of us wanted Savannah in his custody for long, in case he hoped to use the opportunity to pitch to her as a future employee.

We met Savannah at the airport. By "we," I mean Lucas, myself, and Troy. Yes, Troy was still with us, though I had every intention of handing him back to his boss after lunch. Nothing against Troy, but there was something unsettling about a huge half-demon dogging your every step. Savannah, however, took our new shadow in stride, as if there was nothing at all unusual about having a chauffeur/bodyguard—further proof that Cabal royal blood flowed in her veins.

Over breakfast, we answered Savannah's questions about the attacks. She listened with more curiosity than concern. Altruism isn't Savannah's strong suit. I tell myself it's part of being a teenager, but I suspect there's more to it than that.

"Just as long as I don't get kidnapped again," she said. "Twice in one year is enough for anyone. I swear, I must be the most endangered kid on the planet."

"You're special."

She snorted. "Yeah, well, special never seems to bring anything but trouble. Now I know why my mom moved us around so much." She looked up sharply. "We don't have to move again, do we?"

"It's not that kind of problem. All we need to do is find you a safe place to stay while I look for this guy."

"What?" She looked from me to Lucas. "No way. You're kidding, right?"

"Paige can't investigate while worrying about you, Savannah."

Her eyes swung to meet mine. "You wouldn't do this. You wouldn't send me away."

I opened my mouth, but guilt zapped my voice.

"Savannah . . ." Lucas warned.

Her gaze clung to mine. "Remember the last time? You said you wouldn't leave. Not ever."

"Savannah—" Lucas's voice sharpened.

"We can work the case together. You've got all those new spells. You can protect me better than anyone. I trust you, Paige."

A right hook below the belt. I managed a strangled, "I—we—"

Lucas told her who'd be looking after her.

Savannah blinked, then eased back in her chair. "Well, why didn't you say so?" She took a swig of orange juice. "Hey, does this mean I get to skip school?"

After breakfast we returned to the airport to see Lucas off. As Savannah chatted with Troy, Lucas and I discussed my next steps in the case.

"The boy who was attacked first, Holden," I said. "He called the emergency line, too. Don't you think that's odd? That almost every victim had time to call for help before they were attacked? Jacob, I can see, because he had a cell phone. But the others?"

"I'd strongly consider the possibility that they were permitted to make the call, perhaps by prolonging the chase so they could reach a phone."

"But why?"

"It was already too late for help to arrive, so the killer was probably ensuring that the case remained under Cabal jurisdiction, and the victims weren't found by humans first. However, we should concentrate on facts, rather than interpretation. It's too early for that."

"Speaking of facts, I wish Holden saw his attacker." A thought struck me. "What we need is the eyewitness report of someone who *wasn't* supposed to escape. We need a necromancer."

Lucas shook his head. "A good idea, but murder victims are very difficult to communicate with so soon after they pass over, and on the rare occasion when a necromancer manages to make contact, the spirits are almost always too traumatized to recall details surrounding their death."

"I don't mean Jacob. I mean Dana. A good necromancer can make contact with someone in a coma."

"You're right, I'd forgotten that. Excellent idea. I have several necromancer contacts, all of whom owe me considerable favors. On the flight, I'll place some calls and see which of them could get to Miami quickest."

CHAPTER 12

VISITING HOUR

Before taking Savannah to the airport, the Cabal guards had escorted her to our apartment to get more clothing. Benicio had also asked her to pack suitcases for Lucas and me, since we'd arrived in Miami with only one change of clothing. Considerate of him, I'll admit. I'd been too worried about Savannah to think of that myself. The only downside was that this meant Savannah picked out what she thought we should wear.

Lucas had taken his suitcase straight onto the jet without opening it, probably fearing that the look on his face when he glanced inside might make Savannah feel her efforts were underappreciated. Though Lucas owned very little in the way of casual clothing, I suspected every piece of it was in that bag, and not a single item suitable for court. I only hoped she'd thought to grab him some socks and underwear.

When I unpacked my bag, I saw that lack of undergarments wouldn't be a problem for me.

"What did you do, empty my entire lingerie drawer into the bag?" I said, untangling a web of bras.

"Course not. I don't think they make suitcases that big." She tugged a pair of garter straps from the bra-knot. "Do you actually wear these? Or are they just for sex?"

I grabbed the garters. "I wear them."

Of course, when I did wear them it was only because they improved a certain sexual advantage of wearing skirts, one that was very awkward to accomplish with full nylons. That, however, wasn't a tidbit I was sharing with anyone—well, other than Lucas, but he already knew.

"You promised me I'd get stuff like this when I went to high school," she said, lifting a pair of green silk panties.

"I promised no such thing."

"I mentioned it, and you didn't say no. That's the same as promising. Do you know how embarrassing it is changing in a locker room, having the girls see me wearing cotton grannies?"

"All the more reason to keep you wearing them. If it embarrasses you to have *girls* see them, it'd be even more embarrassing to have guys see them. Like a modern-day chastity belt."

"I hate you." She fell back, spread-eagled onto the bed, then lifted her head. "You know, if you won't get them for me, I might sneak behind your back and buy my own. That'd be bad."

"You gonna start doing laundry, too?"

"As if!"

"Then I'm not worried."

Someone knocked at the door. Savannah vaulted from the bed and was out of the room before I could stuff my handful of lingerie into a drawer. I heard Savannah's shout of greeting and knew who it was.

"Paige is in the bedroom putting away her underwear," Savannah said. "It'll take a while."

I grabbed another handful.

"Shit," said a voice behind me. "She's not kidding. What'd you do, rob a lingerie store?"

There stood the world's only female werewolf, a title that sounds more like it should describe a circus freak show than the blond woman in the doorway. Tall and lean, Elena Michaels had a werewolf's typically athletic build, and the kind of wholesome good looks that cause men to say things like, "Wow, if she dolled herself up, she could be a knockout." Those who dared say such things, though, were more likely to find themselves knocked out.

Today Elena wore a T-shirt, cutoff jean shorts, and sneakers, with her long silver-blond hair tied back in an elastic band and maybe, just maybe, lip gloss . . . and looked a helluva lot better than I did after hours of grooming. Not that I'm envious or anything. Oh, did I mention she was thirty-two and looked mid-twenties? Or that she can eat a sixteen-ounce porterhouse steak and not gain an ounce? Werewolves get all the goodies: extended youth, extreme metabolism, sharpened senses, and super-strength. And, yeah, I'm envious.

Still, if I can't have a werewolf's gifts, I'll take a werewolf as a friend. Being part wolf makes them extremely loyal and protective . . . which made Elena the only person to whom I'd entrust Savannah.

Elena surveyed the mess of lingerie scattered across the bed. "I'm not even sure where half that stuff goes."

Savannah zoomed past Elena, jumped on the bed, grabbed a bra, and held it up to her chest.

"This one's mine," Savannah said, grinning. "Can't you tell?"

Elena laughed. "Maybe in a few years."

Savannah snorted. "At the rate I'm going, it'll take a few years plus a few pairs of socks. I'm the only girl in the ninth grade who still wears a training bra."

"I was still wearing one in tenth grade, so I've got you beat." Elena bent down to pick up a negligee I'd dropped. "Expecting to spend a lot of time alone with Lucas, I see."

"I wish," I said. "He's already headed back to Chicago. Savannah packed my clothes, and I do hope there *are* clothes in this bag somewhere."

"At the bottom," Savannah said.

I shoved the last of the lingerie into a drawer, then stuffed the half-packed suitcase into the closet and turned to Elena. I resisted the urge to hug her. Elena wasn't the hugs-and-kisses type. Even fleeting physical contact, like handshakes, made her vaguely uncomfortable, though nowhere near as uncomfortable as they made someone else . . . which made me realize someone was missing from this reunion.

"Where's Clay?" I said. "Waiting in the car? Hoping he can avoid saying hello to me?"

"Hello, Paige," came a Southern drawl from the living room.

"Hello, Clayton."

I popped my head around the bedroom door. Elena's partner, Clayton Danvers, was standing by the window, his back to me, likely not an unconscious gesture. Like Elena, Clay was blond-haired, blue-eyed, and well built. While Elena was attractive, Clay was traffic-stopping gorgeous . . . and had all the charm of a pit viper.

The first time we met, Clay had tossed me a bag containing a severed human head, and things went downhill from there. I don't understand him, he doesn't understand me, and the only thing we have in common is Elena, which causes more problems than it solves.

He finally deigned to face me. "You said Lucas isn't here?"

"He had to zip back to Chicago for his court case."

Clay nodded, clearly disappointed. One could argue that he simply hoped for someone else to talk with, to avoid having to make conversation with me, but the truth was that Clay seemed to genuinely like Lucas, which shocked the hell out of me. Not that Lucas wasn't likable. Just that Clay, well, he didn't much like anybody. His usual reaction to anyone outside his Pack ranged from near-tolerance to outright loathing. I'd landed on the farthest possible end of that scale, though I was slowly inching away from the brink.

"Ready to go?" Clay said, looking behind me at Elena.

"I just got here," she said.

"We have a long drive—"

"And all the time in the world to drive it." Elena walked from the bedroom and looked at me. "We rented a car so we can drive back to New York, take our time, see the sights, make a vacation out of it. If anyone is after Savannah, Jeremy thought it might be wise if we keep on the move for a few days, rather than rush home."

"Good idea. Thank him for me."

She grinned. "Having us out of his hair for a few days is all the thanks he needs."

"Can we stop in Orlando?" Savannah asked.

"You want to go to Disney World?" Elena said.

Savannah rolled her eyes. "Not likely."

I mouthed something to Elena. She grinned.

"Ah, Universal Studios. Sorry. I thought Disney World sounded kind of cool myself, but we could go to Universal, if that's okay with Paige."

"Have fun," I said. "I transferred some money into Savannah's account, so make sure she pays her own way."

From Elena's brief nod, I knew Savannah's money wouldn't be spent on anything but junk food and souvenirs, as it had when I'd given her money for her week with them this summer. I knew better than to argue. Their Alpha, Jeremy Danvers, was very well-off, and the three of them shared everything, including bank accounts. If I insisted on paying, I'd insult Jeremy. If he had his way, Savannah wouldn't even be using her own money for candy bars and T-shirts.

"Got your bag packed?" Clay asked Savannah.

"Never unpacked it."

"Good. Grab it and we'll go."

"You two have a nice trip," Elena said, plunking onto the sofa. "I'm visiting Paige."

Clay made a noise in his throat.

"Stop growling," Elena said. "I'm here, and I want to spend some time with Paige before I leave. Unless you'd prefer I *stayed* here. You know, that might not be such a bad idea. I could stick around, help her out—"

"No."

"Is that an order?"

"Savannah?" I cut in. "There's a Starbucks a few blocks over. Why don't you show Clay where it is, grab us some coffees?" I looked at Clay. "When you get back, you should probably take off. Benicio's stopping by soon, and he made some noises about taking Savannah into protective custody, so I'd rather she wasn't here when he arrives."

Clay nodded, then walked to the door and held it open for Savannah. When it closed behind them, Elena looked at me.

"Taking mediation lessons from Lucas, I see. Sorry about that. I know you have better things to do than listen to us bicker." She shook her head. "We've worked out a lot of things, but he still has trouble with the idea that I need to keep a corner of my life for myself, a corner that doesn't include him."

I sat in the chair across from her. "He doesn't like me. I understand that."

"No, it's not you." She caught my skeptical look. "Seriously. He just doesn't like me having friends. God, that sounds bad, doesn't it? Sometimes I hear myself saying things like that, and they make perfect sense to me, but then I think of how they must sound to others—" She stopped. "So tell me about this case."

"Ouch. You have to work on your 'steering clear of personal issues' segues."

She laughed. "That obvious, eh?"

"As for Clay not wanting you to have friends, I know he's like that, and I know why, so you don't need to worry about it. I'm not going to mail you brochures for women's shelters. I'll admit, at one time, I was a little concerned. Not that I thought he was abusive or anything, but he's, uh, extremely committed—"

"Obsessive."

"I wasn't going to say it."

She laughed and shifted to recline on the sofa, feet on the coffee table. "Don't worry, I say it all the time. Usually to him. Sometimes shouted. Occasionally accompanied by a flying object. We're working on it, though. He's learning to give me some space, and I'm learning that he's never going to be happy about it. Oh, I told him about that idea we had, for the ski trip this winter? He flipped. Then I said it'd be the four of us, not just you and me, and he simmered down, actually said that sounded okay. That's the trick, I think. Suggest something he'll hate, then offer a less painful alternative."

"If that doesn't work, next time you argue about me, remind him you could befriend Cassandra instead."

Elena whooped a laugh. "Oh, that'd put the fear into him . . . though he probably wouldn't believe it. Speaking of believing, would you believe she's still calling me?"

"Are you serious?"

"She somehow got my cell phone number."

"I didn't—"

"I know you didn't, that's why I didn't ask. Problem is, now I have to talk to her, at least long enough to say I don't want to talk to her. When she called the house line, Jeremy would say I wasn't home, and Clay—well, Clay never let her get past hello." Elena swung her legs down and twisted around to sit at the opposite end of the sofa, facing me. "I hate to admit this, but I'm spooked. I mean, she can't want us to be buddies, not after what she did, so what does she *really* want?"

"Honestly? She probably doesn't have an ulterior motive. I think she really wants to get to know you better, and she doesn't see any conflict between that and trying to steal your lover or convince the council to leave you for dead." I shrugged. "She's a vampire. They're different. What can I say?"

"Two words. Serious psychotherapy."

I grinned. "We'll go halfsies and get her a gift certificate for Christmas."

Elena was about to reply when the door opened. Savannah walked in, carrying my key card in one hand and a steaming coffee cup in the other. I was sure that whatever was in that cup, it wasn't hot chocolate, and probably wasn't even decaf, but I said nothing. I doubted Clay realized she was too young for coffee. I only hoped Elena would step in when the wine and whiskey came out.

Savannah held the door open for Clay, who walked through carrying a cardboard cup holder with three cups.

"That was fast," Elena said. "Too fast. What'd you do? Run all the way there? Or drive?"

"It was only half a block."

"Uh-huh."

"He's right," Savannah said. "It was closer than Paige thought, but we're just dropping off your drinks, then we're going to check out the marina while you guys talk."

Elena glanced at Clay, tensed, as if waiting for him to refute this. When his mouth opened, her fingers tightened on the sofa cushion.

"First, we're taking your suitcase down to the car," he said to Savannah. He turned to Elena and handed her a coffee cup. "When you're done here, just come and get us."

She smiled up at him. "Thanks. I won't be long."

He nodded and passed me a cup.

"Tea," he said, then glanced at Savannah. "Right?"

"Chai," she said.

I took the cup with thanks, then laid it down and helped Savannah get ready.

CHAPTER 13

A Fortuitous Collision of Circumstances

Savannah was, as she'd said, already packed, but I wasn't letting her go without an armful of instructions, most of which were some variation on "be good" or "be careful."

Handing Savannah over to anyone, even to people I knew would protect her with their lives, wasn't easy for me. Elena made it easier, though, by arranging a twice-daily check-in time of eleven in the morning and eleven at night. If either of us would be busy at the designated time, we'd forewarn the other, so no one would be left worrying about a call not made or not answered. Yes, it bordered on obsessive-compulsive, but neither Elena nor Clay made me feel I was overreacting, and I truly appreciated that.

I planned to walk down with Elena and see them off, so Savannah and I didn't bother with good-byes. As the door swung shut behind them, I turned to Elena.

"Clay's really good with Savannah," I said.

"Uh-huh."

"You don't think so?"

She plunked down onto the sofa. "No, I'm just waiting for part two of that comment."

"You mean the part that goes 'You know, he'd probably make a pretty good—'"

She held up a hand to stop me. "Yep, that part."

I laughed and plunked into my chair. "Any progress on that front?"

"He's moved from hints disguised as jokes to outright hints. That took a year, so I figure I have another year before he insists on progressing to actual discussion. He's being pretty good about it, though. Taking his time, getting me used to the idea before he pops the question."

"He knows you're not ready."

"Problem is, I'm not sure I'll ever be. I want kids. I really do. I always assumed I'd grow up, marry a nice guy, live in the suburbs, and raise a houseful of kids. But with Clay, well, I always thought a life with him meant giving up all of that. Even the 'growing up' part."

"Highly overrated."

"I think so." She grinned and stretched her legs along the sofa. "Kids, though, well, it's a big step, and not just for the normal reasons. Clay knows I'm not going anywhere, so it isn't a question of commitment. It's the werewolf issue. Two werewolves having a baby? Never been done. Who knows what—" She rubbed her hands over her arms. "Well, I'm just not ready, and right now, I don't have time to worry about it, not with all these recruitment problems."

I put down my chai. "That's right. You met that new recruit this week. How did—"

Two raps at the door cut me off.

"Guess Clay's getting antsy," I said. "At least he tried."

Elena shook her head. "That's far too polite a knock for Clay."

"And it's the wrong door," I said, following the sound. "That'd be our bodyguard."

Elena laughed. I opened the door that joined the two suites and she saw Troy.

"Shit," she murmured. "You weren't kidding."

"I just saw Mr. Cortez's car pull into the lot," Troy said. "Figured you might like some advance warning. I thought I heard"—he leaned into the room and saw Elena—"voices. Hello."

He leaned farther into the room for a better look, and it was obvious he wasn't going anywhere without an introduction.

"Troy, this is Elena; Elena, this is Troy Morgan, Benicio's bodyguard, temporarily on loan."

Elena stood and extended her hand. Troy nearly tripped over his feet to take it. As usual, I don't think Elena noticed the attention, and certainly didn't reciprocate.

"You're a, uh, friend of Paige's?" he said.

"A fellow council member," I said. "She just stopped in for a visit . . . with her husband."

"Hus—" He looked down at Elena's hand and saw her engagement ring. "Oh." He stepped back, reluctantly. "The interracial council, huh? So you're a supernatural. Let me guess—"

"Sorry," I said. "But if Benicio's coming up, we'd better get Elena gone."

Another rap at the door, this time the hall one.

"Come on," Troy said to Elena. "We'll duck out through my room."

"Say good-bye to Savannah for me," I said. "I'll call you tonight."

Elena let Troy usher her into his room. I paused, then opened the hall door and invited Benicio in. His new bodyguard stayed in the corridor. Before I'd even closed that door, the adjoining door reopened and Elena popped her head through. She motioned toward the hall, mouthing "guard." I discreetly waved her inside. Better for her to go out the main door, and arouse Benicio's suspicions a bit, than have the guard see her sneak from Troy's room and raise Benicio's suspicions a lot. I doubted Troy usually had women spend the night while he was on duty.

"Is Savannah here?" Benicio asked, looking around. He saw Elena.

"She was just leaving," I said.

Elena brushed past Benicio with a small smile and a nod. I held the door open, then closed it behind her and turned to Benicio.

"Now, where were we?" I said. "Oh, you brought the case files. Thanks."

I took the files. Benicio glanced at the half-open bedroom door, trying to see through it.

"Is Savannah—"

"Did Lucas get to Chicago okay?" I asked. "He was worried about being late. He cut it pretty close this morning."

"The plane landed at eleven."

"Time to spare, then. Good."

Benicio slipped a look through the bedroom doorway. "I assume Savannah—"

"Is everything in this?" I said, hoisting the file.

Before he could answer, I walked to the window and spread the file on the wide sill, pretending to look through it as I surveyed the parking lot below. I saw Clay and Elena's blond heads bobbing through the scattering of cars, moving fast, Savannah's dark head between them.

"Let's see. Incident reports . . ." Elena, Clay, and Savannah stopped at a car. A convertible, of course. A moment's pause, then Clay tossed Elena the keys and they climbed inside. "Scene photos, medical reports . . ." The car peeled from the lot. "Looks like everything's here. Now, you were saying . . . ?"

"Savannah," he said. "I don't see her here, Paige, and I certainly hope you wouldn't be foolish enough to let her wander around the hotel unaccompanied."

"Of course not. She's staying with friends while I investigate this."

"Friends?" He paused. "The woman who just left, I presume. Perhaps you don't realize how serious this is. You cannot turn Paige over to a human—"

"She's a supernatural. Someone who will take very good care of Savannah."

Benicio paused, only for a moment, processing everything he knew about my supernatural contacts in less time it would take most people to name the capital of France.

"The werewolf," he said. "Elena Michaels."

I'll admit to a moment of disconcertion. The werewolves valued their privacy, which was why I hadn't told Troy who Elena was. When Benicio did his homework, he didn't miss anything.

"Werewolf?" Troy murmured behind us. "She was a werewolf? Shit. Now there's a story that'll buy me a few rounds at the club."

"No," Benicio said. "You won't tell anyone."

Troy straightened. "Yes, sir."

"As a matter of interracial courtesy, we must respect the werewolves' privacy. You may, however, take a few drinks on my club tab, to compensate."

Troy grinned. "Yes, sir."

"I don't mean to criticize, Paige," Benicio said. "And I don't wish to insult your friends, but I must point out that the Cabal is far better equipped to protect Savannah. You lack experience in such matters, and what may seem like a good idea to you is not necessarily the wisest option."

"It wasn't my idea."

"Then who—?" He stopped, realizing the only possible answer. Then he nodded. "If Lucas thinks this is best, we'll leave the girl with them . . . for now. If the situation worsens, though, we may need to reconsider our options."

"Understood," I said. "Now, what can you tell me about this case?"

Benicio ordered a room-service lunch for us, which we ate in the hotel room while discussing the case. If Benicio had any problem discussing Cabal problems with a witch, he gave no sign of it, but was as generous with his information and offers of assistance as I could want. More generous than I wanted, to be honest. I was uncomfortable enough taking a case Benicio had brought to us. I didn't want to work with him any closer than necessary.

There were a few strategic moves I could make that made me feel less like I'd been suckered into working for Benicio. Earlier, I'd notified the hotel that I'd be staying on, and asked them to change the billing to my credit card. They were less than a third full, with no hope of major bookings soon, so after some dickering, we'd agreed on an affordable rate. I didn't tell Benicio that I'd switched the billing. By the time he found out, it'd be too late for him to argue.

I also gave Benicio back his bodyguard. When he protested I argued that with Griffin on grief-leave, Benicio needed one of his regular guards, and my own investigating would be less conspicuous without a half-demon shadow.

Benicio left at one. Lucas still hadn't called about the necromancer. While I waited, I read through the files. I kept my cell phone on the desk, checked for messages twice, and adjusted the ring volume once. A bit anxious for Lucas's call? Nah.

When the phone finally rang, I checked caller ID, and answered with "You found someone?"

"I apologize for taking so long. Two of my contacts were slow in phoning back, then I had to wait for court to recess."

"But you found someone?"

"A fortuitous collision of circumstances. A first-rate necromancer who just happens to be on business in Miami this week." His voice sounded oddly strained, as if forcing cheerfulness. Must have been the connection.

"Perfect," I said. "When can he meet me? Or is it she?"

"Early this evening, as a matter of fact. Very fortunate. The only other possibility couldn't make it until Monday, so this is quite the lucky break."

Did it sound as if he was trying to convince me? Or himself?

"Okay, so tell me about—"

"Hold on." A muffled word or two to someone else. "It appears the recess ended sooner than I expected. Do you have a pen?" He gave me the address and directions. "Now, everything's been arranged. Someone will meet you there. They're expecting you between six-thirty and seven. It's a reasonably good section of town, but I'd still advise that you ask the cab-driver to wait until you're inside. Go to the rear door, knock, and give your name."

"Speaking of names, what's this necro—"

"They're calling me in now. I have to go, but I'll phone you tonight. Oh, and Paige?"

"Yes?"

"Trust me on this one. However things may appear, please trust me."

And with that, he was gone.

CHAPTER 14

THE MERIDIAN THEATER
PROUDLY PRESENTS . . .

"Is this it?" the driver asked.

I leaned forward and read the sign: parking for employees and guests of the meridian. all unauthorized vehicles will be towed at owner's risk and expense. Was I a guest of the Meridian? What was the Meridian? Damn Lucas. I'd left a message on his cell, asking him to call me back with more information, but obviously court was running late today.

The directions he'd provided had taken the cab on a convoluted path through an industrial area when, according to my new Miami map, I could have accessed the same street off a major thoroughfare. Of course, the driver hadn't suggested a shorter route, though I had caught him smiling at the meter once or twice.

The address Lucas gave me was right here. The parking lot. What exactly had he said? There'd be a rear door. To my left was a block-long wall dotted with air vents and barred windows, plus two entrances: a loading dock, and a double set of gray-painted metal doors.

I asked the driver to wait, got out, and walked to the doors. They were indeed solid, with no handles or locks. Beside them was a doorbell marked DELIVERIES. I double-checked the address, and rang the bell.

Thirty seconds later, the door swung open, letting out a blast of shouting voices, rock music, and power tools. A young woman squinted out into the sunlight. She wore cat's-eye glasses, red leather pants, and an ID badge with an obscenity in the name space.

"Hi, I'm—" I raised my voice. "I'm Paige Winterbourne. I was supposed to meet—"

The woman shrieked over her shoulder. "J.D!" She looked back at me. "Well, come in, girl. You're letting out all our air-conditioning."

I excused myself while I paid the cabdriver, then hurried back to the building. As I stepped inside, a fresh song started, volume cranked. At first wail, I winced.

"Isn't that god-awful?" the young woman said, slamming the door behind me. "It's Jaime's warm-up song. 'My Way.'"

"Tell me that's not Frank Sinatra."

"Nah, some dead Brit."

"Recorded as he was dying a long, painful death."

The woman laughed. "You got that right, girl."

A fortyish man appeared, slight, balding, carrying a clipboard, and looking harried to the point of exhaustion. "Oh, thank God. I thought you weren't going to make it."

He grabbed me by the elbow, tugged me into the room, and propelled me through a mob of drill-wielding men working on what looked like a scaffold.

"You *are* Paige, right?" he asked, moving us along at warp speed.

"Uh, right."

"J.D. I'm Jaime's production manager. They didn't send you around the front, did they?"

I shook my head.

"Thank God. It is a zoo out there. We've been sold out since last week, but some moron at WKLT has been announcing all day that we still have seats available, and now we have a line from here to Cuba of very unhappy folks."

A pink-haired woman appeared from behind a heavy velvet curtain. "J.D., there's a problem with the sound levels. The acoustics in here are shit, and—"

"Just do your best, Kat. We'll take it up with the booking agent later."

He pushed me past the woman, then through the curtain. We stepped out onto a side stage, in front of a rapidly filling auditorium. I stopped to gape, but J.D. tugged me along, crossing the stage to the opposite side.

"What kind of—" I began.

J.D. stopped in mid-stride and I nearly bashed into him.

"I don't believe this," he said. "I don't fucking believe it. Tara! Tara!"

A woman scurried up the steps. She could have been J.D.'s twin, carrying a matching clipboard, just as slight and harried, not balding but looking ready to tear out her own hair.

"Front row," J.D. said. "Second seat right of the aisle. Is that not reserved for Jaime's guest?"

Tara consulted her clipboard. "A Ms. Winterbourne. Paige Winterbourne."

"This is Ms. Winterbourne," J.D. said, jerking a finger at me. Then he jabbed the same finger at the sixty-year-old platinum blonde in the second seat. "That is not Ms. Winterbourne."

"I'll get security."

Tara disappeared behind the curtain. J.D. surveyed the theater, now nearly three-quarters full, with a steady stream flowing in.

"I hope they didn't overbook. Houston overbooked and it was an absolute nightmare." He stopped. "Oh, my God. Take a look at what's coming through the door now. Do you see what she's wearing? I didn't think those came in purple. Some people will do anything to catch Jaime's attention. In Buffalo last month— Oh, good. Your seat is clear. Follow me."

He kept his hand on my elbow, as if I might otherwise be swallowed by the crowd. A security guard escorted the platinum-haired grandmother down the aisle. She turned and shot a lethal glare at me. J.D. quick-marched us down the steps.

"Is front row okay? Not too close for you?"

"Uh, no. It's fine. This, uh, Jaime, is it? Is he around? Maybe I could—"

J.D. didn't seem to hear me. His gaze was darting over the crowd, like a sheepdog surveying an unruly mob of ewes.

"We needed more ushers. Ten minutes to show time. I told Jaime—" A watch check. "Oh, God, make that eight minutes. How the hell are they going to get everyone in here in eight minutes? Go ahead, sit down and get comfortable. I'll be out to see you at intermission. Enjoy the show."

He darted into a group of people and disappeared.

"Okay," I muttered. "Enjoy the show . . . whatever it is."

As I sat, I glanced at the people on either side of me, hoping one of them might be this Jaime guy, who I assumed was the necromancer I'd come to meet. To my left was a teenage girl with piercings in every imaginable location . . . and a few I would have preferred not to imagine. On my other side was an elderly woman in widow's weeds with her head bowed over a rosary. Talk about audience diversity. Now I was stumped. I couldn't imagine what kind of show would interest both of these people.

I looked around, trying to pick up some clues about the show from the theater, but the walls were covered in plain black velvet. Whatever the show was, I hoped I wasn't expected to sit through it before I spoke to this Jaime. Maybe after it started, he'd come out and get me. I guessed he was the theater owner or manager. Someone important, from what J.D. said. An odd profession for a necromancer. Unless this Jaime wasn't the necromancer. Maybe he was only the guy who would take me to the necromancer. Damn it! I didn't have time for this. I pulled out my cell phone, called Lucas's number again, but only got his voice mail.

I left a message. "I'm sitting in a theater right now, with absolutely no idea why I'm here, what's going on, or who I'm supposed to talk to. This better be good, Cortez, or I'm going to need a necromancer to contact *you*."

I hung up, and glanced at my neighbors again. Not about to disturb the rosary-widow, I turned to the teen and offered my brightest smile.

"Packed house tonight, huh?" I said.

She glowered at me.

"Should be a great show," I said. "Are you a . . . fan?"

"Listen, bitch, if you raise your hand and get picked instead of me, I'll pop out your eyeballs."

I turned my endangered orbs back to the stage and inched closer to the rosary-widow. She glared at me and said something in what sounded like Portuguese. Now, I don't know a single word of Portuguese, but something in her voice made me suspect that, whatever she said, the translation would sound roughly like what pierced-girl beside me had said. I sunk into my seat and vowed to avoid eye contact for the rest of the show.

Music started, a soft, symphonic tune, far removed from the cater-wauling rock backstage. The lights dimmed as the music swelled. A scuffle of activity as the last people scurried to their seats. The lights continued to fade until the auditorium was immersed in darkness.

More sounds of activity, this time coming from the aisle beside me. The music ebbed. A few lights appeared, tiny, twinkling lights on the walls and ceiling, followed by more, then more, until the room was lit with thousands, all casting the soft glow of starlight against the inky velvet.

A choral murmur of oohs and ahhs surged, and fell to silence. Absolute silence. No music. No chatter. Not so much as a throat-clearing cough.

Then, a woman's voice, in a microphone-amplified whisper.

"This is their world. A world of peace, and beauty, and joy. A world we all wish to enter."

The rosary-widow beside me murmured an "Amen," her voice joining a quiet wave of others. In the near-dark, I noticed a dim figure appear on stage. It glided out to the edge, and kept going, as if levitating down the center aisle. When I squinted, I could detect the dark form of a catwalk that had been quickly erected in the aisle while the lights were out. The woman's voice continued, barely above a whisper, as soothing as a lullaby.

"Between our world and theirs is a heavy veil. A veil most cannot lift. But I can. Come with me now and let me take you into their world. The world of the spirits."

The lights flickered and went bright. Standing midway down the raised catwalk was a red-haired woman, her back to those of us in the front rows.

The woman turned. Late thirties. Gorgeous. Bright red hair pinned up, with tendrils tumbling down around her neck. A shimmery emerald green silk dress, modestly cut, but tight enough not to leave any curve to the imagination. Dowdy wire-rimmed glasses completed the faux-professional ensemble. The old Hollywood "sex-goddess disguised as Miss Prim-and-Proper" routine. As the thought pinged through my brain, it triggered a wave of déjà vu. I'd seen this woman before, and thought exactly the same thing. Where . . . ?

A sonorous male voice filled the room.

"The Meridian Theater proudly presents, for one night only, Jaime Vegas."

Jaime Vegas. Savannah's favorite television spiritualist.

Well, I'd found my necromancer.

CHAPTER 15

DIVA OF THE DEAD

"I'm sensing a male presence," Jaime murmured, somehow managing to walk and talk with her eyes closed. She headed toward the back of the theater. "A man in his fifties, maybe early sixties, late forties. His name starts with an M. He's related to someone in this corner."

She swept her arm, encompassing the rear left third of the room, and at least a hundred people. I bit my tongue to keep from groaning. In the last hour, I'd bitten it so often I probably wouldn't be able to taste food for a week. Over a dozen people in the "corner" Jaime had indicated started waving their arms, and five leapt to their feet, spot-dancing with excitement. Hell, I was sure if *anyone* in this audience searched their memories hard enough they could find a Mark or a Mike or a Miguel in their family who'd died in middle age.

Jaime turned to the section with the highest concentration of hand-wavers. "His name is Michael, but he says no one ever called him that. He was always Mike, except when he was a little boy, and some people called him Mikey."

An elderly woman suddenly wailed, and bowed forward, sucker punched by grief. "Mikey. That's my Mikey. My little boy. I always called him that."

I tore my gaze away, my own eyes filling with angry tears as Jaime bore down on her like a shark scenting blood.

"Is it my Mikey?" the old woman said, barely intelligible through her tears.

"I think it is," Jaime said softly. "Wait . . . yes. He says he's your son. He's asking you to stop crying. He's in a good place and he's happy. He wants you to know that."

The woman mopped her streaming tears and tried to smile.

"There," Jaime said. "Now he wants me to mention the picture. He says you have a photograph of him on display. Is that right?"

"I—I have a few," she said.

"Ah, but he's talking about a certain one. He says it's the one he always hated. Do you know which one he means?"

The old woman smiled and nodded.

"He's laughing," Jaime said. "He wants me to give you heck for putting up that photo. He wants you to take that down and put up the one of him at the wedding. Does that make sense?"

"He probably means his niece's wedding," the woman said. "She got married right before he died."

Jaime looked off into space, eyes unfocused, head slightly tilted, as if hearing something no one else could. Then she shook her head. "No, it's another wedding picture. An older one. He says to look through the album and you'll find it. Now, speaking of weddings . . ."

And on it went, from person to person, as Jaime worked the crowd, throwing out "personal" information that could apply to almost any life— What parent doesn't display pictures of their kids? What person doesn't have photos they hate? Who doesn't have wedding photos in their albums?

Even when she misjudged, she was perceptive enough to read confusion on the recipient's face before they could say anything, backtrack, and "correct" herself. On the very few occasions that she completely struck out, she'd tell the person to "go home and think about it, and it'll come to you," as if their memory was to blame, not her.

This Jaime might really be a necromancer, but she wasn't using her skills here. As I'd told Savannah, no one—not even a necro—could "dial up the dead" like this. What Jaime Vegas did was a psychological con job, not far removed from psychics who tell young girls "I see wedding bells in your future." Having lost my mother the year before, I understood why these people were here, the void they ached to fill. For a necromancer to profit from that grief with false tidings from the other side . . . well, it didn't make Jaime Vegas someone I wanted to work with.

The dressing room smelled like a funeral parlor. Appropriate, I suppose. I looked for chairs, and found one under a bouquet of two dozen black roses. I didn't know roses came in black.

J.D. had escorted me here before being dragged off by his assistant, who'd been muttering something about a man refusing to leave his seat until Jaime summoned his dead mother.

After clearing the chair of roses, I tried calling Lucas again. Still no answer. Avoiding my calls, I suspected. Damn call display. I was phoning home for messages when the door opened and Jaime wheeled in.

"Paige, right?" she said, gulping air. The glasses were gone, and the loosened tendrils of hair that had looked so artfully arranged on stage now clung, sweat-sodden, to her neck and face. "Please tell me it's Paige."

"Uh, yes. I—"

"Oh, thank God. I was running back here and suddenly thought, what if that wasn't her? and I was winking at some strange girl and inviting her to join me backstage, which is exactly what I do not need. My place in the tabloids is ensured without that. So, Paige—"

She stopped and looked around, then opened the door and shouted, "Hello! Did I ask—?"

A tray appeared from behind the door, floating in midair. Presumably there was some flunky behind the door holding it. Or so I hoped. With necromancers, one can never be sure.

She grabbed the tray, then lifted the bottle of single-malt Scotch. "What are you people trying to do to me? I said no booze tonight. I have an engagement. No booze, no caffeine. Like I'm not bouncing off the walls enough as it is." She eyed the bottle longingly, then shut her eyes and thrust it out. "Take it, please."

The bottle vanished behind the door.

"And bring more Gatorade. The blue stuff. None of that orange shit." She closed the door, grabbed a towel, and mopped her face. "Okay, so where were we?"

"I—"

"Oh, right. So I was thinking, what if that's not her? I was expecting the witch. Well, maybe not expecting, but hoping, you know? Lucas called and told me he was sending someone—a female someone—and I thought, oh, my God, maybe it's the witch."

"The—?"

"Have you heard that story?" Jaime continued, her voice muffled as she tugged her dress off over her head. "About Lucas and the witch? Personally, I can't see it."

"You mean, Lucas dating a witch? Well—"

"No, Lucas dating. Period." Jaime shrugged off her bra. "No offense to the guy, really. He's great. But he's one of those people you just can't imagine having a social life. Like your teachers. You see them outside the classroom and it freaks you out."

Now stripped to her panties, Jaime proceeded to slather cold cream on her face, still talking.

"I heard she's a computer geek. Probably some skinny kid with big glasses and an overbite, scared of her own shadow. Typical witch. I can see Lucas hooking up with a girl like—"

"I'm the witch," I said.

Jaime stopped cleaning her face and looked at me. "Wha—?"

"The witch. Lucas's girlfriend. That'd be me."

She winced. "Oh, shit."

The door cracked open and J.D.'s voice floated through. "Got a fire to put out, Jaime. Needs your special touch."

"Just hold on, okay?" she said to me, throwing on a robe. "I'll be right back."

"Hey, it's me," I said, shifting the cell phone to my other ear. "Is your dad there?"

"Paige, nice to hear from you," Adam said. "I'm fine. Midterms went well. Thanks for asking."

"Sorry," I said. "But I'm kind of in a hur—"

A drill screeched outside the dressing room.

"Holy shit, what are you killing?"

"I think they're dismantling the stage," I said. "Is Robert—"

"He's out with Mom. What stage? Where are you?"

"Miami. And, before you ask, I'm here looking for a necromancer. I've found one but she's not quite . . . right, so I was hoping Robert could put me in touch with another one in the area."

"What do you want a necromancer for?" A pause, then his voice dropped. "You're not thinking of . . . you know . . . with your mom? You don't want to go there, Paige. I know you're still—"

"Give me credit. I'm not trying to call up my mother. It's for a case."

"You're working a case and you didn't call me?"

"I just did."

Another earsplitting mechanical yowl, followed by shouts and catcalls.

"Sounds like a party," Adam said. "You said something about a stage? Where are you? A strip club?"

"Pretty close, actually. I just got to see a strip act. Wrong gender, though. Now, tell—"

"Oho, you aren't tossing out that teaser without an explanation. What the hell are you doing looking for a necromancer in a strip club?"

"It's not a strip club. It's a theater. Ever heard of Jaime Vegas?"

"The—" He whooped a laugh. "Are you serious? Jaime Vegas is a necromancer? I can't believe people watch that shit. So she's for real?"

"In a . . . manner of speaking."

"Oh, God, how bad is she?"

"Let's just say showbiz suits her well."

"Hey, now, don't go playing nice. This isn't Lucas you're talking to. What's she like?"

"Flakier than puff pastry."

Another whooped laugh. "Oh, man, I wish I was there. So about this case . . . you changed your mind about working with Lucas?"

"I never said I wouldn't work—"

"Sure you did. When I was up in Portland last month. Lucas was talking about that Igneus case, and I said maybe you could help, and you said—"

"This is just temporary. He's busy, so I'm filling in."

Jaime slid into the room. I lifted a finger. She nodded, grabbed a Gatorade, and perched on the edge of the vanity counter.

Adam continued, "If he's busy, that means you need a partner. I could—"

"I'm fine. You have school."

"Not for the next four days, I don't," Adam said. "No classes until Tuesday. I'll just hop—"

"Stay. If I need you, I'll call. In the meantime, can you ask Robert about nec"—I glanced at Jaime—"that list? It's kind of urgent."

"I will if you promise to call back with *all* the details."

"I'll call you first thing tomorrow. As soon as you wake up. Say, noon?"

"Very funny. I'm up by ten. Call me back tonight. It's only seven o'clock here, remember."

I agreed, then hung up and turned to Jaime.

"Sorry about that. I wasn't sure how long you'd be." I put my cell into my purse and hefted it to my shoulder. "Look, I'm sure this is a bad time for you, right after a busy show and all. I appreciate you taking the time to see me, and the show was . . . great. But you don't need me bugging you with this. Whatever favor you owe Lucas, consider it squared." I stepped backward toward the door and grasped the handle. "Anyway, it's been great meeting you, Jaime, and I wish you all the best—"

"I'm sorry about what I said. I stuck my foot in it so far I'm kicking myself in the stomach right now. After a show, I'm so wired, I just—I don't think."

"That's okay. I—"

"I mean, shit, I can't believe I didn't figure out who you were the minute Lucas told me your name. I knew your mom. Not personally, but I knew who she was, and then I heard about you and Eve's daughter last spring, so I really should have put two and two together, but when I do a show, my brain goes on hold and—" A wry twist of a smile. "And I babble and blather, and make no sense at all, not that you noticed or anything, right?"

"It's okay. Obviously you're busy and you don't need this, so don't worry about it. I have other necromancers I can contact."

She began brushing her hair. "Better necromancers."

"I have no idea whether they're better. I've never worked with you."

She looked up, as if surprised that I hadn't paid her a false compliment.

I continued, "I'm just saying this is probably a bad time—"

"You need me to contact a girl in a coma. Simple. It's ten o'clock and you're not going to get anyone else to do it tonight. Might as well give me a shot, let me repay Lucas."

What could I say to that? Spending the next couple of hours with the Diva of the Dead wasn't exactly my idea of fun, but she seemed calmer now, as the high from her performance wore off. Maybe this wouldn't be so bad after all. Or so I kept telling myself as she dropped her robe and started searching for clothing.

CHAPTER 16

GONE

Following the address I gave, the cab stopped in front of a square block of brick squeezed between a restaurant and a small accounting firm. Unlike its neighbors, this storefront had no obvious signage. It took a minute of searching to see the near-microscopic sign in the window: the marsh memorial clinic.

"Jesus," Jaime said as I rang the after-hours bell. "What is this? A rehab center?"

"A private hospital," I said.

"Shit. Who do you have to kill to get in here?" She caught my expression. "Ah, not *who*, but how many. A Cabal hospital."

A blond woman in her forties opened the door. "Ms. Winterbourne. Hello. Mr. Cortez said you'd be by this evening. Come in, please. And I presume this is Jaime Vegas?"

Jaime nodded.

"Has there been any change in Dana's condition?" I asked.

A brief flutter of emotion rippled the nurse's composure. "I'm afraid not. You're welcome to stay as long as you like. Mr. Cortez asked that this be a private visit, so if you need me, please buzz. Otherwise, I won't bother you. She's in room three."

I thanked her and followed her directions into a side hall. As we walked, Jaime looked around, taking in everything.

"And just think," she said. "This is for the employees. They've probably got a place in the Swiss Alps for the execs. And the family? God only knows. Can you imagine having this kind of money?"

"Remember where it comes from," I said, quoting Lucas.

"I try, but you know, sometimes, you see what a Cabal can do and you think, hmmm, maybe tormenting a few souls now and then wouldn't be such a bad gig. You're dating the guy who's supposed to own all this one day. I'm sure you think about that."

"Not in a good way."

"More power to you, then. I'd be tempted. Hell, I've *been* tempted. Ever met Carlos?"

"Carlos Cortez? No."

"He's the youngest. Well, you know, the youngest of the legit—uh, of Delores's kids. Carlos is the hunk of the litter. Takes after his mother, who's gorgeous . . . and as vicious as a rabid dog. Carlos got the vicious genes, too, but seems to have missed out on Benicio's brains, so he's not very dangerous. Anyway, I met Carlos at a club a couple years back, and he showed some definite interest. There were a few moments there when I was tempted. I mean, here's a guy with money and power, wrapped in a damn near perfect gift box. What more could a girl want? Okay, maybe someone who doesn't have a reputation for nasty bedroom games, but everyone's got their hang-ups, right? Honest to God, that's what I thought. I'm standing there, looking at this guy and thinking, hmmm, maybe I could change him."

"Probably not."

"No shit, huh? I don't learn my lessons well, but that's one I've committed to heart. Take it or leave it, 'cause you ain't gonna change it. But that still didn't keep me from thinking about Carlos. Power and money—if Calvin Klein could bottle the scent, he'd make a fortune." She tossed a grin my way. "Just think, we could've been sisters-in-law. We'd certainly have livened up family reunions."

I pushed open a door marked with a small 3. "They're probably lively enough as it is."

Jaime laughed. "I bet. Can you imagine—"

She stopped as we stepped into the room. It was twice the size of my apartment bedroom. A leather couch and two matching recliners were grouped around a coffee table just inside the door. Past that was a king-size bed. A girl with long blond hair lay in the middle of it, a sunflower-patterned quilt pulled up across her chest. Her eyes were closed. Bandages encircled her neck. To one side, machines bleeped discreetly, as if trying not to wake her.

My breath hitched. How could anyone—? How could her mother—? Goddamn it! Why, why, why? I closed my eyes, swallowed, walked to Dana's bedside, and took her hand.

"Holy shit," Jaime whispered. "She's a kid."

"Fif—" My throat dried up. I tried again. "She's fifteen. But she looks small for her age."

"Fifteen? Jesus Christ. When Lucas said 'girl,' I thought, you know, he meant a woman. I should have known better. He says girl, he means girl."

"Is that a problem?"

Jaime inhaled, gaze glued to Dana. "Tougher, yes. Not to communicate. I mean"—she tapped a manicured nail against her forehead—"up here. What do the doctors say?"

"She's stable. As to whether she'll regain consciousness, they don't know."

"Well, we might find that out tonight. If she's crossed over, I'll know it."

Jaime rolled her shoulders, approached the bed, and gripped the side rail. She stared down at Dana, then shook her head, opened her oversize purse, and pulled out what looked like a jumbo makeup bag.

"I'll call you in when I'm ready," she said, not looking up.

"I'm an old hand at this," I said. "Well, not exactly an old hand, but I've helped out at a few summonings. Here, pass me the censer and herbs and I'll set them up while you—"

"No."

The word came out sharp enough to make me jump. Jaime clutched her tool bag closed, as if I might pry it from her hands.

"I'd rather you waited in the hall," she said.

"Uh, sure. Okay. Call me then."

I walked to the door, then glanced back to see her still holding the bag closed, waiting. I pushed open the door and stepped into the hall.

Well, I said necromancers were queer beasts. Jaime might look a far cry from your typical spacey-eyed necro, but you have to wonder about a woman who'll strip in front of a stranger, yet draws the line at letting the same person watch her perform a summoning ceremony. Not that I minded being relegated to the sidelines. I knew what was in that Gucci makeup bag, and it wasn't designer lip liner.

To summon the dead you needed artifacts of death. In that kit, there'd be everything from grave dirt to scraps of moldy grave clothes to, well, dead things . . . or, at least, travel-size pieces of them. The tools-in-trade of a necromancer. Made me really happy to be a witch, casting spells surrounded by sweet-smelling herbs, pretty gemstones, and antique filigreed chalices.

About ten minutes later, Jaime called me in. When I entered, she was sitting beside the bed, holding Dana's hand. Most necromancers leave their tools out during a summoning, but Jaime's makeup bag had vanished, along with its contents. Only the censer remained, burning vervain, which necromancers used when contacting either traumatized souls, such as murder victims, or the souls of those who didn't realize they were spirits.

"It didn't work?" I asked.

"It worked." Jaime's voice had faded to a strained whisper and her face was pale. "She's here. I haven't—" Her voice strengthened. "I haven't made contact yet. I think it'd be easiest on her if I used channeling. Do you know how that works?"

I nodded. "You let Dana speak through you."

"Right."

"So I'll ask her the questions and—"

"No, no," Jaime said. "Well, yes, you'll ask the questions, but I'll relay them to her, and let her speak through me. She doesn't take over my body. That's full channeling, and if a necro ever suggests that, find someone else. No necro in her right mind ever gives herself completely over to a spirit."

"Got it."

"Now, for the first part, making contact, I'll do that on my own. It's easier that way. I'll establish contact and . . . explain things." She swallowed. "I'll tell her what happened, where she is. She may know, but . . . with kids . . . there can be some resistance to the truth."

Damn it, I hadn't thought of this. We weren't just asking Jaime to contact Dana. We were asking her to tell the girl that she was lying in a hospital bed, comatose.

"I'm sorry," I said. "If you don't want to do this, I totally understand—"

"I'm fine. She'll figure it out sooner or later, right? Now, she's almost certainly not going to remember a play-by-play."

"Trauma amnesia," I said. "Lucas told me about it."

"Good. I'll make contact now. This may take a while."

Twenty minutes ticked by. During that time, Jaime sat ramrod straight, eyes closed, hand clutching Dana's, the occasional twitch of her cheek the only sign that something was happening.

"Okay," Jaime said finally, in a cheerful chirp. "Now there's someone here who's going to help us catch the guy who did this to you, okay, kiddo?"

"Good." The response was pitched an octave higher than Jaime's voice.

"Her name is Paige, and she's a witch, just like you. Do you know what the Coven is?"

"I . . . I've heard of it . . . I think."

"It's a group for witches. Paige used to be in the Coven, helping witches there, but now she works outside the Coven, so she can help all witches." That was a nice way of putting it. I mentally thanked Jaime for the positive spin. "What I want you to do is tell her everything you remember, then she'll ask you some questions, and we'll catch this guy before you wake up."

So Dana was okay. Thank God. I relaxed for the first time since walking into the room.

Dana asked when she'd be waking up.

"Any day now," Jaime said. "Your dad is supposed to be here soon—"

"My dad? I knew he'd come. Is my mom there?"

"She's been in and out," Jaime said. "Taking care of you."

"And they'll be there? When I wake up?"

"Sure will. Now, can you tell Paige what you saw?"

"Sure. Hi, Paige."

I opened my mouth, but Jaime answered for me. "You won't be able to hear Paige, hon. I'll have to relay her messages. But you'll get to see her when you wake up. She's been pretty worried about you."

Dana smiled through Jaime, the smile of a kid who wasn't used to people giving a damn. I'd make sure her dad knew about Dana's situation with her mother and, if he was the kind of father Benicio said he was, Dana would never have to spend another night on the streets. If he didn't, well, then I'd see to it myself.

"I'll try," Dana said. "But . . . I don't remember it so well. It's all jumbled up, like something I saw on television a long time ago and can't really remember."

"That's okay, Dana," Jaime said. "We know you won't remember much, so if you don't, we understand, but if you do remember something, anything at all, that'll be great."

"Well, it was Sunday night. I was coming home from a party. I wasn't loaded or anything. I'd had a joint, but that's it, just one joint I shared with this guy I knew. So I was walking home through the park—I know that sounds dumb, but around there, the park seemed safer than the roads, you know? I was being careful, staying on the path, looking, listening. And then . . ."

Her voice trailed off.

"Then what, Dana?" Jaime prompted.

"Then . . . I think I must forget what happens next because all I remember is this guy was suddenly standing right behind me. I must have heard him coming, maybe I tried to run, but I don't remember."

"Ask her—" I began.

Dana continued, "I know you're going to want to know what the guy looked like, but I didn't really see him. I know I should have . . ."

"Hey, if it was me," Jaime said, "I'd have been freaking so bad, I wouldn't remember a damn thing. You're doing fine, kiddo. Just take it slow and give us what you can."

"He grabbed me, and next thing I know, I'm on the ground, way off the path, in this forest. I was kind of awake, but not really, and I was so tired. I just wanted to sleep."

"Drugged?" I asked.

Jaime relayed the question.

"I—I guess so. Only, it didn't feel . . . I just remember being tired. I don't even think he had me tied up, but I didn't move. I didn't want to move. I just wanted to sleep. Then he put this rope around my neck, and I blacked out, then I was here."

"I want to talk about the phone call you made," I said.

"I made a phone call?"

"To the emergency line," I said. "The Cabal—the place where your dad works."

"I know what you mean, but I don't remember. Dad made my sister and me memorize it, and I know I'm supposed to call them first, so I must have."

I prompted her with a few questions about her attacker's voice, regional accent, word usage, anything that might have stuck in her mind more than a physical description, but she could tell me little more than that he didn't sound like he came from "around here."

"Oh, there was one thing he did say that seemed weird. When he started choking me. It seemed like he was talking to someone, but there wasn't anyone there. Like he was talking to himself, only he used a name."

I perked up. "Do you remember it?"

"I think it was Nasha," Dana said. "That's what it sounded like."

"Ask her what exactly he said," I said, and Jaime did.

"He said he was doing this for this person, this Nasha," Dana said.

"Ritual sacrifice," I said.

Jaime nodded. We continued to prod Dana's memory, but she'd obviously been only partially conscious when she'd heard her attacker speak. Next we moved back to her attacker. He was likely supernatural, and may have done something to indicate his race, but Dana couldn't recall anything. As the daughter of a witch and a half-demon, she was familiar with both spell-casting and demonic shows of power, but her attacker had demonstrated neither.

"That's great, hon," Jaime said when I indicated that I'd run out of questions. "You've been a big help. Thank you very much."

Dana smiled through Jaime. "I should be thanking you. And I will, when I wake up. I'll take you guys out for lunch. On me. Well, on me and my dad."

"Su—sure, kiddo," Jaime said, gaze flicking away. "We'll do that." She glanced at me. "Can I send her back now?"

I nodded, and capped my pen. "Tell her I'll see her when she wakes up."

A few minutes later, Jaime stood and rubbed her shoulders.

"You okay?" I asked.

She made a noncommittal noise and reached for her handbag. I stifled a yawn, then stepped into the bathroom to splash cold water on my face.

"So, do you have any idea when she'll regain consciousness?" I said as I came out.

"She won't."

I stopped and turned slowly. Jaime was fussing with something in her purse.

"What?" I said.

Jaime didn't look up. "She's crossed over. She's gone."

"But you—you said—"

"I know what I said."

"You told her she was fine. How could you—?"

Jaime's gaze snapped to mine. "And what was I supposed to say? Sorry, kid, you're dead, you just don't know it yet?"

"Oh, my God." I sunk into the nearest chair. "I'm sorry. We didn't mean—I didn't mean—putting you through that—"

"Comes with the territory. If not me, then someone else, right? You need to catch this bastard, and this was the best way to get information, so . . ." She rubbed her hand over her face. "I could really use a drink. And some company. If you don't mind."

I scrambled from the chair. "Sure."

CHAPTER 17

TWO-FOR-ONE SPECIAL

Though I was still in shock over Dana's fate, my feelings had to take a backseat to Jaime's. She was the one who needed support, and I was happy to provide it.

I'd seen a jazz bar down the road, the kind of place with big plush booths you could get lost in and a live band that never played loud enough to challenge conversation. We could go there, have a few drinks, and talk through our difficult evening, maybe come to a better understanding of one another.

"No, I am so serious!" Jaime shrieked, waving her cosmopolitan and sending a tidal wave over the glass. "This guy was sitting in his seat, with his pants undone, dick sticking out, hoping that'd get my attention."

The blond guy on Jaime's left leaned into her. "And did it?"

"Hell, no. A four-inch dick? I don't even slow down for that. Zipped right past him . . . and hoped he zipped up before the old lady beside him had a stroke."

"Would eight inches do it?" asked the dark-haired guy on her right.

"Depends on the face that goes with it. Now ten . . . ten and we'd be talking. Twelve, and I'd summon his fucking dog if he asked me."

A roar of laughter. I stared into my mojito and wished I'd made it a double Scotch, neat. I didn't drink Scotch, but suddenly, it seemed like a really good idea.

Around us, music pulsed so loud it rippled Jaime's cosmo puddle. I thought of wiping it up, but decided to wait until another stoned dancer stumbled off the floor and fell onto our table. It'd happened twice so far and was bound to happen again. I only hoped he or she would be wearing enough to soak up Jaime's spilled drink.

We'd been here nearly two hours, having never come within half a block of the jazz club. Jaime had heard the thumping music from outside and dragged me in for "just one drink." I'd had two. She was on number six. For the first two, she'd ignored all attention from the bar's male patrons. By the third, she'd begun sizing up the interested parties. When number five arrived, she'd made her selection from a quintet of stockbroker types who'd been watching us from the bar, and had waved over the two cutest and offered them seats on either side of her, squashing three into a bench made for two.

Though I'd kept my gaze on my drink, sending clear "I am so not interested" vibes, one of the remaining trio had decided the leftovers didn't look too unappetizing and slid in beside me. I wanted nothing more than to return to my quiet hotel room and mourn for Dana by planning my next step in finding her killer. Yet here I was, trapped against the booth wall, listening to Jaime's war stories, nursing my second mojito, and fending off the wandering hands of my unwanted companion. And I was starting to get a little pissed.

The guy beside me, Dale—or was it Chip?—wriggled closer, though we were already closer than I liked getting to anyone I wasn't sleeping with.

"You have really nice eyes," he said.

"Those aren't my eyes," I said. "Look up. Way up."

He chuckled and lifted his gaze to my face. "No, I'm serious. You have beautiful eyes."

"What color are they?"

"Uh . . ." He squinted in the darkness. "Blue?"

They were green, but I wasn't helping him out. I'd already repeated the "I'm seeing someone" line until it sounded like a challenge. Nearly as often I'd told Jaime that I really should be going, but she pretended not to hear me. When I tried again, she launched into another ribald story.

Nice to see she'd recovered from her traumatic experience at the hospital. I'd begun to suspect "traumatic" was an overstatement. Mildly disturbing maybe, on a par with realizing you'd left the house wearing brown shoes with a black dress. Nothing that couldn't be cured with a few cosmopolitans and some wicked thumping bass.

"Excuse me," I said. "I need to—"

"Use the little girls' room?" he said, and laughed as he slid from the booth.

"Hold on, boys," Jaime said. "The ladies need to freshen up."

"Uh, no," I said as she extricated herself from the booth. "I'm leaving."

"Leaving? Already? I haven't finished my drink."

"That's okay. You stay, have fun."

She clutched my arm, more for balance, I think, than to keep me from going. "You're abandoning me? With these three?"

She cast a leering grin at the men. Dale blinked, then staggered to his feet.

"Hey, no, babe," he said, bleary eyes fixed in my general direction. "I'll drive you."

"Oh, I bet you'd like to," Jaime said. "But Paige already has a guy. A friend of mine. And you don't want to mess with him." She leaned into Dale's ear. "He's connected."

Dale frowned. "Connected?"

"Like the Kennedys," Jaime said.

"More like the Sopranos," I said.

Dale sat down.

"You stay and enjoy yourself," I said to Jaime.

"No can do. I told Lucas I'd look after you in the big bad city."

"Uh-huh. Well, I appreciate that, but—"

"No buts. My prodco got me a room way the hell out in the burbs and I am not going all that way tonight. I'm getting a room at your hotel. So come on, girl."

She started to steer me from the table. One of her companions leapt up.

"Can we give you a lift—?"

"Ooops, sorry about that. I might not get to finish my drink, but I can't forget my nightcap." She turned and sized up the two men. "Decisions, decisions."

The blond grinned. "Two-for-one special."

"Tempting, but I'm too old for that shit. One per night." She looked them over. "Hmmm, this is tough. Only one way to do it." She pointed at the dark-haired one. "Eenie-meenie . . ."

Once out of the taxi, and away from Jaime and her "date," I called Lucas, but only got a cellular service recording saying he was out of range. Odd. I left a "call me" message, then phoned Adam and filled him in on the case. By that time, it was nearly midnight even in California, and Robert had gone to bed. It didn't matter. Getting that list of necromancers was no longer high priority. Whatever Jaime's personal shortcomings, she'd done her job with Dana.

I hadn't slept since arriving in Miami, and my brain seemed to protest this lack of rest by making sure my sleep that night wasn't sound. I dreamed of being back in the hospital room, watching Jaime release Dana back to the realm of the dead. She dropped the hand she'd been holding, letting it fall back to the sheets. I stared at that hand, expecting to see chewed fingernails and a frayed braided bracelet. Instead the hand was plump and wrinkled, and bore a familiar gold watch.

"Mom?"

"She doesn't want to talk to you," Jaime said. "You lost the Coven. She handed it to you on a silver platter, and you still screwed up."

"No!"

I shot from my chair, stumbled, and fell into a bed smelling of hotel laundry soap. I pushed into the pillow and moaned. Suddenly, the bed tilted and I grabbed with both hands, struggling to stay on. I saw Lucas sitting on the edge. He had his back to me, and was peeling the label from an empty champagne bottle.

"One month," he said. "You knew what I meant."

He stood and the bed tumbled into a yawning pit of black. I started to scream, but the sound turned to a happy shriek.

"Cortez! You're getting champagne—get that bottle away from the bed!"

The scene cleared. Another hotel room. Three months ago. We were crossing the country at a snail's pace, with nowhere to go, nothing to do but enjoy the trip. The day before, Maria had wired Lucas the insurance money from his stolen motorcycle, and tonight he'd insisted on using part of it to get us a room with a Jacuzzi tub, a fireplace, and an adjoining suite for Savannah.

We were in bed, where we'd been since arriving late that afternoon. Room-service plates littered the floor and, from somewhere in the mess, Lucas had pulled out a bottle of champagne, which was now frothing onto the sheets . . . and me. As I laughed, he shook the last bits of foam onto me, then grabbed glasses, filled them, and handed me one.

"To one month," he said.

"A month?" I sat up. "Oh, right. One month since we beat the Nast Cabal and saved Savannah, an act which we may live to regret. Technically, though, you're a few days early."

Lucas hesitated, face clouding for a split second before he nodded. "I suppose I am."

The memory fast-forwarded a few hours. I was nestled in bed, champagne still singing in my head. Lucas's warmth pressed against my back. He stirred, mumbled something, and slid his hand between my legs. I shifted and rubbed against his fingers. A drowsy laugh, then his finger slipped inside me, a slow, soft probe. I moaned, my flesh tender from the long night but the slight ache only accentuating another deeper ache. He pulled his finger out and tickled a fingertip across the top of my clitoris. I moaned again and shifted my legs apart. He started a slow, teasing exploration that made me clutch the pillow.

"Lucas," I whispered.

Another laugh, but this one clear, no signs of sleepiness. I forced myself to shift from sleep to waking, and still felt a warm hand stroking me from behind.

"Lucas?"

A low laugh. "I should hope so."

I started to flip over, felt his hand disengage, and reached down to grab it.

"Don't stop," I said.

"I won't." He leaned over my shoulder, and slid his finger back inside me. "Better?"

"God, yes." I arched my back against him. "How—how'd you get here?"

"Magic."

"Mmmm."

"A good surprise?"

"The best."

He laughed softly. "Go back to sleep, then. I have everything under control."

"Mmmm."

As for falling back to sleep, naturally I did no such thing. Afterward, I propped myself up on Lucas's chest and grinned.

"These surprise visits are getting better all the time."

He returned a crooked smile. "I take it my unexpected arrival isn't completely objectionable, even if I did disturb your sleep?"

"Disturb away. It is a surprise, though. What happened with your case?"

"It ended this afternoon. Once the prosecution confirmed that its new witness resided in a cemetery, they decided to move straight to closing arguments."

"A definite advantage to working in a human court. They never subpoena dead witnesses."

"This is true. So, I'm here to help, if you want me."

"Hell, yes," I said, grinning. "In every possible way. So you're staying?"

"If that's all right with—"

"It's great. I can't even remember the last time we spent more than a weekend together."

"It *has* been a while," Lucas said softly, then cleared his throat. "My schedule lately has been busier than I anticipated, and I realize this isn't an ideal arrangement for a relationship—"

"It's fine," I said.

"It's not what you expected."

"I didn't expect anything." I flipped off him and sat up. "No expectations, remember? Take it one day at a time. That's what we agreed."

"Yes, I know that's what you said, but—"

"It's what I meant. No expectations, no pressure. You stay for as long as you like."

Lucas pulled himself up. "That's not what—" He paused. "We need to talk, Paige."

"Sure."

I felt Lucas watching me in the darkness, but he said nothing.

"What do you want to talk about?" I asked after a few moments.

"About—" He held my gaze for a moment, then looked away. "About the case. What happened tonight?"

"Oh, God." I thumped onto the pillow. "You have some strange friends, Cortez."

A quarter-smile. "I wouldn't classify Jaime as a friend but, yes, that's one way of putting it. So tell me what happened."

I did.

CHAPTER 18

A THEORY

At seven, still talking, we moved the conversation from the bed to the restaurant downstairs. Dining that early meant we got the best seats, a table in the corner of the atrium.

By nine, the tiny restaurant was full, with a line at the door. We were on our third cup of coffee, breakfast long since done, which earned us plenty of glares from those waiting at the hostess station, but not so much as an impatient glance from our server, probably owing to the size of the tip Lucas had tacked onto the bill.

"Nasha?" Lucas said when I told him the name Dana's attacker had invoked. "It doesn't sound familiar."

"I passed it on through Adam to Robert, to get his opinion. I'd called him yesterday to ask—uh, about some council stuff."

"And a list of alternate necromancers, I presume?"

"I—uh—" I inhaled. "I'm sorry. I know you said to trust you, and I really tried . . ."

A smile tickled his lips. "But gave up somewhere between Sid Vicious and the private strip show. Either of which, understandably, would strain the bounds of the deepest trust."

"Actually, it was *after* the striptease."

His smile broadened. "Ah, well, in that case, you outlasted any reasonable expectation of faith. I'm flattered. Thank you."

"Still, I should have listened to you. You were right. Jaime did just fine."

"She is very good, though sometimes I think she'd prefer otherwise. Have you ever heard of Molly O'Casey?"

"Of course. Top-notch necro. Died a few years back, didn't she?"

Lucas nodded. "She was Jaime's paternal grandmother. Vegas is Jaime's stage name."

"I thought it might be. She doesn't look Hispanic."

"She isn't. Her mother chose the name when she started Jaime in show business, as a child. As Jaime tells it, her mother was a flaming racist, and had no idea Vegas was Spanish. To her, 'Vegas' meant 'Las Vegas,' a good omen for a child with a stage career. Years later, when she found out the name's origin, she almost had a heart attack. Demanded Jaime change it. But, by then, Jaime was eighteen, and could do as she liked. The more her mother hated the name, the more determined she was to keep it."

"There's a story there," I said softly.

"Yes, I imagine there is."

We sipped our coffee.

"I thought you were in Chicago," said a voice above my head.

I turned to see Jaime pulling an empty chair from a table behind us. The trio at the table looked up in surprise, but she ignored them and clattered the chair down beside me, then dropped into it. She was wearing a silk wrapper and, I suspected, little else.

"Isn't this romantic," she said, snarling a yawn. "The happy couple, all brushed, scrubbed, and chipper." She dropped her head onto the table. "Someone get me a coffee. Stat."

Lucas swept a lock of her hair off his muffin plate, then gestured to the server, who stopped mid-order and hurried over with the pot. Jaime stayed facedown on the table.

"Is your, uh, guest joining us?" I asked Jaime.

She rolled onto her cheek to look up at me. "Guest?"

"The guy? From last night?"

"Guy?"

"The one you took back to your room."

She lifted her head. "I took a—?" She groaned. "Oh, shit. Hold on. I'll be right back."

She stood, took three steps, then turned.

"Uh, Paige? Did I get a name?"

"Mark—no, Mike. Oh, wait. That was the blond. Craig . . . or Greg. The music was pretty loud."

She pressed her fingers to her temples. "It still is. Greg, then. I'll mumble."

She staggered across the atrium.

I turned to Lucas. "Interesting lady."

"That's one way of putting it."

Jaime got rid of her "guest," and joined us for the rest of her coffee, then went back to her room for more sleep. She had a show in Orlando that night, so, in case we didn't see her again, we thanked her for her help.

Lucas unpacked while I phoned Robert about the "Nasha" connection. After four rings, the machine picked up.

"That's probably one clue that's not going to help us much anyway," I said once I'd left a message. "I'd really hoped to get more from Dana."

"She's probably blocked what little she did see. We may want to shift our focus to ascertaining how the killer selected his victims."

"Damn, of course. He obviously targeted runaways with Cabal parents, but how would he find out something like that? Maybe the parents had a connection, because of their shared circumstances. Like a support group. Do the Cabals offer stuff like that?"

"They do, but separately. They strongly discourage interaction with the employees of other Cabals."

"What about therapists or social workers? Would they share them?"

Lucas shook his head. "What I believe we're looking for is someone who has obtained access to employee files at the Cortez, Nast, and St. Cloud Cabals."

I looked across the room at my laptop. "They're all computerized, aren't they? So someone hacked into the system . . . and I cannot *believe* I didn't think of that."

"You wouldn't because you aren't familiar with Cabal record-keeping procedures, and the amount of personal detail they keep. You won't find many corporations who keep records of their staff's personal situations. Nothing in a Cabal employee's life is sacred. If someone's mother-in-law has a gambling problem, the Cabal knows about it."

"For leverage."

"Not just leverage, but security. If that mother-in-law gets in trouble with a loan shark, her half-demon son-in-law may use his powers to permanently solve the problem. Likewise, a runaway Cabal child could be a potential security threat, so they keep track of them, and probably know more about their whereabouts than their parents do. As for hacking into the system, while it's possible, Cabal security *is* top of the line."

"Everyone thinks their security is top of the line," I said. "Until someone like me slips in the back door."

"True, but the systems are protected by both technical and supernatural means. To hack them would require a supernatural with an inside knowledge of Cabal security systems."

"Someone who worked in the computer or security departments. Probably someone who was fired in the past year or so. The old 'disgruntled employee' theory."

Lucas nodded. "Let me phone my father. See whether we can find anyone who'd fit that theory."

Lucas had no trouble getting the Cortez Cabal employee list. Benicio knew that while Lucas might love to keep a copy of that list for his own investigations against the Cabals, he would do the honorable thing and destroy it as soon as it had served its stated purpose. Getting the other Cabal HR departments to cooperate wasn't nearly so easy. Benicio didn't tell them Lucas would be accessing the list, but they didn't want *any* Cortez getting his hands on their staff records. It took two hours just to get a list of dismissed employees' names and positions.

Those lists were surprisingly short. I thought the Cabals were holding out on us, but Lucas assured me they looked accurate. When you hire only supernaturals, and you find ones who work out, you bend over backward to keep them. If they don't work out, it's better to make them disappear rather than hand them a pink slip . . . and not just to avoid paying severance. A pissed-off supernatural employee is a lot more dangerous than your average disgruntled postal worker.

Once we narrowed the list down to employees in the computer and security departments, we had two names from the Cortez list, three from the Nasts, and one from the St. Clouds. Put those together and we had five possibilities. And no, there was nothing wrong with my math skills. Two plus three plus one should equal six. So why did we have a list of five names? Because one appeared on two rosters. Everett Weber, computer programmer.

According to the Cortez files, Everett Weber was a druid who'd worked as a programmer in their Human Resources department from June 2000 to December 2000, on a six-month contract. That didn't qualify as a dismissal, but people often take contract jobs expecting them to turn into permanent positions. We needed to find out how amicable Weber's leaving had been. And we needed details of his employment with the Nasts. Lucas phoned Benicio again. Seventy minutes later, Benicio called back.

"Well?" I said as Lucas hung up.

"Preliminary reports from the Human Resources department indicate that Weber's contract ended without rancor, but my father will investigate further. It's not uncommon for managers to be less than forthcoming when confronted with a potentially unreported employee problem. As for the Nasts, Weber worked in their IT department from January of this year until August, in a contract position."

"Another six-month contract?"

"No, a one-year contract that ended after seven months, but the Nasts refuse to elaborate."

I slammed my laptop shut. "Damn it! Do they want this guy caught or not?"

"I suspect the problem is coming from both sides. My father would be reluctant to let the Nasts know we're raising questions about someone in particular. Otherwise Weber may disappear into Nast custody before we can question him, a definite possibility considering he's currently residing in California."

"And the Nast Cabal is based in Los Angeles, meaning they'd beat us to him."

"Precisely. My father's suggestion, and one I would second, is that we proceed to California ourselves and investigate Everett further, before we press the Nasts for details."

"Sounds good, but—"

The ring of my cell phone cut me off. I checked the call display.

"Adam," I said. "Before I answer, what part of California are we heading to?"

"Close enough to Santa Cruz that you can ask him to join us."

I nodded and clicked on the phone.

An hour later we were back at the airport, picking up tickets purchased for us by the Cortez Corporation. This was, of course, Benicio's doing, though it was one step down from what he'd really wanted, which was for us to use the corporate jet. When Benicio offered the tickets instead, Lucas—eager to stop arguing and start investigating—had accepted. Neither of us was happy about the obvious manipulation, but the truth was that we could ill afford to be crisscrossing the country like this. Dana and Jacob deserved better than a low-budget investigation, and we'd make sure they got it, even if it meant accepting transportation expenses from the Cabal.

Of course, Adam didn't mind playing host and tour guide, not when it came with the opportunity for excitement. I've known Adam for half my life, long enough to accept that he's the kind of guy who does as little as he can get away with—unless the "doing" involves straight-up ass-kicking action. Today, with the prospect of some less-than-legal adventuring, he was keen enough to actually meet our plane on time.

Adam was twenty-four, and good-looking in a wholesome California way with a perpetual tan, light brown hair sun-streaked blond, and the well-built body of a surfer. Like his stepfather, he was a half-demon. Robert had long since suspected Adam was the most powerful subtype of fire demon—an Exustio—but it had only been last year that he'd finally incinerated something and proved Robert right. That marked the culmination of seventeen years of increasing powers, dating back to childhood, when Talia had gone seeking answers for Adam's early displays of power, not content to accept a psychiatrist's explanation that Adam's literally hot temper was only adolescent acting-out. Her search had led her to Robert Vasic, who'd eventually given her the answers she sought . . . and fallen in love with her.

"So what's the plan?" Adam said as we climbed into his Jeep.

"We're starting right at the source," I said. "A home invasion, if we're lucky."

"Sweet."

"I thought you'd think so."

CHAPTER 19

LESS-THAN-LEGAL
ADVENTURING

Everett Weber lived outside Modesto, in a small farmhouse, an ugly cinder block with a freshly mowed lawn and tidy yard, but with woodwork years overdue for a paint job. Probably a rental, owned by whoever owned the surrounding vineyards. Like most renters, Weber was quite willing to keep the place neat but wasn't about to dip into his own pockets for repairs.

Weber worked at a place in Silicon Valley, so we hoped that at one P.M. on a Friday, that's where he'd be. From Lucas's preliminary background check, Weber appeared to live alone. Add in the fact that his house was on a dirt road, with no neighbors for a half-mile in any direction, and a daytime break-and-enter wasn't as risky as it sounded.

The remote location made it perfect for a B&E but more difficult to get up close and check for occupancy. We called the house from the road, and no one answered the phone, but that didn't necessarily mean Everett wasn't there. After some skulking around, Lucas proclaimed the house empty, and we met at the back door, whereupon we discovered that every window came complete with bars and security decals. After a quick check, Lucas declared the decals legit. Weber had a security system, and it was activated.

"No disarming spells in your repertoires, I suppose?" Adam whispered as we huddled near the back door.

Lucas pulled a small kit from under his leather jacket. "No, but I do have this."

"Cool." Adam crouched beside Lucas as he worked. "Now this you didn't learn in law school."

"You'd be surprised," Lucas murmured. "No, this comes from having Cabal contract employees as clients. As you might expect, the Cabals don't contract them for their typing skills. In some cases, an exchange of skills proves more valuable than financial remuneration." He fiddled with a mess of wires. "There. Now comes the difficult part. I need to cut these three at the same time or I'll set it off. However, if I do cut them, it's easily discovered, and Weber will know his system was breached. This may take a few minutes." He reached into his kit. "First, I need to—"

Adam reached down and grasped the mess of wires. A spark, then they disintegrated to ash.

"Or we could just do that," Lucas said.

"Damn those spontaneous electrical fires," Adam said.

"Been practicing, I see," I said.

Adam grinned and wiped the ash from his hand. He grabbed the door handle.

"Wait," I said.

I cast an unlock spell. Adam opened the door. We paused, but no alarm sounded. Lucas finished replacing the wires, then waved us inside.

We soon understood why Weber put a security system on a rented farmhouse. Any money he'd saved on rent, he'd invested in electronics, with multiple computers, a plasma TV, and a hi-fi system that I'm sure rocked the neighbors even a mile away.

While Adam and Lucas started searching, I headed for my area of expertise: the computer. I quickly discovered that Weber applied the same standard of security to his hard drive as he did to his house. Although he was the only person living there, he had the computer password-protected. It took nearly thirty minutes to crack that, only to find that all his data— even his e-mail—was encrypted. I burned the files onto a CD for later.

Since Lucas and Adam were still searching, I returned to Weber's computer to search for a specific piece of information: a credit card number. Seeing how careful Weber was with his files, I assumed this search would be futile. Well, I was wrong. Five minutes of hunting and I found a cookie containing an unencrypted credit card number. Later I could hack into the credit card company system and search his records, in hopes that if he was our killer, he'd used his card for traveling.

After another hour, we declared the house thoroughly searched. Lucas and Adam hadn't found anything. We could only hope that decrypting Weber's files and checking his credit card records would prove more fruitful.

We retreated to Santa Cruz, where Adam lived with his parents. I was eager to get Weber's credit card records, but Adam's mother, Talia, insisted that we have dinner first and, having been on food-free mental superdrive since breakfast, I had to agree that my brain needed nourishment before I did something as dangerous as hack into credit card companies.

We had fettuccine Alfredo alfresco, on the multilevel deck that covered half the backyard. Talia and Robert ate with us to hear about the case. As usual, Adam's initial recitation had left out half the details and mangled the rest, so they'd waited to hear the real story from the source.

Talia was one of the few humans who lived within the supernatural world. That was her choice, to accept the dangers of that knowledge in order to better understand her son and husband, and play a full role in their lives. Over the last few years, Robert's health had begun to fail, and Talia had been picking up the slack. Robert was only sixty-eight, but his physical condition had never been what one would call robust, forcing him even from an early age to take the scholarly approach to helping other half-demons, acting as a resource and a confidant. Talia, who was twenty-seven years younger, had embraced the midlife career change. As for Adam taking over Robert's work, well, let's just say no one expected him to be sitting behind a desk, reading demonology texts, anytime soon.

Adam bit off a chunk of bread and chewed it as he talked. "So that's it. We broke, we entered, we found zip."

"I hope you were careful—" Talia began, then stopped. "Yes, I'm sure you were. If there's anything Robert and I can do . . ."

"Lend us your Miata?" Adam said. "The Jeep's been making a funny noise."

"The Jeep's been making funny noises since you bought it, and the last time you drove my car, you buggered up the convertible roof, but if there's anything *else* we can do . . ."

"You asked about a demon named Nasha," Robert said, speaking for the first time since the meal had begun.

"Oh, that's right," I said. "I completely forgot."

"Well, I would have relayed an answer through Adam, but I was stalling to give myself more time, and possibly find a better answer. There's no mention in any text of a demon named Nasha. It's quite likely the poor girl misheard, but I can't even find a name that phonetically resembles Nasha. The closest is Nakashar."

"Nakashar's an eudemon, isn't he?" Adam said as he peeled an orange.

"Very minor. Outside of the Babylonian archive journals, he's not even mentioned."

I looked up, surprised Adam knew this.

Adam continued, "So it's not likely to be Nakashar. Eudemons can be summoned, but they won't interfere in our world. Sacrificing to them is like bribing a meter maid to get out of a speeding ticket. We're talking about a druid, though, right? So we should be looking at Celtic deities. What about Macha?"

"Of course," Robert said. "That would make sense, wouldn't it?"

"I know zilch about the Celtic pantheon," I said.

"Not surprising. Although they are often classified as demons, they aren't included in demonology texts because only druids can communicate with them. They don't fit the classic definition of either eudemon or cacodemon. If you ask them, they'll tell you they're gods, but most demonographers are uncomfortable with that appellation, and prefer to label them 'minor deities.' The study of Celtic deities—"

"—is fascinating," Talia cut in with a smile. "And I'm sure everyone would love to hear about it . . . another time."

Robert chuckled. "Thank you, Lia. Let's just say that Macha is a likely suspect. She's one of the three Valkyrie aspects of the Morrigan, and she certainly does accept human sacrifices. That's one piece of evidence to support your theory, then. Now, I know you want to get back to work. Adam? If you can help your mother with the dishes—"

"Oh, don't torture him," Talia said. "I'm sure he wants to help Pa—" She caught a look from Robert. "Or perhaps first he can show Lucas that motorcycle."

"That's right." Adam turned to Lucas. "Remember I was telling you about that guy my friend knows? Bought an Indian, took it apart, and couldn't figure out how to put it back together? Well, his wife's making him sell it, so I had him e-mail me some pics. Looks like a big metal jigsaw puzzle, but I thought you might like to take a look. You could probably get it cheap, store it here until you guys get a place."

"You boys go on, then," Robert said. As they left, he motioned for me to stay behind.

"Okay," I said when they were gone. "Since when does Adam know about minor eudemons and Celtic deities?"

"Surprised?" Robert smiled. "I think that was the idea. He's been studying for a few months now, but probably didn't mention it because he wanted to astound you with his sudden brilliance."

I moved to the chair beside Robert's.

"It's never been easy for him," Robert continued. "Hearing everyone talk about your accomplishments. I'll admit, I've been guilty of lauding your achievements in the past few years, hoping it would encourage him to take on a more active role in the council."

"He's talked about it," I said. "But it's never gone beyond talk. With added power comes added responsibility."

Robert smiled. "And added work, both of which lack a certain appeal for Adam. In the last few years, though, he's been looking at where you were, and where he was—a college dropout, tending bar—and it bothered him enough to re-enroll at college, but I think he was still able to justify it, tell himself you're an anomaly and no one else can be measured along the same yardstick. Then he met Lucas, and saw what he's doing with his life. I think he's realized that if he continues down this route, he'll be left behind, the friend who watches from the sidelines, buys the beer, and listens to the war stories."

"So boning up on demonology is step one in a bigger plan."

"I wouldn't say a 'plan' per se. Adam has ambitions, but he hasn't figured out where to channel them." As Talia returned for another armload of dishes, Robert smiled up at her. "Now, his mother knows how she'd like to see them channeled. Into book-reading and studying, hands-off work like his old man."

"Nothing wrong with that," Talia said. "Unfortunately, for Adam, it would require heavy sedation and fireproof chains. Being involved means being *involved*, the more dangerous the better."

"It's not that dangerous," I said. "Not really."

Talia laughed and patted my shoulder. "You don't need to whitewash it for me, Paige. I knew my son was never going to lead a quiet life working in an office. In some cases, biology really is destiny. He has power. Better he should use it for good. Or, at least, that's what I keep telling myself."

"He's got a first-rate defense system," I said.

"Exactly. He'll be fine." She exhaled and nodded. "He'll be fine. Now, Paige, go find what you need to stop this guy, and if you need our help, just ask."

I'd hacked into this credit card company's files before—the last time being only a few weeks ago when Lucas needed information for a case. They hadn't changed any of their security parameters since then, so I popped into the system easily. Within twenty minutes I had Weber's credit card transaction records. Nothing on them indicated that he'd visited any of the target cities in the last six months. That, however, might only mean that he was smart enough not to make hotel reservations or dinner purchases with his credit card. Or he might have used a different card.

Lucas slipped into the study as I finished. When I told him I'd struck out, he decided to make some phone calls and see whether we could find another way to place Weber out of town on the days of the attacks. These calls were best made from a pay phone, so he took Adam and left. Did he really need Adam to chauffeur him around Santa Cruz? No, but if he'd left him, I'd have spent the next hour with Adam breathing down my neck as I tried to crack Weber's data files. So Lucas took him along.

It took me about thirty minutes to determine the encryption program Weber had used on his files. Once I knew what he'd used, I downloaded a cracking program and translated them into text. For the hour I waded through the boring detritus of an average life: e-mail jokes, online dating postings, bill payment confirmations, Christmas card address labels, and a hundred other mundane bits of data raised to the value of top-secret information by a paranoid mind and a shareware encryption program.

At ten-fifty, my watch alarm went off. Time to check in with Elena. I phoned her, talked to Savannah, then returned to my work. The rest of the files on the disk appeared to be work-related. Like most professionals, Weber's day didn't end when the clock struck five, and for contract employees, the drive to translate that contract into a full-time job often means bringing work home to impress the company with your throughput. He had plenty of data files on his computer, and a folder filled with programs in SAS, COBOL, and RPG. The mind-numbing side of programming: data manipulation and extraction.

I looked at the lists of data files. There were over a hundred on the disk and I really didn't want to skim through each one. Yet I couldn't just put them aside based on assumptions about the content. So I whipped up a simple program to open each file and write a random sampling of the data into a single new file. Then I scanned the new file. Most of it looked like financial data, not surprising given that Weber worked in the accounting division of a Silicon Valley company. Then, a third of the way down the file, I found this:

```
Tracy Edith
McIntyre          03/12/86     shaman      NY5N34414
Race Mark
Trenton           11/02/88     sorcerer    YY8N27453
```

Morgan Anita
Lui-Delancy   23/01/85   half-demon   NY6Y18923

Now, Silicon Valley companies may employ some pretty young people, and some pretty strange people, but I don't think teenage supernaturals made up a significant proportion of their staff. I found two other similar lists farther down. Three files with information on the teenage children of supernaturals. Three Cabals had been the victims of a killer targeting their youth. Definitely not a coincidence.

My sampling program had pulled off only the first eighty characters in each record, but the information in those records extended well over that. As with most data files, though, all you saw were strings of numbers and Y/N indicators, meaningless without a context. To read and understand these files, you needed a program that extracted the data using a record key.

Ten minutes later, I'd found the program that read the Cabal files. I ran it, then opened the file it created.

Criteria A: age<17; living with parent(s) = N; current location city NOT blank, current location country = USA

ID	Name	Age	Cabal	P.Race	State
01-645-1	Holden Wyngaard	16	Cortez	shaman	LA
01-398-04	Max Diego	14	Cortez	Vodoun	NY
01-452-1	Dana MacArthur	15	Cortez	hd/witch	GA
02-0598-3	Colby Washington	13	Nast	half-demon	SC
02-1232-3	Brandy Moya	14	Nast	half-demon	AL
02-1378-2	Sarah Dermack	15	Nast	necro	TN
03-083-2	Michael Shane	16	StC	half-demon	CA
03-601-2	Ian Villani	14	StC	shaman	NY

```
Criteria B: living with parent(s) = Y; parental marital
status IN [D,W,S]; employee is custodial parent = Y;
parental occupation = bodyguard, department = CEO
```

ID	Name	Age	Cabal	P. Marital Stat.
01-821-1	Jacob Sorenson	16	Cortez	Widowed
03-987-1	Reese Tettington	14	St. Cloud	Divorced

At my elbow was a piece of paper with three names on it—the names of the teens killed from the other Cabals, the only information we had about them. I'd already memorized that list, but still looked over now, needing to be sure I wasn't imagining things. I read the names.

Colby Washington.

Sarah Dermack.

Michael Shane.

I grabbed my cell phone and called Lucas.

CHAPTER 20

A MESSAGE OF HOPE

"H oly shit," Adam said after I'd explained what I'd found. "Well, the
Cabals can fire up their electric chair. Case closed."

"An economically efficient solution," Lucas said. "But I believe, in a
case with such a potentially life-altering—or life-ending—conclusion, it's
not unfair for the accused to expect a few luxuries, such as a trial."

"The guy made lists of teenage Cabal kids, and half the kids on those
lists are now dead. Screw due process. Hell, I'll fry him myself, save the
Cabals the cost of electricity."

"While we appreciate your enthusiasm, I believe we'll begin by talking
to Weber—"

"Interrogate him? Hey, I picked up some good torture tips from Clay.
I could—"

"We'll begin by *talking* to him," Lucas said. "Without the added incentive
of physical, mental, or parapsychological duress. We'll mention the files—"

"And say what? Do you have a reasonable explanation as to why we
found lists of dead kids on your computer? Lists created *before* they died?
Oh, yeah, I'm sure there's a logical—"

I clapped a hand over Adam's mouth. "So, we'll talk to Weber. Tonight?"

Lucas checked his watch. "It's past midnight. I don't want to frighten
him—"

Adam yanked my hand down. "Frighten him? The guy's a serial killer!
I say we scare the living shit out of him, and—"

I cast a binding spell. Adam froze in mid-sentence.

"We'll confront him in the morning," Lucas said. "To be certain, however, that nothing happens in the meantime, I'd suggest we return to his
house, confirm that he's still there, and keep watch until morning."

I agreed, then broke the binding spell, and closed my laptop. As Adam
recovered, he glared at me. I cut him off before he could complain.

"Are you coming with us? Or will our lack of murderous activity be
too great for you to handle?"

"I'm coming. But if you use another binding spell on me—"

"Don't give me any reason to and I won't."

"Remember who you're talking to, Sabrina. One touch of my fingers and I could stop you from ever using a binding spell on anyone ever again."

I snorted and opened my mouth to reply, but Lucas cut me off.

"One other small matter, before we leave," Lucas said. "My father has left over a half-dozen messages on my phone, looking for updates. Should I provide one?"

"Do you think it's safe?" I asked.

Lucas hesitated, then nodded. "My father may be overprotective, but he does trust my judgment and my ability to defend myself. If I tell him we wish to speak to Weber before taking him into custody, he'll accept that. I'll ask him to assemble an apprehension team."

"What?" Adam said. "We don't even get to take the guy down?"

"The Cabal team is trained to handle that, and I'll let them do their job."

Adam sighed. "Well, I guess a stakeout is still pretty cool."

"Jesus," Adam said, slumping into the driver's seat. "How long have we been sitting here? Why isn't it light out yet?"

"Because it's only five A.M." I said.

"No way. Your watch must have stopped."

"Didn't Lucas suggest you bring a magazine? He said it'd be boring."

"He said tedious."

"Which means boring."

"Then he should have said boring." Adam shot a mock glare at Lucas, who sat beside him, watching Weber's house through binoculars.

"Boring means something which is dull," Lucas said. "Tedious implies both long and very dull, which, I believe you'll agree, this is."

"Yeah? Well, remind me to pack my pocket dictionary next time you two drag me along on one of these 'tedious' adventures."

"Drag?" Lucas said, arching an eyebrow. "I don't recall any arm-twisting involved."

"Hey, brain-flash," Adam said. "Why don't I slip out for a closer look? Make sure he's still there."

"He is," Lucas said. "Paige cast perimeter spells at both doors."

"Yeah, well, no offense to Paige, but—"

INDUSTRIAL MAGIC • 431

"Don't say it," I said.

Adam opened the driver's door. "I'll go check."

"No," Lucas and I said in unison. When Adam hesitated, door still open, I added, "Close the door or we'll put my spell-casting ability to the test."

He grumbled, but closed it. Another two hours passed. Two hours during which I had cause at least every ten minutes to wish we'd left Adam behind. Finally, at seven-thirty, a light went on in Weber's bedroom. Adam lunged for the door handle. Lucas put out a hand to stop him.

"We're not jumping him the moment he gets out of bed," I said. "There's no rush."

Adam groaned and sank into his seat.

We'd prepared our plan of action before leaving the Vasics. I'd remembered what the gang punks in the alley had said on seeing us, which also reminded me of my own impression the first time Lucas showed up on my doorstep, clean-cut and funereally earnest in his department-store suit. With the right choice of clothes and a couple of books from Robert's library, we were set.

Lucas and I gave Adam time to sneak around and cover the rear door, then we climbed the front steps. Lucas rang Weber's doorbell. Two minutes later, a thin, dark-haired man answered. Weber matched his Cortez Cabal employee photograph, right down to the black shirt.

"Good morning," Lucas said. "Do you know where you'll be spending eternity?"

Weber's gaze dropped to our Bibles. He mumbled something and tried to shut the door. Lucas grabbed the edge and held it fast.

"Please," I said. "We have an important message for you. A message of hope."

Now, we really didn't expect Weber to let us in. My religio-babble was only intended to give Lucas time to ready his knock-back spell, which would send Weber reeling away from the door so we could get inside. But as the words left my mouth, Weber's eyes widened.

"You're the ones," he said. "The ones Esus said would come."

I blinked, but Lucas nodded and murmured an affirmation. Weber ushered us inside, then cast a nervous glance out the front door before closing it.

"Go on in," he said, wiping his palms against his pants. "Sit down. Oh, wait, let me clear that chair. I'm sorry the place is such a mess. I've been—"

"Busy," Lucas finished.

Weber nodded, head bouncing like a bobble dog's. "Busy, yes. Very busy. When Esus told me . . . well, I wanted to run, but he said I shouldn't, that it would only make things worse."

"He's right," Lucas said.

"He's always right." Weber cast a nervous glance around. "He said it's not safe here. He said you'd take me someplace safe."

My gaze shot to Lucas, trying to gauge his reaction, but he gave none.

"That's right," Lucas said. "Just let me call our driver."

Lucas reached into his breast pocket for his cell phone, to call the extraction team. Obviously Weber wouldn't be comfortable talking here, so there was no use trying. Time to skip to the next phase and take him in for questioning.

Lucas only had time to press the first button when a sharp crack rang out, followed by a tremendous crash. A metal canister hit the floor between us. Lucas lunged, grabbing me by the shoulders and throwing us both to the ground. The canister began to smoke.

"Cover your—" Lucas began, but the sound of breaking wood drowned him out.

I turned to see the front door slam open and three men dressed in black barrel through. All three turned their guns on us, then disappeared as smoke filled the room.

CHAPTER 21

THEY ALWAYS GRAB THE GIRL

Someone started shouting orders, but I was doubled over, hacking my lungs up, unable to hear anything but my own coughing. I pulled my shirt over my nose, but it didn't help. My eyes teared up from the gas; between that and the smoke, I was blinded. Fingers grabbed my arm and tugged me forward. Trust Lucas to keep his calm, whatever the situation.

I stumbled behind Lucas's dark shape. A doorway loomed before us. As we moved through it, the smoke lessened, but my eyes still streamed tears. I wiped my free arm across them. Lucas kept pulling me, presumably toward the back door and clean air.

"Paige!" Adam's voice. Through the smoke I could make out his outline running toward us.

"Get outside," I rasped. "It's—"

He charged. The hand on my arm wrenched me backward. I tripped and spun to see that it wasn't Lucas holding me. It was Weber.

I punched at Weber, but my fist glanced off his shoulder. His other hand sheared down. I felt something hit me between the ribs. Heard Adam's bellow of rage. Lucas lunged through the door and cut Adam off in mid-charge. The stink of sulfur and burned flesh overwhelmed the fading smell of the gas. Lucas gasped in pain. I tried to wrench myself from Weber's grip, but he held me fast.

"Nobody move!" Weber screeched, his voice shrill with panic. "I've got the girl."

A split second of clear, if near-hysterical, thought. Of course he'd grab the girl. They always grabbed the girl. But why did I have to be the girl?

Then cool steel pressed against my throat, and I stopped thinking. The blade pressed into my throat, and blood trickled down my neck. In that moment, it seemed that even to breathe might be fatal, that with the slightest movement some vital artery would be severed. As I held my breath, I became aware of another pain, sharper and lower. My rib cage. I pressed the spot. Blood seeped through my fingers. I'd been stabbed. The thought hit me so hard I rocked, and in rocking felt the knife nick my throat again. I closed my eyes and began to count, fighting against panic.

"Move the knife away from her throat," Lucas said, his voice even but strained.

"She—she's my hostage."

"Yes, I know," Lucas said slowly. "But if you wish her to remain a viable hostage, you cannot take the chance of accidentally wounding her, so please lower that—"

A loud scuffle cut him off, as the men from the other room barreled into the kitchen. I didn't dare look to confirm that, could only stare at the empty space in front of me. Weber tensed, and the blade dug into my throat again.

"Stand down!" Lucas shouted over the clamor. "He has a hostage. Put your weapons down!"

"Everyone against the wall," a man barked.

"Don't pretend you don't know who I am," Lucas barked back. "I gave you an order. Lower your weapons!"

"I take my orders from the Nast—"

"You'll take your goddamned orders from me or you'll be regretting it into the next life! Now stand down."

A moment of silence, then the pressure on my throat lessened.

"I want a helicopter," Weber said. "I want—"

"You want to get out of here alive," Lucas said, his voice returned to its usual soft, reasonable tones. "The house is surrounded by professional snipers. The moment you step into their line of sight, they will shoot."

"I—I have a hostage."

"And they are trained to handle that. You'll be dead before you have time to hurt her."

Weber hesitated, knife trembling against my throat. Adam tensed, but Lucas kept a restraining hand on his shirt. Lucas's lips moved in an incantation. Then he stopped as Weber lowered the knife.

"Good," Lucas said. "Now you need to—"

"Esus, god of water's great gift!" Weber shouted, sliding his fingers along the knife's blade and flicking my blood to the floor. "Esus, hear me!"

"You don't want to do this," Lucas said.

Weber's eyes rolled back and he started speaking in another language. I counted to three, then threw myself forward. He caught me, one arm going around my neck. My feet flew out as he yanked me back. Adam lunged at Weber. The knife shot to my throat. Weber yelled a warning, but Adam kept coming. The knife bit through my skin. Then Adam stumbled, thrown off balance by Lucas, who'd this time had the presence of mind to use a knock-back spell rather than touch Adam.

"Everybody stay back!" Weber shrieked.

"We will," Lucas said, motioning Adam to move behind him. "Now, lower that knife—"

"Esus!" Weber shouted. He wiped the dripping blood from my neck and flung it to the kitchen floor. "Take this offering and deliver your loyal servant!"

Weber paused, but nothing happened. I looked at Lucas. He met my eyes and I could see his fear, but he motioned for me to stay calm and wait. Weber ran through his supplication twice. Then he waited. We all waited, the hum of the refrigerator the only sound.

"He's not answering," Lucas said softly. "He won't interfere. Now, if you want to negotiate, you need to lower that knife. I won't talk to you while you have a knife at her throat."

Weber looked at the ceiling one last time, then lowered his gaze to Lucas. "If I lower the knife, they'll shoot me."

"No, they won't. They have their weapons down, and they won't take the chance that you can get your knife back to her throat before they aim and fire. Lower the knife . . ."

As Lucas continued reasoning with Weber, the knife blade quavered against my throat. One slip, one push too hard against the skin, and . . . oh, God, it hurt to breathe. Blood now soaked the front of my shirt, wet and clammy against my skin. Where had I been stabbed? Beneath the heart, I knew, but what was there? What organs?

And then I thought: Goddamn it, you're standing here sniveling and hoping your boyfriend saves you before you bleed out. Typical witch.

I closed my eyes and whispered a spell. Though the words of the two men covered mine, every syllable pressed my throat against the knife blade. I ignored the pricks of pain and kept casting. As the last words left my mouth, the knife went still. I swallowed and prayed it wasn't a coincidence. I counted to five, waiting for the knife to resume shaking. It didn't. Another swallow, then I concentrated my all on holding the binding spell and very slowly eased sideways, away from the knife.

"Don't—" Weber started, then realized he couldn't move his hand. "What the—?"

Weber's other hand shot forward to grab me as I side-lunged out of his reach. The spell snapped. I saw the knife blade swing down. As I twisted and dove for the floor, the knife slashed through the side of my stomach. Then Lucas grabbed me, knocking the knife away, as Adam launched himself at Weber. Weber screamed. The stink of scorched flesh filled the tiny kitchen. The Cabal SWAT team leapt into action. And it was all over.

CHAPTER 22

LAYING THE BLAME

Of the next hour I remember only images and snippets that whizzed past at MTV speed. Lucas stanching my wounds. Adam pacing behind us. The SWAT team leader barking orders. A man examining my wounds. Adam snapping questions. Lucas reassuring me. A weight on my chest, slowly bearing down. Gasping for air. Lucas shouting orders. A door slamming. Road rumbling beneath tires.

The next time I came to, I was lying on some kind of bed that vibrated and swayed. I struggled to open my eyes, but could only pry them open a slit. When I inhaled, the air was sharp, metallic. I felt a light pressure around my mouth. An oxygen mask. A surge of panic made my head hurt. I dipped toward unconsciousness again and fought my way back.

A soft jolt and the vibrations ceased.

"Finally."

Lucas's voice, distant and muffled. A squeeze on my forearm. I felt the warmth of his fingers, resting on my arm. Then his breath tickled my ear.

"We're here," he said, still sounding as if he was a room-length away. I had to concentrate to make out the words. ". . . you hear me?"

A clang, then the whoosh of an opening door and the dim light turned midday bright. Lucas's grip on my arm tightened.

"What are you doing here?" he said, voice cold.

Another voice answered. Familiar . . . Benicio. "I came in with the team. Our team. The one you requested. How is she?"

A clatter, and the low murmur of other voices. My bed jerked. Lucas's fingers brushed my forehead as my bed lifted. A jolt, a murmured apology, and I was tugged into the sunlight. A few bumps, then the squeak of wheels and the rush of air. Lucas's hand found mine and gripped it as we moved.

"You're upset," Benicio said, his voice low.

I managed to open my eyes enough to see Lucas at my side, walking fast, Benicio beside him, leaning in for privacy.

"And that surprises you?" Lucas clipped his words, voice colder than I'd ever heard it.

"I don't blame you for being angry, but you know I had nothing to do with this."

"It was all a misunderstanding. Or a coincidence. Have you decided yet? If not, may I suggest you choose misunderstanding? It provides more opportunity for prevarication."

Benicio reached for Lucas's free arm. "Lucas, I—"

Lucas swiped at his father's hand, catching it and knocking him back. Benicio's eyes went wide. Lucas's face twisted as he spun to say something, but as he wheeled around, he noticed my eyes were half-open and stopped in mid-turn. He bent over me, nearly tripping as he tried to keep pace alongside the stretcher.

"Paige? Can you hear me?"

I tried to nod, but had to settle for fluttering my eyelids. He squeezed my hand.

"You're okay," he said. "You're in a hospital—a private hospital. Robert arranged it. They need to . . ."

I slid back into unconsciousness.

The cuts on my neck proved the least of my injuries. The blade had left only shallow gashes that required no more than a quick cleaning and small bandages. I'd sustained two other injuries—one serious but relatively painless, the other minor but painful as hell. The chest wound had cut my lung, collapsing it. The doctors had inserted a chest tube, cleared out the blood, and reinflated my lung, which now seemed fine, although they had to keep the chest tube in for a day or two. The abdomen cut had sliced only through muscle—well, okay, undoubtedly more fat than muscle, but the doctors said "muscle" so I'm sticking to their version. Though the wound was superficial, every time I moved, it was like getting stabbed all over again.

The next morning I opened my eyes to see Adam hunched over a psychology textbook, highlighter in hand. I reached up to rub my face and nearly toppled the IV stand onto the bed. Adam grabbed it just in time.

"Shit," he said. "I finally convince Lucas it's safe to leave for a few minutes and you decide to wake up. If he comes back, close your eyes, okay?"

I managed a weak smile and opened my mouth to speak, then made a face. I pointed to the water. Adam poured me a glass. He started to put in the straw, but I grabbed the glass and took a gulp. The water hit my parched throat and bounced back, dribbling out my mouth.

"That's attractive," he said, reaching for a tissue.

I snatched it before he could do anything as humiliating as wipe my face. He picked up something from the dresser.

"Brought you something." He handed me a stuffed beanbag bear dressed in a black witch's hat and dress. "Remember these?"

"Hmmm." I struggled to focus, still woozy. "Right. The dolls." A small smile, as the memory surfaced. "You—" I wet my lips and tried again. "You used to buy them for me. Gifts."

He grinned. "Every ugly wart-faced witch doll I could find. Because I knew how much you loved them."

"Hated them. And you knew it. Used to lecture you on sensitivity and stereotyping." I shook my head. "God, I was insufferable sometimes."

"Sometimes?"

I swatted him and laughed, then gasped as pain shot through my stomach. Adam grabbed for the call button, but I lifted my hand to stop him.

"I'm okay," I said.

He nodded and sat down on the side of the bed. "You had us pretty worried. At the house everything seemed okay, but then, boom, you blacked out and your blood pressure dropped—" He shook his head. "Not a good scene. I was freaked, and Lucas was freaked, which only freaked me out even more, 'cause I figured this guy doesn't scare easy and if this scares him, there must be a reason to be scared and—" Another shake of the head. "It wasn't good."

"Paige."

I looked up to see a figure in the doorway. The voice told me it was Lucas, but I had to blink to double-check. Pale and unshaven, he was still dressed in the suit he'd worn for the missionary ruse at Weber's house, but the jacket and tie were gone. His shirt was wrinkled and splattered with coffee stains. One sleeve of his shirt was charred at the forearm, with bandages peeking through the gaping hole. That was the drawback to working with Adam—when he got mad, you had to stay out of his way, or you paid the price in second-degree burns.

"I'll be outside," Adam said, shifting off the bed.

He slipped out the door. As Lucas approached I saw that the stains on his shirt weren't coffee brown, but rust red. Blood. My blood. He followed my gaze.

"Oh, I should change. I—"

"Later," I said.

"Do you want to call Savannah? I can—"

"Later."

I held out my hand. He took it, then reached down to hug me.

An hour later, I was still awake, having persuaded the nurse to hold off on my pain medication. First I needed answers.

"Are they holding Weber in L.A.?" I asked.

Lucas shook his head. "My father won that battle. Weber is in Miami, with a trial date set for Friday."

"I don't get that," Adam said. "Why bother? They know the guy's guilty. What are they going to do, say 'Whoops, we didn't issue a proper warrant' and let him walk?"

"He's entitled to a trial," Lucas said. "It's Cabal law."

"But is it a *real* trial?" I asked.

"A Cabal trial mirrors a human law trial at its most basic level. Lawyers present the case to judges who determine guilt or innocence and impose sentence. As for Weber being released on a technicality, it's unlikely to the point of impossible. The concept of civil rights is much more narrowly defined in a Cabal court."

"You don't need to worry about this guy, Paige," Adam said. "He's not coming back out."

"That's not—" I turned to Lucas. "Has he confessed?"

Lucas shook his head. His gaze slipped to the side, just barely, but I'd been with him long enough to know what this meant.

"There's something else, isn't there?" I said. "Something's happened."

He hesitated, then nodded. "Another Cabal teen died Friday night."

I bolted upright, sending shock waves of pain through me. Lucas and Adam both sprang to their feet, but I waved them down.

"I'm sorry," Lucas said. "I shouldn't have blurted it out like that. Let me explain. Matthew Tucker was the nineteen-year-old son of Lionel St. Cloud's personal assistant. When Lionel came to Miami for the meeting Thursday, Matthew came along with his mother. On Friday night, while we were watching Weber's house, a group of the younger Cabal employees decided to go clubbing, and Matthew joined them. After a few drinks, they wandered out of a nightclub district and into a less savory neighborhood. The group split up, and everyone thought Matthew was with someone else. When they returned without him, the Cabals sent out search teams. They found him shot to death in an alley."

"Shot?" Adam said. "Then it's not our guy. Stabbing and strangulation. That's his MO."

"The Nast Cabal has since confirmed that their second victim, Sarah Dermack, was shot."

"Did this Matthew call the emergency number?" Adam asked.

Lucas shook his head. "But neither did Michael Shane, the St. Cloud victim."

"Was Matthew on Weber's list?" Adam asked.

"No," I said. "And if he lives with his mother, who's not a bodyguard, he doesn't seem to satisfy the criteria. He's also older than the others. But still, it does seem—"

"Like something completely different," Adam cut in. "The guy was in the wrong place at the wrong time and got shot."

"What are the Cabals saying?" I asked Lucas.

"Almost to the word, exactly what Adam just said."

Our eyes met and I saw my own doubts reflected back.

"So we have questions, then," I said. "If the Cabals aren't going to ask them, we need to do it ourselves. That means we need to go to Miami and talk to Weber."

Lucas went quiet. Adam looked from him to me.

"My opinion?" Adam said. "You both take this 'protecting the innocent' thing way too far, but if you've got questions, then you'd better get them answered before it's too late. Yeah, I know you don't want to take Paige to Miami, and I can totally understand that, but Weber's locked up. He's not going to hurt her."

"It's not Weber he's worried about." I turned to Lucas. "How does your father explain what happened?"

At first, Lucas didn't respond, seeming reluctant to give his father's rationales a voice. Then he took off his glasses and rubbed the bridge of his nose. "His explanation is that he has no explanation. He assumes that, in mentioning Weber's name to the Nasts, he inadvertently provided them with the impetus to begin their own investigation, which culminated in the SWAT raid."

"I suppose that makes sense," I said. "I know you think your father did this intentionally, but you were in that house, too. He'd never put you in danger like that."

"Paige is right," Adam said. "I don't know your dad, but from the way he was acting yesterday, this was as much a shock to him as it was to you."

"So it's settled," I said. "We're going to Miami."

"On one condition."

The hospital I was in was a small private clinic, far less opulent than the Marsh Clinic in Miami, but serving a similar purpose. This one was run not by a Cabal, but by half-demons. Doctors, nurses, lab techs, even the cook and janitor were half-demon.

San Francisco, like several other big American cities, had a sizable half-demon enclave. Half-demons had no central body like the witch Coven or werewolf Pack. As with most distinct groups in a larger society, though, they recognized the comfort and advantages of community, and many who didn't work for a Cabal gravitated toward one of these half-demon cities.

One of the major advantages to living near other supernaturals is medical care. All the major races avoid human doctors and hospitals. Of course, supernaturals can be and have been treated in hospitals. If you get hit in a head-on collision, you can't tell the paramedics you want to be flown to a private clinic hundreds of miles away. In most cases, such hospital stays are uneventful. But sometimes they aren't, and we do what we can to avoid taking this chance.

Lucas's condition was that, since I needed ongoing medical care, I must transfer to another hospital. Therein lay the problem. Miami was Cortez Cabal territory. The nearest non-Cabal supernatural-run hospital was in Jacksonville. Not only was that a six-hour drive from Miami, but it was run by sorcerers. If a witch was injured in Jacksonville, she'd stand a better chance of recovery by going home and treating herself than by showing up at a clinic staffed by sorcerers.

Benicio wanted me to recuperate at the high-security condo/hospital reserved for family, but Lucas refused. Instead I'd go to the Marsh Clinic and Lucas would stay with me. He'd order all my meals from restaurants and he'd administer my medication, which the San Francisco clinic would provide. The Marsh Clinic would give me a bed and nothing more. If my recuperation hit a speed bump, an outside doctor would be flown in.

Adam switched the phone to his other ear. "Elena's letting you stay up how late? Does Paige know this, 'cause, as a friend, I should tell her." He shot me a grin. "Uh-huh, well, I don't know . . . Bribery works, though." He paused. "Oh, no. No way. This calls for a T-shirt, at least. And none of those cheap three-for-ten-dollars tourist shirts, either."

I'd made my morning call to Elena early today. At eleven we'd be in the air, and I didn't want to worry her by not phoning. On Saturday morning, Lucas had been an hour late phoning because I'd been in surgery, and Elena had been ready to pack her bags and fly out to find us.

I finished brushing my hair and surveyed the results in the mirror on my hospital bed table. After two days in a hospital bed, it wasn't good. A hair clip was my only hope. And maybe a hat.

We were leaving within the hour. Lucas was in a conference with my doctor, getting last-minute nursing instructions and medication.

On the phone, Adam continued to tease Savannah and, although I couldn't hear her end of the conversation, I knew she was lapping it up. From the moment Savannah met Adam, he'd been the subject of a serious girlhood crush. I thought it would wear off after a few months, as adolescent crushes usually do, but a year later Savannah showed no signs of wavering in her affections, which were displayed through endless teasing and insults. Adam handled the situation admirably, acting as if he had no idea that she saw him as anything more than a pesky substitute big brother. Lucas and I did the same, never saying or doing anything that would embarrass her. She'd outgrow it soon enough. In the meantime, well, there were worse guys she could have a crush on.

"Uh-oh," Adam said. "I hear Paige coming back. Last chance. T-shirt or I tattle. No?" He turned from the phone. "Hey, Paige—!" He paused. "Medium? Not likely. I'm a large." Pause. "Ouch. Nasty. Hanging up now." Another pause. "Yeah, okay. Say hi to Elena and Clay for me. And get to bed early."

He hung up my cell phone, then thumped onto the edge of the bed, making my hand bounce and brush mascara on my forehead. I glared at him, grabbed a tissue, and erased the damage.

"You're doing okay, aren't you?" he said. "After everything . . . you're doing pretty good."

"Better than I was a few weeks ago, you mean, right? I know. I just needed a kick in the pants, and this case did it."

"Not just that," he said. "I mean, in general, you're doing good. You had a rough couple months settling in, but now, and this summer when you guys stopped by, I thought, she's happy. Really happy."

"I've still got a few things to figure out, but yes, I'm pretty darn happy."

"Good."

As I zipped up my makeup bag, Adam slid off the bed, walked to the window, and looked out. I watched him for a moment.

"Still mad about Miami?" I said.

He turned. "Nah. Sure, I'd love to help and, yeah, I'm a bit pissed at being left behind, but Lucas is right. His dad already made a point of introducing himself to me and dropping hints about post-college 'employment opportunities.' I'm probably better off avoiding the Cabals until I get my shit together. Which reminds me . . . you were saying last month that we need to do something about Arthur."

"Definitely. We need a necromancer on the council, and it does no good to anyone to have one who's never around. That whole fiasco with Tyrone Winsloe? Arthur didn't even return our calls until it was over. I've been hinting that he should find a replacement, but he ignores me."

"Guy's a miso—what do they call it? Doesn't like women? Not gay, I mean, but . . ."

"Misogynist."

"Yeah, that's it." Adam perched on my bed. "So I was thinking, maybe I should talk to him instead. What do you want me to do?"

Advice flew to my lips, but I bit it back. "What do you think?"

"Maybe if he's ignoring us, we should ignore him. Just get a replacement and let him find out about it whenever he bothers showing up at a meeting. How's that?"

I stifled the urge to give my opinion. Difficult bordering on painful. "We—*you* could do that. Maybe ask your dad if he has any suggestions for a replacement."

I noticed Lucas walk past the door—for the second time. God forbid he should interrupt a conversation. When I called out to him, he popped his head in.

"Ready if you are," I said.

He disappeared, then returned, pushing a wheelchair.

"That better not be for me," I said.

"You're quite welcome to attempt walking. However, if you pass out halfway to the front door, you may wake up back in this bed, recuperating, while I interview Weber in Miami."

I glared at him and waved the chair over. Adam laughed.

"Oh, hey," Adam said. "Before I forget, what do you want to do about that motorcycle?"

Lucas helped me into the wheelchair. "I should wait. It's hardly a necessary expenditure—"

"Tell your friend yes," I said to Adam. I looked up at Lucas. "You want it. I know you do. Take the bike and if you don't want to use your insurance money, consider it an early Christmas gift from me. I know you don't have a place to work on it yet, but you will sooner or later."

"Probably sooner," Adam said, grinning. Then he looked over my shoulder at Lucas and the grin vanished. "The, uh, housing market's good right now, I mean. It's always slow in fall, so maybe you'll find a place."

"No rush," I said. "We're still settling in."

Adam looked at Lucas again and I craned my neck, trying to intercept the look that passed between them, but it vanished before I could catch it. Lucas reached for his satchel.

"Here, let me take that," Adam said. "You get the girl, I'll carry the bags." A quick grin. "Not exactly fair, but I won't be doing the grunt work forever. You just wait." He looked at me. "As soon as I get home, I'm asking Dad about those necro replacements for Arthur. I'll have that all set up by the next meeting."

I smiled. "Great. I'll leave you to it, then."

Adam accompanied us to the airport, where we thanked him for all his help, and I promised to keep him updated on the case. Then we said our good-byes and boarded the plane.

CHAPTER 23

HIGHLY INAPPROPRIATE

We took the Cortez jet back to Miami. Like staying in their hospital, using their jet was a question of safety versus, well, safety. Was I in greater danger on their plane or on a commercial flight? I'd have been happy taking my chances on a regular plane. Not that I expected to be attacked in mid-flight by Cortez hitmen, but because it was in my nature not to make a fuss where my own health was concerned. Lucas disagreed and, considering I couldn't yet sit upright for longer than a few minutes, he was probably right.

Back in Miami, Benicio was scrambling to make peace with Lucas in the only way he could—by arranging for us to see Weber. Although Weber was being held in Cortez custody, each Cabal had assigned a guard. Such cooperation would be heartwarming, if they hadn't done so only to safeguard their own interests in the prisoner. No one, not even the son of a CEO, was getting near Weber without approval from every Cabal.

I thought our request was simple enough. We'd promised to comply with any security precautions. We were on the same side. Moreover, without us, they wouldn't have Weber. Yet, as quickly became obvious, that was probably more a deterrent than an asset. The Cortez Cabal had scored a major coup when we found Weber, and the other Cabals seemed to be refusing our request out of pure spite.

We spent the next day at the clinic, working through the case details while Benicio lobbied the Cabals on our behalf. Lucas had managed to track down the ingredients for a healing poultice and a healing tea. I prepared them myself, and he didn't argue—both were witch magic, requiring witch incantations, and although he knew the procedures, I was better at them. That's not ego talking—witches are better at witch magic, just as sorcerers are better at sorcerer magic. This was also my first field test of a stronger healing spell that I'd learned from the tertiary-level grimoires I'd found that spring. I cast it on the poultice, where it was supposed to not only speed healing, but act as a moderate-strength topical analgesic. To my delight, it worked even better than I expected. By the end of the second day, I was out of bed, dressed in my normal clothes, and feeling more like someone under house arrest than a patient.

Dana's father hadn't yet arrived. Getting word to Randy MacArthur was proving nearly impossible. As for Dana's mother, well, the less I thought about her, the better, or I'd pop stitches. While I was at the clinic, I assumed the role of surrogate visitor. Dana was beyond knowing or caring, but I did it anyway.

That night I persuaded Lucas that I was well enough to go out for dinner. To stretch the excursion out as long as possible, I'd ordered dessert. Afterward, we lingered over coffee.

"Your dad seems to be really pushing for us on this," I said. "You don't still think he had something to do with the raid, do you?"

Lucas sipped his coffee. "Let's just say that, while I don't discount the possibility of his involvement, I admit I overreacted. You were hurt, I was frightened, and I lashed out at the most convenient target. It's just . . . I have some serious trust issues with my father."

I slipped him a tiny grin. "Really? Go figure."

Before Lucas could continue, his cell rang. After two nos, one thank-you, and one "We'll be there," he hung up.

"Speak of the devil?" I said.

He nodded. "The answer is still no. Worse yet, it seems likely to be a permanent no. They've moved the trial to tomorrow."

"What?"

"They say they've rescheduled because both sides are ready earlier than expected, but I suspect our sustained efforts to obtain an audience helped sway their decision."

"So they're blocking us by bumping up the trial." I leaned back in my chair, hiding a grimace as the movement pulled at my torn stomach muscles. "That's it, then. We're screwed."

"Not yet. As my father pointed out, if Weber is found guilty, there's always the option of appeal. At least this will give us the opportunity to hear the entire case. If the prosecution presents concrete evidence linking Weber to the attacks, we may deem an appeal unnecessary."

"And save everyone, including ourselves, a lot of grief."

"Precisely. Likewise, if they've found nothing new and they fail to address alternate possibilities—that Weber was working with the real killer, or unwittingly obtained the information for him—then we have grounds for appeal." He sipped his coffee. "How are you feeling?"

"Well enough to go to the trial, if that's what you're asking."

The session was set to begin promptly at eight; Lucas assured me this was normal for a Cabal trial. Unlike human murder trials, a Cabal session never stretched for weeks or months. Their court days ran from eight a.m. to eight p.m. and every effort was made to finish within a day or two.

We arrived by cab just past seven. The court and holding cells were almost exactly what I'd first expected the corporate offices to be, a renovated warehouse hidden deep in an industrial ghetto. Lucas had the driver drop us at the sidewalk behind one of the shabbier buildings.

Normally, I'd have insisted on paying the driver, but today I let Lucas. The last thing he needed was a squabble over cab fare. Every stress of the past few days was etched on his face. As he turned from paying the driver, I noticed his tie was crooked. I had to do a double take, certain I was mistaken.

"Hmm?" he said, catching my look.

"Your tie's crooked."

His hands flew up to adjust it.

"Here, let me." I stood on tiptoes to fix it. "You need to get some sleep tonight. In a real bed. We're moving to a hotel."

"Not until you're better."

"I am better," I said. "I look better, don't I?"

A small smile. "Better than better."

"Well, then—"

"Oh, look," a voice said behind me. "If it isn't the geek crusader."

Lucas stiffened. I stifled the urge to sling a fireball over my shoulder. Lucas didn't need this. A fireball would be justified. Inappropriate, but justified.

I turned to see a slim, well-built man in his early thirties, his model-caliber face marred by a sneer. Behind him stood William Cortez, which led me to hazard a guess at the identity of the younger man: Carlos.

"There must be a protest march going on somewhere," William said. "I'm sure they'd be more appreciative of your talents, Lucas. Leave the real work to the grown-ups."

I clenched my jaw to keep from reminding him who'd done the "real work" of bringing in the killer, and risked their lives to do so.

"Paige, you've met William," Lucas said. "And this is Carlos. Carlos, Paige. Now, if you'll excuse us—"

"Not bad, little brother," Carlos said as he checked me out. "Got to hand it to you. Better than I expected. You must have some hidden assets after all."

"Oh, Lucas has hidden assets," William said. "About five million of them, and that's just the guarantee. Hold out for the big gamble, and he has a half-billion more."

Carlos laughed. "No shit. That kind of dough, any loser can get laid, huh? A few blow jobs is a small price to pay for a shot at Cortez cash."

"Not necessarily," I said. "From what I hear, it can be too high a price." I met Carlos's gaze and smiled. "At least with some of the Cortezes."

His eyes hardened. "Like hell."

"If you say so."

I let Lucas lead me away. We'd gone about five steps when he leaned down.

"Dare I ask?" he whispered.

"Jaime."

He started to laugh, but choked it back. "Jaime and Carlos?"

"No," I said. "Jaime and *not* Carlos. She decided five million wasn't enough."

His laugh escaped then, a burst of laughter that made me grin and squeeze his hand. I glanced back to see Carlos glaring after us. Guess I hadn't made a new friend. Too bad.

"To be honest, I suspect it's far less than five million by now," Lucas said as we walked. "At the rate he goes through money, I'd say Carlos is down to about five dollars. He'll have to hold out for the inheritance."

"I thought five million *was* the inheritance."

"No, the trust fund." His lips curved. "Silence falls, as she refrains from stating the obvious, namely that her impoverished boyfriend is not as impoverished as she believed. Remember that next time you challenge me for paying cab fare."

Lucas pulled open the back door to the warehouse, and we stepped through into a lobby that would be the envy of any small-town courthouse. A few people milled about, but Lucas looked neither left nor right, just led me toward a set of interior double doors.

"Somehow I suspect you're no more able to pay the cab fare now than you were ten minutes ago," I said. "No trust-fund-dipping from this

Cortez. You could be kidnapped by demon guerillas and still refuse to use any of it for the ransom."

"True." He smiled down at me. "But if you're ever kidnapped, I'll make an exception."

A swarthy young man in a suit and cap appeared at Lucas's side. "Mr. Cortez, sir?"

"Yes?" Lucas said.

"I work for the St. Clouds. Mr. St. Cloud's driver."

"Rick, isn't it?"

The man smiled. "Yes, thank you, sir. I just wanted to say we appreciate it, what you did, catching this guy. Griffin's inside. He'll speak to you himself, but I wanted to add my thanks. And, uh—" His gaze flicked to the double doors. "To say there's a back way in there, if you'd rather take that."

"Back way?" I said.

"Uh, yes, miss. Past the others. The Nasts and a few of the St. Clouds are in the waiting area. There's another way into the courtroom. You and Mr. Cortez might be more comfortable using it."

"Thank you," Lucas said. "But we'll be fine."

"Yes, sir."

The man backed away and slipped into a side hall. I glanced up at Lucas's taut face. All the tension he'd expelled on our walk into the building had returned double-strength. Once we walked through those doors, it was only going to get worse.

Lucas needed a distraction. As I glanced down the two side halls, I had an idea. Highly inappropriate but, sometimes, a little impropriety is exactly what you need.

"Nearly forty-five minutes left," I said. "We'll be sitting all day. No need to rush in there."

"Do you feel well enough to take a short walk?"

"Not what I had in mind."

I tugged him toward the nearest side hallway. His brows lifted, but when I didn't answer, he followed. I turned at the first branch, walked to the third door and opened it. An office. I tried the fourth. Locked. A quick unlock spell and the door opened into a large storage closet.

I flicked on the light. "Perfect."

"Dare I ask?"

"If you have to ask, you really *are* tired this morning."

He hesitated, then smiled.

"Well?" I said, backing into the closet.

He strode through the door, kicked it shut behind him, and cast a lock spell. I stepped back, but he grabbed me and pulled me to him in a deep kiss.

"Damn," I said, gasping as I pulled back. "I've missed that, Cortez. Last night I was wondering how much weight my hospital bed held. Should've conducted a test."

"Perhaps tonight."

"Uh-uh. Tonight we're springing for a hotel and a bed for two."

"Are you sure you feel up to it?"

I showed him how up to it I felt. After a few minutes of kissing, I slid my hands between us, unbuttoned his shirt, and ran my hands down his bare chest.

"You know, Carlos got me thinking," I said. "If I'm going to be a CEO wife—"

"Co-CEO, wasn't it?"

"Sorry. Co-CEO. It's going to cost me a lot of blow jobs, isn't it?"

Lucas laughed. "Yes, a lot, I'm afraid."

"Then these few days in the hospital have put me behind on my quota. I have some serious catching up to do." I traced a finger down his chest and slipped it under his waistband. "The doctor said no bending, but he didn't say anything about kneeling."

Lucas's breath caught.

I grinned up at him. "Well?"

"As loath as I am to refuse, you *are* still recovering." He reached down and hiked my skirt up to my hips, lips going to my ear. "May I suggest something less taxing for now?"

I pushed my skirt down. "Uh-uh. It's a blow job or nothing." I stepped backward toward the door. "Of course if you're not interested . . ."

He pulled me to him, then pressed my hand to his crotch. "Interested enough?"

"I'm not sure," I said, tracing my fingertips across the bulge in his pants. "It's a bit hard—"

"A bit?"

"—a bit *difficult* to tell." I undid his belt, then his slacks, and slid my hand inside. "Umm, let's see. Yes, I'd say that's interested enough."

I lowered myself to my knees and set about distracting him.

Afterward, we talked quietly, delaying our exit from the room. At seven forty-five, I pulled away.

"Fifteen minutes," I said. "We should get inside."

"In a moment." He kissed me. "I love you."

"Of course you do. You have to. It's the law."

A smile. "Law?"

"Any girl who gives a guy a blow job in a broom closet is entitled to at least one 'I love you.' Whether you mean it or not, you're morally and legally obligated to say it."

He laughed, then kissed the top of my head. "Well, I do mean it. You know that."

"I do. And I also know that if we don't get into that courtroom before the session starts, they'll have an excuse to not let us in at all."

CHAPTER 24

SIGNED, SEALED, DELIVERED

As Lucas pushed open the door into the waiting area, a wave of appropriately somber conversation rolled out. Then it stopped and every head turned to watch us enter. There were at least a dozen men, ranging in age from mid-teens to post-retirement, all in suits that would have paid our rent for three months, and all of them sorcerers. It reminded me of the day I'd joined the previously all-male computer club in high school. One step through that door and the icy stares nearly froze me in my tracks.

Lucas, now feeling more himself, simply gazed about the room, nodded once or twice, then put his hand against the small of my back and propelled me through the crowd.

A straight-backed, silver-haired man in his seventies stepped into our path. My gaze snagged on the black band around his suit jacket arm.

"What do you think you're doing?" he hissed. "How dare you bring her here?"

"Paige, this is Thomas Nast, CEO of the Nast Cabal. Thomas, this is Paige Winterbourne."

Thomas Nast. My eyes returned to the black band on his arm. For his son, Kristof. This was Savannah's grandfather.

"I know perfectly well who she is, you—" He bit the word off with an audible click of his teeth. "This is a slap in the face to my family and I won't stand for it."

Lucas met the old man's glare with a level gaze. "If you are referring to the events leading to your son's demise, may I point out that your family was the instigator in the matter. By pursuing custody in such an unconventional manner, Kristof contravened intra-Cabal policy."

"My son is dead. Don't you dare imply—"

"I'm not implying anything. I'm stating fact. The escalation of events leading to Kristof's death was entirely of his own devising. As for his death itself, Paige played no role in it. If there had been any evidence to the contrary, you would have brought it forward at the inquiry this summer. Now, if you'll excuse us . . ."

"She is not going to sit in our courtroom—"

"If it weren't for her, none of us would be sitting in that courtroom. Good day, sir."

Lucas led me around Nast and through the next set of doors.

The courtroom seated maybe fifty people, tops, and was half-full when we entered. As Lucas looked around for good seats, a door at the front of the room opened and Benicio walked through. His timing was too perfect to be coincidental. He'd been waiting for us. Why, then, wouldn't he meet us in the other room and escort us past the Cabal gauntlet? Because he knew better. Lucas would not have appreciated his father protecting him from Thomas Nast and the others, for the same reason that Lucas refused to slip in the back door. Lucas chose his path, quite literally, and accepted the consequences of it.

Benicio caught Lucas's eye and waved him to an empty row right behind the prosecution bench. When Lucas nodded, a glimmer of surprise crossed Benicio's face. He hovered at the end of the aisle, as if not quite sure Lucas really intended to join him. We walked to the front and I slid in first, letting Lucas follow so he could sit beside his father.

"Good to see you, Paige," Benicio said, leaning over Lucas as we sat. "I'm glad you could join us. You seem to be making a speedy recovery."

"Not as speedy as she'd like," Lucas said. "But she's doing well."

"It may be a long day," Benicio said, and I steeled myself for a considerate "suggestion" that I forgo the trial. "If you need anything—a cushion, a cold drink—just let me know."

As I nodded my thanks, the front doors opened again and Griffin walked in, accompanied by Troy and a man I didn't recognize but could guess, by his size, was a fellow guard. Troy led Griffin to our row, where Benicio stood and ushered him in to sit with us. Troy and the other guard took seats on opposite ends of our row.

While Lucas and I talked to Griffin, both front doors opened almost simultaneously. Through one, Weber stumbled in, blinking at the sight of the crowded courtroom. He was dressed in a regular shirt and trousers. Although he wasn't handcuffed or chained, there was a gag across his mouth. That might seem cruel, but a druid's power is the ability to call upon his deities, so the gag was an understandable precaution.

As the guards led Weber to his seat, three sixtyish men walked through the other front door. The judges. Last night Lucas had explained the basics of the Cabal justice system. Cases are presented not to a single judge or a jury, but to a panel of three judges, and the majority vote carries. The judges work a five-year term and the same three are used by all four Cabals, in a circuit-court arrangement. The men—always sorcerers, therefore always male—are selected by an intra-Cabal committee. They are lawyers nearing the end of their careers, and are paid very handsomely for their term, meaning they can retire at the end of it, so they are not beholden to the Cabals for later employment. Fifty percent of their payment is withheld until after the term is completed, and any judge found guilty of accepting bribes or otherwise compromising his position forfeits that portion. All this is intended to make the judges as impartial as possible. Is it perfect? Of course not. But to give the Cabals their due, they'd taken reasonable steps to ensure a fair justice system.

To keep the trials short, they are a bare-bones affair in every respect. Opening and closing arguments are limited to ten minutes each. The lack of a jury means there's less need to explain every step in detail. Expert witnesses are allowed only when necessary—no Ph.D.-whores being paid to claim that DNA identification is a faulty science. Even regular witnesses don't always need to take the stand. Noncritical ones, like Jaime, have their statements taken beforehand and answer questions posed by each side.

Breaks were as basic as the session itself, with a single fifteen-minute morning recess. By then I was already feeling the effects of my rushed recuperation. Lucas insisted I take painkillers, and I had to agree. Without them, I'd have been done by lunch. As it was, let's just say it wasn't the most comfortable morning I'd ever spent. To get through it, I concentrated on paying attention and taking copious notes. Lucas and I shared a steno pad, which we passed back and forth, marking down pertinent points, elaborating on one another's notes, and exchanging written comments on the progress of the trial.

For lunch, a caterer delivered sandwich trays and we had thirty minutes to eat while standing in the lobby. Benicio ate with us, and the three of us managed to carry on a reasonably normal conversation. Benicio only slipped up once, suggesting that we join him for dinner the next night . . . a dinner that would also include three prominent foreign shareholders who just happened to be in town. Lucas handled it with a gentle reminder that, with the way the trial was progressing, we'd likely be busy preparing Weber's appeal.

After lunch, Lucas called the hotel where we'd stayed earlier. Our former room was still unoccupied and the manager offered it to us at the same rate. When Benicio heard our plans, he phoned the Marsh Clinic and arranged to have all our belongings moved to the hotel, so I could go directly there and rest after the trial. A considerate move, and only the latest of many, which prompted me to admit that perhaps Lucas had inherited more from Benicio than his natural talent for lying.

The trial did not go well. Weber had retained his own counsel. When I'd first learned this, I'd been relieved. As the trial progressed, though, I found myself wishing he'd let the Cabals assign him a lawyer. As much as I hated to give them credit, I saw nothing grievously unjust in their system and, had they provided Weber's counsel, I'm sure he would have had competent representation, which was more than he had now.

There were two ways to play this case. One: stress the circumstantial nature of the evidence. Two: plead insanity. Weber's lawyer chose both. And that presented a problem. The first says Weber didn't do it. The second says he did, but he can't be held responsible. Using both says he did kill those teens, but you can't prove it and anyway, he was crazy, but not crazy enough to leave any hard evidence.

At six o'clock, the lawyers presented their closing arguments. At six-twenty, the judges retired to council. At six-thirty they returned with a verdict.

Guilty.

The sentence: death.

Weber, not surprisingly, panicked, and had to be forcibly escorted from the room, screaming muffled invocations from behind his gag.

As one of the judges said some final words, I took the notepad and drew a question mark, to which Lucas wrote "no change." We'd heard no further evidence to damn or acquit Weber, and none of our concerns had even been raised. So we would proceed with his appeal.

The judge thanked the witnesses and counsel, and court was adjourned. Benicio leaned over and whispered that he'd be right back, and asked us to wait. Then he escorted Griffin to the front of the courtroom. The other guard followed, but Troy stayed at his post in our row. Benicio, Griffin, and the other guard walked to the door through which Weber had just been taken. Before Griffin stepped through, he turned, caught our attention, and mouthed a thank-you. Then they were gone.

"You must be exhausted," Lucas said, handing me my purse from the floor.

"I'm okay," I said. "Do we need to launch the appeal today?"

Lucas shook his head. "I'll tell my father that we plan to go ahead and he'll relay the message to the Cabals. Tonight we rest and try to put it out of our minds."

I glanced up to see Benicio slip back into the courtroom, accompanied by his new guard.

"There he is," I said. "That was fast."

"Good," Lucas said. "Earlier, he offered to drive us to the hotel and, if you don't mind, I'd like to accept. Then we can tell him our appeal plans on the way, rather than delay our departure by doing so now."

"If it gets me to a bed sooner, I'm not arguing."

Lucas looked up as Benicio eased into our aisle. "Paige and I would like—" He stopped. "What's wrong, Papá?"

Benicio shook his head. "Nothing. You were saying?"

Lucas studied his father's face. At first, I could see no sign of anything wrong. Then I noticed it, the slightest tilt to Benicio's head, not quite meeting Lucas's eyes as he spoke to him.

"I'm sure Paige can't wait to get out of here," Benicio said. "Why don't we—"

A cough. We looked up to see William and Carlos standing on my other side.

"Thomas Nast wants to speak to you, Father," William said.

Benicio waved him away. William's lips tightened.

"We'll wait for you in the car, Papá," Lucas said. "We can discuss the appeal on the drive."

"Appeal?" Carlos said. "For who?"

"Everett Weber, of course."

Carlos laughed. "Hell, little brother, I didn't know you'd taken up necromancy."

Lucas's eyes cut to his father. Benicio rubbed his hand across his mouth.

"He doesn't know, does he?" William said, lips twitching in a smug smile.

"Know what?" Lucas said, gaze never leaving Benicio's.

"That execution sentence?" Carlos said. "Signed, sealed, and delivered."

I blinked. "You mean . . . ?"

"Everett Weber is dead," William said. "If justice was done, it would be done swiftly. Father and the other CEOs agreed on that before the trial began."

Lucas turned to Benicio. "Before the trial began . . . ?"

"Of course," William said. "Do you think he'd let you embarrass us by trying to set a child murderer free? Can't ever leave well enough alone, can you, Lucas? Saving the innocent, saving the guilty, it doesn't really matter, as long as you stick it to the Cabals. Thank God Father didn't tell them you wanted an audience before the trial or who knows what kind of hornet's nest you'd have stirred up."

Lucas stared at his father, waiting for him to deny any of this. Benicio only dropped his gaze. I stood. Lucas looked at Benicio one last time, then followed me into the aisle.

We weaved around clusters of sorcerers and headed into the parking lot. More Cabal clusters out here, having a smoke or getting a dose of Miami sun before jetting home. As we passed one group, a young man caught my gaze. I glanced into a pair of big blue eyes and felt a jolt of recognition. I paused, but Lucas didn't, his attention elsewhere, and I hurried to keep up.

We continued through the packed parking lot in silence. As we walked, I tried to push past my shock and think clearly. Weber was very likely guilty, so his execution, while unnecessarily swift, was probably not unjustified. It might still be possible to speak to him, through a necromancer, and reassure ourselves that he was indeed the killer. As I was wondering whether I should mention this to Lucas yet, a voice hailed us.

"Lucas? Hold up a sec."

I tensed and turned to see a young man striding toward us. Tall and lanky, a year or two younger than me, blond hair tied back in a ponytail, gorgeous big blue eyes. As I saw those eyes my heart skipped. He was a sorcerer, of course, but it was more than that. This was the same young man whose gaze I'd met just a moment ago, whom I now realized I didn't recognize, but felt like I should. Then I noticed the black armband and the recognition clicked. He reminded me of Kristof Nast. Kristof's eyes. Savannah's eyes.

A few paces behind him was another young man, late teens, also wearing an armband. He met my glance with a scowl, then looked away.

"Hey, Lucas." The first young man stopped and extended his hand. "Good to see you."

"Sean, hello," Lucas said, distractedly, his gaze wandering.

"Good work you did, catching that freak. Course, no one's going to send you a thank-you card, but most of us do appreciate it."

"Yes, well . . ."

Lucas turned toward the road, clearly eager to go, but the young man didn't move. His eyes flicked to me, then dipped back to Lucas. Lucas followed the path of his gaze, then blinked.

"Oh, yes, of course. Paige, this is Sean Nast. Kristof's son."

"And that's—" Sean turned to his reluctant companion and waved him over, but the younger man scowled and scuffed his shoe against the pavement. "That's my brother, Bryce."

These were Savannah's half-brothers. I quickly extended my hand. Sean shook it.

"This isn't a good place," he said. "And I know you guys are busy, but we're staying in town for a few more days, and we thought maybe—"

"Sean?"

Sean shot a glare in his brother's direction. "Okay, okay, I thought maybe—"

"Sean!"

"What?" Sean spun on his heel, then his eyes went wide.

As I turned, I saw a suit jacket thrown on the hood of a car. Someone eager to shed his formal trappings. Then I saw pants, and shoes, and a hand protruding from the jacket sleeve. Red drops dripped from the outstretched fingers and over the car's left headlight, leaving a glistening trail before plinking into the small pool of blood below.

CHAPTER 25

POINTING FINGERS

We ran to the body. I remember that first view as a series of close-up snapshots, as if my brain couldn't comprehend the whole. The hand splayed palm-up, a rivulet of blood trickling down the index finger. A black band around the biceps of his suit coat. His eyes closed, long blond eyelashes resting on a smooth cheek, a cheek still too young for shaving. Tie loosened and stained red, merging with the wet stain on his white dress shirt, the stain growing. The stain growing . . . blood still flowing . . . heart still pumping.

"He's alive!" I said.

"Grab his other arm," Lucas said to Sean. "Get him on the ground."

The two lowered the boy off the car hood and onto the pavement. Lucas and I dropped to our knees on either side. Lucas checked for signs of breathing while I felt his pulse.

"He's not breathing," Lucas said.

Lucas started CPR. I ripped off the boy's shirt and used it to mop up the blood, trying to see the source so I could staunch the bleeding. I cleared away enough blood to see three, four, maybe five stab wounds, at least two pumping blood. The wet shirt quickly turned sodden. I looked up at Sean and Bryce.

"Give me your shirts," I said.

They stared at me, uncomprehending. I was about to ask again when I saw the shock in their eyes and realized they hadn't budged since we'd begun.

"Have you called for help?" I said.

"Call—?" Sean's voice was distant, confused.

"Nine-one-one or whoever. Somebody, anybody, just call!"

"I have it," Lucas said. "Take over here."

We switched places. I put my hands over the boy's chest and leaned forward to pump, but his skin was so slick with blood that my hands slid off. I stabilized my balance and pushed his chest, counting fifteen repetitions.

I pinched the boy's nose, bent over his mouth, and exhaled twice. Lucas gave instructions to the dispatcher. I pumped the boy's chest again. The blood seemed to have stopped flowing. I told myself I was mistaken. I had to be.

As I swiveled back to his mouth, Lucas took over chest compressions. I leaned over the boy. As my lips touched his, something hit me, a full-bodied smack like an airbag going off. For a second, I was airborne. Then I crashed backward to the pavement. Pain ripped the breath from my lungs in a ragged gasp and everything went black for a split second.

I recovered just in time to see a blond man dive at me, face twisted with rage. Before he could reach me, Lucas slammed into him, knocking him to the ground. As I scrambled away, the blond man's hand shot up, fingers outstretched toward me, but Lucas pinned both his arms down, which for a sorcerer was as effective a power-buster as gagging was to a druid. The man struggled but, as he quickly learned, Lucas was a lot stronger than he looked.

"My son—she was—"

"Trying to save his life," Lucas said. "We've called an ambulance. Unless you know CPR, let us—"

The screech of tires cut him off. An unmarked minivan whipped into the parking lot. Before it even stopped, two paramedics leapt out. I tried to stand, but the force of the blow had set my stomach wound ablaze. Lucas knelt beside me.

"Can you get up?" he asked.

"I'm trying," I said. "Doesn't look like it, I know, but I am trying."

He put his arms around me and lifted me gingerly. "We can't do anything here. Let's get you inside."

As Lucas stooped to put my arm around his neck, I saw the blond man kneeling beside the boy, gripping his hand. The crowd around him parted and Thomas Nast walked through. The old man stopped. He swayed. Two or three men lunged to steady him, but he pushed them away, walked over, looked down at his bloodied grandchild, and dropped his face into his hands.

With the scene unfolding outside, the courthouse was empty and still. Lucas led me to a sofa in a back room and helped me lie down. Once I was comfortable, he slipped out, spell-locking the door behind him. Moments later, he returned with a paramedic. The man examined me. He found my stitches strained but not burst, and advised bed rest, painkillers, and a formal checkup in the morning.

When the man left, I forced myself to acknowledge the obvious. If the paramedic had time to look after my minor injuries, that could only mean one thing.

"He didn't make it, did he?" I whispered.

Lucas shook his head.

"If we'd called sooner—"

"It didn't matter. By the time we got to him, it was already too late."

I thought of the boy. Savannah's cousin. Yet another member of her family she'd never met, didn't even know existed. And now, he didn't.

A commotion in the hall cut my thoughts short, the thunder of footsteps and angry voices. Lucas started a lock spell, but before he could finish, the door banged open and Thomas Nast strode through, Sean at his heels, eyes red.

"You did this," he said, bearing down on Lucas. "Don't tell me you didn't."

Lucas's hand shot out and waved a circle as he murmured the words to a barrier spell. Nast hit it and stopped short. Sean caught his grandfather's arm and tugged him back.

"He didn't do anything, Granddad," Sean said. "We told you that. Lucas was doing CPR on Joey, then had to call for help, so Paige took over."

Nast's face contorted. "This witch touched my grandson?"

"To help him," Sean said. "Bryce and I didn't know how. They were there and—"

"Of course they were there. They killed him."

"No, Granddad, they didn't. Bryce and I followed them from the courthouse. We were right behind them the whole time. They didn't do anything."

The door opened again and two men came in. The first waved a notepad—our notepad—dropped in the parking lot.

"This is yours, isn't it?" he said to Lucas. "I saw you writing in it during the trial."

Lucas murmured an affirmation and reached for the pad, but the man snapped it out of his reach. Sean Nast snatched the pad from behind and peered at it, then glanced up at us.

"You were preparing an appeal," Sean said. "You didn't think Weber did it."

By then all the Cabal CEOs, including Benicio, had crowded into the small room, and Lucas had to admit we had questions about Weber's guilt, which led to the obvious question of why no one had been apprised of our suspicions. Lucas would never lower himself to "I told you so" even when so richly deserved. I might have filled in the blank had Benicio not done so himself. His admission won him no brownie points for honesty, and the other Cabals jumped on him, accusations flying.

That only opened the floodgates to more finger-pointing. Within minutes, everyone had a theory on who was behind the murders, and they all involved another Cabal. The Cortezes had covered up Weber's innocence because the real killer was one of their own. The Nasts lived nearest to Weber, so they'd planted evidence and launched the SWAT attack, again to hide the real killer in their midst. The Boyds were the only Cabal the killer hadn't attacked, so they were obviously behind it. And the St. Cloud Cabal? Well, no evidence pointed to them as the culprits, which was only proof that they were.

In the midst of all this, Lucas quietly retrieved our notepad and helped me sneak out the door. My incision still felt as if it had been ripped open and stuffed with hot coals, so I had to lean heavily on Lucas, and our progress was slow. Once again we made it halfway across the parking lot before someone hailed us.

"Where do you think you're going?" William called.

"Don't stop," I murmured to Lucas.

"I wasn't going to."

William strode around and blocked our path. "You can't just run out on this."

"Sadly, no," I said. "But I can hobble, and believe me, I'm hobbling as fast as I can."

Lucas started to skirt his brother, but William stepped in front of us.

"Move," I said. "Now."

William glared at me. "Don't you—"

"Don't *you*," I snarled back. "I just saw a boy die because you people executed the wrong man. I'm mad as hell and my pain medication ran out hours ago, so get out of my way or I'll blast your ass back into that courtroom."

A whoop of laughter, and Carlos sauntered over to us. "Whoo-hoo. You've got a real spitfire there, Lucas. I gotta hand it to you. You done good."

"She's had a difficult day, William," Lucas said. "I'd get out of her way."

William strode toward me. "No little witch is going to—"

I flicked my fingers and he stumbled backward.

Carlos laughed. "The girl knows sorcerer magic. Maybe you should listen to her, Will."

"Maybe Lucas shouldn't be teaching her tricks," William said, bearing down on me again. "Sorcerer magic is for sorcerers."

"And witch magic is for witches," I said.

I recited an incantation and William inhaled sharply as the air was sucked from his lungs. His mouth opened and closed, struggling to breathe. I mentally counted to twenty, then ended the spell. He doubled over, gasping.

"Shit," Carlos said. "Never seen witch magic like that."

"And, on that note, we'll take our leave," Lucas said. "Good night."

He led me around William and out of the courthouse parking lot.

"We need to stay on this case," I said as Lucas lowered me onto the hotel room bed. "Now more than ever. If the Cabals keep bickering, the killer will have a heyday."

"Um-hmm."

Lucas bent to tug off my pumps. I pulled my leg back to do it myself, but he waved me away and removed them, then folded back the covers. I started unbuttoning my blouse. He nudged my hands aside and did it for me.

"Weber didn't just coincidentally create that list of potential victims," I said. "He did it for someone. He had access to the files and knew how to extract the data. If we can contact his spirit, he should be able to lead us to the killer . . . or point us in the right direction."

"Um-hmm." Lucas tugged off my skirt and folded it.

"I know a few good necros. We can call one in the morning."

Lucas tucked my legs under the covers. "Um-hmm."

"First thing we need to do is—"

I crashed into sleep.

I was in a forest, doing a ceremony with Lucas. Someone banged on a door, which, of course, seemed odd under the circumstances, but my brain, perhaps recognizing I was asleep, overlooked the illogic, and my dream-self yelled at the intruder to leave us alone.

Another triple knock, louder this time. The forest evaporated and I clawed up from bed. Lucas's arms went around me, gently restraining.

"Shhh," he whispered. "Go back to sleep."

Another knock. I jumped, but he ignored it.

"They'll go away," he said.

And they did. I snuggled against his bare chest. Sleep tugged at me. I surrendered and felt myself drifting under again when the bedside phone buzzed.

"Ignore it," Lucas whispered.

Five rings. Then silence. I relaxed again, stretched out—*Da-da-di. Da-da-di.*

"Isn't that . . ." I mumbled into a yawn.

"My cell phone." A sigh rippled through him. "I should have turned it off. I'll answer it and get rid of him. Perhaps I can reach—" He twisted and sighed again. "Of course not."

He slid from the bed and retrieved the cell phone from his suit coat. When his tone changed, I knew it wasn't Benicio. I propped myself up on the pillow. His gaze shunted to me, brows knitting. I mouthed, "Who is it?"

"Yes, well, your timing is . . . interesting," he said into the phone. "Just a moment, please." He covered the mouthpiece. "It's Jaime."

"Did you call her?"

He shook his head. "She heard what happened today and thinks she might be able to help. She's outside."

I pushed back the covers and swung out my feet. "Perfect. Not my first choice, but the sooner we can contact Weber, the better."

He opened his mouth, as if to argue, then snapped it shut, and told Jaime he'd be right there.

CHAPTER 26

WAKING THE DEAD

Since we'd missed dinner and it looked as if we weren't going back to bed anytime soon, Lucas went to get us something to eat. He was gone before I finished dressing. A quick hair-brushing and face wash and I was presentable, but nothing more. When I saw Jaime pacing the living-area carpet, my first thought was "Geez, she looks almost as bad as I do."

Dressed in jeans and a T-shirt, no makeup, Jaime was hardly the picture of showbiz celebrity. Though I'd originally guessed her age at late thirties, Lucas said she'd passed forty a couple of years ago. Today, she looked it. Maybe dressing down was intentional, a disguise to avoid recognition . . . although she hadn't struck me as the type who *would* try to avoid recognition.

I walked into the room, trying not to stagger.

"Jesus, are you okay?" she said.

She hurried to help me, but I waved her back.

"Of course you're not okay," she continued. "I heard what happened in California. I should have thought—I can talk to Lucas if you want to go back to sleep."

"I'm fine." I considered the sofa, but the recliner seemed as if it would offer more support. "So you heard about the trial?"

Jaime hovered until I was seated, then dropped onto the sofa. "Cabal gossip flies faster than a spooked spirit. I asked the guy who took my deposition to call me when a verdict came in, but I still haven't heard from him. Probably never will. I'm necromancer non grata with the Cabals."

"Really? With your grandmother, you should be prime recruitment material and, God knows, they hate to offend anyone they can use."

Jaime twisted her rings. "Well, I'm not quite the necro my nan was. And, of course, my high profile doesn't sit well with the Cabals. When I started hitting the big time, they wanted me to shut up and shut down. Lucas helped me with that. They leave me alone now."

The door lock clicked. Lucas pushed the door open with his foot, both hands occupied with a tray of food. Jaime watched him struggle for a moment, then jumped up and went over to help.

"Mmm, that smells great," I said. "Soup?"

"Seafood chowder. Not quite the caliber you're accustomed to, but it was this or split-pea."

"Good choice." I picked up a crystal glass of ruby red liquid. "Wine?"

"Not when you're taking these," he said, plunking my medication bottle on the tray. "It's cranberry juice. Dessert is crème brûlée—a more appetizing alternative to pudding."

I grinned up at him. "You're the best."

"No shit," Jaime said. "Last time I was sick, the guy I was seeing brought me a bottle of ginger ale . . . and expected me to pay him back for it."

Lucas took a mug and a second crème brûlée from my tray and laid them in front of Jaime. "If you'd prefer something else, the kitchen is open for a few more minutes." He placed cream and sugar containers beside the coffee. "And, no, you don't have to pay me back for it."

"I am definitely dating the wrong guys."

Lucas started unwrapping his sandwich, then paused. "Should we eat on the road?"

"Ten minutes isn't going to make a difference. Eat your sandwich, then we'll go."

"Go where?" Jaime said.

I explained the evidence against Weber, and how we were certain he'd obtained those lists for the killer. "The only way we're going to find out who wanted those lists is to talk to Weber. So you can help us by doing that, if that's okay."

"Well, umm, sure. Anything I can do. I thought we'd start by contacting Dana again but, well, I guess contacting this Weber guy makes more sense. We know where he's buried, right?"

"Oh, I'm sure they haven't buried him yet," I said.

"They have," Lucas said. "Cabal policy. They inter their dead immediately."

Jaime nodded. "Otherwise, it's like propping open the door to Tiffany's and going home for the night."

Lucas caught my confused look. "Supernatural remains are considered extremely valuable necromantic relics."

"Yep," Jaime said. "Other people go to the black market for DVDs and diamonds. Us necros get to buy decomposing body parts. Another reason why I give thanks every day for this incredible gift I've been given."

She scraped the last bit of custard from the ramekin and licked the spoon. "Okay, this wasn't quite what I had in mind for my evening, but let's do it. Time to wake the recently deceased."

Jaime had just finished her final Orlando show when she heard the news about Weber. She'd then rented a car for the two-hundred-mile trip to Miami, so we now had a vehicle. Lucas drove because he was the only one who knew where to find the cemetery. But, as I soon discovered, that wasn't the only reason. When we hit the outskirts of Miami, Jaime put on a sleeping mask. At first, I thought she was taking a catnap. Then I realized that allowing a necromancer to know where the Cabal buried their dead would be a serious security breach. Not that I could imagine Jaime skulking around a moonlit cemetery with a shovel, but I gave her bonus points for blindfolding herself rather than put Lucas in an awkward position.

The Cabal didn't bury their dead in a municipal cemetery . . . or any recognizable cemetery at all. Lucas drove past the city limits, then made so many turns that I was lost even without a blindfold. Finally he pulled off the road and headed down a thin strip of land flanked on both sides by swamp. A mile later, the road ended. I squinted out the window.

"This is the cemetery?" I said.

Lucas nodded. "It's hardly conducive to graveside visits, but the alligators tend to discourage trespassers."

"Alligators?" Jaime tugged down her blindfold. "Jesus, we're in the middle of the fucking Everglades!"

"The periphery, to be precise. The Everglades are comprised primarily of saw-grass plains, not swampland as you see here. This would be Big Cyprus Swamp, which is technically located outside the Everglades National Park."

"Okay, let me rephrase that, then. Jesus, we're in the middle of a fucking swamp!"

"Actually—"

"Don't say it," Jaime said. "We're not in the middle of a swamp, we're at the edge, right?"

"Yes, but we will be going into the middle, if that makes you feel better."

"Oh, believe me, it does." She peered out into the dark tangle of trees, hanging moss, and stagnant water. "How the hell are we going to get to the middle?"

"We need to take the airboat." He glanced at me. "If you do see an alligator, your new shock spell should be ample deterrent."

"Great," Jaime muttered. "And what are us nonspell-casters supposed to do? Run for our lives?"

"I wouldn't advise it. The average alligator can outrun the average human. Now, Paige, if you could cast a light spell, we'll work our way down to the boat."

CHAPTER 27

SORRY, ΠO VIRGIΠS HERE

After hot-wiring the airboat, Lucas persuaded us it was safe to come aboard, and we set off for the cemetery. The trip reminded me of a Tunnel o' Horrors ride I'd taken once, the kind where you're traveling along in pitch black. Nothing jumps out at you, but that doesn't make it any less terrifying, because you spend the whole time tensed, waiting for the big boo. I've never much seen the attraction of intentionally scaring yourself silly, but at least with those rides, you know nothing in there can hurt you. Not so with the Everglades. It's dark and it stinks, and you're zooming under tree branches hanging with moss and vines that tickle across the back of your neck like ghost fingers. Everywhere you look, you see trees and water, miles of them in all directions. Of course, there's not much danger of drowning. The gators'll get you first.

Don't ask me how Lucas knew where he was going. Even the combination of my light spell and the boat's headlight illuminated no more than a dozen feet in front of us. Yet, despite the lack of obvious markers, Lucas expertly guided the boat through twists and turns. After about twenty minutes, he eased off the throttle.

"What's wrong?" I asked.

"We're here."

"Where the hell is here?" Jaime said, leaning over the side of the boat. "All I see is water."

Lucas steered another few yards, inched the boat sideways, then hoisted up a tie line. I directed my light-ball over his head and saw grass leading up onto a hillock that rose from the water like the back of a sleeping brontosaurus.

"Can we get out?" I said.

He nodded. "Stick to the path, though. And try to avoid stepping in the shallow water."

"Let me guess," Jaime said. "Piranha?"

"Not this far north. There are, however, water moccasins, coral snakes, and cottonmouths."

"Let me guess: They're all poisonous."

"Very."

"Anything else we should know about? Lions and tigers and bears, maybe?"

"There are, I believe, still a few black bears in the swamp, but not in this immediate area. As for feline predators, while I've heard of bobcat sightings, I've personally only seen a panther."

Fortunately, we didn't encounter any alligators, water moccasins, bears, or panthers. I heard a splash now and then, but it was probably a large fish. If not, well, sound carried at night, so it was likely miles away . . . or so I told myself.

The path wound through a few acres of soil just dry enough to walk on, like ground after spring thaw, when you can't decide whether to switch to shoes or stick with boots. The perimeter was ringed with cypress trees, those gnarled, drooping, moss-festooned specters that characterized the Everglades. As the ground rose and dried, the plant life gave way to grasses, hardwoods, and the occasional cluster of white orchids.

Lucas pushed back a curtain of willow branches and ushered us into a semicleared patch.

"Cabal cemetery number two," he said. "Reserved for executed criminals and the unfortunate victims of what the Cabal likes to call 'collateral damage.'"

"I see they saved a few bucks on headstones," I said, peering over at the unmarked ground. "How the heck are we going to find— No, hold on, there's some freshly turned earth, so that must be where they buried Weber. Oh, wait, there's another new grave over there . . . and that stuff looks pretty fresh, too. Damn. They must employ full-time gravediggers."

"The ground here dries very slowly, so most of these aren't as new as they look, though I suspect all three have been dug this month. As for finding Weber's grave, it isn't really necessary. In communicating with the recently deceased, relative proximity is as satisfactory as absolute."

"'Close enough' counts in horseshoes *and* raising the dead." Jaime wiped her palms against her jeans. "Okay, time for the gross stuff. Can you guys take a walk while I set up?"

We wandered over to the opposite side of the graveyard. For the next twenty minutes, we sat in the darkness, doing battle with swarms of mosquitoes and near-invisible biting gnats that Lucas said were called, quite appropriately, no-see-ums.

Finally Jaime called us back.

Although we were within a few yards of Weber's assumed burial site, we had no intention of actually doing anything with his body. Communicating with the dead, fortunately, did not require raising the dead. Necromancers could indeed return a spirit to its physical body but, having seen it done once, I never wanted to witness it again. Instead, most necromancers communicated with the spirit world in other ways. Earlier Jaime had decided she'd use channeling again, as she'd done with Dana. Channeling was more difficult than other forms of communication, but it would allow us to communicate directly with Weber.

Again, Jaime lit a censer of vervain, since Weber probably fell into the category of a traumatized spirit. Beside the censer of vervain was another of dogwood bark and dried *maté*. This was a banishing mixture, used to drive away party-crashing spirits. When you summon in a graveyard, uninvited ghosts are a definite possibility. For now, this mixture would be kept unlit, but Jaime had an open book of matches right below it, ready to use.

Once we were ready, Jaime closed her eyes and invited Weber's spirit to join us. It wasn't a simple "Hey, come on out." Inviting a spirit required long inducements, and we settled back, knowing this could take a while.

After about two minutes, the ground vibrated. Jaime stopped mid-invocation, hands raised.

"Uh, tell me no one else felt that," she said.

"The ground out here can be a little unstable," Lucas said.

I glanced at him. "Like 'eroding into the swamp at any moment' unstable?"

"No, the Cabal has taken precautions to ensure the cemetery won't sink into the Everglades until it reaches full capacity. Minor shifts, though, are not to be unexpected. Please continue."

Before she could, the earth rumbled again. I pressed my hand to the ground, which vibrated like a twanged piano tuner. Jaime grabbed her matchbook and lit the censer holding the repelling herbs. The ground gave a tremendous shake, so violent I would have toppled sideways if Lucas hadn't caught me. Behind Jaime, an oak seedling quavered, then vaulted into the air. The ground ripped open, clods of dirt spewing like volcanic lava.

"Jesus fucking Christ!" Jaime said, scuttling toward us. "I *know* I didn't do that."

A strip of turf ripped back, like a peeled sardine can, opening a deep rectangular pit. From the bottom of the pit came scratching, scrabbling sounds.

"I would strongly suggest we don't wait to see what that is," Lucas said.

We all scooped up a handful of Jaime's equipment. As we turned to run, the thing in the pit rose to the top and, despite Lucas's advice, even he stopped to look. A body levitated over the grave. It was an old woman with long gray hair, dressed in a hospital gown. Her flesh had desiccated rather than decayed, reminding me of those bog mummies from England.

The body rotated ninety degrees, until its feet pointed at us. For a moment, it hovered there. Then, suddenly it sat upright, eyes flying open.

"Who dares disturb my eternal rest?" boomed a deep male voice with a Scottish burr.

Jaime backpedaled past us. I started to follow, then noticed Lucas hadn't moved. I tugged his jacket.

"Hey, Cortez, I think that's our signal to run."

"While I have no aversion to the general concept, it may not be warranted."

"Dinnae whisper, mortal!" the corpse rumbled. "I asked you a question. Who dares—"

"Yes, yes, I heard that part," Lucas said. "However, considering that we did not disturb you, but rather you have answered an invitation extended to another, I believe it is you who must identify yourself."

"Are you crazy?" Jaime hissed. "Leave it alone!"

"I repeat," Lucas said. "Please identify yourself."

The corpse's head snapped back with a sickening crack, then twisted in a full circle, the flesh around its neck splitting, banshee wail ripping through the Everglades.

"Ah, *The Exorcist*, if I'm not mistaken," Lucas murmured. "One must admire an entity with a full appreciation of contemporary pop culture." He raised his voice to be heard above the wailing. "Your name, please."

"My name is war! My name is pestilence! My name is misery and pain and everlasting torment!"

"Perhaps, but as a form of address, it is rather unwieldy. What do your friends call you?"

The thing stopped its head-spinning and glowered at Lucas. "I have nae friends. I have worshipers. I have devotees. And, thanks to you, today I have one fewer of those."

"Esus," I said.

The corpse turned toward me and sat up straighter. "Aye, thank you." It glared at Lucas. "The witch knows who I am."

"And, apparently, you know who we are," Lucas said.

"I am Esus. I know all. I know you, and I know the witch, and I know the necromancer." He peered over at Jaime. "Caught your show. Nae bad, but it could use a wee oomph."

Esus's voice had lost its orator boom and settled into an odd blend of Scottish and American idiom—the speech of an ancient spirit who liked to keep up with the times.

Jaime eased up beside us. "So you're a . . ."

"A druid deity," I said. "Esus, god of woodland and water."

"I like the witch," Esus said. "I'll talk to the witch."

"And we'll talk to Everett Weber," Lucas said.

"No, you willnae. I gave you a chance to speak to Everett and what did you do? Nearly got the poor bastard shot by a bunch of Cabal cowboys. But did I interfere? Nae. I stood down and let my acolyte be taken into custody, because I trusted you to get him out of there." The corpse threw up its hands. "But, och, he's out of there now. After he's dead!"

"That's true." I sidled as close to the reanimated corpse as I dared. "But, being all-knowing, you also know that wasn't our fault. We did our best with the information we had."

Esus's sigh blew bits of withered flesh out the corpse's torn neck. "I know. But I still cannae let you talk to Everett. He's a wee bit traumatized right now, being suddenly dead and all."

"Understandable," I said. "But we really do need to speak to him, and now is the best time."

"Nae can do, lassie. Ask all you want, but I'm nae changing my mind. Of course, whatever Everett knows, I know, so you could ask me. It'll cost you, thocht."

"Nuh-uh," Jaime said. "No deals with the devil. I've learned my lesson on that one."

The corpse glowered at her. "I am nae the devil. Or a demon. Or some skittering spook. I am . . ." Esus crossed his arms. "A god."

"Very well, then," Lucas said. "What would you like?"

"What do you think I'd like? What do all gods like? Sacrifice, of course."

"I'll give up booze for a week," Jaime said.

"Ha-ha. You could use a wee bit of that humor in your show. Far too much of that touchy-feely stuff for me. A good corpse joke now and then would liven things up. As a druid god, I demand true sacrifice. Human sacrifice." He looked at Lucas. "You'd do."

"I'm sure I would. No human sacrifices."

"A goat, then. I'll take a goat."

Jaime looked around. "Would you settle for a gator?"

"No live sacrifices," Lucas said. "Of any kind. In return for clear and comprehensible answers to our questions, I will offer you a half-pint of blood."

"Yours?"

"Of course."

Esus pursed his lips. "A full pint."

"Half before and half after."

"Agreed."

Esus dictated instructions for setting up the sacrificial circle. Then I helped Lucas draw the blood. Not for the squeamish. I'd put in plenty of volunteer hours at blood donor clinics, but our methods that night were, shall we say, a tad more primitive, involving a penknife and a bra. As a tourniquet, there's no better suited item of clothing, nor one that is less likely to be missed. And if it got bloodstained, well, I never turn down an opportunity to freshen my lingerie wardrobe.

Once the blood was drawn, I untied the makeshift tourniquet and repositioned it over the wound. Lucas held his arm up to slow the flow, then turned to Esus.

"Sufficient?" Lucas said.

"Red silk," Esus said. "Bonny. Dare I assume there are matching panties?" His gaze slid down me, grin turning to a leer, which, considering he was in the shriveled corpse of an old woman, was less than flattering. "Maybe I asked for the wrong sacrifice."

"Sorry, no virgins here," I said.

"Ne'er been that keen on virgins myself. And I'll take red silk over white lace any day. Tell you what, dump sorcerer-laddie here, and you and I—"

Lucas cleared his throat. "What can you tell us about the killer?"

"Afraid of a wee competition, senor?"

Lucas raked a pointed look over Esus's current corporeal form. "No, not really."

"Och, I'll find a better body, of course." Esus turned to me. "Blond or brunette?"

"I kinda like what I've got," I said. "Sorry."

"Oh, I can do that, too. Dinnae see the attraction, but—"

"We had a deal," Lucas said. "Now, we found records of Cabal children on Everett's computer and a program that selected potential victims. What we want to know is—"

"Who bought the data," Esus said. He closed his eyes and intoned a low hum, dragging the note out for a few seconds. "That which you seek can be found in a land inhabited by neither the dead nor the ever-living. Like you, yet nae like you. A hunter, a stalker, an animal heart in a—"

Lucas cleared his throat. "Perhaps we should define clear and comprehensible."

"Perhaps we should define dull and boring." When Lucas only stared at him, Esus sighed. "Have it your way. He's earthbound. Human. Now that's information that Everett himself couldnae give you because he ne'er saw the man. I caught a glimpse of him at the courthouse, when he killed that bairn. Damned Cabal shamans put up a barrier to keep me outside, so I couldnae help Everett. I was trying to find a kink in the armor when the dobber grabbed the bairn. Didnae get a good look at him, thocht."

"Why not?" Jaime said. "I thought you were all-seeing."

"All-knowing, nae all-seeing," he snapped. "I'm a god, nae Santa Claus."

"But if you're all-knowing—" she began.

I elbowed her to silence. I doubted gods, even minor Celtic deities, appreciated having their shortcomings pointed out.

"What *can* you tell us about him?" I asked. "From the glimpse you got?"

"Male, corporeal human form, light hair, average size, and fast as Thor's thunderbolt. Stabbed that poor bairn so fast he didnae have time to scream. Your man has killing experience, and lots of it. In the auld days, priests made a dozen sacrifices to me every spring, and none of them was as good at it as this fellow."

"Back to the files, then. How did that come about?"

"The way most jobs come about. Networking. After the Nasts fired Everett—oh, and do you know why they fired him? Because some sorcerer's laddie wanted the job for his co-op. Obviously, Everett wasnae happy. He was looking for a wee bit of revenge, maybe shooting his gob off too much. This guy found out, called and asked Everett if he wanted to make some cash hacking into Cabal employee files. Everett figured the guy was looking to recruit Cabal employees. Happens all the time."

I nodded. "Then he asked for employee files for the Cortez, Nast, and St. Cloud Cabals."

"Nae, he wanted all four. The Cortez and Nast ones Everett could get easily enough, having worked for them. He knew a fellow in the St. Cloud computer department, so he could buy those files. But he had nae idea how to get the Boyd file. This guy didnae care. He said the other three would be good enough; he'd take care of the Boyds later."

"Everett gets the three files, and then . . ."

"Then he wants Everett to extract the information on employees' bairns. And that's when he knew the guy was nae recruiting."

"No kidding," Jaime muttered.

"Look, I'm nae defending Everett. He fucked up. But he's nae saint and he's nae hero. He got greedy and he got scared and between the two, he convinced himself that there could be some innocent reason why a bodie would want a list of runaway Cabal bairns. When those bairns started dying, we both knew he was in trouble. If the Cabals didnae get him, the killer would, tidying up his loose ends. When I saw you were heading in Everett's direction, I told him to go quietly, because I knew your reputations, and figured you would hunt down the truth."

"Sorry," I murmured.

"Och, couldnae be helped. Once the Cabals had a suspect, they were nae letting anything as inconvenient as the truth get in their way. I should have foreseen that."

"How did he get the list to this guy?" I asked.

"Very cloak-and-dagger. The dobber isnae stupid. He communicated by phone, gave nae way to contact him, told Everett where to leave the printouts. When Everett dropped off the lists, there was cash waiting for him."

"So there were two lists," I said. "One of Cabal runaways—the easy marks. Then one of personal bodyguards' kids, to prove that if he could get that close to the bodyguards, he could get that close to the CEOs themselves. From there he jumped straight to the families—"

"Nae, there was a third list. Everett did it separately. After the guy found out there were only two names on the second list, he wanted the bairns of the CEOs' personal staff."

"Then Matthew Tucker *was* a victim," I said. "But, still, to jump from a secretary's son to a CEO's grandson seems a megaleap."

"It's likely his original intention was to remain with the third list," Lucas said. "However, the convergence of Cabal families for the trial provided him with the perfect opportunity to escalate faster."

"And now that he's hit the top, that's where he'll bide," Esus said. "Going back to killing the kids of mere employees now would be admitting he bit off more than he can chew. Here on in, it's a CEO family or nothing. You'd better watch your back, senor."

"I doubt he'll jump to an adult while he still has a decent pool of teen-age victims to choose from. He's striking at young people for a reason, and not just because they're easier targets."

"He wants it to hurt," Esus said. "Your man is hurting because of something the Cabals did, and he wants to hurt them back."

Lucas prodded Esus with more specific questions about the dates and times of phone calls, et cetera, then we gave him his final half-pint, and bade him farewell.

CHAPTER 28

GO-BETWEEN

If Esus hadn't insisted on Lucas's blood, I'd have gladly given the second half-pint, for reasons both personal and practical. On the practical side, we had no food or drink to boost Lucas's blood sugar after his "donation," and he had to navigate the boat back to the dock. Though I couldn't drive a boat, I could drive a car, and insisted on doing so from the dock to the edge of Miami, where Jaime removed her blindfold and took over. We managed to stay awake until about two seconds after we collapsed into bed at a little past four.

Since it was so late when we'd returned to the hotel, Jaime slept on our hotel room sofa. When I awoke late the next morning, I found a note from Lucas. He hoped to find some tangible evidence connecting Weber to the killer, either in his phone records or personal effects, the latter of which had been shipped by the crateload to Miami for pretrial searching.

Beside the note, Lucas had left a glass of water, two painkillers, and the ingredients for a fresh poultice for my stomach. Though I hated to admit it, I needed that . . . otherwise, I don't think I'd have been able to climb out of bed that morning. As it was, I still had to lie in bed for twenty minutes, waiting for the pills and the tertiary healing spell to take effect. Once I could move, I showered, dressed, then slipped into the sitting area of our suite, expecting Jaime to still be asleep. Instead, she was reading a magazine on the sofa.

"Good, you're up," she said. "Let's go grab something to eat."

"Fuel up before you head back on the road? Good idea."

"Uh, right." She grabbed her brush, leaned over, and began sweeping it through the underside of her hair. "You like Cuban?"

"Not sure I've ever had it."

"You can't leave Miami without trying some. I saw this funky little place near the clinic."

"The clinic?"

"You know, where Dana is."

Jaime continued to brush her hair from the bottom, which effectively covered her face and any untoward gleam in her eye. She started to work on a nonexistent tangle. I waited. I gave her ten seconds. She only took four.

"Oh, and since we'll be in the neighborhood, we can stop in and see how Dana's doing. Maybe try contacting her again."

Jaime tossed her hair back and brushed the top, allowing her to slant a glance my way, and gauge my reaction. I'd wondered what had driven her back to us. Somehow I doubted she'd really heard the news about Weber and thought "Oh, I should rush back to Miami and help out." Last night she'd mentioned wanting to contact Dana, and now I realized this was probably the real reason she'd returned, that she felt guilty over having misled Dana and wanted to talk to her again. This couldn't help the case, but if it would help put Dana's—and Jaime's—soul at peace, well, there was little I could do here until Lucas came back. So I placed my eleven o'clock phone call to Elena, then left with Jaime.

"She's not there," Jaime said, tossing down her amulet beside Dana's still form. "Goddamn orientation training."

"Orientation?" I said.

"That's what I call it. Other necros have fancier terms. Gotta make it sound all mystical, you know." Jaime rubbed the back of her neck. "After a spirit crosses over, you have a day or two, sometimes three, to contact them, then the ghost Welcome Wagon snatches them up and shows them the ropes. During that period, the spirit is on hiatus. Some kind of psychic door slams and you can scream your lungs out, but they can't hear you."

"I've heard of that," I said. "Then, afterward, you can contact them, but it's harder than it would be in the first couple of days."

"Because they've learned how to 'just say no' to pesky necros. After that, we're as welcome as encyclopedia salesmen. You have to pester them until they listen just to get rid of you. Unless *they* want something, and then they'll drive *us* nuts until we listen." Jaime raked her hands through her hair. "This makes no sense. If she's in training, then why—" She twisted her hair into a ponytail. "You wouldn't have a clip, would you?"

"Always," I said, digging in my purse. "With this hair, it pays to be prepared. A drizzle of rain or shot of humidity and it's ponytail time."

"So the curl's natural?"

"God, yes. I wouldn't pay for this."

She laughed and fixed the clip in her hair. "See, now, *I* would. That's the irony, isn't it? Girls with curly hair want straight and girls with straight hair want curly. No one's ever happy." She glanced in her compact. "Decent enough. Ready for lunch?"

I returned my chair to its place across the room. "What were you saying earlier? About something not making sense?"

"Hmm? Oh, don't mind me. I never make sense. Don't forget, you wanted to check in with the nurse before we leave."

According to the nurse, Randy MacArthur was expected in two days. That made me feel better. Dana might not be coming back, but it would help her to know that her father had been there for her. We hadn't told anyone that Dana was gone. If keeping quiet meant she'd be on the respirator long enough for her father to see her "alive" one last time, then she deserved that much.

As we walked from the clinic, I noticed a balding man across the road on a bench, reading the newspaper. As we headed down the road, he watched us over his paper. Nothing unusual about that—I'm sure Jaime got more than her share of lingering looks. When we'd gone half a block, though, I happened to glance over my shoulder and saw the man strolling on the other side of the road, keeping pace with us thirty feet or so behind. When we turned the corner, he did the same. I mentioned it to Jaime.

She glanced back at the guy. "Yeah, I get that sometimes, usually from guys who look like that. They recognize me, hang around a bit, work up the courage to say something. There was a time, I'd have killed for the attention. Now, some days, it's just—" She shrugged off the sentence.

"More than you bargained for."

She nodded. "That's the bitch of celebrity. You spend years chasing it, dreaming of it, starving for it. Then it happens and the next thing you know, you hear yourself whining about the lack of privacy and you think, 'You ungrateful bitch. You got what you wanted, and you're still not happy.' That's where the therapists come in. Either that or you self-medicate your way into Betty Ford."

"I can imagine."

Her gaze flicked toward me and she nodded. We walked in silence for a minute, then she checked over her shoulder.

"Let's, uh, skip the Cuban place, if you don't mind," she said. "We'll drive someplace else, lose the admirer."

"Sure. Does this happen a lot?"

"Is three or four times a week a lot?"

"Are you serious?"

She nodded. "Now, I have to admit, most aren't middle-aged admirers, just folks who want me to contact someone for them. I don't do private consultations, but people don't believe me. They think they just aren't offering enough money. There was this woman once, a friend of Nancy Reagan's. You remember Nancy . . . or are you too young for that?"

"She had a thing for psychics." I'd read this somewhere, having been in preschool during the Reagan administration, but I doubted Jaime would appreciate a reminder of our age difference.

"Well, Nancy had this friend— Is this where we're parked?"

"Next lot."

"Jesus, my memory lately . . . I swear, the holes are getting bigger."

We walked into the parking lot. Though it was midday, tall buildings surrounded the tiny strip of land, wrapping it in shadow.

"What? Buggers too cheap for electricity?" Jaime said, squinting into the half-filled lot. "Hey, our city has only the second-highest crime rate in the nation. When we hit number one, we'll celebrate by springing for security lights."

"I'd cast a light spell," I murmured. "But I hear footsteps."

As Jaime shoulder-checked, a car door slammed. We both jumped.

"I didn't see a car turn in here, did you?" I said.

She shook her head. I glanced around, but saw no one.

"Let's just—" Jaime began.

The slam of a second door cut her off. She followed the noise and swore under her breath.

"Walk fast and don't look," she whispered. "Two very big guys bearing down fast."

"How big?"

"Huge."

I stopped and turned around. "Hey, Troy."

Troy lifted his sunglasses onto his head. "Hey, Paige. Morris, this is Paige."

The temp bodyguard was the same one who'd been at the courthouse yesterday. He was several inches shorter than Troy, broader in the shoulders, and black, which ruined the whole bookend-bodyguard effect. Morris did, however, share Griffin's stone-faced demeanor, responding to the introduction with a nod so abrupt I thought it might be a hiccup.

Across the lot, our middle-aged stalker headed for a Mercedes. Troy lifted a hand in greeting. The man waved back, confirming what I'd only just suspected, that he was a Cabal employee sent to follow not Jaime, but me.

I completed the introductions by identifying Jaime. Troy smiled and shook her hand.

"The celebrity necro," he said. "Pleased to meet you."

"Uh, thanks," Jaime said, surreptitiously tucking in the back of her T-shirt. "So I'm guessing you guys are Cabal security?"

"Benicio's bodyguards," I said. "And I'm guessing the boss is in the SUV waiting for me."

"Yeah, different city, same plan. I told you, he likes routine."

"Benicio Cortez? Here?" Jaime glanced at the Cadillac SUV. "Oh, shit."

"It's more like 'aww, shit,'" I said. "Now comes the boring part. I have to send Troy back to say I want Benicio to come here, then he'll insist I come there, and poor Troy will get his daily dose of jogging by running between us."

Troy grinned. "True, but the good part is that it's definitely not routine. Most times, when I say Mr. Cortez wants to speak to someone, they trip over me running to get to him."

"It's getting late, so let me make this easy on you. Wait here and I'll see what he wants."

I walked to the SUV, tapped the rear window, and motioned for the driver to lower it. Instead, Benicio opened the door.

"Come around the other side and get in please, Paige."

"No, thanks." I held the door open and stepped into the gap. "Let me guess: The clinic called you when I showed up, then you had one of your security guys hang around outside and follow me when I left."

"I wanted to speak—"

"I'm not done. My point was that you knew the moment you got that call that Lucas wasn't with me, and he'd already told you he wasn't happy about your approaching me in Portland. So now, when he's probably never been more pissed off with you, you decide this is a good time to follow me into an empty parking lot, corner me, and strong-arm me into talking to you."

"I would like to speak—"

"Am I talking to myself? Did you hear anything I just said? No, forget it. You go ahead and talk, and then Lucas will find out about it, and you can save yourself one place setting at Christmas dinner for the next umpteen years." I tried to stop there, but couldn't help adding, "Do you have any idea how upset he is right now?"

"Having my phone calls automatically blocked was a good clue. I want to explain myself, but I can't do that if he won't speak to me. So I hoped perhaps I could speak to you instead."

I shook my head. "I won't be your go-between."

"I'm not asking for that. What I'm saying is that I recognize you're a full partner in Lucas's life and in this investigation, and I'm speaking to you as such. You're an intelligent young—"

"Don't," I said. "Don't insult me and don't play me. You have something to say? Fine. But you'll say it to both of us. You'll follow me back to the hotel and I'll take you to Lucas. We'll tell him you met up with us outside the clinic and, seeing he wasn't with me, you asked if you could speak to us both at the hotel."

"Thank you."

"I'm not doing it for you."

CHAPTER 29

THE USUAL SUSPECTS

Instead of having Benicio follow us, I decided to ride with him and let Jaime follow us in her rental car. I had questions, not about why he'd betrayed Lucas, but about the investigation. When Lucas saw his father he'd be too upset to ask about the case, so I'd do it for him.

Benicio confirmed that the Cabals had resumed their investigation. After Joey Nast's death, they'd changed tactics. No longer content to follow the clues, they'd rounded up the usual suspects—anyone known to have a beef with the Cabals—and were trying to "extract" clues.

"Extract?" I said, the blood draining from my face. "You mean torture."

Benicio paused. "The Cabals do employ intense interrogation techniques. I would hesitate to use the word torture . . . But you must understand, Paige, the pressure that the Cabals are under. Not just the pressure, but the fear, the feelings of impotence. Do I think this is the best way to proceed? No. But I'd be hard-pressed to find members of my board who agree. The Nasts are in charge of the investigation now."

"Because of Joey."

"Correct." He gazed out the side window for a moment, then turned to me. "Until last month, the Nasts' New York office was in the World Trade Center."

"Did they lose—?"

"Twenty-seven people, out of a staff of thirty-five. The Cabals—we place ourselves above such things. We may kill one another but, as supernaturals, we have little to fear from the outside world. If we are attacked, we have the resources to strike back. But what happened last month . . ." He shook his head. "There's no revenge for that, and the Nasts are damned if they're going to be victimized again." He looked at me. "You can't concern yourself with our side of the investigation, Paige, because you can't stop it."

"I can if I find the killer."

He looked at me, then nodded.

⚜

I didn't lie to Lucas. As he so often reminds me, I'm horrible at it. The best I could do was omit damning details about my encounter with Benicio, and slant the story so he'd draw the conclusion that his father had expected Lucas and me to be together. Did he buy it? Probably not, but since I was obviously intent on brokering peace, Lucas decided not to stall the negotiations with a fresh injury complaint.

Once I'd secured Lucas's approval, I phoned down to Benicio in the lobby and invited him up. Since this was family business, I suggested Jaime take Troy and Morris to the hotel restaurant for coffee. Troy agreed, but Morris decided to wait in the hall.

Less than a minute after I hung up, Benicio rapped at the door. Lucas opened it. Before he could get in so much as a greeting, Lucas cut him short.

"Having renewed the investigation, Paige and I are committed to using all available resources. If you agree to communicate only for the purpose of sharing our findings, I will accept your calls. I trust that whatever leak led to the raid on Everett Weber's house has been repaired."

"You have my word—"

"Right now, I could have your blood oath and still not believe you. Perhaps instead you will take my word. If you lie to me again and another person dies because of it, we are through."

"Lucas, I want to explain—"

"Yes, I know you do, which leads me to my next request. I don't want to hear your explanation. I know perfectly well what happened. You made an executive decision. To your mind, Weber was obviously guilty and I was questioning that simply because it is my nature to question. Therefore, given the choice between indulging your son's quixotic whims and saving the Cabal from embarrassment, you chose the Cabal."

He paused. Benicio opened his mouth, but nothing came out.

Lucas continued, "I would like copies of the crime-scene reports for Matthew Tucker and Joey Nast."

"Uh, yes, certainly. I'll courier them over right away."

"Thank you." Lucas walked to the door and opened it. "Good day."

"Are you angry with me?" I asked after Benicio left.

He blinked, his surprise at the question answering. "For what?"

"Bringing your father here."

Lucas shook his head and put his arms around my waist. "I needed to get those case files, but I have been, I'm afraid, avoiding making the call."

"How are you holding up?" I asked.

"Besides feeling like an idiot? After twenty-five years of experience, I consider myself a reasonably good judge of my father's capacity for deception, and yet I never once suspected he wasn't lobbying to get us an audience with Weber. I can't believe I was that stupid."

"Well, I certainly don't know him anywhere near as well as you do, but I never doubted his intentions, either. He knew you were upset about the raid, so naturally he'd want to get back in your good books by going to bat for you on Weber. It made sense to me."

"Thank you," he said, kissing the top of my head.

"I'm not just saying that to make you feel better."

A crooked smile. "I know. That's one thing I can count on, that you always tell me the truth. With my father, I know he's not the most trustworthy of men, but I—" He paused. "I can't help wanting a closer relationship, like we had when I was young. I feel like we *should* have that again and, somehow, that the onus for reestablishing it falls to me."

"It shouldn't."

"I know that. Yet sometimes . . . I know it must be difficult for him, being who he is. He doesn't have anyone he can trust, not even his family. He can barely stand to be in the same room as his wife. His relationship with their sons is almost as bad. I know that's at least partly, if not primarily, his own fault, yet sometimes, when I'm with him, I want to compensate for that."

He eased us down onto the sofa. "My father called me when I was on the plane to Chicago. We talked. Really talked. He didn't make a single reference to the Cabal or my future in it. He just wanted to talk about me, and about you and me, how we were doing, how happy he was to see me happy, and I thought—" Lucas shook his head. "I was an idiot."

"He's the idiot," I said, leaning over to kiss him. "And if he doesn't see what he's missing out on, then I'll take his share."

Someone rapped at the door.

"Whoops," I said. "Forgot Jaime. She probably wants to grab her stuff and take off."

I opened the door.

"So what's next on the agenda?" Jaime said as she walked in. "Lunch is out, I guess, but maybe I can grab takeout for us."

"That would be . . . very nice," I said. "But what about you? When's your next show?"

"Show? Oh, the tour. Right." She opened her purse, pulled out lipstick, and walked to the mirror. "Next stop Graceland. Well, Memphis actually, but I might as well just hold it at Graceland, 'cause half the people in the audience are going to ask me to summon Elvis. I just give them some song and dance about how he's up in heaven enjoying fried peanut-butter-and-banana sandwiches and singing for God. Pisses him off to no end, but you gotta give the folks what they want, and no one cares what he's really doing."

"What *is* he really doing?" I asked.

"Sorry, kids, that's the X-rated show. Let's just say he's happy. Where was I? Right, Memphis. I don't do my Elvis schtick until Halloween, which means I have six days to myself. I'm supposed to be rehearsing but, hell, like I couldn't do that shit in my sleep."

"So instead, you're . . . ?"

"Taking some much-needed downtime and building up good karma credits helping you guys. I figure I'll hang around here, and if you need a necro, I'm ready and willing."

"That's very generous," Lucas said. "But we probably won't need—"

"Sure you will," Jaime cut in. "Every murder case needs a necro. And if you want someone to make phone calls or run errands, I'm your gal Friday."

Lucas and I exchanged a look. I could understand Jaime wanting a few days off. She'd looked exhausted yesterday, and although she'd bounced back, these spurts of energy seemed forced, as if she was running in high gear to keep from collapsing.

"So, what are you guys—" Jaime began, then she caught a glimpse of herself in the mirror and stopped mid-sentence. She yanked the clip from her hair and tried gathering it again, but her hands trembled so badly she couldn't keep it together long enough to get the hair clip on. She crammed the clip into her pocket. "Can I borrow your brush, Paige?"

"Um, sure, it's right—"

She was already in the bathroom. Lucas lowered his head to whisper something to me, but Jaime popped out of the bathroom, wielding the hairbrush with harsh strokes.

"So where are we at? Any fresh leads?"

Lucas glanced at me. I shrugged discreetly. If Jaime was offering to help with the investigation, I saw no reason to refuse, and no reason not to fill her in.

"Lucas was checking Weber's phone records. Since that's how Esus said he was making contact with the killer, it seemed a good place to start." I looked at Lucas. "Please, tell me it was a good place to start."

"It wasn't a bad place to start, though I'd hesitate to call my findings overwhelmingly encouraging. Once I applied the approximate time range,

I came up with a reasonably definitive list of five phone calls. The last two took place in the past week, presumably after the killer took a hard look at the second list and decided to expand his criteria. Both calls came after the killings began. The first, received on the eighth, came from Louisiana, where he was likely preparing for his attack on Holden. The second came the following day, from California, presumably arranging to pick up the final list. Both calls were made from pay phones."

"And the earlier calls? Before the attacks? Tell me they all came from the same place."

"From the same region, though, again, all from pay phones. The first was made in Dayton, Ohio, the second in Covington, Kentucky, and the third near Columbus, Indiana. Triangulate those points on a map and in the middle you'll find Cincinnati."

"So he's from Cincinnati?" Jaime said.

"It's reasonable to assume he was residing there, at least briefly, before the killings began. By making the calls from three smaller cities, it would appear he was avoiding a deliberate link with Cincinnati."

"So should we head up to Cincinnati? Start asking around the supernatural community?"

"There isn't a supernatural community in Cincinnati." I glanced at Lucas. "Is there?"

"While there may be a few supernaturals living in the region, there is no 'community' to speak of. The Nasts recently considered locating a satellite office there for that very reason." He caught my frown and explained. "Cabals prefer to expand into virgin territory, where they don't have many resident supernaturals to contend with."

"So there's nobody in Cincinnati to ask." Jaime sighed. "Shit. It couldn't be that easy, could it?"

"There's still the motivation lead," I said. "Esus thinks we're looking for a supernatural with a vendetta against the Cabals. The only other reasonable motivation is money. Pay me a billion bucks and I'll stop killing your kids. But the Cabals haven't received any blackmail notes." I paused. "Unless they have and they're just not telling us. Damn, I hate this."

"I feel reasonably safe in saying that no extortion attempts have been made," Lucas said. "Now that one of Thomas Nast's grandsons is dead, a killer with any knowledge of Cabals would know he can't buy his way out of this. As Esus said, it's personal."

"Then, when you put the clues together, we have a serious lead here. Adult male, living in the Cincinnati area, has reason to want revenge on the

Cabals—not one, but all the Cabals. There can't be many supernaturals who fulfill that criteria."

"So we just ask the Cabals—" Jaime looked over at Lucas. "It's not that easy, either, is it?"

"Probably not," he said. "I'm afraid that if I give the Cabals too much information, we'll have a repeat of the Weber incident."

"Or a sudden epidemic afflicting male supernaturals living in Ohio," I said.

"Precisely. We'll start instead by canvasing my contacts. If a supernatural has reason to be this angry at the Cabals, someone must have heard of it."

"There's nothing we outsiders like better than gossip about the big bad Cabals," Jaime said. "I could make a few calls of my own."

"Excellent idea," Lucas said. "First, though, let me talk to a local contact. He publishes an underground anti-Cabal newsletter, and he's always my best source of Cabal rumor."

"He lives in Miami and puts out an anti-Cabal newsletter?" I said. "He'd better hope your father never finds out."

"My father knows all about Raoul. In such matters he follows Sun Tzu's maxim about keeping your friends close and your enemies closer."

"Uh-huh," I said. "Okay, well, is this Raoul someone I can meet?"

"He's a shaman, not a sorcerer, so he'll have no aversion to discussing matters with a witch. In addition, we may be able to find some, uh, interesting reading material in his bookstore."

"Spells?"

A tiny smile. "Yes, spells. Remember, though, that by bringing you to the source of the spells, any that you care to acquire must be purchased by me, and therefore count toward my accumulated total option choices."

I grinned. "You got it."

"Spells don't help me," Jaime said. "But I could use a book to read. Mind if I tag along?"

That was fine with us, so we grabbed our things and left.

CHAPTER 30

LITERARY HAUNTS

R aoul was on vacation. According to his assistant, he hadn't taken so much as two consecutive days off in five years but now, when we needed him, he'd decided it was time for a monthlong European holiday. I suspected this wasn't a coincidence—he'd probably heard of the Cabals' latest "investigative" tactics, and feared he'd be next on their list.

Although Raoul was gone, he wasn't out of contact. That's the life of the self-employed—you can never really be away, or you might come home to find your business in shambles. Even lying in my hospital bed, I'd checked my e-mail and followed up on anything critical—well, anything my customers considered critical. Raoul hadn't left a phone number, but he was available by e-mail. His assistant sent off an immediate "Call Lucas Cortez" message for us.

"Can we check out the grimoires?" I said. "Wait, let me guess. He keeps those locked up, meaning they aren't available until he comes back."

"I'm afraid so."

I sighed. "Strike two. Well, let's go find Jaime."

Although the building was larger than most used bookstores, every available inch of space was in use, leaving a maze of narrow, serpentine aisles flanked by ten-foot-high shelves. The occasional murmur or shoe squeak indicated other shoppers, but they were lost among the stacks.

"Guess we should split up," I said. "Should we lay a trail of bread crumbs?"

"Perhaps, though I may suggest a more prosaic solution. Do you have your cell phone?"

I nodded. "Whoever finds her first, calls. Got it."

I tracked Jaime to the horror section and told her about Raoul.

"Shit," she said. "There's no luck like bad luck, huh? Guess we should get back to the hotel then, and Lucas and I can tap into the gossipmonger circuit."

I looked at her empty hands. "You didn't find anything?"

"Not what I was looking for."

She turned to leave, but I put a hand on her arm.

"We can spare a minute. What were you looking for?"

"Stephen King. Now, every bookstore *must* have him. But he's not here."

I scanned the shelf, which appeared to be arranged alphabetically by author. "You're right. That's strange. Did you want his latest? Maybe it's in general fiction."

"I'm actually looking for *Christine*, which should be under horror."

"Let's check the map up front, maybe ask the clerk." I started walking. "Isn't *Christine* the one about the possessed car?"

"That's it. I've been wanting to reread it ever since this show I did a couple months ago. A guy had this car that he swore was possessed, just like in the book. I don't do private consultations, but my prodco was filming the show, and they thought it'd be cool if we checked out his car in the parking lot. Oh, here's the map."

I scanned the map. "Aha. Here's our problem. King gets his own shelf in the Popular Authors section."

As we walked to the section, Jaime continued her story. "So this kid—he's maybe your age—has this gorgeous 1967 Mustang convertible. First thought: 'Uh-oh, call DEA.' The kid didn't look like any trust-fund brat, so where'd he get a car like that? When I ask him, he gets all nervous. Says his grandpa left it to him. And sure enough, it really is haunted. Guess who by?"

"The grandfather," I said.

"Bingo. The old guy jumped me the second I got within sensing distance, so spitting mad he could barely communicate. Seems he *did* leave the car to the kid. But on one condition. He wanted to be buried in it. No one else in the family would listen, but the kid promised to do it."

"And then he stiffed him."

Jaime laughed. "Yeah, the kid stiffed the stiff. Took the car, took the money, and plopped Gramps into the cheapest casket he could buy."

"So what'd you do?"

"Told the kid the truth. Either he buried Gramps in the car or he had to live with a permanent pissed-off hitchhiker. Oh, here it is."

The King section took up two eight-foot-long shelves, and the books weren't alphabetized. As I skimmed the titles, I glanced at my watch.

"We can skip this," Jaime said. "No biggie."

"Another minute or two won't matter. Oh, I forgot to call Lucas. He can help."

"Why don't I just grab something else."

As if on cue, a book tumbled from the top shelf and landed between us. Jaime picked it up.

"*Salem's Lot*." She shook her head. "Not one of my faves. You ever read it?"

"I started to, because I thought it was about witches. When I found out it was vampires, I stopped. Not keen on the vamps myself."

"Who is? Damned parasites." Jaime stood on tiptoes to put the book back. The moment she released it, it jolted out and fell to the floor.

"I think it's lonely," I said with a laugh. "Looks like it's gathering some dust up there."

Again, Jaime put the book back. This time, before she could let go, the book slammed into her palm hard enough to make her yelp. Then it tumbled to the floor.

"Maybe there's some kind of catch up there," I said. "Here, I'll find a new place for it."

As I bent for the book, it spun out of my reach. Jaime grabbed my arm. "Let's go," she said.

A book flew from the shelf, hitting her side. Another book sailed from a lower shelf, then another and another, pelting Jaime. She doubled over, arms wrapped over her head.

"Leave me alone!" she said. "Damn you—"

I grabbed her arm and propelled her out from the hailstorm of books. As we moved, I looked down at the novels strewn across the aisle. They were all copies of *Salem's Lot*.

The moment we were out of the Stephen King section, the books stopped flying. I speed-dialed Lucas and told him to meet us at the door.

"Ghost?" I whispered to Jaime as I hung up.

She nodded, gaze tripping from side to side, as if ready to duck.

"I think it's over," I murmured. "But we'd better scram, before someone notices the mess."

Again, Jaime only nodded. I rounded a corner, and looked down the unfamiliar aisle.

"Classics," I said. "Wrong turn. Let's back up—"

A book shot straight out from the shelf and clipped Jaime in the ear. More flew out, pummeling her from all sides. I shoved her out of the way, catching a few books myself, each striking harder than one would think possible for a slender paperback. One hit me in the knee. As I pitched forward, the book flopped to the floor. *The Iliad* . . . the same as every other book flying from the shelves.

I righted myself and kept propelling Jaime forward until we reached the front door. Lucas took one look at my expression and hurried over.

"What happened?" he whispered.

I motioned that we'd tell him outside.

On the way to the car, I told Lucas what had happened. Jaime stayed silent. Strangely silent, not chiming in with so much as an "uh-huh."

"Seems the bookstore had a resident ghost," I said. "I've heard of things like that happening. A necromancer is sitting in a bar, having a drink, minding his own business, and all of a sudden a spirit realizes there's a necro in the house and goes wild, trying to make contact. Like a shipwreck survivor spotting a rescue boat."

Jaime nodded, but kept her gaze straight forward, walking so fast I could barely keep up.

"It certainly does happen," Lucas said. "But I suspect that's not what we had here"—he shot a pointed look at Jaime—"is it?"

She nibbled her lower lip and kept walking. Lucas tugged my arm, indicating for me to slow down. When Jaime got about twenty feet ahead of us, she glanced over each shoulder, realized we weren't with her, then turned to wait.

For a minute we just stood there, looking at each other. Then Lucas cleared his throat.

"You have a problem," he said to Jaime. "I presume you came to us for help with that problem. But we aren't going to drag it out of you."

"You have more important things to do. I know that. But I think it . . . it might be related."

"And I assume you are going to explain what 'it' is as soon as we get back to the hotel?"

She nodded.

CHAPTER 31

UNDELIVERED MESSAGE

The hotel room door was still shutting behind us when Jaime started talking.

"I've got a haunter," she said. "And it's a strange one. I was going to tell you guys, but I know you're busy and I wasn't sure what was going on—I'm still not." She perched on the arm of the armchair, still talking. "It started Wednesday afternoon, before my Orlando show. At first I figured it was Dana, that she knew she was dead and wanted to pay me back for lying to her." Jaime twisted her rings. "I shouldn't have done that . . . not that I could have told her she was dead—it's not my place, right? But I went overboard with the reassurances. They just came out automatically, like I was doing a show."

She glanced from Lucas to me. When neither of us spoke, she continued, "That's what I do with my shows, in case you haven't guessed. I make it up. No one wants to hear the truth. Fanny Mae wants to make contact with her dead hubby, and the guy's standing beside me screaming, 'Worried about me? You fucking whore, you weren't worried about me when you hopped into bed with my brother an hour after my funeral!' You think I'm going to tell her that? I tell her the same thing I tell everyone else. He misses you, but he's happy and he's in a good place. And you'd think, you'd really think, that after I've given the same damned message for the thousandth time, that people would wise up, but they don't. Tell them what they want to hear and they never complain."

She inhaled and shifted down onto the seat. "When this spook came knocking, I figured it was Dana, so I came back here to talk to her. But she was gone, and my haunter wasn't, so obviously it isn't her."

"Can't you contact it?" I said.

Jaime shook her head. "That's what's so weird. I can't make contact. Not only that, but it's behaving . . . well, it's just not following ghost-necro protocol." She looked at me. "Do you know how this works? How a spirit contacts a necro?"

"Vaguely," I said. "Most necromancers I know don't really talk about it."

"Typical. They act like it's some big trade secret. Way I figure it, my friends—the supernaturals, at least—*should* know how it works. Otherwise, they see me mumbling to myself and staring at blank walls, they're going to figure I've lost it. There are two main ways a spook says hi. If he knows the proper procedures, he can manifest, and I get sight and sound. If he doesn't know the tricks, then all I get is audio—the old voices-in-my-head. Any ghost should be able to do the latter. But this one can't."

"So it's throwing things instead?"

"It is now. Up until today, it's just been hanging around, like a mental stalker. I know it's there. I sense it all the time, as if someone is looking over my shoulder, and it's"—she lifted a hand to show her trembling fingers—"making me nervous. Then to start poltergeisting? That's just—well, I'm spooked, and I'll admit it."

"True poltergeist activity is rare, isn't it?" I said.

"Extremely rare. When I was younger, I did some ghost-buster work to pay the bills. Number one haunted-homeowner complaint? Poltergeists. I went out on dozens, if not hundreds of calls. I found exactly three real poltergeists. The rest of the time, it was clever kiddies looking for attention. I'd tell the people some cock-and-bull about the ghosts wanting to see the family spend more time together, and that usually fixed the problem. Real poltergeist activity, though, means a ghost has found a way to move things in our dimension, and that's a very special talent."

Lucas frowned. "So how does a ghost who can't even contact a necromancer manage to manipulate objects cross-dimensionally? I see the problem. Have you considered the possibility that this isn't a human-based entity at all?"

"Maybe a minor demon," I said. "Or a nature spirit."

"Could be, I guess," Jaime said. "But I'm a necro. I talk to the dead, like my title says. If it ain't dead, why's it bugging me? You guys are the spell-casters—the conjurers—so it should be trying to talk to *you*. And I'm pretty sure the message is for you, anyway. Until the bookstore, it backed off whenever you two were around."

"Because it thought you were going to convey the message," I said. "But maybe the message is to tell us to start conjuring, so it can communicate. When it realized you didn't understand, it bumped it up a level in the bookstore. So let's try some group conjuring. Among the three of us, it has to find someone it can talk to."

Jaime looked up at the ceiling. "You hear that, Casper? We're going to try making contact, so you can back off now."

After a moment of silence, I asked, "Did it stop?"

Jaime shook her head. "I think the contact problem goes both ways. I can't hear it and it can't hear me. Let me grab my kit and see if we can fix that."

As Jaime opened her suitcase, Lucas's cell phone rang.

"Yes, I'm certainly interested," he said after an exchange of greetings. "However, it may be another week or so before we can see it. Will that be a problem?" He paused. "Good. Thank you." Another pause. "No, I haven't had a chance yet and, ultimately, it is her decision, but I would very much like to see it." Pause. "Yes, I'll let you know as soon as we return to Portland."

He signed off, then pulled out his DayTimer from his satchel and made a note as Jaime set up her implements on the floor. This time, she didn't bother asking us to leave.

"A real séance," she said as she finished. "Now all we need is sleeping bags and a pillow fight. When I was young, I was never allowed to go to sleepovers, in case the kids tried a séance. Might have given them more than they expected."

We settled onto the floor.

"I'll be casting a general summoning spell," Lucas said. "A mild one, I should say, nothing likely to conjure up anything dangerous."

"I'll do my communication spell," I said. "It's for mental communication with the living, but it might help."

"Mental communication?" Jaime said. "Witches can do that? Cool."

"Not really. It only works if the other party is expecting it and only if they're some distance away, so really, what's the point? Save a few bucks on cell phone charges? The reception is crappier than the cheapest cell provider."

We all settled in, did our thing . . . and nothing happened.

"Hey!" Jaime yelled at the ceiling. "An hour ago you were tearing apart a bookstore trying to get my attention, and now you can't be bothered to say hello? Do you know who you're talking to? The most famous necro in the U.S. of A. Not only that, but a former Coven Leader and the son of a Cabal CEO. Three powerful supernaturals, waiting with bated breath to talk to you."

Across the room, Lucas's DayTimer fell from the table.

"I think that means it isn't impressed," I said.

The DayTimer cover flipped open.

"I believe that's a sign," Lucas said. "Shall I . . . ?"

"Go stand by it and watch," I said. "We'll keep working."

Jaime did her invocation while I cast.

"Nothing," Lucas said before I could ask. "Perhaps—"

The pages started to flip.

"Seems we have a time delay from the ghost world," I said.

"It's turned to the first *D* page in my address book," Lucas said. "If the spirit is referring to a specific person on this page, I'm not making the connection. My supernatural contacts are coded in another section. These are all humans."

My purse slid off the chair by the door, unzipping as it fell and scattering the contents on the carpet. A moment later, my PalmPilot spun.

"A tech-savvy spook," Jaime said. "Maybe it wants to communicate by text messaging."

"Or, more likely," Lucas said, "it's *not* tech-savvy or, at least, can't operate an electronic organizer. I believe the message we're supposed to receive is that the correct name is located, not in my address book, but in Paige's."

"How would it know what's in there?" I said, crossing the floor to pick up my Palm.

"Perhaps it doesn't know, so much as assume. Who might you know whose last name starts with a *D*? Presumably a supernatural."

"That could be a dozen people, maybe more. There's— Wait, we've had other clues. The bookstore. Of all the books in one section, it only knocked down copies of *Salem's Lot*."

"Witches?" Lucas asked.

Jaime shook her head. "Vampires—but if the spook doesn't know its pop culture, it might think witches."

"It was also knocking down copies of Homer's *Iliad*," I said.

"Oh, great," Jaime said. "We move from *Who Wants to be a Millionaire* to 'Final Jeopardy.' Where are we going to find an egghead who's read *The Iliad*?"

"Uh, right here," I said. "Well, I had to. Required reading for college English."

"It was on my curriculum as well," Lucas said.

"Okay, the high-school dropout reveals herself again," Jaime said. "Hey, I knew the Stephen King answer. That oughtta get me a nice parting gift. So what's *The Iliad* about?"

"The Trojan War," I said.

"With the horse," Jaime said. "I knew that. Any supernaturals in the story?"

"There's an enchantress, Circe—no, that's *The Odyssey*."

"Unless, again, the spirit is mistaken about its literary references," Lucas said. "If it believed *Salem's Lot* was about witches, and the sorceress was from *The Iliad* . . ."

"Let's start there, then," Jaime said. "Witches whose last names start with *D*. You're a witch, so the ghost might assume you know—"

"Cassandra," I said, thumping my Palm down. "Cassandra the Prophetess, from *The Iliad*. Cassandra DuCharme, from the interracial council."

"Let me guess," Jaime said. "This Cassandra is a witch."

"Vampire."

"Even better." Jaime looked to the ceiling. "Is that it? Do we win?"

No response.

"If it can't hear us, it'll need some other prompt," I said. "Hold on."

I grabbed my pen and notepad from the spilled contents of my purse, tore a sheet from the pad, and wrote CASSANDRA. I laid the sheet on the table. Again, the spirit gave no response.

"Well," Jaime said. "Three possibilities. One, we're flat-out wrong. Two, the spook has simmered down because we finally got the message. Three, it's illiterate."

"If the message *is* Cassandra, I still don't know what that means," I said.

"Why don't you call her," Lucas said. "See whether she can shed some light on this."

CHAPTER 32

PADDLING UPSTREAM
DURING A HURRICANE

I used our hotel room phone to call Cassandra. This was moderately indiscreet, and normally I'd have been more cautious, but the truth was, phoning from the hotel was the best way to ensure she'd answer. Cassandra was a call-screener, and not one who just ignored calls from strangers. She almost always let her machine pick up, then phoned back at her leisure. The only way to persuade her to answer was to pique her curiosity. A call from a Miami hotel just might do that.

Cassandra answered on the second ring.

"It's Paige," I said.

The line went silent and I could fairly hear Cassandra's annoyance buzzing down it. Short of "accidentally" pulling out the phone cord, though, there was little she could do. Well, she could hang up, but that would be crass, and Cassandra would never be crass.

"What is the problem, Paige?" she asked, voice dripping icicles.

"I had a question—"

"Oh, of course you do. Why else would you call? Just to chat, say hello? Hardly. Very presumptuous of you, Paige, to come asking for favors after what you've done to me with Elena."

"I haven't done—"

"I don't know what you've been telling her about me but, let me assure you, I will set her straight. I understand you feel threatened in your friendship with her, but—"

"Cassandra," I said sharply. "I haven't said anything to Elena about you. Why would I? If she's not taking your calls, then I'd suggest you ask her why not. Or better yet, ask yourself."

"What's that supposed to—"

"It has nothing to do with me, that's all I'm saying. Believe me, I have better things to do than sabotage your friendships. No one else's world revolves around you, Cassandra."

"Did you call me to insult me, Paige?"

"No, I called to see how you're doing."

"Very funny."

"No, I'm serious. I'm in the midst of a murder investigation and your name came up—"

"Oh, and you suspect me, do you? How . . . thoughtful."

"No, I don't suspect you," I said through gritted teeth. Sometimes, carrying on a conversation with Cassandra was like paddling upstream during a hurricane. "The victims had all their blood and I'm sure you wouldn't waste a free meal. I'm calling because your name came up, so I was concerned. Has everything been okay there?"

"Are you saying I'm in danger? How long did you know this before you deigned to call?"

"About two minutes."

A pause, as her brain whirred to think up some way to turn my concern into a slight.

"What's going on there?" she asked.

"A murder investigation, like I said. There have been several deaths—"

"And you haven't notified the council?"

I counted to three. Across the room, Lucas pointed to the minibar. I rolled my eyes.

"It's not council business," I said. "It's Cabal—"

"Well, then, it can't concern me, can it? Cabals will have nothing to do with vampires. So obviously I'm neither a suspect nor a potential victim."

"Guess not," I said. "Must be a mistake. I'll see you at the next council—"

"Don't blow me off like that, Paige. If my name came up in this investigation, I want to know more about it. What's happening?"

I squeezed my eyes shut. I'd tweaked her curiosity and now she wouldn't let me off the phone without a full explanation. I didn't have time for that.

"Like you said, it must be a mistake—" I began.

"I didn't say that."

"Sorry for bothering you. If I hear anything else, I'll let you know. Thanks. Bye."

I dropped the phone into the cradle and collapsed onto the sofa.

"Jesus," Jaime said. "She sounds like a piece of work."

"Next time we have to make contact, I'll trade you," I said. "Your spook for my vamp."

"Think I'll stick with the spook. So it seems maybe my haunting isn't related to the case after all. This spirit saw me with you last week, you know Cassandra, and it wants to relay a message to her. Although, from what I heard, I can't imagine anyone *wanting* to talk to her."

"She's not that bad," I said. "We just don't get along."

"Maybe, but she *is* a vampire. Gotta be a whole passel of spooks in the next world because of her, just biding their time waiting for her to show up. Maybe that's the message: When you die, we're gonna kill you . . . or something like that. Course, they'll be waiting a long, long time."

"Not for Cassandra," I said. "She's an old one. Probably less than fifty years left on her quasi-immortality warranty."

"That doesn't matter, though, right? If anyone's waiting for her on the other side, they'll be disappointed, since vamps don't go there."

Both Lucas and I looked up. "They don't?"

"Hoo-ha, look at that. The necro knows something the whiz kids don't. Vamps are dead already, remember? So where do the dead go when they die? There's a stumper. All I know is there are no dead vampires in the ghost world. My opinion? *This* is their afterlife. When their time card runs out, poof, they're gone. And that's your undead lesson for today. Now it's time to get back to work. Or should I grab takeout first? We missed lunch and it's almost dinnertime."

"You have contact calls to make," I said. "My only contacts are council members, who know next to nothing about Cabal business. So I'll get dinner. What does everyone want?"

"What I want is for you to take a break," Lucas said. "You've been—"

"I'm fine."

"When I saw you dashing through the bookstore, Paige, you looked pale enough to *be* Jaime's ghost. And, as well as you might think you're hiding it, don't think I've failed to notice that you wince every time you sit or stand. As for dinner—" He lifted his cell phone. "Room service. Wonderful invention. Go lie down. Please."

"But I—"

"Paige . . ."

"The files on Joey and Matthew," I said. "We still haven't read them—"

He handed me the files. "Read them in bed, then."

I hesitated, then took the files and left them to their phone calls.

I fell asleep reading the files and didn't awake until after nine. Lucas, having suspected I'd drift off, had ordered me a sandwich and salad earlier. He'd also removed my clothing, probably assuming I was down for the night. When I got up, I thought of redressing, but it seemed a waste of effort, so I just pulled on my kimono. Decent enough. It wasn't like I hadn't seen Jaime in less.

Jaime had reserved the adjoining room, and was in it finishing her calls, but when I awoke, she came over to fill me in. Both she and Lucas had canvased their contacts and found no one who'd heard so much as the vaguest rumor about a supernatural living in Ohio who'd recently had contact or trouble with the Cabals. Even Raoul hadn't been able to help. Lucas was disappointed, but not surprised. When you lived so far off the Cabal grid, it was unlikely you'd have any opportunity to clash with them.

Knowing the Cincinnati connection might be a false lead, Lucas and Jaime had broadened their questions to include any supernatural targeted by the Cabals in the past two years. That led to a list of twenty names, plus half a dozen promises to call back with more information. Of those names, though, neither of us could see any whose beef against the Cabals was great enough to launch a murderous rampage. The most common complaints were being refused Cabal employment, or being harassed because *they* refused Cabal employment. No one would ever kill teenagers over something like that. We hoped that when the other contacts called back with their lists, we'd see more likely possibilities.

"And until then?" I said. "I didn't see much in the crime-scene files, but we should probably go through them together. Let me grab—"

Lucas put a restraining hand on my knee. "Tomorrow. We've done enough today, and I believe we've earned ourselves an hour or two of respite."

"We could order in a movie," Jaime said.

I said nothing, but Lucas caught my underenthused look. He pushed to his feet, crossed the room, and tugged the scroll tube from his suitcase. When he glanced over at me, I grinned.

I turned to Jaime. "Would you mind if we skipped the movie? My brain's still whirring, and I really need a more active distraction. Lucas and I have this spell we've been dying to practice."

"Spell-casting practice?" she said. "Sounds like work to me."

I grinned. "Never, especially not when it's a new spell. You can never have too many spells."

She laughed. "You kids are such keeners. You're so cute. So what does your new spell do?"

"Lowers a target's core body temperature, inducing moderate hypothermia."

Jaime looked from Lucas to me. "Uh-huh. Okay, I gotta ask: What the hell do you guys need a spell like that for?"

"We both have a limited range of lethal spells."

"And . . . that's a bad thing?"

"It can be. Don't worry. We're both very responsible spell-casters. We'd never misuse our power. Oh, hey, if you don't mind sticking around though, we could use a target."

"Target?"

"Well, we can't know for sure whether the spell works without a target." Jaime stood. "I hear my television calling. You kids have fun."

"We will."

Lucas waited for Jaime to leave, then plunked down beside me.

"Alone at last," he murmured.

I snatched the scroll from him, unwound and read it. "So how are we doing this? Straight-up spell-casting? Or fun and games?"

"Do you need to ask? The decision, though, should really be yours. If you're too tired, or too sore—"

"Oh, I feel fine." I grinned. "Fine enough, anyway. Strip spell-casting okay?"

"Better than okay." He looked down at my kimono. "Although you would appear to be at an initial disadvantage."

"You arguing?"

A slow grin as he pulled me to him. "No, not at all."

We didn't get the spell working, having exhausted our—or my—store of energy before a successful cast. It didn't matter. It used to matter. Success or failure at spell-casting practice used to matter a lot, to both of us, and we'd both admitted to hours or even days of frustration following a failure. But now that we almost always practiced together, it had become a game rather than a test. And, no matter whether we cast a new spell successfully or not, practicing together did have one definite advantage—it meant we never left a session feeling frustrated.

CHAPTER 33

I'm Not Dead Yet

We awoke at seven. Jaime popped over minutes later, and from the looks of things, hadn't slept more than an hour or two. While Lucas picked up breakfast, I took a quick shower. I'd just stepped out when someone rapped at our door. Lucas probably, with his hands full again.

"Could you grab that?" I called to Jaime.

I dressed, then opened the bathroom door to find Jaime standing there.

"Vampire at the door," she said.

"Seriously?"

"Seriously."

I sighed. "Please tell me it's not Cassandra."

"Short auburn hair? Looks about my age? Perfect makeup? Designer outfit?"

"Shit," I said, leaning against the wall.

"How about I don't invite her in?"

"Unfortunately, that doesn't work. Cassandra goes where she pleases, invited or not, wanted or not. Crosses, holy water, icy glares, nothing keeps her out."

"I heard that, Paige," Cassandra called from the main room. "Stop hiding in the bathroom and tell me what this is all about."

I walked through the bedroom into the living area. Cassandra was lounging by the window, taking in the sunlight and, sadly, not bursting into flame.

I turned to Jaime. "Cassandra, this is—"

"I know who she is," Cassandra said. "I have a television."

"Oh, but you two had already introduced yourselves— No, wait . . ." I looked at Jaime. "You didn't know her name. So how'd you know she was a vampire?"

"Easy. It's like you witches and sorcerers can recognize one another. I'm a necro. She's dead. So I can tell. Only dead things walking around are vamps. Well, there are zombies, but they don't smell like French perfume."

"Don't be ridiculous," Cassandra said, fixing Jaime with a glower. "I'm not dead."

"Of course you are. So you came all this way—?"

"I am *not* dead."

Jaime slanted me an eye-roll. "Sure, whatever. Now—"

The hall door opened. Lucas walked through, then stopped. He looked at Cassandra, then down at his tray of breakfast for three.

"Don't worry," Jaime said. "She doesn't eat. Well, she does, but even you aren't that hospitable."

"Ah, Cassandra, I presume," he said, laying the tray on the dinette table.

"Cassandra, this is Lucas Cortez," I said. "Lucas, Cassandra DuCharme."

Cassandra's gaze skimmed over Lucas, assessing and dismissing him in a millisecond. Anger darted through me, not so much at the insult as at the coolly confident way she did it, with a look that said, if she had wanted him, she could have him. Now I knew how Elena felt.

"Cassandra's just leaving," I said. "Seems she took a wrong turn on her way somewhere else."

"I'm not leaving until I get an explanation."

"First, we don't owe you an explanation. Second, if I thought you'd leave once we gave it, I'd tell you in a heartbeat. We're very busy, and as much as I appreciate your interest—"

"You said my name came up in reference to this case. I want to know who, how, and why."

"Don't know, don't know, and don't know," Jaime said. "It didn't tell us."

"It?"

"The spook."

Cassandra crossed her arms. "Spook?"

"Ghost," I said. "Or maybe not—we haven't determined that yet. A spiritual entity of some kind has been pestering Jaime and it has something to do with you. That's all we know."

"Me? Why on earth would a ghost want to communicate with me?"

"Maybe because you put him there," Jaime said. "Dinner coming back to haunt you. Literally."

Before Cassandra could answer, our room phone rang.

"Jesus," Jaime muttered. "Grand Central Station."

Lucas picked up the extension from the side table. He announced himself, then waited. His gaze flicked to me, a slight frown on his lips.

"Yes, of course, perhaps we—" He paused. "Oh, well, certainly then. Come up." Lucas hung up and turned to me. "That was Sean Nast."

"Savannah's—Kristof's son?"

"Yes, he has something to tell us, about the case. He was phoning from the lobby."

"You want me to skedaddle?" Jaime said.

"No need. He knows from the trial that you've been working with us. But perhaps . . ."

He looked at Cassandra.

"I'm not going anywhere until I get some answers," she said.

"Yes, I understand, but given the animosity between the Cabals and vampires—"

"It's not animosity," Cassandra said. "To have animosity, you have to acknowledge that the other party exists. You needn't worry. I will be as the Cabals wish me to be: invisible. Since no one can outwardly recognize vampires"—she shot a pointed look at Jaime—"there's no need for him to know what I am."

A knock at the door. Lucas opened it. Sean Nast walked in, followed by a man who could only be a Cabal bodyguard. Sean turned to his guard.

"Wait outside," he murmured.

"Mr. Nast said—" the guard began.

"Please," Sean said.

The guard nodded and retreated into the hall. Lucas closed the door behind him.

"Granddad's getting paranoid," Sean said. "I feel like I'm twelve again."

"Sean, this is Jaime Vegas," Lucas said. "Jaime, Sean Nast, Thomas Nast's grandson."

Sean grinned. "Hey, my frat watches you on *The Keni Bales Show* every month."

As they shook hands, Sean's gaze flicked to Cassandra.

"Sean, this is Cassandra," Lucas said. "Cassandra, Sean Nast."

If Sean noticed the lack of a surname for Cassandra, he gave no sign of it, only shook her hand with a "Pleased to meet you," then turned to us.

"Tyler Boyd is missing." He glanced at me and added, "That's the Boyd CEO's youngest son. He's seventeen."

"He's missing? Since when?"

"We aren't sure. Tyler went to his hotel room around eleven last night. When he didn't show up for breakfast, his dad sent someone to get him. His bodyguard was in the room, dead, and Tyler was gone. Mr. Boyd called Granddad and the Cabals have been out searching ever since."

"Good," Lucas said. "My father has excellent shaman trackers."

"That's the problem. They didn't call your dad, or anyone in your Ca—your family's Cabal."

"What?" I said. "But he went missing here, right? In Miami?"

"And the Cortezes have all the resources here, I know. It's crazy. I am so fucking—" He glanced at Jaime and Cassandra. "Sorry. I'm just fed up with their crap. Joey's dead and now Tyler's missing and all the Cabals can do is bicker about who's to blame and who's trying to take control of the investigation. Without your dad's trackers and CSIs, all we have is a bunch of VPs and bodyguards milling around the city, hoping to bump into Tyler."

"So you want me to call my father."

Sean rubbed his hand over his chin. "Yeah, I know you're on the outs with him, and I hate to ask, but I don't know what else to do. I tried phoning his company switchboard but, of course, they just kept routing me to some junior, junior assistant who won't even relay a message. If you have your father's direct number, I'll make the call."

"Your family wouldn't appreciate that. Better let me handle it."

"I'm not worried about what my family thinks. You can tell your dad I'm the one who told you to call."

"I'll call him, because he has the resources to process the scene and search for Tyler. I won't, however, tell him it was at your instigation. You're angry, with good reason, but that's not a decision you want to make right now."

"I don't care—"

"Lucas is right," I said. "Not only don't you want to start a rift with your family, but you don't want to widen the one between your Cabals. It'll only make things worse."

Sean nodded. "Okay, but after you make the call, will you come to the Boyds' hotel with me? I came here because I wanted to get your dad involved, but also because I wanted to get you two involved. So far you've done a hell of a lot more than the Cabals."

"We'll certainly go," Lucas said. "But I believe it would be best if we arrived independently. Why don't you give Paige the hotel address while I phone my father?"

When Lucas was gone, Sean glanced at Jaime and Cassandra, neither of whom was making any attempt to pretend they weren't listening. He obviously had something else to say to me, so I offered to walk him down to his car. The bodyguard followed us to the elevator. While we waited, Sean gave me the address for the Boyds' hotel.

"So, you, uh . . ." Sean said as we stepped onto the elevator, "you've got someone with Savannah, right? She's someplace safe?"

"With friends," I said. When I saw him hesitate, I added, "Supernaturals."

"Good, good. I figured that. I tried mentioning it to my uncle, that someone should ask whether she's being protected, since she's a potential target. I can't mention it to Granddad. After . . . after what happened with my dad, he . . . well, we aren't allowed to talk about Savannah. My uncle wouldn't ask Benicio about her, either. I think they . . ."

"Would rather pretend she doesn't exist? After last spring, I'm just as happy if they do."

He shoved his hands in his pockets and rocked on his heels. I should have kept my mouth shut. Nothing stops a conversation deader than reminding someone that his family is responsible for sending your life swirling down the gutter.

The elevator doors opened. I motioned for Sean to wait as I jotted down an e-mail address.

"This is Savannah's," I said. "If you ever want to say hi, introduce yourself, this might be the easiest way to do it. If you'd rather not, I understand."

He took the paper. "I'll do that. I'd like to . . . make contact. It's not right, ignoring her." He folded the sheet into quarters and tucked it into his wallet. As he did, he looked down at a tattered photograph in his ID holder. "You wouldn't have a picture of her, would you?"

"Sure do." I took out my wallet, and flipped through my card holder, which was filled with photos. "Someday I need to break down and buy a purse-size photo album, like those little old ladies who show you all their grandchildren while you're waiting in line at the bank."

I took out two. One was Savannah on her first-ever horseback ride that summer; the other was Savannah, Lucas, and Adam shooting hoops near our place last month.

"Cute kid," he said, smiling. "Definitely got Dad's eyes."

"You can keep that one," I said, pointing to the horseback photo. "I have it on file at home."

He thanked me and we said our good-byes.

I returned to our room to find Cassandra and Jaime sitting at opposite ends of the sofa, Jaime reading her latest magazine, Cassandra coiled to pounce the moment I walked in.

"So the killer is targeting Cabal families?" she said. "The Nasts first, and now the Boyds?"

I gave her a very brief rundown of the events to date.

"The grandson of a CEO?" Her frown deepened. "So it's a revenge crime."

"Uh, yes. That's what we—"

Lucas opened the bedroom door.

"Did you get hold of your father?" I asked.

Lucas nodded. "He's on his way to the hotel with a team. I told him we'll be arriving shortly, and he's promised to clear the way for us. That should be simple enough. I suspect anyone with the authority to challenge him will already be out searching for Tyler. Shall we go?"

Cassandra stood and picked up her purse.

"Uh-uh," I said. "This is very serious—"

"I realize that, Paige. You're looking for a missing person. A vampire is a far better tracker than a shaman."

I hesitated and glanced at Lucas. He nodded.

"Good," Cassandra said. "You can explain the rest of this matter on the way."

CHAPTER 34

PREDATORY INSIGHT

Lucas had rented a car the morning before, so we no longer needed to borrow Jaime's. She stayed behind in the hotel room and promised to call if anyone else showed up. Now, normally, if we have a guest in the car, I'll sit in the backseat. It's only polite. But Cassandra brings out the rude in me, so I slipped into the front passenger seat and left her to wrinkle her Donna Karan in the cramped rear.

It took us an infuriating forty-five minutes to reach the Boyds' hotel. Not only was it on the other side of the city, but we hit gridlock in a construction zone and might have been even later if Lucas hadn't navigated an alternate route down back roads.

On the way, I gave Cassandra a fuller overview. When we pulled into the hotel parking lot, she was still asking questions.

"I'm sorry to interrupt," Lucas said. "At the risk of offending you, Cassandra, I must ask that you, again, not reveal—"

"I have no intention of letting them know what I am."

"Thank you."

"It might be even better if Cassandra waited here," I said. "Until we start searching."

"Good idea. Cassandra, if you—"

The door banged shut. She was already striding toward the building.

"Or maybe not," I said.

"If we don't impede her involvement, perhaps she'll satisfy her curiosity faster."

"And go home faster?"

He gave a small smile. "That would be the idea."

Troy met us in the parking lot, then escorted us into the hotel, which looked more like a luxury condo complex than any temporary lodgings I'd ever seen.

From the outside of Tyler Boyd's second-floor suite, one would never guess a murder had recently been committed there or that a crime-scene team was ripping the room apart. Only when the door opened did the noise within escape.

Two men were working in the living area, one taking photos and the other running a handheld vacuum over the sofa. A third man appeared from a back room, carrying what looked like a laptop case. He exchanged a hasty hello with Lucas, then hurried out the door.

The murdered half-demon guard lay sprawled across the remains of the coffee table, covered in glass shards and wood splinters. His head was twisted to the side, face fixed in a grimace. I fought the urge to look away from that dead stare. Beside me, Cassandra leaned over the corpse, eyes studying it with detachment. I tried to emulate her, to see this body not as a person but as a piece of evidence.

At first I thought the guard's throat had been cut. Then I saw a length of wire draped over his neck and realized he'd been strangled with it.

"Our coroner believes that was done postmortem."

Benicio's voice came from behind us. He looked at Cassandra. His gaze passed over her with curiosity, and perhaps a little interest, but when we didn't introduce her, he didn't ask. Maybe he trusted Lucas's judgment. Or maybe, knowing his son's eclectic collection of contacts, he didn't want to ask.

"Dennis has already made some preliminary observations." Benicio called the security chief from another room. "Dennis? Would you please share your findings with Lucas and Paige? And answer any questions they might have?"

"Of course, sir." Dennis motioned to the dead guard. "We think he was approached from behind and possibly injected with something. That would explain why he didn't fight back."

"Didn't fight?" I looked at the shattered table. "Oh, I see. The damage is from him falling."

"Falling very hard." Lucas knelt and prodded a black chunk by the guard's hand.

As I crouched I caught a familiar scent, one that brought back memories of Girl Scout summer camp. Burnt firewood. Pieces of charred wood surrounded the guard's clenched hands.

"An Aduro," I said. "He grabbed for the table as he fell and burned it, meaning he wasn't dead when he collapsed."

Cassandra examined the wire embedded in the guard's neck. "No blood."

"Which indicates it was done postmortem," Dennis said. "Plus the fact that it's unlikely anyone could have garroted a man his size, with his powers."

"What about Tyler?" I said. "Did he escape or was he taken?"

Dennis waved us to the bathroom. We stepped inside. Benicio stayed in the doorway, looking on. Across the room, a slight, red-haired man examined the window ledge with some kind of electronic scanner. The window itself was broken. There were a few bits of glass on the inside, but most presumably had fallen out.

Lucas turned around to look at the broken doorjamb. "So either Tyler was in here when the killer arrived, or he managed to get in here before being attacked. Then the killer broke into the bathroom, but—" Lucas turned to the window. "Tyler was already gone, out that window. Simon? Any indication that the killer staged the window break?"

The red-haired man shook his head. "No, sir. There are blood smears on one shard. I'll need a sample from the Boyds' lab to match it, but the DNA is definitely from their family, so I'm assuming it's Tyler's. There are no signs of struggle or blood in the bathroom. I found Nike prints on the ground below, imprinted hard, indicating someone jumped from this window."

"So we're assuming Tyler fled," Lucas said. "That's logical. I doubt the killer would take him out of the hotel. Too risky. He's always killed on-site before. He's not likely to change his methods now."

Benicio's cell phone rang. After a few clipped words, he hung up. "Tyler's been found." He saw my expression and added, "He's alive."

"Was he chased?" I said. "If he was, then the killer could still be in the area—"

"He's not," Cassandra said. "He's moved on."

"What?"

The barest eye-roll, as if her conclusion was so simple it shouldn't require an explanation. "He's a hunter. He strikes at the easy targets. When they're no longer easy, he finds another."

"So you think he chased Tyler—" I began.

"The moment the boy escaped, your killer abandoned him. As Lucas said, he kills on-site. He'll hang a girl in a tree or drape a boy over a car, but that's only for outrage value. He's a hunter. He kills them where he finds them, and he kills efficiently. When that other attack was interrupted, he left the boy alive rather than risk discovery. He's not about to chase this young man through the streets of Miami."

"By moved on, you mean—" I looked at Lucas. "To another member of a central family. That's what Esus said. With Joey Nast, he reached the top level, and he'll stay there now."

Cassandra nodded. "Anything else would be a regression. However, with each step he takes, he makes it more difficult for himself. He'll need to take advantage of every possible moment when security might be lax, such as—"

"Such as when the Cabals believe the killer is stalking another victim. When they're all out searching for him. Lucas? Who are the other teens? Are there any in your family? Nephews—"

"I have an eleven- and a twelve-year-old grandson," Benicio said. "Hector's boys. I tripled their guard as soon as Griffin's son was killed, and I've moved them to a secure location outside of Miami. As for others, Lionel St. Cloud has one boy, Stephen. He's eighteen. Then there are a few more teenage Nast grandsons, and Frank Boyd has several nephews around Tyler's age."

"Stephen St. Cloud," Lucas said. "He's already hit the Nasts. If he can't get to a Cortez, he'll go for a St. Cloud."

"I'll call Lionel—"

"Where are they staying?" Lucas asked.

Benicio hesitated, finger poised over his phone keypad. "The Fairfield over in South Beach. Just wait while I—"

We were already out the door.

"Why the hell didn't you tell us what you were thinking?" I said, twisting in my seat to glare at Cassandra as Lucas pulled away from the hotel parking lot.

"But I did."

"You knew the killer had moved on the moment you saw that Tyler had escaped, but you said nothing. Then, when you did bother to tell us he'd moved on, you had to be prodded to explain what you meant by that. This isn't a game, Cassandra."

"Isn't it?" she said. "Your killer might disagree."

"You know what I mean. You should have told us immediately, warned us—"

"So you'd have left a few minutes earlier? I intended to explain myself, Paige. I simply didn't see the need to rush."

"You—"

Lucas glanced over, telling me to ignore Cassandra, but I couldn't.

"A young man might be dead and you didn't see the need to rush!"

Her green eyes met mine, sculpted eyebrows arching. "Well, if he's dead, there's certainly no reason to hurry, is there? If you mean that you might have saved him had I told you sooner, I can hardly imagine that sixty seconds would make a difference one way or the other. Yes, a young man is in danger. Yes, he might die. Tragic, but certainly nothing that doesn't happen every hour of every day."

"Oh, well, then that makes it okay."

"I didn't say it did, Paige. I was merely pointing out that death is a tragedy but, ultimately, an unavoidable one. You can't save everyone, as difficult as that may be for you to accept."

"I'm not—" I snapped my jaw shut, swallowed the rest of the sentence, and forced myself to face the windshield again.

Lucas's cell phone rang. He handed it to me.

"Paige Winterbourne," I answered.

A slight pause. Then Benicio asked, "Is Lucas there?"

"He's driving. Did you get in touch with Lionel St. Cloud?"

Another pause, as if considering whether to insist I pass him over to his son. "Yes, I called him, and he tried to call Stephen, but there's been no answer. Both of Stephen's uncles came to search for Tyler, but we did manage to find a cousin still at the hotel. He reports that Stephen's room is locked and no one's answering the door. Now, Paige, I've dispatched my search team to the Fairfield. They may be a few minutes behind you, but they will be there quickly. I—" He paused. "The killer may still be at that hotel. I don't want Lucas going inside."

"I understand that," I said. "I can ask him to stay out while I go in, but—"

"I mean for you to both stay out, at least until you're accompanied by the search team. An extra minute or two isn't going to make much difference."

"So I've heard," I said. "But I'm not willing to take that chance. Just tell your team to hurry and meet us inside."

I pressed the disconnect button. As I was passing the phone back to Lucas, it rang. He reached over and turned it off.

After another minute, we moved into the center lane. To our left stood a large Spanish-style villa. A discreet sign near the palm-flanked drive announced we'd arrived at the Fairfield.

CHAPTER 35

Unnatural-Born Killer

The Fairfield wasn't nearly as opulent as the Boyds' hotel, though I suspected the price was still at least double what we were paying. It had that kind of graciously understated atmosphere that doesn't come at an understated price. Stephen St. Cloud's room was on the third floor. When the elevator was slow in coming, we took the stairs.

We emerged at the far end of a quiet corridor. At the opposite end, a dark-haired man in his twenties lounged by the elevators. He didn't glance over until we stopped outside Stephen's room. Then he did a double take, and strode toward us, glowering.

"Good morning, Tony," Lucas said.

"What the hell are you doing—"

"My father sent me. Have you been able to get into Stephen's room yet?"

"Not unless I can walk through walls. We need a locksmith."

"No," I said. "You just need a witch."

I cast my top-level unlock spell. The last words were still leaving my mouth as Cassandra reached for the door handle. When I finished, she pushed it open and walked inside, leaving us in the hall.

"No dead bolt or chain," I said, checking the lock mechanism as I walked through. "Gotta love these cardlocks. Any witch could walk right in."

Cassandra strode from the living area into the bedroom. We'd barely made it out of the front hall when Cassandra walked from the bedroom and brushed past us on her way to the door again.

"I have it," she said. "Let's go."

"Guess that means he's not here," I said. "I don't see any signs of a struggle, so he seems to have left on his own. Tony? Any idea where he might have gone?"

Tony glanced at me, then turned to Lucas.

"What?" I said. "Is my voice pitched outside a sorcerer's range? Lucas, please, interpret."

"Do you know where Stephen might be?" Lucas asked.

"Out grabbing breakfast, I guess. Everyone else left to search for Tyler, and Step was bitching about being left behind. He hates being treated like a child."

"So he pulled a snit fit and took off," I said. "Very mature. Please tell me he has a bodyguard with him."

"Does he have a bodyguard?" Lucas interpreted for the invisible witch.

"Uh, yeah," Tony said. "Me."

We stared at him.

Tony shrugged. "Well, his dad needed Step's regular guard to help in the search, so he told me to watch him, make sure he stayed in his room."

"Which you did admirably," I said.

Tony glared at me. "He's eighteen, an adult. I don't know what all the fuss is about. If you'll excuse me, I have work to do."

"Don't worry," I called after him as he stalked off. "We'll find Stephen ourselves. But thanks for offering to help us look."

Cassandra popped her head back through the doorway. "Are you two coming?"

In the few seconds it took us to reach the door, she'd made it to the elevator and pushed the button. A minute later we were heading for the main lobby. Cassandra paused partway there, head turning from side to side, eyes narrowing. I don't understand how vampires track people, and I've never dared ask Cassandra. All I know is that it's not by scent, yet it's like tracking by scent in that they pick it up at the source and the trail fades over time.

Cassandra wheeled and strode back down the hall. I looked at Lucas, shrugged, and hurried to catch up. As she shoved past a middle-aged couple, the man muttered an epithet after her. Not stopping, she glanced over her shoulder, eyes meeting his. The man looked away fast, his arm going around his wife's waist as he picked up their pace.

Cassandra veered into a side hall. I turned the corner as she pushed a door clearly marked EMERGENCY EXIT. Before I could call a warning, she flung the door open. Sunlight flooded in, momentarily blinding me. I braced for the alarms, but none came.

Cassandra walked through, letting the door swing shut behind her. Lucas grabbed it before it hit me. We stepped outside. When the sun-blindness cleared, I found myself at the edge of a half-filled parking lot.

"Damn," I murmured. "You can't track him if he took a car."

Ignoring me, Cassandra marched into the parking lot. From the front of the building came the squeal of tires peeling into the lot.

"The search team?" I asked Lucas.

"I doubt they'd make their arrival so obvious, but they should be here by now. I should fill them in. Will you be all right?"

"I'll get a speed-walk workout," I said. "But I'll be fine. You go on."

I went after Cassandra. She'd stopped about twenty feet from the door.

"Can you—?" I began.

She started off again, darting between two minivans. I sighed and broke into a jog. She moved fast, taking a roughly diagonal path across the parking lot, weaving around cars. When I stepped behind her, she wheeled so fast I jumped back. Her eyes narrowed, and I was preparing a retort when I noticed her gaze was fixed somewhere behind me. I turned but saw nothing.

"Someone's here," she said.

In a hotel parking lot, that didn't strike me as strange, but before I could say so, she strode past me and backtracked a row. Then she stopped and surveyed the lot.

"Maybe we should—" I began.

She disappeared between two cars. I looked around. Beyond the distant road noise, the lot was still and quiet. I cast a sensing spell. Nothing. Not even Cassandra, who should have been within range. Damned spell. I really needed more practice.

I stood on tiptoes. Sunlight glinted off Cassandra's auburn hair as it bobbed between the cars. As I headed toward her, I heard the soft fall of footsteps behind me. I slowed, but didn't turn. Instead I glanced at my reflection in the side of an SUV. The gap behind me was empty.

I was turning my attention back to Cassandra when a shadow flickered past, the metal side of the SUV darkening for a split second. I whirled, casting my sensing spell as I turned. This time the spell caught something, but farther off, to my left. At the same moment I heard the clack of women's shoes to my right and the equally purposeful footfalls of the person approaching from my left. On my right, the footsteps stopped as Cassandra emerged from between two cars.

"There you are," she said. "You have to keep up, Paige. I can't be—"

I turned left. Again, it was who I expected. Lucas covered the distance between us, expression blocked by the sun.

"Strange," I said to Cassandra. "I sensed Lucas, but not you."

She frowned.

"With my spell, I mean. It didn't pick you up."

"Yes, well, your spells aren't exactly foolproof, Paige."

"Or it could be the whole undead thing, I guess."

Her lips tightened. "Now, don't you start on that, too. I am not . . ."

As she spoke, I saw Lucas's face and my gut tightened. I didn't hear the rest of what Cassandra said.

"They found him, didn't they?" I said.

Lucas nodded, and I knew they hadn't found Stephen alive.

Stephen had been killed in his car, shot in the temple, then placed in the reclined driver's seat, with sunglasses on and a ball cap pulled down to cover his wound. To anyone walking past, it would look as if he was dozing in his car. Odd, but not alarming.

I told Lucas that I'd had the feeling I was being followed. Cassandra concurred, and Lucas deployed the team to search the lot while we stayed with the body. If I hadn't said anything, would Cassandra have mentioned her suspicions? I doubted it, yet not because I thought she'd intentionally prevent us from finding the killer. Why would she? She didn't care. And that, really, was the crux to understanding Cassandra. She didn't care.

An hour later, the team concluded that the killer was gone. I'd have liked to stay, to hear their findings, but it's difficult enough to conduct a clandestine crime-scene investigation in a hotel parking lot without having onlookers.

"You've been quiet," Lucas murmured as we headed for our car.

"Thinking."

When I didn't go on, he said, "Share?"

I motioned that I'd discuss it in the car. I waited until we were on the highway before speaking. I told myself I was collecting my thoughts, but I think I was waiting to see whether Cassandra would speak first. She didn't.

"He's a hunter," I said. "He strikes fast, leaves the bodies where he killed them, uses the most convenient method, and changes plans if things get complicated. An experienced killer."

"Yes, as Esus said—" Lucas began.

He noticed I'd directed my comment to Cassandra, and stopped. She continued staring out the side window. Either she was ignoring me, which wouldn't be surprising, or I'd drawn the wrong conclusion, which, given my track record of late, wouldn't be surprising either.

"He's an expert stalker, too," I said. "Dana never heard him coming. Joey didn't have any warning. Even a druid god didn't hear him attack. I'm sure he was following me in the parking lot, but I only heard the odd footfall, saw one flash of movement. And I couldn't pick him up with my sensing spell."

Lucas glanced across his shoulder at me. "So you're suggesting that Esus may have been mistaken, that our killer may indeed be noncorporeal, a demon or another entity."

"I wouldn't call it a demon," I said. "Though some may argue the point. The kind of entity I'm thinking of lives right here in our world. The killer took down a two-hundred-plus-pound trained bodyguard. Felled him like a tree. That doesn't happen by jabbing him in the back with a hypodermic. He'd still have had a moment or two to fight. This kind of killer has a special way to incapacitate his victims. But so far, he's only used it twice—on Dana and this guard. That's why both had neck injuries. To cover the marks. Marks that are very difficult to detect, but ones that I'm sure every Cabal autopsy looks for."

"A vampire bite," Lucas said.

Cassandra nodded. "That would be my interpretation as well."

I bit back the urge to scream, "And when the hell were you going to say so?"

Lucas turned into our hotel parking lot. "The only problem with that scenario is that I can't imagine what grudge a vampire could possibly bear against a Cabal."

"I'm sure you couldn't," Cassandra murmured.

Lucas's eyes flickered to the rearview mirror. "No, Cassandra, I can't. But if you can, perhaps you could tell us."

For a moment, she said nothing. Then she sighed, as if put upon once again to explain the obvious.

"Cabals will have nothing to do with vampires," she said.

"Precisely," Lucas said. "They have a strict policy against dealing with either werewolves or vampires, which is why I can't imagine . . ." He stopped, then looked through the mirror at Cassandra. "Or, perhaps, that is not so much the argument *against* such a possibility as *for* it."

"For money and power, the Cabals are the biggest game in town," I said. "Maybe someone's tired of being kept off the playing field."

CHAPTER 36

Stand-in Mother-in-Law

We returned to our hotel room. Jaime heard us come in and zipped over for an update.

"So my spook wasn't trying to get you to contact Cassandra," Jaime said, popping the top off a Diet Pepsi. "It just wanted to tell us that we're looking for a vampire."

"Probably," I said. "*Salem's Lot* is about vampires, and Cassandra would be the vampire I know best. So that fits the theory. This does change the possible motivation, though. It doesn't take nearly as much to send a vamp on a killing spree. They're already expert killers—it's not as big a deal for them. I'd say we now have two more likely motivations. One, a vampire tried signing up with the Cabals or cutting a deal with them, got rebuffed, and decided to show them why you don't mess with the undead. Two, a vampire is just pissed off in general at the Cabal no-vampire policy and is making a statement."

"A crusading vampire?" Jaime said. "The only vamps I've ever met aren't exactly the altruistic type." She glanced at Cassandra. "Exhibit one."

Cassandra gave her a cool stare. "Ah, yes. And remind me again why you're here? More to do with a nagging spirit than a nagging conscience, if I recall correctly."

Jaime flushed. "Well, I've solved that problem and I'm still here, aren't I?"

"So your ghost is still being quiet?" I asked.

"So far, so good."

"Cassandra," Lucas said. "If we are dealing with a vampire, then this is your area of expertise. Given Paige's two possible motivations, should we consider both equally or concentrate on a revenge scenario?"

"Vampires are capable of crusading for a cause," she said, easing onto the sofa. "Though typically only one that benefits vampires, as this one would. You'd be looking for a young vampire. As with any race, the youngest are the most idealistic, the most likely to work for change. The older ones know their energies are better spent pursuing more realistic, individualistic causes." She slanted a look at Lucas and me. "You'll learn that soon enough."

"Not if I can help it," I murmured.

"The pursuit of righteousness is romantic, immature, and, ultimately, self-destructive, Paige. One would think you'd have learned that lesson this spring with Samantha."

"Savannah," I said. "And the only thing I learned was that the purest form of evil isn't something like a Cabal. It's the person who's willing to sacrifice another to save herself."

Jaime's gaze followed our exchange with interest. Before she could comment, Lucas spoke.

"So, having decided that both avenues are equally likely, may I suggest we pursue both? The fact that we are likely now dealing with a vampire explains why none of my contacts heard of such a situation, since vampires have little contact with other supernaturals. That means I'll have to go directly to the Cabals for information or, more accurately, through my father, who can ask about specific instances where a vampire may have had Cabal contact. Meanwhile, perhaps Cassandra could help Paige contact the vampire community, assess the general mood and any Cabal-related rumors."

"I don't believe I offered to help," Cassandra said. "This isn't my problem."

"No?" Jaime said. "Isn't that why you serve on the interracial council? So if a vamp goes rogue, you can take him out? Every race does it, monitors their own. We have to."

"This isn't the same. You're asking me to *betray* my own. To sneak Paige into their midst and gather information to be used against us."

"No," I said. "We're asking you to sneak me in to gather info that can be used to help you—all of you. Cabals don't like vamps now. How do you think they're going to react when they find out it's a vampire who has been killing their kids?"

"I'm not concerned about retaliation."

"Good. Then you can go home, Cassandra. I can get what Lucas wants without you."

Cassandra's lips curved as she reclined against the cushions. "You need to work on your bluffing, Paige. Your technique is far too obvious."

I grabbed my purse and headed for the bedroom.

"It won't work, Paige," Cassandra called after me. "Your only other vampire contact is Lawrence and he's been in Europe for two years. You'll be lucky if he remembers your name. He certainly won't rush back here to help you."

As my fingers grazed the bedroom door handle, I stopped. I knew I should take the high road, phone my contact, and ignore her taunts. But I couldn't, not with Cassandra. I flipped open my Palm, clicked on my phone book, found an entry, strode back, and held it up for Cassandra.

She read it and blinked. And, in that small reaction, I took more pleasure than I liked to admit.

"Aaron?" she said. "When did he give you—"

"After we rescued him from the compound. He told Jeremy and me that anytime we needed something vampire-related, we could call him."

"Jeremy might not appreciate your calling in a joint favor that doesn't benefit werewolves."

"Which is why I'll phone him first. But we both know he'll tell me to go ahead."

"Werewolves rescuing vampires?" Jaime murmured. "Someday, you have got to tell me this story. Well, Cass, looks like she's trumped you. Time to lay down your cards and go home."

"Is she here for a reason?" Cassandra said.

"I don't want to bicker with you, Cassandra," I said. "I appreciate what you did this morning, helping us hunt for Stephen, but please, go on home. We can handle this."

As my tone softened, the fire leached from her eyes. She sighed and reached for my Palm.

"Let me call Aaron," she said. "Save your marker for another time."

I hesitated. "Maybe that's not such a good idea. Unless I seriously misread things, Aaron seemed pretty miffed with you back at the compound."

"It was a misunderstanding."

"The last time he saw you, you turned him over to an angry Romanian mob and fled for your life. Call me crazy, but I don't think there's much wiggle room for misunderstanding there."

Across the room, Jaime snorted a laugh. Cassandra glared at her, then turned back to me.

"I didn't hand him over to the mob," she said. "I simply left him there. I knew he could handle himself. Anyway, none of that matters now. We're back on good terms."

"Such good terms that you don't have his phone number?"

She plucked the Palm from my hand, marched into the bedroom, and closed the door.

⚜

Two hours later I was boarding a plane for Atlanta, to meet with Aaron. Unfortunately, I was not alone, having been unable to convince Cassandra that she had better things to do. I tried to be gracious by saying I'd understand if she preferred to fly first class. My kindness, though, only provoked a similar outpouring of generosity, and she treated me to a first-class seat next to hers.

I'd brought my laptop and, as soon as we were seated, set to work catching up on my business e-mail. Cassandra stayed quiet until the plane lifted off.

"I hear from Kenneth that you're trying to start a new Coven," she began.

"Not really," I mumbled, and typed faster.

"Well, that's good."

I stopped, fingers poised above the keyboard. Then, with great effort, I forced them back to the keys and resumed typing. Do not rise to the bait. Do not rise—

"I told him I couldn't imagine you'd do anything so foolish."

Type faster. Harder. Do not stop.

"I can understand why you'd want to. It must be very hard on your ego. Getting kicked out of your Coven. And as Leader, no less."

I willed my fingers back to the keyboard, but they ignored my brain's command, and kept clenching into fists instead.

"I suppose it was very satisfying for you, those few months as Coven Leader. You'd obviously want to recapture that sense of importance."

"It was never about being important. I just wanted to—"

I stopped and resumed typing.

"You just wanted to do what, Paige?"

The flight attendant stopped by. I ordered a coffee. Cassandra took wine.

"You wanted to do what, Paige?" Cassandra repeated when the server was gone.

I turned to look at her. "Don't needle me. You always do this. You're like one of those sitcom mothers-in-law, poking and prodding, feigning interest, but only looking for a soft spot, someplace to sneak in an insinuation, an insult."

"Isn't it possible that I'm not feigning interest? That I really do want to know more about you?"

"You've never been interested in me before."

"You've never been interesting before. But you're finally growing up, and I don't just mean getting older. In the last year or so, you've matured into an intriguing individual. Not necessarily someone I'd choose to be stranded on a desert island with, but conflict of opinion can make for more interesting relationships than common interests. If I challenge your opinions, it's because I'm curious to hear how you defend them."

"I don't want to defend them," I said. "Not now. Your questions feel like insults, Cassandra, and I don't want to deal with them."

To my surprise, she didn't say another word. Just sipped her wine, reclined her seat, and rested for the remainder of the flight.

CHAPTER 37

DISCONNECTED

Vampires are a race of city dwellers. That may seem obvious, since it's far easier to kill undetected in a city with hundreds of annual unsolved murders, rather than in a small town that might see a single homicide a year. In truth, though, that's not a major factor in their choice.

Real vampires aren't the marauding bloodsuckers you see on late-night TV, racking up a dozen victims every night. A real vampire only needs to kill once a year, though they must feed more often than that. Feeding is easy enough—if you ever pass out in a bar and wake up the next morning with a hangover that seems worse than normal, I'd suggest you check your neck. You may not find the marks, though. Unless you know what you're looking for, vampire bites are nearly impossible to see, and the aftereffects are no more debilitating than donating blood on an empty stomach.

Since a vampire bite is rarely fatal, it would be easy enough for vamps to live outside the city and commute for their annual kill. It might even be safer. The problem is that pesky semi-immortality. When you don't age, people notice. It may take a while, but they eventually start to ask what brand of moisturizer you're using. The smaller the town, the more people pay attention, and the more they talk. In a big city, a vampire could stay in one spot for fifteen to twenty years, and never hear more than a few snide Botox comments. Plus, there's the whole boredom issue. Small towns are great for raising a family, but if you're single and childless, Saturday nights on the front porch swing get a little dull after the first hundred years.

So, vampires like the city life. In North America, they also prefer the sunshine belt, with over half of the continent's vampires living below the Mason-Dixon line. Northern winters probably lose their appeal pretty quickly when you realize you could lie on the beach all day and never risk so much as a sunburn. And it's much easier to bite someone in a tank top than to gnaw through a parka.

Cassandra had arranged to meet Aaron in a bar on the south side of Atlanta. I'd never been to Atlanta, and our quick taxi ride from the airport to the bar didn't provide much opportunity for sightseeing. What I noticed most was how modern it was. It looked, well, it looked like a northern city, very high-tech, very efficient, very un-Southern. I'd expected something like Savannah or Charleston, but I saw little that reminded me of either. I suppose if I'd considered my history first, I'd have known better than to expect much Old South in Atlanta. General Sherman took care of that.

The taxi drove us to a neighborhood best described as working-class, with row houses, postage stamp–size lawns, and streets lined with ten-year-old cars. The driver pulled up in front of a bar sandwiched between an auto-supply store and a Laundromat. The sign on the door read LUCKY PETE'S BILLIARDS, but the BILLIARDS part had recently been stroked out.

Cassandra paid the driver, stepped from the car, looked at the bar, and shook her head. "Aaron, Aaron. Two hundred years old and you still haven't developed an iota of taste."

"Seems fine to me. Hey, look, the sign says Fridays are Ladies' Night. Cheap beer after four. Is it past four?"

"Unfortunately, yes."

I spotted Aaron on my first survey of the bar. I would say, with some certainty, most women would spot Aaron on their first survey of any bar. He's at least six feet two, broad-shouldered, and tanned, with sandy-blond hair and a ruggedly handsome face. Aaron sat at the end of the bar, engrossed in a beer and a cigarette, and ignoring the glances of a secretarial quartet behind him. As Cassandra approached, she took in his muddy work boots, worn jeans, and mortar dust–coated T-shirt.

"How nice of you to dress up for me, Aaron," she said.

"I just got off work. You're damned lucky I even agreed—" He saw me and blinked

"This is—" Cassandra began.

"Paige," Aaron said. "How're you doing?"

"Good." I slid onto the stool beside his. "How have you been?"

"Keeping out of trouble." A quick grin. "Mostly. And watching my back a little better. Still damn embarrassing, getting kidnapped like that. Beer?"

"Please."

He motioned to the bartender. "I won't ask you, Cass. There's nothing here you'd touch. Probably not even the patrons. Are you going to pull up a stool or just stand there?"

"This hardly seems the place for a private conversation," she said, then wheeled and headed for a booth near the back.

Aaron shook his head. I ordered my beer and he took a refill on his. As he pushed aside his empty glass, he noticed his cigarette in the ashtray and stubbed it out.

"It's not enough that I'm a vampire, I gotta kill people with second-hand smoke, too." He pushed the ashtray up beside the empty beer glass. "I heard a rumor about you hooking up with the Cortez boy. That true?"

I nodded, took my beer from the bartender, and laid down a five. Aaron waved it back and exchanged his fresh beer for a ten, with a murmured "no change."

"Thanks," I said.

"I owe you more than a cheap beer. Now, this Cortez, it's Lucas, right? The youngest? Doesn't work for the family?"

"That's right."

"Well, that's good, because someone was trying to tell me it was the next older one. You don't wanna get mixed up with those Cabal guys. But, now, Cassandra said she wanted to talk about a Cabal situation, and since you're here, I'm assuming you're involved. But if you're with Lucas, and he doesn't work for the Cabals . . ."

"Let's go sit with Cassandra and I'll explain."

I told Aaron the story. When I finished, he leaned back and shook his head.

"Fucking unbelievable. We need that kinda trouble like we need a stake through the heart. You find this loser, you make sure the Cabals know the rest of us had nothing to do with it." He took a gulp of beer. "I guess you want to know whether I have any idea who might be behind it. I'm also guessing you've already checked out John and his gang."

"John?" I said.

"John, Hans, whatever he's calling himself today. You know who I mean, Cass."

"Oh," Cassandra said, lip curling. "Him."

"Well, you've told Paige about him, right? His little anti-Cabal crusade?"

My head snapped up. "Anti-Cabal crusade?"

She frowned. "When did he start this?"

"Oh, only about a decade or so ago."

"This is the first I've heard of it."

Aaron shook his head. "No, it's just the first time you've heard it and paid attention."

"What is that supposed to mean?"

Aaron turned to me. "Guy's name is John, but he calls himself Hans; thinks 'John' isn't a proper name for a vampire. He's one of the New Orleans vamps."

"Oh."

Aaron grinned. "That explains everything, doesn't it? John's got this burr about Cabals. It goes with the whole mentality of those guys. They're vampires, so they're 'special' and they should rule the frigging supernatural world. If it wasn't for that damned writer . . . It's gone straight to their heads. I wouldn't be surprised if they were behind this."

"Any idea where we can find them?" I asked.

"I can get John's address but it might take a day or two. He's not exactly on my Christmas card list. But if you're in a hurry, his posse hangs out at the Rampart in New Orleans." He looked at Cassandra. "But you check it out for her, Cass. Don't be taking Paige in there."

"Vamps only?" I said.

"Nah, just not a very nice place. I'll put out some feelers, too, see if I can pick up any rumors."

I pulled out my notepad to give him my number.

"Hold on," he said, and took out his cell phone. "Safer this way. Every damned piece of paper I stuff into my pockets winds up in the washing machine. I can tell you where I was when I heard Lincoln had been shot, but do you think I can ever remember to empty my pockets before doing laundry? Not a chance."

I dictated my phone number and Lucas's, and Aaron entered them into his cell directory. Then he returned the phone to his jacket, lounged back in his seat, and cracked his knuckles.

Cassandra sighed. "What is it, Aaron?"

"Hmmm?"

"Whenever you do that"—she waved at his hands—"it means there's something on your mind. What is it?"

He paused, then looked over at me. "The Rampart. It's a problem, and it's been a problem for a while, which brings up something else. The interracial council. I know you have Cass, but maybe you'd consider taking another vamp—"

"Excuse me?" Cassandra said.

"Oh, get your back down. I mean a second vampire, someone who'll bring forward vampire concerns, like the Rampart. I'll do it, but if you know of someone better, that's cool. There aren't enough vamps to have our own governing body, and the council used to perform that role—"

"Used to?" Cassandra said. "If anyone has concerns, I'll take them to the council."

Aaron turned and met her gaze. "Cass, you stopped doing that years ago. Decades. You're not . . . You're not part of anything anymore. You're disconnected."

"Disconnected?"

"I'm not trying to give you a hard time. There have always been two vampire delegates for a reason, one as a resource and one as an ombudsman. Now that Lawrence is gone, you've taken over his old role and, well, someone needs to do yours."

When she didn't respond, he touched her elbow, but she yanked her arm back.

"I am *not* disconnected," she said.

Aaron sighed, and looked at me. "Think about it."

I nodded. We finished up and left.

CHAPTER 38

THE NEW ORLEANS VAMPIRE SITUATION

I switched the cell phone to my other ear and walked into a quieter corner of the airport. "We have a flight for New Orleans leaving in an hour, so I'll be stuck there overnight."

"Perhaps I should have come along," Lucas said. "I haven't accomplished much here. My father convened an intra-Cabal meeting this afternoon, and he says that no one recalls any dealings with vampires. That, of course, is preposterous. Even if no vampires have approached them, they must have encountered one or two in the course of business. Either they think I'm stupid or they just can't be bothered to lie more creatively."

I let out an oath.

"My sentiments exactly. Now, my father *has* admitted to one recent Cortez Cabal encounter with a vampire. Apparently one tried to arrange a private meeting with him in July. The request was denied, of course, and the matter ended there."

"What did this vampire want to speak to him about?"

"No one bothered to ask. As soon as they found out he was a vampire, they didn't care to hear anything else. Not a reason, not a name, nothing. And as much as I'm predisposed to think my father is withholding information, I must admit that this is exactly how Cabal employees are trained to deal with vampires."

"Can I just say 'arghh!' When this is over, we don't ever have to work with these nice people again, right?"

"You have my word on that. Perhaps then, one good thing will come of this. It might persuade you to join me in future *anti*-Cabal work."

"Hey, no one needed to convince me. I was always willing to help. You just had to ask."

Silence buzzed down the line. Cassandra appeared at my shoulder to say that the plane was boarding. I motioned that I'd be right there.

"I have to go," I said to Lucas.

"I heard. About working together, I was always under the impression—that is to say—" He paused. "You need to run, but I'd like to discuss this later. And don't forget to call me when you get to New Orleans."

"I won't."

Cassandra had said little since we'd left Aaron. Again, she bought me a first-class ticket. I knew Cassandra had money, lots of it, and I doubted she ever flew coach, but it was still a nice gesture. She also offered me her in-flight meal, which I refused, though I did accept her package of cocktail nuts. By the time I finished dinner, she was on her second wine, which told me something was wrong. I'd never seen Cassandra drink more than half a glass at a sitting.

When the flight attendant came by with dessert, I looked at the gelatinous square they called lemon meringue pie, and opted for a tea instead. Cassandra motioned to her wineglass for a refill.

"How long have you been attending council meetings, Paige?" Cassandra asked as the attendant left. "Five, six years?"

"Almost twelve."

"Twelve years, then." She fingered the stem of her glass. "You've always had a good memory, so perhaps you'll remember better than I can. When's the last time we investigated a vampire concern?"

"In '98. Dallas, Texas. We had a report of a killer draining his victims' blood. Turned out it was a human killer, though, so I suppose that doesn't really count as a vampire concern." I paused. "Let's see, before that it would have been '96. A vacationing Russian vampire was raising a ruckus—"

"Yes, yes, I remember that. I meant when did I last bring a *concern* before the council?"

"Like what Aaron was talking about? A situation that's worrying vampires in general?"

"Exactly."

I took my tea from the attendant and pulled out the bag. "You've never done that."

"Oh, come now, Paige. Of course I have." She leaned back in her seat. "Never mind. You were only a child, and you were always goofing off with Adam—"

"Hey, I never goofed off in a meeting. Don't you remember all those times Robert gave Adam shit for not paying attention like I did? Drove Adam crazy. Then he'd take it out on me afterward, teasing me about brownnosing—" I stopped, noticing Cassandra's attention had wandered to her wineglass. "Point is, I paid attention. I took notes. Quiz me if you like. Dates, places, I can name them. In twelve years, you've never brought a vampire concern to the council."

"That didn't strike you as odd?"

I shrugged. "Numbers-wise, vampires are rare, and you're all pretty self-sufficient, so I figured you didn't have concerns. It never bothered anyone else, so it didn't bother me. Lawrence didn't bring up concerns when he was your codelegate."

"That's because Lawrence was so old, he didn't care about anyone but himself." She fluttered her hands over her table. "Took off to Europe and never even bothered to tell us he wasn't coming back. I may be self-centered, but I'd never do that."

I sipped my tea.

Cassandra looked at me sharply. "Well, I wouldn't."

"Okay. Sure. Now about this bar, the Rampart—"

"I must have brought a concern to the council in the past twelve years. What about the Gulf War draft? Several vampires had taken on the identity of American citizens and they were worried about being called for the draft—"

"There was no draft for the Gulf War. That must have been Vietnam." She frowned. "When was Vietnam?"

"Before I was born."

Cassandra snatched up her napkin and folded it precisely. "Well, there's been something since then. I only remember *that* one because it was historically significant."

"Probably."

By the time we reached New Orleans, it wasn't yet eleven, still too early for bar-hopping. As I phoned Elena for my nightly check on Savannah, Cassandra directed the taxi to the Empire Hotel, her local favorite. After we checked in, I called Lucas, letting him know I'd arrived safely, then showered and got ready.

When we went downstairs, Cassandra had the doorman hail us a cab.

"This bar," I said. "The Rampart. Aaron has a problem with it?"

Cassandra sighed. "That's just Aaron. For a man who looks like he doesn't spend much time thinking, Aaron spends far too much time at it. Thinking and worrying. He can be the worst mother hen you can imagine."

"So he's overreacting about the Rampart? About it not being safe for me?"

"The Rampart is safe insofar as any bar is safe these days. It's a favored hangout for local vampires, nothing more."

"No offense, but if vamps like hanging out there, it doesn't sound like the safest place for anyone with a pulse."

"Don't be ridiculous, Paige. Dogs don't piss in their beds and vampires don't hunt where they live."

Cassandra strode toward a cab pulling to the curbside. I hurried after her.

Cassandra explained more about the Rampart on the drive. This might seem dangerous, having such conversations within earshot of humans, but supernaturals haven't needed to rabidly monitor their discussions since the nineteenth century. These days, we keep our voices down and watch what we say, but if the odd "demon" or "vampire" escapes, people jump to one of three logical conclusions. One, they misheard. Two, we're discussing a movie or book plot. Three, we're nuts. If our taxi driver overheard any of our conversation, the biggest danger we faced was that he'd ask where this "vampire bar" was located, not so he could alert the proper authorities to a nest of bloodsucking murderers, but so he'd have another destination to add to his list of recommendations for visiting Goths and Anne Rice fans. After all, this was New Orleans.

Speaking of Anne Rice, while I'm sure she's a lovely woman, there are many in the supernatural world who blame her for the New Orleans vampire situation. Roughly coinciding with the popularity of Ms. Rice's novels, the influx of vamps to the city rose astronomically. At one point in the late eighties there had been nine vampires in New Orleans . . . in a country that historically sees a national average of fewer than two dozen. Some had emigrated from Europe just to move to New Orleans. Fortunately, three or four have since left, and the population has averaged five or six over the past decade.

The problem with the New Orleans vamps isn't overpopulation. It's that they all share a similar mind-set, the same mind-set that drew them to the city in the first place. For these vampires, seeing their cultural popularity skyrocket with Ms. Rice's books was like a rock singer seeing his face on the cover of *Rolling Stone*, the ultimate moment of self-affirmation, when they could say "See, I'm just as cool as I always thought I was." And for the vampires of New Orleans, life has never been the same since.

The Rampart wasn't just a vampire bar in the sense that it attracted vampires. It was actually owned by vampires. As Cassandra explained: John/Hans and two others had bought the place years ago. They'd kept it small and exclusive, a place they could make their own and amuse themselves playing bar owners.

The taxi driver stopped in an industrial district. Security lights dotted every building except the one beside us, which was swathed in a blackness that seemed almost artificial. As I opened the door, I saw that it was indeed artificial. The brickwork and the windows had been painted black. Even the lone street lamp had been wrapped in black crepe paper and the bulb broken or removed.

"Early Gothic Nightmare. How original," Cassandra said as she climbed from the car. "Last time I was here it looked like a perfectly normal bar. No wonder Aaron is getting his shorts in a twist. He can't stand this sort of thing."

"Well, their taste in decor may be criminal, but unfortunately they aren't violating any council statutes. At least they're keeping it low profile. I don't even see a sign."

"I don't even see a door," Cassandra muttered. "They've probably painted it black like everything else. Now where was it the last time ... ?"

As her gaze traveled along the building, a limo pulled up and belched three giggle-wracked young women onto the curb. Two wore black leather miniskirts. The third was dressed in a long white dress that looked more suited for a wedding than girls' night out. A beefy bodyguard grabbed the bride's elbow to steady her and led the trio toward the building. As the limo reversed, its headlights illuminated the four. The "bride" turned into the lights and squinted.

"Hey," I said. "Isn't that—what's her name—she's a singer."

The quartet had just vanished around the building when a Hummer pulled up and disgorged two young men in undertaker suits. They followed the same path as the bridal party.

"So much for keeping a low profile," Cassandra muttered.

"At least we found out where the door is," I said.

Cassandra shook her head and we circled the building in search of an entrance.

CHAPTER 39

KEEPING UP WITH THE TIMES

When we got to the other side, we still couldn't find a door.

"This is ridiculous," Cassandra said, pacing along the building. "Are we blind?"

"I don't know about you," I said. "But I can't see in the dark. Should I risk a light spell?"

"Go ahead. From the looks of those fools going inside, I doubt they'd notice if you lit up the whole neighborhood."

Before I could begin the incantation, an ivy-covered trellis moved and a shadow emerged from behind it. A girl, no more than a teenager, stumbled out, her white face and hands floating, disembodied, through the air. I blinked, then saw that she was dressed in a long black gown; together with her black hair it blended into the backdrop of the building.

When she saw us, she swayed and mumbled something. As she staggered past, Cassandra's head whipped around to follow, eyes narrowing, the green irises glinting. Her lips parted, then snapped shut. Before she tore her gaze away, I followed it to the girl's arm. Black gauze encircled her bare forearm. Around the edges, blood smeared her pale skin.

"She's hurt," I said as the girl reeled onto the road. "Wait here. I'll see if she needs help."

"You do that. I think Aaron is right. You should wait outside."

I stopped. My gaze went to the girl, tottering along the side of the road. Drunk or stoned, but not mortally wounded. Whatever was going on inside might be worse, and I couldn't rely on Cassandra to handle it. I reached past her and tugged on the trellis.

"I meant it, Paige," Cassandra said. "See to the girl. You're not coming in."

I found the handle, pushed the door open, and squeezed past Cassandra. Inside, the place was as dark as its exterior. I touched walls on either side, so I knew I was in a hallway. Feeling my way along, I moved forward. I got about five steps before smacking into a wall of muscle. A beefy face glowered down at me. The man shone a flashlight over us, and smirked.

"Sorry, ladies," he said. "You got the wrong place. Bourbon Street is that way."

He lifted his flashlight to point, swinging it near Cassandra's face. She swatted it down.

"Who's in tonight?" she demanded. "Hans? Brigid? Ronald?"

"Uh, all three," the bouncer said, stepping back.

"Tell them Cassandra's here."

"Cassandra who?"

He shone the flashlight beam in her face. Cassandra snatched it from his hand.

"Just Cassandra. Now go."

He reached for his light. "Can I have my flash—?"

"No."

He hesitated, then turned, banged into the wall, cursed, and headed off into the darkness.

"Fools," Cassandra muttered. "What are they playing at here? When did they do all this?"

"Uh, when's the last time you visited?"

"It can't be more than a year—" She paused. "Maybe a few years. Not that long."

The door opened so fast that the man behind it nearly fell at our feet. Mid-forties, not much taller than my five feet two, he was pudgy with soft features and gray-flecked hair tied back with a velvet ribbon. He wore a puffy shirt straight out of *Seinfeld*, the top three buttons undone, revealing a hairless chest. His pants were ill-fitting black velvet, tucked into high-top boots. He looked like a middle-aged accountant heading off to a *Pirates of Penzance* audition.

He righted himself and blinked owlishly into Cassandra's flashlight beam. I gestured toward the exit. He didn't seem to see me, but stood gawking up at Cassandra.

"Cass—Cassandra. So—so good of you—"

"What the hell are you wearing, Ronald? Please tell me Fridays are Masquerade Night here."

Ronald looked down at his outfit and frowned.

"Where's John?" Cassandra said.

"J—John? You mean Hans? He's, uh, inside." When Cassandra turned toward the door, Ronald jumped in front of it. "We didn't expect—we're honored of course. Very honored."

"Get your tongue off my boots, Ronald, and get out of my way. I came to speak to John."

"Y—yes, of course. But it's been so long. I'm just so pleased to see you. There's a blues bar just a few blocks over. Very nice. We could go there, and Hans could join us—"

Cassandra shoved Ronald aside and reached for the door handle.

"W—wait," Ronald said. "We weren't ready for you, Cassandra. The place, it's a mess. You don't want to go in there."

She tugged open the door and walked through. I grabbed it before it closed. Ronald blinked at me, as if I'd materialized from nowhere.

"I'm with her," I said.

He grabbed the door edge, then paused, uncertain. I tugged it open enough to slip through into what looked like another, longer hallway. Ronald scurried after us. He passed me and jostled Cassandra's heels. At a glare from her, he backed off, but only a step.

"I—I think you'll like what we've done here, Cassandra," Ronald said. "It's a new age for us, and we're taking advantage of it. Adapting to the times. Refusal to change is the death knell of any civilization—that's what Hans says."

"Step on my heels again and you'll hear a death knell."

She stopped before another door, waved me forward. I slipped past Ronald.

"I want you to wait out here," Cassandra said.

I shook my head. "You go, I go."

"I won't be responsible for you, Paige."

"You aren't," I said, and pushed open the door.

Beyond the door was a cavernous room, just barely illuminated by a dull red glow. At first, I couldn't make out the source of the lighting, but then I noticed that the faux Grecian pillars were pieced with tiny holes, each letting out a thin ray of red light, like an infrared pointer.

One glance around and I knew the designation "bar" no longer applied to the Rampart. It was a club, probably a private one. The only furnishings were a half-dozen couches and divans, most of them occupied. Areas on either side of the room had been cordoned off with beaded curtains. Only the occasional murmur or muffled laugh broke the silence.

On the nearest sofa, two women were curled up together, one semireclined, holding her hand out, the other bending over whatever her companion held. Cocaine, maybe methamphetamine. If Hans and his bunch had opened an exclusive drug club, they were treading dangerous ground for people who had to stay below the radar. I wasn't sure whether this violated the council's statutes, but we'd need to look into it after this investigation was over.

One of the women on the divan leaned over her partner's arm. I tried to glance over discreetly, to see what kind of drugs they were using, but the woman wasn't holding anything. Instead, she stretched out her arm, empty palm up, forearm braced with her other hand. A dark line bisected the inside of her forearm. She clenched her fist and a rivulet of blood trickled down. Her companion lowered her mouth to the cut.

I stumbled back, hitting Cassandra. She turned sharply, mouth opening to snap at me, then followed my gaze. She wheeled on Ronald.

"Who is that woman? I don't know her."

"She's not"—Ronald lowered his voice—"not a vampire."

"Not a—?" I said. "Then why is she . . . ?"

"Because she wants to," Ronald said. "Some like to give, some to receive. Hardly a new fetish, but they've become more open about it. We're simply taking advantage—"

Cassandra stomped off before he could finish. She strode to the nearest curtain and shoved it back, to the yelps of the surprised guests within. She swung around, letting the curtain fall, and headed for the next cubicle. Ronald scrambled after her. I stayed where I was. I'd seen enough.

"You're not seeing the beauty of it, Cassandra," Ronald whispered. "The opportunities. Hiding in plain sight, that's the ultimate goal, isn't it? Other races can do it. Why shouldn't we?"

Cassandra shoved back another beaded curtain. I looked away, but not fast enough. Inside was the singer, in her mock bridal ensemble, splayed across the center of the couch, arms outstretched, her two female companions each attached leechlike to an arm, her dress shoved up around her hips while her male bodyguard crouched before her, pants down . . . and I don't need to describe anymore. Suffice to say, I hoped to wipe the scene from my memory before it reappeared at an inopportune moment, and ruined a perfectly good round of bed games.

Cassandra whirled on Ronald. "Get these people out of here now."

"But—but—they're members. They've paid—"

"Get them out and consider yourself lucky if money is all you lose."

"M—maybe this wasn't such a good idea, maybe we made an error in judgment, but—"

Cassandra brought her face down to his. "Do you remember the Athenian problem? Do you remember the penalty for their 'error in judgment'?"

Ronald swallowed. "Give me a minute."

He hurried to the singer's cubicle and pushed his head through the beaded curtain. I caught the words "police," "raid," and "five minutes." The quartet came barreling out so fast, they were still pulling on their clothes as they raced past me.

A minute later, as the last stragglers stumbled for the exit, a door opened at the far end of the room. In strode a tall woman in her late twenties. Her face was too angular to be pretty, with features better suited to a man. She wore her blond hair long and straight, an uncomplimentary style that left one with the fleeting impression that she might be a guy in drag, yet her black silk baby-doll revealed enough to reassure any confused onlooker that she was indeed gender female. Even her feet were bare, toes painted bright red, as were her fingernails and her lips. It looked as if she'd put on her lipstick in the dark, and smeared it. As she moved into the semilit room, I saw that it wasn't lipstick at all, but blood.

"Wipe your mouth, Brigid," Cassandra snapped. "No one here is impressed."

"I thought I heard harping," Brigid said, gliding into the center of the room. "I should have known it was the queen bitch—" A tiny smile. "Whoops, I meant queen bee."

"We know what you meant, Brigid. Have the guts to admit it."

Cassandra's gaze slid from Brigid and riveted to a young man following Brigid so closely that he was almost hidden behind the statuesque vampire. He was no more than my age, slightly built and pretty, with huge brown eyes fixed in a look of bovine befuddlement. Blood dribbled down the side of his neck, but he seemed not to notice, and stood there, gaze fixed on the back of Brigid's head, lips curved in an inane little smile.

"Get him out of here," Cassandra said.

"You don't give me orders, Cassandra," Brigid said.

"I do if you're fool enough to need them. Send him home."

"Oh, but he is home." She reached down and stroked his crotch. "He likes it here."

"Don't be boorish," Cassandra said. "Find another dupe to charm when I'm gone."

"I don't need to charm him," Brigid said, hand still on the young man's crotch. He closed his eyes and began rocking. "He stays because he wants to stay."

Cassandra thrust the young man toward Ronald. "Get him out of here."

Brigid grabbed Cassandra's arm. When Cassandra glared at her, she dropped it and stepped away, lips drawn back. She saw me and her eyes glimmered. I tensed, binding spell at the ready.

INDUSTRIAL MAGIC • 541

"You bring your human along and I can't bring mine?" Brigid said, eyes fixed on mine.

"She's not human, which you'll discover if you continue what you're doing."

Brigid's blue eyes gleamed brighter. Charming me, or trying to. The power rarely worked on other supernaturals, but to be sure, I took the opportunity to field-test yet another of my new spells: an anticharm incantation. Brigid yelped.

"Stings, doesn't it?" Cassandra said. "Leave the girl alone or she'll move onto something even less comfortable."

Brigid turned to Cassandra. "What do you want, bitch?"

Cassandra smiled. "Undisguised hate. We're making progress. I want John."

"He's not here."

"That's not what your bouncer said."

Brigid flipped her hair off her shoulder. "Well, he's wrong. Hans isn't here."

Cassandra turned on Ronald, who backed up against the wall.

"He was in the back room, with Brigid and the boy," Ronald said.

"Let me guess," Cassandra said to Brigid. "He told you to come out here and create a diversion while he slipped out the back door. Come on then, Paige. Time to hunt a coward."

CHAPTER 40

ΠEVER UΠDEREStiMATE tHE POWER OF VAMPiRE EGO

The back door of the Rampart opened into an alley.

"What about Ronald and Brigid?" I said, hovering in the doorway. "They might know something, and the moment we're out of sight, they're going to bolt, too. Two birds in the hand are definitely worth more than one in the bush."

Cassandra shook her head, gaze traveling along the alley. "They'd never betray John. Without him, they wouldn't survive." She turned left. "This way."

"You picked up his trail?"

"No, but I'd go this way."

We looped behind a body shop and came out into a warren of dilapidated row houses that looked as if they'd been boarded up since I was in grade school. At the end of the lane, Cassandra stopped and studied the houses. A bottle clinked. I jumped.

"If you hear someone, it's not him," she said.

"Someone else is out here?"

"Lots of someones, Paige. Abandoned doesn't mean empty."

As if to underscore this, a woman's laugh floated down the street. A bottle sailed from a second-story window and smashed on the road, adding to a puddle of broken glass.

Cassandra walked to the far sidewalk and traversed the row of houses, with me at her heels. I felt silly tagging along after her and, worse yet, useless, but there was nothing else I could do. My sensing spell wouldn't work for finding a vampire, and if he wasn't going to give himself away by making noise, there was no use searching on my own.

Two houses from the end, Cassandra peered up at the building. She grabbed the rusted railing and started climbing the steps to the front door. Halfway up, she stopped. She looked at the door, tilted her head, then wheeled. I ducked out of her way, but she stayed on the step and gazed out into the street. After a moment, she turned back to the house, studied it, then shook her head and marched down. At the road, she passed the last house with only the briefest glance and crossed the road. I jogged after her.

"Is there anything I can do?" I asked.

"Yes. Stay out of my way."

I threw up my hands, and walked back to the house she'd first approached.

"I didn't say wander off," she called after me.

"I'm not wandering. Something about this house caught your attention, so I'm checking it out while you search the others."

"He's not in there."

"Good. Then it won't hurt for me to check."

"The last thing I need is to be worrying about you stepping on someone's dirty needle."

"I'm not a child, Cassandra. If I do step on a needle or get mugged, I preabsolve you of all responsibility. You search that side of the road while I double-check your hunch back here."

Cassandra huffed something under her breath and stalked off. I climbed the steps to the row house. The front door was boarded over, but someone had kicked a large hole at the bottom. I crouched and crawled through.

The smell hit me first, triggering memories of a stint volunteering in a homeless shelter. Inhaling through my mouth, I looked around. I was in a front hall. Peeling wallpaper hung from the walls, mingling with strips of flypaper polka-dotted with mummified bug bodies. I cast a light spell and shone it along the hallway floor. The carpet had long since been torn up, leaving bare underlay. As I moved forward, I pushed the trash out of the way with my foot. Though there were no needles, there was enough broken glass and rat droppings to make me glad I'd changed out of my open-toed sandals before leaving Miami.

From the hall, I had three destination choices: upstairs, the living room, or the door at the end, which presumably led into the kitchen. I cast a sensing spell from the foot of the stairs. It might not work on vampires, but in a place like this, the living were of equal concern. When the spell came back negative, I headed for the living room. No sign of a vampire there, or anything large enough to hide one. Same with the combined dining/kitchen area. Even the closets were bare, all doors and shelves having been stripped off, presumably to feed the fire pit in the middle of the living-room floor.

As I headed for the stairs, something whispered across the upstairs floor. The sound was too soft for footsteps . . . unless the feet belonged to the large furry rodents who'd left their calling cards in the debris below. I walked halfway up the stairs and launched my sensing spell. It came back

negative. Now that I thought about it, that was strange. Recent rat droppings meant recent rats, and my spell should have picked them up. I suspected I knew the reason for the sudden outflux. Rats don't just flee a
sinking ship—they flee stronger predators, too.

I prepped a knock-back spell and climbed to the top landing. The
house was still and silent. Too still. Too silent. The preternatural stillness
reminded me of earlier that day, when I'd thought the killer had been
stalking me in the parking lot.

From the top of the stairs, I could see into all four rooms. I wanted to
be at the front of the house, which narrowed my choices to two, one of
which was the bathroom—too small for what I had in mind. I peeked in
the front bedroom, making sure it was empty, then stepped inside and cast
a perimeter spell across the doorway. Problem was, I'd never tried this
spell with a vampire, so I couldn't rely on it now. When this was over, I'd
have to test my whole array of sensory spells on Cassandra. Not that she'd
ever offer herself up as a guinea pig, but there were ways around that.

Next I readied a fresh knock-back spell. "Readying a spell" means to
start the incantation, so it can be launched with a few final words. Spells
are wonderful weapons, but on a speed-of-use scale, they rank down
there with bows and arrows. If the arrow isn't already in the bow when
you get jumped, you're in trouble. The other problem, though, is that you
can't pause mid-incantation indefinitely. Lucas and I had once spent a
weekend experimenting with this, and concluded that you could ready a
spell for about two minutes. After that, you had to prep it again. This
being my first practical application of that research, I was re-readying my
spell every sixty seconds, just to be sure.

I crossed to the front window. It was boarded up, but someone had
pried loose the middle board to let in sunshine. I stood sideways, so I
could see both the window and the doorway, then I redirected my light
spell behind me, for backlighting.

Once my eyes adjusted to the darkness of the street below, I could
make out Cassandra's figure walking down the empty road, Pradas click-
ing impatiently against the asphalt, Dolce & Gabbana coat snapping
behind her. How many people were huddled behind other windows along
this street, drawn there by our earlier noise and now watching as this
impeccably dressed, attractive forty-year-old woman strode unaccompanied down their street? Talk about an easy mark. Yet no one came out.
Maybe they didn't dare.

Judging by Cassandra's angle and purposeful stride, she was heading
here, presumably having found nothing farther down. That meant my

hunch about John's whereabouts was probably correct, and it meant I had to move fast.

I turned my back to the door and adjusted my light-ball until I could see the reflection of the door in the window glass. Then I took out my cell phone. I readied a new spell, called our apartment, and started talking before the machine picked up.

"Hey, it's me. I'm still in New Orleans. Cassandra got a lead on a vamp and she's following him now. He was supposed to be at this bar, but he ducked out the back door. Can you believe that? Mr. I'm-an-Evil-Vampire running out the back." I paused, then laughed. "No kidding. Vamps, huh?"

Through the reflection in the window I saw a shape cross the doorway. I prepped a fresh spell and continued talking into the answering machine.

"I bet he is," I said as the shape crept closer. "Probably hiding in some cubbyhole hoping the rats don't get him. Guys like this, it's a wonder they haven't died out—"

I cast the rest of the binding spell, then whirled to see a man frozen in mid-lunge. Slender, early thirties, black hair slicked back into a ponytail, white linen shirt, flowing knee-length black leather coat, and matching leather pants. Mascara, maybe. Eyeliner, definitely.

"John, I presume," I said. "Forgot that vampires really do cast a reflection, didn't you?"

His brown eyes darkened with fury. Below, the front door clicked shut.

"Up here," I called. "I found him."

Cassandra's heels clicked double-time up the stairs. As she rounded the corner, she looked almost concerned. Then she saw John and slowed.

"Like my statue?" I said. "The not-so-cunning vampire swooping down on his not-so-unsuspecting prey."

"I see your binding spell has improved." She looked at John and sighed. "Let him go."

I released the spell. John fell on his face. Cassandra sighed again, louder. John scrambled to his feet and brushed off his pants.

"She trapped me," he said.

"No," I said. "Your ego trapped you."

John adjusted his coat, then scowled at a line of grease across his white shirt.

"This better come out," he said.

"Hey, I didn't do that," I said. "That's what you get crawling around dumps like this."

"I wasn't crawling. And I didn't duck out the back door. I—"

"Enough," Cassandra said. "Now, John—"

"I prefer Hans."

"And I prefer not to have to chase you through abandoned buildings, but it seems neither of us gets our wish tonight. I came to speak to you about—"

"The Rampart." John rolled his eyes and slouched against the wall, then noticed his shirt creased and adjusted his slouch. "Let me guess, you've been to see Saint Aaron. Such a waste of a gorgeous vampire. I could reform him, of course." He grinned, all teeth. "Show him the error of his ways, or the way to delicious errors. Show him what that perfect body—"

"You're not gay, John. Get over it. Now, I don't know what beef Aaron has with the Rampart, but I know nothing about it and I saw no cause for concern myself."

John straightened. "Oh?"

"The matter I came to discuss involves the Cabals."

"The Cabals?" John's brows knitted. "What about the Cabals?"

"This"—she flourished a hand at me—"is Paige Winterbourne. You've met her mother."

Recognition sparked in John's eyes, but he dowsed it and shrugged.

Cassandra continued, "Of course, I don't expect you to remember a nonvampire, but Paige's mother was the Leader of the American Coven. Though I'm sure you don't follow spell-caster gossip, Paige is involved with Lucas Cortez, Benicio Cortez's youngest son and heir."

From John's expression none of this was news to him, but he gave no sign of it and let Cassandra continue.

"Young Lucas has some ethical disputes with his father's organization and is actively involved in anti-Cabal activities. That's why Paige approached me. As a fellow council member, she's well aware of my strong anti-Cabal stance."

I nodded, though the thought of Cassandra taking a strong stance on anything had me struggling to keep a straight face.

"Paige wanted me to join their little crusade, but I'm hardly about to join forces with spell-casters. She then told me that you and your . . . associates have formed your own anti-Cabal league. Naturally, I'm intrigued, though I cannot understand why you wouldn't have approached me about this yourself."

"I—we—didn't someone tell you? I asked Ronald—"

"For now, I'll accept that excuse, though I wouldn't suggest you try it again. As for this campaign, I hear that you've been quite busy. Busy and successful."

John hesitated, then shrugged. "Not surprising, really. They're such an easy target."

"But this latest assault? Truly inspired."

Again, John hesitated, and I saw by his expression that he had no idea what Cassandra was talking about. He coughed to cover his confusion, then pressed on. "Yes, well, it was a team effort. Months of planning. We were pleased with the results, though, and we hope to build on that success for our next effort."

"I'm sure you will."

Cassandra walked to the window and looked out, regrouping and plotting her next move. I left her to it. That fake phone call had tested the limits of my deceptive abilities.

John shot up the sleeves on his coat. "We've let these Cabals go on too long. It was an amusing exercise to watch, but they've forgotten their place in the supernatural world. We should have taken a hand in the Cabals right from the start, demanded tribute, something to remind them who's in charge. Not that I blame you—"

Cassandra looked at John. He lifted his hands and stepped back.

"Not at all. You were misled, like the rest of us. When they said they didn't want vampires joining up, we didn't care. Why should we? Vampires certainly aren't going to punch time cards for spell-casters. We just didn't see where that would lead."

"Where that would lead . . ." Cassandra murmured. "Yes, of course. I'm assuming you're referring to the recent problems we've had with the Cabals."

"Sure. Right."

Cassandra glanced at me, my cue to play the clueless outsider.

"What problems?" I said.

Cassandra waved to John, as if to grant him the floor.

"Well, the, uh, general problems they have with vampires. They know we could rise against them at any time. Too long we've lain dormant, complacent with our place in the world—"

Cassandra strode to the door and disappeared into the hall. John hurried after her.

"Did you hear something?" he asked.

"No, I've heard enough. Paige? Come on."

I followed her from the house.

CHAPTER 41

UNDERSTANDING CASSANDRA

"I hope we're leaving because you have an idea," I said as we walked along the street.

"He doesn't know anything."

"How do you know? You barely prodded him."

"What was I supposed to do? Rip out his fingernails? I'm over three hundred years old, Paige. I have an excellent understanding of human and vampire behavior. John knows nothing."

I glanced back toward the row house.

"Don't you dare," Cassandra said. "Really, Paige, you can be such a child. An impetuous child with an overdeveloped sense of her own infallibility. You're lucky that binding spell held John or I would have had to rescue you yet again."

"When have you *ever* rescued me?" I shook my head, realizing I was being deftly led away from my goal. "Forget John, then. What about the other two? We should stop by the Rampart, see if you can pick up their trail—"

"If John doesn't know anything, they don't know anything."

"I'm still not convinced John doesn't know anything."

She muttered something and walked faster, leaving me lagging behind. I took out my cell phone. She glanced over her shoulder.

"I'm not standing here waiting for a cab, Paige. There's a restaurant a few blocks over. We'll phone from there."

"I'm not calling for a cab. I'm phoning Aaron."

"It's three A.M. He will not appreciate—"

"He said to call him when we finished talking to John, whatever the hour, and see whether he's found any other leads."

Cassandra snatched the cell phone from my hand. "He hasn't. Aaron spent the last seventy years in Australia, Paige. He's barely been back for two years. How could he possibly know anything about us? About the vampires here?"

"He knew about John and the Rampart." I peered at her through the darkness. "You really don't want me asking other vampires for information, do you?"

"Don't be ridiculous. I took you to Aaron. I brought you here. I chased down John—"

"*I* chased down John. You walked right past him."

"John doesn't know anything."

"But you do."

"No," she said, meeting my eyes. "I don't."

I knew then that she was telling the truth. She didn't know anything . . . and that's why she was blocking and snapping at me, because these were her people, she represented them, and she should have known something. Known about the Rampart, known about John's anti-Cabal crusade, known who'd had run-ins with the Cabals. But she didn't. That was the problem.

"Lucas and I can handle this," I said, my tone softening. "You don't need to—"

"Yes, I do need to. You were right. As council delegate I need to help solve this before the situation gets worse for all involved." She handed me my cell phone. "Go ahead. Call Aaron."

I shook my head. "It can wait until morning. Let's go back to the hotel and get some sleep."

Of course, I didn't want to sleep. I wanted to plot my next move. I wanted to call Lucas and get his opinion. I wanted to call Aaron and see whether he'd uncovered anything. Most of all, though, I wanted to shake Cassandra until her fangs rattled.

I did none of this. I could hardly track fresh leads at this hour, so there was no reason not to phone Lucas and Aaron in the morning. As for Cassandra, well, let's just say I was having trouble working up a good dose of righteous indignation. For once in my life, I think I understood Cassandra, or some minuscule part of her.

Aaron was right: Cassandra was disconnecting. A modern term for an ancient vampire affliction. When a vampire begins to pull back from the world, it's a sure sign that she's coming to the end of her life. I'd always thought it was intentional. You know you don't have much time left, so you begin to withdraw, make peace with yourself.

I'll admit, if I knew my time was coming, I'd throw myself into the world like never before, and spend every minute with those I loved. Yet it made sense that vampires might be more reflective, might isolate themselves, as they saw the end coming and realized the full cost of their existence. Even if they killed only one person a year, that added up to hundreds of victims over a lifetime. Hundreds who'd died so they could live. As that life draws to an end, they must look back and question their choice.

Seeing Cassandra deny her disconnection, fight to pretend that she's just as much a part of the world as ever, I understood that the process must be as involuntary as any other part of aging. I've said that Cassandra didn't care about anyone but herself, and she'd been that way my entire life. Although I was sure she'd never been the most altruistic person, if she'd always been as self-centered as she was today, she'd never have been granted a seat on the council. Perhaps, as she grew older, she'd begun finding it more difficult to care, as the years and the faces blurred together, her own self and life the only constant. Yet she'd told herself she wasn't affected by it, that she was still as vibrant and vital as ever. Could I really blame her for that? Of course not.

What about my mother? Could I blame her? She must have seen the signs with Cassandra. Why didn't she say anything? When Cassandra's codelegate, Lawrence, had taken off for Europe, sinking into the final stages of his decline, my mother should have insisted on getting a second, younger vampire delegate. If she had, maybe none of this would have happened. We'd have known which vampires were having trouble with the Cabals. Yet my mother had done nothing. Why? Perhaps for the same reason I sat on the hotel bed, staring at the door, knowing I should go out there and confront Cassandra, yet unable to do so.

Fear glued me to that bed. Not fear of Cassandra herself, but fear of offending her. I've never been very good at respecting my elders. Everyone deserves my basic respect, but to earn extra requires more than just having lots of candles on your birthday cake. My mother raised me to be Coven Leader, meaning I grew up knowing that my "elders" would someday be my subordinates. Yet there's a big difference between kowtowing to a seventy-year-old witch and showing respect to a three-hundred-year-old vampire. I couldn't just walk out there and say, "Hey, Cass, I know you don't want to hear this, but you're dying, so get over it."

Something had to be done. It made my gut churn to admit that my mother may have made a mistake, but if she had, I couldn't perpetuate it simply to avoid disrespecting her memory. If Aaron wanted a place on the council, then he should have it. I wouldn't tell Cassandra that now—that would be kicking her when she was down. But we did need to talk.

Cassandra stood in the living area, staring out the window. She didn't turn when I walked in. As I watched her, my resolve faltered. This could wait until morning.

"Bathroom's all yours," I said. "You can have the bedroom, too. I'll pull out the sofa."

She shook her head, still not turning. "Take the bedroom. I don't sleep very much anymore."

Another sign of a dying vampire. I watched her stare out the window. She looked . . . not sad, really, but somehow smaller, dimmer; her presence was confined to that corner of the room instead of taking over the whole of it.

"Can we talk, then?" I said.

She nodded, and walked to the couch. I took the chair beside it.

"If you want to speak to John again, I'll help you," she said. "I will warn you, though, that he's likely to send us on a wild-goose chase." She paused. "Not intentionally. He simply puts too much credence in gossip."

"Well, maybe Aaron can help us sift through John's bullshit. Aaron seems to have a good network of contacts."

Cassandra stiffened, almost imperceptibly, then nodded. "Aaron was always very good at that, immersing himself in our world. Helping others. Keeping order. It's what he does best." A small smile. "I remember, we were in London when Peel began recruiting his bobbies, and I told him, 'Aaron, finally, a career for you.' He'd have been horrible at it, of course. If he caught a hungry child stealing a loaf of bread, he wouldn't have arrested him, he'd have helped him steal more. He's a good man. I—" She paused. "So we'll talk to John again, then. Aaron should be able to get an address for us later today."

"I can probably get it tonight. If he owns the Rampart with Brigid and Ronald, then one of them has to have their address in the public record system. I'll also call Lucas, tell him I won't be coming back to Miami just yet, see whether he wants to join us."

Finding John's address was even simpler than I'd hoped. It was in the phone book. Just to be sure, though, I hacked into public records and double-checked. It may seem that supernaturals, particularly vampires, would avoid leaving a paper trail and, in most cases, they do. Few supernaturals will list themselves in the local phone books, as John had. Yet when it comes to such highly regulated matters as the issuing of liquor licenses, it's more dangerous to provide false information. Vampires carry valid driver's licenses and file their taxes like everyone else, though the name on their paperwork may or may not be their true birth name, depending on how they prefer to keep their identity current. Some pick a victim in their age range and take over his identity for a while. Others pay supernatural forgers to create fresh documents every decade or so. Like Cassandra, John apparently chose the latter route.

Next I called Lucas. As I'd expected—and hoped—he did want to join us. We discussed whether Cassandra and I should wait for him before visiting John, but he didn't think his presence would help. He'd catch the next flight to New Orleans, and we'd meet up after lunch.

By this point, it was after six, so sleep was out of the question. I fixed a fresh poultice for my stomach and cast a fresh healing spell. It helped. A few hours of sleep might have helped more, but I didn't have time for that. The painkillers might have helped, too, but I'd left them back in Miami, and not by accident. This trip, I needed to be clearheaded.

At seven, we went to a bistro down the road, where I had beignets and café au lait while Cassandra drank black coffee. After breakfast, Cassandra tried calling Aaron, but he wasn't answering his cell, so she left a message. Then we hailed a cab and headed out to interview the vampire again.

CHAPTER 42

EMBRACING ONE'S
CULTURAL HERITAGE

We stood on the sidewalk in front of John's house. Cassandra looked up at it and sighed.

"You weren't really expecting a brick bungalow, were you?" I said. "At least it's not as bad as the Rampart." I peered through the wrought-iron fence. "Oh, I didn't see that . . . or that. Is that what I think—oooh." I pulled back. "You may want to wait outside."

Cassandra sighed again, louder, deeper.

Now, I have nothing against Victorian architecture, having grown up in a wonderful little house from that very era, but John's place was everything that gives the style a bad name, plus a good dose of Southern Gothic. It looked like the quintessential haunted house, covered in ivy and peeling paint, windows darkened, spires rusting. On closer inspection, the disrepair was only cosmetic—the porch didn't sag, the wood wasn't rotting, even the crumbling walkway was crumbled artfully, the stones still solid enough that you wouldn't trip walking over them. The yard appeared overrun and neglected, yet even a novice gardener would recognize that most of the "weeds" were actually wild-looking perennials.

"This used to drive my mom crazy," I said, pointing at the lawn. "People paying to make their yard look like an abandoned lot. No wonder the neighbors have high walls. He has some nice gargoyles, though. I must admit, I've never seen them anatomically correct."

Cassandra followed my gaze, and shuddered.

"It sure is dark in there," I said. "Or are those blackout blinds? No, wait. It's paint. He's blacked out all the windows. Can't be too careful with those fatal sunbeams."

"The man is an idiot, Paige. If you doubted that last night, this house should seal the matter. We're wasting our time."

"Oh, but it's so much fun. I've never seen a *real* vampire's house before. How come your fence doesn't have wrought-iron bats?" I grabbed the gate and swung it open, then stopped dead. "Hey, I missed those. Forget the bats. *That's* what you need outside your condo."

Cassandra stepped into the gate opening, looked inside, and swore.

"I didn't think that word was in your vocabulary," I said. "Guess now we really know why the neighbors put up high fences."

There, flanking either side of the walkway, were a pair of raised fountains. The base of each was a shell-shaped bowl filled with water and lily pads. Standing in each bowl was a masculine version of Botticelli's famous *Birth of Venus*. The man stood in the same pose as Venus, left hand coyly drawn up to cover his chest, right hand down by his genitals, yet instead of covering them, he held his optimistically endowed penis, pointing it upward. Water jetted from each penis and over the path into the basin of the twin statue opposite. The water didn't flow in a smooth stream, though. It spurted.

"Please tell me there is something wrong with his water pressure," Cassandra said.

"No, I believe that's the desired effect." I followed the path of the water over the walkway. "So, are we supposed to duck or run through between spurts?"

Cassandra marched around behind the left-hand statue, following a path undoubtedly created by countless delivery men.

"Hey," I said as I ducked between the statues. "That looks familiar."

Cassandra fixed me with a look.

"No," I said. "Not *that*. The face. Check out the statue faces. It's John, isn't it? He had them modeled after himself."

Her gaze flicked down. "Not entirely."

I grinned. "Cassandra, you and John? Say it isn't so."

"May I never be so desperate. I meant that if he was that gifted, I'd certainly have heard about it. The vampire community isn't that big."

"And neither, apparently, is John."

We climbed onto the porch, then both stopped to stare at the door knocker, an iron Nosferatu-style vampire head, teeth bared.

"You know," I said. "We might not be giving John enough credit. All this could be a clever example of reverse psychology. No one would ever suspect a real vampire would be stupid enough to live like this."

"One would hope that *no* person would ever be stupid enough to live like this."

She lifted the door knocker.

"Hold on," I said, putting my hand out to stop her. "Is this really such a good idea?"

"No," she said, wheeling and heading down the steps. "It is not. I saw a nice little boutique on the corner. Why don't we do some shopping, wait for Aaron to phone back—"

"I meant it might not be wise to announce ourselves. If he bolted last night, he might do the same again."

"Only if we're lucky."

"I think we should break in."

"Quite possibly the only suggestion that would make this excursion even more unbearable. If this involves crawling through a broken basement window, may I mention now that these pants are dry-clean-only, I didn't bring another change of clothes, and I'm certainly not going to—"

I finished murmuring an unlock spell and opened the door. Inside, all was dark and silent.

"It's daytime," Cassandra murmured. "He'll be asleep."

Guess I should have known that. I needed to brush up on my vampire lore.

The house was cool, almost cold compared to the warm fall day outside. I could chalk up the drop in temperature to an otherworldly chill from stepping into the abode of the undead, but I suspected John just had his air conditioner cranked too high.

I cast a light spell and looked around. The walls were covered in crimson velvet-flocked wallpaper, and decorated with paintings that probably violated obscenity codes in a dozen states.

"I didn't know goats could do that," I said, casting my light over one picture. "And I'm not sure why they'd want to."

"Could you dim that thing?" Cassandra said. "Please?"

"Sorry, it's a single-wattage spell," I said. "But I could blindfold you. Hey, look, there's a leather hood right there on the coatrack. Oooh, check out the cat-o'-nine-tails. Think John would notice if I scooped it?"

"You're enjoying this far too much."

"It's just so refreshing to see a vampire who fully embraces his cultural heritage." I waved my light-ball toward the stairs. "Shall we see whether we can wake the undead?"

Cassandra shot me a look that said she was seriously reconsidering her thirty-and-up policy. I grinned back and headed for the stairs.

Upstairs we found more red velvet wallpaper, more paintings of questionable artistic merit, more S&M-themed knickknacks, and no John. There were four bedrooms. Two were furnished as sleeping quarters, but seemed to be used only as dressing rooms. The third could best be described as a museum of vampire-fetish, and is best left undescribed in further detail. The fourth door was locked.

"This must be his," I whispered to Cassandra. "Either that, or the stuff in here is even worse than the stuff in the last room."

"I doubt that's possible." Cassandra's gaze darted toward the fetish room. "Perhaps, though, I should wait in the hall. In case John returns."

I grinned. "Good plan."

I cast a simple unlock spell, assuming it was a normal interior door lock, the type that could be sprung with a hairpin. When that failed, I moved to my next stronger spell, then to the strongest. Finally, the door opened.

"Damn," I murmured. "Whatever he's got in here, he really doesn't want anyone to see."

I eased open the door, guided my light-ball around the corner, and found myself looking into . . . an office. An ordinary, modern home office, with gray carpet, painted blue walls, fluorescent lighting, a metal desk, two computers, and a fax machine. A whiteboard on the far wall held John's to-do list: pick up dry cleaning, pay property taxes, renew cleaning contract, hire new dishwasher. Not a single mention of sucking blood, raping the local virgins, or turning his neighbors into undead fiends. No wonder John didn't want anyone coming in here. One glance through that door and all his image-building would be for naught.

I stepped out and closed the door behind me.

"You don't want to go in there," I said.

"Bad?"

"The worst." I looked along the hall. "So he's not here, and it doesn't look like he's slept up here in a while. So where does a culturally faithful vamp sleep? You didn't see a mausoleum out back, did you?"

"Thank God, no. He seems to have had the sense to draw the line at that."

"Probably because he couldn't get the building permit. Okay, well . . ." I looked at her. "Help me out here. I'm not vamp-stereotype savvy."

She paused, as if it pained her to answer, then sighed. "The basement."

✦

We stood in the center of the basement. My light-ball hung over the only object in the room, a massive, gleaming, ebony black, silver-trimmed coffin.

"Just when you thought it couldn't get any worse, huh?" I said. "At least it's not a mausoleum."

"He's sleeping in a box, Paige. It doesn't get any worse than that. A mausoleum, at least you could fix up, add some skylights, perhaps a nice feather bed with Egyptian cotton sheets . . ."

"He might have Egyptian cotton sheets in there," I said. "Oh, and you know, it might not be as bad as you think. Maybe he doesn't sleep in there. Maybe it's just for sex."

Cassandra fixed me with a look. "Thank you, Paige. If those pictures upstairs weren't enough to taint my sex life for weeks, that image will certainly do it."

"Well, at least we know he's not having sex in there right now. I think it'd need to be propped open for that. So what's the proper etiquette for rousing a vamp from his coffin? Should we knock first?"

Cassandra grabbed the side of the coffin and was about to swing it open when her head jerked up.

"Paige—!" she called.

That was all I heard before a body struck mine. As I pitched forward, pain shot through my torn stomach muscles. I twisted and caught a glimpse of a naked thigh and a swirl of long blond hair. Then a hand grabbed me from behind and a head plunged toward my neck.

I reacted on instinct, not with a spell, but with a move from a barely remembered self-defense class. My elbow shot up into my attacker's chest and my other hand slammed, palm first, into the nose.

A shriek of pain and my attacker stumbled back. I scuttled around, binding spell at the ready, and saw Brigid huddled on the floor, naked, cupping her nose.

"You bitch! I think you broke my nose."

"Stop whining," Cassandra said, reaching down to help me up. "It'll heal in the time it takes you to get dressed." She shook her head. "Two vampires laid low in two days by a twenty-two-year-old witch. I am embarrassed for my race."

I could have pointed out that I was twenty-three, but it wouldn't have had the same alliteration. At least Cassandra had some vague idea of my age. Most times she was doing well if she bothered to remember names.

Behind us, the coffin creaked open.

"What the hell is—" John grumbled, yanking a sleep mask from his eyes. "Cassandra?" He groaned. "What did I do now?"

"They broke in, Hans," Brigid said. "They were prowling around, looking at everything—"

"We weren't prowling," Cassandra said. "And we were trying very hard *not* to look at anything. Now get out of that coffin, John. I can't speak to you when you're in that thing."

He sighed, grabbed both sides, and pushed himself up. Unlike Brigid, he was, thankfully, not naked, or I'd have been unable to resist vocalizing comparisons with the statues out front. Though John was shirtless, he wore a pair of billowing black silk pants, cinched at the waist. I assumed they were supposed to look debonair, but I was having serious MC Hammer flashbacks.

"We need some information," Cassandra began. "Last night, we weren't entirely forthright with you for security reasons. But, after we spoke to you, it was obvious that I may have underestimated your . . . stature in the vampire world."

"It happens," John said.

"Yes, well, here's the situation. A vampire has been killing Cabal children—the children of Cabal employees."

"Since when?" John said, then coughed. "I mean, I heard about that, of course."

"Of course. As of yet, the Cabals don't realize that they're hunting for a vampire. The interracial council would like to keep it that way, to catch the perpetrator quietly. We know the Cabals don't like vampires. We don't need to give them an excuse to come after us."

"Let them," Brigid said, stepping forward. "They want a war, we'll give them a—"

John hushed her with a wave. As he watched us, I realized that, as I'd hoped, Cassandra had indeed underestimated him. Playing the fool didn't mean he was one.

"If you catch him, what are you going to do with him?" John asked. "I'm not going to help you find a vampire so you can kill him. I could argue he's doing us a favor."

"Not if the Cabals find out."

John paused, then nodded. "So I assume you want to know who has a beef with the Cabals."

"Shouldn't she already know?" Brigid said, slanting a look at Cassandra. "That's her job as our representative, isn't it? To know who's been naughty and who's been nice?"

Cassandra met Brigid's sneer with a solemn nod. "Yes, it is, and if I have been remiss in performing my duties, I apologize. As of now, expect me to do so, and if I do not, you may petition the council to have me removed. As well, I may consider seeking a codelegate."

"We'd appreciate that, Cassandra," John said. "We've all talked about this. We'd like a second delegate on the council. I'd be willing, of course."

"I . . . appreciate the offer," Cassandra said. "Right now, though, we need to resolve the most pressing concern. If you know anyone who has had a problem with the Cabals—"

"First, I want your word that whoever is responsible won't be executed."

"I can't do that. Council law—"

"Fuck council law."

Cassandra glanced at me. I shook my head. This we couldn't do. We both knew that the killer had to go to the Cabals. To do otherwise would be to risk having them turn on both the vampires and the council. All we could do now was negotiate with them to minimize the fallout.

"We can't promise absolution," Cassandra said. "But we'll make sure he's treated fairly—"

"No deal."

"Perhaps you fail to understand the importance of this. The more children this vampire kills, the uglier this will get. We need to stop him—"

"Then stop him," Brigid said. "You shouldn't need us. And I don't think you do. I think this is all a little act for your council buddies, so they don't find out the truth."

Cassandra's eyes narrowed. "What truth?"

"That you knew exactly what was going on. You knew how bad things were. You want us to tell your little witch friend here so you can claim you didn't know a thing about it. Well, you can't possibly be that out of touch—"

"I'm afraid she is," said a voice behind us.

We turned to see Aaron step into the basement, followed by Lucas.

"Cassandra doesn't know what's been going on," Aaron said. "But I do."

CHAPTER 43

EDWARD AND NATASHA

"Hello, Aaron," Brigid said, sliding up to him and running a finger down his chest. "You're looking good . . . as always."

Aaron lifted her finger off his shirt and let it drop. "Put some clothing on, Brigid."

She smiled up at him. "Why? Tempted?"

"Yeah, to cover my eyes."

Brigid sniffed and swung to Lucas. "So this is the Cabal crown prince, is it?" She looked him up and down. "Nothing contact lenses and a better wardrobe couldn't fix."

She took a step toward him.

"No, thank you," Lucas murmured.

"Brigid?" John said. "Please, get dressed."

"Don't bother," Cassandra said. "If Aaron has what we need, then we'll leave you two to your immortal slumber."

She headed for the door.

"Hold on," John said. "I may have details Aaron doesn't. My deal still stands."

"Deal?" Aaron said.

I nodded. "He wants us to promise not to execute the killer or hand him over to the Cabals."

"Ah, fuck, Hans, you know we can't do that. They'll come after us, hunt us down."

Brigid laughed. "You think we're afraid of the Cabals? We're vampires. The gods of the supernatural world, impervious to harm—"

"Yeah, until someone chops off our heads, then we're worm food like everyone else. Hans, maybe you've got Brigid believing that vamp-superiority crap, but I know you're smarter than that."

"We don't need this," Cassandra said. "If you have a name—"

"I do, but Hans may know more. I want to find this guy before he kills another Cabal kid."

"Why?" Brigid said. "Who cares about another dead Cabal brat?"

"The Cabals do."

John hesitated, then nodded. "Let's talk."

At Cassandra's insistence, we moved out of the basement. John suggested the backyard, so we waited for him there. Like the front yard, the rear was surrounded by a high fence. Here, though, the fence had been erected by John, not his neighbors. The yard was almost as big a shock as the home office, which is probably why he kept it hidden.

It was small, no more than a few hundred square feet. Instead of grass, it had rock gardens and koi ponds surrounded by gravel paths. In the center of the yard was a pagoda with a teak table and chair set, where we waited for John.

Brigid had already made it clear that she wouldn't be joining us. Apparently, she took her role as a "true" vampire very seriously, never venturing outside during the day. I suspected this was why John chose to have the meeting outdoors, so he could speak without her interruptions.

As we waited, Lucas explained how they'd found us. Aaron had called him early this morning, thinking we'd be sleeping in after our night chasing John. They decided to hook up and come to New Orleans together. Lucas knew we were heading to John's house, but didn't have the address. Aaron had the address.

I was anxious to hear Aaron's findings, but before I could ask, John returned. He was dressed in black leather pants and a white linen shirt. Still pretty Goth, but not as theatrical as last night's attire. I suspected there were a lot of theatrics to John's image. Last night he'd gushed about Aaron, but when the man showed up in person, Brigid had been the only one vamping it up.

"It's Edward, isn't it?" Aaron said as John pulled out a chair.

"That would be my guess," John said. "I don't know him well enough to say for certain—"

"*No one* knows them well enough to say for certain," Aaron said.

"Them?" I asked.

"Edward and Natasha. They're a couple. Been together a very long time."

"I've heard those names," I said. "In the council minutes. They're immortality questers."

"Did the council investigate them?" Lucas asked.

"Investigated and exonerated, if I remember correctly," I said. "It was at least thirty, forty years ago. Another vampire expressed some concern about their questing—no outright allegations, just a bad feeling. Anyway, Edward and Natasha weren't breaking any codes, just searching for answers, like most questers."

"Well, it's gone beyond bad feelings," Aaron said. "Seems rumors have been circulating about them in the vamp community for a while, saying they've gotten into some nasty shit up in Ohio." Aaron caught my look. "Yeah, they've been living in Cincinnati. Lucas told me that's where you figure the killer's from. I'd say we've got ourselves a suspect."

"Is this connected to their questing?" I asked.

"Possible," Lucas said. "They may have uncovered a ritual requiring supernatural blood."

"Then where's the Cabal connection? Sure, it's a great way to find supernaturals—just hack into the Cabal employment records—but you think they'd stick to the periphery, with runaways like Dana. Attacking a CEO's family is only going to raise the stakes."

"That could be a side effect of the killing itself," Lucas said. "After Dana and Jacob, Edward saw the chaos he was creating and couldn't resist a bigger challenge."

"Or maybe the ritual wasn't working and they thought Cabal royal blood might help."

"Not they," John said. "Only Edward."

Cassandra shook her head. "Those two don't do anything alone."

"They do now," Aaron said. "No one's seen Natasha for months. Rumor is she'd finally had enough, that things got too bad, and she took off."

"I find that hard to believe," Cassandra said. "They'd been together for over a century. After that long, you don't just—" Her gaze flicked toward Aaron. "What I mean is, it seems unlikely that those two would separate."

"Well, one way or another, she *is* gone," John said. "And I doubt Edward's happy about it."

CHAPTER 44

QUEST FOR IMMORTALITY

Next stop: Cincinnati, Ohio. Using Edward and Natasha's known aliases, as provided by Aaron, Lucas had found two Cincinnati area addresses for the vampires. There, we hoped to find either more evidence or some clue as to their current whereabouts. Aaron offered to come along, and Cassandra was in for the long haul, so all four of us were going, which seemed an expensive proposition . . . until Lucas led us to the private airstrip at the Lakefront Airport.

"I wondered how you two got to New Orleans so fast," I said as we approached the Cortez jet.

Lucas's gaze slid away and he shifted our bags to his other shoulder. "Yes, well, after I spoke to you, my father called and when I told him we were pursuing a lead, he offered the use of the jet. It seemed a wise idea, allowing us to bypass the schedules and restrictions of commercial flight." He shifted the bags again. "Perhaps I should have—"

"You did the right thing," I said. "The faster we can move, the better."

"I don't see what all the fuss is about," Cassandra said as the flight crew scrambled to lower the boarding ramp. "This business about refusing to join your own Cabal makes absolutely no sense. If you want my opinion—"

"I'm pretty sure he doesn't, Cass," Aaron said.

"Well, I was just going to say—"

With impeccable timing, the pilot hailed Lucas to discuss last-minute flight details. A crew member took our overnight bags, then the attendant showed us to our seats. By the time Lucas returned, the plane was taxiing down the runway. The attendant followed him in and took beverage orders, then chatted with Lucas for a moment as the plane lifted off. And if you think this sidetracked Cassandra from voicing her opinion about Lucas's situation, then you don't know Cassandra.

"As I was saying," Cassandra said after the attendant delivered our drinks. "I really fail to understand this whole rebellion of yours—"

"Cass, please," Aaron said.

"No, that's fine," Lucas said. "Go ahead, Cassandra."

"One would think, if you are serious about this Cabal reformation business, then the best position from which to effect change is within the organization itself."

"Ah, the Michael Corleone strategy," I said.

Aaron grinned. "Hey, I hadn't thought of that one."

The light flashed, telling us we could remove our seat belts. After taking his off, Aaron stood and shucked his jacket. Underneath, he wore a T-shirt with the sleeves ripped off. Now, not every guy can pull off the sleeveless T-shirt look, but Aaron . . . well, Aaron could. And the sight temporarily diverted Cassandra from her course. As Aaron reached around the corner to hang his jacket, her gaze slid down his well-muscled arms, and came to rest on his backside. A look flitted through her eyes, more wistful than lustful. Then she jerked her gaze away with a sharp shake of her head.

"Michael Corleone," she said, honing in on her target again. "Do I know him?"

"From the *Godfather* movies," Aaron said as he lowered himself into his seat. "His father was a Mafia don. He didn't want any part of the family business, but finally decided to take over and mold it into a legitimate business. In the end, he became exactly what he'd rebelled against."

"Is that what you're afraid of?" Cassandra asked Lucas.

"No, but the basic premise holds. One man cannot reform an institution, not when everyone working for him is happy with the status quo. I'd face such serious opposition that my authority would be completely undermined and, if I continued, the board of directors would have me assassinated."

"So you pursue individual acts of injustice from outside the organization." Cassandra sipped her coffee, then nodded. "Yes, I suppose that makes sense."

"And I'm sure he's thrilled to hear that his life meets with your approval," Aaron said.

She glared at him. "I was simply clarifying matters for my own understanding."

"Okay, but why do you always have to be so damned antagonistic about it? You never just *ask* questions, Cass. You lob them like grenades."

"Aaron," I cut in. "You said you have two addresses. One in the city and one outside it. Is that an old one and a current one?"

"I'm not sure," Aaron said. "They're under separate aliases, an old one and a current one. According to Josie—"

"Josie?" Cassandra cut in. "Your source is Josie? Oh, Aaron. Really. The woman has porridge for brains. She—"

"I'm not sleeping with her."

"That's not—" Cassandra shot a glare around the cabin. "Where is that girl? What, she serves coffee and disappears until the flight's over? Paige's cup is almost empty."

"Uh, that's okay, Cassandra," I said. "But thanks for thinking of me."

"If you need anything, just press the buzzer by your elbow," Lucas said. "Otherwise, I've asked Annette to stay up front so we can speak freely. Now, about these two addresses. The rural one is under an older alias, but we should check out both. It won't take long."

"It'd be even faster if we split up," Aaron said. "Lucas and I take one, you ladies take the other. That way, we each have a spell-caster for breaking in and a vampire for sneaking around."

"Good idea," I said. "We'll take the rural address, and leave the city one for Lucas, in case he needs to do more than peer in the windows. He's the break-in pro, not me."

Cassandra's brows arched. "And you admit it? That's a first. You really are growing up, aren't you?"

"Cassandra?" Aaron said. "Shut up."

"What? I was praising her—"

"Don't. Please." Aaron looked at me. "I wish I could say she hasn't always been like this, but she has. After a few decades, you get used to it."

"Get used to what?" Cassandra said.

"So," Aaron said. "How do you guys like living in Portland?"

Cassandra and I stood on the side of a country road, our rental car parked behind us. Through the thick brush and gnarled skeletons of dead trees, we could make out a tiny cabin that looked like it predated indoor plumbing.

"Uh, rustic getaway cottage?" I said, double-checking the address Aaron had scribbled into my notepad. "Maybe they preferred life before electricity."

"This is ridiculous," Cassandra said. "I warned you, Paige. Aaron is far too trusting. He hates to believe anything negative about anyone, but that Josie is, bar none, the stupidest vampire ever to walk the earth. Probably gave him the names of her ex-boyfriends instead of Edward's aliases. She—"

My cell phone rang. Thankfully.

"It's Aaron," he said when I answered. "We have the house here. Lucas is scouting it out now, but I talked to the lady next door and she gave me a spot-on description of Edward and Natasha. Says they've been away a lot lately, and she hasn't seen Natasha in a few months, but Edward stops by now and then."

"Want us to come and help search?"

"If you could. Four pairs of eyes are better than two. If Cassandra squawks, tell her she can wait at a coffee shop instead. That'll make her pipe down. She hates to miss anything."

I signed off and relayed Aaron's message to Cassandra.

"So this isn't the right house?" she said. "What a surprise."

She headed for the car. I stayed where I was, peering through the trees at the cabin.

"Wait there," I called back to Cassandra. "I want to check this out first."

I headed for the cabin. Cassandra's sigh was loud enough to be heard from the roadway but, a moment later, without so much as a whisper of long grass, she was beside me.

"The only thing you're going to find here is Lyme disease," she said. "That's not a vampire's house, Paige. It never has been. It's too small, too far from the city—"

"Maybe that's the point," I said. "Immortality questers are notoriously paranoid about security. They need a place to conduct their experiments. Why not here?"

"Because it's a dump. And it's certainly not secure."

"Does it hurt to look?" I said. "It's probably five hundred square feet tops."

Cassandra sighed, then swung in front of me and marched to the cabin.

Ask people what they fear most in life and, if they answer honestly, they'll say "the end of it." Death. The great question mark. Is it surprising then, that people have pursued immortality with a relentlessness that surpasses the pursuit of wealth, sex, fame, or the satisfaction of any other worldly desire?

You might think that supernaturals wouldn't fall into this trap. After all, we know what comes next. Well, okay, we don't know *exactly*. Ghosts never tell us what's on the other side. One of the first lessons apprentice necromancers learn is "Don't ask about the afterlife." If they persist, eventually they'll be unable to contact the dead at all, as if they've been put on a ghost-world blacklist. So we don't know exactly what happens next, but we know this much: We go somewhere, and it's not such a bad place to be.

Yet even if we know that a decent afterlife awaits, that doesn't mean we're in any hurry to get there. The world we know, the people we know, the *life* we know, is here on earth. Faced with death, we kick and scream as hard as anyone else. Maybe harder. The supernatural world is rife with immortality questers. Why? Perhaps because we know, by our very existence, that magical things are possible. If a person can transform into a wolf, why can't a person live forever? Vampires live for centuries, which seems proof that semi-immortality is not a pipe dream. Then why not just become a vampire? Well, without getting too deeply into the nature of vampirism, let's just say it's extremely difficult, even harder than becoming a werewolf. For most supernaturals, finding the holy grail of immortality seems more feasible than becoming a vampire. And a quester needs only to look around to know that being a vampire doesn't cure the thirst for eternal life. If anything, it sharpens it.

I always assumed that vampires were such ardent immortality questers because, having enjoyed a taste of it, they can't help wanting the whole deal. Now, after Jaime told me she'd never heard of a necro contacting a dead vamp, I began to wonder how many vampires knew there was no proof of a vampire afterlife. I've never thought immortality sounded all that great, but if it was a choice between that and total annihilation, I'd take eternal life any day.

"Well," Cassandra said, standing in the cabin doorway. "I think we can safely say there's no secret lab in here."

I squeezed past her. Inside, the cabin was even smaller than it had appeared, a single room no more than three hundred square feet. The door had been secured with a lock good enough to require my strongest unlock spell and there were no windows, which had raised my hopes that something of interest was hidden within. From what I saw, though, the lock was only to keep out teens looking for a party place. There was nothing here worth stealing.

The cabin did appear to be in use, maybe as a retreat for an artist or a writer, someone who needed a distraction-free place to work. Distraction-free it certainly was. The only furnishings were a wooden desk, a pullout sofa, a bookcase, and a coffee table. The desk was empty, and the bookshelf held only cheap reference texts.

I surveyed the bookshelf's contents, then peered behind the unit.

"Please don't tell me you're looking for a secret passageway," Cassandra said.

I turned to the sofa, grabbed one end and pushed, but it was as heavy as most sofa beds.

"Could you—?" I said, gesturing at the far end. "Please."

"You can't be serious."

"Cassandra, please. Humor me. You know I'm not leaving until I move this sofa, so unless you want to be here awhile—"

She grabbed the end and hoisted. We moved it forward just far enough for me to roll up the area rug and look underneath.

"I've always said you were practical, Paige. Whenever someone in the council questioned your ideas, I said 'Paige is a practical girl. She's not given to flights of fancy.'"

"Huh," I said, heaving up the carpet. "Don't remember hearing that."

"Well, you must not have been around. The point is that I have always given you credit for common sense. And now, here you are, searching for a secret room . . ."

The floor under the carpet was a checkerboard of wood panels, each roughly three feet square. The gap between most of the panels was less than a quarter-inch, but one groove looked a shade wider. I ran my fingers along it.

Cassandra continued, "If Edward and Natasha were into alchemy, which I doubt, they would have rented storage space in the city for their experiments. They would not be digging secret rooms under a run-down cabin in—"

My fingertips struck a catch, and the door sprang open.

I peered into the darkness below. "Strange place for a root cellar, don't you think?"

I cast a light spell, then tossed the ball into the hole. Along one side was a ladder. As I shifted to step onto the first rung, Cassandra grasped my shoulder.

"You're not invulnerable, Paige. I am. It might be trapped. I'll go first."

I suspected this offer had more to do with curiosity than concern, but I stepped back and let her go through.

CHAPTER 45

APPETITE FOR ART

As I stepped onto the ladder, my vision clouded for a second, like a mental stutter.

"Someone's coming," I whispered into the hole. "My perimeter spell just went off. I cast one across the front of the property."

Cassandra blinked, as if shocked by this show of foresight. She motioned for me to come down and hide there, but I shook my head, hurried to the door, cracked it open, and peeked out. A young man headed toward the cabin. He struggled to carry an armload of supplies, and could barely see where he was going, let alone see me. When Cassandra peered over my shoulder, I pointed out a path along the left side of the cabin, behind the overgrown bushes.

Cassandra took the lead, as usual. This time, though, it made sense. A vampire's stealth is partly preternatural and partly hunting experience. By following in her footsteps I could move almost as quietly as she could.

Behind the cabin, the land was a patchwork of forest and meadow. The forest alternated between stands of evergreens and deciduous trees. Even the meadow itself seemed uncertain what form it should take, with patches of long grass interspersed with brush and brambles.

"Should we wait it out or come back later?" I whispered when we'd walked far enough.

"Wait it out."

"I'll phone Lucas, then. He's probably wondering where we are."

It turned out that Lucas and Aaron didn't need our help. The house had required little more than a quick sweep, and revealed nothing. With the news of our find, Lucas promised to hurry over and help *us*.

As I hung up, Cassandra glided out from a stand of trees. I hadn't noticed she'd left.

"This isn't going to work," she said. "He'll be there for a while. He's an artist."

"Artist?"

"He's set up in front of the cabin with a half-finished painting of it, although why on earth anyone would want a picture of that in their living room is quite beyond me."

"Wonderful. Well, since it doesn't look as if he'll leave on his own, we'll have to give him a supernatural push. Think a hailstorm would persuade him to call it a day?"

"I'll handle this. Wait here."

Cassandra slipped away without waiting for an answer, which was a good thing because I had no intention of staying behind. As good as Cassandra was, everyone can use backup. So I waited until she was out of sight, then looped around the cabin the other way.

The obvious plan of action was to charm him. Like most vampire powers, charming is a functional skill, another adaptation that makes them expert hunters. At its most basic, charming is extreme charisma. It allows a vamp to walk up to the most street-savvy girl in a bar and, within minutes, have her saying, "Hmm, yes, I think I would like to follow you into that dark alley."

By the time I got close enough to see around the cabin, Cassandra would probably be nearly done "persuading" the artist to leave. If anything went wrong, though, I'd be close enough to help out. When I reached the front corner of the cabin, I readied a cover spell, which would keep me hidden so long as I stayed motionless. When the spell was half-cast, I leaned out and finished the incantation at the same time, so I could watch without being seen.

Cassandra wasn't there. I could see the artist, a balding man in his late twenties, sitting on a folding campstool, his attention riveted to the canvas on his portable easel. A bush a few yards behind the man shimmered, as if ruffled by a sudden breeze. Cassandra? Why was she over there? Oh, probably approaching from the road so he wouldn't wonder where she'd come from.

Cassandra's green shirt flashed between two bushes, now less than a yard behind the artist. Okay, stop playing and come out before you give the poor guy a heart attack.

As if hearing me, Cassandra eased into the open. She stood between the bush and the artist, her narrowed eyes gleaming. She tilted her head, gaze fixed on the back of his head. Then she smiled. Her lips parted, and the tip of her tongue slid over her teeth.

Oh, shit.

I jerked back behind the cabin just as she pounced. There was an intake of breath, half-sigh, half-gasp. Then silence. I wrapped my arms around my chest and tried very hard not to think about what was happening just a scant ten feet away, which, of course, made me think about it all the more. She wouldn't kill him. I knew that. She was just . . . feeding.

I shivered and hugged myself tighter. It wasn't such a bad idea, I told myself. Beyond the obvious debilitating effect of blood-draining, a vampire's initial bite, if done properly, knocked its victim unconscious, so the blood would flow freely. Cassandra's bite would guarantee the artist would be out cold for a few hours. And she did need to eat. But still . . .

"I told you to stay where you were, Paige."

I turned to see Cassandra at the corner of the cabin. There wasn't so much as a blood smear on her lips, but her color was high and her eyes had lost their usual glitter, lids half-closed with the lazy, sated look of someone who's just had a very good meal . . . or very good sex.

"I—backup—wanted—" I managed.

"Well, I appreciate the sentiment, but you should have listened to me. Now come on. We need to check out that basement."

Instead of marching off in the lead, she prodded me forward. When I turned the corner, I saw the artist slumped on the ground. I couldn't suppress a shiver.

"He'll be fine, Paige," Cassandra said, her tone gentler than usual.

"I know."

"You may not like it, but I could argue that some people would feel the same about the chicken you ate for dinner last night."

"I know."

A soft chuckle. "You aren't going to argue the point? *Quelle surprise.*" She patted my back. "Let's get to that secret room. I can't wait to see what they've stashed down there."

Before we went back into the cabin, I cast another perimeter spell. If anyone arrived before Lucas and Aaron, we needed enough advance warning to move the unconscious artist. It may have seemed wiser to move him immediately, but with a vampire bite, the safest way to hide what happened is not to hide it at all. Better for the artist to wake up on the ground by his chair, thinking he'd suffered a blackout.

With Cassandra following, I climbed down the ladder. Then I stood at the bottom and cast my light-ball around four walls, each with a floor-to-ceiling canning shelf. Every shelf was empty.

I slumped against the ladder. "It really is a cold cellar."

"Don't be so hasty," Cassandra said, moving her hands along the far shelving unit. "Here, this one seems looser than the others. Grab the other end."

I took hold of the shelf and, on the count of three, pulled. The shelf didn't move. I walked to the nearest shelf and began examining it, the first wave of disappointment having given way to resolution. Maybe I had been mistaken about this room, but I wasn't leaving until I was certain of that.

I poked and pried at the shelf but it didn't budge. On to the next one.

"That one's firmly fastened," Cassandra said as she inspected the remaining shelf. "It doesn't so much as quiver."

I stopped yanking on the shelf and instead ran my fingers along both sides, where the unit fastened to the wall. It was rammed so tight against the wall that I couldn't even squeeze a fingernail into the gap. I crouched to examine the underside of the lower shelves.

On the second-to-bottom shelf, I found a nail sticking out near the corner. I prodded it. The nail slid into the wood and the shelf snapped hard against my hands.

"A catch," Cassandra said. "Well done again."

Before I could pull it open, my vision clouded.

"Not again," I muttered. "My perimeter spell, with flawless timing."

Cassandra checked her watch. "Aaron and Lucas."

"Or so I hope. I'll check. You go on in."

I scooted up the ladder and out the cabin door. Lucas and Aaron were picking their way through the brambles. I hailed them with a shout.

"Hear you found Edward's hidey-hole," Aaron called as they drew closer. "Way to go."

"We haven't had a chance to look inside yet," I said. "We ran into a few complications."

When they caught up, Lucas's hand brushed mine, then gave it a squeeze.

"Oooh, would that be one of those complications?" Aaron said, jerking his chin toward the fallen artist. "Or just a late-afternoon snack?"

"Both, I think," I said.

"Is she in a better mood now?"

"Actually, now that I think about it, a much better mood."

Aaron's laugh rang out through the quiet meadow. "Oh, yeah, same old Cassandra. I thought that might be the problem. She gets pretty damned testy when she hasn't eaten. That's one big drawback to socializing with nonvamps. Nobody wants to hear you say, 'I'm just popping out for a bite.' If she ever gets bitchier than usual, that's a good time to send her out on a late-night coffee run. Best way to cheer her up." He grinned. "Well, there are other ways, but you don't want to hear about those."

We circled past the artist and headed into the cabin.

CHAPTER 46

A STRANGE PLACE TO TAKE A BATH

I led Lucas and Aaron to the secret room. As I looked around, my first thought was, "That makes sense, and that makes sense, and . . . what the hell is that for?"

The room was just slightly larger than the fake cold cellar, maybe eight feet square. Along one wall was a bookcase, filled with ancient reference books and experimentation journals. The shelves on the opposite wall held vials, beakers, jars, and other scientific equipment. All this was exactly what I expected to see in a quester's laboratory. What I couldn't understand, though, was the claw-footed bathtub that took up a quarter of the floor space.

"I like to read in the bath, too," I said. "But that seems a bit extreme."

"Especially with no running water," Aaron said.

"I would assume it's used as a mixing basin," Lucas said. "Though it seems rather large for the purpose and it would likely have required removing the cabin floor to get it down here. Perhaps it has a greater significance, a relic of some sort."

Cassandra looked up from the journal she'd been reading. "You're both right. It would be used for mixing a compound, then bathing in it. Ingestion is the most common way to take immortality potions, but immersion is also popular."

"Find anything?" Aaron said, looking down over her shoulder. "At least it's not in code."

"It would be better if it was," she said. "A code can be deciphered and broken. Instead, what they've done is put in only enough detail to remind themselves what they did."

"Huh?"

She lifted the book closer to my light-ball. "'March seventh, 2001. Tried variation B again with fresher source material type Hf. No change. April twelfth, 2001. Expanded variation A to include source material type Hm, subtype E. No change.'"

"Shit," Aaron muttered. "Is it all like that?"

Cassandra nodded.

"What's the date on the last entry?" Lucas asked.

"June of this year."

"A month or two before Natasha left him," I said. "Any idea what they were doing at the time? Maybe something changed, made her decide to leave?"

Cassandra handed me the journal. "It's exactly like the other entries. They talk about 'materials' and 'variations' and 'subtypes,' but nothing specific."

I moved beside Lucas and held the journal between us as we read the last half-dozen pages. Then I flipped to the start of the book, which dated back to 1996, and skimmed to the present.

"The only change I see is a gradual increase in ingredient Hf and Hm. It appears on and off in the earlier entries, then becomes a regular ingredient in the last year. Otherwise, the entries are pretty similar—variations A through E, methodologies A through K."

"Let's see what other goodies we have, then," Aaron said. He scanned the equipment shelf. "Lots and lots of unlabeled, half-filled bottles." He grabbed one, pulled out the stopper, sniffed it, and gagged. "I may be invulnerable, but please don't ask me to taste-test anything."

I took the bottle from him and sniffed. "Sulfur." He handed me another one. "Rosemary." I eyed the shelf and named three more from looks alone. "All fairly common potion ingredients. Same with the dried stuff. Half these things you could pick up in any New Age shop."

"Which could mean that this is all they use," Cassandra said. "Or it could mean that they've hidden the more damning ingredients."

"Time to start looking for more cubbyholes," Aaron said. "I'll get the top shelves."

He ran his hand over the highest shelf, which appeared empty. As he swept along it, he dislodged a bottle and sent it crashing into the tub. Cassandra reached into the tub and touched the bottom, beside the broken pieces.

"Dry," she said. "It was empty."

She started to stand, then stopped, and ran a finger along the inside of the tub. With a frown, she leaned farther in, then shook her head and straightened.

"See something?" I said.

She shook her head. "It's been scrubbed clean."

"I believe I've found something here," Lucas said.

He was crouched in front of the equipment shelf. I expected to see another doorway behind the shelf. Instead, he gestured at the shelf itself, which he'd cleared of bottles. When I looked, I saw not a wooden shelf, but a drawer. It seemed too shallow to hold anything. Then Lucas pulled back the velvet cloth that lay over the contents—a row of surgical instruments.

"They, uh, could be veterinary tools," Aaron said. "Some questers use animal sacrifice. It's discouraged, but it does happen."

I met Lucas's gaze. "Hm and Hf."

He gave a slow nod. "Human male and human female."

Cassandra said nothing. When we looked over at her, she was bent over a hole in the floor, where she'd taken off a section of board.

"What's that?" I said.

She slammed the board back into place. "More ingredients. They're . . . human."

Aaron squatted beside her and reached for the loose board, but she held it fast to the floor.

"You don't need to look, either," she said.

"I've lived through Jack the Ripper, Charles Manson, and Jeffrey Dahmer. Nothing under that board is going to shock me."

"It's not going to make you sleep any easier, either." She looked at us. "I'll draw up an inventory of what's in here, and package it if you'd like. For now, I can tell you that they were using body parts, from multiple humans, and they weren't retrieving them from graveyards."

Her gaze skittered toward the tub. She blinked hard and looked away.

"It smells of blood, doesn't it?" Lucas said.

"I caught a whiff of something, and I thought it might be blood, but I can't pick it up again."

Aaron ducked his head into the tub. He inhaled, then shook his head. "Nothing. That's one smell we can always pick up but I'm not—" He stopped. "Scratch that. I caught it. Very faint, but definitely human blood."

"So that's what the tub is for," I said. "They put them in there to . . . harvest what they needed without making too big a mess."

"Could be," Lucas said.

I met his gaze. "But you don't think so."

He picked up the journal and turned to a page near the end. "There are several references this year to immersion in source material Hm and Hf."

"Elizabeth Báthory," Cassandra murmured.

My gut sank, as I understood what they meant.

Elizabeth Báthory was a Hungarian countess who lived in the sixteenth century. According to legend, she'd killed six hundred and fifty young women, most of them peasants, and bathed in their blood because she believed it would grant her eternal youth. After several decades of killing, Báthory was arrested, tried, convicted, and put into a room. Then the door was bricked over.

It has been argued that Elizabeth Báthory was at least part of Bram Stoker's inspiration for Dracula, perhaps even more than the equally sadistic and better known Vlad Dracul, from whom Stoker borrowed the name. In vampire society, it was generally believed that Elizabeth Báthory had been a vampire and that she'd been seeking, not eternal youth, but her youth for eternity—in other words, an immortality quester.

It was also rumored that her experiment had succeeded, that she had found eternal life and that the story of her death had been concocted, not by human officials, but by powerful elements within the vampire community. When they'd discovered her crimes—and, yes, killing six hundred humans *was* a crime even by vampire standards—they'd masterminded her arrest and trial. Then, the vampires themselves walled her up, where she remains to this day, having outlived every vampire who knew where she was imprisoned.

In covering up the success of her immortality experiments, her captors had tried to ensure such crimes would never be repeated. Yet the story, true or not, had been passed down through generations of immortality questers. Most didn't dare replicate Báthory's work but, about every hundred years or so, somebody tried.

"But to bathe in blood," I said. "That would—each time you did it, you'd need to kill how many people? Where would they bury all those—?" I stopped, remembering the strange patchwork terrain out back. I swallowed. "I think I might know."

After uncovering the fourth body, we stopped digging. All four corpses were drained of blood, and all in the ground less than a year, which meant they weren't Edward and Natasha's requisite annual kills. When we looked out over the patchwork of old-growth and new-growth meadow, we knew if we kept digging we'd find many more.

After ensuring that the artist was still unconscious, we returned to the cabin and took what we could for later examination. Then we drove to Edward and Natasha's house in the city and searched it again, now looking for hidden rooms and caches. We found nothing, which didn't surprise us; it was unlikely they'd go to all the trouble of secreting away their materials at the cabin, only to leave some in their house.

Throughout the searches, we'd all been pretty quiet, still shocked over what we'd found at the cabin. As Lucas drove us to the airport, though, my numbed brain finally began to churn through the facts . . . and found a gaping crater in the logic.

"Doesn't it punch a big hole in our theory about his motivation for killing Cabal kids?"

Lucas slanted a look my way, telling me to continue.

"Okay, if Edward's experiments with humans failed, then I can see him testing them out with supernaturals. But what's he taking? Not blood, that's for sure. Or, at least, not enough to bathe in. If he's taking something else, like the stuff that Cassandra found—" I glanced into the backseat at her. "Was it . . . material that wouldn't be missed?"

She shook her head. "Some of it is external, some internal, but everything would have been missed, if not in a visual examination, then at least in the most cursory autopsy. Perhaps he was taking something different, something small enough to be overlooked."

"I doubt that," Lucas said. "Joey Nast was still alive when we found him. I can't imagine the killer had time to excise anything from his body."

"But everything else fits," I said. "We're looking for a vampire killer, possibly from the Cincinnati area. Edward is a vampire from Cincinnati, with killing experience that goes well beyond feeding. According to his neighbors, he hasn't been home in over a week. His longtime lover has left him, which might have sent him over the edge, desperate to find the key to immortality so he can win her back. Even his physical description matches what little Esus saw of him. It all fits."

"All except that one piece," Lucas said. "Edward appears to be our man, so I'd suggest that we consider another theory regarding his motivation."

"Like what?" Aaron said.

"I have no idea," Lucas said. "But I'm open to suggestions."

We all looked at one another . . . and said nothing.

CHAPTER 47

A Most Unwelcome
Intrusion

We boarded the jet. Our first stop would be Atlanta. Although tomorrow was Sunday, Aaron had to work. Well, he didn't have to, but he'd promised a friend he'd take his shift and, since it didn't look like we'd be hot on Edward's trail just yet, he didn't want to break that promise. When we had a line on Edward, Aaron wanted to come back and help out. Being a vampire meant he had a lot of unused sick days, so he didn't expect to have any trouble getting time off his brick-laying job.

When Lucas returned from conferring with the pilot, he suggested we all try to sleep.

"It's not the most comfortable environment," he said. "But I doubt anyone slept much last night, and these next few hours may be our only chance tonight."

Cassandra nodded. "You and Paige should definitely try to sleep. I'm not tired, though, so I'll sit in the rear cabin, if you don't mind."

Lucas escorted Cassandra into the tiny private cabin behind ours.

"Did she sleep at all last night?" Aaron whispered to me when they were out of earshot.

I shook my head. "She says . . . she says she's not sleeping much lately."

His eyes filled with quiet grief, as if this was the answer he'd been both expecting and dreading.

"I'll sit up with her," he said.

As I pulled pillows and a blanket from the closet, Lucas disappeared into the crew area. He returned a few minutes later carrying two mugs of tea. He slid my "forgotten" bottle of painkillers from his pocket. I opened my mouth to argue, then caught his look, nodded, and held out my hand. He shook two into it, then sat beside me.

"How are you doing?" he asked.

"Shaken, but okay. When we heard Edward and Natasha were into dark stuff, I steeled myself for what we thought was the worst—that they were experimenting with humans. But the scale . . . the number of people they must have—"

I gulped my tea and sputtered as the hot liquid burned my throat. Lucas took my mug with a rush of apologies.

"No, that's my fault," I said. "I always tell you to make it hot. I drank it too fast."

I took the mug from his hands. As I moved it to my side table, my hands shook so badly that tea sloshed over the side, nearly burning me again.

"Damn it," I muttered, then managed a small smile. "Guess I'm not so okay after all."

He squeezed my hand. "Completely understandable."

"I know I have to be able to handle this better," I said. "If I'm going to help you, I need to get over my squeamishness. I'm too—"

"You're fine," he said. "I'm not feeling too 'okay' myself. I can guarantee, as a, uh, partner in my endeavors, you'd likely never see anything on this scale again."

"Partner?" I said, my smile turning genuine. "Don't think I didn't notice the hitch in your voice. Don't worry. I have no plans to shoehorn myself into your life that way. I'll be here to help when you need me, but that's it."

"That wasn't— That is to say, I certainly don't mind, if you're interested . . ."

"I'm not. Well, I am, but I can't be, right? Between the council and the new Coven, my plate's already full." I inhaled. "We screwed up. The council, I mean. We should have caught this."

"You can't keep tabs on every vampire—"

"Can't we?" I said. "The Pack does it with werewolves, and there are more of them to police and fewer people to do it. I don't mean we need to be breathing down every vampire's neck, but we need to be more proactive in general. There were rumors. We should have heard them. I can't blame Cassandra for that. It's everyone's responsibility. I want to change things, to start paying closer attention. But I also want to start this new Coven. I *need* to do that. It's what I'm supposed to do."

"Because your mother would have wanted it," he said softly.

"Not just that. I wanted—or I thought I wanted . . ." I rubbed my hands over my face. "I know rebuilding the Coven is important, but some days I feel like there are other things I should be doing, things I'd *rather* be doing, and the Coven . . . I'm not sure it's still my dream, or that it ever really was."

"You'll figure it out."

Lucas leaned over and kissed me, a slow, gentle kiss that calmed the confusion crashing about in my head. After a few minutes, we reclined our seats, curled up together, and let the soft drone of the plane lull us to sleep. When the plane landed in Atlanta, I woke up just enough to hear Aaron and Cassandra's whispered exchange of good-byes. A moment after the cabin door shut behind Aaron, I felt Cassandra tug the fallen blanket up over me. I sensed her standing there, watching me, but by the time I pried my eyes open, she was gone.

When I woke again, the plane had landed in Miami. I knew it had to be past dawn, but the cabin's blackout shades made it nearly pitch black inside. I snuggled in closer to Lucas and pulled up the blanket to ward off the chill of the air-conditioning.

"Cold nose," Lucas said with a sleepy laugh.

I tried pulling back, but he lifted my chin and kissed me.

"That's nice and warm," he said.

"Hmmm. Very nice."

"We're going to have to see my father today," he murmured between kisses.

"Hmmm, not so nice."

Another laugh. "Sorry."

"No, you're right. We need to tell him what we found . . . and we should thank him for the use of the jet." I caught Lucas's look. "You don't still regret taking it, do you?"

He sighed. "I don't know. I worry about how it will be interpreted. Then I worry about whether it's a sign of backsliding. And then I worry about worrying too much, what you must think of it." A quarter-smile. "Self-doubt is not a sexy trait in a lover."

"Depends on the lover. You can be almost scarily self-confident, Cortez. I like being the only one who gets to peek through the chinks in the armor. If you're still worried, though, I do know a good temporary cure."

A crooked grin. "Distraction?"

"Um-hmmm." I slid my hands under the blanket.

"Wait," he said. "I still owe you for the broom closet, and believe I can be adequately distracted by reciprocating that favor."

I grinned. "You never owe me. But I won't argue if you insist."

"I do."

As he shifted forward to kiss me, a seat squeaked . . . only it didn't sound like the seat we were lying on. I lifted my head to see Benicio tiptoeing for the cabin door. Lucas bolted upright and swore.

Benicio stopped, his back still to us. "My apologies. I came by for an update. I was waiting for you to wake up."

"We've been awake, quite obviously awake, for a few minutes," Lucas said.

"Yes, well . . ."

"You couldn't resist eavesdropping on a private conversation," Lucas said. "Until it threatened to become too private."

"I—"

"We're dressed," I said. "You might as well come in and say your piece."

Benicio turned, his gaze glancing off Lucas's glare before veering to rest on the far wall. I got up and stalked past him, out the cabin door and into the serving station, where I turned on the coffeemaker. By the time I returned, I'd had enough time to cool down. I was still pissed, but there was little danger I'd "accidentally" dump Benicio's coffee in his lap.

"I was just summing up our findings," Lucas said as I passed out the mugs.

"I can't believe it," Benicio said. "They wouldn't have gotten away with that here, but in Ohio . . ." He shook his head. "We need more offices in the Midwest. I've said it before."

Lucas stopped, mug halfway to his lips. "The Nasts were looking into a Cincinnati office, weren't they?"

Benicio nodded. "They still are, I believe, but they delayed their plans. They ran into a problem with the area that needed to be cleared up first."

I turned to Lucas. Our eyes met.

"When did they—" Lucas began.

The intercom buzzed on. "Sorry for the interruption, sir, but there's a red-haired woman here and she demands to speak to you. She says—"

"That's fine," Lucas cut in. "She's with us. Let her in."

I glanced back at the still-closed door between the rear cabins. "Guess she stepped out before we woke up."

The main door opened and I caught a glimpse of Benicio's stand-in bodyguard, Morris. Then a woman barreled past, nearly knocking the big man flying. It was indeed a red-haired woman, but not Cassandra.

CHAPTER 48

jUSTIFIABLE HYSTERIA

jaime stumbled past the guard, head bowed, shoulders hunched. As she staggered forward, my first thought was that she'd been drinking. Then I noticed her shoes—one sneaker, one pump with a two-inch heel, both pulled on over bare feet, the sneaker still untied, as if she'd grabbed the first two shoes she could find, yanked them on and ran. Her blouse was misbuttoned and stained with splotches of brown and dark red, and her hair hung in a snarled mess, a clip clinging to one side. She pushed back her hair, revealing a face streaked with makeup and tears.

"Oh, God," I said, rushing forward. "What happened?"

She turned. Four bloodred gouges raked her face from eye to jaw. I gasped.

"I'll call a medic," Lucas said as I guided Jaime to a chair.

"N—no," she said. "Don't, please. I—I'm okay."

She collapsed into the chair, bent her head down almost to her thighs, and gulped air, body shaking. After a moment, she convulsed in one final shudder, then lifted her head and brushed her hair from her eyes. She looked around, a slow, cautious gaze, shoulders tensed, as if expecting something to leap out at her.

"I'll call the medic," Benicio said, rising slowly.

"No!" she snapped. Then she saw who she was snapping at. Her eyes went wide and she dropped her face into her hands with a hiccupping laugh. "Oh, yeah, a fucking breakdown in front of Benicio Cortez. My day is now complete." She tilted her head to the ceiling. "Thank you very much!"

I dropped into the seat beside Jaime and took her hands. She squeezed mine so hard her nails drew blood. I murmured a calming spell. Jaime inhaled a long, shuddering breath, exhaled and relaxed her grip. After one last cautious look around, she sank back into the seat with a relieved sigh.

"Gone," she said. "I thought that might be the problem. Must have thought you two had abandoned us for good."

Lucas explained to Benicio what was going on.

"A ghost who can displace objects but can't contact a necromancer?" Benicio said, frowning. "I've never heard of such a thing."

"Join the club," Jaime muttered. "The poltergeisting was bad enough, but now this—" She pointed at her cheek. "Last time I had a spook reach out and touch me was twenty years ago, when I accidentally disturbed something very old, and very powerful. And, believe me, that one could talk back—in several languages. This one—" She shook her head. "Well, I don't know what this one's problem is, but it's not acting like any spook I've ever met."

"We think it might not be a ghost at all," I said to Benicio. Then I looked at Lucas. "I think it's time to consider exorcism."

He nodded. "Past time, by the look of things. We should—"

"No exorcism," Jaime said.

"Yes, I realize they're unpleasant," Lucas said. "Yet it can't be any worse than what you're enduring now. This has gone far enough—"

"No, it hasn't," she said firmly. "It hasn't gone far enough. Not yet. Whatever this thing is, it has a message it's eager—painfully eager—to deliver to you guys. It's a rough ride, but I'm prepared to tough it out if it'll help solve this case."

"What if it's not trying to help us?" I said. "Look at the way it's acting. That's not normal behavior for a helpful spirit."

"But it has helped, right? It gave us the vampire clue and led us to Cass—" She stopped, eyes going wide. "Oh, my God. Paige is right. It *is* evil."

"I heard that."

I twisted to see Cassandra in the open doorway between the cabins. She stifled a yawn.

I smiled. "Got some sleep?"

"A nap."

"Good."

She started forward, then blinked, seeing Benicio. She slanted a look my way, and I knew she wanted a proper introduction this time.

I gestured toward Cassandra. "Benicio, this is—"

"Cassandra DuCharme," Benicio said, standing and extending a hand. "Pleased to meet you."

Cassandra's brows arched.

Benicio smiled as he released her hand. "When Lucas first raised the possibility that we were dealing with a vampire, I suspected it might have been you I met at Tyler Boyd's apartment. The Cabal keeps very good records on all supernaturals of influence, so I only needed to check our dossiers for your photograph to be sure."

"One advantage to vampire mug shots," I said. "They're never out-of-date."

"I assume you're here to represent the vampires' interests in this matter?" Benicio said.

"Yes," Cassandra said. "Something which, I fear—" She stopped and her gaze swept across the other side of the cabin, her frown growing as she saw no one there. She gave her head a sharp shake. "Which I fear may become—"

She wheeled, one hand shooting up, palm out, as if to ward something off. She scowled at the empty space behind her.

"Huh," Jaime said. "Good to see I'm not the only skittish one this morning."

Cassandra's gaze shot to Jaime, getting a look at her for the first time. "What the hell happened to you?"

"Same thing I think is happening to you," Jaime said. "Without the clawing, bitch-slapping, hair-pulling, and all that fun psychic wounding stuff."

"Jaime's spirit is back," I explained. "It's probably here now. Is that what you're sensing?"

Cassandra cast another look around. "I'm not sure. What—"

Jaime flew forward, nearly onto Lucas's lap. He lunged to grab her, but before he could, she jerked back into her seat so hard she ricocheted off it and would have toppled to the floor if both Lucas and I hadn't caught her.

"What?" she shouted at the ceiling. "We aren't moving fast enough for you? Impatient bitch."

"It's a woman?" Benicio asked.

Jaime flourished a hand at the claw marks down her face. "Either that or a demon with talons. Fights like a woman, I'll tell you that much." She fingered her scalp and winced for effect, then looked at me. "You don't see any bald spots, do you?"

I lifted up in my seat for a better look, then shook my head. "Nothing a good brushing won't fix."

"Thank God. Last thing I need is—"

Jaime's head whipped back so fast her vertebra crackled. Lucas, Benicio, and I all jumped from our chairs, and even Cassandra stepped forward. Twin indentations appeared on the side of Jaime's neck. Before anyone had time to react, the dents punctured through the skin and blood spurted.

Cassandra shouldered me aside. Jaime yelped, her hand going to her neck as she backed away from Cassandra. Blood gushed over her fingers. Lucas reached to grab Cassandra's arm, lips parting to cast a spell. Then he saw that I wasn't trying to stop Cassandra.

"It's okay," I said to Jaime. "Let her—"

Jaime's bloodied hands shot out to push Cassandra away.

"She can—" I began, but Jaime's scream cut me short.

Cassandra reached for Jaime, but Jaime kicked her back. Arterial blood continued to spurt from Jaime's neck. As Lucas dove to grab her, I cast a binding spell, but it failed. Benicio was on the phone, calling for help. By the time a medic arrived, it would be too late, but there was no time to tell him this. I cast the binding spell and, again, in my panic, fumbled it. Lucas grabbed Jaime's arm, but it was slick with blood and she yanked free easily. She was fighting blindly now, kicking and hitting at anything that came close.

"Jaime!" I shouted. "Let Cassandra—"

Lucas tackled Jaime. She fought, but he pinned her down. Cassandra bent over Jaime. Blood sprayed Cassandra's face as she lowered her mouth to the wounds. Jaime screamed and bucked, throwing Cassandra off, but when she jerked upright, the wounds had closed, leaving the tiny punctures invisible from where I stood.

Jaime scrambled to her feet, then hesitated. Her fingers went to the side of her neck.

"Vampire saliva stops the bleeding," I said.

"Oh," Jaime said, face reddening.

She swayed. Lucas caught her before she fell and guided her over to the chair, which I reclined before she sat down. When she tried to sit upright, I gently restrained her.

"Lie down. You lost a lot of blood. Lucas, could you—"

He stepped through the cabin door bearing a large glass and a carton of juice.

"Perfect," I said. "Thanks."

As I helped Jaime drink some of the juice, Benicio asked whether we thought a blood transfusion should be arranged. Cassandra said it wasn't necessary, that the amount of blood Jaime lost would replace itself without intervention. She'd know, I guess, so we took her word for it. When Jaime finished the juice she lay down and closed her eyes.

"They aren't supposed to do that," she mumbled.

"Do what?" I asked.

She yawned. "Kill the messenger."

Another half-yawn, then Jaime's face went slack. I put my fingers to her neck. Her pulse was steady. I pulled the blanket up over her and turned to the others.

"She's right," I said, keeping my voice low. "No matter how upset the ghost might be, it makes no sense to try to kill Jaime. She's the only one it has any hope of communicating with."

"Unless it knew she wouldn't die," Lucas said. "If so, then one could construe it as a message of sorts, telling us that it not only knows *of* Cassandra, but recognizes her by sight and knows that a vampire can stop blood flow."

"It's a vampire," Cassandra said.

"Not necessarily," I said. "It knew that you could stop the bleeding—any supernatural who's studied vamps knows that. As for the bite marks, they were probably intentionally vampirelike, to drive home its point about you."

"They weren't vampire*like*. They were vampire."

"But—"

"I know the bite of a vampire, Paige. I also know that there is one in this room besides me. I've been around long enough that I can recognize my own kind faster than you can recognize a sorcerer."

"If our ghost is—or was—a vampire, that would explain why it can't make contact with Jaime," Lucas said. "It's trying to do the impossible."

I gave a slow nod. "Meaning that necromancers never hear from dead vampires, not because they don't exist, but because wherever they exist, they're beyond contact. So now we probably know one thing about our ghost. That's a start."

"Two things," Jaime murmured, her eyes still closed. "It's a vamp and it's a she."

Cassandra, Lucas, and I exchanged a look.

"Natasha," I whispered. "She's not missing. She's dead."

CHAPTER 49

THE CURSE OF CLEAR VISION

"When Edward attacked Dana, he said he was doing it for some-one," I said. "Someone she heard as 'Nasha.'" I looked at Benicio. "Something stopped the Nasts from putting an office in Cincinnati. A problem that needed to be cleared up first. Would a local pair of serial-killing vampire immortality questers count?"

He gave a slow nod. "A Cabal always investigates the local supernaturals before building a new office. If they have minor concerns, they usually persuade the offenders to relocate. But in a case such as this, on this scale, particularly one that involves vampires . . . the solution would be a permanent one."

"Kill them."

"Let me make some phone calls," Benicio said. "Before we jump to any conclusions."

"So now you think the Nasts will tell you the truth?"

"No, but with this much detail to prompt their memories, I know people who will."

A half-hour later Benicio confirmed our suspicions. The Nast Cabal had learned of Edward and Natasha's murderous hobby, and decided they wouldn't make good neighbors. According to Benicio's sources, the original plan had been to kill both, but the vampires had outwitted several assassins and fled the country. Unwilling to accept failure so easily, the Cabal sent out one last hit man, who'd managed to behead Natasha. The Nasts then made a mistake. They decided not to spend any more money chasing Edward around the globe. By killing his mate, they'd taught him a lesson he'd not soon forget. And he hadn't.

"They killed Natasha, and he wants revenge," I said. "Understandable . . . when it comes to attacking the Nasts. But what do the other Cabals have to do with it?"

Lucas looked at his father. "A vampire asked for a private meeting with you in July. The Nasts executed Natasha at the end of August. Presumably, if several assassination attempts had been made, the Nasts had been chasing the pair for at least a month. I would say that the timing of that request wasn't coincidental."

"Edward wanted to speak to the Cortez CEO?" I said. "But why?"

"Presumably to request sanctuary," Lucas said. "That's not uncommon. If you are pursued by one Cabal, the best place to go for help is to another Cabal. If the Boyds and St. Clouds were being honest with us, I suspect they'd admit to similar requests."

"In other words, he went to each of the Cabals for help, and they each turned him down, wouldn't even find out what he wanted. And that pissed him off enough to start killing their kids? This doesn't make sense."

"No," Cassandra said, her first words since we'd begun. "It wouldn't. Not to you."

She moved to the window and opened the blind. For a moment, she just stared outside. Then she turned back toward us.

"You have to see this from a vampire's point of view. Do I think such a slight is grounds for killing someone's children? Of course not. But I can understand why Edward might. What is the life of those children to him? No more than those bodies in his field. A means to an end. Is he killing them because he wants them to die? No. He's killing them because he wants to cause pain, to hurt those who hurt him. They killed his life partner. I don't think you really understand what that means."

"They'd been together a long time," I said. "Obviously, they—"

"Obviously nothing. What do you consider a long marriage in your world? Twenty-five years is a cause for great celebration, isn't it? Edward became a vampire when Queen Victoria took the throne. He'd been one for less than a decade when he went to Russia and met Natasha, who had just become one herself. They have never been apart since. One hundred and fifty years together, with no one else: no parents, no siblings, no children, no friends. Nothing but each other."

"Now she's gone, and he wants revenge. He'll keep killing until he's repaid every Cabal for her death, by killing children from each."

"No, he'll keep killing until he's dead," Cassandra said. "Nothing else will stop him. I have no idea what his plan is, and he may very well have one, but he won't stop when he reaches the end, because he won't feel avenged. How could he? No hurt he inflicts on the Cabals will match his own."

"Okay," said a sleepy voice from the other seat. Jaime opened one eye. "I get the whole 'eternal love' thing and, as weird as it sounds, I think you're right that my spook is this Natasha chick, but that leaves one big question. Why the hell would she want to help us catch her man?"

"Does she?" Lucas said. "I'm not certain that would be a correct interpretation of her actions to date. The only clue she's given us is the vampire lead, which was undoubtedly meant not to tell us that our killer is a vampire, but that *she* is."

I nodded. "Maybe figuring that if Jaime knew she was a vampire, she'd know the right way to make contact."

"So what does she want?" Jaime asked.

We all looked at Cassandra.

"I don't know her well enough to answer that," Cassandra said. "The only thing I can say, with some certainty, is that she wasn't a passive or unwilling partner in anything Edward did."

"In other words," I said, "she's not suffering a sudden attack of conscience and wants to help us stop Edward before more kids die."

"Definitely not," Cassandra said. "She may be seeking the same thing they sought before her death: protection from a rival Cabal, offering to help you find Edward on the condition that the Cortezes protect him from the Nasts. Or she may be hoping to feed you false information and lead you away from him."

"Doesn't matter either way," Jaime said. "Unless she learns how to carve words in my flesh, she's not telling us anything. Wherever she is, it's out of necro calling range. She's trying her damnedest to change that, but it's not working."

"And where exactly is she?" I said. "Stuck in limbo? Or a demon dimension? Or some separate vampire afterlife? Maybe if we knew . . ."

"We can look into that," Lucas said. "But we may never find the answer. The important question right now is not where is she, but where is *he*?"

We knew Edward was almost certainly in Miami. Why go elsewhere when all the Cabals were right here? But where to find him? At this point, we might as well grab a map of Miami, start tossing darts into it, and conduct our search that way.

Benicio left shortly after that to start working the Edward angle with the Cabals—or the Cabals that weren't already working it. Presumably, the moment the Nasts heard the words "vampire suspect" they'd known exactly who was killing their kids and had started searching for him. Of course, it would have been nice if they'd shared that information, but that would also mean sharing the glory when he was caught—and accepting full blame for letting him slide from their grasp in the first place.

"The only way you're going to catch him is when he goes for his next victim," Cassandra said as she settled onto our hotel sofa. "And the best way to do that is to set a trap."

"Not a bad idea," Jaime said. "One possible target—or two of them—are your nephews, Lucas. I'm sure your dad won't want us using them for bait, but he's got the firepower to make sure they're safe. If you're there, it wouldn't be too bad for the kids. They know you—"

Lucas shook his head. "They don't know me."

"Well, maybe not very well, but you're their uncle. They see you at Christmas, family picnics, whatever. They—"

"I mean, quite literally, they don't know me. We've never met, and it's unlikely they know I exist. Not only do my nephews not know me from a stranger, they barely know my father—that's Hector's way of punishing him for his succession choice."

"Okay," Jaime said. "But, still, this guy's going to go after those kids sooner or later. Hector knows that. I'm sure he'd help if it meant his kids would be out of danger for good."

"Not if that help also meant helping me, or an investigation he considers mine."

Jaime shook her head. "Man, and I thought my family was looped. Well, maybe we can use someone else. What about the older Nast boy? The one who came here?"

"Sean?" I said.

"Right. Sure, he's a bit older than the rest, but I bet he'd be willing to do it. And Ed sure as hell wouldn't turn down the chance to knock off another Nast."

"Perhaps," Lucas said. "But I wouldn't know where to find Sean. Thomas removed him and Bryce from Miami the day Stephen was killed. Every Cabal family member under thirty has been evacuated."

"And it won't take long for Edward to figure that out," I said. "When he does, we won't just need to search Miami for him. We'll have a dozen possible victims, in a dozen different cities, to worry about."

"We need to move fast," Lucas said. "To that end, I do have an idea. An instrument of last resort. A clairvoyant."

"Great," Jaime said. "Only one problem. Finding one of those would be tougher than finding Ed himself."

"Not necessarily. I have one among my contacts."

"Seriously?" Jaime said. "Who?"

"Faye Ashton."

"She's still alive?" Cassandra shook her head. "I'm glad to hear it, but I can't see how she'd be much help. Quite mad."

I shivered. "That's what usually happens, isn't it? To real clairvoyants. Their visions drive them insane. Like the really good nec—" I stopped myself.

"Necromancers," Jaime said. "Don't worry, Paige, you're not telling me anything I don't already know. By the time my nan died, she was hardly the picture of mental stability. It's worse for the clairvoyants, though. If this Faye is well, fey, how can she help?"

"She can, with effort, clear her thoughts temporarily," Lucas said. "I have an open invitation to use her powers, but given the strain it would place on her already fragile condition, I've never accepted her offer. I haven't visited her at all this trip, knowing that she's likely heard about the case and would want to help."

"She's here?" I said. "In Miami?"

Lucas nodded. "In a private nursing home, a Cortez-run mental-health facility."

"So your dad's looking after her?" I said.

"He should. He's the reason she's in there."

The dictionary defines a clairvoyant as someone who can see objects or actions beyond the natural boundaries of sight. That's a near-perfect description of a true clairvoyant. With the right cues, they can see through the eyes of a person miles away. A good clairvoyant can go beyond mere sight and pick up a sense of their target's intentions or emotions. It's not mind reading, but it's as close as any supernatural can get.

A clairvoyant is also the closest thing the supernatural world has to a soothsayer. None of us can truly foresee the future, yet a clairvoyant can make educated guesses about a person's future actions based on their current situation. For example, if they "see" a person nursing a sore tooth, they can "foresee" that person visiting a dentist in the near-future. Some clairvoyants attune this deductive skill to the point where they appear to have the gift of prophecy.

I'd never actually met a clairvoyant. Even my mother met only one in her long life. Like spell-casting, it is an inherited gift, but so few people carry the gene that there are only a handful of clairvoyants born each generation, and they learn to hide their gift right from the cradle. Why? Because their powers are so valuable that anyone who finds a clairvoyant, and reports it to the Cabals, would reap a lottery-size reward.

To a Cabal, a clairvoyant is a prize beyond measure. They are the living equivalent of a crystal ball. Tell me what my enemies are plotting. Tell me what my allies are plotting. Tell me what my family is plotting. A Cabal CEO with a good clairvoyant on staff can double his profits and cut his internal problems in half. And the Cabals fully acknowledge the clairvoyants' value, treating and rewarding them better than any other nonsorcerer employee. So why do the clairvoyants go to extremes to avoid such a dream job? Because it will cost them their sanity.

Good necromancers are plagued by demanding spirits. They're taught how to erect the mental ramparts but, over time, the cracks begin to show, and the best necromancers almost invariably are driven mad by late middle age. To maintain their sanity for as long as possible they must regularly relieve the pressure by lowering the gate and communicating with the spirit world. It's like when Savannah wants something I don't think she should have—after enough pestering, I'll negotiate a compromise, knowing that will grant me a few months of peace before the pleading starts again. Clairvoyants also live with constant encroachments on their mental barricades, images and visions of other lives. When they lower the gate, though, it doesn't quite close properly, and gapes a little more each time.

In effect, the Cabals take the clairvoyants and use them up. The power, and the temptation to use it, is so great that they force the clairvoyant to keep "seeing" until the gates crash down and they are swept into a nightmare world of endless visions, seeing everyone else's lives and losing sight of their own.

That is what Benicio did with Faye Ashton. Lucas's grandfather had taken Faye as a child, then put her aside for safekeeping until she came into her full powers. By then Benicio was CEO. For twenty years, Faye had been the Cortez clairvoyant. A long life span for a clairvoyant, which may suggest that Benicio tried to conserve her powers, but the end result was the same. She went mad, and he put her in the home where she'd lived for the last decade.

Along with some of her powers, she'd retained enough of her sanity to never let Benicio near her again. Lucas, though, was another matter. Not only had she known him since he was a child, but she never turned down the opportunity to help anyone who fought the Cabals. So she'd given Lucas carte blanche to use her powers. Yet he never had. Although she assured him that the occasional "seeing" wasn't going to damage her already ruined mind, he'd always been unwilling to take the chance. Now, though, we had nowhere else to turn.

The nursing home was a century-old manor in a neighborhood where most homes had long since been converted to medical and legal offices, as the cost of maintaining the monstrosities overshadowed their historical value. From the street, the nursing home appeared to be one of the few still used as a private residence, with no signage and a front yard that hadn't been converted into a parking lot.

We parked in the driveway, behind a minivan. At the door, Lucas rang the bell. A few minutes later, an elderly black man opened the door and ushered us inside. When the door closed, it was like stepping into Cortez headquarters. All street noise vanished; I suspected the house had first-rate soundproofing, probably to keep the neighbors from realizing this wasn't a private home.

Inside, nothing disturbed this veneer of domestic normalcy, not a reception desk or nurse's station, not even the usual hospital stink of disinfectant and overcooked food. The front door opened into a tastefully decorated hallway with a parlor to one side and a library on the other. A woman's laugh fluttered down from the second level, followed by a low murmur of conversation. The only smells that greeted us were fresh-cut flowers and fresher-baked bread.

Lucas exchanged greetings with the caretaker, Oscar, and introduced me. As Lucas had explained earlier, both Oscar and his wife, Jeanne, were shamans, a race whose reputation for compassion and stability made them excellent nurses for the mentally ill. This was a long-term care facility, and none of the eight residents were ever expected to leave. All were former Cabal employees. All were here ostensibly because of excellent employee benefits packages, but in reality because the Cortez Cabal was responsible for their madness.

"It's good to see you," Oscar said, patting Lucas on the back as we headed down the hallway. "Been over a year, hasn't it?"

"I've been—"

"Busy." Oscar smiled. "It was an observation, not an accusation. We all know how busy you are."

"How is Faye?"

"No better. No worse. I told her you were coming, so she's ready. Woman's got the strength of a bull. She can be completely catatonic, but the moment I say someone's coming to see her, she pulls it together." He grinned over at me. "Well, unless she doesn't want to see them, in which case she plays possum. I suppose you two are here about those kids being killed."

Lucas nodded. "Does Faye know about it?"

"The damn woman's clairvoyant, boy. Course she knows. We tried to keep the news from her, but she sensed something was up and badgered one of her outside friends into spilling the beans. Been pestering us to get hold of you ever since, but we said, no, Faye, if he wants your help, he'll come get it."

"Has she . . . seen anything?"

"If she had, I'd have tracked you down. Everyone's been careful not to give her any details. That way she won't start fishing around that big psychic pond and strain herself."

"We can provide her with sufficient details to avoid that," Lucas said. "Yet, if you feel it would still be too great a strain—"

"Don't you answer that," called a strident voice. A small, white-haired woman wheeled herself into the doorway. "You send him away, Oscar Gale, and I'll make your life hell. You know I will."

Oscar smiled. "I wasn't going to do that, Faye. You'll be fine. You always are."

Faye reversed her wheelchair, vanishing into the room. We followed.

CHAPTER 50

BLACK HOLE OF HATE

Faye Ashton was a tiny woman who, had she stood, probably wouldn't have topped five feet. I doubted she weighed more than a hundred pounds. Though she was only in her late fifties, her hair was pure white and her face was lined with wrinkles. Her dark eyes danced with energy, giving her face the haunted look of a young spirit trapped within a body that had grown old before its time.

The wheelchair wasn't the result of age or mental infirmity. Faye had been in one since a childhood battle with polio. That was how the Cabal found her. When Faye's father, her clairvoyant parent, had been unable to cope with her growing medical bills, he'd contacted the Cortez Cabal and made them an offer. If they would give Faye the best possible care, they could take her. And they had.

As Oscar closed the door behind us, Faye wheeled her chair in a sharp 180.

"Took you long enough . . . and don't give me any of that crap about not wanting to hurt me. There's not enough left to hurt."

"We had other leads to pursue," Lucas said.

Faye grinned. "Good answer." She looked at me. "You must be Ruth Winterbourne's girl."

"Paige," I said, offering my hand.

She took my hand and, with a shockingly firm grip, pulled me down to kiss my cheek. Then she put her hands on either side of my face and held it in front of hers, eyes searching mine. A sheen of perspiration covered her forehead. After a minute, she released me and smiled.

"Wonderful," she said.

"I think so," Lucas said.

Faye laughed. "You should. You couldn't do better. Now, what do you have for me?"

Lucas told her the details, particularly those about Edward. He also gave her a photo of Edward and Natasha that he'd taken from their house, plus a shirt he'd removed from Edward's laundry hamper. I hadn't known he'd taken either. He must have already been considering contacting Faye.

As Faye listened, the sheen of perspiration spread to her cheeks and jaw, then beaded into rivulets of sweat. The room was cool, with a faint air-conditioned breeze that set goose bumps springing up on my bare arms, but obviously that wasn't enough for Faye. When Lucas finished, I offered to find Oscar and see if we could get Faye a fan or a cold drink.

"It's not the temperature, hon," she said. "It's me. Keeping the old brain clear takes some effort."

I remembered something my mother had done for a necromancer friend when she'd begun losing her battle with the spirit world.

"Can I try something?" I asked. "A spell?"

"You're welcome to try."

I cast a calming spell, then recast it for added strength. Faye closed her eyes. Her lips moved soundlessly, then she peeked one eye open.

"Not bad," she said, then opened the other eye. She smiled and rolled her shoulders. "Well, that gives a bit of relief. What was it?"

"Just a calming spell. Any witch can do one. I'm surprised they don't have a witch here. Shamans are great caretakers, but for a nurse, you really should have a witch."

Faye snorted. "Try telling that to those damned sorcerers."

"I will," I said. "I'll speak to Benicio next time I see him."

Faye's eyebrows shot up, and her lips curved just a fraction, as if waiting to burst into a laugh when I acknowledged the joke.

"She's quite serious," Lucas said. "She'll tell him and, even more shocking, he'll probably listen."

"I have leverage," I said, slanting a look toward Lucas.

Faye threw back her head, laughter filling the room. "You found the bastard's weakness, did you? Clever girl. If you can get me a witch, you'll move to the top of my approved visitors list. Now, let's see what I can do for *you*."

Faye laid Edward's photo on her lap and stared down at it. I took a chair slightly behind Faye, knowing it was always easier to concentrate when your audience was out of sight. Lucas pulled a chair over beside mine.

After a moment, Faye's shoulders dropped and she slouched forward. I glanced at Lucas. He nodded, telling me this was normal. At least ten minutes of silence passed. Then Faye's body tensed. Her mouth opened.

"I have—"

She gasped and her body jerked upright, eyes rolling to the whites. Lucas leapt up. She blinked, recovering, and shooed Lucas away.

"Sorry," she said. "Wrong tactic. I was too open. Got an emotional shock wave."

"You found him?" Lucas said.

"Big black hole of hate? That'd be him. Damn thing nearly sucked me right in." She shivered, then straightened. "Okay, round two coming up. This time, I'll turn off the emotional radar and stick to the visuals."

Faye dropped her head and, this time, took only a minute to hone in on Edward.

"He's sitting on the edge of a bed, staring at the wall. That doesn't help you much. Let me look around. Bed, dresser, television, two doors . . . wait, there's something on the back of the door. A fire escape plan. So we're talking motel or hotel. No surprise there. Details, details . . . I see a window. Looks out over the top of buildings, so let's narrow that down to hotel, something with at least three floors, he's probably on the third or fourth. The room's clean. Not so much as a sock on the floor. Okay, start directing."

"Back to the window," Lucas said. "Describe the buildings you see outside."

"Two. Both concrete, lots of windows. A tall one in the far distance, the shorter one in front of it, maybe fifty feet from the window. Doesn't leave much of a view."

"Any distinguishing marks on either?"

"No—wait, there's a sign on the farther one, on the roof, but it's too far to read."

"Do you see the sun?"

"No."

"Shadows?"

"There's one cast by the window."

"Which direction is the shadow falling?"

Faye smiled. "Clever boy. The shadow slants straight into the room, meaning the window points south."

"Back to the fire evacuation notice. Can you get close enough to read it?"

"Yes, but it doesn't list the hotel name or room number. Already thought of that."

"Does it have the room rate?"

"Ah, yes. One hundred dollars even."

"Good."

Lucas directed Faye around the room some more, but found nothing useful. Though I cast the occasional calming spell, she was starting to sweat again, so Lucas concluded the search.

"One last thing," Faye said. "Let me do a quick read. He's still sitting there, so he must be thinking. If he's planning something, I might be able to give you a heads-up."

She went quiet, dropping her head to her chest again. A minute of silence passed, then she shuddered and her head jerked back, pupils flicking like someone in REM sleep. Lucas laid his hand on her shoulder. After a moment, she shuddered again.

"Sorry, it's that damned black hole again. It's . . . I've never felt anything like it. She meant so much to him." Faye swallowed. "Well, even Hitler loved his dog, right? Doesn't make someone a good person, and this one definitely isn't. Only thing he cared about was her. Okay, let me have another go—"

"Maybe you shouldn't."

"I've got it. Just hold on." She exhaled and let her head fall again. "He's frustrated. The killing—it doesn't help, doesn't fill the void. He needs more. There's one he was saving for last, but he can't wait. He's going to—" Her head snapped back, hitting the wheelchair headrest so hard it jumped.

"Oh." The single word came like a gasp.

Her arms gripped the sides of her wheelchair as her body stiffened, torso rising out of the chair. Lucas and I both jumped up. Before we could reach her, her body went as straight as a board, and she slid from the chair. Lucas lunged and grabbed her before she hit the floor. She convulsed, eyes rolling, mouth open. I grabbed a pen from a nearby table, opened her mouth, and stuck it in to hold her tongue down. Then she stopped. Just stopped, as if frozen in place. Lucas gently lowered her to the floor.

"I'll get Oscar," he said.

"Is she—"

"She'll be okay. This is, I fear, her normal state. Catatonic."

As he left, I rearranged Faye's arms, trying to make her more comfortable, though I knew she was beyond caring. As I adjusted her head, I caught a glimpse of her eyes, wide and unseeing. No, not unseeing. Leaning over her, I saw movement there, her pupils contracting and flickering, ever so slightly, like someone watching television. Only it wasn't a television screen she was seeing, but the tiny screen in her own mind, playing a hundred movies of a hundred lives, all glimmering past so fast her brain could no longer make any sense of them.

I *would* talk to Benicio about getting Faye a witch nurse. It wouldn't cure her, but anything had to be better than . . . this. Yes, that would mean advocating that a witch take a job with a Cabal, something I'd never thought I'd do, but the sad truth was that there were dozens of witches eager for Cabal employment, and if it meant they could help someone like Faye, well, for now, that was the best I could do.

CHAPTER 51

HOTEL SHOPPING

By evening we'd checked out nearly half the hotels in Miami as we'd searched for one with a view that matched what Faye had seen outside Edward's window. We'd started by targeting those hotels with rack rates of a hundred dollars. Tougher than it might sound. It was a nice, even number, and many hotels had at least a few rooms at that rate.

When we first left Faye, we'd called Jaime, who'd offered to split the phone-book list with us. After we found a few possibilities, Jaime suggested she and Cassandra take over the phone calls while we did the footwork. A wise arrangement, except that Jaime and Cassandra found so many hotels with rooms at a hundred dollars that we couldn't begin to keep up.

At eight, Jaime called.

"We're still working on the last batch," I said when I answered.

"That's what I figured. I'm calling to say we're holding the rest of the list hostage. You guys have been at it for six hours, and I know you haven't eaten dinner. Probably skipped lunch, too."

"We just need to—"

"No. Seriously, Paige. Time to call it a day. Better to quit now, get food, get sleep, and get cracking again at daybreak."

As much as I hated to quit, this did make sense. With night falling, we could barely make out the buildings surrounding the hotels. I relayed the advice to Lucas, who agreed.

"Good," Jaime said when I told her. "There's a bar down the road here, advertises full-kitchen service until midnight. I'll meet you there in half an hour. If you keep working, you'll keep me waiting. I can cause a lot of trouble left alone in a bar. Remember that."

We did keep Jaime waiting fifteen minutes, but only because Lucas had another idea that he wanted to pursue immediately. The Cabal had satellite photos of Miami. Maybe with those we'd have more luck picking out the configuration of buildings Faye had described. Cortez headquarters was on the way, so we stopped by, and had copies of the photos in less than twenty minutes.

Despite her threat, Jaime hadn't caused any trouble at the bar. She wasn't alone, either. When I noticed a figure across the table from her, I immediately thought male, then noticed that it was Cassandra. The three of us ordered dinner, while Cassandra nursed her wine.

Jaime had managed to bully Lucas into not examining the photos while we ate, but the moment the plates left the table, he had them out. I tried helping, but we only had one magnifying glass, and the details were too small to see with the naked eye, so I let Jaime talk me into a post-dinner drink.

Halfway through the drinks, Cassandra got off a "celebrity necro" jab at Jaime, who responded by bringing up her favorite issue.

"I'm not dead," Cassandra said, barely ungritting her teeth enough to let the words out.

"Care to test that theory? Let's say you find a guy lying on the ground, and you're not sure if he's dead or alive. How do you tell? Three ways. Heartbeat, pulse, breathing. Here, Cass, give me your wrist, let me check your pulse."

Cassandra glared and sipped her wine.

"Not seeing any condensation on that glass, Cass. Something tells me you're not breathing."

Cassandra's glass rapped against the tabletop. "I'm not dead."

"Geez, you sound like that Monty Python skit. You guys ever see that one? They're cleaning up the plague victims and one keeps saying: 'I'm not dead yet.' Sounds just like you, Cassandra. Well, except he had a British accent." Jaime sipped her drink. "Anyway, I don't see what the big deal is. You *look* like you're alive. Now zombies, there's a nasty afterlife."

"Speaking of zombies," I began, eager to segue off this subject. "I heard some necro in Hollywood raised a real one for that movie, oh, what was it called—"

"*Night of the Living Dead?*" Lucas said.

His leg brushed mine under the table. Last spring we'd tried to overcome a hellish day by watching that movie, before moving on to better methods of distraction. Our first night together. Our eyes met and we both grinned, then Lucas returned to his work.

"No, not that one," I said. "Something recent."

"I heard the rumor," Jaime said. "Makes a good story, but it's not true. The only living dead in Hollywood is Clint Eastwood."

I sputtered my drink. Jaime patted my back and laughed.

"Oh, I'm kidding. But he kinda looks it, don't you think? The man has not aged well."

"I wouldn't say that," Cassandra murmured.

"Well, I would," Jaime said. "And what I want to know is why, in every goddamned movie, he gets paired up with some hot little number a quarter his age."

"Jealous?" Cassandra said.

Jaime snorted. "Yeah, like I want to walk around with an eighteen-year-old guy on my arm. Nothing wrong with having fun, but you gotta keep your dignity. My rule: no guys more than a decade older or five years younger. The whole cougar thing is so . . ." She shuddered and pulled a face.

"Cougar?" Lucas said, glancing up from his photos.

"Women who date significantly younger men," I said.

"Why are you looking at me, Paige?" Cassandra said.

"I wasn't—"

"I can hardly date men my own age, can I?" Cassandra added.

Jaime laughed. "Got a point there, Cass. How old were you when you die—changed? About my age, I'll bet."

"Forty-five."

Jaime nodded. "If I could stop aging at some point, it'd be here. I know, most women—hell, most *people*—they'd go for their twenties, maybe thirties, but I like forty. Got the experience under your belt, but the body is still in perfect working order. A damn fine age for a woman." She lifted her glass. "Take that, Clint."

We ordered another round of drinks, talked a bit longer, then headed back to the hotel.

On the plane we'd agreed to meet Benicio for breakfast the next day, to share progress on the case. Now that we had a solid lead, we hated to waste time on something as trivial as eating. Yet when Lucas suggested that we needed to start our day early, Benicio offered to meet us at our hotel for breakfast at six, and keep his visit short. Not much we could say about that.

When we got to the restaurant, Troy slipped in ahead of us. He cornered the hostess, murmured something, and passed her a folded bill. A minute later, the hostess returned and escorted us to the patio. Our table was in the far corner. The three closest tables sported RESERVED tent cards.

I supposed that was what the extra tip was for, guaranteeing our privacy. Since the restaurant was almost empty at this hour, it was a request easily accommodated. Troy and Morris took the next nearest table.

After we ordered our meal, I asked Benicio about hiring a witch nurse for Faye.

"A calming spell, hmm?" he said, unfolding his napkin. "Never could get that one to work myself. Do you think it would help the other residents as well?"

I hesitated, not because I wasn't ready with an answer, but because the thought of Benicio Cortez practicing witch magic . . . well, it was enough to render even me momentarily speechless.

"Er, yes," I said. "I think it would. That's just an educated guess, of course. You'd have to test it on the others."

He nodded. "I'll hire a witch part-time for Faye then, and if she can help the others, we'll make it a full-time position. Now, my contacts in the witch community are, as you might guess, quite poor. We'll discuss this later, but I may need your help finding someone qualified—"

"I'm sure you can do so without Paige's assistance, Papá," Lucas said. "Witches apply for Cabal positions all the time. Human resources should be able to provide all the contact names you need."

"Perhaps, but if I have any questions, Paige, may I call you?"

I glanced at Lucas, who gave a soft sigh, then the barest nod.

"If it means getting a good witch nurse for Faye, you can call me," I said.

Benicio opened his mouth with what I was sure was another "request," but was diverted by the arrival of our coffee. We spent the next minute in silence, each fixing our drinks.

"So, Paige," Benicio said after his first sip of coffee. "How do you like Miami?"

A new topic. Thank God. I relaxed into my chair. "Can't say I've had much time for sightseeing, but I've certainly enjoyed the sunshine."

"Miami has its charms, though the pace isn't to everyone's taste. Nor the violence. Before you go, Lucas, you should take Paige for a drive, show her where you grew up." He turned to me. "It's a beautiful area. A fraction of Miami's crime rate, the safest streets in Florida, an excellent school system—"

"Any news regarding the case?" Lucas asked.

There wasn't. We told Benicio that we were pursuing a lead, but he didn't press for details, only offered us full use of the Cabal resources, should we need them. We spent the rest of breakfast discussing what the

Cabals were doing to find Edward. The Nasts, as we'd expected, had been searching for him since Friday. Unfortunately, they hadn't found any clues . . . or any they cared to share.

As we neared the end of the meal, Benicio said, "As I was saying earlier, Lucas should take you on a tour of the area. Now, I know, I have a vested interest in wanting my son living closer than Oregon, but there is Savannah to consider. You've already had one bad experience keeping custody of her and, although you handled that very well, it was the *second* attempt, was it not?"

"Second attempt, but same person . . . who is not going to be making any more."

"Maybe so, but now the news of Savannah's desirability has spread across the supernatural world. You must consider that—"

"Both Paige and Savannah are quite happy with Portland," Lucas said.

"I understand, but before you put down permanent roots, you must give the matter serious thought. You don't want to buy a house in Portland only to realize six months from now that it's unsafe for Savannah."

"I know that," I said. "Which is why I'm not house-shopping until we've been there a year."

"Oh?" Benicio frowned. "I thought you had a house picked out. Lucas said . . ." His voice trailed off as he saw my look of confusion. "Oh, I see he hasn't mentioned it."

"No, I had not," Lucas said, his voice tight. "But thank you for doing so for me." He turned to me and lowered his voice. "I'll explain later."

We finished the meal in silence.

"What house?" I said before the hotel room door closed behind us.

"I believe I mentioned a potential arrangement with my last client, who, feeling indebted—"

"What house?" I said, throwing my purse onto the sofa. "The condensed version."

"You're understandably upset—"

"Hell, yes, I'm upset. You're making long-term plans for us and I have to hear it from your *father*?"

"It's not as it sounds. When he first called me in Chicago, he wanted to talk about our apartment. He didn't think it was right, me expecting you and Savannah to live there because I refuse to dip into my trust fund. I told him the apartment was short-term. He wouldn't listen, so I said that I had a lead on a house in Portland."

"Why didn't you tell me? We haven't discussed this, Lucas." I thumped down onto the couch and rubbed my temples. "If this was meant to be a surprise—"

"No, certainly not. I would never presume anything like that. Once this was over, I planned to show you the house and, if you liked it, then it would be yours to take at the offered price, whether you chose to share it with me or not."

"Whether I chose—? What the hell is that supposed to mean?"

He sat on the couch beside me, close but not touching. "I would have mentioned it, but I wanted to get through this first. It seemed unfair to discuss long-term plans now, when you were getting your first glimpse of what a life with me might entail—the . . . familial issues."

"So, you think I'm going to turn tail and run?"

He managed a wry smile. "I'm surprised you haven't already."

"No, I'm serious. Is that really what you think? That I care so little for you that I'd—" I shifted down the couch, away from him. "I knew all about your 'familial issues' when we got together, Lucas."

"Yes, but you may have been unprepared for the impact it could have on our lives. I would completely understand—"

"Would you?" I said, springing to my feet. "You'd understand if I walked out the door? Said 'Sorry, not for me'? Just like you'd understand if you showed me this house and I said, 'I'll take it . . . now where are you going to live?'"

"I don't want to pressure you, Paige. Of course, I don't want you to leave, and, yes, I want to get this house with you, but if that's not what you want—" He reached for my arm, but I yanked it back.

"You have no idea how I feel about you, do you?"

When he hesitated, I strode to the door. Then I paused, hand on the knob. I couldn't do this. Not now.

"Come on," I said. "We have work to do."

The Cabal photos of Miami had given Lucas a half-dozen possible hotels, which we now needed to check. As for our spat, neither of us mentioned it, though the heavy silence in the car said we were both thinking about it. As much as I wanted to resolve the problem and get past it, I told myself it was better to ignore it for now. Plenty of time to fix things later.

On the fourth possibility, we found a match. A five-story mid-price hotel, with a southern view that matched Faye's description.

We were walking up the side alley, heading for the front of the building, when Lucas's cell phone rang.

"That was Oscar," he said when he hung up. "Faye's awake and very upset. All he can make out is that she wants to see me—immediately."

"Damn," I said.

"If she has new information on the case, it almost certainly relates to Edward's whereabouts, which we've probably found, rendering her information welcome but potentially unnecessary. At this point—" He looked up at the hotel. "I'm loath to walk away, however briefly, from the best lead we've had."

"I could go talk to Faye," I said. "But if Edward's in this hotel, I'd rather back you up."

"And I'd rather have you backing me up."

"What about sending Jaime? She's good with people, and it sounds like she's had some experience with Faye's type of condition, with her grandmother."

"Good idea."

Lucas called. Jaime was still in bed, but once she had woken up enough to understand what he was asking, she agreed to speak to Faye. If it was important, she'd call me back. So Lucas turned off his phone, I switched mine to vibrate, and we headed into the hotel.

"Sure, yeah," the young desk clerk said, head bobbing as he looked at the photo Lucas held. "Room three-seventeen. That's him."

"He's still checked in?"

"Right."

"Has he gone out yet this morning?"

"Not this way." He checked his watch. "And not this early. He usually heads out around noon, comes back after my shift."

Lucas wrote down a phone number. "If he comes down, wait until he's gone, then call this number. But only after he's left. Don't do anything to make him suspicious."

"Sure." The young man's head bobbed. "Okay. Sure."

Lucas strode through the front doors, face grim.

"Time to call the SWAT team?" I said.

"I'm afraid we have more immediate concerns. Right now that clerk is on the phone to Edward, warning him we're here."

"What?"

Lucas rounded the building corner, walking so fast I had to jog to keep up. "I introduced us as NSA, told him we needed to find this man immediately. The first thing he should think, given the current climate, is 'terrorist.' But he doesn't ask any questions, even after I tell him not to raise the man's suspicions, implying he's dangerous. He tells us what we want to know and gets us out of there fast so he can call Edward, collect whatever reward Edward offered for warning him."

"And once Edward gets that call, he'll grab his things and bail."

"Precisely. Now—" He stopped halfway between the front of the hotel and the side door. "I want you to stand here. Cast a cover spell. If he comes out, don't do anything. Let him go, but watch where he heads, then get me. I'll be around back watching that door."

I nodded, but Lucas had already broken into a jog, heading toward the rear. I stood against the wall opposite the hotel, and hid behind a cover spell.

Less than two minutes later, the side door opened. A man stepped out. He wore a baggy windbreaker, sweatpants, sunglasses, and a ball cap pulled low, but none of that left any question that it was the man from the photograph: Edward.

Edward stepped out from behind the door and looked both ways. When his gaze passed over me, I resisted the urge to hold my breath, and concentrated instead on staying perfectly still. He eased the door shut. Then he lowered his knapsack to the ground, bent, and opened it. As he crouched there, I couldn't help thinking how easy it would be to trap him in a binding spell. All I needed to do was break cover for a second and—

Edward pulled a gun from the knapsack and my idea died mid-thought.

He fiddled with the gun, then tucked it into the pocket of his windbreaker, hoisted his knapsack onto his back, and headed toward the rear of the building. Damn it! If only Lucas and I had practiced my long-range communication spell more, I could warn him. He'd be hiding, but not under a cover spell, since his cast wasn't reliable yet. I reassured myself that Lucas knew better than to pop out of hiding the moment he heard someone. Not that he'd even hear Edward. The man walked across the gravel like it was a foam cushion, not so much as rattling a stone underfoot. He stuck to the shadows, glancing over his shoulder with every few steps. Right before he reached the back of the building, he turned left and seemed to walk right through the wall I stood against.

I counted to three, then broke cover and leaned out to see an adjoining alley farther down. I took one slow step. The crunch of gravel under my feet resounded like thunder. I quickly recast my cover, but Edward didn't return. Again, I broke cover. Again, I took a single step. Again, the gravel crackled underfoot.

This wasn't working. After a moment's thought, I cast a light-ball and tossed it down the alley, praying Edward didn't pick that very moment to look behind him. When Lucas saw the ball, he peered around the corner. I gestured to the side alley. He nodded, darted across the alley, and pressed himself against the far wall. Then he inched to the opening and peeked down it. As he pulled back, he waved me forward.

When I got to the adjoining alley it was empty. Lucas motioned that Edward had slipped into a corridor farther down.

"He has a gun," I mouthed, pantomiming a pistol with my hand.

Lucas nodded and we set off in pursuit.

CHAPTER 52

THE TARGET

We hurried along the passage, then peeked into the cross-alley Edward had taken. It ended at a street. Edward stepped onto the sidewalk and turned right. We hustled to the end of the alley and looked out. Edward was poised on the curb of a busy road, as if debating whether to dodge through traffic. Lucas motioned for me to get into a better viewing position and cast a cover spell. I did.

After a moment on the curb, Edward wheeled and headed left along the sidewalk. At the first stoplight, he joined a small crowd and waited, rocking on the balls of his feet. When the light changed, he wove through the other pedestrians, then darted into the first door on the other side.

I broke cover.

"He went into a coffee shop," I said. "Lying low?"

"Perhaps. I'll take a look. Once I verify he's there, I'll call for backup. Best not to try taking him in on our own, not when he's armed."

"But he's in a public place. He wouldn't dare shoot—"

"Are you sure?"

"You're right. In that case, though, I'm not sure I even want you peeking in the window. We need a spell. What about that glamor spell? The one you used with Savannah, to make me look like Eve."

"It only works if the viewer wants or expects to see someone else. I don't know how much information that desk clerk gave Edward, but I suspect he knows who he's watching out for. I believe we're down to the most obvious, and least satisfactory, choice. Arm myself with a good spell, slip in there, and hope for the best."

"Arm *ourselves*. I'll cover you."

Edward wasn't in the café. Lucas even popped into the men's washroom to be sure, but came out shaking his head. I did a visual sweep of the room. Next to the bathrooms was a short hall with three doors.

Two were marked staff only. The third had a push bar on it—a back exit.

We peeked out the rear door, then stepped into the alley. The empty corridor stretched a half-block in either direction.

"Damn," I muttered.

Lucas surveyed the ground. Water dripped from a leaky eaves trough. During the cool night, a puddle had formed but now, in the heat of morning, it was drying fast. There were several footprints in the hardening mud, but only one still had water pooled between the tread marks. Lucas gestured in the direction the print pointed.

A dozen yards down, the alley branched off, heading farther away from the street. Lucas motioned for me to wait, then peered around the wall. A second later, he pulled back, brows knitting, and motioned for me to look.

I glanced around the corner. Edward was there, less than thirty feet away. I started to pull back fast, then noticed he'd stopped with his back to us. His knapsack lay at his feet and he was pulling out a map. Lucas tugged me back, then bent down to my ear.

"Go into the shop," he whispered. "Call my father."

I leaned over to his ear. "What if he leaves?"

"I'll follow and call you."

We'd let the café rear exit close behind us, so I had to walk all the way around the building. I was still in the alley when my phone vibrated. I glanced over my shoulder, but Lucas hadn't moved. I picked up the pace to get to the sidewalk, where I could answer without fear of my voice carrying to Edward. Before I was there, the phone stopped. I'd just set foot on the sidewalk when it vibrated again. I checked the number, but didn't recognize it.

"Hello?"

"Where are you?" Jaime's voice, words rushing out.

"We're—"

"Get over here now. Stop whatever you're doing, grab Lucas, and get over here."

"We can't. We're following Edward. We have him on the run—"

"Shit! No, leave him. Just back off and leave him alone. Where are you? I'll get the Cabal to send someone. Get back here—no, just get someplace—"

"Slow down, Jaime. What's—?"

The line buzzed, then Cassandra came on.

"Paige? Listen to me. We're with Faye. She knows who Edward's next target is. It's—"

I knew what she was going to say even before the name left her lips. I hit disconnect and fumbled to shove the phone back into my pocket, but it slipped and fell to the sidewalk. Ignoring it, I raced back into the alley.

CHAPTER 53

COUP DE GRÂCE

W hen I reached the alley behind the café, Lucas was gone. Edward was on the move. Of course he was. He knew who was chasing him. He wasn't running from Lucas; he was luring him in.

I raced down the adjoining alley, where we'd last seen Edward. I didn't worry about how much noise I made. If Lucas heard me, he'd come running, away from Edward, which was exactly what I wanted.

When I rounded the first junction, I saw Lucas. He was walking carefully, looking from side to side, his back to me. I opened my mouth to shout to him, then stopped. If Edward was lying in wait around the next corner, any disruption could spook him. I wasn't about to spook a vampire with a gun.

I jogged down the alley. A few yards from Lucas, as I ran under a fire escape, a shadow moved overhead. I whirled and looked up to see Edward, crouched on the fire escape.

"Lucas!" I yelled.

As I raced toward Lucas, I realized that we were in a blind alley, with only an alcove adjoining at the end. I wheeled just as Edward leapt to the ground. He raised his gun. I side-lunged into his firing path, and started casting a binding spell. Edward trained the gun on my chest.

"I'll fire before you finish," he said. His sunglasses were gone, and his eyes were as flat and emotionless as his voice. He looked over my shoulder at Lucas, who'd also frozen mid-incantation. "You, too. Cast and I'll shoot her."

"Paige," Lucas said. "Step aside. Please."

"So he can shoot you? You're the one he's after. That was the message Faye was trying to give us. You're the target."

"Do you really think I won't shoot because you're in the way?" Edward said.

Yet he didn't. He lifted the gun, as if considering firing over my shoulder at Lucas, then lowered it back to my chest, clearly not comfortable enough with his marksmanship to try for anything but a torso shot. He might not care about adding me to his body count, but he wouldn't take the chance that, in the time it took to shoot me, Lucas could cast a spell and escape.

"Do you know what Benicio will do to you if you kill Lucas?" I said.

"Same thing everyone else wants to do. Hunt me down and kill me. Do you think I care? I stopped caring the day I came back to my hotel room and found those Cabal assassins had finished their job."

"We—"

"I walked into that room, and do you know what I saw?" His gaze skewered mine. "Her head on the bedpost. My wife's head on the bedpost!"

I tried to summon up some sympathy, but all I could think about were the dozens of bodies buried behind that cabin.

A soft breeze fluttered down the alley, coming from behind us. Though I didn't dare peek over my shoulder, I knew there was a three-story wall behind Lucas. No breeze could come through that. Was I casting without knowing it? I'd done that once before, under stress. Could I do it again? But no, I couldn't rely on magic. Not now. I plowed ahead.

"So you took what was dearest to them," I said. "But when Benicio finds out—"

"Are you listening? Have you heard a word I've said? I don't care!"

"But you wanted immortality—"

"I wanted eternal life with my *wife*. Without her, it doesn't matter."

A gust of wind whipped through the alley, making us all freeze. It came again, not so much a wind now as a quaking, as if the air itself was heaving, churning.

Edward stepped to the side fast and raised the gun at Lucas. I pitched sideways, throwing myself into his path, but the air around us vibrated so violently that I lost my balance and fell to one knee. As I twisted, the still-healing knife wounds blazed and I gasped.

"Don't move, Paige," Lucas said, his voice tight. "Please, don't move."

I shifted my eyes, straining to see Edward. He had the gun pointed at my chest.

"Don't do this," Lucas said. "She hasn't done anything to you. If you let her go, I can promise you—"

Edward swung the gun toward Lucas. "Shut up."

"Listen to him, Edward," I said. "If you stop now, you can be with Natasha."

"Natasha is gone!"

"No, she's not. She's a ghost."

His lips twisted. "You lying bitch. You'd say anything to save him, wouldn't you?"

He started to turn the gun on me. Then the air around us crackled and popped, and he swung the gun back toward Lucas.

"I told you, any magic and—"

Behind Lucas, the air darkened, then the backdrop shattered, like a mirror breaking. Light streamed through. A woman's figure appeared in the light. Edward looked up. He blinked.

"Nat—? Natasha?"

She reached for him. Edward took a slow, cautious step forward. Then suddenly, Natasha's body jerked ramrod straight. The hole shimmered around her. Her eyes went wide and her mouth opened in a silent scream, and she tumbled back into the yawning hole, arms still stretching toward Edward.

"No!" Edward shouted.

The gun jerked, then fell from his hand as he raced for the portal. I saw the gun fall. I swear that is the first thing I saw, and in that moment I knew Lucas was safe. Then Lucas toppled backward, a dark hole in his breast pocket. Then, only then, I heard the shot echoing through the alley.

I twisted around. Lucas was still falling into the hole. The light swallowed his head, then his chest, and finally his feet.

I dove in after him.

CHAPTER 54

THROUGH THE BACK DOOR

I was jumping on a bed, leaping as high as I could, shrieking each time my feet struck down. Someone was singing. My mother? No, a younger voice, struggling to sing without laughing.

Five little monkeys jumping on the bed.
One fell off and bumped his head.
Momma called the doctor and the doctor said,
"No more monkeys jumping on the bed!"

"Again!" I screamed. "Again!"

"Again?" the voice laughed. "If you break your mother's bed, she'll have both our hides."

I threw my chubby fists in the air as I jumped, then lost my footing and collapsed face-first into the pillows. Hands reached down to pick me up, but I pushed them back, got up, and whirled around, bouncing.

"Again! Again!"

A dramatic sigh. "One more time, Paige. I mean it. This is the last time."

I giggled, knowing this would be far from the last time.

Five little monkeys . . .

I groaned and the dream faded, but I could still hear the song, that same person singing it. The voice tickled a memory, but it evaporated before I could seize it.

I opened my eyes, but could see nothing. A cold, damp darkness enveloped me and I shivered. I blinked and tried to clear my fogged brain. I was lying on my side. I reached out and touched something cold but smooth and solid. As I ran my hand across it, I felt bumps and sharp edges. Rock. I was lying on rock.

Four little monkeys jumping on the bed . . .

I squeezed my eyes shut, but the tune kept playing in my head. What was that song? Now that I heard it, I could say every word by heart, as they bubbled up from my subconscious. An image came to mind. Me, no more than two years old, jumping on my mother's bed as someone sang.

"No more monkeys jumping on the bed!"

Three little monkeys—

"Oh, God, stop!" I said, cradling my booming head.

The song stopped.

A voice sighed, that same dramatic sigh I'd heard in my dream. "Well, it was either that or scream until you woke up. Be glad I took the musical approach."

I scrambled up and looked around. My eyes had adjusted enough that I could make out dim shapes around me, but none looked remotely human. I blinked hard and focused. Scattered around me were huge boulders, rising up from the stone bed on which I lay.

"Rock," I said. "It's all rock."

"Weird, huh? We have some very strange places here. Looks like you landed in one of them. Let's just hope nothing nasty pops out."

My head whipped around, searching for the source of the voice, but I saw only rocks.

Two little monkeys . . .

"Stop that," I said.

"Hey, I'm trying to jar your memory. You used to love that song. Savannah did, too. Both of you, crazy for it, though I think you just liked the excuse to jump on the bed."

Savannah? How did she know—? I swallowed, making the only association I could.

"Eve?" I said.

"Who else? Don't tell me you've forgotten."

When I didn't answer, she said, "Oh, come on. You must remember your favorite babysitter. I looked after you every Wednesday night for nearly two years. If I couldn't make it, you wouldn't let your mom get anyone else. You'd cry so hard she had to cancel the Elders meeting and stay home."

Eve paused. When I still said nothing, she sighed. "You really don't remember, do you? Damn. I usually leave more of an impression."

"Where are you?" I said.

"Hold on. I'm working on that part. Just give me a—" A shimmer of movement to my left. The shape winked, then started coming into focus. "Almost there. This ain't easy, let me tell you."

An audible pop. And there stood a grown-up version of Savannah, a tall, exotically beautiful woman with a wide mouth, strong nose and chin, and long, straight black hair. Only the eyes were different, dark instead of the bright blue Savannah had inherited from Kristof Nast.

She hunkered down before me, then touched the ground and shivered. "Damn cold. You sure picked a helluva place to pop through. If I'd known, I'd have dressed warmer." She caught my eye, her wide grin a mirror of Savannah's. "Ghost humor." She looked down at her clothes: jeans, sneakers, and a dark green embroidered blouse. "You know, I used to really like this blouse, but after wearing it for a year straight . . . Time to figure out how to change clothes." She sized up my ensemble. "Not bad. Could have been worse."

"I'm not—I'm not a ghost. I didn't—"

"Die? Jury's still out on that one. All I know is you're here, and if you're here, you should be dead." Eve shook her head. "Never expected you to go all Romeo and Juliet on me, Paige. I know, once you commit yourself to someone, you go all the way, like you did with Savannah, but, really—" She waved at our surroundings. "This is too far."

"Lucas," I said, scrambling up.

"Easy, girl. He's right over—" Eve stood. "Now where . . . ? Oh, there."

I hurried past her. As I skirted an outcropping of rock, I saw Lucas's shoes. I raced around a large boulder to find him lying on his back, eyes closed. I dropped down beside him, fingers going to his throat, feeling for a pulse.

"Uh, you won't find that, Paige," Eve said behind me. "Not on yourself, either. Part of the passing-over package deal. You can jog all you want and never run out of breath. First time in a week your stomach hasn't hurt, I'll bet."

I touched Lucas's cheek. His skin was warm. I leaned down, bringing my face to his, and gently shook his shoulder as I called his name.

"You could try kissing him," Eve said. "But I don't think that works in real life . . . or real afterlife."

I glared at her. She held up her hands.

"Sorry, not the time for quips." She walked around Lucas and knelt on his other side. "He's okay, baby. This is normal. It's death shock. Takes a day or two to recover. Normally, you'd come through into one of the waiting areas, where there are people to look after you, but you guys took the back door."

"D—death shock?"

I looked down at Lucas's chest. His shirt was whole. I slid my hand under it, but found no bullet hole.

"No, he's okay," I said. "He didn't get shot. He just fell through the rift, like I did."

Eve said nothing.

I turned to face her. "He didn't get shot. Look, no hole."

She nodded, eyes not meeting mine. I swallowed hard, then pulled up my blouse. On my stomach, where Weber had stabbed me, the skin was now smooth and unblemished.

Eve bent over Lucas and adjusted his glasses, which had slipped in the fall. "No need for these here, but they still pass through. Weird, huh?" She leaned back for a better look, then straightened the glasses again and brushed strands of hair off Lucas's forehead. "Poor kid. All these years, being Ben's son was the only thing that protected him, and now it's what killed him." She shook her head. "Did Lucas ever tell you we met?"

I struggled to focus, then nodded. The memory flashed and a tiny smile tweaked my lips. "He said 'encountered' was a more accurate word than 'met.'"

Eve laughed. "That's Lucas, isn't it? Got to be precise." She rocked back on her heels. "How long ago was that? Shit, it has to be four, five years. He couldn't have been more than twenty. Tried to confiscate some of my grimoires. But I caught him. Trounced him good, too."

"So he said."

Eve's left brow shot up. "He admitted it? Well, that's real strength, isn't it? Not being able to knock someone down, but being able to admit it when you're the one who hit the floor. He's a good kid. Good for Savannah, too. You both are." She looked from me to Lucas, then thumped down and pulled her knees up. "Ah, shit, what are we going to do?"

"We need to go back."

"Hey, I'm with you on that one, but it's easier said than done. Normally, it's a one-way ticket, but you guys didn't take that train in, so maybe we can find a way—" Her head snapped back and she glared at something over my head. "Goddamn it, you're worse than a bloodhound. Track me down no matter where I hide." She waved her hands. "Shoo. I'm busy. Go away."

I craned my neck to look behind me, but there was no one there.

"Of course I'm helping her get out of here," she snapped. "What, you want our daughter raised by wolves?"

I hesitated. "Kristof?"

"Yeah. You can't hear him?"

I shook my head.

Eve laughed. "Ha! Hear that, Mr. Almighty Cabal Sorcerer? You can't even project far enough into this dimension for her to hear you. I broke right though. In living color."

"Dimension?"

"Dimension, level, layer," she said, "It's complicated."

"So the real ghosts are all in your layer? The one Kristof's in now?"

"Nah, they're scattered everywhere. That's the bitch of it, really. You pass over, thinking you'll see everyone who left before you, and you don't, because they're not all in your dimension. Some of us, the magical races, can blur a layer or two, see through to the other side, like Kristof's doing. But to pass through—" She grinned in Kristof's direction. "That takes a real spell-caster."

"So my . . . my mother. Is she here?"

Eve shook her head. "Sorry, baby. Not in this layer or in mine. There are others, though. I just haven't figured out how to see through them."

Her gaze shot up again. "Yeah, yeah, funny guy. Go find someone else to pester. I need to talk to Paige."

A pause.

"Is he leaving?" I asked.

"Nah, just sitting there. Being quiet, though, which is the best I can hope for. Now, let's see what we've got here. That vamp bitch Natasha somehow ripped open a hole in her layer. I have no idea how she did that. Hell, I didn't even think vamps *had* a layer. It's all very strange. Almost makes me wonder if the Fates *let* her open it up, so she could suck her fiend-partner into hell with her."

"Uh-huh."

"Nice theory, but it doesn't help you out, right? Point is, you guys fell through by accident, and we need to get you back. Now, since you came through here, this spot must be important. A portal, if you want to get all Trekkie about it."

I looked around.

"Damned ugly place to stick one, isn't it?" she continued. "Which is probably the point. No one comes here sightseeing."

"So, can you break through?"

Eve shot a glare behind me. "Finish that sentence at your peril, Kris." She paused. "That's what I thought." She turned to me. "No can do. Not yet anyway. We need a necromancer."

"Good, I know just where to find one."

"Jaime Vegas?" Eve made a face. "Not my first choice, but I guess any necro will do. Between her and me, we should be able to rip this thing open enough for you to go through."

"*Lucas* and me."

"Uh, right. Now, I can't say it'll work for sure, because I know there's no way for *me* to go back permanently. Believe me, I've tried."

Her eyes cut to Kristof and, for a split second, I caught a glimpse of something in those eyes that sent a shiver down my spine, and reminded me of who and what Eve was. She locked glares with the air behind me.

I suspected whatever Kristof said, it had something to do with Eve trying to cross back into the world of the living. From the way she said it, I guessed she'd been trying damned hard to return to life and, for a moment, I wondered at that. She seemed happy and comfortable enough. It wasn't like she was in some kind of hell dimension. So why fight to return to life?

Even as the question flitted through my brain, I thought of my own situation. I was here, in the afterlife, and not for one second did I consider staying. Why? Because my life was on that other side and, no matter how pleasant it might be to live in a world free of pain and discomfort, I wanted to finish my "real" life before I embarked on my afterlife. That real life, though, included Lucas. It had to.

"So if you can't get back," I said, "then you think maybe we . . . ?"

"I don't know, but I'm sure as hell gonna try. You're a special case, so there's gotta be a way."

"Okay, so let's do it. You're a ghost, so you contact Jaime—"

"It's not that easy. First, we have to find her."

. "Find her? She's in Miami."

"Obstacle number one, though it's not as bad as it seems. Miami exists here, too, only it's not quite . . . well, it's different. Distance isn't a problem. It's all very . . . relative."

"Uh-huh."

Eve shook her head. "I can't explain. Even I don't understand it all yet. Obstacle number two, though—" She looked down at Lucas. "We can't carry him."

"I'm not leaving him here."

"Well, then we have a real problem. He'll wake up in a day or two, but by then, the Searchers will have found us, and once they do, you're taking up permanent residence. Now, we can—" She stopped and looked up at Kristof, then nodded. "Kristof is offering to stay here with Lucas."

When I hesitated, she looked back toward Kristof. "You ripped the poor girl's life apart. That doesn't encourage trust, Kris." She looked at me. "It's okay, Paige. If Kristof says he'll watch Lucas, he will. He has nothing to gain if you and Lucas don't make it back to Savannah. He knows now this is what I want, what I wanted from the start, for Savannah to be with you. He won't interfere again."

Eve stood. I squeezed Lucas's hand, took one last look at him, then followed Eve across the rocky plain.

CHAPTER 55

PRIMEVAL SWAMP

We hiked across the rocky plain for what must have been two hours. One problem with the ghost world? Serious lack of public transportation. Yet, even with all that walking, I didn't suffer so much as sore feet. I suppose that renders motorized vehicles unnecessary. That and the fact that, here, you have all the time in the world to get wherever you're going.

Normally, I guess, travel in the ghost world is like a Sunday stroll, relax and enjoy the scenery. Where we were, though, there was no scenery to enjoy, unless you were a geologist. Rock, rock, and more rock. Not exactly the Elysian fields I'd hoped for. Of course, this was a temporary stay—the more temporary, the better—but I couldn't help being curious, if only to take my mind off the worries that were gnawing through my gut. This was the afterlife, the greatest mystery in the world unfolding before me. Yet my attempts to get more information from Eve were blocked with witticisms and non sequiturs. I can, however, be somewhat persistent, and finally she was forced to address the issue.

"I can't tell you anything, Paige. I know you're curious, but if we're going to get you out of this world, then the less you know—"

"The better," I finished.

"The better for *me*, too," she said. "I'm already in the Fates' bad books, and once they find out—"

"So the Fates are real?"

"Oh, yeah, only they don't just sit around spinning yarn—" She shot me a mock glare. "Stop that. You're going to trick me into talking, and then they'll find out and I won't just be up to my neck in shit anymore, I'll be drowning in it. Believe me, they *will* find out—hopefully just not until you're gone."

"How will they find us? Those Searchers you mentioned?"

Eve kept walking.

I continued, "If I need to be on the lookout for these things, then I have to know what to look for."

"No, you don't. If you see them, they've already seen you, and we're both going down. Not a whole lotta laws in this place, but we're breaking most of them."

"What if—"

I stopped and stared. The rocky plains ended less than a dozen yards in front of us. Beyond that was . . . nothing. They didn't end in a cliff or a wall of darkness or anything so dramatic. They just ended, like hitting the last page in a book. I can't describe it any better than that.

"Well, come on," she said.

I couldn't move. There was something indescribably terrifying about the view in front of me, the yawning nothingness of it.

"Oh, hell," Eve said. "It's just a way station."

She grabbed my elbow and propelled me forward. When we reached the end of the plain, my brain went wild, digging in its mental heels. That response shot down to my legs and they stopped moving. Eve sighed and, without a word, stepped behind me, and pushed.

I'd been tricked. In that last second before Eve shoved me through, I realized the truth. Eve wasn't helping me. She didn't want me going back to Savannah. She hated me, hated what I was doing to her daughter, hated how I was raising her. This was her revenge. She was—

"There," Eve said, stepping beside me. "That's not so bad, is it?"

I looked around. Fog surrounded me, a strange, cold, bluish mist.

I rubbed my upper arms. "So what is this place? A way station between what?"

"Between planes, the nonearthly realms of the ghost world, like where you landed. From here I can transport us to another plane, or to any place on earth. Well, our version of earth."

"But how—"

"Think of it as a cosmic elevator. A modern one, though. No elevator attendant on duty. Can't just walk up and say 'Miami, please.' Don't I wish. No, it's strictly do-it-yourself, and you have to figure out the right incantation to get to each place, like breaking a code. Different place, different code."

"So I assume they don't like ghosts traveling."

Eve shrugged. "They aren't totally against it, but they'd rather you found a place and stuck to it, at least for a while. Frequent commuting is not encouraged. It confuses the older ghosts, seeing new faces popping in and out all the time."

"But you know the codes."

She grinned. "Not as many as I'd like, but I'm racking up far more frequent flier miles than the Fates would like. They've rapped my knuckles a few times. Not about using the codes, because, technically, that's allowed, but they don't always approve of the methods I use to get them."

"Uh-huh."

"And that's all you need to know about that. Now hold on."

Eve murmured an incantation in a language I'd never heard. Then she turned and walked back in the direction we'd come.

"It didn't work?" I said as I hurried after her. "So now what—"

"More walking, less talking, Paige."

I took one more step and my foot sank into what felt like a steaming pile of horseshit. I yelped and jumped back. I looked down. Warm, slimy mud oozed into my sandals.

"Gross, huh?" Eve said. "Come on."

I followed. The mist still swirled around us. I opened my mouth to ask Eve something, then caught a whiff of the air and gagged. In grade school, a sadistic teacher had forced our class on an educational tour of a sewer plant. It had smelled like this, only better. One more cautious step, and a wave of humid heat washed over me. Then the mist cleared.

I looked around. The first association that clicked was: the Everglades. But it wasn't. It had the same smell, the same feel, the same general look, but everything was multiplied a hundredfold. I touched the nearest overhanging fern. The leaf was bigger than I was. Massive twisted trees loomed overhead, pale moss dangling all around them, like a tattered wedding dress on a bridal corpse. An insect the size of a swallow buzzed past. As I turned to get a better look at it, something deep within the swamp shrieked. I jumped. Eve laughed and steadied me.

"Welcome to Miami," she said. "Population: a few hundred . . . none of whom you want to meet."

"This is Miami?" I said.

"Weird, huh? Watch this."

She murmured an incantation, then rubbed her hand in front of us, as if cleaning glass. There, in the spot she'd cleared, was a tunnel view of a city street, neon signs blazing. A pair of headlights rounded the corner and headed straight for us. I locked my knees so I wouldn't bolt. The car zoomed to the edge of the "window," then disappeared.

"That's your Miami," she said, then pointed at the swamp. "This is ours."

She swiped her hand over the image, and it dissolved. I took a few steps, shoes squelching in the mud.

"Stick close," she said. "I'm serious about there being things out there you don't want to meet."

I looked around and shook my head. "So all the cities are gone in the ghost world?"

"Nah. Miami's special."

"What are the other cities like? Do they look like ours?"

"Kind of. That's the cool thing. They look like the real ones, but they're stuck in the past, at some important point in their history, their heyday or whatever."

I looked around. "So Miami's heyday was back when it was a primeval swamp?"

Eve grinned. "All downhill from there, huh? Or maybe it's a metaphorical thing."

"You said ghosts live in the other cities. What if you lived in Miami while you were alive? Would you have to relocate?"

"Mostly, yes. But those things I was mentioning, the ones that live here? Rumor has it that they used to be—" She grimaced and made a zipping motion over her mouth. "No more questions, Paige."

"But shouldn't I know—"

"No, you shouldn't. You don't need to. You just want to. God, I'd forgotten how curious you are. When you were little, I swore your first word wasn't 'Momma,' it was 'why.'"

"Just one last—"

"One last question? Ha! Do you have any idea how many times I fell for that one?" She started walking. "One last question. One last game. One last song."

"I just—"

"Stop talking and get moving or you'll learn more about this swamp than you ever cared to know."

CHAPTER 56

BLINDSIDED

Eve knew her way around the ghost-world Miami from her frequent visits over the last two weeks. What had lured her to this hell swamp? Us. She'd been keeping tabs on Lucas and me since we'd arrived in Miami, as she'd been periodically checking in on Savannah while she was under Elena's care. Apparently, she'd been doing this since her death, reassuring herself that her daughter was safe, and now keeping track of her guardians as well. It was a strictly visual supervision, but only because she hadn't figured out a way to extend her protectorship to a more active form. Not surprisingly, the Fates frowned on the whole guardian-angel routine. Interfering with the living was forbidden. Even checking in on loved ones, as Eve was doing, was discouraged. To make the full transition to ghost life, you had to break all ties with the living world. Eve was having some difficulty with the concept.

We had to walk two miles to get to where our hotel would be in the living world. I hoped Jaime was there. Otherwise, we were in for a long hunt.

Two miles wasn't relatively far, given the size of Miami, but when you were walking through a swamp, up to your ankles in muck, blazing a trail through the vegetation with fire spells, every few yards seemed like miles. Fortunately, Eve had forged some paths earlier, including one to our hotel. Otherwise the vegetation would have been impassable. Already, in the half-day she'd been gone, the vines had wound over her trail, the lush vegetation filling in so fast you could almost see it growing.

As we hacked through a particularly overgrown area, I thought I *did* see the vegetation growing, as ferns a few yards ahead swished in the still, fetid air. Then I saw a shape move behind the fronds.

"Shit!" Eve said.

The figure shambled forward, taking shape in the dim light. I made out a vaguely humanoid form, then everything went dark. I bit back a yelp, and started casting a light spell. Eve grasped my forearm and leaned down to my ear.

"It's me, Paige. I did it."

Did what? Before I could ask, I remembered that Eve was also a half-demon, having been sired by an Aspicio. An Aspicio's power is sight, and its progeny can inflict temporary blindness.

"What?" I hissed. "Don't—I can't see!"

"That's the idea."

Mud squelched as the thing moved through the swamp, coming closer with each step. I blinked hard, but saw only darkness.

"Eve!" I whispered. "Stop this. I'm not a little girl anymore. I've seen things, lots of things. Demons, corpses, *reanimated* corpses—multiple reanimated corpses. Whatever's out there, I can handle—"

I stopped mid-sentence, mouth open, frozen, not in fear, but in a binding spell. Eve's hair tickled my ear as she leaned down over me.

"Maybe you can handle it, Paige, but you don't need to."

I glared at her—or in the direction I assumed she was.

"Don't worry," she whispered. "I've dealt with these things before. Most times if you just stand still, they'll go away."

Stand still? Did I have a choice? I couldn't see. I couldn't move. I couldn't speak. I could hear, though. I was frozen there, blinded, listening to the squelching of some unknown horror as it shambled toward me. Then another sense kicked in. Smell. A sickly sweet smell, worse than the stink of the rotting vegetation. My gut clenched.

As the thing drew close, I caught a faint, papery sound, like dry leaves rustling in the breeze. The noise took on a rhythm, then a clear sound, a steady, raspy "ung-ung-ung." The hairs on my arms shot up and I struggled against the binding spell. The smell grew stronger, until it was so overwhelming, I felt the gag reflex in my throat. But, caught in the binding spell, I couldn't gag. My mouth filled with bile. I fought harder against the spell, but it didn't crack.

"Ung-ung-ung."

The sound was so close now I knew the creature was right in front of us, just off to my left, where Eve stood. The noise stopped, replaced by a dry snuffling.

"It's okay, Paige," she whispered. "Just let it sniff you, and it'll—" A chomping sound. Then a gasp. "You fucking—!"

She cast a spell, something I didn't recognize. A high-pitched shriek rent the air, then a bellow, and fast footfalls through the mud.

"You'd better run," Eve said. "Goddamned—"

"Ung-ung-ung!" The cry, loud now, came from somewhere to our left, immediately followed by another to our right.

"Holy shit," Eve whispered.

She snapped the binding spell and I stumbled forward, my sight returning just in time for me to see the ground rushing up. Eve grabbed my arm and yanked me upright. I made out three, maybe four humanoid shapes rushing at us before Eve whipped me around and we started to run.

We raced, slipping and sliding and scrambling, through the swamp. Apparently unaccustomed to moving fast, the creatures were having just as much trouble. We retraced our steps through the path we'd cut coming in, which made it easier.

As we rounded a corner, Eve skidded across a muddy patch. I caught her before she fell.

"I hate running away," she muttered as we plowed forward again. "Hate it, hate it, hate it."

"Should we stop and fight?"

"As soon as we get enough of a head start to cast. They're falling behind, aren't they?"

"Seems like it."

"Good. Fucking bastards. I can't believe they attacked me."

"Look on the bright side," I said as we tore around another curve. "At least they can't kill us."

Eve's laugh rang through the swamp. "This is true. Being dead has its—"

Eve's body jerked, as if someone had yanked her legs out from under her. Her lips parted in an oath, but before any sound came out, she was sucked into the swamp.

"Eve!" I shouted.

Something grabbed my left foot. I pulled my right foot back to kick it, but a tremendous yank pulled me off balance, and the swamp sailed up to swallow me.

Chapter 57

Busted

Before I had time to panic, the swamp vanished, and I was plunked down onto a cold, hard surface. Back to the rocky plain? I looked around, but a mist surrounded me. Unlike the cold fog in the way station, this was warm and almost tangibly soft. As I child, I'd often lain on the grass, stared up at the clouds, and wondered what they'd feel like. The mist around me was almost exactly what I'd imagined. A sudden image of clouds and harps and trumpeting angels sprang to mind. Had I died—again—and gone to heaven?

"Ah, shit," Eve muttered somewhere beside me. "Busted."

Okay, not heaven. Whew. Monotonous bliss was not what I had in mind for my eternity.

As the mist withdrew, it contracted, growing denser. For a split second, something like a face appeared in the mist. Then it stretched into a pale ribbon, twisting as it wended toward the roof and disappeared.

"Damn Searchers," Eve muttered. "There's gotta be a way to outsmart them. Gotta be." She glanced over at me. "Don't worry. Everything will be okay. Just keep quiet and let me do the talking."

The mist now completely gone, I looked around. What I saw was so overwhelming that, for a moment, I could only stare, uncomprehending. The room we were in—no, it wasn't a room, there couldn't be a room this large. The bluish-white marble walls seemed to extend into infinity, the dark marble floor stretching to meet it like the earth reaching to the horizon. The vaulted white ceiling and huge pillars gave it the look of a Grecian temple, but the mosaics and paintings decorating the walls seemed to come from every culture imaginable. Each frieze portrayed a scene from life. Every part of life, every celebration, every tragedy, every mundane moment seemed to be pictured on those walls. As my gaze passed a bloody battle scene, a rearing horse's front leg moved, infinitesimally. I blinked. The rider's mouth opened, so slowly that the casual glance would miss it.

I was about to say something to Eve when the floor began to turn.

"An audience has been granted," Eve muttered. "About time."

The floor rotated until we were faced with an open space at least as inconceivably huge as the one on the other side. Across the expanse, vines hung from the ceiling, thousands, tens of thousands of them, suspended from every inch of space. The sight was so incongruous that I blinked and rubbed my thumb and forefinger over my eyes. When I looked again, I saw that they weren't vines at all, but pieces of yarn, colored every shade in the rainbow, and all exactly the same length.

"What the—?" I began.

"Shhh," Eve hissed. "Let me talk, remember?"

It was then that I saw the woman. She stood on a dais, behind an old-fashioned spinning wheel. Neither young nor old, ugly nor beautiful, thin nor fat, short nor tall, she was a perfect average of everything female, a middle-aged matron with skin the color of honey and long graying dark hair.

Her head down, she pumped a length of yarn from the wheel until it looked the same length as those hanging all around her. Then in a transition so fast and seamless it seemed a trick of the eyes, the woman aged fifty years, becoming an elderly crone, back bent, long hair as coarse and gray as wire, the simple mauve dress now white with the palest hint of violet. Her sunken eyes gleamed, dark and quick, like a crow's. One wizened hand lifted the length of yarn. The other, wrapped around a pair of black scissors, reached up and snipped it off. A man—so pale he looked albino—appeared from the jungle of dangling yarn, took the newly cut piece, and disappeared back into the dark depths of wool.

I looked back at the crone, but in her place stood a child no more than five or six, so small she couldn't see over the spinning wheel. Like the others, she had long hair, but hers was gleaming golden brown, and her eyes were cornflower blue. Her dress was an equally vivid purple.

The girl threaded the wheel, standing on tiptoes to reach it. Once it was ready, she changed to the middle-aged woman, who began to spin the yarn.

Beside me, Eve sighed loudly. "See? Even the Fates aren't above petty sadism, making us sit here and stew."

The woman, now the old crone, pinned Eve with her sharp eyes. "Petty? Never. We're enjoying a rare moment of peace, when we don't need to worry what you're up to."

She clipped the yarn. As the albino man retrieved it, the girl appeared. Before she could load the wheel, she stopped, her head cocked, a frown flitting across her pretty face. The albino appeared, holding a length of yarn in his hands. The girl nodded gravely, then morphed into the middle-aged woman, who took the yarn. She slid it through her fingers, then closed her eyes. A single tear squeezed out as her fingers slipped up the yarn nearly to the top. The woman became the crone, who looked at the tiny length of yarn pinched between her fingers.

"So young," she murmured, and clipped it off.

She handed the tiny piece of yarn back to the albino, who took it and walked into a hallway to our left. The old woman turned into the girl.

"So this is the problem we heard about," the girl said, her voice high and musical. "And you're involved, Eve? Shocking."

"Hey, I didn't—"

The girl smiled. "Didn't do anything? Or didn't cause the original problem? We're well aware of your innocence in the latter, but we'd beg to differ on the former. Exactly how many rules have you broken today, Eve? I'm not sure I can count that high."

"Sarcastic deities," Eve muttered. "Just what every afterlife needs."

The girl changed into the woman. "We'll discuss your transgressions later, Eve. Right now—" Her voice softened as her gaze moved to me. "We have a more distressing situation to contend with. Not that you're to blame, child, but we must fix this immediately. We'll send you back, of course. You'll still remember your visit. We hate to tamper with memory, and we see no need for it in your case." A smile. "You're not the type to turn this experience into a bestselling memoir. Now, all we need—"

"Is Lucas," I said.

Eve elbowed me. I ignored her.

"We need Lucas. We left him—"

The woman shook her head. "He can't go, child. He died. He must stay here."

"No, he didn't—"

"We know you don't want to believe that, but—"

"Wait," I said, lifting my hands. "I'm arguing the fact, not the interpretation. The bullet hit Lucas and he fell into the portal."

"We know what happened."

"Then you know it takes longer than that split second to die after being shot in the chest. Therefore, when he fell through the portal, he wasn't dead."

The woman shook her head, smiling. "Always the logical one, aren't you? I'm afraid it's a matter of semantics, child. The shot would have killed him. We know that."

My heart seized in my chest, but I pushed on. "Okay, you know that because you know it was his time, but—"

"His time?" the old woman said as she appeared. She swept a hand at the yarn jungle behind her. "It's never anyone's time, girl. We don't make that decision. What happens happens, and what happened was that Lucas Cortez died—"

The middle sister cut in. "Which is a tragedy, of course. But here he'll be able to continue his work. There's good and evil in this world, too. We can use Lucas here and, when you die, you will join him. You'll be together. That's already been determined. That's why you came through to the same dimension. You just have to wait—"

"I won't wait. If he stays, I stay."

The woman's lips curved in a sympathetic smile. "That's not a choice you really want to make. It won't go the way you hoped."

"I'm not hoping for anything. I'm making a statement of fact. Lucas stays, I stay."

"Don't do this," Eve hissed in my ear. "You can't trick them."

"It isn't a bluff."

The crone appeared. "Whether you go or stay isn't your decision to make, girl."

"But if you send me back, I can make it my decision. You've said there's no predestination, so I can choose my own time of death."

"Doesn't matter. Even if you kill yourself, there's no guarantee you'll ever see him again."

"Of course there is. You said so yourself. It's been decided—we'll be together. I suppose you could change things, but that would be petty, and you said you're never petty."

The woman appeared with a sigh. "I do so prefer the ghosts who cower and quake in our presence."

"Oh, she's awful, isn't she?" Eve said. "Been like this since she was a child. Always questioning everything and everybody. No respect for authority. My advice? Send her and Lucas back and spare yourselves sixty, seventy unnecessary years of grief."

"Thank you, Eve, for considering our feelings in the matter. However, your bias in the matter is well-known. You want Paige for your daughter's guardian."

"Have you considered that, Paige?" asked the old woman, popping back to fix me with that soul-piercing stare. "If you stayed here, you'd abandon Savannah, after all you've—"

The middle sister cut in. "No, that's not fair. We won't make you

choose, child. The decision must be ours. That is the only truly equitable—" She stopped, head tilted. "Yes, sister, that's an idea."

The woman vanished, then the child appeared, then the crone, then the
three began flipping so quickly I couldn't tell who I was seeing. Snatches
of conversation flew past, meaningless, out of context. Then the middle-
aged woman took over.

"Eve, you want Paige and Lucas as Savannah's guardians. Would you
be willing to barter for it?"

Eve lifted her chin, meeting the other woman's gaze squarely. "I am.
You want me to obey the rules, right? Send them back—both of them—
and I'll do it."

The woman smiled and shook her head. "Obedience without accep-
tance is meaningless. When you understand the rules, you'll obey them.
Until then—" She shrugged and waved at the yarn hanging behind them.
"You make your own mistakes. You determine your own fate. We don't
do that for you."

Eve frowned. "Then what's the price?"

"You will owe us a favor. A chit, which we may call in whenever we
wish."

"I'll do it."

"Are you sure?"

"No, but I'm agreeing anyway. Do this for me, and I'll owe you one.
Now, we left Lucas—"

The Fate cut Eve off with a wave. "We know." She closed her eyes and
the three forms flipped past in a blur, then returned to the middle sister.
"There. Lucas is back in the living world. Paige, we'll see you again someday, hopefully after a long and—"

"Wait!" Eve said. "Don't I get to say good-bye?"

"Yes, after I do. Now, Paige, turn around."

I did. Twenty feet away, the air shimmered, like heat rising off hot
asphalt.

"That's the portal. When you're done with Eve, just walk through it. Be
quick, though. I've sent Lucas back to where he left, and he'll likely be disoriented. There was no danger there a moment ago but—well, be quick."

I looked back at the Fates. "Thank you."

The woman nodded. "You're welcome. Just remember the cardinal
rule of leaving the afterlife." She morphed into the child, who grinned.
"Don't look back."

I smiled, turned, and headed for the portal. Eve walked beside me.
Neither of us said anything until we reached it. Then I turned to her.

"Thank you," I said. "For everything."

"Hey, you're raising my kid. I owe you everything. Tell Savannah . . . No, I won't waste our last minute with that. You know what to tell her. And I won't tell you to take good care of her, because I know you will. So I'll settle for telling you to take care of yourself. You grew up good, Paige. Maybe more 'good' than I'd like, but I'm still proud of you." She leaned over, kissed my forehead, and whispered, "Have a good life, Paige. You deserve it."

"I—"

She took my shoulders, turned me around, and pushed me into the portal.

CHAPTER 58

BAD GUY DEAD?

I came to in the alley. When I opened my eyes, I saw only darkness. I blinked and the world took focus as my eyes adjusted. It took a moment for my numbed brain to understand why it was dark out, to make that most obvious deductive leap. Night. It was nighttime. How long had we—? The thought slid from my brain. Too much effort. I tried lifting my head, but that also seemed like too much work. Everything was so . . . heavy. The very air had a weight that went beyond the dampness of a wet Miami night.

I yawned and closed my eyes. As I drifted toward sleep, my brain replayed snatches from the last eight hours and I shot upright, remembering everything.

"Lucas?" I scrambled to my feet. "Lucas!"

Pitching forward into the darkness, I stumbled over something and fell to my knees. My hands felt for the object that had tripped me, praying that it was Lucas. I touched the cold rough surface of broken concrete. Staying on all fours, I felt around wildly. When I overreached, pain shot through my abdomen, the first twinge I'd felt since jumping through the portal. The sudden shock of the pain made me stop long enough to think. I closed my eyes, took a deep breath, and cast a light spell. After casting, I kept my eyes closed, telling myself that when I did look I'd see Lucas, but still afraid . . . I opened my eyes. He wasn't there.

"Lucas!"

I flew to my feet, waving the light-ball about. He had to be here. They promised, they promised, they—

My light illuminated an outstretched hand near the end of the alley. Lucas lay on his back, arms out, face to the sky, eyes closed. He's sleeping, I told myself. Sleeping like I was. Then I saw the blood on his shirtfront.

As I shot forward, an image raced through my mind, a scene from some half-remembered movie where a man had been granted a wish and, before he could use it, his wife died. So he made the obvious wish. He wanted her alive again. But he hadn't been specific, hadn't said he'd wanted her as she'd been before the accident, and the last scene had been of her mutilated body lurching toward the front door.

"You weren't specific!" I shouted to myself, my mental voice reverberating through my head. I said I wanted Lucas to be sent back to this world with me and the Fates had done exactly that. They'd brought him back as he'd been when he left it—shot through the heart.

People always say that after someone dies, the first thing they think of is everything they regret not having told them. My own regrets were enough to bury me alive, but they never crossed my mind, not in the ghost world, when I'd refused to believe he was dead, and not now, when I was certain he was. Instead, the only thought going through my head at that moment was that his death was my fault. I'd had the chance to save him, to deal with Fate, and I'd been my usual impetuous self, demanding something before thinking it through.

As I knelt beside Lucas, his eyelids flickered. My breath caught. For a long moment, I didn't breathe, certain that somehow my dropping to the pavement had caused a vibration that made his eyelids move. Fingers trembling, I touched the side of his neck.

"Mmmm," he murmured.

My hands went to his shirt and I fumbled with the buttons, then gave up and ripped the sodden fabric. Beneath the bloodied hole, Lucas's chest was unmarked. Unable to believe it, I touched the spot where the bullet should have gone through, and felt his heart beating as strong as ever. I dropped my head onto his chest, and all the fear and anxiety I'd repressed in the ghost world bubbled forth in a chest-wrenching sob.

When I gasped for breath, a distant sound made me stop and listen. It came again, a soft rhythmic scraping against the concrete. A pale shape floated into the darkness a few yards away. I tensed and waved my light-ball higher, until it cast a dim glow down the length of the alley. A ghostly white wolf stood at the other end, head tilted as if as surprised to see me as I was to see it. Our eyes met. The wolf dove back into the darkness.

"Did you just see . . . ?" Lucas croaked, lifting his head and squinting into the darkness.

"I think so."

"Then are we . . . back? Or still on the other side?"

"I have no idea. I'm just glad you're okay." I gave him a fierce hug, then pulled back fast. "Did that hurt? You *are* okay, aren't you?"

He smiled. "I'm fine. Just a little stiff . . . like someone hit me in the chest with a bullet."

"You remember?"

"I remember a lot of things," he said, then gave a confused frown. "Including things I really ought not to remember, considering I was unconscious at the time. It was very . . . strange. I was—" His lips curved in a slow smile. "Oh."

"Oh what?"

"I just remembered how I got back here." His smile broadened to a lazy grin that lit up his eyes. "The Fates. You talked to the Fates. You told them—" He paused, and the grin dissipated, eyes sobering. "I must say, though, you were taking a serious risk, Paige. If they'd called your bluff—"

"Bluff?" I squawked. "You think I was bluffing? I couldn't tell a lie to save my own life, let alone someone else's. I can't believe you'd think—"

He tugged me down to him in a kiss. "I had to check." A smile. "Just in case."

"Well, you shouldn't have to, and if you think you do, then that's my fault. No more head games. You're stuck with me. I even followed you into the next world. Now that's commitment . . . of the scariest stalker-chick kind."

His grin broadened. "Are you sure I'm alive? Because if this is my afterlife, I must have been a very good boy."

"The best," I said, bending over him.

As our lips met, Lucas reached up and pulled me down on top of him. I entwined my fingers behind his head and kissed him with ferocity that surprised me and sent a chuckle rippling through him. He returned the kiss full-strength, his lips parting mine, the tip of his tongue tickling mine. We kissed for a few minutes, then his hands slid to my rear, pulling me against him—

"Uh, sorry to interrupt," a voice wafted from down the alley. "But if any clothing is about to be shed, could you toss it this way?"

I jumped off Lucas so fast I nearly kneed him in a place I really didn't want him injured.

"Elena?" I said.

She peeked out from the end of the alley, her face a pale blob in the blackness.

"Uh, yeah. I am so sorry, guys, but I thought I'd better cut in before it was too late."

"So that was you. The wolf."

"Sorry if I startled you. I'd been by here about a half-dozen times tonight, so when I picked up your scent, I figured it was the old trail, from this morning. Then there you were."

I walked forward. She hadn't moved from her spot behind a garbage bin.

"Why are you—" I began, then grinned. "Oh, wait. You weren't kidding about the clothes, were you?"

Lucas had been coming up behind me, but now stopped in mid-stride.

"That's okay, Lucas," she said. "I'll stay back here. But if anyone has a spare piece of apparel . . ."

Lucas already had his shirt half-unbuttoned. He handed it to me and I took it to Elena.

"Always the gentleman," she said as he turned his back. "Thank you. I promise I'll get it back in one piece— Oh." She fingered the bloodied bullet hole, eyes widening. "What happened?"

"Got shot through the heart," I said. "But he's fine now."

"Uh-huh," she said, brows arching. "That must have been some healing spell."

"It's a long story. I'll explain later. So what the heck are you doing here, anyway?"

"Looking for you two," she said as she shrugged on Lucas's shirt. "When you missed your eleven o'clock check-in yesterday morning, I started to worry. I phoned your cell and left messages, then I kept phoning and finally someone answered—a guy who found your phone lying in an alley near here. Not a good sign. So we caught the next flight for Miami."

Elena tugged down the shirt, craning her neck to see how far it fell.

"Everything's covered." I leaned around the corner. "Lucas? She's decent."

"So long as I don't bend over," she said with a sigh. "I really have to start leaving my clothing in more convenient places."

"Or you could buy a big fanny pack," I said. "Strap it around your waist before you Change."

"Don't laugh. I've actually considered that."

"Where's Clayton?" Lucas asked. "I assume you didn't come alone."

"Oh!" I said. "Savannah. Did you—"

"She's with Jeremy at a hotel near here. Very worried and mad as hell about being left out of the search. You should call right away. I have my cell phone . . ." She grimaced. ". . . which is with my clothing. Sorry."

"Fanny pack," I said.

"No kidding. Now, Clay . . ." She looked around. "We split up to cover more ground. I should have howled for him before I Changed back, but I was so surprised seeing you two here that I completely forgot."

"You could howl now," I said.

She fixed me with a look. "No, thank you."

"Can you whistle?" Lucas asked.

"A much less embarrassing choice," she said. "Now let's just hope he recognizes it."

Elena put her fingers in her mouth, but only managed a squeal that sounded more like a stuck pig. A laugh sounded behind us.

"You sure howling wouldn't have been less embarrassing, darling?" Clay asked as he rounded the corner into the alley. He lifted a bundle of clothes. "Forgot something?"

"Thank you." Elena took the pile, rooted into her jeans pocket, and handed me her cell phone. "Just hit redial for the hotel."

I spoke to Jeremy, then to Savannah. I told them we were fine and we'd be there in a few minutes. By the time I hung up, Elena was walking out from an adjacent alley, twisting her hair back in a ponytail. Lucas and Clay were talking off to the side.

"We're too late, darling," Clay said as Elena approached. "They finished without us."

She glanced at me. "Bad guy dead?"

I nodded. "Bad guy dead."

"Damn," she muttered. "Well, that's good, of course . . ."

"But not much fun."

She grinned. "I'll survive. So what happened?"

"His dead lover tore open a portal into the ghost world and we all jumped through. Well, Lucas fell in, I jumped in after him, and Edward jumped in after her. We came back, which is good. He didn't come back, which is also good . . . except that it means that in punishment for his crimes he gets exactly what he wanted all along—eternal life with the woman he loves."

"Uh-huh. I think I'd better get the uncondensed version after we get back to the hotel. Oh, wait, you guys must be starving. First stop: food."

"What time is it?" Lucas asked, tapping his watch and frowning at it.

"Mine stopped, too," I said. "I don't think they survived that return trip."

"It's just past four A.M.," Elena said.

"You might have some difficulty locating a restaurant," Lucas said.

"Don't worry," Clay said. "We'll find food. We always do."

We stood at the take-out counter of a twenty-four-hour Cuban restaurant. Neither Elena nor Clay had ever eaten Cuban, so they were soliciting opinions and advice from Lucas. After placing the order, we took our coffees into the dining area to wait. After a few minutes, I realized we were getting a lot of attention. The restaurant had only eight other patrons, but every eye had slid our way a couple of times and, by the time my coffee was half-finished, I swear every busboy and cook had peeked out from the kitchen. Now, I'll admit, Elena and Clay made an eye-catching couple, but this seemed a tad excessive. The next time someone looked our way, I followed his gaze to Lucas's shirt.

"Uh, Lucas?" I said.

When I had his attention, I tapped my fingers against my left breast. He arched one eyebrow, lips curving in a slow grin. I rolled my eyes and discreetly pointed at his shirt. His gaze slid down to the bloody bullet hole.

"Ah," he said. "Perhaps I should wait outside . . . in the alley or someplace suitably dark."

"I'll come with you," I said. "Elena? Can I borrow your cell? I should call Cassandra, let her know we're okay, in case she's noticed we've been missing for eighteen hours."

"Not likely," Clay muttered. "Ten bucks says she hasn't noticed you've left the hotel room yet."

"That, I believe, is a wager I just might win," Lucas said. "In fact, I'll raise it to twenty and postulate that she's not only noticed, but started looking for us."

Clay shook his head. "Hate to take advantage of youthful optimism, but, sure, you're on. Twenty bucks it is."

It turned out that we didn't need Elena's cell phone after all. Lucas's was still working—though I really hoped no one had called while we'd been in the ghost world, or they'd have racked up a hell of a long-distance charge.

Cassandra wasn't at the hotel. She was out, with Aaron, looking for us, and had been since early the previous afternoon.

"How'd you know that?" I whispered to Lucas when Jaime told me the news.

He only gave a small smile and waved for me to continue talking to Jaime, who'd just returned to the hotel an hour ago, too exhausted from her nights of haunting to continue the search. I told her I'd track down Cassandra via Aaron's cell.

"Better call Benicio first," she said. "He's going nuts. I swear, the city's crawling with supernaturals tonight looking for you two. I heard he called in every Cortez security force in the country. We notified him as soon as we realized you guys were missing." She paused. "Hope that was okay."

"It was. Thanks. Will we see you later? Or are you taking off already?"

"Taking off?"

"Back on tour. Now that everything is over—"

"Over? What about Edward?"

"Oh, right. Sorry. Let me back up."

I told her what she didn't know. Then she told me what I didn't know. When Elena and Clay came out of the restaurant, Lucas and I were huddled together, talking quietly as we tried to absorb the news.

"What's up?" Elena said.

"We have a problem," I said.

"What?"

"Bad guy *not* dead."

CHAPTER 59

STANDOFF

Last time I'd seen Edward, he'd been running for the portal, so we assumed he'd jumped through right after us. He hadn't made it. Less than an hour after we disappeared, Edward phoned John in New Orleans asking to be put in contact with Cassandra. John had the good sense to hand over Aaron's number, rather than try negotiating with Edward himself. When Edward finally got in touch with Cassandra, he demanded that she, as the vampire delegate to the council, negotiate on his behalf with the Cortez Cabal.

This made no sense to me. If Edward knew Natasha was waiting on the other side, why would he want to bargain his way out of a death sentence? Turned out he didn't. As Cassandra explained, Edward knew he'd be executed for his crimes, and he accepted that . . . so long as his punishment ended there. In a Cabal court, there is a sentence worse than execution: execution plus an afterlife curse, which sends your soul into limbo. For a vampire, the threat held little power, since most assumed they didn't have an afterlife. Can't curse a soul that doesn't exist. But now Edward knew better. Natasha still lived, in some form, in some place, and he wanted to be with her. Maybe this was why Natasha had been trying to contact Jaime, to somehow negotiate with us or pass along a message to Edward, telling him to stop and accept execution before he went too far. But now he had gone too far. In killing Lucas, he'd ensured that his death would come with every curse Benicio could dream up. His only hope was to negotiate an ironclad settlement before Benicio knew his beloved youngest son was gone.

The problem was that Cassandra knew nothing about portals and Cabal curses, and didn't even know for certain that we'd found Edward. She knew only that we were missing and he might be to blame. So she did the obvious: demanded to know where we were, whereupon Edward realized everyone knew we'd disappeared, which meant any hope of negotiating with the Cabals had also disappeared, which meant he didn't need Cassandra to mediate for him. So he'd hung up.

Not surprisingly, no one had heard from Edward since. My first thought was that it was still over. Edward would go into hiding, no more Cabal kids would die, and the problem would be resolved, however unsatisfying that resolution might be. Again, Jaime knew differently. When Edward had been trying to persuade Cassandra to negotiate for him, his terms were that he would stop the killings if the Cabal reopened a portal for him. Of course that made no sense to Cassandra, and Edward hung up before she could demand an explanation. Once I told Jaime what happened, though, she knew exactly what he'd meant.

Once a portal to the ghost world had been ripped open, it remained "hot" for about forty-eight hours. That meant, with the right materials, it could be reactivated. As for what material such a reopening required, Jaime knew only that it involved a sacrifice—a human sacrifice. Yet she also knew it wasn't as easy as selecting a random victim from the street. She had an idea where she could find details on the ritual, and promised to do so immediately. While I'd explained the situation to Elena and Clay, Lucas had called his father. We talked for another couple of minutes, then set out for our respective rental cars, which were parked in a lot near Edward's hotel. We got less than a block before a familiar black SUV squealed a U-turn in front of us.

"How the hell . . . ?" I said.

"Cell phone tracking, I would presume," Lucas murmured.

As the SUV pulled to the curbside, I turned to say something else to Lucas, then saw the bloodstained bullet hole on his shirt.

"Shit!" I said. "Your shirt. A jacket, does anyone have—"

No one did, but it didn't matter. Before the SUV even stopped rolling, the rear door opened and Benicio flew out. And, of course, the first thing he saw was that bullet hole.

Benicio stopped in mid-stride, gaze glued to that bloodied hole in Lucas's shirt. All color drained from his face. He took one unsteady step toward his son. Lucas hesitated only a split second, then met Benicio in an embrace.

As the two hugged, Elena slipped off to the side, then returned, grabbed Clay's arm, and tugged him away, motioning to me that they'd wait around the corner to give us privacy.

Lucas tried to explain away the hole, but it was too late. Benicio had already been to see Faye and she'd told him that Lucas was Edward's next target. She hadn't known Lucas had been shot, but the moment Benicio saw that shirt, he knew, and there was no sense fudging the facts. We did, however, gloss over our afterlife visit, saying only that we'd fallen through the portal and reawakened here. Later, Benicio would undoubtedly press for details, but for now he didn't care. Lucas was safe. That was all that mattered.

"So now we still need to find Edward," Lucas said. "He'll probably lie low—"

Benicio shook his head. "He'll want to reopen the portal."

"We did . . . entertain that possibility," Lucas said. "We have Jaime looking into it now."

"And I'll get our researchers on it right away. For now, though, my first priority is you. I've made arrangements for you and Paige to be flown to the safe house, where you'll—"

"No, Papá," Lucas said quietly.

Benicio met his son's gaze. "Don't argue with me on this, Lucas. You are going—"

"I am going to continue what I started. As long as Edward is free, I still have a job to do."

"Your job is done. It ends here, Lucas. I have never interfered before—"

Lucas gave him a look.

Benicio's mouth set. "Not with this, I haven't. I have never tried to stop these crusades of yours or dissuade you from them." He stepped back. "Do you think I don't know how often your life is in danger, Lucas? Do you know how many nights I've spent worrying? Wondering what kind of trouble you'll get into next? But I have *never* said a word. You jaunt off to Boston to take on Kristof Nast over a witch, and I say nothing. You fly to California to confront a potential serial killer, and I say nothing. But now I am saying something. This time, my name isn't enough to protect you, so I'm damned well going to do it myself. You are going to that—"

"No, Papá."

They locked gazes and for a minute, just stood there, staring at one another. Then Lucas gave a slow shake of his head.

"No, Papá. This is my fight, just as much as anything else I've ever done. You're right. All the 'risks' I've ever taken haven't been risks at all, because of you and who I am. That has always kept me safe. So now, when I am—possibly for the first time—in real danger, do you honestly expect me to hide behind you? What kind of man would that make me?"

"A safe one."

Lucas met his father's glare with an unblinking stare. After a moment, Benicio turned away. From his profile, I could see his jaw working, struggling to rein in his anger. Finally, he turned back to Lucas.

"You're taking Troy," he said.

"I don't need a bodyguard, Papá," Lucas said.

"You—"

"He already has one," drawled a voice behind us.

We turned to see Clay heading our way. Although they'd been twenty feet away, and around the corner, they couldn't help eavesdropping—one drawback to a werewolf's enhanced hearing.

"I've got it covered," Clay said. "He needs a bodyguard; he's got me."

Benicio looked at Clay. Then his gaze slid to Elena, who was coming up behind Clay. He gave the barest nod, as if making the mental connection.

"Clayton Danvers, I presume," Benicio said. "Your reputation precedes you."

"Then you know your son is in good hands."

Benicio hesitated only a moment, then looked at Lucas. "You'll keep your cell phone on?"

Lucas nodded. "And keep you updated."

With that, Benicio let us go. A relatively easy victory. Too easy. When Benicio was gone, Lucas told us to expect to be tailed to the hotel by another car, one carrying a Cortez security team. And we were. So Benicio had assigned long-distance bodyguards. An inconvenience, but better than having Troy oversee our every move—and relay our every move back to Benicio.

We took the food back to Jeremy and Savannah, and filled them in.

After we'd finished, Jeremy walked to the nearest window and parted the curtains. "We have about an hour of darkness left. Elena . . ."

"Get back to the alley and get sniffing," she said. "Do you guys have anything belonging to Edward?"

"A shirt taken from his clothes hamper," Lucas said. When Elena gave him an odd look, he explained, "We needed a personal item for a clairvoyant."

"Clair—? You mean like—?" Elena stopped and shook her head. "My world was so much less confusing when it only had werewolves. A worn shirt is perfect." She shot a grin at Clay. "Even you could track from that."

"Yeah? Well, in that case, you won't mind me coming along . . . unless you're afraid I'll find him first, show you up."

Her grin broadened. "Never."

"Good. So—" Clay stopped and looked at Lucas. "Or maybe you'll need to handle this one on your own, darling. I promised Lucas's dad—"

"Go on," Lucas said. "Even my father would admit I'm safe here. Edward could hardly break in and overpower all of us."

Both Clay and Elena looked over at Jeremy, waiting for permission. I still find that very strange, the idea that Pack werewolves don't act without their Alpha's approval. And stranger still that they don't seem to mind. I'm sure it helps that Jeremy never makes a big deal out of it—he'd never jump in when they're in the middle of making plans and yell, "Hey, I never said you could do that!" Instead, he does what he did now, intercepted their questioning looks with the barest of nods.

After visiting Faye, we'd left Edward's shirt in our rental car. Lucas gave Clayton the keys and told him where to find the shirt.

"Paige?" Elena said as they headed for the door. "You want to come along?"

Of course I did, but I also knew it wouldn't score me any points with Clayton.

"You two go on," I said. "I should wait here for Jaime's call."

"Can I go?" Savannah said, jumping up.

A chorus of nos answered her. She scowled and thumped back onto the sofa.

"Have you tried the *arepas*?" Lucas asked her. "These are stuffed with chicken, and those over there are beef."

She sighed, but allowed Lucas to put some *arepas* on her plate and explain how they were made.

Next, Jeremy suggested that we invite Cassandra and Aaron to join us, so we could all discuss a plan of action. I'd intended to propose this myself, but had been waiting for Elena and Clay to leave. I suspect Jeremy had been waiting for the same thing, knowing neither of them would be pleased at the prospect of working with Cassandra.

Jeremy also suggested that Jaime join us. This was a more difficult decision to make. Aaron and Cassandra already knew the werewolves; Jaime did not. The Pack had only rejoined the interracial council last year, after more than a century of cutting themselves off from the rest of the supernatural world. Elena might joke about her world being easier when it contained only werewolves, but there was a lot of truth in that. For the Pack, coming back to the council meant a trade-off between gaining allies and giving up the layer of protection that came with isolation.

Outside of the interracial council, few supernaturals could name the members of the Pack, and even fewer could put names to faces. Jeremy was happy to keep it that way, and I didn't blame him. In this case, though, he weighed the danger of identifying themselves to Jaime against the help she could provide with the portal, and decided she had to join us.

At six, Jaime phoned to say she had something, and was coming right over to explain it. Aaron hadn't returned our messages yet, likely having turned off his cell phone while they hunted for us, so we left another, giving him the hotel address, and told them to meet us here. Moments later Elena called. They'd hit a dead end and were heading back.

While we'd been waiting for Jaime's call, I'd talked to Jeremy about the case, hoping he might see some clue we'd overlooked. After about twenty minutes, I noticed Lucas had gone quiet, looked over, and found he was asleep. I suppose dying does take a lot out of a person. I'll admit, though, that on pretense of removing his glasses, I did surreptitiously check to make sure he was breathing. I'd probably be doing that for a while.

CHAPTER 60

THE LEADER OF THE PACK

When Elena called, Jeremy told them to skip the food run on the way back. Savannah was getting restless, so he was taking her out to hunt down breakfast. They'd been gone about ten minutes when Jaime arrived.

"God, it's quiet in here," she said as I ushered her into the room. "I thought werewolves were supposed to be rowdy—" She saw Lucas asleep on the sofa. "Shit, I'm sorry."

I waved her out onto the balcony, then slid the patio door closed so we could talk. Of course, the first thing she wanted to know was what had happened to us. On the way to the hotel, Lucas and I had decided we'd tell the others the basics of our adventure, but keep the specifics secret. Ghosts are forbidden to reveal details of their world, so we assumed we were expected to do the same. Better to claim we didn't remember what had happened, as we had with Benicio.

"And then, here we were, back on this side. Spit out by the ghost world."

"Nan used to tell stories about things like that, portals opening and the living going through . . . or the ghosts coming out. I'll keep my mouth shut about this one, though. If people knew you guys had passed over and come back—" She leaned over the second-story railing. "Hey, is that your ward? Savannah?"

I glanced down and nodded.

"Then those must be the werewolves," Jaime said.

She leaned out farther for a better look. Elena and Clay had either met Jeremy and Savannah in the parking lot or picked them up on the street, because all four were now crossing the parking lot together. Jaime stared down at them, lips curved in the tiny smile of a woman who sees something she really likes . . . almost always something of the opposite sex.

"That'd be Clayton," I said.

"Ah," she said, tearing her gaze away after one last regret-filled look. "The one Cassandra tried to jump. Damn, can't even be original, can I?"

She peered down at the quartet. "Huh. Now I'd have guessed the blond would have been her choice. He looks a bit like Aaron, and I get the impression that's one ex Cass isn't completely over."

I looked at Clay. "I didn't notice it before, but I guess there is a slight resemblance. In the coloring at least, maybe the build. But that *is* Clayton. So who were you—" I followed her gaze. "You meant *Jeremy*?"

I should point out that there was nothing wrong with Jeremy Danvers. He wasn't what you'd call conventionally good-looking, but he was attractive enough, more striking than handsome, just over six feet tall, and lean, with black hair, high cheekbones, and a slight slant to his black eyes, which suggested Asian blood somewhere in his family tree. If I was surprised, it was because Jaime's choice *was* original. Put Jeremy next to blond-haired, blue-eyed Clayton, and it would be a rare woman who'd notice Clayton wasn't alone. To be honest, I wouldn't have guessed Jaime would be that woman.

"Jeremy Danvers?" Jaime said. "Isn't he the, uh, leader—oh, God, what's the word?"

"Alpha. The lead wolf in a Pack is the Alpha. Werewolves use the same terminology."

"So that guy—the dark-haired one— We *are* talking about the dark-haired one, right?"

"The dark-haired one is Jeremy. He's the Alpha. The blond is Clayton. He was Jeremy's adopted son; now he's the Pack muscle and Jeremy's self-appointed bodyguard. Elena is the woman, of course. She's Clay's partner and acts as Jeremy's representative outside the Pack. Clay and Elena are the Beta wolves, though I don't think they use that terminology."

"Uh, right," Jaime said, gaze once again glued to Jeremy. I suspected she'd be asking me ten minutes from now to explain the relationships again, having not heard a word I'd said about Clayton or Elena. "So he's the leader? I thought the Alpha would be some old guy. He can't be much older than me." She squinted for a better look. "Shit, no, he could be younger than me. He isn't, is he?"

She turned from the view and rubbed her hands over her face. "Ack! Is it just me or was I suddenly channeling the ghost of a love-struck fifteen-year-old girl? Don't ask me where that came from." She inhaled and exhaled. "There, all better. So, uh, how old is he, anyway?"

I grinned. "Too old for someone who doesn't date men more than a decade her senior."

"Bullshit. I mean, that he's that old, not that I won't—it's not a hard-and-fast rule, so if he was that old . . . But he's not. Can't be."

"Werewolves get prolonged youth. He's fifty-three, I think. Maybe fifty-four."

"No way." She sighed. "Damn, everyone else gets cool powers, and I get hauntings. Doesn't seem fair. What the hell does a werewolf need a fountain of youth for, anyway?"

"Same reason vamps have regeneration," I said, holding open the patio door and waving her back inside. "With the hunters, it's all about survival. Prolonged youth means prolonged strength, which means you'll be able to defend yourself longer."

"And look really good doing it."

The door slammed open and we both jumped. Savannah rushed in ahead of Jeremy, with Elena and Clay bringing up the rear.

Seeing Jaime, Savannah skidded to a stop. "Oh, my God! It's—it's you." She shot a glare my way. "You didn't say it was *her*!"

"Jaime, meet Savannah," I said. "A fan."

"Oh, my—I don't believe it. See, Paige? I told you she could really contact the dead and you said"—Savannah switched to the unflattering impersonation every teen uses for adults—"'Only a necromancer can contact the dead, Savannah.' Well, ha! She is a necromancer. This is so cool! You're the best, Jaime. I watch you on *The Keni Bales Show* every month—well, I can't always watch it, because I'm usually in school, but I tape it."

Jaime fairly glowed, sneaking quick glances at Jeremy to see what kind of impression this display of adoration was making on him.

Savannah continued, "I saw your show last month— Whoa, what happened to your face?" As Jaime's hands flew to the scratches down her cheek, Savannah studied her closer. "You don't look so good. Well, not like you do on TV. Are you sick?"

I grabbed Savannah's arm and tugged her aside. "We're still teaching her manners. Normally, we keep her confined to a locked room in the attic, but today she escaped."

"Very funny, Paige. I just meant—"

"Jaime's been going through a very nasty haunting, her reward for helping us out. Now for the proper introductions. Jaime, this is Jeremy Danvers. Jeremy, Jaime Vegas."

As Jeremy shook Jaime's hand, his face revealed nothing more than a glimmering of polite interest—not surprising, given that Jeremy can make Lucas look overemotional. Disappointment darted across Jaime's face. Savannah, obviously thinking Jeremy wasn't nearly impressed enough, scurried back to stand beside her.

"Jaime's on TV," Savannah said.

"TV?" Jeremy repeated.

Elena swung up beside him, grinning. "Yes, TV. Small box, pretty pictures that move . . ." She stage-whispered to Jaime. "He's very old. Not quite used to the industrial age yet." She extended a hand. "I'm Elena." She looked around. "And the rude one who walked past you without saying hello is Clayton."

She paused, waiting for Clayton to offer a belated greeting, but he just kept heading toward the sofa, where Lucas was slowly waking up. He handed Lucas his coffee, sat down beside him, and passed him his glasses from the side table.

"Sorry," Elena muttered. "Just ignore him. Please. You know, I read an article about you a few months ago. At the time, I thought it was pretty interesting. Then when Paige told me who she was working with, the name sounded familiar, so I plugged it into a search engine and realized you were the one I'd read about."

"*You* knew who she was, too, and you didn't tell me?" Savannah sputtered.

"Edward got into a car," Clay announced from across the room.

For a moment, everyone was silent, struggling to fit this statement into the present conversation, then realizing it didn't fit and wasn't supposed to.

"Yeah, yeah," Elena said. "We'll get to that in a second. Don't be so impatient."

We all headed into the room. Lucas was still fighting back yawns, but managed a tired smile for me and shifted over to let me sit down beside him. Clay stayed on his other side and Elena perched on the sofa arm beside him, leaving the armchair for Jeremy. Jaime and Savannah grabbed chairs from the dinette table.

"So Edward got into a car?" I said. "Can't track him that way, I guess. Damn."

"Was it in a parking lot?" Lucas asked.

Clay shook his head. "Street in front of his hotel."

"Did you happen to notice a bus stop nearby?" Lucas asked.

"Oh, very good," Elena said. "Nope. No bus stop, and no street parking. So he must have hailed a cab. Does that help?"

"It might," he said. "I have a contact at one of the taxi companies, who can usually obtain information from the others for a small fee. I'll go call him."

When Lucas slipped into the next room, I turned to Jaime. "How have things been with you since we left? Natasha making any noise?"

Jaime shook her head. "She's gone. Disappeared, probably at the same time she ripped open that portal. Mission accomplished, I guess."

"Maybe, but something happened to her when she opened the portal, and from the look on her face, it wasn't something good. She might not be haunting you now because she *can't*. Someone shut her down, or—"

Lucas reappeared.

I studied his expression. "Not good, I take it."

"Edward did call a cab, one from Peter's company, which made it easy. Unfortunately, he asked to be dropped off in Little Haiti, at the Caribbean marketplace, which doesn't help us at all." He settled onto the couch. "What about this portal ritual, Jaime? Did you have any luck researching it?"

"Yep," Jaime said. "Found exactly what I was looking for. First, though, the warning. I have no idea whether this would even work. Like I told Paige, people don't punch holes into the ghost world every day. Portals and how to reopen them are the stuff,of necro myth. I knew I'd read something about it years ago, going through my nan's books. I had some trouble finding another necro who knew the details, though."

"Do you have the books at your place?" I said. "If it'd help, we could send someone from the Cabal to get them. Save relying on secondhand info."

"I, uh, don't have the books," Jaime said, gaze skittering across the floor. "Back when I left home, I didn't take them. My mother pitched them out."

"That's okay," I said. "We don't need them. You got the information from someone else, so we're good. What did they say?"

"Well, the first three necros I called had no clue what I was talking about. Then I found two who did, and they tried to tell me any necromancer could reopen the portal, no special tools required. But I knew that was wrong. Nan's books were the best there were, the real thing, not like the crap that's out there today." Another wave of regret flooded her eyes. She shook it off. "Anyway, I knew that reopening a portal called for human sacrifice of a specific kind, so I kept calling around and finally found someone who'd read the same book my nan had. We need—"

A knock came at the door. Everyone looked up. Elena's nostrils flared and she leaned over to whisper something to Clay.

"Fuck," he muttered. "Keep talking, Jaime. It's only Cassandra. She can wait. Forever, if we're lucky."

"I heard that, Clayton," Cassandra said as she walked in.

"Who the hell forgot to lock the door?" Clay said.

"You were the last one in," Elena murmured.

"Damn."

CHAPTER 61

BLACK-MAGIC STANDBY

Aaron arrived a few minutes later, having likely been parking the car. He got a warmer reception than Cassandra, but the meet-and-greet phase was cut even shorter this time, now that we were all eager to hear what Jaime had found. First, though, we had to bring Cassandra and Aaron up to speed.

"So now Jaime was about to tell us what Edward needs to reopen the portal," I finished.

"Well, like I said, the key ingredient is the black-magic standby, a good ol' human sacrifice. If Edward performs the sacrifice on the exact spot that the portal opened, it'll reopen for a couple of minutes."

"So what's to say he hasn't done this already?" Cassandra said. "He's a vampire. He could have taken a victim by now and gone through the portal."

"I'm getting to that," Jaime said. "As I told Paige, I knew he needed a specific victim. According to the necromantic ritual book, he needs to shed the blood of someone who passed through the portal."

"What?" Cassandra said. "That's ridiculous. You've made a mistake, Jaime. Obviously, if they passed through the portal, they aren't here to—"

Aaron clamped a hand over Cassandra's mouth. "Continue, please, Jaime."

"Cassandra's right," Jaime said. "Most people who pass through a portal never return, so the ritual doesn't actually mean you need to kill— or rekill—the person who went through. That *would* work, but the ritual means figurative blood—the blood of the closest same-sex relative. That leaves four possibilities, since two of you went through. Someone could use Paige's mother or daughter, or Lucas's father or son. Now, I know Paige's mom has passed over, so unless one of you guys has a kid stashed away—which I seriously doubt—that leaves one possibility."

"My father," Lucas murmured.

"And Edward has how long left?" I said. "About twenty-four hours before the portal closes for good? That leaves him one day to kidnap and kill the Cortez Cabal CEO. Right now, I bet Edward's seriously researching the 'hidden child' theory. It would be near-impossible to get Benicio."

"Perhaps," Jeremy said. "But if he's as determined as he seems, he'll certainly try."

"I should warn him," Lucas said.

As he rose, he brushed his hand against my arm. I looked up and he nodded, almost imperceptibly, toward the bedroom, asking me to join him. I followed. Less than thirty seconds into the call, I understood why he felt the need for a little moral support.

"No, Papá," he said firmly. "I am in absolutely no danger. This is about you—" Pause. "No, my blood—" Pause. "My blood won't—" Pause. "Papá, listen to me. Please. Edward can't use my blood for the ritual."

The lie flowed so smoothly even I almost wondered whether I'd misunderstood Jaime.

"Consider it logically, Papá," Lucas continued. "Why would the ritual require the blood of the person who passed through? That person is gone and, in almost every case, not coming back. In most sacrificial rituals, if the original subject is no longer available, you must use the nearest same-sex blood relative, correct?"

A brief pause. Lucas's lips parted in a silent sigh of relief.

"Yes, that's right," he said. "Therefore *you* are the one in danger. I know you're extremely security-conscious already, but this will require additional protection. For the next twenty-four hours, you should excuse yourself from public life and—"

Lucas stopped and listened, frown lines deepening with each passing second.

"Yes, yes, I do remember your mentioning it, but—" Pause. "In this one case, I believe you have a reasonable excuse for not attending—" Pause. "Yes, perhaps it would be a way to trap him, but—" Another sigh, this one audible. His eyes cut to me. "Let me speak to Paige, and I'll phone you back."

"What's this about trapping Edward?" I said as Lucas hung up.

"My father is scheduled to make an appearance tonight—a semi-public appearance—and he refuses to bow out. He hopes Edward will show up."

"The charity masquerade," I said. "For the New York firefighters."

"Precisely."

"Would Edward know he's there?"

"It's a large event, well covered in the media. The Cortez Corporation is a cosponsor, and my father is expected to attend. Edward would only need to pick up today's paper to see that. That may also explain why the cab dropped him off at the Caribbean marketplace. It would be an excellent place to get costume fixings." He swore under his breath and pinched the bridge of his nose. "Perhaps I can still talk him out of it—"

"You won't," I said. "He's not going to that safe house any more than you are. We have to deal with it. Let's go talk to the others."

As we walked back into the main room, Elena was talking.

"Okay," she said. "This is dead obvious so, since no one else is bringing it up, I know I'm missing something. We're assuming that Edward wants to go back through the portal to get to Natasha. My question is: Why doesn't he just kill himself?"

"I know that sounds easy, Elena, but for a vampire, it's more complicated than that." Cassandra's voice held none of the impatient snap she used with the rest of us. "The only way we can die is by being beheaded."

"Not the easiest method of suicide. Okay, I get it. But why . . ." She hesitated, as if reluctant to question something if no one else was.

"Why not get someone else to do it?" Clay said.

Elena nodded. "Right."

"Because he can't guarantee he'll end up with Natasha," I said as I took my place on the sofa. "We have no idea where she is, whether it was some kind of vampire afterlife, or a side effect of their immortality experiments. The best way for Edward to ensure he'd be with Natasha is to use the portal she opened. In the meantime, we have a new problem."

I told them about Benicio's plan.

"Maybe this is for the best," Cassandra said. "You've done your share—more than your share. Let the Cabals finish this. I would prefer to see Edward taken quietly and allowed a fair trial, but if he's killed while attempting to kidnap a Cabal CEO, there's little I can do about that."

She glanced at Aaron as if for confirmation.

He nodded. "Not much chance they'll behead the guy in the middle of a charity gala. They'll probably settle for taking him into custody; then we could intervene later. If not, well, Cassandra and I can deal with any fallout in the vampire community. Edward has committed enough crimes that I'm not going to put someone else in danger just to make sure he gets a fair trial."

I looked at Lucas. Stone-faced, he was struggling not to argue, but I could see concern simmering in his eyes.

"Your father invited us to the masquerade," I said softly. "Maybe we should go."

"As backup, I hope," Clay said. "Because if you mean what I think you mean—"

I lifted a hand. "Hear me out, okay? Yes, I mean Lucas and I go as guests, that we set ourselves up as bait."

Clay's mouth opened, but Elena shushed him.

"It makes sense, doesn't it?" I said. "Edward thinks we're dead. If he sees us there, it'll throw him off and divert his attention from Benicio. We'd be the easier targets—" I stopped and looked at Lucas. "Unless your dad finds out Edward *can* use our blood. Didn't he have his researchers looking into the ritual?"

"They didn't find anything."

"Good. So he might have a couple of guards tailing us, but he knows Edward's focus will be on opening that portal, not getting revenge by killing you. So he'd assume *he's* the main target. When Edward sees us, though, he'll realize we'd be easier to capture."

"But you're only trading one decoy for another," Clay said.

"True, but it's not an equal trade," Lucas said. "Paige and I know more about vampires than my father does. And we're certainly better equipped to deal with a direct threat than he is. It's been many years since he's needed to defend himself."

"I can pull bodyguard duty," Aaron said. "Watch over you from the sidelines."

Elena glanced over at Jeremy, who nodded.

"Count me in," Elena said.

"*Us,*" Clay said.

"Not sure what I can do, but I'm in, too," Jaime said.

"I'll go as well," Cassandra said.

"Cool," Savannah said. "Do I get to dress up in a costume, too? Or should I help Elena and Clay?"

Everyone turned and looked at her. As her gaze went from my face to Lucas's to Jeremy's, her eyes narrowed.

"No way," she said. "Uh-uh. I'm not staying behind. I can help out. I'm at least as good a spell-caster as Paige—"

"Better," I said. "But you're also thirteen years old. No matter how good you are, I'm responsible for you. Not only might you get hurt by Edward, but you're still a prize for the Cabals."

"You're special, remember?" Elena said, offering a smile. "Just like Jeremy. You two can keep each other company, man the control center, eat lots of pizza, and stay up really late."

Savannah rolled her eyes at Jeremy. "Sucks being special sometimes, doesn't it?"

"It certainly does," Jeremy said.

Benicio was thrilled with our offer to attend the gala as backup for him, though I'm sure he had no intention of letting us watch his back. That was a job for a half-demon employee, not a sorcerer heir, but if it meant Lucas willingly appeared by his side at a public function, Benicio would humor us . . . especially if it also meant he could keep a closer eye on his son.

We devoted the day to preparing for the night. Our first concern was costumes. Though it was by no means our *primary* concern, it did need to be attended to first. Since it wasn't safe for us to be combing costume shops, where Edward might see us, we accepted Benicio's offer to bring materials to us. We left the guys to work on something for Lucas, while Cassandra, Jaime, Elena, and Savannah helped me. Once we came up with an outfit that could be put together quickly, I called Benicio and gave him my material list.

Next Lucas obtained blueprints for the hall and maps of the grounds. We used these to scope out routes Edward could take, plus the best places from which the others could hide and watch us. Then we spent the rest of the afternoon making plans.

At five we started getting dressed. The basis of my costume was a green silk dress. I used the minimal dressmaking skills I'd learned from my mother to sew on scraps and strips of green and brown taffeta. Next, I added real leaves and feathers. Then on to grooming. Cassandra did my makeup in golds and browns. Savannah painted my nails a mossy green. Jaime styled my hair in a messy, upswept do, and added leaves and feathers. Elena held the mirror.

Clayton flung open the bedroom door as Cassandra was zipping up my dress.

"Closed door means *knock*," Elena said, shooing him out.

"You've been in here for two hours," he said. "She can't need that much work." He frowned as he examined my outfit. "What the hell is she? A tree?"

"A dryad," Elena said, cuffing him in the arm.

"Oh, my God," Jaime said, surveying my outfit. "We forgot the bag!"

"Bag?" Clay said. "What does a dryad need with—"

"An evening bag," Cassandra said. "A purse."

"She's got a purse. It's right there on the bed."

"That's a day purse," Cassandra snapped.

"What, do they expire when the sun goes down?"

Elena pushed him out of the room. "Okay, do we still have time for someone to run out and buy something?"

"No!" Clay called back through the closed door. "Car comes in fifteen minutes."

"I'll have to skip the purse," I said. "I can slip my lipstick into Lucas's pocket. He's got his cell phone. That'll have to do."

Jaime opened the door and announced me with due fanfare. I accepted the obligatory gracious compliments from Jeremy and Aaron. Lucas smiled, walked over, and offered his compliments privately into my ear.

"Lucas!" Savannah cried. "Where's your costume?"

"I'm wearing it."

"That's not a costume, that's a suit! The same thing you wear almost every day."

"It's a tux," I said. "And a very nice one."

"But what are you supposed to be?" Cassandra said. "A cocktail waiter?"

"I was going to say James Bond," Jaime said.

"Don't look at me," Aaron said. "I was pushing for a knight costume, but these two"—he gestured at Lucas and Clay—"shut me down."

"And I wisely decided to keep my mouth shut," Jeremy said.

"If he doesn't want to wear a costume, he doesn't have to wear a costume," Clay said. "Hell, he's got a mask. Good enough."

Lucas held up a plain black eye-mask.

"They don't come in colors?" Savannah sighed. "At least you put in your contacts." She looked out the balcony window. "So do you get a limo?"

Lucas shook his head. "A chauffeured car, but not a limousine. My father finds them too ostentatious, even for formal occasions."

"Limos are for high-school graduations," Cassandra said.

"And weddings," Jaime said.

"Not good ones," Cassandra said.

"I like limos," Savannah said.

"So do I," I said, sneaking a grin at Lucas. "Lots of room to . . . stretch out."

He paused, then the corners of his mouth twitched and he reached for his cell phone. "I believe we still have time to request a change of vehicle."

"Uh-uh," Jaime said. "I just spent an hour doing Paige's hair. No limos. Tell you what, though. You guys finish this and I'll rent you a limo for the whole trip back to Portland."

"Cool," Savannah said.

"Uh, right," Jaime said. "Okay, scrap that idea. How about a shorter limo ride and free babysitting?"

"Car's here," Clay said from his spot at the window.

"You guys scoot, then," Jaime said. "We'll meet you there."

CHAPTER 62

Masquerade

The charity ball organizers had chosen a masquerade because of the event's timing—the night before Halloween. The party planners, though, had avoided the usual Halloween fare in favor of something more whimsical, accentuating the fantastical rather than the frightening. The ballroom was ringed with mannequins in incredibly elaborate costumes from children's fiction, from the Queen of Hearts to Puss-in-Boots to the Swan Princess. Paper dragons guarded the door, heads dipping and swaying in an invisible breeze. The buffet tables were floating magic carpets, the food forming the patterns of the rugs. Punch flowed from the mouth of an ice-sculpture phoenix, backlit by a small fire that melted the bird, only to have a fresh one arise from the bowl below. It was a glorious paean to everything magical, and I would have loved it . . . had I not spent every minute worrying about a certain murderous vampire. Mythical creatures make lovely ice sculptures, but far less enchanting enemies.

Most people wore costumes even less definable than mine—rainbow-hued designer dresses and tuxes, intricate body makeup and gorgeous masks—that didn't transform them into any recognizable character or creature. But hey, they looked great, and that, I think, was the point.

Like Lucas, Benicio had opted for the basic black tux. His mask, though, was anything but basic—it was an elaborate red hand-painted devil's face that extended to his upper lip, leaving only his mouth and chin bare. It was gorgeous, and the devil/CEO metaphor was wryly clever, but hardly matched Benicio's normal understated style. After a momentary burst of surprise, Lucas and I had to agree the disguise was good thinking on Benicio's part. Between the simple black tux and the brilliant red mask, there was little chance he'd get lost in the crowd tonight. Keeping an eye on him would be a snap.

Of the Cortez family, the only other members in attendance were William and William's wife. I have no idea what William's wife's name was, because I never met her. From the time we arrived, William found it convenient to be elsewhere, and kept his wife with him, so I know only that she was short, plump, and Hispanic.

As for Benicio's wife, Delores, our invitation apparently revoked hers. Delores was forbidden to attend any function where Lucas might be present. I bet that went over well, informing her this morning that she couldn't come to the event of the season. According to Lucas, Benicio and Delores's marriage had long since become a union of formality. Both lived in their own homes and appeared together only at public events. And if I felt sorry for Delores missing the charity gala, I only had to remind myself that Benicio had instituted the no-shared-events rule eight years ago when Delores tried to poison Lucas at his high-school graduation dinner.

Speaking of wishing Lucas dead, the eldest Cortez son, Hector, had been detained in New York, and was expected to miss tonight's event. A damned shame, really. I knew someday I'd have to face Hector but, in this case, sooner was definitely not better. I had enough to worry about without that.

One thing we *didn't* need to worry about was letting Benicio out of our sight. As I expected, he wasn't letting Lucas out of his. We spent the first half-hour being escorted around the room, introduced to what seemed like every politician and business leader in the state. I know I should have been impressed, but I couldn't help thinking that I was in the same room with quite possibly every person responsible for the Florida election snafu, and the subsequent election of George W. Bush, and somehow I couldn't muster a proper feeling of awe.

As Benicio led us about the room, I kept sneaking glances at Lucas, knowing how much he must have hated this. Given the choice between facing down a gun-toting vampire again and attending a charity ball with his father, I suspect he'd pick the near-death experience. After roughly fifty rounds of being introduced as the next CEO of the Cortez Corporation, he was probably cursing me for bringing him back from the ghost world. Yet he never showed it. Instead he only deflected questions about his future with a smile and a deft change of subject. Finally, when the constant introductions threatened to start us both yawning, Lucas begged leave to take me onto the dance floor.

"Thought you couldn't dance," I murmured as he led me out among the other couples.

"I can't." A small smile. "But I can fake it for a few minutes."

He positioned us where we could both see Benicio and could be easily seen by anyone watching the dance floor.

"Seems you're learning the steps of another dance, too," I said.

"Hmmm?"

"With your father. I saw what you were doing. He introduces you as his heir, you say nothing. You don't deny it, but nor do you say anything that would confirm it."

"I think I've realized that the harder I protest, the harder he pushes."

"And while that might not wear down your resolve, it does wear *you* down."

Lucas pulled me closer and brushed his lips across the top of my head. "Yes, I've noticed that. With you here, I've been seeing it though your eyes, imagining how it must look to you, and I haven't been too pleased with the image I saw reflected."

"Well, the image I see is fine. Always has been."

A soft laugh. "That's good to hear. But I can't continue that way, running away, avoiding him, hoping he'll leave me alone. He won't. I'm his son. He wants some kind of relationship with me, and I think I want the same thing. I need to learn to deal with him on his terms, because he isn't going to change. Yes, if I associate with my father, some people will take that as a sign of backsliding, but I can't worry about that. *I* know I'm not taking over the Cabal. And if you know it, too, then that's all that matters. Which leads me to another area of resolve. Regarding you. Or, I should say, us."

"I hope it's along the same lines," I said. "Standing firm instead of running."

"I've been resolved on that point for four months. Since the first flicker of interest on your part, I knew I wasn't going anywhere without a fight." He paused and frowned, eyes scanning the crowd.

"Talking to two women near the bar," I said. "Can't miss that mask."

"Ah, yes, I see him. Now, what was I . . . ? Resolve. It relates to your participation in my investigations."

"You don't want me there. I understand—"

He pressed his forefinger to my lips. "No, my resolve is to see this conversation through to the end, saying what I want to say without backing down for fear of frightening you off with a proposal that may impose upon your need for independence."

"Uh-huh. Once more, please . . . in translation."

He leaned down to my ear. "I'd like . . . no, I would *love* for you to be my partner, Paige. In my work, in my life, everything. I know you have your own aspirations, and if you don't wish to share my life quite so completely, I understand. But if you do, you are more than welcome to play as large a role in my investigations as you want."

I smiled up at him. "You may regret saying that."

"No, I don't think I will. Is that a yes?"

"It's a 'we need to discuss this more, but I'm definitely interested.'"

He grinned then, a grin so broad Benicio did a double take from across the room.

Lucas noticed his father's reaction and laughed softly. "He probably thinks I just proposed."

I tried to glance over at Benicio, but another couple blocked my view.

"We'd better hurry over and set him straight," I said. "Before he has a coronary."

"No, he looks quite pleased," Lucas said. "I believe he'll be disappointed when he learns I *didn't* propose. He'll have to wait for that. I know better than to push my luck. I'll give it some time before I take that plunge." His grin broadened. "At least a week."

I laughed, but before I could respond, he checked his watch.

"Speaking of time, we're late for our rendezvous with the others. We should go—"

"I'll go. Your dad's not letting you out of his sight tonight. Don't worry, I'll be careful."

"Then I'll track down a couple glasses of champagne for your return."

We disengaged and I slipped from the dance floor.

I found Jaime alone in our agreed meeting place, a nook between the kitchen and the bathroom hall.

"Sorry I'm late," I said. "The others get tired of waiting?"

"More worried than impatient," she said. "Elena didn't like us all hanging out here where we can't see what's going on, so I nominated myself for the job. Not like I can do much else. If I try following them around, I just get in the way. I've *had* stalkers, but never quite developed a talent for it myself, and all four of them are pros."

"Hunters."

She shivered. "Yeah, well, I try not to think about that. Werewolves, uh, they only hunt animals, right? The four-legged variety?"

"Pack wolves, yes. Other werewolves . . . you take your chances."

"Uh-huh. Well, there's nothing to report. No sign of Edward. No Natasha, either. I think I've seen the last of her. Which leads me to something else. I'm really not doing any good here, Paige. If you think I'm helping, I'll stay, but if not—"

"If you want to leave, that's fine."

"No, no. Well, yes, I want to leave, but for a reason. I'm thinking I might be more help if I keep looking into this ritual, call some more people, see whether I missed something. I could go back to the hotel room with Jeremy and Savannah, make my calls, and help them man the control center."

"Manning the control center, hmm?" I said with a grin. "Sure, that sounds like a plan. Go for it."

"I didn't mean that," she said, reddening. "Seriously, I think I'd be more use checking out this lead, don't you? Okay, the control center probably doesn't need extra manning. Maybe I should make the calls from our hotel instead—"

"No, go stay with Jeremy. That's safer all around, and you can bounce ideas off him. He might not know much about necromantic ritual, but he's a smart guy and he's very easy to talk to."

"He is, isn't he? I mean, for a werewolf, and an Alpha werewolf at that, you'd expect the guy to be all high-and-mighty, brawn-over-brains, but he's not, and he just seems like such a—" She buried her hands in her face with a moan. "Oh, God, I'm too old for this shit." She peeked up at me. "Lack of sleep. It's lack of sleep . . . and emotional trauma. I've been traumatized by this vamp-spook, and I'm not thinking straight."

"Exactly."

"Right. So, I'll just go over there and start making my calls. If Jeremy can help, that's great, but otherwise, I'll just do my thing, and he can keep Savannah company. He's great with Savannah, isn't he? I mean, other guys would tell her to go off and play a video game or watch TV, but he pays attention to her and—" She inhaled and exhaled. "Okay. Fine now. Leaving now. If you need me, I'm heading straight to the hotel." She paused. "Well, after I swing by my hotel room for a quick shower—I think I spritzed myself with your hairspray earlier and I'm all sticky. So I'll shower, change my clothes, and then head to their hotel."

"Got it," I said, biting my cheek to keep from smiling.

"First, I'll find Elena and tell her I'm taking off. She seems nice. We haven't really talked, but she seems nice. Down-to-earth."

"She is."

With that, Jaime left, and I headed back to the party. I found Lucas near the buffet tables, holding the promised champagne flutes.

"Your dad hasn't shanghaied you yet?" I said.

"He's heading in this direction, but keeps being waylaid by other guests. In light of my new strategy for paternal relations, I am not using the situation as an opportunity to initiate a game of hide-and-seek, but standing firm and allowing him to make his way here, however long that may take."

I told Lucas about Jaime, and he agreed there was little for her to do here. Between the vampires and the werewolves, security detail was covered.

"I'll admit, I am concerned that Edward has yet to make an appearance," Lucas said. "Given the time constraints he's under, this would be the opportune moment to grab my father, and quite possibly the only chance he'll get before morning."

"Maybe he's having trouble getting past security," I said. "It is tight."

"It *appears* to be tight," he said. "Yet the others had no problem getting past it and they've been skulking about the perimeter for nearly two hours now without incident."

"It doesn't help that this is a masquerade." I looked out over the crowd. "But Elena or Clay would still have scented Edward, or Aaron and Cassandra would have sensed him, so—"

"Champagne, I see." Benicio appeared at Lucas's side and clapped a hand on his shoulder, beaming a smile. "May I assume that congratulations are in order?"

"They are. Paige has agreed to join my investigations on a permanent basis."

Benicio's smile faltered, but only for a second. "Well, that's a start, then. You've made an excellent team so far, and working together will certainly give you more time together, which I know was one of your concerns."

Lucas snuck a look at me. "It was," he murmured.

"And the house?" Benicio said.

"We're buying *a* house," I said. "Maybe the one in Portland, maybe not, but we're definitely buying a house."

"Good, good."

We braced ourselves, waiting for Benicio to start offering advice, but instead he turned to me.

"May I have a dance?"

"Uh, sure."

We walked onto the dance floor.

"Have you considered Seattle?" Benicio asked as we launched into our dance. "If you like Portland, I'm sure you'd like Seattle."

"Portland seems fine, but we'll probably look elsewhere, too, just to be sure."

"As you should. Buying a house is a major commitment. You also have Savannah's security to consider. Has Lucas mentioned that we have a satellite office in Seattle?"

"Really. How . . . surprising."

I caught Lucas's gaze across the floor. He put his fingers into his ears and mouthed "Ignore him." I grinned back.

Benicio plowed ahead, explaining all the benefits of living in a city with a Cortez corporate office. How much safer it would be. How we could share resources. How we could keep an eye on local corporate operations to ensure no serious crimes against supernaturals were "accidentally" being committed. As I listened, I realized Lucas had the right idea. There was only one way to deal with Benicio. Let him talk. Let him "suggest." Don't argue. Don't even answer. Just listen . . . and let it all flow out the other ear.

While we danced, and Benicio talked, I tried to keep an eye on Lucas, but it proved increasingly difficult. Benicio seemed determined to steer me away from Lucas, probably so his son wouldn't notice he was using the opportunity to "advise" me. Soon we were so deep in the mass of other dancers that I lost sight of him.

When we finished our dance, Benicio accompanied me back to where Lucas had been standing. He wasn't there. Benicio lifted one hand, just slightly, and Troy appeared.

"Where's Lucas?" Benicio asked.

"Morris was watching him; I was watching you."

Troy glanced around, then waved Morris over. As Morris approached, Troy slipped away.

Morris admitted he'd seen Lucas head away from the buffet table, but when he tried to follow, couldn't find him.

"I figured he just went to the bathroom. You said not to crowd him, and he was heading in that direction."

Troy returned. "Tim saw Lucas leave, sir. He tried to follow, but Lucas said he needed to use the washroom, so Tim backed off. He's waiting at the end of the hallway. Lucas hasn't come out yet."

"That's right," I said, turning to scan the room so Benicio wouldn't see the lie in my face. "Just before our dance he asked whether I'd seen where the bathrooms were. He probably decided to slip away while we were busy. Now that you mention it, I could use a quick trip myself. If Lucas comes back before I do . . ."

"I'll tell him where you are," Benicio said.

"Thanks."

I hurried off.

I did hope Lucas had gone to the bathroom, but I doubted it. Knowing I was already worried about his safety, he wouldn't take off for something so trivial without telling me. The only thing that would make him leave his post would be spotting Edward or, rather, catching so fleeting a glimpse of the vampire that he knew if he didn't follow immediately, he'd lose him. When he'd seen the Cortez security guard following, he would have used the bathroom excuse to get rid of him.

Edward had already lured Lucas to his death once. Could the same ruse work twice? I told myself it couldn't, that Lucas was too savvy for that. Yet, if the situation were reversed, and I'd seen Edward while Lucas was otherwise engaged, would I say, "Humph, not falling for that one again," and stand my ground? No. I'd realize it could be another trick but, given the choice between protecting myself and catching Edward before he killed again, I'd prep a good spell and proceed with caution. But I *would* proceed. And so would Lucas.

As I surveyed the partygoers, I tried to evaluate the situation logically. The last thing we needed was for me to panic and rush headlong into a back corridor, and straight into Edward's grasp, while Lucas returned from an emergency bathroom visit. First, I should try his cell phone. I reached for my purse . . . and remembered I didn't have one. Nor did I have a cell phone.

I hurried to the bathroom. Standing outside the men's room, I cast a sensing spell within. It picked up one person. Good. Then the door opened and an elderly man walked out. Once he was gone, I cast the spell again, but the bathroom was empty.

"Damn, damn, damn," I muttered.

I had to find Lucas—no, I had to find the others, who would help me find Lucas. As much as I bristled at losing a few precious minutes tracking down the others, I knew the extra effort would be worth it. They could track Lucas in a fraction of the time it would take me.

I shot one last look around the ballroom, then headed into the warren of back halls, where the others were supposed to be prowling. As the noise of the gala settled to a distant murmur, I realized I was entering uncharted—and unoccupied—territory. Time to ready a self-defense spell. I started my suffocation spell, then stopped. Would that work on a vampire? Of course not. They didn't breathe. Fireball spell? Nonlethal, but it could startle him enough for me to make a getaway. Or would it? Fire didn't hurt a vampire. Goddamn it! Why didn't I think of this—

"Hello, Paige."

I jumped and spun around. There behind me was, not a green-eyed, sandy-haired vampire, but a dark-eyed, dark-haired sorcerer. Hector Cortez.

CHAPTER 63

A COWARD'S PLAN

"We need to talk," Hector said, bearing down on me.

Of all the moments Hector Cortez could choose to reenter my life, this was quite possibly the worst. A voice in my head told me to run, forget how bad it would look, forget how embarrassing it would be, get away from him and continue looking for Lucas. But my feet wouldn't obey me. After a lifetime of refusing to run from confrontations, they were damned if they were going to start now.

"I don't believe we've been properly introduced," I said. "Well, we have, but at the time I was bound and gagged, and I don't think you ever expected to see me alive again, so you skipped the formalities. I'm Paige Winterbourne. You're Hector Cortez. I'd say I'm pleased to meet you, but we both know I'd be lying. So your meeting didn't run as late as Benicio expected? Sorry to hear it. Now, if you'll excuse me . . ."

I turned to go. Hector swung in front of me.

"A late meeting? Is that the excuse he used? I didn't have a meeting. I've been exiled in New York for the past two weeks, on my father's orders. Any idea why he'd do that?"

"Besides to keep you from killing Lucas? No, I can't imagine why." I stopped, seeing the hard glint in his eye, the glare of a hawk confronting the sparrow who'd chased him off his turf. "You think *I* got you banished? That I told Benicio that you tried to have me killed in Boston? Well, gee, I'd hope if I did tattle, you'd get something a little worse than an extended New York vacation. No, I didn't tell your father. Now, if you'll excuse me—"

Hector stepped into my path. "I never said you told my *father*."

"What? Oh, so you think I told Lucas and he asked your father to keep you away?" I met Hector's glare with one of my own. "No, I didn't. And I won't. What happened at that house is between you and me, and it stays there. Now get out of my way."

"Is that your plan, then, witch? Hold it over my head?" He stepped closer, looming over me. "I may make a mistake once, but never twice. I'm not getting out of your way, you're getting out of mine. Stay with Lucas, and the only question is when I'll decide to move you aside . . . permanently."

"How about now?" said a slow drawl behind him. "First, though, you gotta move me aside."

Hector turned to see Clayton behind him. His gaze skimmed over the other man with a dismissive twist of his lips. He lifted his fingers to flick Clay aside with a knock-back spell, but Clay grabbed his hand before the first words left his mouth.

"You think you're going to kill Paige to hurt Lucas?" he said, leaning in, putting his face to Hector's. "That sound like a clever plan to you? Sounds like a coward's plan to me."

Hector tried to wrench his hand free, but couldn't so much as twist it in Clay's grasp.

"Who are you?" Hector demanded.

"The question isn't really who, but what," Clay said. "You want to find out? Lay a hand on Paige or Lucas and you will."

Clay clapped his free hand over Hector's mouth, then squeezed his other hand around Hector's fingers. There was a sickening crunch of bone and Hector's eyes bulged, his scream muffled by Clay's hand.

"You think that hurt?" Clay said. "Imagine what I'd do if I was really pissed off."

He shoved Hector away and turned to me. "Come on."

I followed Clay around two corners before he slowed enough to let me catch up.

"He tried to kill you in Boston?" Clay asked.

"You overheard?"

"I was waiting around the corner. Didn't figure you'd appreciate me interfering too soon. So Lucas doesn't know?"

"No, he doesn't, and please don't tell him. Maybe it seems he has a right to know, but—"

"He shouldn't. He worries enough about putting you in danger. If you want to accept the risk, then that's your decision to make, not his. Just take precautions, and if what's-his-name—"

"Hector. He's Lucas's oldest brother."

"Fucked-up family," Clay said, shaking his head. "If this Hector comes after you again, you let me know. Yeah, I know, that's not how you like to handle things, but with something like this, you're not going to get anywhere jabbing each other back and forth. Give one big shove and be done with it."

He looked each way down an intersecting corridor, tilted his head in a quick sniff, then jerked his chin to the left and set out.

"I take it we're following Lucas?" I said.

"Yeah. Well, no. Elena's following Lucas. I'm following Elena. We figure Lucas is following Edward."

"Uh-huh."

"We saw Lucas take off, so Elena sent me to get you while she tracks him."

He rounded another corner, walked a dozen feet, then wheeled and backtracked to an exit door. He opened the door and stuck his head out, then waved for me to follow.

"Wait," I said. "Benicio. Is anyone watching—"

"Aaron."

I was about to step outside when Cassandra hailed us from down the hall.

"Come out and shut the door," Clay said. "Maybe she'll take the hint."

"Hold on. It might be important."

"What's going on, Paige?" Cassandra said when she caught up. "Why aren't you in the ballroom?" She peered out the door. "Clayton? Who are you looking for out here?"

"Elena."

Cassandra rolled her eyes. "What a surprise. The poor woman gets ten feet from you and you're off like a shot—"

"She's following Lucas, who's following Edward," I said.

"Oh."

Clay was already heading into the shadows.

I glanced at Cassandra. "Aaron's watching Benicio. Would you mind helping him? In case Edward circles back?"

I expected her to argue, but she nodded. "Have Elena phone Aaron if you need us."

I jogged to catch up with Clayton. Well, I tried anyway—one does not "jog" in two-inch heels. Instead I stumbled along until I drew close enough to see him standing by the wall, arms crossed, shaking his head. Once he was in sight, I stopped, yanked off my shoes, and broke into as near a jog as I could approximate in my dress.

"Good idea," he said, waving at the shoes in my hand. "But watch your step. Ground's rough."

"Think it's safe enough for a light spell?"

He nodded. After I'd cast the spell, we started off again. We'd gone about twenty yards when Lucas and Elena appeared, walking along a path leading to the parking lot.

"Lost him?" I called.

"Wasn't him," Elena called back. She drew nearer before continuing. "When I caught up with Lucas, he already had his doubts, so I conducted a sniff test. Guy failed, but we decided to trail him a bit farther, just to be sure. Followed him into the parking lot, where he climbed into the back of an SUV and met a woman I really doubt was his wife. We left before the show started."

As she spoke, Lucas kept sneaking concerned looks in the direction of the main building.

"Aaron and Cassandra are watching your dad," I said. "But we should get back inside."

We found Benicio showing an associate's wife around the dance floor. After an uneventful forty-five minutes, we joined the others in a side room, from which we could still see Benicio.

With less than an hour of the event left, the chances of Edward showing up were growing slim. He might try to nab Benicio in the confusion at the end, when everyone poured out to their cars. Yet he had no way of knowing whether Benicio intended to stay until the final moments, so he should still be here somewhere, watching in case Benicio left early. He could try to kidnap Benicio between here and his home, but that would mean taking on an armored car filled with bodyguards. And obviously Benicio's home would be at least as well guarded as his car. Grabbing him here made the most sense. So where was Edward?

Before we returned to the party, I decided to check in with Jaime. The most probable explanation for Edward's failure to appear was that he'd found an easier way to open the portal. If Jaime had uncovered a second ritual, I'm sure she would have called, but it never hurt to check.

Jaime's cell phone rang four times, then her answering service clicked on. That probably meant she was on the line, calling her necromancer contacts. So I phoned Jeremy's hotel room. He answered on the second ring.

"It's Paige," I said. "Nothing to report, I'm afraid. We were hoping Jaime might have something. May I speak to her?"

"Jaime?"

"Uh, right. Redhead? Necromancer? Hanging out in your hotel room right now? And hopefully not being pestered by Savannah . . ."

"Yes, I know who you meant, Paige. But Jaime isn't here."

"Did she leave? Damn it, was she trying to call us? We've been running around—"

"Slow down, Paige. Jaime hasn't been here. Not since she left with the rest of you. Was she heading here?"

"Two hours ago. I know she was stopping by her hotel room first, but . . . two hours?"

"Have you called her hotel room?"

"No, I'll do that now."

"If she's not there, check with the hotel front desk, see whether anyone saw her come in."

I did as he'd suggested. No answer at the hotel room. No answer again on her cell. The desk clerk said he hadn't seen her come in. When I suggested maybe she'd slipped past, he swore he would have noticed, and from his stammer, I guessed he'd been keeping an eye out for this semifamous, fully attractive guest. He offered to run up to her room, and left me hanging on the line before I could respond. Five minutes later he returned saying there was no sign of Jaime. He'd even checked inside her room, which was doubtless against company policy, but I wasn't going to call him on it. I thanked him for his help, then relayed the news to the others.

"Oh, for God's sake," Cassandra said. "The woman has the attention span of a gnat. She probably drove halfway to the hotel, saw a shoe sale, and forgot all about us."

Lucas shook his head. "While Jaime may cultivate the appearance of flightiness, she has far more gravitas than that, and far more dedication. She's stayed with us so far, despite some serious battering."

"Lucas is right," I said. "Jaime really wanted to help, and it would take something far more serious than a shoe sale to distract her from that."

"Ladies' Night at the strip club, perhaps?" Cassandra said.

"Mrrow," Aaron said. "Retract your claws, Cass, before you cut yourself. I'm with Lucas and Paige on this one."

"It's settled, then," Clay said. "Jaime is missing, so someone needs to look for her, and Elena and I are the best trackers. Aaron and Cassandra can stay here and keep an eye out for their fellow vampire. Lucas and Paige? Take your pick."

I looked toward Benicio on the dance floor. "We'd better stay."

"No," Lucas said. "We'll go. My father is well protected by his guards, and Aaron and Cassandra can handle Edward if he shows up, which I'm strongly beginning to doubt. We have a portal that must be reopened using a necromantic ritual, and now we have a missing necromancer. I suspect the two are not unconnected."

"Oh, shit."

"My thoughts exactly."

CHAPTER 64

Missing:
One Celeb Necromancer

In the hotel parking lot, Elena picked up a scent. But it wasn't Jaime's. It was Edward's. She trailed it to an empty parking space, where I found Jaime's designer cell phone lying on the asphalt. Elena and Clay could detect traces of Jaime's scent at the site, but no trail, as if she'd stepped from the car, but gone no farther. And, unless Edward had perfectly retraced his own path, he hadn't gone any farther, either. The logical conclusion: Edward had surprised Jaime getting out of her car; she'd had time to fumble for her cell phone, but dropped it as he overwhelmed her. Then he'd driven off, in her rental car, with her in it.

I cursed myself for not seeing this coming. Yet as Lucas insisted, kidnapping Jaime wasn't the obvious scenario. Reopening a portal was considered a necromantic ritual only because it involved access to the dead. Edward didn't need a necromancer to carry it out. If he had the right victim, he only needed to slit that person's throat over the portal site. Without that blood, he couldn't open the portal at all, not even with a dozen necromancers helping him.

What we had overlooked, though, was the very real possibility that Edward had no idea how to reopen the portal. As Jaime had said, it was an obscure ritual. Edward might not have even known any necromancers to ask about it. Yet he did know where to find one. Given Jaime's celebrity, her involvement in our case had to be all over the supernatural grapevine. Even John in New Orleans had probably known about it. And to find a photo of Jaime, all Edward had to do was run an Internet search, as Elena had done.

Did I think Jaime would tell Edward what he needed to complete the ceremony? Yes, and that's no reflection on her character. What reason did she have not to tell him? She knew Benicio was safely under guard, and if she steered Edward in his direction, she'd be steering him into ours, which was exactly what we wanted. Our main concern was that, after Edward got what he wanted from Jaime, he'd kill her. We could only hope he wouldn't trust Jaime's word enough to kill her before he had the portal reopened.

We planned our attack from both ends, the first end being the gala, where Edward would find Benicio, and the other end being the portal site, where he had to return if his mission was successful. Elena and Clay would join Aaron and Cassandra at the gala; with that kind of supernatural firepower on the alert, Edward would find it nearly impossible to capture Benicio. But, just in case, Lucas and I would stand guard at the portal site.

Lucas drove us back to the neighborhood where the portal had been opened. On the way, I drew a map of the surrounding area, noting all the possible points of entry and all the best locations for perimeter spells. Then we considered places to lie in wait. We were still debating our choices when Lucas's cell phone rang. He checked the call display, then passed it to me.

I didn't even get a chance to say hello before Aaron cut in. "Lucas? Where are you?"

"Uh, it's Paige, and we're still heading to the portal site. Do you want to talk to—"

"No, not if I can help it." His voice sounded strained, and a bit breathless. "Shit! I am so sorry, guys. We fucked up. Fucked up big-time."

"What's wrong?"

I tried to keep my voice steady, but Lucas's gaze shot over the moment the words left my mouth. I mouthed, "It's okay," and pointed at the road.

"We were watching Benicio," Aaron said. "Cass and I. He was on the dance floor. Couldn't miss him with that mask. Then Cass saw his bodyguard leaving. The one with the freaky blue eyes."

"Troy."

"Right, and she wanted me to follow him. She said he sticks pretty close to Benicio, and if he was taking off, something was up. So I went after him while she watched Benicio. I caught the guy sneaking out the back. Tried to get him to talk to me, but he wasn't in a talking mood. We scuffled and just as I took him down, Cass came running out. Said the guy on the dance floor wasn't Benicio."

My gut went cold. "Wasn't—?"

"It was a stand-in. With the mask— Fuck! We saw that mask and we were sure it was him."

"So Benicio's go—"

I stopped myself, but it was too late. Lucas veered the car to the curbside and hit the brakes so hard the seat belt snapped me back against the seat. I passed him the phone.

"Aaron?" he said. "Let me talk to Troy."

Within minutes, Lucas had the whole story, which he relayed to me as he drove hell-for-leather for the portal site. The Cabal researchers *had* found the ritual, so Benicio had always known that Edward could use Lucas's blood to reopen the portal. He'd played along with us because it had seemed the best way to ensure Lucas would be at the masquerade, safely under Cabal guard. As a precaution, he'd brought in a look-alike, who could take his place with that distinctive mask.

When Lucas and I took off after Jaime, Benicio feared the worst. And he'd feared that calling in a full Cabal SWAT team could result in a California-like fiasco, which would only endanger Lucas yet again. This had to be handled delicately. Earlier that day Benicio had sworn to us that if his name was no longer enough to protect his son, he'd do so himself; that was what he'd decided to do.

Benicio had grabbed Morris, told Troy to stay behind in case we reappeared. Then he'd left for the portal site, knowing that was where Edward had to end up. Troy, though, hadn't been about to let his boss take on a murderous vampire aided only by a temporary bodyguard. So he waited until Benicio was gone, then went after him. And that's when Aaron had intercepted him.

Now Benicio was indeed headed to the portal site, with only Morris for backup. But not for long. We were only a few minutes from the site. Aaron, Cassandra, and Troy were also on their way, and Aaron was phoning Elena to tell her to turn around and head over to the portal. In half an hour, we'd have seven supernaturals ready to take on Edward. We only prayed we'd get to him before Benicio did.

We parked as close to the site as we dared. As anxious as we both were to get there, we had to be careful. And there was very likely no need to rush. Benicio might have arrived ahead of us, but if Jaime had told Edward who he needed for the sacrifice, he was probably across the city by now, heading for the masquerade gala. The greatest danger we likely faced was Benicio himself. As Lucas said, it had been years—if not decades—since

Benicio had needed to defend himself. If we came flying down the alley, we might find ourselves on the receiving end of a lethal energy bolt.

Once out of the car, we hurried to the café. I cast perimeter spells at the alley on either side, and across the rear door. That covered the east side. Now on to the west, on the other side of the dead-end alley where we'd met Edward.

We'd gone only a few steps when Lucas lifted a hand to stop me. I followed his gaze down to the ground. A fingerlike puddle snaked around the corner, moving almost imperceptibly, expanding. The puddle shone black in the darkness. Without even casting a light spell, I knew it wasn't water.

As Lucas peered around the corner, I kept my gaze glued to his face, braced for a reaction I prayed I wouldn't see. His eyes closed in a soft wince, and my breath whooshed out. I slipped over to him, and looked.

Morris sat braced against the wall. He was dead. His shirt was ripped apart, and his hands still clutched the bloodied missing half to his throat, a frantic final attempt to save himself. Over the cloth I could see long jagged holes where Edward had ripped at his throat. Then he'd left Morris to bleed out while he turned his attention to the secondary threat: Benicio.

Lucas darted around the corner, moving as quietly as he could. As I set out after him, the whisper of voices fluttered across the still night. We both froze and listened.

". . . won't help . . ." a woman said.

I looked up at Lucas and mouthed, "Jaime?" He nodded.

"You said . . . sacrifice." Edward, his words clipped with anger.

Had Jaime betrayed us? Had she been betraying us all along? I told myself there was no motivation, nothing to be gained by this, but nor did I have time to think it through. If I did, maybe I would find a motive. For now, we had a far more pressing concern.

As we crept forward, the voices came clear.

"I'm telling you it *won't* work," Jaime said. "You can't use him. It needs to be a very specific sacrifice. I was trying to tell you that—"

"You weren't trying to tell me anything," Edward snarled. "You said I needed a sacrifice. *Any* sacrifice."

"Well, I lied, okay?"

"Oh, and now you're telling the truth?"

Lucas motioned for me to pass him. I ducked down before peeking out, then cast a fast cover spell. Jaime knelt before a makeshift altar . . . bound hand and foot. Beside her, Benicio lay on his side, also bound. His eyes were closed. My gut went cold.

"Yes, *now* I'm telling the truth," Jaime said. "Why? Because I'm scared shitless, okay? Maybe I did lie earlier, but that was before you killed a Cabal bodyguard and captured the damned CEO."

A humorless laugh. "So now you take me seriously?"

"Look, you can't kill Benicio, okay?"

Beside me, Lucas exhaled and slumped against the wall. I stifled my own sigh of relief, for fear of breaking my cover spell.

Jaime continued, "It won't reopen the portal."

"Oh, but I could try . . . and I think I will. Just to be sure."

Edward stepped toward Benicio. I broke my cover, a spell flying to my lips. Lucas started to swing around the corner.

"Wait!" Jaime said. "If you kill him, you can't get Lucas."

Edward stopped. Lucas yanked me back behind the wall.

"You need Lucas," Jaime said. "You need someone who went through the portal."

"And what does that have to do with keeping this bastard alive?"

"Think about it. What would happen if you called Lucas and said you have his dad? If you can prove you have his dad? The kid puts his life on the line for total strangers. You think he's not going to come running to save his father?"

"Good," Lucas whispered. "Thank you, Jaime."

I nodded. This was, of course, the perfect plan. Edward wouldn't kill Benicio until he had Lucas, and Jaime knew that when Lucas received that call, he would indeed come running—backed by a small army of supernaturals.

"My phone's gone, but you can use his," Jaime said. "I'm sure he has Lucas on speed dial. Probably right at the top."

Lucas tensed, ready to dash back toward the café so he could answer his phone without being heard.

"In a minute," Edward said. "First, I need to wake this one up . . . at least long enough to make that call for me. After that, though, I think I'll test your word. Better hope you don't fail."

"W—what?"

"All I need him for is to phone Lucas. Once that's done, he'll have outlived his usefulness. And, if his blood does reopen the portal, you'll have outlived yours. Believe me, if you are lying about that, I'll take you with me to the other side. And if you aren't? Well, then, the boy is in for a double surprise when he comes around that corner, though he won't have long to grieve before he's reunited with his old man."

Lucas and I looked at one another. I cast a privacy spell, so I could speak without whispering.

"D—don't answer the phone," I said. "Just don't answer it."

He cast his own spell. "I wasn't going to. If he can't get through, it'll buy us some time. But not long enough to wait for the others. We'll have to handle this ourselves." He laid his fingers on my arm. They trembled against my skin. He squeezed his eyes shut, pushing past the fear. "We can handle it. We have spells, and we have the element of surprise."

"But we don't know what spells work on vampires. We—" I took a deep breath and fought my own panic down. "A binding spell will work. But I need a way to get close enough to cast it without his seeing me. Maybe a distraction. But I don't know what—"

"I might," whispered a voice to our left.

Jeremy appeared beside us. He motioned for us to follow him to the other end of the alley, where Savannah waited.

"Aaron called the hotel for Elena's number," Jeremy whispered. "I thought you could use help, and we were closer than the others. Now what's happened?"

We told him, as quickly as possible.

"Paige was right," he said. "Distraction followed by attack is our best bet. I can provide the first, and assist you with the second."

"Me, too," Savannah said. "I can help."

"Uh-uh," I said. "You're staying—"

"No, Savannah's right," Jeremy said. "She can help me with the distraction."

He told us his idea, then turned to Savannah. "Now, you'll wait with Paige and Lucas. As soon as you see me, you can start, but not until you see me."

She nodded, and Jeremy headed down the side alley to loop around the north building. We returned to our hiding place at the head of the portal alley.

CHAPTER 65

ΠICE DOGGIE

We arrived back at the corner just as Edward finished telling a now-conscious Benicio that he needed to make a phone call. As we waited for Jeremy, I slid off my heels, in case we needed to dash down that alley.

"And if I refuse?" Benicio said.

A slap resounded through the silence. Benicio didn't so much as gasp.

"This isn't some business deal you can negotiate your way out of," Edward hissed. "What do you *think* happens to you if you refuse?"

"You'll kill me," Benicio said calmly. "And if I do call Lucas, and he comes, you'll kill him. Do you honestly think I would exchange my life for my son's?"

Edward gave a short laugh. "So you're offering to sacrifice yourself to save him. Very noble, but it won't work. I'll still find him and kill him."

"But you wouldn't need to. Kill me, use my blood on that portal, and it *will* reopen."

Lucas's eyes went round and his lips formed a silent no. I gripped his arm and looked anxiously down the alley for Jeremy, knowing it was still too soon, that he'd never be ready yet.

"N—no," Jaime said. "It won't work. Don't listen to him. You need Lucas's blood—"

"Try mine," Benicio said, voice still as calm as if he were dickering over the cost of his lunch. "If I am lying, you've lost nothing. As you say, you could probably still capture Lucas without my help, which you'll never get. Kill me, though, and I guarantee your portal will reopen."

Lucas lunged forward, breaking from my grip. At that moment, Jeremy stepped around the other corner. Lucas stopped. Our eyes met, and I knew what he was thinking. Did we still dare try Jeremy's plan? Both of us would have been much happier blazing in there, spells flying. But was that the smart move? The safe move? Savannah looked over at us. Lucas swallowed, then motioned for her to go. As she turned away, he took my hand and squeezed it so hard I heard the bones crackle. I squeezed his back.

As I watched Savannah go, a thousand new doubts skittered through my brain. She was so young. What if she couldn't pull this off? What if she froze up? What if that happened, and we couldn't cast before Edward pounced on her? What if Jeremy couldn't stop him in time? I took a deep breath and closed my eyes. Jeremy thought this would work, and I trusted that he'd never put Savannah in danger.

She stepped into the alley. Edward had his back turned to her, still talking to Benicio. Jaime and Benicio saw her, though. Jaime's eyes widened. I leaned as far from my hiding place as I dared, and, seeing me, Jaime shuttered her look of surprise. Benicio hesitated, then gave a tiny nod, and said something to Edward, keeping him engaged.

I cast a cover spell, then readied a fireball. For the few seconds it took me to prep the spell, I was visible, but the cloak of invisibility fell again the moment I stopped. Behind me, Lucas had a knock-back spell ready—far from lethal, but one of the few spells we knew would work on a vampire.

Savannah crept down the alley. Edward was too intent on Benicio to notice her. When she'd reached the mark we'd agreed upon, she stopped.

"Hey," she said. "Cool altar."

Edward whirled around and stared, momentarily dumbfounded by the sight of a thirteen-year-old alone in an alley at midnight.

Savannah took another step forward. "Is that, like, a Satanic altar? Are you guys gonna call up a demon or something?" She walked over near Jaime and pretended to notice Jaime and Benicio's bindings for the first time. "A sacrifice? Cool. I've never seen anyone get sacrificed before. Can I watch?"

Edward's mouth opened, then shut, as if his brain was still muddling through this. I glanced over at Jeremy, but he was already on his way, creeping along the far wall, out of Edward's sight. He moved as soundlessly as a vampire. Within seconds he was less than a yard from Edward.

Savannah's eyes rounded to saucers, mouth opening in an O of delighted surprise.

"Wow," she said. "Is that your dog, mister?"

Edward followed her gaze, then backpedaled fast. Behind him stood a jet-black wolf the size of a Great Dane. When Jeremy looked up at Edward, his black eyes blended perfectly with his fur, so the effect was one of eerily unrelieved darkness, more like the shadow of a wolf than an animal itself. With Elena, I could easily mistake her for a large dog. With Jeremy, no one getting close enough could make that error. I could tell by Edward's face that he knew this was no stray mutt.

Savannah strolled over and ran her fingers through the ruff around Jeremy's neck. Edward gave a sharp intake of breath, as if expecting her to lose that hand, but Jeremy didn't move.

"He's beautiful," Savannah said. "What's his name?"

She kept her hand on the back of Jeremy's neck. Jeremy looked up, eyes meeting Edward's. He drew his lips back and growled so softly that the sound seemed more felt than heard as it vibrated down the alley.

"Oooh," Savannah said. "I don't think your dog likes you, mister."

She scrunched her face in a thoughtful frown as she studied Jeremy's face. "You know, I think he's hungry." She looked at Edward and smiled. "Maybe you should feed him."

Jeremy pounced.

He caught Edward in the stomach and knocked him across the alley, away from Jaime and Savannah. Lucas and I bolted from our hiding spot and raced down the alley. By the time we got there, Jeremy was on top of Edward and had his teeth buried in his shoulder. Edward kicked and punched, but to no effect. Unfortunately, Jeremy's bite had no effect either. Not a single drop of blood flowed from the wound and the moment Jeremy released his grip, the tears in Edward's flesh knitted together.

Edward's head jerked up, teeth bared, aiming for Jeremy's foreleg.

"Jeremy!" I shouted.

Jeremy yanked his leg out of the way. We didn't know whether the sedative in Edward's bite would knock out a werewolf, but this wasn't the time to find out. Jeremy planted his forepaws on Edward's shoulders to pin him, then slashed at his throat, ripping the flesh in a slice that would have been lethal to anything mortal. Edward snarled in pain, but the moment Jeremy lifted his head from the bite, Edward's neck was whole again.

I turned to say something to Lucas, but he was already hurrying toward the altar. He grabbed the length of rope left over from tying Jaime, and jogged to Edward and Jeremy. As strong as Jeremy might be, unless he could behead Edward, this fight required a pair of human hands.

As Lucas approached, Jeremy lifted his head and met his gaze. Then he sank his teeth into Edward's side and lifted him, to flip him onto his back so Lucas could tie him. Edward slammed his fist into the back of Jeremy's left foreleg joint. Jeremy's leg buckled and his grip on Edward slid.

Beside me, Savannah began to cast. I prepped a knock-back spell, then heard Savannah's incantation and whirled.

"No!" I yelled. "Don't—"

The last words to the spell left her lips as Jeremy regained his hold and tossed Edward up. As Jeremy swung Edward, he moved into the path of

Savannah's binding spell and stopped dead. Edward landed on top of Jeremy. Savannah broke the spell, but Edward already had hold of Jeremy's rear leg. He bit it. Jeremy recovered and twisted, but Edward kept his teeth firmly planted in Jeremy's leg, drawing blood and injecting his sedative. Lucas lunged at the pair. He caught Edward in the side and knocked him away from Jeremy. As the two skidded across the alley, Jeremy stayed where he was, looking around as if confused. Then he snorted, and slid to the pavement.

Lucas and Edward hit the ground fighting, each grappling for a hold on the other. I prepped a binding spell. I knew I couldn't use it while they were tumbling together, but nor could I risk using anything dangerous. I felt useless enough standing there watching. At least the binding spell made me feel I could stop Edward if things went wrong.

The two men were an equal match in size and strength. Lucas had one forearm jammed under Edward's throat, so he couldn't bite, but every time Lucas lifted his free hand to cast, Edward knocked it down.

Edward wrenched away from Lucas and managed to get halfway to his feet before Lucas yanked him down again. They rolled together. When they reached the wall, Edward reared up and twisted. Lucas's head slammed into the brick.

The blow dazed Lucas only for a moment, but in that moment Edward saw his chance. His head arched back, mouth opening. I cast my binding spell—cast it too fast and knew before I even finished that it hadn't worked. Savannah and I both raced toward them, but we were ten feet away, too far to cover the distance in time. As Edward's head swung down for the bite, Lucas recovered and ducked. Edward's fangs still caught the skin of his neck. As Lucas tore himself away, a fine mist of blood sprayed across the alley. The air surrounding Lucas started to shimmer. He dove out of the way. I grabbed Savannah and yanked her backward.

Edward stopped. He saw that first glimmer of the portal and his lips curved in a slow smile.

"Natasha," he whispered.

Lucas pitched himself at Edward, trying to shove him away from the portal. And Edward let him. He knew the portal wasn't about to open. Not yet. He hadn't spilled nearly enough of Lucas's blood. Edward grabbed Lucas by the hair and snapped his head back, teeth arcing down to tear through his throat. Lucas's eyes went wide as he realized his mistake.

"Binding spell!" I shouted at Savannah.

As she cast, I dove for Edward. I caught the back of his shirt and threw myself sideways. I managed to rip him away from Lucas, but not before his fangs made contact. More blood sprayed. The ground began to vibrate.

Edward wrenched away from me. As my grasp on his shirt slipped, Savannah cast her binding spell. Edward froze. Lucas wheeled to grab him.

"No!" I yelled. "Go!"

He hesitated.

"Get away from the portal!"

Lucas's gaze darted from me to his father to the portal, shimmering behind me. Then he turned and jogged toward the other end of the alley.

"Keep holding him," I said to Savannah. "I'll grab the rope."

Something moved behind Savannah. It was just Jeremy waking and lurching to his feet, but the sudden motion startled her and the binding spell snapped. Edward tore free of my grasp. Lucas spun around, saw Edward, and lifted his hands to cast.

"No!" I shouted. "Keep going!"

Lucas hesitated only a second before racing down the alley. Edward shot after him. And I followed, passing Jeremy as he tried to shake off the sedative, growling softly.

Ahead, the two men disappeared around the corner. A moment of silence. Then trash cans crashed like cymbals, the sound not quite drowning out a yelp of pain. I hiked up my skirt and tore down the alley.

I rounded the corner as Edward sprang to his feet, recovering from whatever spell Lucas had cast at him. With a roar, Edward threw himself at Lucas. Lucas backpedaled and lifted his hands to cast again. Then Jeremy skidded around the corner. He whipped past me and launched himself at Edward. As Edward fell, Jeremy clamped his jaws around the back of his neck. Then he pinned him to the pavement, forepaws on his shoulders, mouth still on his neck. I raced in with the rope. Lucas grabbed Edward's hands, yanked them behind his back, and I tied them with the best knots I knew, then let Lucas add his own, just to be sure.

When we'd finished, I turned to Savannah, and nodded. She cast a binding spell on Edward. And it was over.

As Jeremy Changed back, I cared for Lucas, casting a spell to staunch the dribbling blood flow, then wrapping his neck with strips of fabric from my dress. Then, leaving Savannah in charge of the binding spell, we hurried into the alley to free Jaime and Benicio. Lucas headed straight for his father.

Jaime had her head down, but on hearing me, she looked up and flashed a wide grin.

"Hey," she said. "Everything under control?"

"Yes," I said, kneeling behind her. "Thank you so much. You were amazing."

At a noise of assent behind me, Jaime looked up and, from the sudden light in her face, I knew who was standing there. I glanced up at Jeremy and motioned to the ropes.

"Do you mind?" I said. "My fingers are too slippery. Sweating pretty hard, I guess."

He nodded and circled Jaime. "I'll start with your hands. If I pull too tight, just say so."

"Ummm, not yet, okay? Hold on for a minute. I'm still trying to figure out how to escape."

"You don't need to escape, Jaime," he said gently. "It's all over. I can untie you now."

"Oh, I know, and you can, just as soon as I figure out how I *could* have done it. It's humiliating enough to be kidnapped, tied up, and need rescuing. At least I have to be able to say, 'Thanks for setting me free, but I was actually just minutes away from doing it myself.'"

A low chuckle. "I see."

"What do you think of lip gloss?"

"In general? Or as an instrument of escape?"

"Escape. I have some in my pocket and I can almost reach it. What if I'd smeared lip gloss on the ropes? Could I have slid out?"

As Jeremy answered, I felt a hand on my shoulder. I looked up to see Benicio. As I stood, he embraced me.

"Well done," he whispered in my ear.

"I've just called the Cabal, Papá," Lucas said. "They're sending an extraction team."

"Oh, I don't believe that will be necessary."

Benicio pulled back from me. As Lucas and I exchanged a look, Benicio headed for the end of the alley.

"He's quite secure, Papá," Lucas called after him. "Perhaps—"

Benicio lifted a finger, and kept walking. His voice floated back to us, barely above a whisper. Lucas frowned and jogged after him. I followed, trying to hear what Benicio was saying. Then I caught a few words of Latin and knew he was casting. Lucas realized it at the same moment and broke into a run. When we reached the corner, though, Benicio had stopped the incantation. He was leaning over Edward, who lay on his back, staring up, cold-eyed and defiant. Benicio's lips curved in a small smile.

"Vampires are indeed the race of arrogance, aren't they?" he said, his tone pleasant, even congenial. "And perhaps not without reason. You did manage to kill my son once. Almost managed to do it twice. Did you really think you'd get away with it? If you had, I'd have pursued you through every level of Hell to wreak my revenge. As it is, though, things are a bit"—his smile broadened, showing his teeth—"easier."

Benicio lifted his hands and said the last three words of the incantation. As his hands flew down, a lightning bolt severed Edward's head from his neck.

No one moved. We all stood in shock, watching Edward's head roll across the alley.

Benicio lifted his hands again. This time, his voice boomed down the alley, as he cursed Edward's soul for eternity.

CHAPTER 66

FULL CIRCLE

For me, the case truly ended only when it returned to where it had begun: with a teenage witch named Dana MacArthur.

While we'd been tracking Edward, Randy MacArthur had finally arrived in Miami to see his daughter. When the initial flurry of activity over Edward's execution died down, we admitted to Benicio that Dana was gone. Of course, the Cortez Cabal wasn't taking Jaime's say-so, but their necromancers tried to contact Dana and confirmed that she had indeed passed over. So, two days later, Lucas, Savannah, and I stood in a Cabal cemetery and said good-bye to a girl we'd never known.

Since I'd now seen what lay on the other side, Dana's passing pained me less than it might have. Yet I still felt the full weight of the tragedy her death brought for her father and her younger sister, and maybe even her mother. Even for Dana herself, there was tragedy here. She'd gone to a good place, and I was sure she'd be happy, but that didn't mean her life hadn't been cut short, that she hadn't missed out on so much. And for what? To avenge the death of a vampire who had herself killed so many, gone so far beyond the needs of her nature? As I stood in that cemetery, listening to the minister try to eulogize a girl he'd never met, I looked out across the graves and thought of all the other fresh graves in other Cabal cemeteries. I glanced over at Savannah, and thought about Joey Nast, the cousin she never knew. On the other side of the group of mourners, I could see Holden Wyngaard, a plump red-haired boy, now the lone survivor. I thought of the others. Jacob Sorenson. Stephen St. Cloud. Colby Washington. Sarah Dermack. Michael Shane. Matthew Tucker. All gone. And how many tombstones would it take to commemorate the lives of everyone else Edward and Natasha had killed, the scores of humans they'd murdered trying to become immortal? I thought of that, of all those lives, and I couldn't for one second disagree with what Benicio had done. No matter what kind of hell Edward now faced, it was no less than he deserved.

I looked out at the small crowd gathered around Dana's open grave. Her mother wasn't there. I still wondered what had gone wrong in that woman's life to make her abandon her daughter, and I couldn't help but wonder whether having a Coven would have helped. I'm sure it would have, at least for Dana. If she'd had other witches to turn to, she would never have ended up on the streets of Atlanta, and now here.

Yet, as bad as I felt for Dana, I had to accept that the responsibility for starting a second Coven did not lie squarely on my shoulders. I was willing to start one. I would always be willing, and I'd make that willingness known, but I would no longer actively try to convince witches that they needed a Coven. They had to come to see that for themselves. In the meantime, I certainly didn't lack for work. I had an interracial council to reform and a new partnership with Lucas to pursue. Yes, I would have been more comfortable pouring my energy into a dream that started with me, but I think part of growing up is realizing that everything doesn't have to be *mine*. It could be *ours*, and that wasn't a show of weakness or dependence. I liked what Lucas did. I believed in it. I wanted to share it. And, if he wanted to share it back, well, that was damned near perfect.

When the service ended, Benicio leaned over and whispered an invitation to lunch, before we left for Portland. We agreed, and he slipped away to offer final condolences to Randy MacArthur.

The others had all gone their separate ways. The werewolves left Miami the morning after the showdown with Edward. Cassandra and Aaron had followed later that day, after they'd met with Benicio and the other CEOs to discuss possible fallout between the Cabals and the vampire community. Jaime had done her Halloween show in Memphis the night before, then zipped back to attend Dana's morning memorial service before returning to Tennessee for her next show.

As the mourners drifted away from the grave site, I glanced back one last time. Lucas took my hand and squeezed it.

"She'll be okay," he said.

I managed a smile. "I know she will."

"Mr. Cortez? Ms. Winterbourne?"

We turned to see Randy MacArthur behind us, looking uncomfortable in a too-tight black suit. His hand rested on the shoulder of an equally uncomfortable-looking young girl with Dana's long blond hair.

"I—we wanted to thank you," he said. "For stopping him. This—it should never—I don't know how it happened. I had no idea how bad things were—"

"It's okay, Dad," the girl murmured, her red-rimmed eyes fixed on the ground. "It was Mom's fault. Her and that guy. He didn't want kids, and she let him chase Dana off."

"This is Gillian," Randy said. "Dana's sister. I'm going to be looking after her now. Mr. Cortez is giving me a job in town here, so I can stay with her."

"That's great," I said. I tried to catch Gillian's eye and smiled. "You must be what, thirteen? Fourteen? Just starting your second-level spells, I bet."

Gillian looked up at me and for a moment, her eyes were blank, then she realized what I meant. "Spells, no, we don't do that. My mom, I mean. She never . . . well, not much."

"That was, uh, one reason I wanted to speak to you before you left," Randy said. "I know Miss Nast here is about Gillian's age . . ."

It took a moment for me to realize he meant Savannah.

Randy continued, "I know that you're teaching her, and that you used to be with the Coven and you did some teaching there, so I thought maybe you could help Gillian. Long-distance, of course. By phone or e-mail or whatever, maybe visit when you're in town, or we could visit up there. I'll pay you, of course. I hate to impose, but I don't know any other witches. My ex-wife didn't keep in contact with her sister, and I wouldn't even know where to find her, but I really want Gillian to know more, to be able to cast spells, so she can protect herself"—a quick glance at his daughter's grave—"against everything."

"And so she should," I said. "I would love to help her, in any way I can."

"Are you sure?" Randy asked.

I met Gillian's shy gaze with a wide smile. "I'm positive."

WEDDING BELL HELL

Countdown: three weeks

Cross-legged on the bed, I stared at the white blanket of papers around us, another stack in my hand.

"Roses, carnations, or orchids? Chicken, fish, or beef? Music playlist, guest requests, or a mix of both? Photos inside, out, or off-site? Rent a limo, car, or use our own?"

I sighed. I was usually very good at dealing with adversity. I was Paige Winterbourne, daughter of the Coven Leader. Witches knew all about adversity, and I did better than most. At the age of twenty-two, I'd found myself with custody of Savannah Levine, twelve-year-old daughter of a dark witch—her mother dead, her father to follow soon after. Flash forward a couple of years and I'd been kicked out of the Coven, watched my house burn, and been driven from town. I still had Savannah, though. And, as a bonus, I got an amazing guy who wanted to spend the rest of his life with me . . . which was where the current problem started.

I flourished the papers. "We rented the hall, reserved the chapel, picked caterers and florists and photographers and DJs . . . and still the work never stops. Isn't that what we hired all these people for?" I looked over at the page Lucas was studying. "What's that one for?"

"Matchbooks."

"What for? To light the centerpieces?"

"No, as I recall, we have yet to reach the critical 'table arrangement' decision."

"Candles. Or maybe the goldfish bowls Savannah wants. Or your mom's disposable camera idea, to get candid shots—" I slapped my palms to my temples and thumped back onto the bed. "Ack, more choices."

Lucas rubbed my bare feet. After a moment, I peeked through my fingers.

"Do I even want to know about the matchbooks?" I asked.

"Probably not."

"Procrastinate, and we'll only have more work later. Let's get it over with."

"Well, it appears that commemorative matchbooks were included in the cost of our wedding invitation package."

"Bonus. Okay, then, that's settled. On to the next order of—"

"Not so quickly, I'm afraid. We need to decide what we want the matchbooks to say."

"Oh, I don't care. Paige and Lucas. Lucas and Paige. Whichever. Then the date. There, on to—"

"Color."

"Color of—?"

"The matchbook and the text. We also need to select a typeface. And artwork. Plus, they'd like to know if, for an extra hundred dollars—"

"—we can cancel the damned matchbooks altogether?"

He chuckled and resumed my foot massage. I let myself enjoy it before pushing onto my elbows.

"You realize there's only one answer."

"To which question?"

"All of them."

He arched his brows.

"Elopement," I said.

He shifted closer to me, carefully moving the papers aside as he did. "If you really want that . . ."

I sighed. "We can't. Your mother—"

"Has already said it's our choice. Yes, she'd like a church wedding, but considering that I found someone actually willing to marry me, she's not about to quibble over the specifics."

"But she'd be disappointed. And your father wouldn't forgive us."

"Which, one could argue, is all the more reason to elope."

I play-punched his leg. "Things are going well with your dad—far better than I dared hope. If a church wedding makes him happy, it's a small price to pay." I lifted the ledger. "Well, not a *small* price, but worthwhile."

I glanced over at Lucas. "He's still letting us run the show, right? Hasn't insisted on paying again?"

Lucas shook his head. "Just general 'if the costs get to be too much' reminders that his checkbook is available."

"Nothing else, right? No advice, no suggestions . . . ?"

"None."

"Which worries you."

"Terrifies me. But perhaps he realizes this is one area where his interference wouldn't be welcome." He paused. "And, in the more likely event that he's simply lying low, plotting his mode of attack, we have the backup plan."

"We do, indeed. Now, on to the next life-or-death matter." I flourished a page. "Rubber chicken, dried-out beef, or fish that hasn't seen water in a week . . ."

Countdown: one week

Savannah and I were out front planting mums. I wasn't much of a gardener, but I figured that as a new homeowner in a neighborhood with magazine-ready gardens, I should at least make an effort.

"I wouldn't," Savannah said. "If you can't compete, don't join the race, my mom always said. Better a spectator than a loser."

"Dig," I said.

"Like you have time for this crap. What's more important, saving the world from evil or having a pretty garden? It's stupid."

"No, it's 'fitting in.' Now dig."

A horn honked, and I looked up to see a sporty little black car pulling to the curb, passenger window sliding down. Leaning over from the driver's seat was a tall woman in her late forties, her dark hair short and stylishly tousled, broad grin lighting up an unexceptional face.

"You girls look busy," she called.

I smiled and stripped off my dirty gloves. Savannah tossed her trowel onto the sidewalk and bounded over to Lucas's mom, her arms wide.

"Grand—" she began.

"Don't you dare," Maria said, raising a warning finger.

"One more week," Savannah said as she got in the passenger side. "Do you prefer Gran or Granny?"

As Maria eased the car into the driveway, I grabbed my trowel and gloves and followed. When Savannah jumped out and headed for the back door, I stepped into her path.

"Maria's suitcases are still in the car," I said.

Savannah sighed and gestured for Maria to pop the trunk.

Maria hesitated, key fob raised. "Are you sure about this, Paige? I can stay at a hotel. Just drive in to help and—"

"And waste precious time traveling? We have a lot to do. Stay here. Please."

As we headed inside, Savannah was still razzing Maria about becoming a grandmother. It was a dubious connection, but Maria never pointed that out. Just emphatically declared that she was far too young to be the grandmother of a teenager.

"But I've never had a grandmother," Savannah said, making puppy eyes at Maria as we cut through the kitchen. "You wouldn't deprive me of that, would you?"

"Tell you what. If you call Benicio, Grandpa, we have a deal."

"Okay."

Maria laughed as we walked into the living room. "Now, *that* I have to see. Of course it means you also have to start calling our son Dad."

"Certainly not," Lucas said from the couch, not lifting his gaze from his notebook. "I intend to insist on Father, spoken with the proper degree of respect."

Maria bent to kiss Lucas's cheek, then glanced at his notes. "What are you working on?"

"A list," Savannah and I said in unison.

Lucas lifted his gaze, fixing us with a baleful glare. "I'm making note of everything we still need to do for the wedding, organized by date, priority, and probability of enlisting help to complete it."

"It's a list," I said, sliding onto the sofa beside him.

"Watch it or you'll find your name beside every item." He looked up at Maria. "How was your trip, Mamá?"

Maria sat down and regaled us with tales of late-summer construction horror, as crews worked feverishly to finish before winter blew in. She'd driven down from Seattle. When Lucas and I bought the house, deciding to settle in Portland, Maria had moved from Illinois to Washington State, declaring it was "close enough to pester her son, but not close enough to drive him crazy."

It was a joke, of course—few mothers meddled less in their child's life than Maria. She and Lucas were close, but she had her own life—her career as a high-school teacher, boyfriends, a wide social circle, and a string of causes that she championed.

Lucas was telling her about damage my car had sustained in a crater-deep pothole when the doorbell rang.

"Probably the neighborhood beautification council," Savannah muttered. "Come to complain because we left gardening tools unattended on the lawn for ten minutes."

"If so, they're *your* tools," I said, getting up. "Practice your hostess skills on Maria while I answer the door."

While I doubted it was the beautification council at my door, it wasn't impossible. When I'd first seen our house, I'd fallen in love with the neighborhood, which had reminded me of the one where I'd grown up in Boston—quiet streets of modest, immaculately tended older homes. As I'd learned, most of the residents were either retirees or urban professional couples, one with the spare time to landscape and the other with the cash to hire someone. We had neither.

When I swung open the door and saw a fortyish woman in a suit, designer clipboard at the ready, I thought my time had come.

"Miss Winterbourne?" She forced a smile. "You won't be hearing that much longer, will you? By next week, it'll be Mrs. Cortez. Or will that be Winterbourne-Cortez?"

"It will be Winterbourne," Lucas said from behind me. "May I ask—?"

"Winterbourne-Cortez," the woman murmured, marking it onto her pad. "Lovely." She proffered her hand in a shake as brief and light as an air-kiss. "Margory Mills, wedding planner, at your service."

"Wedding planner . . . ?" I glanced over my shoulder at Lucas, who winced, pushing his glasses up the bridge of his nose.

"My father hired you, I presume?"

"He did indeed. A very generous man."

"Yes, well, while we appreciate the gesture, and apologize for any inconvenience the misunderstanding might cause—"

"You want to plan your own wedding," she said, stepping inside and brushing past us. "I understand, as does your father. But you already *have* planned it. All that's left is coordinating the affair so your special day is as perfect as you imagined it."

"Yes, but—" Lucas began.

I caught his attention and cast a privacy spell, so we could speak without Ms. Mills overhearing. "If it makes your dad happy, it's not such a bad idea. There *is* a lot of work still."

We turned to accept Ms. Mills's proposition, but she was already in the living room, introducing herself to Maria and Savannah.

"The troops are rallying, I see," she said. "Splendid. Many hands make light work. Now let's see these wedding plans."

I retrieved the overstuffed file folder while Savannah—after two meaningful looks and a nudge—offered refreshments. Once the coffee and cookie tray were delivered, Savannah retreated to her room while we went over the plans.

"Amazing," Maria said when we finished. "I don't know how you kids did it. All that work. Makes me glad I'd never—" She stopped with a sidelong glance at Ms. Mills. "*Planned* a wedding. This certainly will be lovely, though."

"Of course it will," Ms. Mills said. "First, though, you'll need to complete the wedding party list. I don't see a maid of honor or a best man."

"We're just having bridesmaids and ushers," I said.

"Oh . . ." She looked ready to comment, then snapped her mouth shut. "Well, I presume you have a third usher, to even out the party."

I shook my head. "Savannah's more of a junior bridesmaid and flower girl combined. We wanted to keep the wedding party small."

"I see. Well, on to the dinner then." She perused the menu. "Red wine. I don't believe I've ever heard of that brand . . ."

"It's a local winery. They also have a great nonalcoholic sparkling wine."

"What about white?"

"Well, we're serving beef, to support the beef farmers."

"Some people will still prefer white, and you must cater to all your guests. I'll add a case of that—at Mr. Cortez's expense, of course."

Lucas glanced my way, ready to argue, but I gave a small shake of my head.

"Now, about dinner." She pored over the menu, frowning. "I only see beef . . ."

"That's the primary option, but we also have vegetarian."

"What about kosher? Lactose-free? Gluten-free? Nut-free?"

Lucas shook his head. "There is one lactose-intolerant guest, but he simply avoids dairy products. While we would love to offer meals for every conceivable personal choice and food allergy, it isn't feasible with a guest list of only forty. We've hired a women's shelter to cater and, while they will provide ingredient lists for concerned guests, the menu must understandably be limited."

"Women's shelter? Oh, dear." A brisk note in her book. "No matter. I know an excellent four-star restaurant in Portland that will cater on short notice. We'll have a choice of beef medallions, sea scallops—"

"We've already hired the shelter group," I said.

"And Mr. Cortez will compensate them with a sizable donation, I'm sure. Now, about the DJ. Your father would prefer a live band, and he's told me you both like jazz, so we're flying a lovely quartet from—"

Lucas held up a finger, asking her to wait. Then he took out his phone and dialed.

"Papá? It's Lucas. Your wedding planner is here." Pause. "Yes, the gesture was—" Pause. "Yes, we *are* quite busy—" Pause. "Yes, it was very thoughtful of you. However . . ."

Countdown: three days

"Okay," I said, rounding the bottom of the stairs, cordless phone still in hand. "I've straightened out the hotel. Seems the desk clerk was looking at next month's reservations. The block we reserved for our guests *is* still booked. Crisis twenty-nine averted. Oh, and twenty-seven, too. I've spoken to Petulia's Petunias and convinced them that having lived for three years without a website feedback form, they don't absolutely need one done this week."

Lucas nodded and put his cell phone into his satchel. "And I believe potential crisis twenty-eight is resolved as well. I've cleared up the misunderstanding with that necromancer, assuring him that while I'm happy to investigate his legal case, I cannot represent him, not being a member of the bar in Utah . . . and I cannot begin *any* investigation in the next ten days."

"Good." I collapsed against him. "All bullets dodged so far."

Savannah walked around the corner, shaking her head. "You guys don't need wedding planners; you need life planners."

"Are you volunteering?"

She snorted and headed past us for the stairs.

"While you're up there, get changed for dinner, assuming you're joining us . . ." I backed away from Lucas. "Elena's plane. It's after five, and they said they'd phone when—"

"She called your cell," Savannah yelled back. "The house line and Lucas's line were busy. They're on their way. Oh, and they invited Maria to dinner as well. And yes, I reminded them that means no supernatural talk at the table."

"Thank y—"

"Hey, someone's here," Savannah called from upstairs. "It's a big black SUV."

I stiffened, and Lucas's arm tightened around me, chin jerking up.

"Just kidding," Savannah said, grinning as she hurried past us down the stairs. "It's only Adam."

"Ask him—"

Too late. She was already in the kitchen, making a beeline for the back door.

Countdown: two days

Lucas had asked Benicio to come no sooner than Thursday, which we'd figured was too close to the wedding for him to interfere, yet early enough that he didn't feel like "just another guest."

He was there right after breakfast.

Lucas had said that his parents got along fine, but I'd still been nervous, wondering if—like many estranged couples—they only put on a good show for their child. If that was the case, though, Benicio and Maria were both excellent actors. They exchanged hugs and "How's teaching?" and "How are your grandsons?" chatter . . . and seemed genuinely interested in the answers.

While they were talking, I sent Savannah out to the SUV to offer refreshments to Troy and Griffin, Benicio's bodyguards. Benicio hadn't brought them inside—according to Lucas, that would be rude, suggesting Benicio thought he needed protection in our house. I wanted to invite them in, but wasn't sure that was allowed. Emily Post doesn't cover etiquette for dealing with a guest's bodyguards.

"They'll take coffee," Savannah said as she came back in. "And muffins."

"You're becoming quite the little hostess," Maria said as Savannah set about preparing the tray.

"I feel like I'm stuck in a Jane Austen novel," Savannah grumbled.

"The lowly ward," I said. "Consigned to servitude. When you're done with that, you can report to Maria for your next orders. We'll be showing Benicio the house."

"And this bedroom we turned into an office," I said, walking from the master bedroom into the adjoining area. "It's too small for a second desk, so we're thinking of finishing the basement for a large office, making this room a sitting area or library."

"There's only the three bedrooms?" Benicio said.

"Yes, Papá." Lucas kept his voice soft but words emphatic. "We don't need any more. Not for quite some time."

Benicio smiled. "So you think now, but things may change once you're married." He stepped into the hall. "I noticed a lovely new subdivision going up just outside the city. It has estate-sized lots, and the builder assured me their zoning would allow a second, smaller residence on the property for hired help." He lifted his hands against our protests. "I know you don't want a battalion of employees, but you're both very busy. I'm sure a housekeeper—"

"We have a woman who comes in every week," I said.

"Perhaps, but that must hardly make a dent in your workload, Paige. A housekeeper could do the laundry, cooking, day-to-day tidying." He looked at Lucas. "I'm sure it isn't easy for Paige, especially with you gone so much."

"We do fine," I said.

"Perhaps, but I have someone in mind. A young witch, recently emigrated and in a rather difficult position."

"Father," Lucas said sharply. "That is—"

"I—I'll be downstairs," I said quickly. "Helping Maria and Sav—"

Benicio caught my arm. "My apologies, Paige. That was underhanded of me. Yes, there is a witch, but I'll find her other work. I simply want to make things easier for both of you. Your time is so much better spent on the work you love. We'll speak no more of housekeepers, though."

"Or new houses," Lucas said.

Benicio nodded and let us lead him down the hall toward Savannah's room.

"I did want to ask about your honeymoon, though. How are you getting there? The last thing you need is airport delays. I'm not using the jet this week—"

"No, Papá."

"Have you decided how you're getting to the reception? I hope it's not a limousine. Weddings should be special. Romantic. Perhaps a horse-drawn coach—"

"Benicio?" Maria looked up as she climbed the stairs. "If you want to help, I have something you could do. I know Paige and Lucas wouldn't want to impose by asking . . ."

"Anything," Benicio said.

"It's the reception favors. Savannah and I are making them—putting the candies into the little pillows and tying on the ribbons. Could you give us a hand?"

"Er, yes, I suppose—"

Maria put her hand on Benicio's arm and led him away. "And could you ask the boys to come in and join us? Yes, hardly bodyguard duties, but I know they'll be good sports. We can make a production line of it . . ."

Countdown: nineteen hours

"Black and white," I said, staring down at the brandy snifters stuffed with matchbooks. "Black and white. Could it be any simpler?"

Savannah plucked out a fuchsia matchbook. "Maybe they thought they were doing you a favor. Livening up a seriously boring wedding color scheme."

Elena took a book and turned it over. "Maybe we could bleach them. The matches won't work, but it's a nonsmoking reception anyway. Who'll notice?"

"I'll buy some flowers to match," Jaime said. "Just a few scattered in with the white ones, so it'll look like an intentional accent color."

"It's not that bad. At least everything else is—" Elena stopped and crammed the matchbook back into the snifter. "Savannah? Jaime? Grab a couple glasses and we'll set them out for the rehearsal party."

I snatched a matchbook before they could whisk the glasses away. "Lucas with a K? Who spells Lucas with a K? Where's my phone? Maybe a rush order—"

"I thought you didn't even want matchbooks," Savannah said.

"Well, no, but—" I took a deep breath. "Oh, God, I can't believe I'm panicking over the matchbooks."

Jaime grabbed my arm and motioned for Elena to take the other one. "Savannah, hon? See if you can scare up a bottle of champagne. If anyone complains, tell them it's an emergency."

Countdown: fifteen hours

After three glasses of champagne, the matchbooks could have spontaneously combusted and burned down the reception hall and I wouldn't have cared.

We held the rehearsal party in the hotel meeting lounge. Just finger foods and drinks, decompressing and enjoying the company of friends before the insanity to come.

"—walking around the corner," I was saying. "And Lucas is madly waving me back, but, nope, I'm not retreating because I have this spell."

"Which she'd only mastered the week before," Lucas said, quickly glancing around to make sure his mother wasn't nearby. "But, naturally, she's eager to use it."

Elena grinned. "Naturally."

"Understandable," Lucas said. "Though, perhaps, in hindsight, testing it against a Ferratus half-demon may not have been the most . . . judicious choice."

"So he's barreling around the corner, and I'm standing there, as calmly as can be, reciting my spell. I cast it and— Pfft. Nothing. Here comes this half-demon, high on God knows what, and me planted in his path like a moron going, 'Hmm, that's odd. The spell should have worked . . . '"

Someone tapped Lucas's shoulder. I turned to see Troy.

"Fair warning," Troy murmured to Lucas. "Your dad's making his way over here. He wants to talk to you about the wedding."

"Wedding's tomorrow," Clay said. "Tell him it's too late to bug you about it. Better yet, I can."

Jeremy laid his hand on Clay's shoulder and shook his head. "Let me run interference this time. He wanted to speak to me on another matter."

As Jeremy slipped away, Jaime shook her head. "Is it just a control thing with Benicio?"

"I think he honestly wants to be involved," I said. "Problem is, his idea of involvement *is* control. But if it gets worse, we have a backup plan."

"In the meantime, why don't you guys call it a night," Elena said. "It's getting late. Slip out now and get a good night's sleep. I'll call you a cab."

"Better yet, take your dad's ride." Troy grinned. "He can't complain about that . . . and he can't follow you without his wheels. Come on. I'll talk to the driver."

"Here," Troy said as we crawled into the SUV's leather rear seat. He handed us a bottle of champagne and two glasses. "I've told the driver to take the scenic route. Oh, and—"

He leaned in and pressed the button to raise the black glass divider between the front and rear seats.

"How, uh, private is that?" I asked.

He grinned. "One-way glass and completely soundproof. Enjoy."

Countdown: eight hours

Lucas reached over and brushed a curl off my cheek. I slid across the six inches of mattress between us, and snuggled under his arm, head on his chest.

"How long have you been awake?" he asked.

"Awhile."

"Worrying?"

"A bit."

He adjusted his arm under me, hand dropping to my bare hip. "About the wedding particulars . . . or the generality?"

I tilted back my head to look up at him. "The particulars. You know that. I'm definitely getting married today, and I've been practicing my binding spell, so don't even think of running."

A soft chuckle. "I won't. So I presume, then, that a wedding gift, given now, would not be unreasonably premature?"

I jumped up and swung over him, crouching on all fours and grinning down. "A gift? For me?"

He blew strands of my hair off his face. "No, for my other wife-to-be."

I scrambled off him and hopped from the bed.

"It's in—" he began.

I grabbed a bag from under the bed and handed it to him. "Yours first."

His brows arched, then he pulled himself up until he was sitting, his back against the headboard. He reached into the bag and pulled out an old leather-bound grimoire.

His brows arched higher. "I've been looking for this for—"

"Years," I said, plunking down beside him. "But you didn't have Robert Vasic to dig it up for you. Now, where's mine?"

He opened the book and began leafing through it.

"My gift, Cortez," I said, reaching for the book.

He snatched it away at the last second. As I fell forward, he grabbed me and pulled me to him in a laughing kiss that turned slow and delicious, and all thoughts of my gift slid from my brain until I felt something poke my shoulder.

I turned to see him nudging my back with a manila envelope. I took it, opened it, and pulled out . . .

"A list?" I said, staring down at the handwritten page.

"A to-do list." As I frowned, he plucked it from my fingers. "Step one: Pick a suitable date. Step two: Confirm with all parties. Step three: Select a destination from the choices provided." Still reading, he took three glossy brochures from the envelope and passed them to me. "Step four: Book flights. Step five: Plan itinerary. Step six: Enjoy seven days of hell chaperoning five teenage girls." He laid the paper down. "I thought it was time the Sabrina School had a class outing."

"You mean—" My throat dried up. "A get-together? With the girls? That'd be amazing. Some of them might not be able to afford it, but if I can scrape together—"

"Would I give you a gift you need to pay for yourself? It's been scraped. Or, I should say, reallocated from the fund formerly designated for a suitably ostentatious engagement ring, which the recipient refused to allow her fiancé to purchase."

I kissed him so hard he pulled back, laughing and gasping for breath. Then he lowered me onto the bed and we kissed, bodies entwining—

The alarm sounded.

Lucas glanced over at it. "When is your first appointment?"

"Eleven."

He shut off the alarm, then leaned over me again. "Then I propose we take advantage of the respite—and the empty house—and allow ourselves a well-earned lazy morning." He tickled his fingers up my side. "I'll finish what I began. Then, when you're properly woken, I'll whisk you away to a leisurely breakfast at Angelo's."

"I think I'm going to like being married."

His mouth lowered to mine. I slid my hands down to his—

The doorbell rang.

"Didn't hear it," I murmured against his lips.

"Hear what?" he said, resuming the kiss.

It rang again. I let out a curse. Lucas lifted his head, hesitated, then motioned for me to wait. He crawled from bed, pulled on pants, grabbed a shirt, and padded into the hall as the bell rang again.

I waited two minutes, then pulled on my robe and crept into the hall to hear him arguing with someone at the door, his civility quickly fraying. Yes, the breakfast tray was a thoughtful gesture, and please, thank his father for that. Yes, while the morning at a spa sounded quite nice, we'd already booked our appointments. No, Lucas did not need to consult with his wife-to-be on that. No, we did not need lunch catered for the wedding party. No, we had not changed our mind about the jazz trio . . .

Finally, after physically edging his father's messenger out, Lucas sighed, forehead resting against the closed door. I crept up behind him and put my arms around his waist.

"Time to enact the backup plan?" I murmured.

"I believe so."

Now that Lucas *wanted* to meet with his father, though, Benicio was nowhere to be found. So we enjoyed our breakfast at Angelo's, then headed to the hotel to gather our respective halves of the wedding party and get ready.

Before we parted, I squeezed Lucas's hand. "So I guess the next time I see you will be at the altar."

He leaned down to kiss my forehead. "It's a date."

Countdown: five hours, thirty minutes

I found Savannah with Elena, Jaime, and Talia—Adam's mother—in a corner table at the hotel restaurant.

Talia pulled out a seat for me. "I was just telling Savannah how much I loved the invitations. She did such a great job with them."

"The invitations?" I laughed. "Believe me, Savannah didn't pick those. She said they were the most boring things she'd ever—"

I stopped, gaze crossing over three confused faces and settling on Savannah, who was studiously picking apart a chocolate croissant. I turned to Talia, who had her wedding invitation in hand.

"May I see that?" I said, taking it before she could answer.

On the front of my invitation—my very formal, very simple wedding invitation—someone had sketched a cartoon of Samantha from *Bewitched* and Harry Potter. I stared at it, then burst out laughing.

"Did you do that on all of them?" I looked at her and sobered. "Please tell me you didn't—"

"Only ours," Savannah said. "The humans got the boring plain ones. Well, except Talia."

Talia's brows arched. "Humans? Is that what we are to you? *Humans?*"

"Okay, supernaturally challenged." Savannah ducked Talia's swat, then looked over at me. "So I'm not in trouble?"

"Only if you don't make us one for our keepsake box. Now, we have hair appointments—"

My cell phone rang. It was Lucas, still looking for Benicio.

"Is my mother there?" he asked.

"Not yet. We were just going to swing by and grab her for the salon."

A pause. "Ah. Well, if you see my father . . . anywhere, could you please tell him I'm looking for him?"

Maria was up, but not quite ready. She popped into the bathroom. I could hear low voices from inside, like she'd turned on a radio. As I turned, my gaze snagged on a pair of leather loafers half-hidden under the bed. Men's leather loafers, brand new and very expensive.

The bathroom door opened and Maria hurried out, closing it behind her.

"Oh," I said. "Lucas is looking for Benicio. He wants to speak to him. If you see him . . . anywhere, could you relay the message? I'll just wait in the hall. Let you finish getting ready."

I called Lucas back from the hotel.

"Found him, I presume?" he said.

"Umm-hmm."

A soft sigh, then he started to say something, but stopped mid-syllable. "Ah, he's calling me now. That was prompt."

Countdown: fifteen minutes

I watched my reflection in the mirror, tugging a curl over my shoulder, then brushing it back. Over, back. Over, back. The noise from the tiny chapel was a distant rumble, like the far-off roar of the ocean. I had asked for a few minutes to practice my vows, but I didn't need it. I knew them by heart. Felt them by heart.

The door creaked open and a face appeared above mine in the mirror. For a second, Adam just stood there, staring.

"Now that is a sight I never thought I'd see," he said finally. "Paige Winterbourne in a wedding gown."

I turned and grinned, and he faltered.

"Looks that bad?" I said.

"Awful. Doesn't suit you at all. Take it off and burn it while you still can." He walked over and handed me my bouquet. "You left this in the front room. Lucas found it, and I think the poor guy had visions of a runaway bride, dropping her bouquet and bolting."

"How is he?"

"Happy." Adam swung around me, getting a full view of my dress. "His dad's pretty pleased, too. That was a smart idea Lucas had."

"It was my idea."

Adam rolled his eyes. "Of course."

The door swung open. Savannah popped her head in, then let out a dramatic sigh.

"There you are. You're supposed to be at the front of the church, loser."

"Yeah," Adam said. "Move it, Paige."

"Not her." Savannah grabbed Adam's arm and dragged him out. At the door, she looked at me. "I'll be back for you in a minute."

⚜

I walked into the church to the tune of popping flashes. Elena and Talia led the procession. Savannah was ahead of me, her bridesmaid role having been upgraded to maid of honor. You need a maid of honor if you have a best man. And we now had one, standing beside Adam and Clay at the front of the room. Benicio, beaming brighter than any of the flashbulbs.

And to Benicio's right, Lucas. My destination.

"I think I have rice in my bra," Savannah hissed as we posed on the front step for pictures.

"Join the club," I murmured, teeth clenched in a jaw-aching smile.

Lucas leaned into my ear. "I'll help you with that in the car."

"I bet you will."

Another blinding round of flashes. Then the crowd parted, path opening to the limousine that would whisk us to the reception hall.

As the last of the people moved out of the way, and the opening cleared, I stopped in my tracks.

"Oh, my God," Lucas murmured.

Savannah started to snicker.

"That's very . . . fancy," Elena said.

"Not my idea," I muttered between my teeth.

"Oh, I didn't think it was."

Talia let out a small laugh. "Last time I saw something like that was on TV. Lady Di's wedding, I think."

Lucas and I both turned to see Benicio smiling.

"You never did actually say no to *that* idea," he said.

I looked at Lucas. He shrugged, then swooped me up and carried me down the red carpet to the coach and four waiting at the end.

KELLEY ARMSTRONG is the bestselling author of the Women of the Otherworld series, the Nadia Stafford crime series, and the *New York Times* #1 bestselling young adult trilogies Darkest Powers and Darkness Rising. She lives in rural Ontario with her family.

www.kelleyarmstrong.com

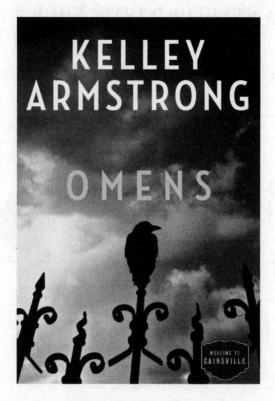

KELLEY ARMSTRONG

OMENS

WELCOME TO CAINSVILLE

NO WEREWOLVES.
NO DEMONS.
JUST GARGOYLES.

Following the epic conclusion of her internationally bestselling Women of the Otherworld series, Kelley Armstrong launches a brand-new series set in Cainsville, a small town as spookily fascinating as Stephen King's Castle Rock or Dean Koontz's Moonlight Bay.

WELCOME TO CAINSVILLE

NADIA STAFFORD ISN'T YOUR TYPICAL HUNTING LODGE OWNER.

SHE'S AN EX-COP WITH A CODE OF JUSTICE ALL HER OWN...

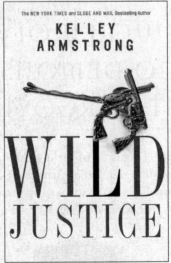

MURDER, ACTION, AND SUSPENSE FROM
THE *NEW YORK TIMES* AND *GLOBE AND MAIL*
BESTSELLING AUTHOR KELLEY ARMSTRONG.

WELCOME TO THE OTHERWORLD.

Bitten

Stolen

DIME STORE MAGIC

INDUSTRIAL MAGIC

HAUNTED

BROKEN

NO HUMANS INVOLVED

PERSONAL DEMON

LIVING WITH THE DEAD

THE NEW YORK TIMES and GLOBE AND MAIL Bestselling Author

KELLEY ARMSTRONG